# CONTENTS

# MICHAEL VEY

## THE PRISONER OF CELL 25

*To Michael*

# PART ONE

# 1

## Chopsticks and Spiders

"**H**ave you found the last two?" The voice on the phone was angry and coarse, like the sound of car tires over broken glass.

"Not yet," the well-dressed man on the other end of the phone replied. "Not yet. But we believe we're close—and they still don't know that we're hunting them."

"You *believe* you're close?"

"They're two children among a billion—finding them is like finding a lost chopstick in China."

"Is that what you want me to tell the board?"

"*Remind* the board that I've already found fifteen of the seventeen children. I've put out a million-dollar bounty on the last two, we've got spiders crawling the Web, and we have a whole team of investigators scanning global records for their whereabouts. It's just a matter of time before we find them—or they step into one of our traps."

"*Time* isn't on our side," the voice returned sharply. "Those kids are already too old. You know how difficult they are to turn at this age."

"I know better than anyone," the well-dressed man said, tapping his ruby-capped pen on his desk. "But I have my ways. And if they don't turn, there's always Cell 25."

There was a long pause, then the voice on the phone replied darkly, "Yes. There's always Cell 25."

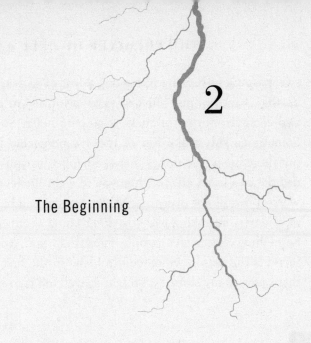

# 2

## The Beginning

It's not like I was looking for trouble. I didn't have to. At my height it just always found me.

My name is Michael Vey, and the story I'm about to tell you is strange. Very strange. It's my story.

If you passed me walking home from school you probably wouldn't even notice me. That's because I'm just a kid like you. I go to school like you. I get bullied like you. Unlike you, I live in Idaho. Don't ask me what state Idaho is in—news flash—Idaho *is* a state. The fact that most people don't know where Idaho is, is exactly why my mother and I moved here—so people wouldn't find us. But that's part of my story.

Besides living in Idaho, I'm different from you in other ways. For one, I have Tourette's syndrome. You probably know less about Tourette's syndrome than you do Idaho. Usually when you see someone on TV pretending to have Tourette's syndrome, they're shouting swear words or barking like a dog. Most of us with Tourette's don't do that. I mostly just blink my eyes a lot. If I'm really anxious, I'll also clear my throat or make a gulping noise. Sometimes it hurts. Sometimes kids make fun of me. It's no picnic having Tourette's, but there are worse things that can happen to you—like having your dad die of a heart attack when you're eight. Believe me, that's much worse. I'm still not over that. Maybe I never will be.

There's something else you don't know about me. It's my secret. Something that scares people more than you would believe. That secret is the reason we moved to Idaho in the first place. But, again, that's part of my story. So I might as well tell it to you.

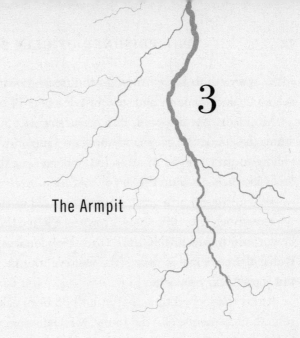

# 3

## The Armpit

**M**r. Dallstrom's office is as good a place to begin as any. Or as bad a place. Mr. Dallstrom is the principal of Meridian High School, where I go to school. If you ask me, ninth grade is the armpit of life. And there I was in the very stinkiest part of that armpit—the principal's office. I was sitting in Mr. Dallstrom's office, blinking like crazy.

You could guess that I'm not fond of Mr. Dallstrom, which would be stating the obvious, like saying, "Breathing is important" or "Rice Krispies squares are the greatest food ever invented." No one at Meridian was fond of Mr. Dallstrom except Ms. Duncan, who directed the Glee Club. She had a picture of Mr. Dallstrom on her desk, which she sometimes stared at with soft, googly eyes. Every time Mr. Dallstrom came over the PA system, she would furiously whack her baton on a music stand to quiet us. Then, after he'd said his piece, she would get all red-faced and sweaty, and remind us of how lucky we were to be led through the treacherous wilderness of high school by such a manly and steadfast defender of public education.

Mr. Dallstrom is a bald, thin scarecrow of a man with a poochy stomach. Think of a pregnant Abraham Lincoln with no beard and a yellow toupee instead of a top hat and you get the picture. He also looks like he's a hundred years old. At least.

When I was in fifth grade our teacher told us that "the easiest way to remember the difference between PRINCIPLE (an underlying law or ethic), and PRINCIPAL (the chief administrator of a school), is that the principal is your PAL." Believe me, Mr. Dallstrom did not put the PAL in principal.

It was the second time that month I'd been called to his office for something someone else did to me. Mr. Dallstrom was big on punishing the victim.

"I believe this is the second time you've been in my office this month," Mr. Dallstrom said to me, his eyes half closed. "Is that right, Mr. Vey?"

That was the other thing about Mr. Dallstrom—he liked to ask questions that he already knew the answer to. I was never sure if I was supposed to answer him or not. I mean, he knew the answer, and I knew the answer, so what was the point? Bottom line, it was the second time I'd been locked in my locker by Jack Vranes and his friends that month. This time they put me in upside down and I nearly passed out before the custodian unlocked my locker and dragged me down to Mr. Dallstrom's office.

Jack Vranes was, like, seventeen and still in ninth grade. He'd been held back so many times, he had a driver's license, a car, a mustache, and a tattoo. He sometimes called himself Jackal, which is a pretty accurate description, since both he and the animal prey on smaller mammals. Jack had biceps the size of ripe Florida oranges and wasn't afraid to use them. Actually, he loved to use them. He and his gang, Mitchell and Wade, watched ultimate fighting, and Jack took Brazilian jujitsu lessons at a gym not far from the school. His dream in life was to fight in the Octagon, where he could pound people and get paid for it.

"Is that right?" Dallstrom repeated, still staring at me. I ticked almost a dozen times, then said, "But, sir, it wasn't my fault. They shoved me inside my locker upside down." He wasn't looking very moved by my plight, so I continued. "There were three of them and they're a lot bigger than me. A *lot* bigger."

My hope for sympathy was met by Mr. Dallstrom's infamous "stare o' death." Really, you'd have to see it to understand. Last quarter, when we were studying Greek mythology and we got to the part about Medusa—a Gorgon woman who could turn people to stone by looking into their eyes—I figured out where Mr. Dallstrom had come from. Maybe it had something to do with my Tourette's, but I blurted out, "That must be Mr. Dallstrom's great-great-great-great-grandmother."

Everyone had laughed. Everyone except for Mr. Dallstrom, who had picked that precise moment to slip into our class. I spent a week in after-school detention, which wasn't all bad because at least I was safe from Jack and his posse, who somehow never got sent to detention no matter how many kids they stuffed into the lunchroom garbage cans or locked in their lockers. Anyway, that had officially put me on Mr. Dallstrom's troublemaker list.

"Mr. Vey, you cannot be stuffed into a locker without your consent," Mr. Dallstrom said, which may be the dumbest thing ever said in a school. "You should have resisted." That's like blaming someone who was struck by lightning for getting in the way.

"But I tried, sir."

"Obviously not hard enough." He took out a pen. "Who are these boys who allegedly stuffed you into your locker?" Mr. Dallstrom cocked his head to one side, his pen wagging impatiently in front of him. I stared at the pen in its hypnotic trajectory.

"I'm waiting, Mr. Vey. Their names?"

There was no way I was going to tell him. First, he already knew who had done it. Everyone knew Jack had put more kids than textbooks into lockers. Second, ratting out Jack was the shortest route to death. I just looked at Mr. Dallstrom, my eyes blinking like crazy.

"Stop twitching and answer my question."

"I can't tell you," I finally said.

"Can't or won't?"

*Pick one*, I thought. "I forgot who did it."

Mr. Dallstrom continued staring at me through those half-closed eyes of his. "Did you now?" He stopped wagging his pen and set it on the desk. "I'm sorry to hear that, Mr. Vey. Now you'll have to take their punishment as well. Four weeks in after-school detention. I believe you know where detention is held."

"Yes, sir. It's in the lunchroom."

"Good. Then you'll have no trouble finding your way there."

Like I said, Mr. Dallstrom excelled at punishing the victim. He signed a tardy excuse note and handed it to me. "Give that to your teacher. You can go back to your class now, Mr. Vey."

"Thank you, sir," I said, not entirely certain what I was thanking him for. I walked out of his office and slowly down the long, empty corridor to biology. The hallway was lined with posters made by the Basketball Boosters' Club with messages like GO WARRIORS, SINK THE VIKINGS—that sort of thing—rendered in bright poster paints.

I got my backpack from my locker, then went to class.

My biology teacher, Mr. Poulsen, a short, balding man with thick eyebrows and a massive comb-over, was in the middle of lecturing and stopped mid-sentence at my entrance. "Glad you decided to join us, Mr. Vey."

"Sorry. I was at the principal's office. Mr. Dallstrom said to give this to you." I handed him my note. He took the paper without looking at it. "Sit down. We're reviewing for tomorrow's test."

Every eye in the class followed me as I walked to my desk. I sat in the second row from the back, just behind my best friend, Ostin Liss, who is one of the smartest kids in the universe. Ostin's name looks European or something, but it isn't. His mother named him that because he was born in Austin, Texas. It was his private curse that she had spelled it wrong. I suspect that Ostin was adopted, because I couldn't figure out how someone that smart could come from someone who couldn't spell the name of the city she lived in. But even if Ostin's mom wasn't the brightest crayon in the box, I liked her a lot. She spoke with a Texan accent and called everyone "honey," which may sound annoying but it wasn't. She was always nice and kept a supply of red licorice in their pantry just because she knew I liked it and my mother didn't buy candy.

Ostin never got shoved into his locker, probably because he was wider than it—not that Jack and his friends left him alone. They didn't. In fact he had suffered the ultimate humiliation from Jack and his friends. He'd been pantsed in public.

"How'd it go with Dallstrom?" Ostin whispered.

I shook my head. "Brutal."

As I sat down, Taylor Ridley, who sat in the desk to my left, turned and smiled at me. Taylor is a cheerleader and one of the prettiest girls at Meridian. Heck, she's one of the prettiest girls in any high school anywhere in the world. She has a face that could be on the cover of a beauty magazine, long, light brown hair and big brown eyes the color of maple syrup. Since I'm being completely honest here, I'll admit that I had a crush on her from the second I first saw her. It took me less than a day to realize that so did everyone else at Meridian.

Taylor was always nice to me. At first I hoped she was nice because she liked me, but really she's just one of those people who is nice to everyone. Nice or not, it didn't matter. She was way out of my league. Like a thousand miles out of my league. So I never told anyone about my secret crush—not even Ostin, who I told everything. Some dreams are just too embarrassing to share.

Anyway, whenever Taylor looked at me, it made my tics go wild. Stress does that to people with Tourette's. I forced myself not to blink as I sat down and pulled my biology book out of my backpack. That's the thing about my tics. If I try real hard, I can delay them, but I can't make them go away. It's like having a bad itch. You can ignore it for a little while, but it's going to build up until you scratch. I've learned tricks to hide my tics. Like sometimes I'll drop a pencil on the ground, then when I bend down to get it, I'll blink or grimace like crazy. I'm sure the kids around me think I'm really clumsy because sometimes I'll drop my pencil four or five times in one class. Anyway, between Mr. Dallstrom and Jack and Taylor, I was blinking like an old neon sign.

Poulsen started up again. "Okay, class, we were talking about electricity and the body. 'I sing the body electric,' said the poet Whitman. Who, pray tell, can explain what role electricity plays in the body?"

He panned the room with his dusty gaze, clearly disappointed with the lack of participation. "You better know this, people. It's on your test tomorrow."

"Electricity runs our heart," the girl with massive braces in the front row said.

"Cor-rect," he said. "And what else?"

Taylor raised her hand. "It signals all of our nerves and thoughts."

"That's right, Miss Ridley. And where does this electricity come from?" He looked around the room. "Where does the electricity come from? Come on, people." It was dangerous when no one was answering because that's when he started hunting out those least likely to answer correctly. "How about you, Mr. Morris?"

"Uh, batteries?"

The class laughed.

"Brilliant," Poulsen said, shaking his head. "Batteries. Okay, Mr. Morris, perhaps it's time you changed your batteries, because clearly they are running down. Where does electricity come from, Mr. Vey?"

I swallowed. "Electrolytes?" I said.

"That would be true, Mr. Vey, if you were an electric eel."

Everyone laughed again. Taylor glanced over at me sympathetically. I dropped my pencil on the floor.

Ostin raised his hand.

"Mr. Liss," Poulsen said. "Enlighten us."

Ostin straightened himself up in his chair like he was about to deliver a lecture, which he was.

"The human body generates an electrical current through chemical concentrations in the nerves in a process called bioelectrogenesis. Whenever a nerve signal is sent, potassium ions flood out of nerve cells and sodium ions flood in. Both of these ions have slightly different charges and so the difference in ionic concentrations inside and outside the nerve cell creates a charge which our bodies process as electricity."

"Bravo, Mr. Liss. Harvard awaits. For those of you who have no idea what Mr. Liss just said, I'll write it on the board. Bio-elec-tro-gen-e-sis."

When Poulsen's back was turned, Ostin turned around and whispered, "What happened with Dallstrom? Did Jack get detention?"

I shook my head. "No, I got detention."

His eyebrows rose. "For getting shoved into your own locker?"

"Yeah."

"Dallstrom's a tool."

"*That* I know."

# 4

## The Cheerleader

That Wednesday felt like one of the longest days in school ever. I had no idea that it wasn't even close to being over. After the final bell rang, Ostin and I walked to our lockers, which were next to each other.

"Want to come over and play Halo?" Ostin asked.

"Can't. I've got detention, remember?"

"Oh, yeah."

"I'll knock on your door when I get home."

Ostin and I lived just two doors from each other in the same apartment building.

"I won't be home. I have clogging lessons at four."

"Ugh," I said. It was hard to imagine Ostin doing any physical activity, but dancing with a bunch of seven-year-old girls wearing black patent leather tap shoes was like a bad car wreck—gross, but you just have to look. "You've got to get out of that, man. If anyone here finds out, you're ruined for life."

"I know. But the clogging teacher's my mom's cousin and Mom says she needs the money and I need the exercise."

"It's still cruel," I said, shutting my locker. "I'll see you tomorrow."

He put out his fist. "Bones."

"Bones," I said, bumping his fist even though I was sick of doing it—I mean, it was okay the first *million* times.


The hallways were crowded with students as I walked with my backpack down to the lunchroom. Ms. Johnson, a young, new English teacher, had just been assigned to supervise detention, which I thought was a good thing. She was reputed to be cool and nice, which, I hoped, meant she might let us out early.

I walked up to her. I had to force myself not to tic. "I'm Michael Vey. I'm here for detention."

She smiled at me like I'd just arrived at a dinner party. "Hi, Michael. Welcome." She looked down at her clipboard and marked my name on her roll. "Go ahead and pick a table."

The smell of lunch still lingered in the air (which was a punishment of its own), and I could hear the lunch workers behind the metal window screens preparing for tomorrow's disaster.

There were three other students in detention: two boys and one girl. I was smaller than all of them and the only one who didn't look like a homicidal psychopath. As I looked around the room for a place to sit, the girl looked at me and scowled, warning me away from her table. I found a vacant table in the corner and sat down.

I hated being in detention, but at least today it wouldn't be a complete waste of time. I needed to study for Poulsen's test. As I got my books from my pack, I noticed that my shoulder still hurt a little from being crammed into my locker. I tugged on my collar and exposed a bright red scrape. Fortunately, I had gotten my fingers out of the way just in time to not have the door slammed on them. I wondered if anyone would call my mom about the incident. I hoped not. She had a stupid job she didn't like and I didn't want to make her day any worse than it already was.

Just twenty minutes into detention, Ms. Johnson said, "All right, that's enough. Time to go."

I scooped my books into my pack and threw it over my shoulder. "See you tomorrow," I said to Ms. Johnson.

"See you tomorrow, Michael," she said pleasantly.

Outside the cafeteria, the halls were now empty except for the janitorial crew that had moved in and were pushing wide brooms up and down the tiled corridors. I stopped at my locker and grabbed the licorice I'd stowed in there after lunch and had looked forward to all day. I peeled back its wrapper and took a delicious chewy bite. Whoever invented licorice was a genius. I loved licorice almost as much as Rice Krispies squares. I swung my pack over my shoulder, then walked out the south door, glad to finally be going home.

I had just come around the corner of the school when Jack and his posse, Mitchell and Wade, emerged from between two Dumpsters. Jack grabbed me by the front of my shirt. I dropped my licorice.

"You ratted us out to Dallstrom, didn't you?" Jack said.

I looked up at him, my eyes twitching like crazy. "I didn't tell him."

"Yeah, right, you little chicken." Jack shoved me backward into a pyracantha bush. Sharp thorns pricked my neck, arms, and legs. The only place that wasn't stinging was where my backpack protected me.

"You're going to pay," Jack said, pointing at me, "big-time." He turned to Mitchell, who was almost as tall as Jack but not as broad-shouldered or muscular. "Show him what we do to snitchers."

"I didn't tell on you," I said again. "I promise."

Before I could climb out of the bush, Mitchell pulled me up and thumped me hard on the eye. I saw a bright flash and felt my eye immediately begin to swell. I put my hand over it, trying not to lose my balance.

"Hit him again," Jack said.

The next fist landed on my nose. It hurt like crazy. I could feel blood running down my lips and chin. My eyes watered. Then Jack walked up and punched me right in the gut. I fell to my knees, unable to breathe. When I could finally fill my lungs with air, I began to groan. I couldn't stop blinking.

"He's crying like a baby," Mitchell said joyfully. "Cry, baby, cry."

Then came Wade. Wade West had yellow hair and a crooked nose. He was the smallest and ugliest of the three, which is probably why he was the meanest since he had the most to prove. "I say we pants him." This was a specialty of Wade's. By "pants" he meant to pull off my pants—the ultimate act of humiliation. Last year in eighth grade, Wade had pantsed Ostin behind the school, pulling off his pants and underwear in front of a couple dozen classmates. Ostin had to run home naked from the waist down, something he had never lived down.

"Yeah," Mitchell agreed, "that'll teach him for ratting us out."

"No!" I shouted, struggling to my feet. "I didn't tell on you."

Just then someone shouted, "Leave him alone!"

Taylor Ridley was standing alone near the school door, dressed in her purple-and-gold cheerleading outfit.

"Hey, check out the cheerleader," Wade said.

"You're just in time to watch us pants this guy," Mitchell said.

"Yeah, shake those pom-poms for us," Jack said, laughing like a maniac. Then he made up his own cheer, which was surprisingly clever for Jack. "Two, four, six, eight, who we gonna cremate?" He laughed again. "Grab him."

Before I could even try to get away, all three of them grabbed me. Despite the fact that my nose was still bleeding and I could barely see out of one eye, I went wild, squirming against their clamplike grips. I got one hand loose and hit Jack in the neck, scoring only a dull thud. He responded by thumping me on the ear.

"Come on, you wimps!" he shouted at Mitchell and Wade. "You can't hold this runt?" They pinned me facedown on the ground, the weight of all three of them crushing me into the grass.

"Stupid little nerd," Mitchell said. "You think you can rat on us and not pay?"

I tried to curl up so they couldn't take my clothes, but they were too strong. Jack pulled on my shirt until it began to tear.

"You leave him alone or I'll get Mrs. Shaw!" Taylor shouted. "She's right inside." Mrs. Shaw was the cheerleaders' adviser and taught home economics. She was a soft-spoken, matronly woman and about as scary as a throw pillow. I think we all knew that she wasn't actually inside or Taylor would have just gotten her in the first place.

"Shut your mouth," Jack said.

Hearing him talk that way to Taylor infuriated me. "You shut your mouth, you loser," I said to Jack.

"You need to learn manners, blinky boy."

"You need mouthwash," I said.

Jack grabbed me by the hair and pulled my head around. "You're going to be wishing you'd kept your mouth shut." He smacked me again on the nose, which sent a shock of pain through my body. At that moment something snapped. I knew I couldn't hold back much longer.

"Let me go!" I shouted. "I'm warning you."

"Ooh," Wade said. "He's warning us."

"Yeah, whatcha gonna do?" Mitchell said. "Cry on us?"

"No, he's gonna wipe his nose on us," Wade laughed. He pulled off my shoes while Mitchell grabbed my waistband and started tugging at my pants. I was still trying to curl up.

"Stop struggling," Jack said. "Or we're going to take everything you got and make you streak home."

"Leave him alone!" Taylor yelled again.

"Mitch, hurry and pull his pants off," Wade said.

A surge of anger ran through my body so powerful I couldn't control it. Suddenly a sharp, electric *ZAP!* pierced the air, like the sound of ice being dropped onto a hot griddle. Electricity flashed and Jack and his posse screamed out as they all fell to their backs and flopped about on the grass like fish on land.

I rolled over to my side and wiped the blood from my nose with the back of my hand. I pushed myself up, red-faced and angry. I stood above Jack, who was frothing at the mouth. "I told you to leave me alone. If you ever touch me again, I'll do worse. Do you understand? Or do you want more?" I lifted my hand.

Terror was evident in his eyes. "No. Please don't."

I turned and looked at his posse. Both of them were on the ground, quivering and whimpering. In fact, Wade was bawling like a baby and moaning, "It hurts . . . it hurts so bad."

I walked over to him. "You bet it hurts. And that was just a little one. Next time you bully me, or any of my friends, I'll triple it."

As the three of them lay there groaning and quivering, I sat back on the ground, pulled on my shoes, and tied them. Then I remembered Taylor.

I looked back over at the door, hoping she had gone inside. She hadn't. And from the expression on her face, I could tell she had seen everything. Bad, bad news. My mother was going to kill me. But there was nothing I could do about that now. I grabbed my backpack and ran home.

# 5

## Hiding the Evidence

By the time I got home, my left eye was nearly swollen shut. I set my backpack on the kitchen table, then went into the bathroom and looked at myself in the mirror. My eye looked like a ripe plum. There was no way of hiding it from my mother. I got a washcloth and wiped the blood off my nose and chin.

My mother usually got home around six thirty, so I heated up a can of SpaghettiOs for dinner, grabbed the blue ice pack she kept in the freezer for her occasional headaches, then held the ice against my eye while I played video games with one hand. I know I should have been studying for my biology test, but after a day like this one, I just didn't have it in me.

I really didn't want to talk to my mom about my day, so when I heard her key in the door, I ran to my room, shut the door, turned out the lights, threw off my shirt, and crawled into bed.

She called for me from the front room. "Michael?" Twenty seconds later she knocked on my door, then opened it. I pretended to be sleeping, but she didn't fall for it.

"Hey, pal, what are you doing in bed?"

"I don't feel well," I said. I pulled the covers over my head.

"What's wrong?"

She turned on my bedroom light and immediately saw my torn shirt on the floor and the blood on it. "Michael, what happened?" She walked over to my bed. "Michael, look at me."

"I don't want to."

"Michael."

Reluctantly, I pulled the covers down. Her mouth opened a little when she saw my face. "Oh my . . . what happened?"

A lump came to my throat. "Jack and his friends wouldn't leave me alone."

"Oh, honey," she said. She sat down on the side of my bed. After a minute she asked, "Did it . . . happen?"

I didn't want to tell her. I didn't want to upset her more than she already was. "I'm sorry, Mom. I tried not to. But they wouldn't leave me alone. They were trying to pull my pants off."

She gently brushed the hair back from my face. "Stupid boys," she said softly. I could see the worry on her face. "Well, they had it coming, didn't they?" A moment later she said, "I'm sorry, Michael. I wish I knew what to do."

"Why won't they just leave me alone?"

My cheek was twitching and she gently ran her thumb over it. Then she leaned forward and kissed my forehead. "I wish I knew, son. I wish I knew."

# 6

## The Morning After

**M**y radio alarm clock went off at the usual time: 7:11. I had my radio set to the *Morning Zoo* show. The hosts, Frankie and Danger Boy, were talking about people who suffered from bananaphobia—the intense fear of bananas.

I gently touched my eye. The swelling had gone down some, but it still ached. So did my heart. I felt like I had betrayed my mom and I worried that we'd have to move. Again. The thought of starting over filled me with dread. I couldn't imagine how hard it would be for her. I went into the bathroom and looked in the mirror. *You look pretty sorry*, I thought. I showered and got dressed, then walked out to the kitchen.

My mother was standing next to the refrigerator dressed in her orange work smock. She was a checker at the local Smith's Food Mart. She was making waffles with strawberry jam and whipped cream. I was glad, not just because I loved waffles, but because it meant she wasn't mad at me.

"How's your eye?" she asked.

"It's okay."

"Come here, let me see." I walked over to her, and she leaned forward to examine it. "That's quite a shiner." She pulled a waffle from the iron. "I made you waffles."

"Thanks."

I sat down at the table, and she brought over a plate. "Would you like orange juice or milk to drink?"

"Can I have chocolate milk?"

"Sure." She went back to the kitchen counter and poured me a glass of milk, then got a can of powdered chocolate from the cupboard and stirred some in. The sound of the spoon clinking against the glass filled the room. She brought the glass over to the table, then sat down next to me.

"So these boys who were picking on you . . ."

"Jack and his friends."

"Do I need to call their parents?"

"I don't think Jack has parents. I think he was spawned."

She grinned. "What about the other boys?"

"They crawled out of the sewer."

"So would it help if I called these sewer creatures' parents?"

I cut a piece of waffle and took a bite. "No. It would just make things worse. Besides, I don't think they'll be messing with me anymore."

"Do you think they'll tell anyone what happened?"

"No one would believe them anyway."

"I hope you're right." She looked across the table. "How are the waffles?"

"Good, thanks." I took another bite.

"You're welcome." Her voice was pitched with concern. "Did anyone else see what happened?"

"A girl."

"What girl?"

"She's in one of my classes. She was telling them to leave me alone when it happened."

The look of anxiety on her face made my stomach hurt. After a moment, she stood. "Well, I guess we'll just cross that bridge when we get to it." She kissed me on the forehead. "I better go. Want a ride to school?"

"No, I'm okay."

Just then there was a knock. My mom answered the door. Ostin stood in the hallway. "Hello, Mrs. Vey."

"Good morning, Ostin. You're looking sharp today."

Ostin pulled in his stomach. He thought my mother was a "babe," which made me crazy. Ostin was fifteen years old and girl crazy, which was unfortunate because he was short, chubby, and a geek, which is pretty much all you need to scare girls our age away. I have no doubt that someday he'll be the CEO of some Fortune 500 company and drive a Ferrari and have girls falling all over themselves to get to him. But he sure didn't now.

"Thank you, Mrs. Vey," he said. "Is Michael ready?"

"Just about. Come on in."

He stepped inside, dwarfed by the size of his backpack.

"Hey, Ostin," I said.

He looked at my black eye. "Dude, what happened?"

"Jack and his friends jumped me."

His eyes widened. "Did they pants you?"

"They tried."

"High school," my mother said. "You couldn't pay me a million dollars to go back." She grabbed her keys and purse. "All right. You boys have a good day. Stay out of trouble."

"Thank you, Mrs. Vey."

"See ya, Mom."

She stopped at the doorway. "Oh, Michael, we're doing inventory at the store today, so I'll be late tonight. I'll probably be home around eight. Just make yourself some mac 'n' cheese."

"No problem."

"You sure you don't want a ride?"

Ostin almost said something, but I spoke first. "We're fine," I said.

"Okay, see you later." She walked out.

"Your mom is so hot," Ostin said as he sat down at the table.

"Dude, shut up. She's my mom."

He pointed to my face. "So what happened?"

"Jack thought I ratted him out to Dallstrom. So he and his posse jumped me behind the school."

"Wade," Ostin said bitterly. "You should have just zapped him."

I put my hand over his mouth. "Shut up. You know you're not supposed to know."

"I know. Sorry." He looked over at the door. "She's gone anyway," he said. His face brightened. "Hey, I got the multimeter from my uncle so we can test you." Ostin had this idea about measuring how many volts of electricity I could generate, which frankly I was curious about too.

"Cool."

"Seriously, dude, I don't know why you hide your power. It's like having a race car you have to leave parked in the garage all the time. Why even have it? You could be the most powerful kid at school. Instead you get beat up."

"Well, Jack and his friends won't be bothering us anymore."

Ostin looked at me in surprise. "Did you do it?"

"Yeah."

"Cool! Man, I wish I had been there to see you hand down the righteous judgment."

I took another bite. "If you were there, you'd have a black eye too. If Wade didn't pants you first."

He frowned at the thought of it. "So does your mom know you used it?"

"Yeah."

"Did she freak?"

"Yeah. But she was cool about it. She's worried that someone might find out, but she doesn't want me to get beat up either. They started it. I just finished it."

"Speaking of, are you going to finish those waffles?"

"There's extra in the kitchen."

"Cool. My mom made gruel for breakfast."

"What's gruel?"

"It's punishment. Really, dude, it tastes like wallpaper paste. I think they feed it to prisoners in Siberian gulags."

"Why does she make it?"

"Because she ate it when she was a kid. But your mom's waffles . . . oh, baby. The only thing better than how she looks is her cooking."

"Dude, just stop it."

Ostin shook his head. "I was born in the wrong house." He threw two waffles on a plate and brought them over to the table, where he drowned them in a sea of syrup. "Did anyone else see you do it?"

"Taylor."

"Taylor Ridley? The cheerleader?"

"Yeah."

"What did she do?"

"She just stared."

"Wow. I wish I had been there." He took a massive bite of waffle, the syrup dribbling down his chin. "Did you study for our biology test?"

"A little. In detention. How about you?"

"Don't need to. It's all right here." He pointed to his head. Ostin had a 4.0 grade point average only because the scale didn't go higher. If his body matched his brain, he'd be Mr. Universe. "Do you have detention today?"

"I have detention for the next four weeks unless you can figure out a way to get me out of it."

"Maybe you should just shock Dallstrom."

"Only in my dreams."

Just then the front door opened and my mom leaned in. "Michael, can you give me a hand?"

"Sure. What's up?"

"Just come outside."

"Need some help, Mrs. Vey?" Ostin asked.

"You stay put, Ostin. I need to talk to Michael alone."

Ostin frowned. I got up and walked outside, shutting the door behind me. "What's wrong?"

"I left the car's dome light on all night and the battery's dead. Can you give me a jump?"

"Sure."

I followed her out of the building and across the parking lot to our car, a ten-year-old Toyota Corolla. She looked around to make sure no one was watching, then she climbed inside and popped the hood. I lifted it the rest of the way up, then grabbed the car battery's terminals. "Go ahead," I said.

The starter motor clicked until I pulsed (which is what I call what I do, pulse or surge) and the engine fired up. I let go of the battery. Mom raced the engine for a moment, then she stuck her head out the window. "Thanks, honey."

I shut the hood. "Sure."

"Have a good day."

She pulled out of the parking lot as I went back inside. Ostin was still at the table finishing his waffles.

"What was that about?" he asked, his mouth full.

"Car battery was dead."

"And you started it up?"

"Yeah."

"That is so cool."

"At least my electricity's good for something."

"It's good as Jack-repellant," Ostin said cheerfully.

I looked at him and frowned. "Stop eating. We're going to be late."

He quickly shoved in two more bites, then stood. I threw my pack over my shoulder, then Ostin and I walked the five blocks to school.

Meridian High School was the fourth school I had been to since we moved to Idaho five years earlier. On the first day of high school, my mother had said to me, "Don't get in trouble—and don't hurt anyone," which I'm sure would have sounded ridiculous to anyone who didn't know my secret. I mean, I'm shorter than almost everyone at school, including the girls, and I never started problems, except by being small and looking vulnerable.

When I was in the sixth grade at Churchill Junior High, a bunch of wrestlers put me in the lunchroom garbage can and rolled me across the cafeteria. It was chicken à la king day and I was covered with rice and yellow gravy with carrots and peas. It took five minutes before I couldn't take it anymore and I "went off," as my mother calls it.

I wasn't as good at controlling it back then, and one of the boys was taken to the hospital. The faculty and administration went nuts. Teachers questioned me, and the principal and the school police officer searched me. They thought I had a stun gun or Taser or something. They went through my coat and pants pockets, and even the garbage can, but, of course, they found nothing. They ended their investigation by concluding that the boys had touched a power cord or something. None of the wrestlers got in trouble for what they had done and all was forgotten. A few months later my mom and I moved again.

# 7

## The Cheerleader's Story

If you've ever had a black eye, you'll know what my day was like. Everyone just stared at me like I was a freak or something. By the end of the day I was walking with my head down and my eyes partially covered by a copy of the school paper—the *Meridian Warwhoop*. Still, the day wasn't all bad. I didn't see Mr. Dallstrom once, and there was no sign of Jack or his friends. I figured I had probably scared them off for at least a few days.

As I walked into biology, my last class of the day, I noticed Taylor Ridley staring at me. I ignored her gaze and sat down.

"Hey," she said. "Are you okay?"

I didn't look at her. As usual my tics started.

She leaned toward me. "Michael."

I didn't even know that she knew my name.

The tardy bell rang and Mr. Poulsen began walking up and down the rows of desks, handing out our tests.

"People, today's test comprises one-fifth of your final grade, so you don't want to rush it. I want complete silence. N'er a word. You know the penalty for cheating, so I won't elaborate, except to remind you that it's an automatic F and an unpleasant visit to Mr. Dallstrom." (*Is there any other kind?* I thought.) Mr. Poulsen walked to the front of the classroom. "When you're done with your tests, bring them to me, then go back to your desks and sit quietly."

I could see Ostin squirming in front of me, happy as a pig in mud. He loved tests. Sometimes, for fun, he'd download them from the Internet and quiz himself. Clearly something was wrong with him. I pulled out my pencil and began.

1. Which definition best describes a chromatid?
   a. Protein/DNA complex making the chromosome
   b. Molecules of DNA with specific proteins responsible in eukaryotes for storage and transmission of genetic information
   c. Five kinds of proteins forming complexes with eukaryotic DNA
   d. Each of a pair of identical DNA molecules after DNA replication, joined at the centromere

*D*, I thought. *D? Or is it A?* I was mulling over my answer when a folded piece of paper landed on my desk. I unfolded it.

*How did you do that?*

I glanced around to see who had thrown it. Taylor was looking at me.

I wrote back, *Do what?*

I looked up at Poulsen, who was at his desk reading a book, then threw the note back. Within seconds the note was on my desk again.

*You know. I saw you do something to those boys.*

I sent her another note.

*I didn't do anything.*

Taylor wrote back.

*You can trust me.*

I was writing another denial when I heard Mr. Poulsen clear his throat. I looked up. He was standing at the top of my row, staring at me.

"Mr. Vey. Those notes wouldn't have something to do with the test we're working on?"

I swallowed. "No, sir."

"Then you picked the wrong time to share your feelings with Miss Ridley."

I blushed while the class laughed. He walked toward me. I was blinking like crazy. "I think I was quite explicit about the rules. Hand me that note." I looked down at the paper. I couldn't give it to him. If he read it aloud everyone would know.

"Wait," Taylor said. "He didn't do anything. I was the one passing notes."

He looked at Taylor and his expression changed from stern disciplinarian to gentle educator. I think even he had a crush on her. "What did you say, Miss Ridley?"

"I wrote the notes, not Michael."

He looked at Taylor in disbelief. She was the model student, incapable of such a shameful act. Then, while he was looking at her, Taylor did the strangest thing. She smiled at Mr. Poulsen with a confident smile, then cocked her head to one side and narrowed her eyes. Suddenly Mr. Poulsen looked confused, like a man who had just been awakened from a nap. He blinked several times, then looked at Taylor and smiled. "Excuse me, what was I saying?"

"You said we have forty minutes left on our tests," Taylor said.

He rubbed his forehead. "Right. Thank you, Taylor." He turned back toward the class. "Everyone keep at it. You have forty minutes left." He walked back to his desk while everyone in our class looked back and forth at each other in amazement. I couldn't believe what had just happened. I looked back at Taylor.

"You can trust me," she mouthed.

It took me the whole class to finish the test. In fact, I ran out of time on the last three questions and just randomly circled letters. Ostin had finished the whole thing in less than fifteen minutes and strutted to the front of the room to turn in his test, unaware that the rest of the class was staring daggers at his back. For the rest of the period I could hear him sneaking cheese puffs from his backpack.

After the bell rang, Ostin and I walked out to our lockers.

"Man, that test was cake," Ostin said. "I can't wait for the next one."

"You're a freak," I said.

Suddenly Taylor grabbed my arm. "Michael, we need to talk."

"No we don't," I said. I kept walking, leaving her standing there.

Ostin looked at me in amazement. "Dude, that was Taylor Ridley you just brushed off."

I looked at him. "So?"

He smiled. "That was so cool."

Taylor ran in front of me and stopped. She looked at Ostin. "Excuse us, please."

"Sure," Ostin said, looking thrilled that Taylor had spoken to him.

After he'd taken a few steps back, she turned to me. "Please."

"I can't," I replied.

"I need to know," Taylor said. "I really, really need to know."

I just looked at her. "What did you do to Mr. Poulsen?"

"I don't know what you're talking about," she said, mimicking what I'd written to her on the note.

"You did *something*," I said. "I saw it."

"Really? Well, so did you."

"Nothing I can tell you about."

"Michael, please. It's important." She grimaced. "I'm begging."

"Dude, she's begging," Ostin said, forgetting that he wasn't supposed to be listening.

Taylor turned to him. "Excuse me," she said sharply.

Ostin wilted beneath her gaze. "Sorry." This time he crossed to the opposite side of the hall.

I looked at her for a moment, then said, "I'd get killed for telling you."

"No one will ever know. I promise." She crossed her chest with her finger. "Cross my heart."

I looked over at Ostin, who was still pretending not to listen. He shook his head.

Taylor looked at him, then back at me and sighed. "Michael, I *really* need to know. I promise, I'll never tell anyone." She leaned in closer. "I'll even tell you *my secret*." She just stood there, staring at me the way Ostin stared at jelly doughnuts. Then she put her hand on my arm. "Please, Michael. It's more important than you can possibly imagine."

She looked so desperate I wasn't sure what to do. Finally I said, "I couldn't tell you here anyway."

"We can go to my place," she said quickly. "I live just down the street. No one's home."

Ostin looked at me in amazement. I could guess what he was thinking. *Dude, Taylor Ridley just invited you to her house!*

"I can't," I said. "I have after-school detention."

"That's okay, I'll wait for you," she said eagerly.

"Don't you have cheerleading or something?"

"Only on Mondays and Wednesdays. And Fridays if there's a game." She looked deeply into my eyes. "Please."

Saying no to the girl you have a crush on is hard enough, especially when she's begging, but I had also run out of excuses. I exhaled loudly in surrender. "Where do you want to meet?"

Taylor smiled. "I'll just go with you."

"To detention?"

"I don't think they'll try to keep me out, do you?"

"I don't know. No one ever tries to get *into* detention. It's like breaking into jail."

Taylor smiled. "Then I guess we'll find out."

"Hey," said Ostin, who had inched his way back into our conversation. "What about me?"

Taylor looked at him. "What about you?"

"I'm Michael's best friend. Ostin," he said, eagerly putting out his hand. Taylor just looked at him.

"He's my friend," I said.

"What do you want?" she asked.

"I want to come with you guys."

"We can trust him," I said.

She looked him over, then turned back to me. "Sorry, but I can't."

I looked at Ostin and shrugged. "Sorry, man."

He frowned. "All right. See you guys later."

As Ostin walked away, Taylor turned to me. "Let's go, you delinquent."

We walked down the hall together, something I never thought would happen in a million years. I wondered if Taylor might be afraid to be seen walking with me—like her popularity quotient might fall a point or two (I wasn't sure how that worked), but she didn't seem to care. She must have said "Hi" about a hundred times between my locker and detention. As usual I felt invisible.

As we walked into the lunchroom Ms. Johnson looked at Taylor quizzically. Taylor was one of those students who was always the teacher's pet: perfect citizenship, always got her homework done, raised her hand to speak, never a cause of trouble. I once overheard a teacher say, "If only I could have a classroom of Taylors."

"Do you need something, Taylor?" Ms. Johnson asked.

"No, Ms. Johnson. I'm here for detention."

"I'm surprised to hear that." Ms. Johnson looked down at her clipboard. "I don't have you on my list."

"I know. I didn't get in trouble or anything. I'm just waiting for my friend Michael."

Ms. Johnson nodded. "That's very kind of you, being supportive of a friend, but detention isn't a place to hang out."

Taylor just looked at her with her big, soft brown eyes. "Please? I really think I can help him change his ways."

I turned and looked at her.

Ms. Johnson smiled. "Well, if you really want to help, I don't see why not. But you can't sit together. We can't have talking."

Taylor flashed a smile. "That's okay, Ms. Johnson. I've got a lot of homework to catch up on." She waved to me. "Be good." She sat down at Ms. Johnson's table, grinning at me.

I'm pretty sure that Taylor was the happiest person to ever go to detention. Frankly, I wasn't hating it too much myself. I couldn't believe that the best-looking girl at school was in detention waiting for me. The lunchroom was at least ten times more crowded than the day before, which meant that there was either a sudden outbreak of misbehaving, or Mr. Dallstrom had had a bad day. I was about to sit at the end of a long table near the back wall of the cafeteria when someone said, "Not there, tickerhead."

I looked up. Cody Applebaum, a six-foot ninth grader, was walking toward the table, sneering at me. "That's my side of the table."

I had no idea what a tickerhead was. "Whatever," I said. I walked to the opposite end of the table and sat down. I opened my algebra book, unfolded the day's worksheet, and began doing my homework. About five minutes into my studying something hard hit me in the head. I looked up at Cody, who was laughing. He had a handful of marbles.

"Knock it off," I said, rubbing my head.

"Knock it off," he mimicked. "Puny wimp. Go tell your mama."

Sometimes I felt like I was wearing a sign that said PICK ON ME.

I went back to my book. A few seconds later another marble hit me in the head. I looked up. Cody was now leaning against the wall on the back two legs of his chair. He raised his fist and bared his teeth like an angry baboon.

"Stop it," I said.

"Make me."

I went back to my studying. Less than a minute later another marble hit me in the head. As I looked up, I noticed a metal trim that ran along the wall where Cody was leaning.

I don't know why I did it—maybe I was still feeling great from finally putting Jack in his place, maybe it was the obnoxious smirk on Applebaum's face, or maybe it was that I was showing off for Taylor. But, most likely, it was the culmination of too many years of being bullied. Whatever the reason, I was done with playing the victim. I slowly reached back and touched the trim behind me and pulsed. Cody let out a loud yelp and fell back off his chair, smacking his head against the wall, then the floor. When Ms. Johnson stood up to see what had happened, Applebaum was lying on his back rubbing the back of his head.

"Cody! Quit screwing around."

He looked up from the ground. "Something shocked me."

"Right, Cody. I saw you leaning back on your chair," Ms. Johnson said. "One more outburst like that and I'm adding two days to your detention."

Cody climbed back into his chair. "Sorry, Ms. Johnson."

I looked over at Taylor. She was looking at me, slowly shaking her head. I shrugged.

Ms. Johnson let us out early again. On the way out of the cafeteria, Taylor said, "Nice spending time with you, Ms. Johnson."

"You too, Taylor." Ms. Johnson glanced over at me. "Hopefully your behavior will rub off on some of the other students."

"I hope so," she said.

Taylor laughed when we were out of the cafeteria. "Stick with me, Vey, maybe my behavior will rub off on you."

"Thanks," I said sarcastically. Actually I was happy to stick with her, but for other reasons.

As we walked down the hall, Taylor asked, "What did you do to Cody?"

"Nothing," I said.

"Same 'nothing' you did to Jack and his gang?"

I grinned. "Maybe."

"Whatever you're doing, you shouldn't do it in public like that."

"You should talk. Besides, Cody started it."

"It doesn't matter," Taylor said.

I turned to her. "It does to me. I'm sick of being picked on and doing nothing about it." I opened the door for her, and we walked out of the school.

"I know. But if you keep doing it, someone's going to figure it out."

"Maybe. Maybe not."

We walked toward the back of the schoolyard. "Where do you live?" I asked.

"It's just through that fence over there and two houses down. So, tell me about the other day when Jack was picking on you."

"You have to first tell me what you did to Mr. Poulsen."

Taylor nodded. "Okay. I'll tell you when we get to my house."

Taylor's house was a tan rambler with plastic pink flamingoes in the front yard and a small grove of aspens on the side. She took a key from her pocket and unlocked the door.

"No one's home," she said. She stepped inside, and I followed her. The house was tidy and nice, bigger than our apartment, but not by much. There was a large wood-framed picture of her family above the living room fireplace. She had two older brothers. Everyone in Taylor's family had blond hair and blue eyes except Taylor.

"Where's your family?"

"My parents are at work. My brothers are in college. I usually only see them on weekends."

"Where do your parents work?"

"My mom works for a travel agency that does educational tours for high school students. My father's a police officer." Taylor turned on the lights and led me to the kitchen. "Want some juice or something?"

"No thanks."

"Go ahead and sit down."

I sat down at the kitchen bar while she looked inside the fridge. I put my hand over my right eye, which was fluttering like a moth's wing.

"How about some lemonade?" she asked.

"Sure."

She poured us both a glass then sat down next to me. "Can I ask you something?"

"Sure."

"Why do you blink like that?"

I flushed. "I have Tourette's syndrome."

"Tourette's syndrome? You mean, like those people who shout out swear words for no reason?"

"That's Tourette's, but I don't do that. I do other things."

"Like blinking?"

"Blinking. Sometimes I make gulping noises. Sometimes I make faces."

"Why?"

I shrugged. "No one really knows why. Tourette's is a neurological thing, so it can affect any part of my body."

"Does it hurt?"

"Sometimes."

She thought it over. "Is it okay that I'm asking you about this? I'm not trying to embarrass you. I just thought, if we're going to be friends, I should know."

What she said made me happy. *If we're going to be friends* . . . "Yeah. It's okay."

Taylor stood. "Let's sit in the family room. You can bring your drink." We walked into the next room, then sat down next to each other on the sofa. I took a drink of lemonade and puckered. "Wow. That's sour."

"My mom must have made it. She makes it really tart." Taylor took a sip. "Yep, Mom."

I set down my glass.

"So," she said, lacing her fingers together, "are you going to tell me what you did to those boys?"

"You said you'd tell me your secret first."

Taylor smiled nervously. "I know I did, it's just . . ." She looked at me with her beautiful brown eyes. "Please. I promise I'll tell you. It's just easier if you go first."

There was something about Taylor that made me feel like I could trust her. "Okay," I said. "What did you see?"

"I heard a loud zap. Then I saw Jack and his friends rolling on the ground like they had been tased."

I shook my head. "That's pretty much what happened."

"How did you tase them?"

As I thought over how much I wanted to share, Taylor said, "My dad has a Taser. He also has a stun gun. He showed me how they work."

My mother had made me promise to never tell anyone about my electricity, but we had never talked about what to do if someone already knew. Or at least thought they did. "I don't know if I should say," I said.

Taylor leaned closer and touched my arm. "Michael, I understand. I really do. I've never told anyone my secret. But I'm tired of keeping this to myself. Aren't you?" Her eyes were wide with sincerity.

I slowly nodded. Ostin was the only person I'd ever told about my electricity, and telling him had been an incredible relief—like a hundred pounds falling off my shoulders. I slowly breathed out. "You know when people rub their feet on the carpet and build up electricity, then touch someone to shock them?"

"Static electricity," she said.

"Right. When I was little I would touch people and it would shock them like that. Except I didn't have to be on carpet. I could be on anything, and I didn't have to rub my feet. Only the shock was much worse. Sometimes people screamed. It got so bad that my mom made me wear rubber gloves. As I got older, it got more powerful. What I did to those boys was nothing compared to what I could have done."

Taylor set down her lemonade. "So you can control it?"

"Mostly. Sometimes it's hard."

"What does it feel like when you shock?"

"To me or them?"

She grinned. "You. I can guess how it feels to them."

"It's like a sneeze. It just kind of builds up, then blows."

"Can you do it more than once?"

"Yes. But I can only do it so many times before I start to lose energy. It takes a few minutes to build it up again."

"Do you have to touch someone to shock them?"

"Yes. Unless they're touching metal, like Cody was today."

She nodded. "That was actually pretty cool. Do you ever shock yourself?"

"No."

"How come?"

"I don't know. Electric eels don't shock themselves." I took another small sip of the lemonade and puckered.

"You don't have to drink it," Taylor said. "I won't be offended or anything."

"It's okay." I set the glass down. "Your turn. What did you do to Mr. Poulsen?"

A wide smile crossed her lips. "I rebooted him."

"You what?"

"You know, like rebooting a computer. I reboot people. I think it's an electric thing, too. The brain is just a bunch of electrical signals. I can somehow scramble them."

"That's weird."

"You're calling *me* weird?"

"I didn't mean it like that. I'm not saying you're weird."

"Well, I am. And so are you. I don't think there's anyone else in the world like us."

"Unless they're hiding it like us. I mean, I sat next to you in class and I never knew."

"That's true."

"When did you first notice that you were different?" I asked.

"I think I was around seven. I was lying in bed one night under the covers when I noticed that there was a bluish-greenish glow coming from my body."

"You have a glow?" I asked.

"Yeah. It's just faint. You can only see it in the dark and if you look closely."

"I glow too," I said. Hearing that she had the same glow made me feel good—like I wasn't so different. Or alone.

"That summer I was playing wizard with some friends and I cast a spell, only they fell to the ground and started to cry. At first I thought they were just pretending. But they weren't. They couldn't remember what they were doing."

"That's why Mr. Poulsen couldn't remember what he was doing," I said.

She smiled. "Yeah. It comes in handy sometimes."

"Does it hurt the person you reboot?"

She seemed embarrassed. "I don't know. It's not like I do it all the time. Want me to do it to you?"

"No. Do you want me to shock you?"

"No." She looked at me seriously. "You know, Michael, my parents don't even know about this. Do you have any idea how good it feels to finally tell someone?"

I nodded. "Yes."

She smiled. "Yeah, I guess you would." She lay back into the cushion. "So your parents know?"

"My mother does. My father passed away when I was eight."

"I'm sorry." Her expression grew more serious. "So what does your mother think of it?"

"I think it scares her. If she knew I was talking to you about it she'd be really upset."

"She won't hear it from me," Taylor said. "I wish I could tell my parents. I've tried a few times, but whenever I ask to talk to them they get nervous, like I'm going to tell them I've done something wrong. I guess I'm just afraid of how they'll react."

"You should tell them," I said.

"I know. Someday I will."

Taylor leaned forward and said in a softer but more excited tone, "There's something else I can do. Want to see it?"

"Sure."

She patted the sofa cushion next to her. "Come closer."

I scooted closer until our bodies nearly touched. I started gulping but stopped myself. "This isn't going to hurt, right?"

"No." She leaned toward me until we were touching. "Now think of a number between one and a million."

"One and a million? Okay." I thought of the last four digits of my phone number.

"Just keep thinking of the number." She reached over and took my hand. Suddenly a big smile came across her face. "Think of the number, silly, not me."

"What, you're reading my mind?" I asked jokingly. It wouldn't take a mind reader to know what I was thinking—the most beautiful girl at school was holding my hand. I focused on my number again.

"Three thousand, nine hundred, and eighty-nine," she said.

I looked at her in astonishment. "How did you do that?"

"I don't know. But I'm pretty sure that it's part of the same rebooting thing. I mean, it's all about electricity, right? Our thoughts are just electricity firing, so when I touch you, your thoughts show up in my brain as well—same projector, different screen."

Her explanation made sense. "So you can really read minds?"

"Yes, but not without touching. If I were to put my forehead against yours I could see even better."

*I wouldn't mind that,* I thought, forgetting that we were still holding hands. A big smile came across her face. I blushed and let go of her hand. "So all you need to do is touch someone?"

She nodded. "I've even been able to read people's minds if they're touching metal—like the way you shocked Cody." She leaned back again. "So what do we do now?"

"First, we need to promise never to reveal each other's power."

"We already did that," she said.

"Right. Second, I think we need to stick together."

She looked at me with a funny expression. I'm glad she wasn't touching me. After a moment she said, "That's a good idea. We should start a club."

"A club? With just the two of us?"

"Unless you know someone else like us."

"Ostin should be in our club. He could come in handy."

"Who's Ostin?"

"He's my friend. You just met him at my locker. He sits in front of me in biology."

"The know-it-all kid."

I nodded. "He's my best friend."

"Does he have powers?"

"No. But he knows a lot about science and electricity. He's really smart. Like mad scientist smart. His mother told me when he was only six years old, their DVD player broke. Before his father could take it in for repair, Ostin had taken it apart and fixed it."

"He's not too smart socially," Taylor observed.

"That's a different kind of smart."

"But can he keep a secret? Because no one can know about this."

"He's kept my secret since I told him."

"How long ago was that?"

"Almost three years. Besides, who is he going to tell? I'm his only friend."

Taylor didn't look completely convinced, but she nodded anyway. "All right, he can be in our club."

"We'll need to come up with a name," I said. "Every club has a name."

"You're right. How about . . . the Power Team."

I frowned. "No, too boring. How about, the Electric Eels."

"Yuck," she said. "Have you ever seen one of those? They look like fat snakes with acne. Besides, shocking people is your thing. You could call yourself Eel Man."

I didn't really care for the name, though I did like that she referred to me as a man. "And you could call yourself the Human Reset Button."

She shook her head. "Let's just stick with our real names."

"Okay. Besides, we don't have to come up with something right now. Ostin's good at this kind of thing. He'll have some good ideas."

We sat a moment in silence.

Taylor stood. "Would you like some more lemonade?"

"No, I'm good."

She looked at the clock above the television set and groaned. "My mom will be home in another half hour. You better go. My parents are kind of strict. I'm not allowed to have boys over when they're not here."

I stood. "I need to get home anyway."

She walked me to the door. "Thanks for coming over."

"You're welcome. When should we get together again?" I tried not to sound too eager. "For our club."

"When's good for you?"

"How about tomorrow night?"

"I can't, there's a basketball game. Aren't you going?"

"Right. I forgot." The truth was, I hadn't ever gone to a school game.

"How could you forget? It's the regional championship."

"I've just had a lot going on lately."

"How about Saturday?"

"Saturday's good during the day. But at night my mom and I are kind of celebrating my birthday."

"Saturday's your birthday?"

I nodded. "But we're really celebrating on Monday, since my mom has to work all day Saturday."

Taylor said, "My birthday is Sunday."

"Really? That's a coincidence."

Her brow furrowed. "Maybe it's not. We were born on nearly the same day and we both have electrical powers. Think about it. Maybe it had something to do with the stars being in alignment or something."

It may sound strange, but I had never considered why I had electrical powers any more than I had wondered why I had Tourette's. "If that's the case, then there would be tens of thousands of people like us," I said.

Taylor shrugged. "Maybe there are."

"I doubt it," I said. "Or we would have at least heard of a few of them. I mean, someone pops a zit and it ends up on the Internet."

"You're right." She thought some more. "Were you born here?"

I shook my head. "I was born in Pasadena, California. How about you?"

"I don't know. I was adopted."

Now I understood why Taylor looked so different from the rest of her family. "So, we'll get together Saturday?" I asked.

"Sure. But first I need to make sure my parents don't have plans. They've been on my back lately for being gone too much. I'll let you know."

"Great."

She opened the door for me. "Bye, Michael."

"See ya, Taylor. Thanks for the lemonade."

"You're welcome. Talk to you tomorrow."

After she shut the door, I took off running. I had just formed an exclusive club with Taylor Ridley. I didn't need to run. I could have floated the whole way home.

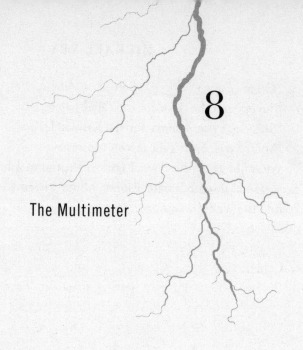

# 8

## The Multimeter

As soon as I got inside the apartment building, I knocked on Ostin's door. He opened it, his face bent in disapproval. "So how's the cheerleader?" he asked snidely.

"I know you're mad you got left out."

"What did you do, make out?"

"Shut up, Ostin. Do you want to come over or not?"

It took him two seconds to get over it. "Yeah, wait." He ran back into his apartment, then returned carrying a small yellow-and-black device and a notepad and pen. "Let's start our tests."

As he was shutting his door, Ostin's mom shouted, "Where you going, Ostin?"

"I'm going to Michael's."

"Be careful," she said.

Ostin looked at me and shrugged. His mom was a little protective. Actually she was a lot protective. I'm surprised she didn't make him wear a helmet to clogging.

"We're having dinner soon. Ask Michael if he wants to eat with us."

He looked at me. "Want to eat with us? We're having fish sticks."

"No thanks." I hate fish sticks.

He turned back. "He's not going to eat with us."

"Dinner will be ready by seven. Don't be late."

"Okay."

He shut his door while I walked down the hall and unlocked my apartment. As soon as we were inside, Ostin opened his notebook and clicked his pen. "All right," he said, using the tone of voice he used when he was doing something scientific. "First things first. Today is Thursday, the fourteenth of April. How are you feeling?"

"Why are you asking me that?"

"I want our experiment to be accurate, so try to be as specific as possible. Are you feeling more or less electric than usual?"

"I don't ever feel electric," I said.

"Okay. Usual," he said, scribbling in his notebook. "Weather is fair. I checked the barometer earlier and it's one thousand seventeen millibars and humidity is negligible." He brought the multimeter over to me, which looked a little like a fat calculator with cables attached. "Okay, clamp these on your fingers."

I looked at the clamps. "I'm not going to put those on my fingers. They're sharp."

"Do you want this to be accurate or not?"

I rolled my eyes. "Okay." I clamped the copper leads around my fingers. They bit into my skin.

"Now, don't do anything until I tell you."

"Just hurry. These things hurt."

"When I say 'go,' I want you to pulse with all your power. Five, four, three, two . . . wait."

"What?"

"I don't know. The screen on this thing just went blank." He pushed some buttons. "Okay. Four, three, two, one, *go!*"

I surged as hard as I could. The snap and crackle of electricity filled the room and there was a spark from my fingers to the clamps.

"Holy moley," Ostin said. He set down the multimeter and began writing in his notebook. "You produced eight hundred and sixty-four volts."

"That sounds like a lot."

"Dude, that's more than a full-grown electric eel. You could paralyze a crocodile with that." His eyes narrowed. "You could kill someone."

The way he said that bothered me. "I'm done," I said. I was taking the clips off my fingers when the front door opened and my mother stepped in. Ostin quickly hid the machine behind his back. I looked at her in surprise. "Mom. What are you doing here?"

"I live here," she said, looking at us suspiciously.

"But you said you were working late."

"You sound disappointed."

"No, I . . . I'm just surprised."

"I had a headache, so they let me come home early." Her eyes darted back and forth between us. "What's going on?"

"Nothing," I said.

"You were doing something. What do you have behind your back, Ostin?"

Ostin froze. "Nothing." His "nothing" sounded more like a question than a statement.

My mother walked up to him and put out her hand. "Let's see it."

He slowly took the multimeter from behind his back and handed it to my mom. She examined the device, then looked up at him.

"What does it do?"

He swallowed. I was hoping he'd make something up—calculate algorithms or something.

"It measures voltage."

"Voltage? You mean electricity?" She looked perplexed. "Why would you . . ." She stopped and looked at me. I could see anger change her countenance. "How long has Ostin known?"

I swallowed. "I don't know. A while."

"Thirty-four months and nine days," Ostin said.

*Shut up*, I thought.

My mother handed the multimeter back to Ostin. "You need to go home now, Ostin," she said. "I need to speak to Michael."

"Okay, Mrs. Vey," he said, eager to get out of our house. "Have a good night."

*Run, you wuss*, I thought.

After the door shut, my mother looked at me for what seemed like a year. Then she said, "Come here." I followed her over to the couch. "Sit."

I sat and she sat next to me. For a moment she just held her head in her hands. The silence was excruciating. Finally she looked up. "Michael, I don't know what to say to you. Do you know how hard this has been, moving away from our home and everyone we know in California, to come to a new city just so that no one would find out about you? I gave up a good-paying job at a law firm to be a checker at a supermarket."

I lowered my head. "I'm sorry, Mom."

"No, sorry doesn't cut it. Who else knows about this?"

"The boys yesterday. And Taylor."

"Who's Taylor?"

"The cheerleader who saw me."

"Did you see her at school today?"

"Yes."

"Did she ask you about what happened?"

I swallowed. "I went to her house."

My mother's eyes widened. "Please don't tell me that you talked to her about what happened."

I slowly nodded.

She threw up her hands. "Michael, what were you thinking? Now we may have to pick up and start over again. I am so tired, I don't know if I can do it."

My eyes welled up. "I'm sorry, Mom. I didn't mean to . . ."

"Michael, it doesn't always matter what you mean to do, it

matters what you do. Please, explain to me, why would you risk everything and tell them?"

For a few moments I just sat there silently. Then, suddenly, it all came out. "I'm sick of having everyone at school think I'm just some wimpy kid who makes funny faces and noises. I'm sick of being bullied all the time. And I'm sick of hiding who I am.

"Ostin is the only friend I have. He doesn't care about my Tourette's or my electricity. He just likes me for me." I looked up into her eyes. "I just want someone to know the truth about me and still be my friend."

She put her head down. Then she took my hand. "Michael, I know it's not easy being different. I don't blame you for feeling this way. It's just that most people can't understand your special gift."

"You think this is a gift, Mom? It's not. It's just another reminder that I'm a freak."

"Michael, don't say that."

"Why? That's what they call me."

"Who calls you that?"

"The kids at summer camp last June. They surrounded me and said, 'Let's see what the freak does next.' And they don't even know about my electricity, they were just talking about all my ticking and blinking."

Her eyes welled up with tears. After a moment she asked softly, "Why didn't you tell me?"

"Because you have enough to worry about."

She looked like she didn't know what to say.

"I'm just tired of everyone picking on me all the time for no reason except they think they can. I'm tired of knowing I could stop them and I don't. You know who I hate more than them for picking on me? I hate myself for letting them. I'm tired of being a nobody."

My mother wiped her eyes. "You're not a nobody, Michael. You're a great kid with a big heart." She kissed my forehead, then said, "I owe you an apology. I was wrong when I said that it doesn't matter what you meant to do. Sometimes we can't know what's right. We can only know that we meant to do the right thing—and that we had the right reason."

"How do we know if it's the right reason?"

My mother looked into my eyes, then said, "If love is our reason we may veer off course sometimes, but we'll never be lost." She put her arm around me. "Michael, I'm sorry for getting mad at you. I was just scared. Ostin's been a good friend, hasn't he?"

I nodded. "The best."

"And he's kept your secret?"

"Yes."

"Then I'm glad you told him. It's best to not keep secrets from our best friends." She crossed her arms at her chest. "Now tell me about this cheerleader."

"I think she's like me."

She smiled. "She likes you?"

"No, Mom, she's *like* me."

"What do you mean?"

"She has powers too."

My mom's expression changed. "What?"

"She showed me. It's been her secret too. She even glows like me."

"She can . . . shock?"

"Sort of. It's like she can shock people's brains. And she can read minds."

"Are you sure?"

I nodded. "She showed me."

She looked down for a moment, then softly said, "He said there might be others . . ."

"What?" I asked.

She shook her head. "Nothing. It's nothing. So, is she cute?"

"She's the cutest girl in the whole school."

"Work that." She smiled at me. "Why don't you go see if Ostin wants to go to Baskin-Robbins with us."

I smiled. "Okay, Mom." I stood and started toward the door.

"Michael."

I turned back.

"When I start thinking about all the hard things in my life, I think of you and I feel lucky to be me. I could not be more proud of you. And I know your father would be just as proud."

I walked back and hugged her. "I love you, Mom."

Her eyes moistened. "I love you more every day. Never forget that."

That night I had a double-decker ice cream at Baskin-Robbins—Bubble Gum and Pralines and Cream. Ostin had a triple-decker. My mother didn't have anything. She just kept looking at me and smiling.

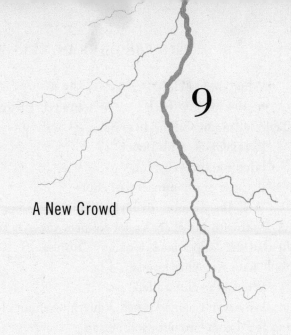

# 9

## A New Crowd

The next day I didn't see Ostin until lunch. I found him sitting where we always sat, at a small round table near the vending machines. It was pizza day and he'd gotten an extra slice. He waved to me. "Michael." I sat down at the table.

"Your eye's looking a lot better," he said.

"Thanks. Where were you this morning?"

"I had a dentist appointment."

"How'd it go?"

"It was just a checkup. Two cavities."

"Probably all the ice cream you ate last night," I joked. "At my last appointment I had three. I can only chew sugarless gum now." I opened my carton of milk. "So we're starting a club."

"Who?"

"Us. You, me, and Taylor."

"What kind of club?"

"It's for people with . . ." I hesitated. I hadn't told him about Taylor. "Unique abilities like mine."

"Excellent. So why Taylor?"

"I don't know. Why you?"

"Because of my intellect, of course."

"Well, there's more to Taylor than meets the eye."

"And with her there's a lot to meet the eye. Her superpower can be that she's super good-looking," Ostin said.

"That's not what I meant," I said.

"What's the club called?"

"We haven't named it yet. Something about electricity. I was hoping you'd come up with something."

"I'll put my computer on it," he said, tapping the side of his head. He took a bite of pizza. Before he'd finished chewing he said, "Hey, we get our tests back in biology today."

"Can't wait," I said sarcastically.

"How'd you do?"

"I don't know. B maybe. If I'm lucky." I didn't have to ask him what he was getting. We both knew he got an A. He could teach the class.

Just then one of the cheerleaders walked up to our table. There was a basketball game today and the cheerleaders always wore their outfits on game day. "Is this seat taken?"

Ostin's eyes were as wide as glazed doughnuts. "No."

"Good." She dragged the chair off to a nearby table.

"Any time, babe!" Ostin shouted after her. "Come back if you need another one. Got plenty of 'em. I'm your chair connection." He turned to me. "Did you see that? She spoke to me."

I nodded. "Yeah, I think that's going somewhere."

He took another couple of bites of pizza. "So what happened with your mom last night? First she's mad as a hornet and then she's taking us out to ice cream."

"She's just afraid that someone will find out about me. That's why we moved from California, you know. And our last apartment."

"Yeah."

"You haven't told anyone, have you?"

"Never."

"Good. Because I'd have to shock you if you did."

He looked at me anxiously. "You're kidding, right?"

"Like an electric eel."

He stopped chewing.

I punched his arm. "Relax, I'm kidding." Then I added, "Sort of."

Just then Taylor walked up to our table. She was also wearing her cheerleader outfit. She looked as pretty as ever. I could feel my tongue knot up, and I started blinking like crazy.

"Hi, Michael. Is this seat taken?"

"No, you can take it," Ostin said eagerly. "I'll even carry it for you."

She looked at him. "No, I mean, may I sit here?"

"Sure," I said. I couldn't believe she wanted to sit by us. She turned to Ostin, who looked like he might hyperventilate with excitement. "Dallas, isn't it?"

"Ostin."

"Right. I knew it was a Texas thing."

"I was just telling Ostin about our club," I said.

Taylor suddenly looked nervous. "Did you tell him anything else?"

"No," I said.

Ostin looked at us curiously. "Tell me what?"

"Nothing," I said.

"Nothing," Taylor said. She turned to me. "Remember when you asked me where I was born? You'll never believe what I found out."

Before she could tell me, two guys walked up to our table wearing letterman jackets. Spencer and Drew. They both played on the basketball team. They were two of the coolest guys at Meridian. "Hey, Taylor," Spencer said. "Whassup?"

She smiled. "Hi, guys."

They sat down at our table.

"This is my friend Michael," Taylor said. The taller of the two reached out his hand. "Hey, I'm Spencer."

The other guy just bobbed his head. "Drew."

"Hi," I said. Ostin looked starstruck.

"So are you guys nervous for the game?" Taylor asked.

"Nah," Spencer said. "It's just another game."

"Not hardly," she said to me. "It's the regional championship. The winner of this game goes to State."

Drew said, "Cottonwood's won their last three games. They have this forward who's on fire."

Ostin looked at him quizzically. "Literally?"

"What?"

"He's literally on fire?"

I kicked Ostin under the table.

Drew looked at me. "Where'd you get the shiner?"

"I got in a fight."

He turned to Taylor. "Hey, this isn't the kid you told us about who kicked Jack's butt?"

"That's him," Taylor said. "I watched him beat up Jack and two other guys. He has a black belt."

"You gotta be kidding me." Drew looked at me in awe. "Dude, you're legend."

I wasn't sure what to say. "Thanks."

"I'm Ostin," Ostin said.

Drew said to Ostin, "You gonna eat both those pieces of pizza?"

"Uh . . ."

"Great." Drew reached over and took one, shoving half of it into his mouth.

Then two more cheerleaders walked up to our table. "Hey, guys. Hi, Tay."

Taylor said, "Hi, Dom. Hi, Maddie."

"Hello, girls," Drew said. "Move over, Houston."

"Ostin," Ostin said.

The girls sat down between Drew and Ostin. Ostin had a blissful look on his face, like he was in heaven—a nervous heaven—but heaven all the same. I was anxious too. I kept turning away to blink, hoping no one would notice.

"We're having a party at Maddie's house after the game," Dominique said. "Are you all coming?"

"Yeah," Spencer said. "We'll be there."

"Can you come, Tay?"

"Yes." She turned to me. "Michael, you're coming to the game, aren't you?"

Her question caught me off guard. "Uh, yeah. Of course," I said. "Wouldn't miss it."

Ostin looked at me like I'd lost my mind.

"Great. You guys want to come to the party after?" Taylor asked.

"Sure," I said.

Taylor turned to the cheerleaders. "Guys, this is my friend Michael."

"Hi, Michael," Dominique said.

"Hi," Maddie said.

"That's Houston," Drew said, pointing at Ostin.

"Nice to meet you," Ostin said.

"Do you have something in your eye?" Maddie asked me.

I turned red. "Uh, no."

"You were just blinking kind of funny."

I wanted to crawl under the table.

"Michael has Tourette's syndrome," Taylor said.

"Oh, I thought you were, like, winking at me," Drew said.

"No. I can't help it."

"Is it, like, contagious?" Drew asked.

"Duh," Taylor said. "Is stupidity contagious?"

Drew looked genuinely baffled. "I don't know, is it?"

Spencer laughed. "You're such an idiot, dude."

"Sorry," Drew said to me.

"It's okay. I was born with it. It makes me blink and stuff."

Dominique said, "I have a cousin with—how do you say it?"

"Tourette's."

"Yeah, Tourette's. His name is Richard, but everyone in his neighborhood calls him King Richard, because he's, like, totally amazing on any board. Skateboard, snowboard, wakeboard—if it's a board, he can rule it."

"That's nothing," Drew said. "Mike here is a little Chuck Norris. The other day he beat up three guys twice his size. You should have seen it. It was awesome."

"That's so cool," Dominique said.

I glanced at Taylor. She grinned.

Ostin just sat and listened, so excited that he didn't seem to notice the loss of his pizza. When the second lunch bell rang, he popped up like a toaster pastry. "Gotta go," he said. "Lovely hangin' with you ladies."

No one at the table acted like they'd heard him.

"Hold on," I said, standing. "I need to go too."

"Hey, stay cool, man," Spencer said to me. "See you tonight?"

"Yeah. Good luck with your game."

"Spencer's made All-State," Taylor said. "He already has college scouts checking him out."

"That's really cool," I said.

He shrugged. "I throw a ball through a hoop. Nothing to it. See ya around, man."

Taylor stood up with me. She put her hand on my arm as we walked away from the table. "Sorry we crashed your table. I didn't plan on that happening."

"No, it's cool. I'm just not used to hanging out with those guys."

"What guys? Spencer and Drew?"

"Yeah. And the cheerleaders."

Taylor nodded. "You mean the popular kids."

"Yeah."

"They're no different than anyone else. Besides, they like you."

"Really?"

"Couldn't you tell?"

"No." I looked at her. "So why did you lie to them?"

"I didn't lie."

"You told them I'm a black belt."

"I told them you *have* a black belt. What's that around your waist?"

I grinned. "That's not what they thought you meant."

"Look, word's gotten out about what you did to Jack. I mean, you took out three kids twice your size. You think that's going to go unnoticed? I was just protecting your secret."

Another bell rang. Taylor sighed. "I've got to go. Can't be late to class. Look, I found out something I need to tell you, but I've got to run. We can talk at the party tonight."

"Okay," I said. "Wait, I don't know where your friend lives."

"You can go with me. Just meet me after the game."

"Where will you be?"

"Cheering." She lightly punched my arm. "See ya."

"Bye."

Ostin was waiting for me outside the cafeteria doors. "Dude, that was epic. Bones." He put out his fist.

I bumped it. "What was epic?"

"Our table became the cool table."

"Yeah. That was weird."

"And they love you. You're in with the in crowd. I can't believe Taylor is, like, all over you."

"No she's not."

"Are you blind? That hottie's got the hots for you, and she is H-O-T, hot."

"We're just friends," I said.

"Whatever, dude. Whatever. So are we really going to the game?"

"And the party after," I said.

"Wow," Ostin said with a broad smile. "What a day."

After school I walked down to the cafeteria but Ms. Johnson had canceled detention because of the game, so I headed home alone.

As I walked out the doors Jack, Mitchell, and Wade were standing there. My first thought was that they were waiting for me, but the surprise on their faces convinced me otherwise. My stomach churned with fear and anger.

Jack threw down the cigarette he was smoking. "What's up, man?"

he said. His tone was different from before—like we were now buddies or something.

I didn't say anything, but kept on walking.

"How did you do that?" he shouted after me.

I spun around. "Do what?"

"Electrocute us."

"You want another demonstration?"

Jack raised his hands. "We don't want any trouble," he said. "We're good, right?"

Wade took a slight step back, and Mitchell looked like he'd wet his pants if I said "Boo!"

"No, we're not good. I'm still on detention because I wouldn't tell on you guys. You need to talk to Mr. Dallstrom and fix that." I stepped toward them, suddenly feeling the liberation of having nothing to hide. I don't know if it was old anger or new confidence, but I said to Jack, "If I have to spend another week in detention . . . " I poked him on his chest and he jumped back, probably anticipating another shock.

"Okay. I'll tell Dallstrom it's my fault."

"Good, because if I have another week of detention, I'm coming after you." I turned to Mitchell. "And you." Then I turned my whole body toward Wade. "And especially you. And if you think it hurt last time, next time you're going to think you were struck by lightning. You understand?"

"Hey, no prob, man," Wade said, his voice quivering.

"We're cool," Mitchell said.

"We better be," I said, turning from them. As I walked away, a large smile crossed my face. I just couldn't help it. I couldn't remember the last time I'd felt that good.

Ten minutes later I knocked on Ostin's door and he answered. "Hey, you're back early."

"They canceled detention. So, can you go to the game?"

"Yeah. My mom was so excited she almost fainted. She said, 'Finally you're doing something normal.'"

"Just be sure to wear your clogging shoes," I said.

"They're tap shoes."

I hit him on the arm. "Just kidding. I'm going home. I still haven't asked my mom. I'll call you in a couple hours."

When my mother got home from work, she hung her sweater in her room, then started boiling water for spaghetti. "So what do you want to do tonight?"

I had been excited to tell her about the game, but now that she was home I was afraid to ask her. I suppose I felt a little like I was letting her down. "I thought maybe I'd go to the school basketball game," I said uneasily. "If it's okay with you."

She turned to me and smiled. "That sounds fun."

"But then you'll be alone."

"I think I can handle that. Do you want me to pick you up when the game's over?"

"Well, we've been invited to a party afterward. It's at one of the cheerleaders' houses."

She looked at me. "So, last night you had no friends, and today you're getting invited to cheerleader parties. What was in that ice cream?"

"It's Taylor."

"She's the cheerleader?"

"Yeah. She's kind of becoming a friend."

I don't know the last time I saw my mother smile that wide. "Is she nice?"

"She's really great." I looked at my mom. We had spent every Friday night together since we moved to Idaho. "You sure you're okay alone?"

She dropped the pasta into the pot. "Are you kidding?" she said, winking at me. "I'm just glad to finally get you out of my hair. Do you know how many books I have to catch up on? Just call when you're ready to leave the party, and let me know where to pick you up."

I smiled. "Thanks, Mom." I gave her a hug. I love my mother.

Neither Ostin nor I had ever been to a school basketball game before. We sat near the floor at one end of the gymnasium. Ostin looked as out of place as a Twinkie in a salad bar. I panned the floor for Taylor, but I couldn't see her.

"These metal bleachers are bruising my butt," Ostin said. "How long do these things last?"

"You're too soft," I said, still looking for Taylor.

"Your girlfriend's over there," Ostin said, pointing to a flock of cheerleaders on the other side of the floor.

"She's not my girlfriend."

"Yeah, right," Ostin said.

I waved to Taylor several times, but she didn't see me. Or at least she didn't act like she did.

The game was close. At halftime, Meridian was down by five points. The drill team had come out to do their thing when I saw Taylor walk over to our side of the gym.

"Taylor!" I shouted.

She didn't even look up. Then she walked up to the end of our bench, where Tim Wadsworth was sitting. Tim Wadsworth was the guy every girl at Meridian dreamed of. He had perfect skin, golden hair with a soft curl, straight teeth, and a body that would make a Greek Olympic statue envious. Mr. Perfection was flirting with Taylor or vice versa. I couldn't tell. As I watched her I got madder and madder. He was holding a Coke and talking to her. Then she took a drink from his cup.

Without even thinking about it I surged.

There were at least twenty people on the bench and they all jumped up at once, like they were doing the wave. Tim also jumped, spilling his Coke all over himself. At first Taylor just looked confused, then she looked down the bench and saw me. She glared.

"Why'd you do that?" Ostin asked, rubbing his butt. "That really hurt."

"Let's get out of here," I said.

We walked down to the floor and started to leave the auditorium when Taylor shouted, "Michael!" I turned around. She stormed up to me, her eyes snapping. She glared at Ostin. "Texas boy, leave."

"Okay," Ostin said, quickly walking away.

She turned back to me. "What was that?"

I was twitching like crazy. "None of your business."

"It is my business when you act stupid and start drawing attention to yourself."

"You're one to talk. You're always the center of attention."

"I'm talking about drawing attention to your power."

"Is it really that you're worried about or is it Tim Wadsworth?"

"Tim Wadsworth?" Her expression softened. "Oh, I get it. You're jealous that I was talking to him."

"No, I'm not."

"Yes, you are."

"No, I'm not."

She smiled. "Hey," she said sweetly, putting her arms out. "Come here." I couldn't believe she had gone so quickly from wanting to hit me to wanting to hug me, but I didn't really understand girls at all. I just went along with it. "You know, Michael . . ."

Touching her felt really wonderful. "Yes?"

Suddenly she pushed me back. "Ha, you are jealous."

She had hugged me just to read my mind. "You tricked me."

"Yeah, well, you just shocked a whole row of people. The custodian is under the bleachers looking to see if there's a loose wire or something."

"Well . . ."

"That's all you have to say?"

Frankly, I didn't know what to say. Suddenly she started to laugh. She was soon laughing so hard she was crying. I just watched her. I was totally confused. "This is so crazy," she said. "Could you imagine if these people around here could hear what we're saying?"

"They'd think we're nuts."

"You should have seen Tim's face when you shocked him. He had Coke dripping from his hair." She looked into my eyes. "I don't remember the last time I had this much fun. I'm so glad I've gotten to know you."

"Me too," I said.

She exhaled. "Well, I've got to get back to cheering or Mrs. Shaw will have my head. But you and Dallas are still coming to the party with me, right?"

"Ostin," I corrected.

"Sorry, I keep getting that wrong."

"Yeah, we'll come. If you still want us."

"Of course I do. It will be fun. Besides, I really have to talk to you about what I found out."

"Great. Where should we meet?"

"Just come down to the floor after the game. See ya." She took a few steps and then stopped. "By the way, you're a lot cuter than Tim Wadsworth."

She spun around and ran back to the floor. I don't know. It may have been the greatest moment of my life.

# 10

## A Suspicious Coincidence

The end of the game was pretty exciting. Meridian was ahead by just one point with three seconds left on the clock when they fouled Cottonwood's best player, sending him to the line to shoot free throws. He must have been pretty nervous because he missed both of his shots badly—one of them by at least ten feet.

Everyone went wild. After the game Ostin and I walked down to the floor. Taylor was surrounded by a couple dozen friends, but she smiled when she saw me. "Ready to go?"

I nodded.

"Angel's dad is going to give us a ride to Maddie's."

"Me too?" Ostin asked.

"Of course."

The four of us walked out to the parking lot. Angel was a pretty Asian girl, and Ostin just stared at her until it was embarrassing.

Finally she stopped and turned to him. "What?"

"Ostin," he said, putting out his hand to shake.

She looked at his hand, then slowly put out her own. "I'm Angel."

"Are you Chinese or Japanese?"

Her brow furrowed. "Chinese."

"Were you born in China?"

"Yes."

He nodded. "What brought your parents to America? Opportunity? Freedom of speech?"

"My parents are American," she said. "I was adopted."

"Oh, you're adopted."

I wanted to smack him.

"Sorry, Angel," I said. "Ostin doesn't get out much."

"Hardly ever," he said.

She shook her head. "It's okay."

"And I think you're the prettiest girl in the world," Ostin blurted out.

"Enough," I said to him.

Angel smiled.

Maddie's home was the last on a long, tree-lined street called Walker Lane, where the rich kids in our school lived. I think her home could have fit our entire apartment building in it and still have had room for an indoor swimming pool, which, by the way, it had. It was the first party I'd been invited to since we moved to Idaho, unless you count Ostin's last birthday party, which was only me and his obnoxious cousin, Brent, who only came because his aunt made him. Brent broke a beaker in Ostin's new chemistry set within five minutes of Ostin opening the box. I thought Ostin would have a mental breakdown.

Angel's dad drove a nice car, a BMW with leather seats the texture and color of footballs. I knew it meant nothing to these kids to ride in a car like that, but I thought it was really cool. So did Ostin. He was grinning like a Cheshire cat, though it also may have been because he was sitting next to Angel. When Mr. Smith dropped us off, I said, "Thank you, sir."

He smiled. "It's nice to see that not everyone's lost their manners. You're welcome, son."

As we walked up to the house Taylor took my arm. "Well played."

"What do you mean?" I asked.

"Nothing," she said. "You're a real gentleman."

The stairway to the house was lined with little pointy trees growing in ceramic pots. I stopped at the door. I don't always notice my vocal tics, but I was gulping loud enough to get Taylor's attention.

Taylor looked at me. "You okay?"

I stopped gulping. "Yeah. I guess I'm just a little nervous."

"It's cool. Don't worry about it. We're just here to have fun."

I took a deep breath. "All right."

She opened the door and we were met by a rush of music and light. The house was filled with kids. Maddie, one of the cheerleaders we'd met at lunch, was standing by the door talking to several basketball players. The only one I knew was Spencer.

"Hey, Tay!" Maddie shouted. The girls hugged. They did a lot of that.

Spencer looked over. "Hi, Taylor."

"You were awesome tonight, Spence!" she said.

"Yeah," I said. "You were awesome."

"Thanks, little dude."

Maddie looked at me and cocked her head. "What's your name again? Trent? Trett?" I suddenly realized that she was thinking Tourette's.

"No. It's Michael."

"Michael. I wonder why I thought it was Trett."

"And I'm Ostin," Ostin said.

She didn't even look at him.

"You have a nice house," I said.

"Yeah." She patted my arm. "Well, have fun." She flitted off.

Ostin was clinging to me like lint to a belly button—at least until he spotted the food table. "Hey, hold the phone, I'll be right back."

Taylor turned to me. "Hold whose phone?"

"It's just a saying. He found the food."

"Good. They'll be happy together."

A moment later Ostin returned carrying a plate brimming with potato chips and brownies. "This stuff is great."

"I see you've made yourself at home," Taylor said.

"My home is nothing like this."

"Would you like a drink?" I asked Taylor, surprising myself at how formal I sounded.

She reciprocated my tone. "Why yes, kind sir. Thank you."

"Come on, Ostin," I said.

On the way to get a soda, Ostin said to me, "I never thought I'd be invited to a party at a place like this."

"I never thought I'd be invited to a party," I said.

The food table was in the middle of a luxurious dining room where lit wall insets held porcelain statues spaced evenly between large, original oil paintings mostly of fruit bowls. In the center of the food-laden table was a large tub of ice, packed with bottled water and cans of soda. Drew walked up to me.

"Hey, it's little Chuck Norris. Give me some," he said, raising his hand.

"Hey, Drew," I said. I set down the cup and we high-fived, clasping hands as we did. He fell to one knee pretending I had him in some kind of kung fu grip. "Don't hurt me, man," he laughed. "Don't hurt me."

I chuckled nervously. "Hey, congrats on the game. You guys played really well."

"We dodged a bullet, man. Cooper is their best free-throw shooter and he tossed two bricks in the last three seconds. We were lucky."

Living alone with Mom, I had never engaged in small talk about sports, so I wasn't sure if I was doing it right. "Well, you know what they say about being lucky . . ."

Drew looked stumped. "No. What do they say?"

"It's better to be lucky than good."

He looked at me for a moment, then laughed. "You're all right, little dude."

"Hi," Ostin said.

"Hey, what's up, Houston?"

"Nothing," Ostin said, trying to sound cool. "Just hanging."

"Houston, we have a problem," Drew said, then burst out laughing at himself.

Just then a mountain of flesh named Corky walked up behind Drew. Corky was the size of a small planet and had an entourage of girls who moved around him like satellites. I knew who Corky was only because he was always being called up onstage at the school assemblies for winning some award or another. The last thing he'd won was the State Heavyweight Wrestling Championship. He took Drew in a choke hold, then released him. "Drew-meister, what gives?"

"Just hanging around the oasis with my little black-belt friend."

Corky looked me over. My head barely came to his chest. "This isn't the guy you were talking about."

"He's the man," Drew said. "Little Chuck Norris."

"He's a shrimp."

"Only on the outside," Drew said. "On the inside he's a powder keg of pain, just waiting to explode on someone."

Corky laughed. "You're pulling my leg, aren't you? I could crush him like a bug."

"I'd like to see that," said Drew. "Battle of the Titans."

Corky pointed a massive finger at me. "You're talking about the little guy?"

Drew put his arm around me. "This is exactly who I am talking about."

He looked at me incredulously. "C'mon, little guy," he said, gesturing for me to follow him. "Let's go outside and spar a little. I want to see what you got."

Drew laughed. "He'll mess you up, dude. I'm not kidding."

"I've got to see this," one of the girls said.

"I really can't. I've got to get Taylor a drink," I said.

"She won't die of thirst," Corky said. "C'mon, I won't hurt you. We're just playing around."

Just then Taylor walked up. "Hi, guys. Hi, Cork." She looked around. "What's going on?"

"Corky wants to engage the little dude in hand-to-hand," Drew said. "Called him out."

Taylor looked at me, then back at Drew. "What?"

Ostin translated. "He heard about Michael's fight with Jack and he wants to see what Michael can do."

"Black belt or not, I'm going to crush him," Corky said.

Taylor glanced over at me with a look that said: *How do you get yourself into these things?* Then, to my surprise, she said, "Awesome. Let's do it." She looked around, then shouted, "Everyone outside! Michael's going to take down Corky!"

I couldn't believe what she was saying. As we walked out amid the river of bodies, I whispered, "Are you trying to get me killed?"

"Trust me."

"That you will get me killed?"

"No, I'm trying to get you out of this mess."

The house emptied as everyone poured out of the house into the backyard. Corky started cracking his knuckles. Ostin grabbed my shoulder. "Dude, you know you can't use your power."

"I know."

"He's going to kill you."

"I know."

Taylor walked to the front of the crowd as if she were the master of ceremonies. "Okay, so here's the deal. First one knocked to the ground loses. Fair enough?"

"Fair enough," Corky said, bobbing a little.

"Taylor . . . ," I said.

She reached into her pocket. "And here's a twenty-dollar bill that says Michael's going to put Corky on his back. Any takers?"

Everyone looked at each other, but to my surprise, no one was willing to bet against her. I mean, the guy could wad me up like a piece of paper and shoot me out a straw. Taylor looked at Corky. "C'mon, Corky. You're going to crush him, right? Where's your money?"

He looked at her hesitantly. "I don't have my wallet . . ."

"In fact, let's make it sweeter. The loser has to wear my skirt to school on Monday."

I looked at her. Now I was sure she was trying to get back at me for shocking Tim at the game.

". . . All day," she continued. "And, he has to carry the other's books and tie his shoes."

To my surprise Corky was suddenly looking very nervous.

"Come on, Corky," Taylor said. "He's half your size. On the other hand, there's only one of you. The last time I saw him, he had three guys on their backs begging for mercy. It was the most amazing thing I've ever seen." Taylor turned back to face the crowd, who had formed a half circle around them. "Who wants to see Corky wearing my skirt on Monday?"

A large cheer went up. I noticed that Corky was sweating. "Hey, I was just kidding around. I don't want to hurt the little guy. Cool?"

I breathed out a sigh of relief. "Cool."

Just then Drew stepped in. "Arrgh," he said in his best pirate, "them be fightin' wards, matie. Wards yu'll be a regrettin'. Li'l Norris be so tough he can kick the back side 'a yar face."

Everyone laughed, which started a barrage of Chuck Norris jokes.

"Little Norris is so tough, when he does push-ups he doesn't push himself up. He pushes the earth down."

"Little Norris is so tough, he can lead a horse to water *and* make it drink."

"Spiderman owns a pair of Little Norris pajamas."

"Little Norris is so tough he can make onions cry."

"What's the matter, Corky?" someone shouted. "Chicken?" Then someone started a chant: "Vey, Vey, Vey."

Now Corky couldn't back out—he'd never live it down. There was no way around it; we were going to spar. It was a classic David and Goliath scenario, except I couldn't use my slingshot. I was going to get killed.

Taylor sidled up to me. "That didn't go the way I thought it would."

"Really?" I said.

"It's not so bad."

"How is this 'not so bad'?"

"Well, no one expects you to beat him. So if you lose, you'll look brave for fighting a monster. And if you somehow win, you'll be a legend."

"I feel much better now," I said sarcastically.

She looked at Corky, then back at me. "Wait. I've got another idea."

"I can't wait to hear it."

"When I say 'go,' run into him as hard as you can and try to knock him down."

"Are you kidding me? He's a freakin' brick wall."

"Trust me."

"I did."

"Trust me again."

"Let's go!" Corky shouted impatiently. "Let's get this going."

"All right," Taylor said, stepping away from me. "When I say 'go,' come out fighting. Ready . . ."

Corky's eyes narrowed into small slits as he leaned forward on the balls of his feet, squaring off the way he did before a wrestling match. After the razzing Taylor gave him, I don't think he was going to hold back.

"Get set . . ."

His fists balled up. I swallowed and tried not to look overly terrified—just a little terrified. I was certain he could smell my fear.

*Don't panic*, I told myself.

"Go!"

I took off running at him, feeling like a pitched baseball about to be smacked out of the park. Shouting like a madman, I slammed into him with everything I had, my face buried into his very solid abs. To my amazement he stumbled backward and fell, crashing to the ground in an azalea bush.

"Yeah!" shouted Drew, running to Corky. "I told you, man! Little Norris rules."

I lifted myself up. Corky was still on his back, covered in white flower petals and looking dazed. Drew pointed his finger in Corky's face. "I warned you, don't mess with the little Norris. The kid's got sweet moves."

The truth is, I was more surprised than anyone, including Corky. I put my hand out to lift him up, which he fortunately ignored, since I'd need a car jack to lift him. He slowly climbed to his feet, wiping off his backside. "Good job, kid."

Taylor walked up to him. "I'm not letting you wear my skirt," she said. "You'll stretch it. But it looks like you'll be carrying Michael's books."

I waved it off. "No," I said, "we were just messing around. He could have crushed me like a bug. Thanks for taking it easy on me."

Corky, still confused about what had happened, looked at me and nodded. "Hey, no problem. I don't know where you learned that junk, but you're pretty good."

Drew put his arm around me. "He's the man. You gotta start hanging out with us, Little Norris."

The crowd gathered around me. A pretty girl with long black curly hair walked up to me. I knew her from math class but she had never acknowledged my existence. "Hi, Michael. I'm Chantel. That was so cool," she said, her brown eyes locked on mine.

"Thanks."

"What school do you go to?"

"Meridian. I'm in your math class."

"Really? I've never seen you."

"I sit right behind you."

"Oh," she said, blushing a little. "Lucky me."

Taylor grabbed my arm. "Come on, Michael."

"We'll catch up later," I said to her.

She smiled and waved. "See you in math."

Everyone was giving me high-fives and patting me on the back as Taylor dragged me off.

"Why do I have to go?" I asked.

"So you don't get a big head," Taylor said.

"Where are we going?"

"Where no one will hear us. Come on, Ostin."

"You got my name right," he said.

We went back inside. Ostin grabbed another brownie from the table and the three of us went upstairs to a bedroom. Inside, Taylor locked the door behind us.

"Where'd you learn that move?" Ostin asked. "That was awesome. You took down gorilla-man without your powers."

"It wasn't me," I said. I looked at Taylor. "Was it?"

She sat down on the bed. "It was sort of you. You did knock him down."

Ostin's eyes darted back and forth between us. "What did she do?"

"The same thing she did to Mr. Poulsen. She rebooted him. Didn't you?"

"What?" Ostin said.

I looked at Taylor. "Can I tell him?"

She rolled her eyes. "You just did."

"Well, you showed him first."

"What are you talking about?" Ostin said, looking back and forth between us.

"Taylor has powers like mine," I said.

Ostin's jaw dropped. "She can shock like you?"

"Not exactly. She can shock people's brains."

"What?"

"She can reboot people."

I didn't have to explain "reboot" to Ostin—he was all about computers. "Ah," he said, a large smile crossing his face. "Like pressing the reset button. I get it. That's why Poulsen looked like he'd been sucker-punched. I just thought he had a brain tumor or something. Then how did you knock Corky over?"

"I didn't, Michael did. I just rebooted him a second before Michael crashed into him. He didn't even know where he was."

"That's awesome!" Ostin said.

"No, it's not," I said. "She shouldn't be using her powers in public like that. Someone will figure it out."

"I know." She looked down, covering her eyes with her hands.

"I need to confess something." She looked up at me. "But first, you need to promise me that you won't get mad, okay? I feel bad enough about it."

"What did you do?" I asked.

"Promise me."

"All right. I promise."

"I won the basketball game for us. At least I might have."

"What do you mean?"

"I rebooted that guy as he was shooting his free throws. That's why he missed so badly."

"That's just wrong," Ostin said.

I looked at her in disbelief. "After what you said to me at the game? What happened to not using our powers in public?"

"I know. I just didn't want to lose. I'm such a hypocrite. I, like, ruined that guy's life."

Ostin started pacing. "People, we need to keep this under control. That's why we need the club, to set standards." His mouth spread in a broad smile. "And I have a name for our club. The Electroclan."

"What's an Electroclan?" I asked.

"It's just a name," Ostin said. "The electro part is self-evident. A clan is a group of people who all have the same . . ."

"I like it," Taylor said before he finished. "It's catchy."

"I told you he was good at this," I said.

I could tell by his crooked smile that Ostin was feeling pretty good about himself. First Taylor had remembered his name, now she liked the name he'd come up with for the club. "Now we need bylaws and a mission statement."

"What kind of bylaws?" Taylor asked.

"Like, for instance, who we can tell about our powers," Ostin said.

"Which would be *no one*," I said.

"And when we can use our powers," Ostin said.

"That's easy for you," Taylor said. "You don't have powers."

"Yes I do. Advanced intellectual powers."

"They're not electric."

"You're wrong. Technically, all thinking is electric. The brain con-sists of about a hundred billion cells, most of which are neurons whose primary job is shooting electrical impulses down an axon, and—"

"All right," I said, "we get it."

"So, I'm just as powerful as . . ." He suddenly looked down, then over at me. "What was I saying?"

I looked at Taylor and she grinned.

Ostin turned red. "You rebooted me, didn't you?"

"Well, you're just so powerful."

"You can't do that," he said. "You don't know if that damages someone's brain. It could burn brain cells."

"Relax, Ostin," I said. "You've got plenty to burn." I turned to Taylor. "He's right, you know. We shouldn't be using our powers on each other."

"I was just fooling around."

"All right," I said. "Rule number one: No using powers against each other."

"And we need a mission statement," Ostin said, though this time not quite as confidently.

"We need a mission," I said.

"I think I have one," Taylor said, moving closer to me. "To find out why you and I have powers. I've discovered something that might be important."

I sat down on the bed next to her. "What?"

"Okay, you were born in California, right?"

"Pasadena."

"Get this . . . so was I."

"Really?"

"I asked my parents. I was born at Pasadena General Hospital. So I went online and tried to find our birth records. They have the records of births for the last forty-two years. In all that time just eleven days are missing. Guess which days."

"Our birthdays?" I ventured.

"Exactly," Taylor said.

"That's weird," I said.

"Statistically, an improbability," Ostin said. "You two born at the same hospital nearly the same day with the similar mutant variation."

"Mutant variation?" I said.

"For lack of a better term."

"Find a better term," Taylor said. "I like power."

"Clearly," Ostin said, loud enough for us to hear.

"I mean the word *power*. We have similar powers." She looked at Ostin. "I'm not a mutant."

"Technically," Ostin said, "you are."

"Yeah, well, you're a geek."

"Doesn't change the fact that you're a mutant."

"If you say that again I'm going to reboot you."

I stood up. "Stop it, you two. Ostin, quit calling us mutants or I'll shock you."

He blanched.

"Why would the records be hidden?" I asked.

"Same reason I hide my diary from my mother," Taylor said.

"Because you'd get in trouble if she found it," I said. I smiled at Taylor. "I think you're onto something."

"Except we've hit a dead end," she said. "The records are gone."

"There's more than one way to skin the proverbial cat," Ostin said, still sounding a little abused. "The county recorder's office will have vital statistics for . . ."

"Can you even speak English?" Taylor said.

"Excuse me. The government has records of all the deaths and births during that time period even if the hospital doesn't."

"Excellent," I said. "So we just look up those births and see where they lead."

"I'll do it," Ostin said. "I'll look them up and analyze them for our next club meeting. When should we meet again?"

"You have your birthday party tomorrow," Taylor said, "and I have mine on Sunday. Monday I have cheerleading practice. How about Tuesday?"

"Works for me," Ostin said. The only thing Ostin ever had on his calendar was clogging and the Discovery Channel.

"Good with me," I said. "Then the first meeting of the Electroclan is hereby adjourned until next Tuesday."

"Good," Ostin said. "I hope there's some of those brownies left."

The three of us walked back downstairs. I glanced at my watch. It was around ten thirty. I said to Taylor, "I need to call my mom for a ride home."

"Don't you have a phone?" she asked.

I felt embarrassed. "No. Things are kind of tight right now."

"You can use my cell phone," she said. She flipped it open and handed it to me. I pushed the buttons, but the screen kept dissolving into static. "What's wrong with your phone?"

She looked at it. "I don't know, nothing was wrong with it earlier. Let me try it." I handed it back. She pushed a few buttons. "It's fine. Maybe it's you."

"Maybe you better dial."

"What's your number?"

"Two-zero-eight, five-five-five, three-nine-eight-nine."

She dialed the number. After a moment she said, "Hello, Mrs. Vey, this is Taylor Ridley. I'm calling for Michael." I put my hand out for the phone, but she didn't surrender it. "Thanks, we're having a good time." Long pause. "That sounds really fun. When are you doing it? Okay. I think that will be fine. I look forward to meeting you too. Here's Michael." She handed me the phone with her hand over the mouthpiece. "Your mom invited me over tomorrow night for cake and ice cream."

"You're coming?"

"If it's okay with you."

"Sure." I put the phone to my ear. "Hi, Mom. Yeah, that's okay. Sorry, I just have a bad connection. Well, it's just me, okay. We're over on Walker Lane. Walker Lane. It's the last house. You can't miss it, the house is huge. Okay. Bye."

I handed Taylor her phone. "That's so weird," I said. "I've never had that problem before."

"Maybe your electricity is increasing," Taylor said.

"Tomorrow, we'll check your voltage again," Ostin said.

I felt like an old car battery when he said that.

Ostin said to Taylor, "Hey, if you're coming over to Michael's, we can have another meeting."

I looked at Taylor.

"Fine with me," she said.

"Fine with me," I said.

Ostin smiled. "Great. Bones." He put out his fist.

I put out my fist.

"I don't do that," Taylor said.

I admired how easily she'd gotten out of that. I'd have to remember to do that next time.

# 11

## Birthday Wishes

Saturday morning my mother got up early and made my second favorite breakfast: hot chocolate and crepes, both of them topped with whipped cream and chocolate syrup. My birthday was the one time of year that my mother said nothing when I filled my plate with more whipped cream than crepe.

She made herself a simple crepe with butter and powdered sugar then sat down next to me. "I'm sorry I have to work today. Are you sure you're okay with celebrating after school on Monday?"

"I don't care what day we celebrate," I said with my mouth full.

"And we'll have cake and ice cream tonight. Do you and Ostin still want to go to the new aquarium on Monday?"

"Yeah. And can we go to PizzaMax for dinner?"

"Whatever you want. It's your day." She smiled at me and her eyes got all sparkly. "I can't believe you're fifteen. Another year and you'll be driving. You've grown into such a fine young man. I am so proud of you."

My mom always got emotional on my birthdays. "Watermark moments," she called them. Whatever that means.

"Thanks," I said.

"Wait, I have a present." She ran out of the room and came back a moment later carrying a small rectangular box wrapped in tissue paper. "I know we usually wait until we have cake to open presents, but I wanted to give this to you now. It's special."

I pulled off the wrapping to expose a dark blue velvet box. I opened it. Inside was a man's watch.

"Wow."

"It was your father's," she said.

I lifted it out of the box, admiring it.

"Do you like it?" she asked.

"A lot. It's cool."

"Well, you're a man now, so I wanted to give you something special. Turn it over; there's something on the back."

I turned the watch around. It read, I LOVE YOU FOREVER—MOM.

"I had it engraved," she said.

I hugged her. "Thanks, Mom."

"You're welcome."

I couldn't imagine a better gift. I wanted to tell her that she was the best mother in the world. I didn't. I should have.

# 12

## The First Meeting

About an hour after my mother left for work, Ostin knocked on my door. He was carrying the multimeter and his notebook. He noticed the can of whipped cream on the counter. "Dude, did you have crepes?"

"Yes."

"Any left?"

"In the fridge. You can microwave them."

He heated up the remaining crepes, then piled them high with powdered sugar and whipped cream while I played a video game.

"That was a cool party last night," he said.

I nodded, intent on my game. "Yeah, it was."

"Especially when you knocked Corky over."

I didn't say anything.

"Taylor's really a babe. You know she likes you."

"She likes everyone."

"I don't mean it like that. I mean she *likes* you. I read this book on body language. And I was watching her body."

"Yeah, I bet you were."

"No, for scientific purposes."

"I bet," I said.

When he'd finished eating the last of the crepes, he came over to the table. "Okay, let's see if there's been a change in your electrical status."

I paused the game. After the cell phone incident I was curious to find out myself. "Let's do it."

"Wait, what's that?" he said, pointing to my new watch.

I held up my arm. "It's a watch my mom gave me this morning for my birthday."

"What's it made of?"

"I think silver."

"Hmm," he said. "Silver has high conductivity, even more than copper. That's why they use it in satellites and computer keyboards." Ostin always vomited up everything he knew about a subject.

"So?"

"Well, you should probably take it off. It might throw off our readings."

"All right." I unclasped it and laid it across the kitchen counter. Then I clipped the multimeter's cables to the ends of my fingers.

Ostin looked down at the machine. "Ready? Three, two, one, go!"

I surged.

Electricity sparked from the copper ends. "Whoa!" Ostin cried. He set down the machine and began scribbling in his notebook.

I unhooked the clips. "What was I?"

"Dude, you're not going to believe it."

"What?"

"This thing goes to a thousand volts and it's saying ERROR. You're definitely becoming more electric."

I sat down on one of the kitchen bar stools and put my watch back on. I wondered what that meant: more electric. "Do you think it will stop?"

"I don't know. No wonder Taylor's cell phone didn't work." He set down his notebook. "So is Taylor really coming over for cake and ice cream?"

"She said she was. Then afterward we can have our first official meeting of the Electroclan."

"That's sick," Ostin said. "Real sick."

Ostin and I played video games most of the day except when we took a break and walked to the 7-Eleven for Slurpees.

Around five o'clock Ostin's dad came and got him for dinner. After he left I made myself macaroni and cheese again, then lay on the couch and read from one of the books I'd been assigned in my English class—*Lord of the Flies*. I read until Ostin came back an hour later. We still had time for a few games of Halo before my mother got home.

Mom got home at the usual time, a little after six thirty. I could tell from her eyes that it had been a hard day. Still, she smiled when she saw me. She was carrying a chocolate butter-cream cake from the supermarket's bakery. "I got your favorite cake," she said as she walked in. "Hi, Ostin."

"Hi, Mrs. Vey. How was work?"

"It was work," she replied. She set the cake down on the counter. She looked at the multimeter but didn't say anything about it.

"Did you boys get some dinner?" She spotted the dishes in the sink and the pan still on stove. "Oh, you did. Mac and cheese."

"Sorry, I didn't do the dishes," I said. "I got distracted with the game."

"That's okay, it's your birthday."

While my mother was changing her clothes, the doorbell rang.

"Michael, would you get that?" she shouted from her room.

"Got it, Mom."

I paused the game, then opened the door. Taylor stood in the hall-way holding a wrapped package. I immediately started blinking.

"Happy birthday," Taylor said. She held out the present. "This is for you."

"Wow. Thank you." I felt dumb that I hadn't gotten her anything. "Come in."

"Thanks."

Ostin stared in awe, as if we'd just received an angelic visitation, which wasn't far from the truth.

"Hi, Tex," she said.

I knew she was kidding, but I don't think Ostin did. He was a genius about everything but girls.

"Hey, Taylor," he said. He'd pretty much given up on correcting everyone. As he was fond of saying, "I don't care what you call me as long as it's not late to dinner." I think he meant it.

My mother walked out from her room. She smiled when she saw Taylor. "You must be Taylor," she said.

"Hello," Taylor said. She walked up and shook my mother's hand. "It's so nice to meet you."

"It's nice to meet you, too." My mom glanced over at me standing there, holding the wrapped package.

"Taylor brought me a present," I said.

"How thoughtful. Michael, will you get the ice cream from the freezer?"

"Sure."

My mom led Taylor over to the table. I hoped she wouldn't interrogate her, but, of course, she did.

"So Ridley's an interesting name. Is it Scottish?"

"No, it means 'cleared woods' in Old English. So I'm like a vacant lot."

My mother laughed. "Have you lived around here for a while?"

"I've lived in the same house my whole life."

"Do you have any brothers or sisters?"

"I have two older brothers. They both go to college. So it's kind of like being an only child."

"Well, we're happy you could come tonight. Just go ahead and sit down, and I'll get the cake."

"Thank you, Mrs. Vey."

My mother walked back into the kitchen, where I was scooping ice cream into bowls. "What a cute girl," she whispered to me. "Well done."

"C'mon, Mom. She's just a friend."

My mom just smiled. She put sixteen candles on the cake—one extra for good luck—lit them, and carried the cake to the table.

The three of them sang "Happy Birthday" to me, and we sat around the table for the next hour and talked and laughed. Taylor and my mother really seemed to hit it off.

I was surprised at how talkative Taylor was. She even told us her favorite birthday story. "When I was five, my mom made this *Beauty and the Beast* cake with all these plastic trees and they caught on fire so we had a big forest fire on our kitchen table until my dad blew it out with the fire extinguisher. He's a little extreme that way. It put out the fire but ruined the cake, so my mom ended up putting candles on Twinkies."

We all laughed except for Ostin, who, no doubt, would have done the exact same thing as Taylor's dad.

"When is your birthday, Taylor?" my mom asked.

"Sunday."

She turned to me. "Michael, why didn't you tell me? This should have been a joint party."

"It's just cake," I said.

Taylor said, "So, Michael, are you going to open my gift?"

"Yes." I peeled the paper back, then opened the box. Inside was a black hoodie with our school's name printed on the front.

"Do you like it?" Taylor asked. "I thought you could, like, wear it to the games."

I held it up. "It's awesome. Thanks."

"Cool," Ostin said. "My birthday is in October."

My mother smiled. "That's a very sweet gift."

Taylor grinned happily. "It's nothing."

We sat around and talked until nine, when my mother started gathering up the dishes. "I think I'm going to call it a night. Taylor, do you have a ride home?"

"My dad's going to pick me up."

"Well, it was very nice meeting you. I hope we'll be seeing you again."

She smiled. "Thank you, Mrs. Vey. I'm glad you invited me."

"You're very welcome. Good night, Ostin."

"Good night, Mrs. Vey. Thanks for the cake."

My mom walked over to me and kissed my forehead. "I love you. Happy birthday."

"Thanks, Mom. I love you too."

She walked off to her bedroom.

When she was gone, Taylor said, "Your mom is really nice."

"She's a babe," Ostin said.

"Dude, she's my mother. You've got to stop saying that."

"Sorry."

Taylor laughed. "Well, she is. I hope I'm that hot when I'm a mom."

I wished my mother had heard what Taylor said. Lately she had been saying that she thought she looked old.

Ostin said, "So, let's get our meeting started. Who's going to call it to order?"

I looked at Taylor.

"I think you should be the president," she said to me.

"Why me?"

"Because I said so."

"I second that," Ostin said.

Somehow her reasoning seemed a little ironic, but I wasn't about to fight her on it. "Okay, I call the first meeting of the Electroclan to order." I looked at Taylor. "Now what?"

"We need to follow up on our last meeting."

"We need minutes," Ostin said.

"No more than thirty," Taylor said. "My dad's coming to pick me up."

"No, minutes is what they call the notes from the last meeting," I said.

Ostin rolled his eyes.

"Sorry," she said.

Ostin started. "In our last meeting Taylor shared her discovery that you were both born in the same hospital in Pasadena, California, a very unlikely coincidence. Then Ostin pointed out that the fact that both of you having this mutan—"

Taylor looked at him and he stopped.

". . . power is a statistical improbability. And third, the hospital records of said hospital, for the eleven days around your birth dates beginning April sixteenth, appear to have been conveniently expunged."

Taylor looked at me. "Does he always talk like this?"

"Pretty much," I said. "*Expunged* means erased." I only knew because Ostin loved using that word. "Thanks, Ostin."

"I have something very important to add to the record," Ostin said.

"Go ahead," I said.

"I discovered something very disturbing. During those eleven days there were two hundred and eighty-seven births in Pasadena County."

"What's so disturbing about that?" Taylor said.

Ostin looked at her. "May I continue?"

"Sorry."

"Fifty-nine of those babies were born at Pasadena General Hospital, where you two were born. As I looked over the records, I came across something very, very peculiar." He paused just to make sure he had our attention. "Forty-two of the children born during that time didn't live more than two days."

"What?" Taylor and I said almost in unison.

"I checked the same time period the month before and there was *only one* baby that didn't live."

"Forty times the number of . . . ?" I couldn't say it.

"That is so sad," Taylor said. "Did it say what happened to them?"

"Unknown causes." Ostin scratched his head. "But it gets stranger. Only seventeen of the babies born at Pasadena General lived, and that includes you two."

I leaned forward on my chair. "You're saying that out of fifty-nine births only seventeen babies survived?"

"Precisely." Ostin knit his fingers together. "It couldn't be a coincidence. A forty-two-hundred-percent increase in death in an eleven-day period and the records of those eleven days disappear. I'm guessing that whatever caused those deaths has something to do with whoever destroyed the records."

"We need to find out what was different about those eleven days," Taylor said.

"My thinking exactly," Ostin said. "Just give me a few days to get to the bottom of it."

Ostin told Taylor about my most recent voltage test and a few minutes later we adjourned our meeting. A little after nine thirty, Taylor's dad called from our parking lot and I walked her out. Her father was driving his police cruiser, which seemed to me kind of strange, as I always just thought that police cars were for picking up bad guys, not your kid. I guess I had never known anyone who had a police officer for a parent.

Taylor's dad looked pretty tough. His window was down and his arm was hanging out of it. He smacked the side of the car as we approached.

"Dad, this is Michael."

"The birthday boy," he said. "Why aren't you in your birthday suit?"

Taylor rolled her eyes. "Dad, why do you try to embarrass every boy I'm with?"

He leaned back into the car. "It's my job."

"Sorry about that," Taylor said. "He loves to harass boys. When I'm old enough to date he's going to be a nightmare."

"It's okay," I said. "Thanks for coming over. And for the gift. It was really cool."

"Thank you for inviting me." She smiled. "Actually, I guess I should thank your mom."

"She's braver than I am," I said. "Hey, we're going to have my real birthday party Monday after school. We're going downtown to the aquarium and then out for pizza. Want to come?" Somehow the invitation sounded dumb as it left my mouth.

"I'd love to."

"Really?" I guess I was still getting used to the idea that she liked being with me. "We're leaving around four thirty."

She frowned. "I'm sorry, that won't work. I have cheerleading until five."

"We can wait," I said.

"Are you sure?"

"We could even pick you up at school."

"That sounds good. You sure it's okay with your mom?"

"She'll be thrilled. I can tell she likes you."

Taylor smiled. "Okay. I'll see you at school." She climbed into the patrol car. "Thanks again."

"Have a happy birthday tomorrow," I said.

"Thank you. Good night."

"Good night, Mr. Ridley," I said.

"Night, Michael."

Her father drove off. The police car's siren chirped, then its lights flashed for just a second. Taylor waved to me from the back window. Hands down it was my best birthday ever.

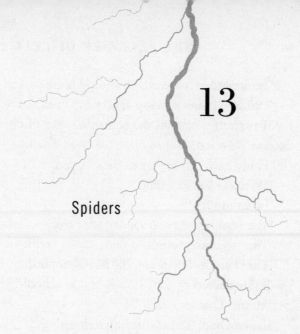

# 13

## Spiders

I've never cared much for Mondays. If I were the king of the world, I'd have Mondays removed from the calendar. Of course the problem in that is that Tuesday would become the new Monday, which would defeat the purpose. Then again, if I were king of the world I probably wouldn't hate Mondays. Notwithstanding, this was one Monday I was looking forward to. I was celebrating my birthday with my mom, Ostin, and Taylor at PizzaMax. What could be better than that?

As I suspected, my mother was thrilled to hear I had invited Taylor, though I'm not sure if she was more excited that Taylor was coming, or that I had actually gotten up the courage to ask her. We were eating breakfast when I said, "So we need to pick Taylor up at the school, okay?"

My mother smiled. "No problem."

"I was thinking I should get her a present. Do you know what girls like?"

She smiled at me wryly. "I should hope so, I'm a girl."

"I know. I mean one my age."

"Trust me, we're all the same. We like clothes and jewelry. And flowers."

"I only have twenty-six dollars," I said.

"Does she have an iPod?"

"I think so."

"You could get her an iTunes gift card. We have them at the store."

"That's a cool present," I said.

"That way every time she listens to a song she bought with it she'll think of you."

"Mom."

She laughed. "I'm just trying to help."

Ostin had another dentist appointment that morning, so after breakfast my mom dropped me off at school. I can't believe the difference a weekend can make. Somehow I went from zero to hero. People I didn't even know said hi to me in the hall, and the basketball team, who previously didn't know I existed, had taken to calling me "Little Norris." I'd be lying if I said I didn't like it.

That afternoon I was standing in line for hot lunch when Ostin marched up to me. "Dude, we need to talk."

"Hold on, I'm getting my lunch."

"This is more important than food."

Those were words I never thought I'd hear from Ostin's mouth. "You're serious."

"As a heart attack, dude. And we need Taylor."

I looked around. "I don't know where she is."

"She's over there," he said, pointing across the crowded lunchroom. That's when I first realized Ostin had Tay-dar. I don't know why he was so much better at finding her than I was, but he definitely was. Taylor was sitting at a table with five other girls. "You need to get her. Now."

"You go get her," I said.

"She won't come with me. She doesn't even remember my name."

"Yes she does. She's just teasing you."

"You're the president of the Electroclan," he said. "It's your responsibility."

I wondered what good it was being president of something if you're always being told what to do by the members. I relented. "All right."

"I'll meet you in the courtyard."

I left the lunch line and walked up to her table. Taylor was in the middle of telling a story, and one of the girls nudged her when she saw me approach. Taylor looked up at me. "Hi, Michael."

I felt awkward with all the girls looking at me. I did my best not to twitch. "Uh, can I talk to you?" I fumbled for an excuse. "About biology."

She looked at me quizzically. "Sure. What's up?"

"Can I talk to you in private?"

"Wooo," one of the girls said.

"Shut up, Katie," Taylor said, standing. "I'll be right back." We stepped away from the table.

"What's going on?"

"Ostin says he needs to talk to us. He says it's important."

"Important?"

"He skipped lunch to talk to us."

"It must be important. Where is he?"

"He's in the courtyard."

We walked together to the school's outer courtyard. Ostin was sitting alone on a bench, a little hunched over as if hiding. He stood when he saw us. He was clutching a piece of paper.

"Hi, Ostin," Taylor said. "What's up?" Had he not been so grim I think he would have been overjoyed that she got his name right.

"Everyone sit down," he said gravely.

We sat on both sides of him.

"Remember our last meeting? We were wondering about what might have happened around those days you were born."

"The eleven days," I said. "When all the babies died."

"Exactly. What I did was look through the newspaper for anything out of the ordinary that began the day or week before April sixteenth. Everything looked pretty usual until I found this." He held up a sheet of paper. "It's a newspaper article from the *Los Angeles Times*."

He read it out loud.

> PASADENA—Scientists from Elgen Inc., an international medical equipment provider, announced today the discovery of a new method of body imaging, which they claimed will "render current MRI (Magnetic Resonance Imagery) technology obsolete."
>
> The new machine, called the MEI (Magnetic Electron Induction), was created at a cost of more than $2 billion and, according to its developers, "has the potential to deliver benefits of diagnosis and treatment once considered an impossibility." Dr. C. James Hatch, Elgen Inc.'s CEO, said, "This new technology will have the same effect on current medical technology that the X-ray machine had at the turn of the 19th century."
>
> Current MRI technology uses radio waves to generate images of organs and tissues. In closely guarded technology, the MEI creates electrically charged molecules that are 1,200 to 1,500 times more visible than current MRI readings. This method is the first of its kind to employ electrons to create an enhanced view of the body.
>
> "This new technology will benefit every known discipline of medicine and possibly many that have not yet been pioneered," said Dr. John Smart, one of the machine's inventors and professor emeritus at Harvard Medical School. "This technology may very well pave the way to new disciplines in health studies."
>
> The MEI technology has received FDA approval for limited human testing and is currently being installed in Pasadena General Hospital. Human testing is planned to begin April 16 of this year.

Ostin set down his paper. "Now here's the clincher. Twelve days later a small article ran in the *Times* saying that the MEI experiment had been temporarily suspended due to some minor technical malfunction."

"Hmm," I said. "What are the odds that all those babies started dying the day the machine was turned on and ended the exact same day they turned it off?"

"Impossible odds," Ostin said. "Crazy impossible. The machine must have something to do with it."

"You mean they put all those babies through the machine?" Taylor asked

"No, they wouldn't do that. I'm guessing that something went wrong and the machine's waves traveled through the walls."

"And if the machine was somehow responsible for those deaths," Taylor said, "the people who owned the machine wouldn't want others to find out about what happened to all those babies or they could be sued for millions."

"Hundreds of millions," Ostin said.

"Wow," Taylor said. "Think about it, they've been hiding this from the public for fifteen years. If they knew that we knew . . ."

"That," Ostin said, looking even more worried, "is why I needed to talk to you." He turned to Taylor. "How did you look up those first hospital records?"

"On the Internet."

"Where?"

"On my computer," Taylor said.

"At home?"

"Yes. Why?"

He combed his fingers back through his hair. "I was afraid of that."

"What's wrong with that?" I asked.

"Hopefully, nothing. But they might have set up spiders."

Taylor asked, "What's that?"

"Spiders comb the Web looking for references to certain topics or inquiries. They could have programmed their computer to alert them whenever someone looks up a certain topic."

"Such as birth records at Pasadena General during those eleven days," I said.

Ostin nodded. "Exactly," he said breathlessly. "You need to clear off anything on your computer connected to that search, cookies and everything. If they track you down . . ."

"What would they do?" Taylor asked.

"They've already killed forty people. With more than two billion dollars of research at stake, who knows?"

Taylor suddenly blanched. "Oh no."

"What?"

"Something happened Saturday while I was at your party. What was the name of that company again?"

"Elgen Inc."

Taylor suddenly looked pale. "Meet me at my locker." She sprinted off toward the building. She had already opened her locker by the time we caught up to her. She pulled out a glossy, trifold brochure and handed it to me. The piece looked like a recruitment brochure for some kind of fancy school. The cover of the brochure had a picture of well-dressed, smiling students walking in front of a beautiful building.

Taylor said in a hushed voice, "This guy came over Saturday night and met with my parents. He said he was from a very special school in Pasadena, California. He told my parents that nationally this school only selects seventeen students a year and that I had been recommended by an anonymous source for entry. They said it was the most prestigious boarding school in the country and those who attended were guaranteed a full-ride scholarship to the university of their choice: Harvard, Yale, anywhere.

"My parents were way excited, but told him that they could never afford the tuition. The man said not to worry about it, that they were offering me a full scholarship, including books, room, and board. All I had to do was show up."

Ostin looked jealous. "But you're only in ninth grade."

"That's what my parents said, but the man claimed that starting their students young is one of the reasons their students are so successful and that any student enrolled in their school could pretty much name their college and salary. My parents told him they needed to think about it, because they didn't want me to be away."

"What's the name of the school?" I asked.

"The Elgen Academy of Pasadena."

"Elgen?" I looked again at the brochure.

Taylor looked afraid. "What have I gotten myself into?"

"You've got to erase everything off your computer as soon as you can," Ostin said.

I shook my head. "If it's them it's already too late for that. You better tell your mom and dad."

"Tell them what? That their daughter has superpowers and some big corporation is hunting her down?"

"If that's what it takes," I said.

She leaned back against her locker and slid down until she was sitting on the ground. Her eyes began to fill with tears. I sat down next to her. Without looking at me she said, "I'm scared."

"Listen," I said. "My mother has been in tough spots before. She'll know what to do. We'll pick you up from cheerleading and we'll figure it out tonight."

Taylor wiped her eyes. "Okay. That's a good plan."

"Trust me, it will be okay." I looked at the brochure again. "May I keep this?"

She nodded. I folded it up and put it in my pants pocket.

Just then a voice came over the PA system. "Michael Vey to the front office. Michael Vey."

Taylor looked at me with wide eyes.

"What's that about?" Ostin asked.

"I have no idea."

# 14

## A Change of Plans

I walked to the front office about as enthusiastically as a man on his way to the electric chair— and with about as much hope. I was ticking like mad—blinking and gulping. As I stood in the waiting room, the school secretary, Mrs. Hancock, walked out of Mr. Dallstrom's office. She greeted me with a smile. "Hello, Michael," she said. "Mr. Dallstrom will be right with you."

I swallowed. I was afraid that was the reason they were calling me. I had no idea why Mr. Dallstrom wanted to see me—I hadn't been shoved in a locker for days.

A moment later he came to his door. He was smiling, which looked frighteningly out of place, like lipstick on a pig.

"Michael, come in."

"Yes, sir." I followed him inside his office. He sat back in his chair and smiled again.

"Have a seat," he said, gesturing to the chair in front of his desk. "How's school going?"

I looked at him, wondering if some alien being had taken over his body. I slowly sat down. "It's fine."

"Great. I just wanted to tell you that your detention has been canceled. I'm sorry about that little misunderstanding. And Mr. Vranes and his cohorts will be doing their time. I guarantee they won't be bothering you anymore."

"Oh." It was all I could think to say. "Thank you."

He stood and walked around his desk to me, putting his hand on my shoulder. "Michael, we're proud that you're a member of our student body."

Now I was certain I was being punked. "You are?"

"Absolutely we are." Mr. Dallstrom leaned back against his desk. "Michael, I have some terrific news. Two of Meridian's pupils have been awarded the prestigious C. J. Hatch Scholarship to the acclaimed Elgen Academy in Pasadena, California. And you are one of them." He stuck out his hand. "Congratulations."

I gulped. How had they found both of us? I timidly offered my hand. When I could speak I asked, "Why me?"

"Why not you?" Mr. Dallstrom said. "Elgen Academy selects their elite student body using a closely guarded process that involves scholarship, citizenship, and character. I am told that this is the first time in the academy's illustrious history that two students have been invited to the academy from the same city—let alone the same school. We are very proud indeed."

"I don't know what to say."

"Say hurray!" he said. "This is the chance of a lifetime! The academy's board will be contacting your parents directly and extending the offer. I'm certain that they'll be as proud and excited as we are."

"It's just my mom," I said. I was suddenly very afraid for her.

"And, Michael, the best part is that your good fortune is shared by the entire student body of Meridian High. If you and the other student accept this remarkable offer, our school will be given a two-hundred-thousand-dollar grant to use however we best see fit. We could restock our library, refinish the basketball court floor, procure new music stands, buy new wrestling mats, and still have plenty to go around." He leaned forward. "This is the biggest thing ever to happen to Meridian High. Your picture will hang proudly on our Hall of Fame."

"What if I can't go?" I said.

His expression fell. "And pass up this incredible, once-in-a-lifetime opportunity?" He leaned forward, looking at me with an expression that was oddly both friendly and threatening. "I'm sure we can count on you to do the right thing."

I swallowed. "Yes, sir."

"I better let you get back to class. Don't want to stand in the way of our greatest student. Do you need a tardy slip?"

"Uh, no. I don't think the bell's rung yet."

"Right you are. You can go. Have a great day."

I walked out of his office more terrified than I had gone in.


Ostin and Taylor were waiting for me outside fifth-period biology. Taylor didn't look like she felt well.

"Are you okay?" I asked.

She had a hand on her right temple. "I'm just upset."

"What happened?" Ostin asked. "Why did they call you down to the office?"

I was still processing everything, and I didn't want to upset Taylor any more than she already was. "I'll tell you later."

Ostin's brow furrowed. "Did you get in trouble?"

"I'll tell you later," I repeated.

"Let's just go to class," Taylor said. "I need to get my mind off of this."

"Good idea," I said.

Taylor didn't say much during biology. Actually she didn't say anything. She looked like it was all she could do to not go running out. More than anything I wanted to reach over and hold her hand. I didn't blame her for being afraid. I was afraid. Actually, I was terrified.

I had no idea who those people were and what they would do.

I met Taylor in the hallway after class. "Are you all right?"

She nodded but said nothing. Ostin walked up. He looked as nervous as we were.

"You remember the plan?" I asked Taylor.

She nodded again.

"Okay," I said. "We'll pick you up at five."

"I'll meet you at the front of the school," she said.

"Are your parents home?" I asked.

"They don't get home today until after five. Why?"

"Just in case my mother needs to talk to them."

"I hope not." She sighed. "I'll see you later."

"See you."

She turned and walked off to the gymnasium.

Ostin and I walked in the opposite direction out of the school. We hadn't even left the schoolyard when I said to him, "I don't feel right about this. Maybe we should stay with her."

"That would seem weird."

"So?"

"If she'd wanted us to stay she would have asked."

"Yeah," I said. "You're probably right."

"So what did Dallstrom want?"

"I've been offered a scholarship to Elgen Academy."

Ostin blanched. "Oh no."

"It gets worse. They've bribed Mr. Dallstrom. They've offered the school two hundred thousand dollars if Taylor and I go."

"You'll have to change schools—Dallstrom will make your life miserable if you don't go."

"I know."

"When are you going to tell your mom about all this?"

"I'm more worried about *what* to tell her. What if she wants me to go?"

"This is bad," Ostin said, shaking his head. "Really bad."

We walked the rest of the way home in silence.

*   *   *

My mother got home from work later than she had planned—just a few minutes before five. She called as she opened the door, "Michael, Ostin, you guys ready?"

"We're over here, Mom." We were sitting in front of the television watching the Discovery Channel. It was Shark Week.

"When is Taylor done?"

"She has cheerleading until five."

"It's almost five now," she said. "We better hurry."

Mom, Ostin, and I climbed into the Toyota and drove over to the school. My mom pulled up to the school's front steps and put the car in park.

"Where are we meeting her?" my mom asked.

"She said she'd be in front," I said.

"Maybe they're running late," Ostin said. "Or she went back inside."

My mother said, "You two run in and see what's up."

I opened my door. "C'mon, Ostin."

We ran up the stairs into the school's main lobby but Taylor wasn't there. We walked down to the gym. Inside, groups of cheerleaders were practicing stunts. I looked around but I couldn't see Taylor. "Where is she, Ostin? Use your Tay-dar."

"She's not here," he said.

"She has to be."

"She's not."

Mrs. Shaw, the cheerleader adviser, was on the other side of the gym. I walked over to her. "Excuse me, Mrs. Shaw. Do you know where Taylor Ridley is?"

She looked up from her clipboard. "Taylor said she wasn't feeling well, so she left early."

"She walked home?"

"I don't know. She might have called her parents."

"Thank you," I said.

Ostin and I walked out of the gym.

"That doesn't make any sense," Ostin said. "Why didn't she call?"

Just then I spotted Taylor's friend Maddie. She was wearing

gym clothes and walking down the hall texting. I called out to her. "Maddie!"

She looked up and smiled. "Hi, Michael. How are you?"

"Fine. Have you seen Taylor? It's really important that I find her."

"She left practice early. She had a really bad headache."

"Did you see her leave?"

"Yeah."

"How was she acting?"

"Well, she was upset because of her headache."

"Was she alone?"

She looked at me with an idiotic grin. "I'm not telling on her."

"This isn't a *thing*," I said. I looked at her phone. "Look, will you call her? Please."

"She never answers her phone. I'll text her."

"Great. Just ask her where she is."

"Sure." She thumb-typed a message. Less than a minute passed before her phone buzzed. "She's at home."

I felt some relief. "Tell her I'm here to get her and ask if I should come over."

She began typing. Her phone buzzed again. "She says she's sorry she forgot to call. She's not feeling well and will have to pass on tonight, but happy birthday." She looked at me. "I didn't know it was your birthday. Happy birthday."

"Thanks." I turned to Ostin. "At least she's okay," I said.

We walked back to the car and climbed in. My mom looked confused. "Where's Taylor?"

"She went home early," I said. "She had a headache."

She looked as disappointed as I felt. "That's too bad. Maybe next time."

# 15

## The Man Who Wore
## Sunglasses at Night

None of us spoke much as we drove downtown. I have to admit that Taylor's absence had dulled my excitement. I think even Ostin was upset.

When we got to the aquarium, my mother looked at me and smiled sadly. "Let's have a good time, okay?"

"Okay," I said.

Even though it was a weekday, the aquarium was running a Family Night Special so the place was crowded. The busiest exhibit by far was the sharks, with their cold, unblinking eyes and their teeth bared beneath them, gliding through the water just inches from the tank's glass, as if death were only a few inches away from you. I suppose that's how I felt about everything right now, as if something bad were circling me, just waiting to bite. I soon discovered that Ostin was feeling the same way.

"Do you think Taylor's safe?" he asked me.

"I don't know."

"Do you think we are?"

"Not if she isn't."

It was hard keeping my mind on the exhibits. The three of us wandered over by the electric eels. *Electrophorus electricus* are ugly creatures with pocked skin as if they'd all grown up with a bad case of acne.

There were three eels in the tank, and the largest was about six feet long with a dark gray back and an orange underbelly. There was a voltage meter connected to the outside of the tank with a red needle that occasionally bounced around as the eels sent out surges. Out of curiosity I slid my hand over the metal corner of the tank and pulsed a little. The voltage meter jumped with my charge. Then, to my surprise, the eels in the tank all swam to me as if I had summoned them. Maybe I had. I turned back to see if my mother had seen this but she was looking through her purse. As I looked at her I wondered if I should tell her about my invitation to the academy. I wanted to but I wasn't even sure where to start. A few minutes later I walked over to her.

Before I could say anything, Ostin said to my mother, "Did you know that electric eels are not really eels?"

"Really," she replied, no doubt prepared for Ostin's upcoming monologue. My mother always looked genuinely interested in what Ostin had to say, which was probably one of the reasons he had a crush on her—which, by the way, still grossed me out.

"They're a species of gymnotiformes, also known as knife fish. Biologically, they're closer to the carp or catfish than the eel. And they breathe air, so they have to come to the surface every ten minutes."

"I didn't know that," my mother said.

"They are at the top of the food chain, which means they have no natural predators. In fact, even a baby electric eel can paralyze an alligator with its shock."

I knew most of this already. For obvious reasons, I had always taken great interest in electric eels. When I was nine I used to write "EEM"—secret for "Electric Eel Man"—on the corners of my papers, as if it were my secret identity. Still, I let Ostin talk. I think he would explode if he didn't.

"They're basically a living battery. Four fifths of their body is used in generating or storing electricity. They can produce a charge upward of six hundred volts and five hundred watts, which is powerful enough to be deadly to a human. Though some experts claim they've produced up to eight hundred volts."

"I'd hate to take a bath with one," she said, smiling.

"Or give a bath to one," I said.

She looked at me and grinned. When I was three years old, I accidentally gave her a shock while she was bathing me. It knocked her over. It was pretty much showers after that.

"Eels use their electric shock to stun or kill their prey, but they can also use low voltage like radar to see in murky waters. It's called electrolocation. It's how they find food."

"Speaking of eating," my mother said, "is anyone getting hungry?"

That was one way of shutting Ostin up. "Is that a trick question?" he asked.

"I'm hungry," I said.

"Good," she said. "I'm starving. Off to PizzaMax."

The pizzeria wasn't actually called PizzaMax. Its real name was Mac's Purple Pig Pizza Parlor and Piano Pantry, which is as dumb as it is long, but they have awesome pizza. My mother and I ate there the first week we lived in Idaho, and a few weeks later when she asked me where I wanted to eat, I only remembered the Mac's part. The name stuck.

We ordered six pieces of cheesy garlic bread, an extra-large Mac's Kitchen Sink pizza, which has everything you could imagine on it (except anchovies—gross!), and a cold pitcher of root beer.

While we were eating, my mom asked me, "What do Taylor's parents do?"

"Her dad is a police officer. Her mom works at a travel agency."

My mom nodded. "She's a really nice girl. I hope she comes around again soon."

"I hope she does too," I said.

"Still like your watch?" my mother asked. I think she just wanted to see me smile again.

I held up my arm so she could see that I was wearing it. "Love it."

I could tell this made her happy. She looked into my eyes. "Are you feeling okay?"

"Yeah," I said.

"You're kind of quiet tonight."

I was never very good at hiding things from my mother. "I guess I just have a lot on my mind."

"Are you still upset about Taylor?"

I shrugged. "A little."

She put her hand on my shoulder. "Things don't always go as planned, do they? But in the end they seem to work out."

"I suppose so," I said. I hoped so.

We had been at PizzaMax for nearly an hour when Ostin excused himself to go to the bathroom. My mother smiled at me, then slid around the vinyl seat of our booth to get closer.

"Honey, what's wrong? You're really ticking."

I slowly looked up at her. "Mr. Dallstrom called me down to his office today."

Her brow fell. "Oh. What happened?"

"Nothing happened. I got offered a scholarship."

A smile crossed her face. "What kind of scholarship?"

"It's to this really prestigious school in California."

Her smile grew even larger. "Michael, that's wonderful. What's the name of the school?"

I was relieved to see her happy. "The Elgen Academy."

Her smile immediately vanished into a look of fear. "Did you say Elgen?"

Her expression frightened me. "Yeah."

"In Pasadena?"

"How did you know that?" I asked.

She turned pale, like she was going to be sick.

"Mom, what is it?"

"We need to go," she said, her voice quivering. "We need to get Ostin and leave now."

"Mom, what's wrong?"

"I can't tell you here . . ." She looked at me intensely, her eyes dark with fear. "Michael, there's more to this than you know. Your father . . ."

Just then Ostin returned. "I'm ready for another frosty mug of root beer," he said.

I looked up at him. "We've got to go," I said.

"Right now?"

"Right now," my mother said. "Something's come up."

It was dark outside when my mother paid the bill. We were walking out to the car when Ostin said, "Wait. I forgot my jacket."

"Hurry," my mom said to him as he turned to run back inside. We continued walking to the car.

My mother was unlocking our car door when a man appeared between our car and the truck next to it. His clothes were dirty and worn and his face was partially cloaked in a dark gray hoodie. He said to my mother, "Excuse me, do you have a dollar?"

My mother looked at him, then said, "Of course." My mother always helped others. She lifted her purse.

When my mom's head was down, the man pulled a gun from the hoodie's pouch. "Just give me the purse."

My mother dropped her keys on the ground.

"Okay," she said, her voice pitched. "You can have it. You don't need the gun."

"Shut up!" he said. "Just give it to me and shut your mouth. If anyone screams, I shoot."

"Don't talk to my mother like that," I said.

He pointed the gun at me. He looked nervous and was shaking. "I'll shoot you first."

"Please," my mother said, "just take the money." She handed her purse to him. "Just take it. There's credit cards and cash, you can have it all."

He cautiously reached out and took the purse from her, the gun still shaking in his hand. He backed off again. "I want the car too," he said. "Give me your keys and back away."

"I dropped the keys," my mother said. "They're right there. I'm going to pick them up."

"You don't move," he said, pointing the gun at my mother's chest. "You," he said to me, "give me the keys."

I looked at him, then my mother.

"Bring them to me now and I won't shoot your mother."

"Okay," I said. I crouched down and lifted the keys, then slowly walked toward him. About a yard away from him, I turned back and looked at my mother.

"What are you doing?" he said angrily. "Give me the keys."

My mother guessed what I was thinking. She shook her head.

I looked back at the man. Maybe I had watched too many super-hero movies, but if ever there was a moment to use my power it was now. I could stop him from taking our car and my mother's purse. I was handing him a ring of metal. All I had to do was surge.

I took another step forward, then slowly reached out with the keys. His hand shot out and grabbed them. The instant he touched the key ring there was a loud snap and a yellow spark that briefly lit up everything around us. The man screamed out as he collapsed to the ground. I had never shocked anyone so hard before, and there was a pale mist of smoke in the air.

The man wasn't moving, and for a moment I wondered if I had killed him. It seemed that time stood still. I looked at my mother, wondering how she'd react. She was staring at the man on the ground. The silence was broken by a deep voice.

"Well done, Michael."

I quickly turned around. I have no idea where he came from, but a man was now standing just a few yards from us. He was sharply dressed in a tan suit with an orange silk tie. Even though it was dark, he wore thick-framed sunglasses. His hair, dark brown with sideburns, was nicely styled. He looked at the mugger, then back up at me, and lightly clapped. "Really, that was impressive.

What was that—nine hundred, a thousand volts?"

I looked at my mother, then back at him anxiously.

"Who are you?" my mother asked.

"A friend, Sharon. A friend and an admirer of Michael's. And his gift." My mother and I exchanged glances. "Yes," he said, smiling, "I know all about it. As a matter of fact, I know more about it than you do."

Just then the thief groaned, and I looked down at him. He was struggling just to lift his head. As I watched him anger flooded through my body. If I had ever wondered if my electrical powers were somehow connected to my emotions, there was no doubt of it now as I felt power surging through me like I had never felt before. I looked down at my hands. Electricity was sparking in blue arcs between my fingers, something I'd never before experienced.

"It's an emotional reaction," the man said. "Fear, anger, hate—the powerful stuff causes your nervous system to react. It's peculiar isn't it? Normal people respond with adrenaline—but special people like you react electrically."

My mother put her hand on my arm. "Michael, we need to go."

I didn't move. "How do you know all this?" I asked.

The man took a step forward. "Michael, we've been looking for you for a long, long time . . . almost since you were born."

"Michael," my mom said.

"Why?" I asked.

"To reunite you with the others."

"Others?"

"You're not alone, Michael. There's more of your kind than you think. More than just your friend Taylor."

His mention of Taylor startled me.

"I'd like to introduce you to some of them right now. Behind you is Zeus."

Suddenly a young man was standing next to my mother. He was good-looking but unkempt. He had long, greasy, blond hair and wore a Levi's jacket with the sleeves cut off and no shirt underneath. Even though he was only my age he had a tattoo on his chest of a lightning bolt. My mother looked at him anxiously.

"And this is Nichelle."

A young woman stepped up behind the man. She wore black clothing and dark, thick makeup, mostly black or dark purple, the way the Goth kids do. Both kids looked about my age, though Zeus was taller than me.

"Zeus, show Mrs. Vey what you can do."

He smiled darkly. "Glad to." He lifted his hands, and electricity flew from his fingers to my mother in blue-white strikes. My mother screamed and collapsed just like the man I had just shocked.

"Mom!" I dropped to the ground next to her, cradling her head in my arms. "Why did you do that?" I shouted.

"She'll be okay," the man said. "It just took the wind out of her."

My eyes darted back and forth between the three of them. "Who are you?"

"I'm your friend," the man said softly. "Nichelle?"

The girl started toward me. As she approached I noticed that the Zeus guy took a few steps back, as if he were afraid of her.

As the girl neared me I started to feel different. Everything was out of place, the man, the two kids, my mother on the ground, it was all like a bad dream. I felt weaker. The electricity stopped arcing between my fingers. Then I began to feel dizzy. I looked at the girl, and she looked into my eyes with a strange, emotionless stare. I couldn't make sense of any of it—who these people were and why they were there. More importantly, what they wanted with us.

With each step the girl took toward me, my dizziness increased. Then my head began to pound like a bass drum. I put my hand on my forehead as my vision began to blur.

"Take it easy on him, Nichelle," I heard the man say. "He's not used to it."

Suddenly I heard Ostin's voice, blending into what seemed like a collage of other sounds. I looked down at my mother. She was still, but gazing at me. I saw her lips move but I couldn't hear her. I couldn't hear anything other than the loud buzzing in my ears. I think she said *I love you*. It seems like that's what she said. It's the last thing I remember before passing out.

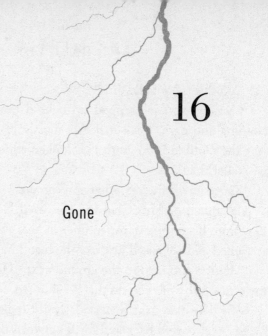

# 16

## Gone

**W**hen I woke, I was in a bed with aluminum side rails. I was lying beneath clean, white sheets and there was an IV taped to my arm. I felt as if I had been drained of all my energy and every joint of my body ached, throbbing like a bad toothache. It took a moment for my eyes to adjust to the light above me. I groaned out, as if expulsing a nightmare. Ostin appeared at my side.

"Michael?"

I turned my head toward him. He was standing in front of closed blinds that glowed from the daylight behind them. Next to him were his mother and father. Ostin's father was in charge of maintenance for the county's parks and recreation, so he was rarely home. I was surprised to also see him in the room. I looked around for my mother but didn't see her.

"Where am I?" My tongue stuck to my dry mouth and it was difficult to speak.

"Honey, you're in the hospital," Mrs. Liss said. Her face was pinched with concern.

"How did I get here?"

"Paramedics," Ostin said.

"You passed out," Mrs. Liss said. "The doctors were afraid you had a stroke."

"Where's my mother?"

"Do you remember what happened?" Mr. Liss asked.

It hurt my head to think about it. "There was a guy with a gun. Then this man with two kids. One of them shocked my mother."

"Shocked?" Mr. Liss said. "What do you mean?"

I looked at Ostin. "Did I dream that?"

He shrugged. "I only saw the gunman."

"Is my mother okay?"

Ostin didn't answer.

I turned to Mr. and Mrs. Liss. "She's okay, isn't she?"

Mrs. Liss walked closer and put her hand on mine. Her eyes were filled with tears. "I have some bad news, honey. Your mother's gone."

I looked at her blankly. "What do you mean?"

"The police believe she's been kidnapped," Mr. Liss said.

My heart froze. *Kidnapped?* "Why would someone kidnap her?"

"We don't know."

My body's pain was nothing compared to the agony I now felt. Tears filled my eyes. How could this have happened? My mother had spent her life protecting and caring for me, and now I had failed to protect her. I had let her down. Why couldn't they have just taken me? I wanted to fall asleep and wake up again in my own house, talking to my own mother. I wanted something to make sense. I wanted the nightmare to end.

# 17

## Lieutenant Lloyd

That afternoon the police came to interview me. Mr. Liss had gone to work, leaving Ostin and his mother still with me. There were two policemen, both in uniform. The officer who did most of the talking was older, with gray hair.

"Michael, I'm Lieutenant Lloyd of the Boise Police Department. This is Detective Steve Pearson."

Detective Pearson waved from behind. "Hello, Michael."

"Hey," I said.

Lieutenant Lloyd said to Ostin and his mother, "We have some questions for Michael. Would you mind waiting outside for a few minutes?"

"Of course," Mrs. Liss said, putting her hand on Ostin's back. "Let's go, Ostin."

Ostin looked at me sympathetically. "See ya, buddy."

After we were alone, Lieutenant Lloyd walked to the side of my bed. He must have noticed my ticking because he said, "Don't worry. We're here to help."

He grabbed my bed's railing with one hand. "I'm really sorry about what's happened to your mother, son. The good news is we have the man who held you up in custody. We're just trying to put the pieces together. I need you to tell me everything you remember about what happened."

I closed my eyes. Remembering what had happened was like pulling a Band-Aid off a bad cut. "I remember some," I said.

"Please tell us what you remember."

I rolled my tongue around inside my mouth. It felt thick and heavy. I was blinking pretty hard. "My mom had taken us out for pizza for my birthday. We had just finished eating and were walking out to our car . . ."

"You and your mother?" Detective Pearson asked.

I nodded. "Yeah. My friend Ostin was with us, but he went back inside to get his jacket."

"Go on," Lieutenant Lloyd said.

"My mom was unlocking the car when this guy was there."

"The guy with the gun?"

I nodded.

"Clyde Stuart," Detective Pearson said. "His name is Clyde Stuart. Where did he come from?"

"I don't know. He was just between the cars. Neither of us saw him at first."

"What did he do?" Lieutenant Lloyd asked.

"He asked for some money. When my mom went for her wallet, he pulled out a gun and asked for her purse."

"Then what?"

"He told us to give him our car keys. I handed them to him."

"Anything else?"

I shook my head. "That's it."

Lieutenant Lloyd looked at me with a perplexed expression, then turned back to his partner. Detective Pearson said, "What we can't figure out is what happened to the suspect."

I realized the gap in my story. My eyes darted nervously between them. "What do you mean?"

"He was incapacitated when we arrived on the scene," Pearson said. "He claims the keys shocked him."

I blinked several times. "I don't remember."

"Stuart was acting like he'd been hit by a Taser," Lieutenant Lloyd said. "We had to carry him into the police cruiser."

"Taser?" Pearson said. "It was more like he was struck by a bolt of lightning."

"Maybe he was," I said.

Lieutenant Lloyd wrote something on his pad. Then he said, "We're wondering if the gunman had an accomplice. Was there anyone with him?"

"No."

"Did you see anyone else around?"

"There was a man."

Lieutenant Lloyd looked up from his pad. "What man?"

"I don't know. Just a man. He was dressed in a suit. And he had a boy and a girl with him about my age."

"Did he come from the pizza place?"

"Maybe. I'm not sure."

"What did he look like? His face?"

"I'm not sure about that either. He was wearing sunglasses."

"At night?" Pearson asked.

"Yeah. I thought it was weird."

"What else do you remember about him?" Lloyd asked.

"He had short, dark brown hair. He looked . . . rich."

"Definitely didn't look like Stuart," Lloyd said, jotting down more notes in his pad. "Did you see them take your mother?"

"No. I fainted or something."

"Fear will do that," Pearson said.

I didn't think it had anything to do with fear, but I said nothing.

"Do you have any idea why someone would want to kidnap your mother?"

I shook my head. "No. Why don't you ask Stuart?"

"We've interrogated him but he's tight as a clam. We know he's hiding something, but whomever or whatever he's protecting has got a real hold on him. Apparently he's a lot more afraid of them than he is of us."

"Will you find her?"

Lieutenant Lloyd looked at me sympathetically. "We'll do our best. I promise." He saw the anguish on my face and added, "We're not done with Stuart yet. I've still got a few tricks up my sleeve." He took a card from his front pocket. "Take this. It has my office and cell phone number. If you think of anything else just call me." The two policemen started to leave the room. Lieutenant Lloyd stopped by the door. "Oh, by the way, the gun Stuart had was empty."

"Empty?"

"No bullets. I thought it might make you feel a little better to know that he wasn't intending to shoot you."

*He might as well have*, I thought.

The policemen walked out. Ostin rushed in as soon as they left. "Do they know where your mother is?"

"No." I lay back in bed. "What did you see?"

"Hardly anything. When I got to your car, you and that man were lying on the ground and your mom was gone. I didn't see anyone else. I ran back to the restaurant and told them to call the police."

"There were three people besides the gunman," I said. "A man in sunglasses and two kids our age. The man knew my name. He knew my mom's and Taylor's names. He knew about my power."

Ostin scratched his head. "How could he have known all that?"

"I don't know."

"He brought his kids?"

"I don't think they were his. And they had electrical powers. At least one of them did. The man called him Zeus. He's the one who shocked my mom."

"He could shock like you?"

"Sort of. Except his electricity left his body. Like lightning." I leaned forward. "There's something else I remember. He seemed afraid of the girl."

"What did she do?"

"I don't know. But the closer she got to me the dizzier I felt. Then I passed out." I combed my hair back from my face. "They're not going to find my mother."

"Don't talk that way."

"Have you heard from Taylor?"

"No, not yet."

I lay back in bed. "At least she's safe. It's a good thing she didn't come with us."

# PART TWO

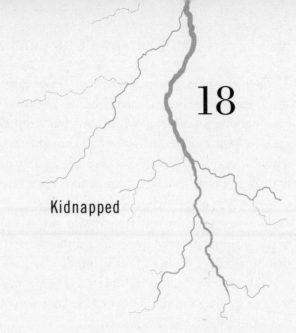

# 18

## Kidnapped

Taylor shook with fear in the backseat of the utility van. Her head still ached, as did her hands, which were strapped in front of her with plastic ties. She felt as if she'd been drugged. A leather strap crossed at her waist, holding her tightly to the seat, and her legs were bound at her ankles with leather shackles fastened to the floor. The van appeared to have been designed for this very purpose—transporting prisoners. On top of her fear, she felt carsick and wondered if she might throw up.

It had all happened so fast. She had been at cheerleading practice for only a few minutes when she came down with an excruciating headache and had to sit down. After ten minutes Mrs. Shaw suggested she go home. That was when Taylor first noticed the scary-looking girl watching her from the gym door. At first she went outside and sat on the concrete steps waiting for Michael, hoping the pain would go away. She noticed that the scary girl followed her at a distance.

Then the pain got so severe that Taylor knew she couldn't wait any longer, so she began walking home. She was crossing the school's back parking lot when a white van pulled up beside her—the van she was held captive in. Taylor had thought the van was one of the school's food-service vehicles, and she hadn't paid much attention until it stopped, the side door swung open, and the scary-looking girl—the same girl who now sat in front of her—stepped out. Taylor's first thought was *Why is that girl wearing a dog collar?* Her headache immediately intensified until she fell first to her knees, then to all fours, dizzy and disoriented.

"Take it easy!" someone shouted. Then a man got out from the front of the van and stood next to her. "Are you okay?"

"I don't think so," Taylor said.

"Let me give you a hand."

Her head was spinning, and the buzzing in her ears was so loud that she didn't resist the two men picking her up and carrying her inside the van, blindfolding her, and strapping her down to the back-seat.

Then someone put something over her mouth and nose. That's the last thing she remembered. She wondered if anyone had seen her being kidnapped and called the police. Maybe her father was coming for her right now. She desperately hoped so, but doubted it. The whole thing had taken less than thirty seconds. She had been taken without even a scream.

Heavy rock music played from the front of the van. Earlier, when Taylor woke, her captors were arguing over whether to listen to classic rock or rap. They flipped a coin to decide. Classic rock had won out, and Aerosmith was playing, adding to her headache.

The scary-looking girl sat alone on the bench in front of her. The girl was about her age, though a little shorter. She had short black spiky hair streaked with purple, black makeup, and she wore a black leather collar around her neck, studded with what looked like real diamonds. She had earbuds in both ears, the white cord running down her neck.

For the last hour Taylor had tried to reboot the driver, even though she knew it would likely result in crashing the van. A crash would, at least, draw outside attention, and she'd rather take her chances with an accident than with these people. But her attempts to reboot him were only met with pain—a sharp prick in her temples. Taylor decided to ignore the pain and try rebooting again with all her might. She pressed the thought, but the pain just grew. It was like sticking pins into her own head. She finally groaned out and stopped.

The girl in front of her turned around and removed one of the buds from her ear. "I'd tell you to stop doing that except it feels kind of good."

"Doing what?" Taylor asked, her head still throbbing.

"Whatever it is that you do to people's brains."

Taylor looked at her. "How do you know what I'm doing?"

"I can feel it. But you're wasting your time. It doesn't hurt me and it won't get past me."

"Who are you?"

"Nichelle," she said. "I'd shake your hand, but"—she paused and smiled—"you're tied up." Her smile fell into a dark glare. "Actually, I wouldn't shake your hand anyway, and the better question is, what am I?"

"What are you?"

"I'm your worst nightmare. Just think of me as an electrical vampire. And girl, I could feed off you all day." The girl put the earbud back in and turned around.

Taylor had never before felt so helpless or afraid. She thought of Michael and his mother waiting for her; she thought of her parents. They probably hadn't noticed her absence yet, thinking that she'd gone with Michael and his mother. It wouldn't be until late that evening that they started worrying. Her mother would be a wreck and her father would be following up on every resource available to a police officer, but by then she'd be long gone, maybe even out of the state. She wanted to be home with all of her heart.

"Why does my head hurt?"

"That's me. Letting you know I'm here." She smiled. "I can increase the pressure if you like."

"No thank you."

"I thought you might say that." Nichelle turned completely around and looked into Taylor's eyes. The pain started increasing, higher, then higher.

Taylor shouted out, "Stop. Please."

The girl was enjoying herself. "Hurts, don't it."

Taylor's eyes filled with tears. "Yes."

The pain stopped. "See, I'm what an electrician would call a ground wire. I just soak up all those lovely powers of yours until we can get you to where you're going."

"Where are we going?"

"You'll see. Don't want to ruin the surprise."

"Why do I feel so sick?"

"Funny you should ask. The scientists at Elgen wondered that same thing. They think it's because your body has become so used to high levels of electricity that you don't feel normal without it. That's what makes me so darn annoying."

"Elgen? Are we going to the Elgen Academy?" Taylor asked.

"So you don't want to be surprised, eh? Okay then, we're going to the lah-bor-a-tory," she said, purposely drawing out the word like she was a mad scientist. Taylor couldn't tell if she was trying to sound comical or scary, but it didn't matter. Either way, it was scary.

"What are you going to do to me?"

"Same thing scientists always do with lab animals—poke and prod around, and when they're done, they'll dissect you like a frog in a middle school biology class."

Pure fear passed through Taylor. "Why? I haven't done anything."

Nichelle shrugged. "Why not?" She leaned back. "You ask too many questions. They're hurting my ears. Like this . . ."

Suddenly a painful, high-pitched squeal tore through Taylor's head. She started crying. "Stop it. Please, stop it."

"Say 'pretty please.'"

"Pretty please."

"'With a cherry on top.'"

Taylor sobbed. "With a cherry on top."

Nichelle smiled. "Good girl." The pain ceased. "Now, no more talking. You just be real quiet there, and in the future, should I ask you something, you will refer to me as 'Master.' You got that?"

Taylor just looked at her.

The girl's eyes narrowed. "I asked you a question."

Taylor's head started filling with the noise. "Yes, Master."

"Very good."

Nichelle gave Taylor a big grin, turned back around, replaced the earbud, and lay back. "I love the abductions," she muttered. "It's the only time I can do whatever I want without getting in trouble. It's been a long time since any fresh Glows have been brought in."

A voice up front said, "Knock it off, Nichelle."

She pulled out an earbud. "You're no fun. It's boring back here. I could make her bark like a dog or do something really embarrassing."

"Just leave her alone."

She turned around and said to Taylor, "These old dudes have no sense of humor. By the way, you should have seen what I did to that boy you led us to. Vey. He had a lot of electricity in him. Much more than usual. When I shut him down, I almost killed him. He's probably still in the hospital."

"You have Michael?"

"I can't hear you," she sang. She winked. "You didn't say 'Master.'"

"I'm sorry," Taylor said quickly, afraid she might hurt her again. "You have Michael, Master?"

Nichelle smiled. "No. The little guy's friend showed up and we had to go. But we'll have him soon enough. We took a little insurance. You and his dearest mumsy."

"You have Mrs. Vey, Master?"

"Yes, we do."

A sharp voice came from the front. "Nichelle, just shut up."

Nichelle leaned toward Taylor. "Now look what you did. You got me in trouble." She turned back to the front. "Oh, chill. It's not like she'll ever get the chance to tell anyone." She shook her head.

"Idiots," she said under her breath, once again replacing the earbud. "No more talking," she said to Taylor. She leaned her head against the interior metal wall of the van.

Taylor tried to keep from crying. She was in pain and frightened. She wondered if what the girl had told her about the laboratory was true. Would they really cut her open? As frightened as she was to find out, she had to know. She leaned her head against the van's wall to read Nichelle's mind. She saw images of the school from the brochure, she saw other youths her age, some of them well dressed and laughing, and she knew Nichelle hated these kids. She saw something she didn't understand—she saw herself at the school interacting with the other students as if it had already happened. Was she seeing the future? Then she saw other youths lying on the ground, some in pain, others crying in a dark place that looked like a dungeon. She sat back up, unable to continue. Everything she saw in Nichelle's mind terrified her.

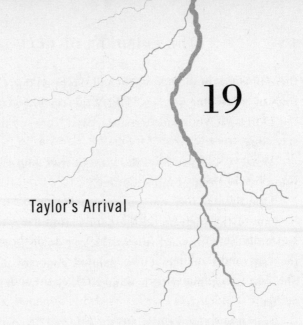

# 19

## Taylor's Arrival

The van drove through the night, and Taylor slept for most of the ride, waking only when a voice came over the two-way radio up front or when the van stopped for gas. Taylor was given no food and only a bottle of water that Nichelle held for her to drink, purposely spilling a good portion of it down the front of Taylor's shirt and jeans.

"Gross, you wet yourself," she said.

The ride was mostly through desert until early the next morning, when they came again into city traffic.

Around 2:00 p.m. the van pulled into a driveway with a guard booth and a tall gate lined with razor wire. The driver rolled down his window and showed the guard a badge, and the gate opened. They drove around to the back of the building, where a large over-head garage door lifted, and the van pulled inside. When the over-head door had closed behind them, the men climbed out and one of them opened the side door. Nichelle stepped out, then leaned against the van, stretching her legs. "Hurry this up. I have to pee."

"Don't get your knickers in a twist," one of the men said. "Just stay close."

"What would you boys do without me?" she said. "Ain't it awful? Can't live with me, can't shoot me."

"Don't tempt me," one of them said.

One of the men undid the bands around Taylor's feet and waist and pulled her forward. Taylor ducked down as she stepped out of the van to the orange-yellow painted concrete floor of the garage. She was trembling with fear, and felt like her legs might give out on her.

"Hatch says to take her into the infirmary to get checked out," the guard at the door said to the driver.

Nichelle and one of the drivers took Taylor inside the building and down a well-lit corridor to a room at the end of the hall. The sign on the door said EXAM ROOM B. Upon their entrance, a tall woman with cropped yellow hair, thin-rimmed glasses, and wearing a white lab coat looked up from her desk.

"This is Taylor Ridley?" she asked the man.

"Yes. Sign here," he said, thrusting out a clipboard. The woman signed the document, then handed the clipboard back to the driver. "Muchas gracias," he said, and walked away.

The doctor looked up at Taylor. "So you're Taylor."

Taylor swallowed. "Yes, ma'am. Where am I?"

"I'll ask the questions," she said sharply. "You're in my office. I'm Dr. Parker, the resident physician at the Elgen Academy." The woman turned to Nichelle. "Tell Miss Ridley what will happen if she doesn't cooperate."

"She knows," Nichelle said. "Don't you?"

Taylor nodded.

The doctor walked up to Taylor and cut off her plastic cuffs with a pair of surgical scissors. Taylor rubbed her wrists.

"Thank you," Taylor said.

"Remove your clothes," the doctor said.

For a moment Taylor just stood there, then a sharp pain pierced her skull. "Stop! I'll do it," Taylor said quickly.

She undressed down to her underwear. She didn't know if they'd make her take everything off, but she wasn't going to until they made her. To her relief, they didn't.

"Lay your clothes on the chair."

"Yes, ma'am."

The doctor lifted a tablet computer from her desk. "Relax," she said in a tone that only made Taylor more uncomfortable. "We're just giving you a routine physical examination to see how healthy you are. Step onto the scale."

Taylor did as she was told. The doctor checked the number on the scale and wrote on her pad. Most of what the doctor asked Taylor to do was no different than when her mother took her to her own doctor for her annual physical, with one exception. She had Taylor stand against the wall and grasp two chrome bars. Then the doctor put on a thick pair of sunglasses. "I'm going to ask Nichelle to leave for a moment," she said. "Are you going to behave yourself? Or do I need to bring in a guard?"

"I'll behave, ma'am," Taylor said, looking at the ground.

She nodded to Nichelle. "Stay close."

"Okay." Nichelle walked out of the room.

The doctor said to Taylor, "This device tests your electrical pulse."

Taylor remained silent as the doctor attached sensors to Taylor's body. After a moment the doctor explained, "The electric children have a secondary pulse. Actually, it's more like an EKG. I made Nichelle leave because she distorts the readings."

When the doctor was done running the test, she punched a series of numbers into a machine that spit out a roll of paper. "I shouldn't be surprised by this," she said. "Your readings are identical to your sister's."

"I don't have a sister," Taylor said.

The doctor looked at her with a peculiar smile but said nothing. She walked to her desk and pushed the talk button on the intercom. "Nichelle, come in, please."

Nichelle walked back into the exam room. Taylor immediately recoiled with fear.

The woman gave Taylor a thin cloth jumpsuit. "Put this on."

Taylor stepped into it and zipped it up, noticing the plastic zipper and snaps.

"Nichelle," the doctor said, "it's time for Miss Ridley's interview. Take her to her cell."

# 20

## A Surprise Visit

I was released from the hospital around six o'clock. A social worker from the state had come to my room to talk with me, and it was agreed that for the time being I would stay with the Lisses. We stopped at McDonald's for dinner, then drove to Ostin's house.

Mrs. Liss had always been nice but tonight she was especially kind. As we walked into the apartment, Mrs. Liss said, "Michael, honey, you can get your things and bring them over. You and Ostin can share a room for the time being."

"I'd like to stay in my own room for now, if that's okay."

She thought about it. "It is just down the hall. I guess that'll be all right. Take this with you." She took a bag of red licorice from her pantry and handed it to me. "It will help."

"Thanks."

"Want me to come over with you?" Ostin asked.

"Thanks, but not now."

He patted me on the back. "I understand." He's probably the only fifteen-year-old in the world who would.

I walked down the hall. I unlocked the door, walked into the dark apartment, and flipped on the lights. Since we moved to Idaho I had spent a lot of time alone, but the apartment had never seemed so quiet and empty. I looked down at my birthday watch, then I twisted it around on my wrist.

My eyes teared up. Where was she? I went into my mother's bedroom. There was a picture on her nightstand of the two of us at Zion National Park in southern Utah. It had been a beautiful day, and Kolob Arch could be seen in the distance behind us. As I picked up the photograph I wondered if I would ever see her again. My heart ached. I lay on her bed and cried.

Sometime in the next hour there was a knock on the door. I wiped my eyes and walked out. I had assumed it was Ostin, but to my surprise Taylor's dad and a woman I guessed was her mother stood in the hallway. They looked very upset.

Officer Ridley spoke first. "Hi, Michael, we're Taylor's parents. Could we speak with you?"

I looked at them nervously, reacting with my usual tics. I assumed they were here to talk to me about my mother. "Sure," I said, stepping back from the door. "Come in."

Mrs. Ridley's eyes were puffy. Taylor's father put his arm around her, and they walked inside, shutting the door behind them.

"Is Taylor okay?" I asked.

Mrs. Ridley began to cry. Mr. Ridley said, "When was the last time you heard from Taylor?"

"Yesterday afternoon. She was going to go with us to the aquarium. But when we got to the school, she was gone."

Mrs. Ridley began to cry harder.

"What's happened?" I asked.

"You haven't heard from her?" Mr. Ridley asked.

"No, sir."

He looked at me suspiciously. "Then you didn't know that Taylor ran away?"

My heart froze. "No. Why would she do that?"

He shook his head. "You know, I'm tough on her sometimes. I just . . ." He paused, overcome by emotion. "I told her that if she didn't start spending more time at home she would have to give up cheerleading." He rubbed his palm over his eyes. "She texted her good-bye."

"We just didn't see it coming," Mrs. Ridley sobbed.

"She won't return our texts," Mr. Ridley said. He took his wife's hand. "We wanted to ask you a favor. We just want her home and safe. Will you please tell her that we love her, and we would really like to talk to her?"

"If I hear from her," I said. I felt sick but knew I couldn't show it. "But I'm sure she has a lot of other friends she'd contact first."

"Then you have no plans to see her?" Mr. Ridley asked. There was a strong inflection in his voice.

"No. I haven't heard from her since yesterday."

They were both looking at me with a peculiar gaze. Finally Mrs. Ridley said, "An hour ago she sent another text that said 'Tell Michael I'll see him soon.'"

Chills went up my spine. When I could speak I said, "I don't know what she meant by that, but if I hear from her I'll call you. I promise."

They both sat looking at me, and I guessed they were trying to decide whether I was telling the truth or not. Finally Mr. Ridley said, "Thank you, Michael." They stood and walked to the door.

Mrs. Ridley stopped in front of my door, blotting her eyes with a Kleenex. "I don't know if you know this, but Taylor was adopted."

"She told me."

"The counselors told us that sometimes adopted children can carry a sense of abandonment. We tried to fill that, but I guess we failed."

"I don't think you failed," I said. "There must be some kind of misunderstanding."

"That's kind of you to say, Michael. Taylor thinks a lot of you. I think if you told her that we love her, she'll believe you. I think she might come back."

"I don't know what's going on, but I do know that Taylor loves you both. I'll let you know if I hear from her."

"Thank you," Mrs. Ridley said. Mr. Ridley put his arm around her and led her out of my apartment.

As soon as they were gone I ran down the hall and knocked on Ostin's door. Ostin answered the door holding a half-eaten toaster strudel. He read the panic on my face.

"What's wrong?"

"They've got Taylor."

# 21

## Dr. Hatch and the Twin

The cell Taylor was placed in was windowless and rectangular, with the walls, ceiling, and floor lined in a soft, pinkish rubber coating that resembled the material that pencil erasers are made of. Mounted to each wall were surveillance cameras, speaker boxes, and other sensors designed to monitor the cell's occupant's activities. On one wall were two chrome bars that stuck out about six inches from the wall—similar to the testing apparatus in the exam room.

In one corner of the room there was a porcelain toilet and sink. The only thing that looked normal was the bed, which was on a wood frame.

Taylor walked over to the bed. There was no metal of any kind used in its construction. The mattress was filled with down feathers. The bed had one other difference she didn't fail to notice: leather restraining straps.

The room was lit by fluorescent lighting concealed behind thick plastic plates. There was neither a thermostat nor switches in the room of any kind, and she had no control over light, heat, or air. The people watching her from the cameras would decide when she would have lights and how hot or cold she would be. She had no control over anything.

Taylor turned on the sink and was grateful that water came out. She still felt nauseous from the car ride, and she washed her face in the cold water. Then she went and lay on her bed, looking up at the ceiling.

She wasn't sure what time it was. She wasn't even sure what day it was. Mrs. Shaw would be furious with her for missing cheer. Taylor shook her head. Had she not been so afraid, she would have laughed at the thought. If only Mrs. Shaw was the worst of her worries. Besides, everyone would know by now that she had been abducted. They had to, didn't they? Her friends would be calling one another, they'd organize search parties. Wouldn't they?

She thought of how worried her parents must be. Just a few days earlier they had scolded her for being gone from home too much. The argument had ended with her slamming her bedroom door. She regretted how she had acted. She'd give up everything she had to be home right now. Even cheerleading.

As Taylor lay on top of the bed thinking, she heard a quick burst of air followed by a sharp metallic click. Her door opened. Nichelle stepped inside, followed by a tall man in a suit and tie. He wore over-sized black-rimmed glasses with dark lenses that concealed his eyes, similar to the glasses the doctor had put on during her tests.

"Sit up," Nichelle barked.

Taylor sat up on the bed. The man walked to the center of the room. "Hello, Taylor," he said. "You're a sight for sore eyes."

Taylor stared at him, her heart pounding fiercely.

"He said 'hello,'" Nichelle said. A sharp, piercing scream entered Taylor's head.

Taylor grabbed her ears and let out a small scream. "Stop!"

"Stop it," the man said sharply to Nichelle. "Go."

Nichelle frowned. "Yes, sir." She walked out of the room without looking at Taylor.

"I'm sorry about that," the man said. "Nichelle gets a bit Draconian."

"I hate her," Taylor said. She immediately regretted this, wondering if she'd be punished.

To her surprise, the man just nodded. "Be assured that you're not alone in that," he said. "Most of the students here do." He smiled warmly. "Let's start over. I'm Dr. Hatch. You are at the Elgen Academy. I hope your trip here wasn't too unpleasant."

Taylor looked at him incredulously. "Why have you kidnapped me? You can't hold me here. My father will find you and—"

He raised his hand. "Your adopted father, Dean Charles Ridley of the Boise Police Department, thinks his little girl has run away. In fact you have already texted him twice today telling him how much you dislike him, and how you never intend to go home as long as he's there."

Hearing this made her heart ache. Taylor began to cry. "Why are you doing this to me?"

"Taylor, I'm sorry it had to begin this way. I really am. But once you see things for what they really are, I promise you won't be upset anymore." He stepped toward her and crouched down to look into her face. "Do you know how long I have been looking for you? You're a very special girl. Not just because you're a Glow, but because you have something that we can't learn from the other Glows."

"What's a Glow?"

"That's our term for the electric children. You all give off that faint glow. Surely you've noticed it."

She didn't answer.

"Of course you have. Anyway, that's why I wear these glasses." He took them off and held them up so Taylor could see. "We invented them right here. They are designed to magnify that glow. I can spot one of you a mile away. Actually, one point seven miles to be exact." He rubbed his eyes, then he looked into her eyes and smiled. "Taylor, you're a very special girl, and part of something that's bigger and more exciting than you can imagine. We have a chance to change the world. I don't mean slap a Band-Aid on it; I mean throw the past out and start fresh. We could create a society where everyone has enough to eat, sufficient medical care, and housing. A world where life is about personal growth and expression, not survival. No more wars. No more hunger. A world where all your needs are met. And you can be a part of its creation."

"What are you talking about?"

"We are creating a world of people just like you—a race of superior beings." He let the statement ring off in the silence. "Taylor, do you know why you are electric?"

"Because your machine didn't work right."

He nodded. "Very good. Exactly. You see, some people, particularly some investors, saw that as a failure. But they missed the bigger vision. We discovered something much, much more valuable. You know, many of the great inventions of our day were accidents. Microwave ovens, penicillin . . ." He smiled. "Even potato chips."

Taylor said, "You killed all those babies."

Hatch stood. "I didn't," he said sharply. "The machine did. Accidentally. Accidents with machines happen every day, don't they? Let's keep things in perspective, Taylor. During that time frame, more babies died in car accidents on the California roads than were harmed by our machine. But you don't hear an outcry about that, do you? You don't accuse the car salesmen or automotive engineers of being mass murderers, do you? Of course not. Accidents are the price of civilization. Blood oils social progress. Sure, it was awful, but was it worth it? Believe me, it was." He looked carefully into her eyes to see if she was buying his argument. He decided she wasn't. "Still, it was unfortunate. And that's where you can help us—and help save the lives of future babies. Would you like to help save babies' lives, Taylor?"

Taylor swallowed.

"Would you?"

"Yes," she said softly.

"I thought so. You're a good girl. I like that about you." He leaned toward her. "We want to study you to see why you lived and they didn't. You can help us learn what the difference is between your body and theirs. If we can isolate that factor, we can create electric children without endangering their lives. And you, Taylor, hold a very special key to that discovery—something that the other Glows can't help us with. Do you want to know what that is?"

Taylor slowly nodded.

"You did well in science," Hatch said. "I've seen your transcripts. You got an A minus on Mr. Poulsen's last biology test. Not bad. So you know that one of the tools we scientists use to study genetics is identical twins. Especially those who have been separated from each other at birth. It teaches us things about genetic influences versus environmental factors—what you're born with compared to what you pick up along the way. You, Taylor, are one of those identical twins."

"I'm not a twin," Taylor said.

*"Au contraire,"* Hatch said with an amused grin. "I'd like you to meet someone." He turned back toward the door. "Nichelle, please ask Tara to come in."

At his command, a girl stepped into the room. Taylor froze. The girl looked exactly like her. Before she could say a word, Tara walked up to her and smiled. "Hi, sis."

Taylor's eyes darted back and forth between Hatch and Tara. "I don't understand."

Hatch smiled. "Ah, the learning begins. There are a lot of things you don't understand yet," Hatch said. "But you will." He smiled at Tara. "Have a seat, Tara. Just there on the bed."

"Thank you."

Hatch's voice became softer, almost gentle. "Taylor, you were born a twin. When your biological mother, a teenage girl named Gail Nash of Monrovia, California, gave you up for adoption, Tara was the first to be adopted. She went to a home right here in Pasadena just three miles from the academy—right here in our own backyard. We found her almost nine years ago."

He looked at Tara, who nodded enthusiastically. "Nine years this coming June."

Taylor just stared at the girl in astonishment. Could this be some kind of trick?

"You, Taylor, on the other hand, were adopted by a family in another state. And everyone knows how inefficient government bureaucrats can be. Your records were lost in the transfer between state agencies. You vanished like a grain of rice in a rice paddy. We might never have found you had you not come looking for your birth records."

Taylor felt sick. Ostin was right: She had exposed them.

"There were seventeen electric children. We had located them all except for two. You and Michael Vey."

Taylor jumped when he said Michael's name.

Hatch smiled. "Yes, you know Michael, don't you?"

She didn't answer.

"Don't worry. You did him a favor by leading us to him. We might never have found him without you."

She felt even worse. "He's here?"

"Not yet. But he soon will be. In fact, he doesn't know it yet, but he's about to start planning his trip to see us." He turned to Tara. "That's all for now. Why don't you come back a little later and show Taylor around."

She stood. "Okey-dokey." She smiled at Taylor. "It's so exciting to finally see you. You're going to love it here. We're contributing to the world in a way you never dreamed possible. And Dr. Hatch is the smartest man alive." Tara looked back at Hatch and he nodded his approval.

"There are some really cool benefits to being here, like, we're not treated like children. Also, we have family vacations twice a year. I've been all around the world. And we get cool presents." She flashed her diamond watch. "How many fifteen-year-olds have a twenty-three-thousand-dollar diamond Rolex watch?"

"Thank you, Tara," Hatch said. "You can tell her all about it later."

"I've gotta go. I'm so glad you found us. I've waited years for us to be together. Ciao!"

She walked out of the room.

"Beautiful girl," Hatch said. "Of course, you know that, since you're an exact replica." He leaned forward, his face taking a gentle demeanor. "So let me tell you what you can expect while you're here. Over the next few days we'll be doing some general kinds of physiological testing. Basic stuff—blood work, an electrocardiogram, and a full body scan. We also have some special tests we've designed to help understand your special gifts. Nothing painful; we just want to make sure you're healthy. The doctors out there don't understand special individuals like you, and so they miss things. We've already saved the lives of some of your colleagues."

"I just want to go home."

Hatch moved closer to her. "Taylor, I know it's hard right now. You've been plucked from all you know like a rose from a weed patch. Change is always hard, but that doesn't mean it's not good. Usually the hard things in our life lead to good."

Taylor wiped her eyes. "You're not going to let me go home?"

"Look, just five minutes ago you didn't even know that you have a sister, and now you do. And soon your friend Michael will be joining us. You need to stop thinking of this as an abduction, and think of it as a long-awaited homecoming—a family reunion, if you will. *This* is your home."

"For how long?" Taylor asked.

Hatch looked at her with a perplexed gaze. "For the rest of your life."

# PART THREE

# 22

## The Revelation

One thing I knew about Ostin, if he didn't understand something, his brain attacked it without ceasing, comparing facts and calculating figures with the intensity of a computer-processing chip. Around nine thirty at night his breakthrough came. He was lying on the couch in my front room, staring at the ceiling as I paced from one side of the room to the other like a caged leopard.

"I just don't get it," I said. "How did they know who I am? How did they know about our powers?"

Ostin was quiet for another minute, then he suddenly shouted, "That's it!"

"*What's* it?"

He jumped up from the couch. "I've been trying to figure out why they came after you at all. You weren't looking for those records." He looked at me, his eyes wide with excitement. "It's because they don't care about the records."

"What do you mean?"

"They're not trying to hide the information about what their machine did. They're looking for the survivors. And when they found Taylor, they found you!"

"I'm not following you."

"Look, these guys have all the records of every baby who survived. What if those other children all had powers like yours and Taylor's? If they discovered that their machine gave those babies special powers, that could be worth billions."

"That's a big 'if,'" I said.

"Is it? You said the other kid, Zeus, shocked your mother, right? So we know there's at least one other"—he spoke the word cautiously—"mutant.

"The only other people we know who were born at that hospital at that time have electrical powers. So, statistically, we're batting a thousand. There were seventeen children who survived. Maybe they all have powers."

He paused, waiting for the last of the puzzle pieces to come together. Then he pounded the palm of his hand with his fist. "It was a fake." Ostin looked at me the way he did when he solved a difficult math problem. "The whole thing with the gunman was fake. It was a test."

"Why would they do that?"

"Because you don't pick up an electric eel without getting shocked. They first had to see what you could do. You said the man in the sunglasses appeared after you shocked the gunman, right?"

"That's right. And he said, 'Well done, Michael.'" I stopped pacing. "You might be on to something. He knew my name and what I did. And Clyde . . ."

"Who's Clyde?"

"He's the gunman. I remember thinking that he looked really nervous, like he didn't want to be there. He was shaking like crazy. And his gun didn't even have bullets." I looked down. "But then why did they take my mom and not me?"

"Maybe they wanted to take both of you, but didn't get the chance. You said you heard me coming, right?"

"Right."

"But they were gone by the time I returned. They must have run out of time. They already had your mother, so they took her and ran."

"Which means they're probably still looking for me."

"They don't have to," Ostin said.

"What do you mean?"

"They have your mother. They know you'll come looking for them." He looked in my eyes. "Whoever took your mom took Taylor. So if we can find one of them, we can find the other."

I suddenly had a flash of inspiration. "Wait. I think I know where Taylor is."

"Where?"

"The academy."

I ran into my bedroom and found the brochure Taylor had given me from her locker. I brought it back out to the front room and spread it open on the counter. "Here. It's got to be the place. Or at least it's connected."

Ostin looked at the brochure. "Five-thirteen Allen Avenue, Pasadena, California." He looked up. "I think you're right. I'm betting that the Elgen Academy is really just for kids with electrical powers."

Ostin's logic made sense to me. Why else would they offer a scholarship to me when there were hundreds of kids with better grades? "You could be right," I said.

"Now what?" Ostin asked.

"We tell the police," I said.

Ostin shook his head. "No way. They'll never believe us."

"Why wouldn't they?"

"Think about it. Two teenagers walk into a police station and tell them that a secret agency is kidnapping mothers and cheerleaders?"

Hearing it like that did sound crazy.

"But we have proof," I said.

"No, we have a hunch and some articles on the Internet. They'll think we're crazy. And even if we somehow convinced them to look into it, this is a multibillion-dollar company. If they find anyone snooping around, they'll just move your mom and Taylor to someplace else and then we'll have nothing." Ostin stood and began to pace. "We need to know more about our enemy. But it's not like they're going to have a Facebook profile. Where do we learn more?"

"Clyde, the gunman," I said.

"But he's in jail."

"Lieutenant Lloyd could get us to him."

"Why would he do that?"

"He said their first interrogation was worthless. Maybe I can convince him that I might be more effective." I brought out the card Lieutenant Lloyd had given me. "I'm going to call him." I immediately went to the phone and dialed Lloyd's cell phone number.

A gruff voice answered. "This is Boyd."

His full name was Boyd Lloyd? No wonder he went by Lieutenant. "Lieutenant Lloyd, this is Michael Vey."

"Michael. What can I do for you?"

I had been so eager to call him that I had dialed without thinking about what I was going to say. "I, uh, just had a thought. You said you had spoken to the gunman, but he didn't say much."

"No, he was as tight as pantyhose on a hippo."

"I was wondering if maybe he would talk to me."

"You want to speak with Clyde?"

"Well, maybe seeing me might make him talk."

There was a long pause. "Frankly, we couldn't do much worse than we did with his last interrogation. Hold on, I'm going to call my partner. May I call you back at this number?"

"Yes," I said. "Bye." I hung up the phone.

"What's up?" Ostin asked. "Why did you hang up?"

"He wants to talk to his partner."

About ten minutes later my phone rang. "Michael, it's Lieutenant Lloyd."

"Yes, sir."

"I spoke with my partner. He thinks there's a chance it might work—a small chance, but worth trying. So if you're willing to face Clyde, I say let's go for it."

"Thank you, sir."

"What time are you available?"

"Any time is good. I'm not back to school yet."

"Then how about I pick you up in the morning."

"Yes, sir."

"I have your address on the police report. I'll come by around ten."

"I'll be ready. Thank you."

"Thank you, Michael. We'll keep our fingers crossed. I'll see you tomorrow."

"Bye." I hung up then turned to Ostin. "We're in."

"Well done," Ostin said. "You know, you could always just shock Clyde again."

"The man helped kidnap my mother. Whatever it takes," I said. "Whatever it takes."

# 23

Clyde

I didn't sleep well that night. I had a nightmare about my mother sitting in a cage at the zoo surrounded by laughing hyenas and calling for me to help her. Ostin woke me when he knocked on my door at seven. I answered the door still in my pajamas. He was dressed for school.

"What's up?" I asked groggily.

"Not you," he said. "My mom told me to come get you for breakfast."

I rubbed my eyes. "Okay. I'll be right there."

I went back to my room and put on my robe, then walked down the hall to the Lisses' and let myself in. Breakfast was on the table and Ostin and his father were already eating. Mrs. Liss had made wheat toast with a fried egg in the middle.

Mr. Liss was reading the paper and dipped it a little to look at me. "Good morning, Michael."

"Good morning," I replied.

"That's your plate," Ostin said.

I sat down next to him.

At the sound of my voice, Mrs. Liss came out of the kitchen. "Good morning, honey. How did you sleep?"

"Not very well."

"That's understandable. You just make yourself right at home."

I poured myself a glass of orange juice.

"There are hash browns, too," Ostin said, pushing a plate my way. "With cheddar."

"Thanks."

"Is there anything else you want?" Mrs. Liss asked. "Do you need some ketchup or Tabasco sauce for your egg?"

"No. I'm good," I said.

Mr. Liss glanced at his watch and set down his paper. "I've got to go." He stood, looking at us. "You boys take it easy." Mr. Liss had an unusually deep voice that made everything he said sound like an order.

"Yes, sir," I said.

"See ya, Dad," Ostin said.

Mr. Liss grabbed his jacket and keys from the counter, kissed Mrs. Liss, then walked out. When he was gone Mrs. Liss said, "I forgot the salt and pepper." She walked back to the kitchen.

Ostin said in a hushed voice, "I wish I could go with you to the police station."

"Me too."

"Are you nervous to see him?"

"Yeah." I took a drink of juice.

Mrs. Liss walked back in. "Here you go, darlin'." She salt-and-peppered my egg for me even though I didn't want it. "So, Michael, do you feel up to going to school today?"

"Not yet," I said. "Lieutenant Lloyd is going to pick me up at ten. We're going down to the station to talk to the man they put in jail."

Her brow furrowed. "Oh? I didn't know that. Would you like me to go with you?"

"No, I'll be all right."

"How are you on clothes? Do you need some laundry done?"

"I'm okay for now." The truth was, I'd been wearing the same clothes for three days.

"Well, whatever you need, just ask. I'll just be your mama until your mama gets back."

"Thank you," I said, grateful for how she'd said it.

Ostin finished eating, then went and got his backpack. "I better get going." I walked to the door with him. "Good luck," he said. "Bones."

"Bones," I replied. We bumped fists and then he walked off down the hallway.

"Thank you for breakfast, Mrs. Liss."

"You're welcome. Please let me know when you get back from the police station."

"Sure thing." I went back to my apartment and showered and dressed. Then it was time to go outside to the parking lot to wait.

I was sitting on the curb when Lieutenant Lloyd pulled up in his police cruiser. He rolled down his window. "Good morning, Michael."

The morning sun was high above the mountains and I shielded my eyes with both my hands. "Hi."

"How are you?"

I shrugged. I know he was just being friendly but it was kind of a stupid question. "I've been better."

He nodded sympathetically. "Come sit in the front seat."

I climbed into the car, put on my seat belt, and we drove downtown.

The drive to the jail took about twenty minutes. I was ticking a lot. Lieutenant Lloyd didn't say anything about it, but I'm pretty sure he noticed because he asked me again if I really wanted to do this. I guess taking a minor into the jail is pretty unusual, and he was probably having second thoughts about it. I told him I was positive it was the right thing.

When we arrived at the jail, I went through all the security, metal detectors and all, then followed Lieutenant Lloyd down a long corridor, passing other police officers on the way. At the end of the hall were two doors. He led me through the door on the left into a darkened room. "This is the observation room," he explained. "This is where we watch what's going on in the interrogation room."

There was a large two-way mirror as well as two monitors mounted to a console. The gunman, Clyde, was sitting in a chair on the other side of the glass, his hands handcuffed behind his back. Seeing him filled me with anger.

"This is Detective Muir," Lieutenant Lloyd said, gesturing to a man sitting in front of the bank of monitors. "He'll be recording everything."

I turned back. "You record what happens inside?"

"Every word," he said.

I hadn't thought about that. I wouldn't be able to speak freely.

Lieutenant Lloyd looked into my eyes. "You're still sure you want to do this?"

"I'm sure," I said.

"You're a brave young man," he said. "Okay, then. We have Stuart in handcuffs, but if you feel threatened at all, let me know." He patted his gun belt. "I have my Taser."

*Me too*, I thought. "I'm ready."

As we started to walk out I brushed by the recording console and pulsed. Suddenly all the screens in the room went blank.

"Wait," Muir said. "We just went down."

Lieutenant Lloyd groaned. "What timing."

"It's like we got a power surge or something," Detective Muir said, flipping a few switches. He spent the next five minutes trying to get the system back up.

Finally Lieutenant Lloyd asked, "Does the phone still work?"

"Yes."

"We'll use the intercom on it. We won't be able to tape it, but at least we'll hear what's going on."

We walked back out to the hallway. Lieutenant Lloyd unlocked and opened the interrogation room door, and we stepped inside. The room was rectangular with bare white cinder-block walls. Clyde sat at the opposite end of a long, wooden table. He wore an orange jail jumpsuit with the name STUART and a number printed above the left breast.

"Hello, Clyde," Lieutenant Lloyd said.

Stuart didn't look at Lieutenant Lloyd, but glared at me.

"I'm sure you remember who this is."

He said nothing.

"Let me help you remember. This is Michael Vey. He's the son of the woman you helped kidnap."

He scowled. "I know who he is."

"Good. Because you owe him an explanation."

Clyde turned his body sideways. "I don't owe him nothin'."

Lieutenant Lloyd shook his head. He whispered to me, "Like I said, he's not cooperating."

"Maybe if I talked to him alone."

He thought about it for a moment, then said, "I was afraid it might come to that." He walked up to Clyde. "I'm leaving Michael alone with you. Don't try anything crazy."

Suddenly Clyde's expression changed from anger to fear. "No! You can't leave him alone with me. I have rights against cruel and inhumane punishment. I have rights!"

Lloyd looked at him like he was crazy. "I was saying, I'm leaving him alone with you. But I'm watching you carefully through the glass so don't get any ideas. . . ." Lieutenant Lloyd turned back to me and shook his head. "Be careful," he whispered. "The man's nutty as a bag of trail mix. Good luck."

When the door shut, Clyde looked up at me and our eyes met.

"Where's my mother?"

His lips pursed. I stood up and took a few steps toward him. I knew the police were listening so I chose my words carefully. "Do you need something to jog your memory?"

"You stay away from me, electric boy."

"What did you call me?"

"I know all about your kind, you glowing freaks."

"My kind?"

He scowled. "Yes, your kind." For the first time I noticed the scars running up his arm. He followed my gaze, then looked back up at me. "Yeah, that's from one of you. You Glows are all alike."

"How many are there of us?"

"Too many. One of you is too many."

"I only did what I did because you pulled a gun on my mother. *You* made me do it."

"That's because they made me do it."

"Who made you?"

He didn't answer.

"You know, I can reach you from here," I said, which wasn't true but he didn't know it.

He sneered at me, then said, "Hatch."

"What's a hatch?"

"Hatch isn't a *what*, you idiot. He's a *who*."

"Who is Hatch?"

He didn't answer.

"Is Hatch the guy with the sunglasses?"

"They're not sunglasses. It's how he sees the Glows." He said the word as if it were bitter on his tongue.

"What's a . . . Glow?"

"You're a Glow."

"Who were those other two kids with him?"

"Glows. Zeus and Nichelle."

"I saw what Zeus does. What does Nichelle do?"

"She's Hatch's protection against Glows." His face bent in a dark grin. "Oh, you're going to like her. Trust me. She's the nastiest of the whole stinking, nasty bunch of you."

"How long have they known about me?"

"Since you were a baby. They just couldn't find you. You and the other."

I guessed he was talking about Taylor. "Where is she?"

"You'll have to ask Hatch."

"Where did they take my mother?"

"How would I know that? They left me."

"Where did they plan to take my mother?"

"You'll never find her," he said, and a dark smile crossed his face. "You have no idea what you're up against, glow worm. They have private jets and hidden compounds. They're all over the world. Your mother could be anywhere by now."

"Where is Hatch?"

He looked away.

"Where is Hatch?" I said louder. I began rubbing the table. "Do you need some persuasion?"

"What are you going to do, kill me? You'd be doing me a favor. They're going to kill me anyway. You'll see. To them we're all expendable. Even the Glows."

I decided to change my tactic. "If I can stop Hatch . . ."

He interrupted me with laughter. "You think you can stop Hatch? The U.S. Marine Corps couldn't stop Hatch."

"If I can stop Hatch, I'll be able to prove that they forced you into this. Help me find my mother and I promise I'll testify for you and get you out of here."

Clyde's laughter only increased. "You think I want to go out there with them? I'm safer in here."

I leaned forward and whispered, "Is Hatch at the school in Pasadena?"

He looked down.

"Is Hatch at the school in Pasadena?" I repeated.

Without looking up he said, "It's not a school."

"Is that where he is?"

He looked up. "You'll find out soon enough."

I looked at him for another moment, then over at the mirror. "I'm done," I said.

When I turned back, Clyde was smiling. "Hatch is waiting for you, you know. He's been waiting a long, long time. He really wants you."

Just then the door opened and Lieutenant Lloyd walked in. "All right, Clyde."

"You know who this kid is, don't you?" Clyde shouted. "He's a Glow. He can shock you worse than that Taser you're wearing. He can kill you. He can kill all of us. They're going to take over."

I looked up at Lloyd and shrugged.

"Shut up," Lieutenant Lloyd said.

"They're going to take over the entire world!"

"Save it for the judge," Lieutenant Lloyd said.

As I walked out of the room Lieutenant Lloyd put his arm on my shoulder. "Sorry, kid. That's what I was afraid of. Ever since we brought him in he's been ranting about hatches and glow worms." He shook his head. "The man's insane."

# 24

Jack

Ostin came to my apartment directly from school. I was on my knees filling my backpack with clothes.

"What are you doing?"

"Packing. They're in Pasadena."

"Clyde told you that?"

"Sort of. The man in the sunglasses is named Hatch."

"Hatch?"

"And you were right. There are more of us electric children."

"Did the police hear all that?"

"Yeah. But they just think Clyde's crazy."

Ostin sat on my bed. "So now what?"

"I'm going to Pasadena."

"How do we do that?"

"What do you mean, 'we'?" I said.

"You can't go alone. What if you need help?"

"This isn't a video game, Ostin. It's real danger. If something goes wrong, we can't just push a reset button."

"Which is precisely why I need to go. What good is being here without my best friend?"

I looked at him. "Thanks."

"So how do we get there?"

"Jack."

Ostin's eyes widened. "Jack the bully?"

"Yeah, he's perfect. He's got his own car."

"There's no way my mom will let me go with him driving."

"Your mom can't know."

"You're right. She'd freak no matter what." He looked down. "What makes you think Jack will drive us?"

"He owes me." I rubbed my hands together and they made the crackling sound of electricity. "I think I can persuade him."

# 25

Tara

Taylor was sitting on her bed eating supper when she heard her door unlock. A voice from a speaker said, "Enter."

The door opened, and Tara walked into the room. She was smiling. "You finally got some food, huh?"

Taylor looked up. In spite of her mistrust of the place, she felt a natural kinship to Tara. "Yeah. What's with all the bananas?"

"High in potassium. It's good for us." She shook her head and her smile grew. "Crazy, huh? You must feel like you fell down the rabbit hole."

"The rabbit hole?"

"You know, *Alice in Wonderland*. But really, it's not as bad as you think."

"I've been kidnapped, tied up, tortured by some deranged Goth chick, and locked in a cell, and you say it's not so bad?"

"You're right, Nichelle's pretty awful, isn't she?" She swayed a little. "As far as the cell, it's just temporary. It's just until you see that they mean you no harm. They have a lot of experience with this."

"Kidnapping?" Taylor asked.

Tara shook her head. "Look, sis, I understand why you're so upset. I really do." She walked over and sat on the bed next to her. "And I'm sorry if I don't seem more sympathetic, but I'm just so happy you're here. My own sister. I've waited for this day for so long."

"How long have you known you're a twin?" Taylor asked.

"Nine years—since Dr. Hatch found me. He promised me that someday he'd find you. And he did."

"I didn't even know I had a sister."

"It's kind of cool, isn't it?"

Taylor pushed away her tray. "I'm sorry, I'm just scared and I don't know what I'm doing here."

"I really do understand," Tara said. "But it will be okay. Trust me. They just want to know why we're so different. The research they do here will save millions of lives someday. And they take really good care of us. Really good care. We even have our own concierge service."

"What's that?"

"You know, like at fancy hotels. You can ask for pretty much anything and they'll get it for you. Clothes, front-row concert tickets and backstage passes, gadgets—almost anything, within reason. I mean, if you asked for a jet, they'd probably say no. But I asked for a diamond bracelet once and they got me one."

"Why would they do all that?"

"Because we're the special ones. Out of billions of people in this world there're only seventeen of us. Well, actually, thirteen of us now."

Taylor wondered what she had meant by that.

"We're like royalty. Try it. Just ask for anything."

"Okay. I want to go home."

Tara sighed. "Except that. Taylor, give it a couple weeks. If you are still so unhappy, then I'm sure they'll let you go."

Taylor looked at her with surprise. "Really?"

"Of course. I don't have a lock on my door. I come and go as I wish. The thing is, they have to protect themselves, too. They have a lot of money invested in all this and they're working with kids. It's a big risk. Does that make sense?"

Taylor looked down for a moment. "Yeah, I guess it does. But then why did they kidnap me?"

"They didn't want to. They invited you to come to the Elgen Academy, didn't they? And everything they promised was true, the best schooling, and the college of your choice. In fact, when you turn sixteen, you can have any car you want. A Ferrari, a Rolls-Royce, Maserati, anything. But your adopted parents wouldn't let you go, would they?"

"No."

"They don't even know about your powers, do they?"

"No."

"Exactly. They have no idea how special you are."

"How do you know all this?"

"Because you're my sister." Her eyes moistened with emotion. "I've waited a long, long time for you."

Taylor felt a little better. "So, are you . . . electric?"

She nodded. "Of course."

"What can you do?"

"Well, we're twins, so my powers are like yours, but a little more refined. I've had years to practice them here." She sat back on the bed. "Okay, want to see something?"

"Sure."

"Okay. Here goes." Tara closed her eyes.

Suddenly, Taylor felt a warm rush of happiness flow through her. Taylor laughed. "How did you do that?"

"Cool, isn't it? I've learned to stimulate the part of the brain that produces serotonin—kind of a happy drug. I can also do the opposite, but you don't want to feel that."

"What do you mean 'the opposite'?"

"I can make you feel the negative emotions. Like rage or incredible fear."

"How much fear?"

"Black-widows-crawling-all-over-your-body fear."

Taylor bristled.

"Like I said, you don't want to feel that."

Taylor shook her head. "No, I'll pass on that."

"You'll learn, too. Part of our education at the academy is working with scientists to develop our powers. They have also found that eating certain things enhances our abilities."

"Like bananas?" Taylor asked.

"Yeah. You can have all the banana shakes you want. Banana cream pie, banana smoothies, the list goes on. Also, minerals help. We take special supplements three times a day. We also avoid refined sugar. It gets in the way of things. Once I gave up soda pop for a month and I doubled my stretch."

"Stretch?"

"That's some of the jargon they use here. You'll learn it. Stretch is how far you can push your powers. One boy here has such a powerful stretch he can reach airplanes."

"What does he do to airplanes?" Taylor asked.

Tara shook her head. "Nothing," she said.

"So can you read minds?" Taylor asked.

Tara's expression fell. "No. Can you read minds?"

Her reaction worried Taylor. "Uh, no. I mean, I just thought with what you can do, you might be able to."

"No. None of us can read minds. I think Dr. Hatch would freak out if someone could. I mean, just imagine what they could do."

Taylor nodded. "What about Nichelle?"

Tara grimaced. "No one here likes Nichelle. She's a beast. Just stay close to Dr. Hatch and she'll keep her distance. She used her power on me once, and Dr. Hatch disciplined her."

"Why didn't you just do something to her?"

"Our powers don't work on her. She's like a vampire. She sucks our power."

"That's what she told me."

"Yeah, she thinks it's cool. She's such a loser. The thing is, around

us she's powerful but in the outer world she's nothing. Like Kryp-
tonite can kill Superman, but you and I could wear it for jewelry.
In the outer world she's just another Goth. Anyway, it's against the
rules to use our powers without Dr. Hatch's permission. And we're
never allowed to use our powers on each other. Just the GPs."

"What's a GP?"

"You'll find out."

"What time is it anyway?"

"It's around ten. Bedtime. So you better get some good rest. We
have a busy day tomorrow."

"Doing what?"

She stood. "I don't want to ruin the surprise, but trust me, you're
gonna love it." She leaned forward and kissed Taylor on the forehead.
"Sleep tight, don't let the bedbugs bite." She walked out and the door
clicked locked behind her.

Taylor lay back on her bed and looked up at the camera's blinking
red light. *Wasn't worried about the bedbugs*, she thought.

# 26

## Harry Winston

Taylor only knew it was morning because a nasal voice over the room's speaker told her it was time to wake up. She was still lying in bed when the lock clicked and Tara walked in. Her arms were full of clothing. "Get up, sleepyhead."

Taylor sat up rubbing her eyes. "I didn't sleep much last night."

"Well, you'll have to nap later, because right now we have a lot of fun to get to."

She laid the pile of clothes at the foot of Taylor's bed. "Fortunately we wear the same size in everything so you can borrow my things for now."

Taylor looked down at her smock. "You mean I don't have to wear this thing?"

Tara stared at her. "You're kidding me, right?"

Taylor shrugged. "I don't know."

"Wow, you've got this place all wrong. This isn't a prison. That's just an examination smock. We all wore them on our first day when they were establishing baselines. But that was yesterday. Today's your lucky day. Dr. Hatch said to take you shopping for a new wardrobe. And guess where?"

Taylor shrugged.

"The Miracle Mile."

"Huh?"

"Rodeo Drive, Beverly Hills. Heard of it? If you're anything like me—and you are—you are going to have the time of your life."

"I don't have any money," Taylor said.

Tara laughed. "You don't need money here. Now get dressed."

Taylor looked through the clothes Tara had brought. None of them looked as if they'd even been worn. "Wow. These are some expensive brands." She picked up a pair of jeans.

"You can keep whatever you like; I'll just get more. Actually, you'll get whatever you need today." Tara held up a blouse. "I love this one, it looks great with my . . . our complexion. Do you like it?"

"Yeah."

"Try it on."

Ignoring the video cameras, Taylor slipped off the smock and put on the blouse.

"You look ridiculously beautiful," Tara said. "You're the most beautiful girl in this place." She laughed. "Oh, that's kind of like complimenting myself, isn't it?"

Taylor grinned. "Yeah, it is."

After Taylor was dressed, the two girls walked outside the cell to an elevator. Tara put her finger on a fingerprint sensor pad. The screen turned green and the elevator door slid open.

"We'll stop by the cafeteria and get some breakfast on the way out," Tara said. She pushed the button for floor one, and they ascended two levels to the main floor. "This way to the cafeteria," she said.

The cafeteria looked less like a school cafeteria than a restaurant in a fancy hotel. They were met at the door by the restaurant's maître d', a short, Italian man with silver hair and a black tuxedo. "Good morning, ladies. You both look *bellissima*."

"Yes we do," Tara said. "Thank you for noticing."

"Thank you," Taylor said.

"What will it be today? Crab Benedict and banana-and-candied-walnut oatmeal are today's chef specials."

"I just want a banana smoothie," Tara said. "We're in a hurry."

"I guess, me too," Taylor said.

"Will you be having that to go, then?"

"Yes," Tara said. "And fast."

"Yes, very well." He ran back through the kitchen doors and just a few minutes later a waiter brought out their smoothies in plastic goblets with small, silver spoons. Tara took both glasses and handed one to Taylor. "Let's go, sis. We're burning daylight."

"Where are we going?"

"I already told you. Shopping."

"Outside?"

"Well, duh?"

Taylor looked around. "No one is going to stop me from leaving?"

"Why would they do that?"

"Dr. Hatch said—"

"Oh," Tara interrupted. "That reminds me. Dr. Hatch is going to meet up with us a little later. He said he has a surprise for you." Her eyebrows rose. "So get excited. His surprises are epic. He doesn't do things small."

Taylor followed her out the front door. It was the first time Taylor had seen the sun for several days. Her instinct told her to bolt, but she was still surrounded by fences, and Tara's happiness and reassurances had calmed her some. A Rolls-Royce Phantom was waiting for them at the curb. The driver stood at the back door, holding it open for them. "Good morning, ladies."

"Morning, Griff," Tara said.

"Good morning," Taylor said.

"Welcome to the academy, Taylor," the driver said. "My name is

Griffin. If I can do anything to make your day more pleasant, please let me know."

Taylor wondered how he knew her name. The two girls climbed into the backseat. Taylor had never been in such a luxurious car. The interior was all leather, glass, and highly polished burled wood. A glass partition separated them from the driver. In the center console was a telephone. Taylor's heart jumped. "Can I call my parents?"

Tara shook her head. "We'll have to ask Dr. Hatch. But it's probably too soon. There's still too much of that still in you."

"Too much of what?" Taylor asked.

Tara pointed to the world outside the compound. "That."

The drive from Pasadena to the palm-tree-lined streets of Beverly Hills was only twenty-five minutes. It was a bright day, and the sidewalks were crowded with both the glamorous and those seeking it.

Griffin parked the Rolls in a reserved spot on South Santa Monica Boulevard, then followed a few yards behind the girls as they shopped.

"Why is he following us?" Taylor asked.

"Duh," Tara said. "Someone's got to carry our bags."

Rodeo Drive started at the Beverly Hills Hotel and stretched on for nearly a mile. Tara explained that the district took up three city blocks and had over a hundred boutiques, hotels, and salons. Every fashion designer worth visiting had a shop in the neighborhood. In the first block they passed stores Taylor had only heard of: Lacoste, Juicy Couture, Chanel, Hugo Boss, and Giorgio Armani.

Tara pulled Taylor toward Juicy Couture, a tall glass store with a window display of mannequins in jewel-studded tracksuits with purses patterned with Couture's trademark crowns slung over their shoulders. Tara wanted to look at the swimsuits and pulled a floral print tankini from the rack.

"What do you think of this?"

Taylor looked at the price tag. "Two hundred and thirty dollars for a bathing suit?"

Tara shrugged. "I know. A bargain, right?"

They crossed Brighton Way and continued down Rodeo Drive. Tara pulled Taylor into Salvatore Ferragamo. At Tara's insistence, Taylor selected a pair of sunglasses in red and Tara got the same ones in purple.

Outside a store called Dolce & Gabbana, Tara squealed, "They have their new collection in! Come on!"

A woman standing near the front of the store smiled as the girls entered. "There are two of you! Which one of you lovely ladies is Tara?"

"I'm Tara," Tara said, curtseying. "This is my twin, Taylor."

"Twice the charm. It's such a pleasure meeting you, Taylor. How may we serve you ladies?"

"We're here to dress Taylor up," Tara said.

"Our pleasure." The woman snapped her fingers in the air. "Marc, bring Tara and Taylor some sparkling water." She turned back to the girls, smiling unctuously. "This way, please."

Taylor whispered to Tara, "She knows you?"

"Of course. I'm one of her best customers."

The woman led them to dressing rooms, where her staff delivered outfit after outfit of gorgeous fabrics and light dresses. They spent more than five thousand dollars and the salesladies waved happily to them as they walked out, the girls' arms heavy with shopping bags, which they surrendered to Griffin.

Taylor trailed behind Tara all morning as they walked through Tara's favorite stores: Bebe, Gucci, Chanel. Even though they were the identical age, Taylor thought Tara acted more like a twenty-one-year-old than a fifteen-year-old. She knew her way around the stores, and if they didn't already know her, all she had to do was say that she was with the Elgen Academy and the employees tripped over each other to help them.

At Tara's urging, Taylor purchased nine pairs of jeans, six skirts, four pairs of shoes, eight shirts, two leather jackets, and three bags of accessories. Just for fun, Tara picked out three identical outfits.

Taylor was nervous about all the money they were spending. She had once used her mother's credit card to download an album with-out asking, and she'd been grounded for a week. "Whose credit card are we using?" Taylor asked.

Tara held it up. "American Express Black card. It's mine. I just have to ask first. But they've never turned me down. I think it has like a two-hundred-thousand-dollar limit."

Taylor's jaw dropped. "You've got to be kidding."

"Nope. Far cry from Preston Street, eh?"

Taylor looked at her. "How do you know where I live?"

"I asked, of course." Tara smiled. "Sis, you just don't understand how excited I've been to have you here. You coming *home* is the greatest thing that's ever happened to me."

The way Tara said "home" scared her. Taylor wasn't sure how to respond to Tara's excitement. Finally she just said, "Thank you."

A few minutes later Taylor was looking at a diamond necklace displayed in the window of Tiffany & Company when Tara said, "Dr. Hatch said to not buy any jewelry."

"I was just looking."

"No problem," she said. "He'll be here soon anyway. He wanted to meet us around one. Which is"—she looked at her watch—"almost a half hour from now. Are you ready for a break?"

Taylor nodded.

"Good. Because I want to show you something." Tara led her to Via Rodeo, where they wandered through the cobblestone roads, pausing at the fountains and wrought-iron lamps and arches. Griffin still followed, but at a distance.

"This is so beautiful," Taylor said.

"It's European," Tara explained. "Have you ever seen the real thing? Europe?"

"No. Someday." Taylor's parents had promised to take her on a tour of Europe the summer after she graduated from high school. Something that even with her mother's professional discounts, they'd still have to save and sacrifice for. Thinking of her parents made her heart ache.

Tara touched her shoulder. "No? You will. You are going to love our vacations." They walked past a crowd of tourists posing in front of a fountain and crossed the street toward the Beverly Wilshire.

"Are you having fun?"

Taylor nodded, even though she was still afraid.

"Told you you'd like it. Only one thing I'm disappointed about. I usually see celebrities. I guess you can't have everything." Before Taylor could respond, Tara asked, "Are you hungry yet?"

Taylor figured they had spent more than ten thousand dollars on clothes. "Are you sure we're not going to get in trouble for spending so much?"

"We might get in trouble for not spending enough. This is what we're supposed to do."

"I just can't believe this," Taylor said, feeling confused.

"Believe it. It's the way it is all the time. Dr. Hatch always says special people should have special things." Her face lit. "You like sushi, don't you?"

"I'm not sure. I've never had it. But I've always wanted to try it."

"I've got a place for you."

They walked a couple of blocks to a Japanese restaurant. Urasawa. The restaurant's lobby was crowded and Tara pushed her way to the hostess counter, which embarrassed Taylor immensely.

"A table for three," Tara said.

The hostess, a middle-aged Japanese woman, looked at her dully. "Do you have reservations?"

"No," Tara said confidently. "We're with the Elgen Academy."

The woman slightly bowed. "My apologies; *gomen nasai.* Right this way." She whispered into a nearby waitress's ear, then grabbed the menus and immediately led Tara and Taylor to a table near the back of the restaurant. "We reserve this table for celebrities," the woman said. "Welcome to Urasawa."

As they sat down a kimono-clad waitress brought out a plate of *gyoza.*

"This is amazing," Taylor said. "I can't believe they just let us in."

Tara looked at the menu. "Of course they did."

Taylor looked at the empty seat. "Is Griffin going to eat with us?"

Tara crinkled her nose. "No. Why would he do that?"

"Then who's the third seat for?"

"Hopefully, that seat would be for me," Dr. Hatch said. He was standing next to the table, dressed casually in light slacks and a polo shirt.

Tara smiled. "Hello, Dr. Hatch."

Taylor bristled at the sight of him, but faked a smile.

"May I join you?" he asked.

"Of course," Tara said.

He pulled out a chair and sat down. "So how goes the shopping? Having fun?"

"We've spent about ten thousand dollars so far," Tara said.

"Only ten?" Hatch said. "Come on, girls, you need to pick up the pace. Shop like you mean it."

Taylor looked at him in wonderment. Dr. Hatch lifted a pair of chopsticks and helped himself to one of the dumplings. "Hmm," he said. "Fabulous."

The waitress returned with a large platter of sushi, tempura, and *yakiniku*. The waitress bowed to Dr. Hatch. "Dr. Hatch, *youkoso*."

"*Domo arigato gozaimasu.*"

Tara and Dr. Hatch attacked the food while Taylor fumbled with her chopsticks.

"This is great sushi," Tara said. "Not as good as that place we ate at in Tokyo last summer . . . But it's still good."

"Kyubei," Hatch said. "Wonderful restaurant. One of the few places that still serves puffer fish."

"You went to Tokyo?" Taylor asked.

"Oh, yeah. We go everywhere. Last year the family went on a trip to Japan, Beijing, Hong Kong, and Taiwan."

"I've always wanted to travel," Taylor said.

Dr. Hatch handed Taylor a fork. "Chopsticks can be such a bother. Please, enjoy. The *unagi* is especially delicious."

Taylor speared a piece. "What's this?"

"Eel," Tara said. "It's my favorite."

Taylor took a tiny bite while Tara and Hatch watched her expectantly. "What do you think?" Hatch asked.

"It looks gross, but it's pretty good."

Hatch smiled. "Things aren't always what they seem," he said.

Taylor sensed he wasn't talking about food.

"Bet you didn't have sushi this good in Idaho," Tara said.

"I didn't have it at all. Sushi's kind of expensive."

"That's too bad," Tara said.

"It's not a big deal," Taylor said defensively. "It's just food."

"Taylor's right," Hatch said. "It is just food. And besides, want is a thing of the past." He smiled at her. "From now on you're going to experience things you've only dreamed of. And you're going to travel to places you've only imagined: Bali, Nepal, Moscow, Paris, Rome. And that's just the beginning. We have a student traveling right now from London to Dubai. It's a brave new world, Taylor. A brave new world with endless opportunities."

He gestured with his chopsticks. "Think of it. Every day billions of people wake up to lives of desperation—some just hoping to survive another miserable day. Those few with enough to eat are hoping their lives might mean something—hoping their dreams and existence won't just blow away with the sands of time. But not you. Not anymore. What we do at the academy, what you do as one of the chosen, will endure. Someday people will read books about you. You will be talked about and discussed just like the early pioneers and explorers in today's textbooks. You are Christopher Columbus, Marco Polo, and Neil Armstrong, all in one."

"Why would they talk about me?" Taylor asked.

"Because you are a pioneer in a very real sense. You are the prototype of the next great species. You will be more famous than you can possibly imagine."

Taylor didn't know what to say. She had always wanted to be famous.

After another half hour Hatch said, "Are you girls almost done eating? Because I have a surprise for Taylor."

Tara smiled. "Lucky girl. Dr. Hatch has the best surprises."

"Are you ready?" Hatch asked.

"I guess so," Taylor said.

Hatch stood and raised his hand. The waitress rushed over. "*Hai,* sir."

"Put it on our tab, thirty percent tip."

"Yes, sir. Thank you, sir."

They walked out of the restaurant. A black Cadillac Escalade with tinted windows was idling out front. Two black-suited men with ear radios and aviator sunglasses stood next to the car. Hatch waved to them. "We're just going to walk. It's only a few blocks from here."

"What's a few blocks?" Taylor asked.

"Have you ever heard of Harry Winston?" Hatch asked.

"Harry Winston the jeweler?"

"Exactly," he said, looking impressed. "How do you know Harry Winston?"

"It's in that song, 'Diamonds Are a Girl's Best Friend.' They say, 'talk to me Harry Winston.'"

Dr. Hatch laughed. "Brava! Very good, Taylor. You're much too young to know that though."

"My mom liked that song. I mean, likes that song." It bothered her that she had used the past tense.

Hatch nodded. "Did you know that Harry Winston acquired, then gave away the most famous diamond in history? It's called the Hope diamond and it's more than forty-five carats. Today it's on display at the Smithsonian Institution in Washington, D.C. What's most impressive to me is that not only did he acquire a gem once owned by King Louis the XIV, but he also had the guts to cut it. He had the courage to improve it. That's how you make history. You cut against the rough." He looked up. "And here we are," he said, raising his hands.

The store was composed of smooth gray stone. A simple brass sign out front read HW, and below that, HARRY WINSTON.

A man opened the door for them. "Hello, Dr. Hatch."

Hatch waved the girls ahead. "Ladies. After you."

Taylor had never been in such a luxurious place before. The floors were carpeted in rich chocolate hues and the walls were a dark mahogany. It was cool inside and windowless, the room lit by large wall lamps. The atmosphere was hushed, as if they'd entered a museum or library.

"This is *the* place to buy jewelry. It's where the stars come when they're up for an Oscar," Tara said.

"And you," Hatch said to Taylor, "are a star."

An older gentleman with silver hair whisked across the room to greet them. "Ah, Dr. Hatch," he said with a French accent. "It's so good to see you again. I have the necklaces you requested right over here."

"Thank you. Tara, I'm going to spend a little time with Taylor. Why don't you find yourself some earrings."

"Yes, sir."

"This way, Taylor," Hatch said.

The jeweler led them to a small private room. In the center of the room there was a round, polished marble desk with a mirror and a magnifying glass. "Shall I bring in a preliminary selection?"

"Please," Hatch said, matching the Frenchman's formal tone and winking at Taylor. The man nodded and left the room.

He returned a moment later carrying three boxes, which he laid reverently in front of Taylor, lifting the lids off one by one. "I would like to show you a sampling from our classic selection. First, the Loop Necklace." He held it out for her to examine. "This elegant piece is made up of three hundred and fifty-eight round diamonds. It is immaculate."

"It's beautiful," Taylor said.

"Would you like to see it on?" Hatch asked.

"Really? Sure." Taylor held her hair off her neck while the jeweler placed the necklace on her. He fastened the necklace, then slid a small oval mirror across the table toward her so she could look at herself.

The necklace felt heavy and cool. Each diamond glistened like it was on show.

"Wow . . ." She touched the necklace. She couldn't believe she was wearing it.

"Show her the next one," Hatch said.

"The next one?" Taylor asked.

The man nodded as he unclasped the necklace Taylor was wearing. "Certainly. The Baby Wreath Necklace consists of one hundred seventeen round and marquise-cut diamonds for a total of twenty-five carats. The pendant is set in platinum." The necklace was shorter and thicker, the diamonds set in an intricate pattern of holly-shaped links.

"Do you like it?" Hatch asked.

"It's cool," Taylor said.

"And the one I've saved for last. Nightlife. Made up of sixty round and pear-shaped diamonds for a total of thirteen carats within a platinum setting."

Taylor gasped when she saw it. The brilliant diamonds hung from a delicate-looking platinum chain, the different diamond cuts alternating in a stunning pattern.

Hatch turned to Taylor. "Anything stand out?"

Taylor smiled in spite of herself. "This one. Definitely." She touched the necklace delicately.

The jeweler nodded approvingly. "A beautiful piece," he said.

"We'd like to try it on, please," Hatch said.

The man lifted the necklace out of its case and handed it to Hatch. Hatch put it around Taylor's neck. The white diamonds glistened against her tan skin like they were alive. Taylor had never seen anything so beautiful in her life. She wondered what her friends would think if they saw her now. But rather than joy, the thought brought her sadness. She missed her friends and she felt guilty for enjoying herself.

"What do you think?" Hatch asked.

"It's the most beautiful thing I've ever seen."

"How much is this trinket?" he asked.

"Just a minute, sir." He turned over the tag. "That piece is one hundred sixty-eight."

"One hundred and sixty-eight dollars?" Taylor asked.

The jeweler almost choked.

"No," Hatch said. "One hundred sixty-eight *thousand* dollars."

Taylor suddenly felt very uncomfortable. "That's like wearing a house."

"Fortunately not quite as heavy," Hatch said, smiling. "But do you like it?"

"Of course. It's incredible."

"Good. Then it's yours."

She looked up at him in amazement. "What?"

"It's our welcome-home gift to you."

Taylor was speechless. "You're kidding."

Hatch put his hand on her arm, touching her bare skin. "I would never kid about something as important as that. We are so glad you've come home."

As he spoke his thoughts coursed through Taylor's mind. A chill rose up her spine and the depth of the darkness filled her with such terror she was suddenly nauseous. Taylor shuddered and pulled away.

Hatch looked at her curiously. "Are you okay?"

Taylor swallowed. "Sorry. I guess I'm not used to sushi."

He nodded. "Of course. It's an acquired taste."

"Would you like the necklace wrapped up or will you be wearing it out?" the jeweler asked.

Hatch looked at Taylor. "Taylor?"

Taylor unfastened the necklace. "I don't mean to sound ungrateful, sir. But you've already done enough. I'm really not used to all this."

"I understand." He turned to the man and handed back the necklace. "Put this on hold. The young lady would like to think about it."

"Very well, sir," he said, disappointment evident in his voice. He returned the jewelry to the display case.

"Can we just go back?" Taylor asked.

"Absolutely. You came in the Rolls?"

"Yes," Taylor said.

Hatch took out his phone and pushed a button on it. "Pick us up outside Harry Winston." He slid the phone back in his pocket. "Come on, Tara."

Tara took off the pearl earrings she was trying on and said to the woman helping her, "Sorry. Out of time."

The three of them walked outside, where the Rolls was waiting for them. The black Escalade was parked behind it. Griffin opened the door and Taylor climbed in first. Hatch sat down next to her. Tara sat in the front next to the driver.

Hatch said, "You know, Taylor, everyone in the family is very excited to meet you."

Taylor swallowed. Then she forced out, "I'm looking forward to meeting them as well."

"I hoped you'd say that, because I've asked the chef to prepare a special dinner in your honor—a personal favorite of mine, beef Wellington. I hope your stomach is a little more agreeable with that than the sushi."

"I was raised on casseroles and pizza. I'm afraid I'm just kind of an average girl."

Hatch frowned. "No, Taylor. You're anything but average." His expression lightened. "But don't worry, we're not all china and crystal, we eat pizza and hamburgers, too. However, tonight is a very special occasion and requires a special cuisine." He leaned back and smiled. "The lost daughter has returned."

# 27

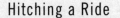

## Hitching a Ride

Jack lived about twelve blocks from my home, in a poor neighborhood. I found his address in the school directory, then went to see him.

Jack's house was at the end of a short, dead-end road called Leslie Street: an aged box of a home with chipped aluminum siding and faded cloth awnings. The front window had been broken and was covered with cardboard that was kept in place with duct tape. The yard was overgrown with weeds and pyracantha bushes. There were at least six cars at the house, some of them parked on the grass or on the road in front, most with flat tires and rusted bodies. Only one or two of them looked like they might actually run.

I climbed three steps to the Astroturf-covered porch. The doorbell had yellowed masking tape over it with the word BROKE written in marker. I opened the rusted screen door and knocked on the wood door behind it. A minute or so later Jack answered. He was wearing a T-shirt with the sleeves cut off, exposing his muscular arms and shoulders, as well as his tattoo. I forced myself not to blink. "What do you want?" he asked.

"I need to talk to you."

"I'm listening."

The TV was blaring behind him and I wondered if someone else was inside. "Not here. I need to talk to you someplace more private."

"Why?"

"I just do."

He looked at me for a moment, then stepped out on the front porch, shutting the door behind him. "Go ahead. My old man can't hear you."

"I need a ride."

"You think I'm your chauffeur now?"

"To Pasadena."

His face looked even more distressed. "Isn't that, like, in California?"

"Yeah."

"Man, what is this, a shakedown? I went to Dallstrom like you said. I'm not going to let you keep bullying me. I'll go to the teachers and tell them what you did."

"Calm down," I said. "I'm not here to bully you. You're the only one I can go to with this."

"Why not your old man?"

"I don't have a father."

"Then your mother?"

"Don't you watch the news?"

"No."

"My mother was kidnapped. I'm pretty sure she's in Pasadena. That's why I need a ride there."

"Why don't you call the police?"

"It's complicated. They can't help."

"Dude, I'm not driving all the way to California."

I reached into my pocket and pulled out a wad of bills I had taken from mom's secret stash. "Look, I've got money. I'll pay you three hundred dollars. It's all I've got."

He eyed the money. I could tell he was wavering. "Where'd you get that kind of dough?"

"It's my mom's emergency stash."

"Three hundred bucks, huh? When do you need to go?"

"As soon as possible."

"Just us?"

"And my friend Ostin."

"What if I bring someone? To help drive."

"Who?"

"Wade."

I hated Wade even more than Mitchell, but if it got me to California sooner, I'd deal with it. "Okay."

"What do we do after we're there?"

"You drop us off and you're done. That's it."

"No ride back?"

"No. I don't know how long we'll be."

Jack looked over at his car, a restored 1980 Chevy Camaro with a navy blue body and yellow racing stripe. "And you want to leave today, huh?"

"As soon as possible. I just need to get some things from my house. And pick up Ostin."

He scratched his stomach, then slowly exhaled. "Okay. I'll call Wade. Where do you live?"

"Not far. Over by the 7-Eleven off Thirteenth East. We'll meet you in the 7-Eleven parking lot in an hour. Deal?" I reached out my hand but he just looked at it fearfully.

"I'm not going to shock you."

He took my hand and we shook. "Deal."


I walked back to the apartment and knocked on Ostin's door. "We leave in an hour."

He looked at me as if I'd spoken in Chinese. "Leave? Where?"

"California. Didn't you think I was serious?"

"With Jack?"

I nodded. "Yeah." I purposely didn't say anything about Wade.

Ostin looked anxious enough without being thrown in the car with his archenemy.

He looked back over his shoulder. "Man, my mom's going to be so chapped at me. She's going to ground me until I'm fifty."

"Ground you from what?" I asked. "Homework or clogging?" We both knew that Ostin pretty much spent all his time in his room anyway.

"From hanging out with you."

"Yeah," I said. "Well, I wish my mom was around to ground me." I slid my hands in my pockets. "Like I said, you don't have to go."

"I never said I wasn't going," he said. "Let me get a few things. I'll be right there."

About ten minutes later Ostin knocked on my apartment door, then let himself in. He had a backpack that was mostly filled with junk food like potato chips and cheese puffs.

"What did you tell your mom?"

"I told her I was going to hang out with you."

"She's going to be worried out of her skull," I said. "She'll probably call the police."

"I thought of that. I taped a note to your door. It says I went to Comic-Con with you and my uncle."

"Will she believe that?"

"I don't know, but that's where my uncle is this week. He's so hard-core he never takes his cell phone, so my mom can't check."

"Brilliant," I said. I picked up my bag. "Ready?"

"Let's do this."

I looked out to make sure no one was watching, then I locked our apartment door and we walked down the hall and out the building.

The 7-Eleven was only fifty yards from my home. Jack wasn't there yet so we went inside and got cherry cola Slurpees and sat on the curb to wait.

"What if he doesn't come?" Ostin asked.

"He'll come. Besides, I'm paying him three hundred dollars."

"Where did you get three hundred dollars?"

"My mom's emergency fund." I rubbed one foot with the other. "If there ever was an emergency, this is it."

About fifteen minutes later Jack's Camaro pulled into the parking lot and up to the gas pumps.

"There he is," I said.

Ostin squinted. "Who's that in the car with him?"

"Wade."

Ostin's eyes widened. "You didn't tell me Wade was coming."

"Sorry. It was part of the deal."

"I hate Wade."

"It's no big deal."

"You don't understand. I really, really hate Wade. Like, if he were in a shark tank and reached up to me for help, I'd throw chum in the water."

Ostin has a great imagination.

"Look," I said, "we don't have a lot of options. Wade can help drive. Besides, he's not going to do anything to you. He's afraid of me."

Ostin just shook his head. "This just keeps getting worse."

Jack and Wade both climbed out of the car. Jack walked up to me. "I need money for gas."

I took the roll of bills out of my pocket and counted out a hundred and fifty. "Here. Half now, half when we get there."

He stuck his jaw out a little. "Fair enough."

Wade looked at Ostin and smiled. "Hey, I know you. I didn't recognize you with your pants on."

"Stay away from me."

"Relax," Wade said. "That was before I found out your friend's a Taser." He smiled and went inside the store. Ostin and I carried our packs over to the car. Jack opened the trunk and we put our things inside. Jack finished filling the car with gas about the time Wade came back out. He had pork rinds, mini-doughnuts, beef jerky, and a six-pack of Red Bull. "Let's go, boys."

"Sit in back," Jack said to Wade.

"What?"

"I want to talk to Michael."

"But . . ."

"Back, now."

Wade scowled, threw Jack the bag of jerky, and climbed in the backseat. Ostin stared at me with the look of a man climbing into a snake pit, but he got in anyway.

I shut my door and Jack fired up the Camaro. I think he'd taken off the muffler to make it louder, because it roared like a jet. He looked over at me and smiled wryly. "California, here we come."

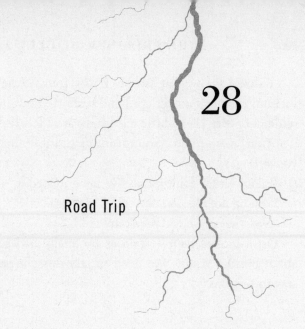

# 28

## Road Trip

A few minutes after we were on the highway, Jack turned to me, offering his open bag of beef jerky. "Here, help yourself."

I took a piece. "Thanks."

He set the bag to his side. "If you want more, it's right here." He rubbed his chin. "So, how long have you been shocking people?"

After all the years I'd spent hiding my power, it was strange talking so openly about it. "Since I was a kid," I said. "Like two or three."

"Do you know how much it hurts?"

I shook my head. "Not really. I've never been shocked."

From the backseat came Ostin's first words since he'd climbed into the car. "You've never been shocked?"

"I don't think I can be," I said.

"So, you could like grab a power line and it wouldn't hurt you?" Wade asked.

"I don't know. But, when I was four, I chewed through the vacuum cleaner's power cord and it shorted out in my mouth. I just remember it tickled a little and afterward I felt really good."

"Wait," Ostin said. "You mean it's possible that electricity makes you stronger?"

"Like I said, I don't know. I've never tested it."

"You could, like, eat batteries," Wade said.

"No," I said. "They'd break my teeth."

Ostin looked happy again as he finally had something to think about besides Wade. "We need to test this," he said. "I'll think of a way to test this."

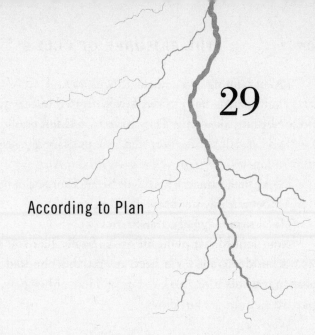

# 29

## According to Plan

**H**atch sat back in a tucked leather chair in his plush, mahogany-paneled office at the academy. Four flat-screen television monitors played on one wall. All were set to different channels, but all of them were covering the same story. In the past hour, two British Airways jets leaving London's Heathrow Airport had crashed shortly after takeoff, strewing wreckage across miles of coastland. He watched it all with a knowing smile.

His phone buzzed. "Sir, your phone call."

"Is the line secure?"

"Yes, sir."

"Put him through."

Hatch lifted the receiver. "Hatch."

The voice was gravelly and coarse with a slight British accent. "I just heard the news. Well done."

"Just as planned."

"BA is claiming mechanical difficulties."

"That's a little hard to swallow with two wrecks within the same hour, but not surprising. They have to tell the public something. So far there are also three terrorist groups claiming responsibility, but they're late to the party—we gave British Airways a specific schedule a week in advance. There will be another accident each day they don't meet our payment schedule."

"Has any money been transferred yet?"

"Not yet. But it will. We're offering them a bargain. Those 747-800s are going for a little over three hundred million dollars each, not to mention the lawsuits and loss of business. British Air can pay the ransom or shut down."

"Who's next?"

"Emirates airline. As soon as they saw the British Airways crash they responded to our demand. First payment is seventy-five million. With all that oil money they won't even miss it."

"Where's our boy?"

"Still in London. As soon as we get payment we'll move him to Rome."

"Very well. Take good care of him."

"We have a whole contingency with him. He's got more security than the queen."

"Too bad we don't have a few more just like him."

Hatch smiled. "We might. We found the last Glow."

"You found Michael Vey?"

"Yes. And we ran a diagnosis of Vey's E patterns. He has the strongest el-waves we've come across yet. He could be the most powerful Glow of them all."

"Promising. Where are you keeping him?"

"We don't have him yet. But we have his mother. And he's on his way to Pasadena right now. He has the idea that he's going to rescue his mother. He'll be disappointed to learn that she's not here."

"Will he cooperate?"

"You know what it's like bringing in these Glows when they're older. But he's been living just a little above poverty, and like I said, we have his mother. He'll be persuaded."

"Inform the board the moment you have him."

"Of course."

Hatch set down the phone. He loved it when a plan came together. And everything was going according to plan.

# 30

## Chickens and Eagles

Upon their return to the academy, Tara and Griffin helped Taylor carry her purchases to her new room on the third floor of the building—a beautiful, well-lit suite across the hall from Tara's. The room had wood floors with a thick Persian rug and a two-hundred-year-old antique French armoire across the room from her four-poster bed. The room was much larger and nicer than hers at home and had its own bathroom and walk-in closet.

Taylor noticed that the windows didn't open and were made of something other than glass. Tara had assured her that it was for her protection, not to keep her in, but Taylor still had her doubts.

While she was thinking about where to put her new clothes Tara walked in. "Need any help?"

"I'm just deciding where to put it all."

Tara picked up one of Taylor's new skirts. "I think we should share clothes just for the fun of it. I've always wanted to do that but no one here is my size." She turned back to Taylor. "So are you excited about your party tonight?"

"I guess."

"You don't sound excited."

"I'm still homesick."

Tara walked over next to her. "I know. But once you get to know everyone, you'll feel a little better."

Taylor sat on her bed. "I don't know about that. I really just want to go home. Don't you miss your family?"

"What do you mean?"

"The family who adopted you."

"Oh. They're gone."

"Gone?"

Tara sat on the bed next to her. "Well, I started coming to the academy when I was six. I'd stay here all week, then sleep at home on the weekends. It was a good arrangement. Then one day there was an accident. My parents' house caught fire and they didn't get out. Fortunately I wasn't there, or I probably would have died too."

Taylor was stunned. "That's horrible. Do they know what caused the fire?"

"The fire department said it was an electrical fire. Ironic, huh?"

Taylor had a sick feeling about it. All the fun of the day drained away. She thought about the man visiting her house and talking to her parents. She hoped one day her house wouldn't catch fire too.

"What if it wasn't an accident?"

Tara squinted. "What do you mean?"

Taylor saw the look on Tara's face and decided against pursuing it. "Nothing," she said. "So the state let you stay here?"

"Fortunately, in the school contract, there was a clause that in case something happened, Hatch received guardianship. I was so young at the time I don't remember much. I've lived here most of my life. This is my family. That's why I am so excited for you to join us."

"How many live here?"

"Nine, counting you."

"Will Nichelle be there?"

"Yeah. But just ignore her. That's what we all do." Tara started counting on her fingers. "There's Quentin, he's the cute blond, you'll like him. And he's a flirt. There's Bryan, he's Puerto Rican, big muscles, but he's really immature. Kylee, who I love, she was my best friend until you came along. I think she might be a little jealous of you, so I'll give her some special attention tonight. Zeus. He's kind of cute, but I need to warn you that he kind of smells. But don't say anything to him about it."

"I don't usually tell people they stink when I first meet them," Taylor said.

Tara grinned. "It's not really his fault. Because of his electric makeup, he can't bathe without shocking himself. Anyway, he's really sensitive about it."

Taylor nodded.

"Then there's Grace. She's really shy, so it will take a while before you get to know her. And there's Tanner. He's out of the country right now on an assignment."

"How many of us are there?"

"There were seventeen of us in the beginning, but there's only thirteen of us left. And some of them aren't in the family."

"What do you mean, 'left'?"

Tara frowned. "Don't worry about it."

Taylor looked down. Hearing that four of them had disappeared scared her as much as anything else that had happened to her. "Do they all have powers?" she asked.

"Every one of them."

"What kind?"

"All sorts. We don't really talk about that. I mean, of course we know. Like Zeus can shoot electricity like lightning, Bryan can burn through things, and Kylee's like a magnet, which means you don't ever give her your credit card because she ruins them, and everyone knows what Nichelle can do. But it's more of a gossip thing. Dr. Hatch says we don't talk about it because it's like in the business world, employees don't talk about each other's paychecks because it causes problems." Tara glanced up at the clock on the wall. "Is that really the time?"

"I think so."

She grabbed Taylor's hand. "Come on. We can't be late."

The girls hurried downstairs to the main floor. The other youths had already arrived and the dining room was loud with chatter. The dining room tables had been brought together to form one long rectangle, large enough to seat the whole family. Taylor and Tara were the last to arrive and every eye followed them in.

A handsome blond boy stood as they entered and smiled at them. "Wow, I'm seeing double."

"I'm Tara," Tara said.

"And that makes you Taylor," he said, slightly bowing. "I'm Quentin. I'm the student body president. Welcome to Elgen Academy."

"Hi," Taylor replied shyly. "I mean, thank you."

"Welcome to the family." He took her arm. "Let me introduce you to the rest of the gang. That's Bryan."

"Woo hoo," Bryan said, pumping his fist in the air. "I'm number one." He punctuated his claim with a loud belch.

"Number-one dork," Quentin said.

"I told you," Tara whispered to Taylor. "Immature."

"And that's Zeus."

Zeus bobbed his head. Taylor noticed that he was seated with spaces between him and the others, and she remembered what Tara had said about his smell.

"That's Kylee and Grace."

"Hi," Kylee said tersely.

Grace looked at her but said nothing.

Quentin said to Taylor, "Don't take it personally, Grace is a little shy. She's that way to everyone at first." He looked at Nichelle, who was sitting alone at the far end of the table. "You've already met Nichelle," he said. Nichelle glared at Taylor.

"There's also Tanner, but he's out of the country. You'll meet him in a couple of weeks. Since you are the guest of honor, Dr. Hatch asked me to seat you at the head of the table. He will sit to your right. And Tara," Quentin said, "Dr. Hatch requested that you sit on Taylor's left side."

"Whatever you say, boss," Tara said.

Tara led her to the front of the table and Taylor sat down. Bryan said, "Hey, you guys look alike."

"We're twins, idiot," Tara said.

"You're such a dork," Kylee said to Bryan, rolling her eyes.

Taylor looked around. She caught Zeus staring at her. He looked away. She thought he was cute. A moment later Dr. Hatch walked into the room.

"Sorry I'm late, everyone. I was just finishing up a call." He sat down at the head of the table. "You've all met Taylor?"

"I introduced her around," Quentin said.

"Thank you, Quentin. Now I expect you all to make her feel right at home."

"Where are you from?" Kylee asked.

"Idaho."

"Where's that?"

"Kylee, don't embarrass yourself with your ignorance," Dr. Hatch said flatly.

Taylor said, "Idaho's on the other side of Washington, above Utah, west of Montana."

"Thank you, Taylor," Hatch said. "I guess I'll have to talk to Miss Marsden about her geography lessons." Hatch lifted a small brass bell next to his plate and shook it. Waiters immediately appeared with platters of food.

The chef had prepared a remarkable feast, though Taylor wasn't very hungry after the lunch they'd had. The servers brought in trays full of beef Wellington, Yorkshire pudding, and roasted lamb with vegetables and potatoes. Taylor filled her plate, but mostly just picked at it as she glanced back and forth at each of the others. Quentin was definitely in charge, and the most popular of them all. She guessed that Kylee and Tara had a crush on him, and Zeus seemed jealous of him.

"Do you find the cuisine agreeable?" Hatch asked her.

"Yes, sir. It's very good."

"It's not pizza, but hopefully it's easier on your stomach than the sushi."

"Yes, sir."

"I think you'll like the dessert as well. We're celebrating some favorable news we got out of the UK today, so everything is English. In keeping with the theme, dessert is an English trifle."

"Yum," Kylee said. "Yum, yum, yum."

"You're such an idiot," Nichelle said.

"And you're an ugly, psycho freak," Kylee said.

"Ladies," Hatch said. "Enough."

"Sorry," they both said to Hatch, but not to each other.

When they had finished their meals, the waiters brought out the trifles, as well as cake, fruit, and pudding served in tall crystal chalices that looked like parfait glasses.

"This is delicious," Taylor said.

"Overall I'm not a huge fan of English cuisine," Hatch said, "but they do some things right."

As the group was finishing dessert, Hatch looked at his watch, then again rang the brass bell. The head server immediately appeared.

"Yes, sir."

"Pour the champagne, please."

"Right away, sir."

The server walked back into the kitchen, then returned with a dark green and black teardrop-shaped bottle. He moved quickly around the table, pouring a small amount of the sparkling amber liquid into each glass. Taylor had never tasted champagne before. She watched the bubbles stream upward in clean bright lines. "You drink champagne?" she asked Tara.

Tara smiled. "Of course. We're treated like adults here." She leaned close to Taylor as if sharing a secret. "Quentin told me this champagne is more than thirty-five hundred dollars a bottle."

Taylor couldn't comprehend it. "That's like three hundred dollars a glass," she said.

Just then Hatch rose from his seat.

"Ah," he said, sniffing his drink. "What an aroma. A 1995 Clos Ambonnay. Simply divine." He extended his glass in front of him. "I'd like to raise a toast to the newest reunited member of our family, Taylor."

Everyone lifted their glasses, including Kylee, who hadn't said anything since Hatch's reprimand.

"To Taylor. May our dreams be her dreams, and may all her dreams come true."

"Here, here," said Quentin.

Everyone began tapping glasses, except Nichelle, who just took a long drink.

"In honor of this special occasion, and other good news, I have a very special treat. I have secured front-row tickets for tonight's Colby Cross concert at the Staples Center."

Everyone cheered.

"Colby Cross?" Taylor said. "She's my favorite singer."

"I know," Hatch said as he stood. "So we'd better be on our way. The limos await."

At Hatch's lead everyone stood and followed him out of the room, Zeus and Nichelle leaving last.

As they climbed into the car Taylor said to Tara, "I can't believe we have front-row seats to Colby Cross!"

"I told you Dr. Hatch would take good care of you. You have nothing to worry about."

Taylor sighed. "It's just the way everything started—being kidnapped was really scary."

"I know. I think he's trying to make up for that. Just keep an open mind, sis. You'll be glad you did."

Taylor sat back into the leather seat and for the first time since her abduction she really smiled. Maybe Tara was right. Maybe what she'd read in Dr. Hatch's mind was false. After all, he'd been nothing but generous and kind. Maybe if her parents had known how well the students were treated they would have wanted her to come. She didn't know what to believe anymore. "Front-row seats," she said again. "It's just so hard to believe."

"Believe it," Tara said. "It's your new life, Taylor. First-class, front-row everything."

A half hour later the limos pulled up to the front of the Staples Center and everyone got out. Once inside the arena an usher checked their tickets, then escorted them to the front row.

As the group was walking to their seats a large, muscular man, with his arm around a woman, bumped into Zeus.

"Hey, watch it," Zeus said.

The man looked over his shoulder and grinned. "Dude, you stink. Take a shower."

The woman laughed.

Zeus turned red. "Is that your girlfriend or is Farm Town missing a goat?"

The man stopped and turned around. "What did you say?"

"Did I stutter? I called your girlfriend a goat."

The man flushed with anger. "You're gonna die, loser." He came at Zeus, grabbing him by the arm. "I'm gonna—" Bolts of electricity shot out of Zeus's fingers. The man cried out and dropped to the ground like a bag of concrete. His girlfriend screamed.

Zeus kicked the man in the side. "Like that, loser?" Suddenly Zeus bent over in pain. "Aargh . . ."

Hatch stood above him with Nichelle at his side. Hatch's face was red with fury. "Thank you, Nichelle."

"Glad to help, sir."

Just then two security officers arrived on the scene. The larger of the two asked, "What's going on?"

The man's girlfriend pointed at Zeus. "Him!" she screamed. "He shot my boyfriend."

Hatch stepped forward. "Excuse me, officers, but I witnessed the entire exchange. The man was acting peculiar, then he just collapsed." Hatch looked at Tara and slightly nodded.

Suddenly the girlfriend began screaming at the top of her lungs "Snakes! There are snakes everywhere!" She began flailing wildly. "Get them off me! Get them off me!"

The guards looked at each other. One pulled out his radio. "Requesting backup near section AA. Also medical assistance, possible drug overdose." While one of the guards struggled to restrain the woman the other said to Hatch, "Thanks for your help."

"Don't mention it."

When the security guard had turned away, Hatch grabbed Zeus by the arm and pulled him aside. "Out to the car. Now."

"But the concert . . ." He doubled over again. "Sorry. It won't happen again."

"No, it won't. Now go."

Zeus staggered toward the exit. Hatch shook his head.

"Totally against family policy," Tara said. "Boy, he's gonna get it when we get back."

"What will Dr. Hatch do to him?" Taylor asked.

"Nichelle will punish him for a while. She just loves doing that. Then he'll lose privileges for a few weeks and probably be grounded to his room for a few days."

Hatch walked back to the group, Nichelle at his side. "Sorry about that," he said to Taylor. "Zeus knows better than to use his gift to hurt others."

Taylor looked at Nichelle, and Nichelle's eyes narrowed as she glared back at her.

"Let's not let Zeus's unfortunate decision put a damper on things. Our seats await."

Their seats were perfect, front row and center, unlike anything Taylor had ever dreamed she would experience. In spite of everything, she was giddy with excitement. When Colby came onstage, the arena erupted in smoke and pyrotechnics, and everyone jumped to their feet. Taylor couldn't believe how close she was to the singer.

Colby started the concert with one of Taylor's favorite songs, "Stay With Me." Several times the singer came to the front of the stage and reached out her hand and Taylor actually got to touch her.

After an hour and a half the stage lights darkened for intermission.

"Nichelle," Hatch said, "go get Taylor and me a couple of Cokes."

"Okay," she said, glaring at Taylor. After she left, Hatch leaned over to Taylor. She noticed he had put on his dark glasses. "Are you having a good time?"

"More than I can say. Thank you, Dr. Hatch."

"You're welcome. We're just so pleased to have you with us."

"I'm pleased to be here. I don't know how to thank you."

"It's my pleasure, really. But now that you ask, could I ask a small favor of you?"

"Of course."

"I'd like to see your gift in action. Sometime during Colby's next few songs, I want you to reboot her—when I tell you to."

Taylor looked at him. "I'm sorry. What?"

He smiled. "Just for fun. No one will know."

Taylor swallowed. "I don't know . . ."

Hatch's expression turned serious. "I'm asking you to do something for me, Taylor."

Taylor swallowed again. She felt uncomfortable with the request, but after all that Hatch had done for her, she didn't dare disobey. *It's not really that big of a deal*, she told herself. After all, hadn't she done the same thing at the basketball game? "Okay," she said hesitantly. "Just tell me when."

Hatch's expression lightened. "I'll tap you on the sleeve."

The applause was even louder when Colby came back onstage but this time, instead of excitement, Taylor felt dread. She took a deep breath. What Hatch had asked her to do was wrong, but what choice did she have?

Colby sang a few more songs and Hatch just watched quietly, smiling and even clapping. Every now and then he looked over at Taylor. Taylor began to hope that maybe he had forgotten or changed his mind. He didn't. Colby was in the middle of Taylor's favorite song, "Love My Love," when Hatch tapped Taylor's arm. Taylor looked at the singer.

"Now," Hatch said firmly.

"Yes, sir." Taylor cocked her head. It was a fast song and Colby's voice suddenly screeched, then stopped in the middle of the chorus, as if she'd forgotten what song she'd been singing. For a few seconds she just looked around, unsure of where she was, while the band kept on playing. Then she grabbed the microphone and started singing, starting again with the first verse. At the end of the song there was a strange hesitancy in the arena, followed by the usual thunderous applause.

"Wow," Colby Cross said into the microphone. "Never had that happen before. I just kind of blacked out. Early onset Alzheimer's, huh?"

"That's okay, Colby! We love you!" a boy shouted from a few rows back. Colby laughed at herself and the crowd applauded again.

Taylor looked over at Hatch. He was smiling and nodding approvingly. "Well done," he said. "Well done."

Taylor sat quietly for the rest of the concert, even when everyone stood for an encore. She felt sad. She had betrayed someone she admired.

After the concert, they returned to the limos. Dr. Hatch switched cars, presumably to talk to Zeus, so Taylor, Tara, Bryan, Kylee, and Nichelle sat in the back, Bryan switching places with Dr. Hatch.

Taylor desperately wanted to talk to Tara but didn't want to talk in front of the others, so she was silent the whole way home, even when Bryan and Kylee got in a brief argument about who was a better singer, Colby Cross or Danica Ross, and they asked her for her opinion. "They're both good," she finally said.

"Yeah?" said Kylee. "At least Danica doesn't forget the words to her own songs."

The comment made Taylor's stomach hurt. She was glad when Nichelle threatened to silence both of them if they didn't shut up.

That night, as Taylor was getting ready for bed, Tara walked into her bedroom. Tara was already in her silk pajamas.

"So, what's up?" Tara asked.

"What do you mean?"

"Do you always get depressed after seeing your favorite singer?"

"No."

"Then what's wrong?"

Taylor sat down on her bed, her hands clasped between her legs. "Do you know when Colby was singing "Love My Love" and suddenly stopped singing?"

Tara smiled. "That was you?"

She nodded. "Dr. Hatch made me do it."

Tara looked at her. "Is that all?"

"Is that all? I embarrassed her in front of thousands of people."

Tara shook her head. "C'mon, she's a celebrity. They paid her a million dollars to sing for three hours, I think she'll get over it. And besides, no one cared. You heard that guy yell from the crowd—they loved it. It made her seem more human."

Taylor sighed. "I guess you're right."

"Dr. Hatch was just seeing you in action. Think of it as a cheerleading tryout. And you passed."

"Does he do that often?"

"What?"

"Test you."

"No. Just now and then to make sure you're on board."

"What if you're not?"

Tara's expression changed. "You know, you can make this good or bad, it's up to you. It's about attitude."

"No, it's about hurting someone else."

"Dr. Hatch doesn't hurt people just to hurt people. You saw how mad he was at Zeus for shocking that guy. Dr. Hatch is just . . . careful."

"Does he ask you to do things?"

"Yeah. I mean, not much lately. More earlier."

"And it never bothered you?"

"Nope."

"Really? Never?"

She looked suddenly pained. "Once. But you get over it. At first you might hate it but before you know it, you'll volunteer to do it." She forced a smile. "Why do you care? We're better than them."

"Them?"

"You know, people."

Taylor looked at her. "We're people. My parents are people."

"Taylor, they're not your parents. And we're not people. We're special."

"Maybe you are, but I'm just a cheerleader."

"I know it's hard being different, but it's like the story Dr. Hatch tells us about the chickens and the eagle."

"What story?"

Tara's face grew animated. "Oh, you're going to like this. It goes like this: A farmer once found an abandoned eagle's nest with an egg inside. Out of curiosity he took the egg home and put it under one of his chickens. The chicken hatched the egg and took care of the eagle like it was just another chick. As the eagle grew it walked around the coop with the chickens, pecking at the ground the way chickens do.

"One day a wise man saw the eagle in the coop. 'How do you keep the eagle from flying away?' he asked the farmer. The farmer said, 'It's easy, because the eagle thinks he's a chicken.'

"The wise man said, 'But it's not. And it's wrong to keep it in this coop. Eagles are majestic birds and destined to fly.' The farmer said, 'Not this one. He's sure he's a chicken.' The wise man said, 'No, once an eagle always an eagle.'

"He then went out to the henhouse, picked up the eagle, and threw him in the air. 'Fly, eagle!' he said. But the eagle just fell to the ground. He tried it again, throwing the eagle higher. 'Fly, eagle!' but the eagle just fell again and went back to pecking in the dirt.

"Then the wise man carried the eagle to the top of the henhouse and pointed the eagle toward the sun. 'You are not a chicken, you're an eagle. You were meant to soar high above the chickens. Now fly!' and he threw the eagle up into the air. Suddenly the eagle stretched out its wings and took off into the sky."

Tara looked into Taylor's eyes. "You, me, all of us electric children are those eagles. Dr. Hatch is the wise man. If you just want to keep on pecking through life with the chickens, it's up to you, sis. So what will it be, eagle or chicken?"

"But I like the chickens," Taylor said.

Tara grinned. "Come on."

Taylor sighed. "Of course I want to be an eagle."

"Good. Then stop worrying so much about the chickens. They don't matter. Eagles eat chickens. It's not because eagles are bad, it's just how they're made." Tara stood, then kissed Taylor on the top of her head. "Have a good night."

"You too."

"Light off?" Tara asked.

"Sure."

Tara switched off the light and closed the door. Taylor lay back looking at the ceiling. "I miss the chicken coop," she said softly.

She wanted to talk to someone who would understand. She wanted to see Michael. She wondered when she would see him again.

# 31

## The Road

Ostin sat in the backseat of the Camaro, pressed up against the side, reading a book. I could tell he was still mad that I hadn't told him about Wade. For the most part Wade kept his distance, listening to his iPod and playing his DS.

A couple of hours into the drive Wade asked, "What are you reading?"

"A book," Ostin said. "Ever seen one?"

"Ever seen a fist?"

"Knock it off," Jack said.

"Porky," Wade said. "Oink, oink."

"Stop it," Ostin said.

"Never seen a hog read before. Are you gonna eat the book when you're done?"

"Shut up."

"Oink, oink."

"Hey, Wade," Jack said. "Ever wonder what a thousand volts would feel like on your tongue?"

His grin disappeared. "No."

"Then keep your mouth shut."

Wade sat back and put his earbuds back in. I looked in the rearview mirror. Ostin looked pretty miserable. I felt bad for him. For his sake, I wished he hadn't come.

I turned to Jack. "Thanks."

"Sorry about that." A few minutes later Jack asked, "You an only child?"

"Yeah. How about you?"

"I've got two brothers and a sister."

"Are you the oldest?"

"No, I'm the youngest. I'm the only one still at home. One of my brothers is in Iraq. He's a Marine." He said this with obvious pride.

"That's cool."

"Yeah, he's really cool. He even got a medal for bravery."

"How about your other brother?"

His smile fell. "He's in prison."

I wasn't sure how to respond. I didn't know anyone in prison. I wanted to ask what he'd done but it didn't feel right. I didn't have to.

"He got really messed up on drugs. He and a guy were stealing snowmobiles to get money for drugs when the owner came out. The guy with him had a gun and he shot the man. My brother didn't even know that he had a gun, but the way the laws are, he's also guilty. So he'll be in prison a long time."

"Do you see him very much?"

"Nah, he's in Colorado. I only see him once a year." His voice lifted. "My sister's doing real well, though. She married a guy who owns a chain of tanning salons. They have a real nice home and two little kids."

"Do you see much of her?"

"Nah, she doesn't have much to do with the family. She got

married young to get away. That's because my folks used to fight a lot before my mother left."

I now understood why Jack locked kids in lockers. I'd probably be doing the same if I came from a home like his.

"What about you? What happened to your dad?"

"He had a heart attack."

"Was he old?"

"No. My mom said he had a 'bad ticker.'"

"That's too bad."

I looked back. Wade's eyes were closed and he was still wearing his earbuds. I wasn't sure if he was sleeping or just listening to music, but I figured that either way he couldn't hear me.

"What's Wade's story?"

"Not good. His parents were alcoholics. His old man used to beat the tar out of him until the state took him away. He lived with foster parents until they put him with his grandma, but she don't really want him. She's not shy about telling him, either. You'd think an old lady would be nicer, but that prune could strip the bark from trees with her tongue. So he just hangs with me most the time. I'm kind of like his only family."

"He's lucky to have you," I said.

Jack looked at me with a peculiar expression. "Thanks, dude." Then he looked back to the road. I swear his eyes were moistening. I turned away so I wouldn't embarrass him.

It took us four hours to reach Winnemucca, Nevada. We stopped at a gas station to fill the Camaro's radiator with water, then we ate dinner at Chihuahua's Fiesta Restaurant. I got a burrito, Jack and Wade got two, and Ostin got the taco platter. We ate quickly, then got back on the road.

"So how do you do it?" Jack asked me.

"Do what?"

"Shock people."

I shrugged. "I don't know. It's like asking how you sneeze. It just happens."

"But you can control it . . ."

"Yeah. Usually."

"Why didn't you shock us when we shoved you in the locker the first time?"

"Because I'm not supposed to use my power. My mother didn't want anyone to find out. She was afraid something might happen."

"Like what?"

"Like what did. That's why they took her."

"I didn't tell anyone," Jack said.

"I know. It wasn't you."

"So you know who took her?"

"Some corporation."

"This is like a James Bond movie," Jack said. "What are you going to do when you get there?"

"I'm going to find my mother."

"Hate to say it, but even if she's there, it's not like they're going to just let you in. If they kidnapped her, she's going to be guarded."

"I know. I'm making this up as I go."

"I get it," Jack said. He took a drink from his Red Bull and looked back at his watch. "We've got another ten hours. If we drive through the night we'll be there by morning."

"Then let's drive through the night."

"I need to pick up some more Red Bulls." He reached in back and thumped Wade on the head, waking him.

He pulled his earbuds out. "What?!"

"Get some sleep. You're driving from Bishop to Pasadena."

# 32

## Another Simple Request

That night Taylor had a dream. She was down on a football field cheering while her parents were in the stands looking for her. She kept shouting, "I'm down here!" But they couldn't hear her for all the noise. She awoke crying.

A half hour later someone knocked on her door. One of the servants, a young, dark-haired woman who spoke broken English, handed her an envelope.

"Excuse me I bother you," she said. "Bless you."

Taylor opened the envelope.

*Family Meeting*
*Library. 9:00 a.m. sharp. Attendance mandatory.*
*Be dressed casually, we will be leaving the academy.*
*—Dr. Hatch*

*Now what?* she thought.

Taylor got dressed, then crossed the hall to find Tara, but she had already left her room. Taylor didn't know where the library was but saw Quentin waiting for the elevator.

"Hey, Quentin."

He turned, his usual smile on his face. "Hey, Tara."

"I'm Taylor."

He stopped and looked at her. "Of course you are. Sorry. I'll figure it out eventually." He put his hand on her back. "Do you have any birthmarks or anything I should look for?"

"Afraid not."

"It shouldn't be too hard. You're prettier than she is."

Taylor rolled her eyes. "Yeah, right. We're identical."

They stepped into the elevator and Quentin pushed the button for the first floor.

"No, there's something different about you. I swear it."

Taylor ignored the comment. "Are we going to the library?"

"Yes. Just follow me."

A few seconds later the elevator door opened.

"After you," Quentin said.

"Thank you." Taylor stepped out into the hall, followed by Quentin.

"Do we have family meetings a lot?"

"No. Just on special occasions."

"So, do you know what it's about?"

"Yes. But I can't tell you. Doctor's orders." He grinned. "But you'll be glad you went."

They arrived at an open door and walked in together. "If you want, let's hang out today," Quentin said. "And by the way, you can call me Q. It's easier."

"Thanks, Q."

"Any time. Talk to you later."

Tara was already inside the library. She was standing next to Dr. Hatch and they both looked at Taylor as she entered.

Taylor was sure they had been talking about her.

Bryan was the last to arrive, his hair sticking up on the side of his head as if he'd just rolled out of bed. Tara left Hatch's side and sat down next to Taylor. "Morning, sis."

"Morning."

"Good morning, everyone," Dr. Hatch said.

"Good morning, Dr. Hatch," they said in unison.

"I have an announcement." He turned to Taylor. "Taylor, since all of you were born around the same time, having individual birthday parties got to be a little ridiculous. So we started having one large family celebration instead. Sometimes we have great activities here at the academy and sometimes we travel to other places."

"Yeah, deep sea fishing off Costa Rica, man," Bryan said.

"My favorite was riding bikes through Tuscany," Quentin said.

"That was cool," Tara said to Taylor. "That was last year."

Hatch smiled. "We've had some good times. I was thinking that since Taylor missed the family party, well, since she's missed the last fourteen, it's only fair that we have one especially for her."

Everyone cheered except Nichelle, who never looked happy. Hatch reached into his coat pocket and brought out an envelope. "So this morning we are going to the Long Beach Arena for the X Games Motocross finals."

Bryan jumped up and high-fived Quentin.

"Oh yeah, oh yeah."

Zeus sat quietly in his seat, looking angry. Taylor guessed he had been grounded from the activity.

Hatch added, "And of course, we have VIP seating. We're so close to the action you can smell the fear."

"All right," Bryan yelled. "Smell the fear, this is going to rock!"

There was a chorus of thank-yous, which Taylor joined. "Thank you, Dr. Hatch."

Hatch smiled at Taylor. "Nothing's too good for family," he said. Then he added, "For my eagles."

What he said bothered her. She knew that Tara had told him about their conversation the night before.

"You know it," Bryan said. "We're eagles! Chickens peck, eagles fly!"

"So let's fly," Hatch said. He stood and raised his hands. "The limos await. Pick up your box breakfast on the way out."

Everyone jumped up except Zeus, who was slumped back in his chair, his legs spread, and his hands clasped between them. Zeus looked up at Hatch penitently, but Hatch walked past him without a word.

On the way to the cars, Taylor asked Tara, "What are the X Games?"

"Are you kidding?" Tara said. "Don't they have television in Idaho? The X Games are only the coolest thing in the world. They've been sold out for months."

Quentin walked up behind her. "So, Taylor, you want to sit by me at the games?"

Both Tara and Kylee frowned.

"Sorry, Quentin," Dr. Hatch said. "I will have the honor of sitting next to this birthday girl."

"Sorry, sir."

The kitchen staff was waiting outside in the parking lot and handed each of them a boxed breakfast as they climbed into the limos. Inside the box was a carton of orange juice, a bagel, an egg and sausage croissant, a cup of yogurt, and, of course, a banana. Taylor spread cream cheese over the bagel, then sat back and watched the scenery. She was in such a different world—half dream, half nightmare. She was feeling more confused each day.

Her mother always told her that she was special—that she was going to leave her mark on the world. And here she was—a new life had been unfolded before her filled with opportunity, growth, wealth, power, and privilege. Just like her mother promised. So why did it all feel so wrong? She looked at Tara and Quentin. They weren't bad. Maybe Tara was right. She needed to trust more and give Dr. Hatch a chance. After all, he had gone out of his way to welcome her. Didn't all his efforts warrant a little consideration? Was he really so bad? She thought back to the time at Harry Winston's, when she saw a glimpse inside Hatch's mind. Could she have been mistaken? What if she was brainwashed?

She closed her eyes. It seemed just too much for her to figure out. Sure, she was living a dream, but if it were up to her, she'd wake from it. Deep in her heart she wanted her little home, her friends from school, and her family. And all the front-row seats, gourmet meals, and diamond necklaces in the world weren't going to change that.

The limos drove in through a special VIP entrance, and the youths walked to the stadium through a background of X Game contenders gearing up and revving their motorcycles.

Dr. Hatch showed his pass to a security guard and they were led out to the competition. Hatch was wearing his glasses again and he stood at the gate and watched as they filed past. "Nichelle, sit on the far end of the row, please."

She frowned. "Yes, sir."

"Taylor, Tara, you sit next to me."

Taylor faked a smile. "Thank you." She had been hoping he'd leave her alone. She was afraid he might ask her to do something again.

They slid down the metal bench to their seats as the sound of the motorcycles filled the air like a swarm of angry bees. "What's the X stand for?" Taylor asked.

"It's short for *extreme*," Tara said.

Taylor nodded. It certainly was. The motocross jumping competition was one of the most amazing things she had ever seen. Each of the riders took a turn following a course of jumps, hills, and ramps, performing stunts off each one. They not only jumped from ramp to ramp, but the riders would do acrobatics in the air. The first rider took her breath away. He was more than eighty feet in the air when he did a handstand on his motorcycle's handlebars.

"That's incredible," she said.

"That's for sure," Hatch said. "One mistake and you're finished."

"Watch," Tara said. "This next guy is my favorite. He's the first rider to do a double backflip on his motorcycle."

Standing right in front of them was a squad of cheerleaders, or at least an X Games version of them. They were more like beautiful dancing girls in bikinis. Still, seeing them filled Taylor with longing. She wished she were cheering.

Hatch watched Taylor watch them. "Do you miss that?"

She looked over. "Excuse me?"

"Do you miss your cheerleading?"

She nodded. "Yes."

He smiled sympathetically. "It's too bad the academy doesn't have enough students to field a team. I guess it's just one of the sacrifices of being special. We do, however, have some very interesting connections. If, in a few years, you'd like to be a cheerleader for the Dallas Cowboys football team, I could pull some strings and make it happen."

Taylor looked at him in amazement. "Really?"

"I know that's little consolation in the meantime, but still, you must admit that there are some overriding benefits to being a part of the academy."

"Yes," Taylor said.

"Indeed," Hatch said. He looked down at his watch. "It's almost lunchtime. Taylor, what will you have to eat? They have ice cream, pizza, sodas, hot dogs."

"I'd like a hot dog," Taylor said.

"Great. And you, Tara?"

"I just want an ice cream."

He handed Tara a hundred-dollar bill. "Please get us two dogs, a beer, and whatever you want."

"Yes, sir."

When Tara was gone, Hatch leaned toward Taylor. "I've been meaning to talk to you. I wanted to apologize."

"For what?"

"I'm really sorry about how all this started. I can understand why you might think we're terrible. I just hope you understand by now that our objectives are all in your best interest, as well as the world's."

"I understand. Tara's explained it," Taylor said, even though she wasn't sure how much she believed.

"Good. The truth is, if you're going to change the world, you don't always have the luxury of time or convention. You can't make omelets without breaking a few eggs, can you?"

"I guess not."

"No, you can't. Now tell me about your friend Michael."

Hearing him say Michael's name filled Taylor with dread. "What do you want to know?"

"What's he like?"

"He's nice."

"I noticed from his report that he's spent a fair amount of time in school detention. Is he a troublemaker? Rebellious?"

She didn't want to talk about Michael but she wasn't sure how to avoid it. "No. He's a good kid. I think he's just unlucky."

"Unlucky," Hatch repeated. "Well, his luck is about to change."

Taylor didn't know what to say. Just then Hatch reached into his coat pocket and pulled out his cell phone. "Hello?"

Taylor looked back out over the grounds, happy for the interruption. After a few more minutes Tara returned with the food. "There you go," she said, handing Taylor two hot dogs and a beer. "Give this to Dr. Hatch."

Taylor handed him the beer and dog. She unwrapped her own hot dog and lost herself in the competition. After a few more competitors, Taylor turned to Tara. "This is really cool!" she shouted over the noise.

Tara smiled. "The coolest. Didn't I tell you?"

Taylor was applauding an amazing jump when Hatch leaned over to her. "See that next rider? The one in the yellow jacket?"

She nodded. "He's really cool."

Hatch said, "He's currently tied for first and this is his last chance to score. I don't want him to win."

Taylor looked at him, wondering why he was telling her that.

"I don't want him to win," he repeated.

"Then hopefully he won't do his best."

"Hope isn't a plan," Hatch said. "It's blind faith in luck. It's chance. Winners don't ever leave things to chance. So when he's in the middle of his jump, I want you to reboot him."

Taylor just looked at him. "But he'll crash."

"That's a distinct possibility."

"It could kill him."

"That's also a possibility, but that's the risk you take in these types of sports. Why do you think all these people are here?"

Taylor's forehead furrowed with concern.

Hatch leaned back, his expression changing some. "I'm not asking much, Taylor. I just want to see if you have what it takes to fit in with us."

Taylor swallowed. Below her the rider rode up to the platform at the top of the ramp. He had removed his helmet and was waving to the excited crowd while cameras flashed around him. He blew a kiss to a woman holding a baby, who Taylor guessed was his wife, then he pulled his helmet back on and began revving his engine. Dr. Hatch leaned back and sipped his beer.

Tara looked at her, then leaned close. "You gotta do it, Taylor. He's not kidding."

"He's asking me to kill someone."

"He's asking you to prove your loyalty. Chicken or eagle, sis?"

"I can't do it."

Tara looked at her nervously. "You have to."

"No, I don't," Taylor said.

"You don't understand. You have to do what Dr. Hatch says."

"What if I don't?"

Tara's eyes widened with fear. "You don't want to find out."

The motorcycle took off. It dipped low, then shot off the end of the ramp, sailing sixty feet in the air. Camera flashes popped as the bike sailed through the sky. The rider twisted back and was in the middle of his second flip when suddenly the bike went awry. The crowd screamed as the bike landed sideways on the opposite ramp, flipping tail over front while the rider flopped across the ground behind it until he slammed into a retaining wall below a long row of bleachers. The rider lay motionless. The woman he had blown a kiss to was running toward him as emergency crews sprang into action, accompanied by the sound of a siren.

Hatch stood and looked at Taylor, then Tara, his face bent in anger. "We're going," he said fiercely, brushing past Taylor. "Nichelle, with me."

The entire family stood. As they slid down the bench Taylor said to Tara. "What happened? I didn't do that."

Tara was furious. "All he asked for was a show of faith. Was that too much?"

"He asked me to kill someone."

"So what."

"So what?" Taylor said. "How can you say that?"

Tara turned on her. "They're just *people*!"

The limousines were waiting where they'd been dropped off and the drivers jumped out at their approach, opening the car doors. Even though no one spoke to her, Taylor could feel everyone's anger directed at her. She wondered how they all knew. Hatch didn't say a word the whole way back.

At the academy the driver opened the door and Hatch climbed out, followed by the other three girls. "Tara, go to your room and wait for me."

Tara furtively glanced at her. There was fear in her eyes, and they began welling up with tears. "Yes, sir," Tara said, and quickly ran off. Taylor was afraid for both of them.

Hatch pointed at Taylor. "You come with me."

Nichelle looked at her, a half smile crossing her face. Taylor shivered. "Yes, sir," she said. Taylor followed Hatch to the elevator. He pushed a button marked D and they descended. When the door opened, they stepped out into a dark corridor. Taylor followed Hatch while Nichelle quietly followed a few yards behind her. They stopped in front of a heavy metal door. Hatch turned to Taylor. "Would you like to explain to me what happened?"

"Nothing, sir. I didn't do anything."

"Precisely." He shook his head. "After all I've done for you . . . all

I asked for was a simple demonstration of loyalty and gratitude and this is how you thank me."

Taylor was terrified. "But he fell . . ."

Hatch tapped his glasses. "I can see when you use your powers. Tara decided to step in for you. I will deal with her later."

"She was only trying to protect me."

"Yes. And deceive me."

"It's my fault."

"Yes, it is. If you had acted with integrity none of this would have been necessary." He opened the door to expose a large, dark room. "I'm so very disappointed in you, Taylor. I extended a hand of friendship and you bit it. I had sincerely hoped we could do this the easy way. I guess I was wrong." He grabbed her by the arm and pulled her into the room.

"You're hurting me," Taylor said.

"You have no idea what hurt is. But you will. Nichelle, Miss Ridley needs a little lesson in gratitude—about an hour's worth to begin with. Oblige me."

A sadistic smile lit Nichelle's face. "I'd be happy to."

Nichelle stepped inside the dark room and Hatch shut the door behind the girls. He could hear Taylor's screams even before he reached the other end of the corridor.

# 33

## The Lesson

Taylor was curled up on her side, shaking with pain. Her clothes were soaked with sweat and her face was streaked with tears. "Please stop," she sobbed. "Please."

"I'll stop when Dr. Hatch tells me to stop."

"You're one of us. How could you do this to us?"

"It's what I do."

"You hurt others?"

"We all do what we were born to do. Out there, I'm no one. If it weren't for the academy I'd be flipping hamburgers somewhere. But in here, I'm a VIP."

"You're a sellout."

Nichelle sneered. "Aren't you the saint? In the end, everyone sells out. Even the saints."

"You're wrong," Taylor said, her voice strained. "Some people would rather die than hurt others."

"Well, you might just get your wish." She walked over and slapped Taylor on the head. "Did I hear you're a cheerleader?" She cleared her throat. "Were a cheerleader?"

Taylor didn't answer.

"I hate cheerleaders. Stuck-up, shallow imbeciles." She crouched down next to Taylor. "Don't you know how stupid you look out there shaking your pom-poms?"

"At least I'm not hurting anyone."

"No? How about all those girls who wanted to be cheerleaders and weren't pretty enough or popular enough? You think you're so good. It's easy to be good when everyone's kissing your feet—when you have perfect skin and teeth." She grabbed Taylor by the hair and lifted her head. "In here you're no one, cheerleader. You remember that. You can't even walk unless I say so. If they let me, I could drain you like a bathtub and watch you die. So how about a cheer for me? Because in here, I'm the star quarterback."

"Until they don't need you anymore," Taylor said. "Then you'll be thrown out with the rest of the trash."

Nichelle yanked Taylor's hair. "Don't push your luck, cheerleader," Nichelle growled. "I don't always stop when they tell me to." She let go of Taylor's hair and Taylor fell to the ground. "Oh, they'll always need me. As long as there're mutants like you out there, they'll need me." Nichelle stood up. "And our session isn't over yet. So just sit back and enjoy yourself." She smiled darkly. "I know I will."

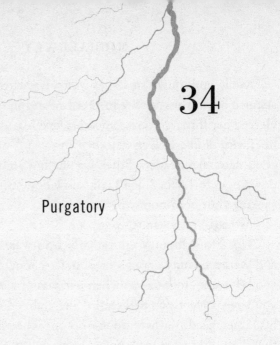

# 34

## Purgatory

Taylor was still unconscious when she was taken by gurney from the holding room into a reinforced cell. She had no idea what time it was when she woke, or how long she'd been out. She was lying on her stomach on a vinyl mat that was too short for her. Her head was throbbing and she groaned with pain. She couldn't see much—the only light in the room was a series of small red diodes blinking from the security cameras—and she was even more afraid than before. She thought of her home, her mother and father and brothers, and began crying. "I want to go home," she said to herself.

"I know," a boy's voice said softly.

She was startled by the voice. She tried to crawl away but couldn't. She couldn't move.

"Be still. I'm not going to hurt you." He gently touched her. She could feel his skin against hers and she entered his mind. It was peaceful and soft and safe.

Taylor looked up. Her eyes had adjusted some to the darkness, and she could see kneeling next to her was an African-American boy. He appeared to be about her age, though he was much larger than her. He was kneeling next to her and gently stroking her back. She could see the pale glow of his skin. He was one of them.

"Please don't hurt me," Taylor said.

"I won't hurt you, Taylor. I'm a friend."

"You know my name."

"Yes."

"Who are you?"

"My name is Ian."

"You're one of them," she said.

"I am one of you, not them."

"Where are we?"

"We're on Level D. This is where they put the disobedient ones. We call it Purgatory."

"Who's 'we'?"

"There are three of us who won't obey Hatch. Four, counting you. So what did you do? Or I should ask, what didn't you do?"

"Hatch wanted me to cause an accident at the motorcycle show. I could have killed the rider."

"That's one of Hatch's tricks."

"Tricks?"

"First, he tries to buy you. He makes you feel obligated so he can manipulate you by guilt. If you're stronger than that he tries to get you to do something wrong. Something small at first, then he increases it. Once you cross the line, he has you. He will hold it over you forever and he keeps upping the ante. You're lucky you're down here. Because if you were still up there, you'd be a murderer."

"My sister Tara's not a murderer."

"Yes she is. Tara, Bryan, Zeus, Quentin, Grace, Kylee, Nichelle, Tanner. They've all sold out. That's why they're up there and we're down here."

"She's my sister."

"She's your twin," Ian said. "She was younger than most of us when they started with her. She couldn't fully grasp what she was being asked to do until it was too late."

Taylor tried to move but the pain made her groan out.

"Just stay still. Nichelle's drained the juice out of you. It takes a while to come back." He left her side, then returned with a cup of water. "Have something to drink. It helps."

Ian guided the cup to Taylor's lips. She drank thirstily.

When she had finished drinking she asked, "Did they do this to you?"

"Yes. Many times. But not as bad. I think they mostly keep me here because my powers aren't as aggressive, so I'm not as valuable to them. That and because I'm blind."

"You're blind?"

"My eyes are. I'm not."

"I don't understand."

"I can see, just not with my eyes. I see the same ways sharks and electric eels see: through electrolocation. Instead of using light waves to see, I use electric waves."

Taylor remembered learning about that in biology.

"Electrolocation has its advantages. Like, it doesn't matter if it's day or night, and I can see through solid objects. You can too, of course—as long as the object permits light waves to pass through them, like glass or ice; but most solids don't. I can see through anything electrons can pass through."

"You can see outside these walls?"

"I can see outside the school. Unless Nichelle's around. Then I'm blind."

"Can you see me?"

"Yes. You look just like Tara." Ian sat back on his haunches. "I have no way of comparing my sight to yours, since I've never seen through my eyes. But I have a pretty good idea of the difference between your sight and mine. I can also see Glows and I can see how power is used."

"Like Hatch's glasses," Taylor said.

Ian nodded. "Yeah. They studied me to learn how to make them. You know, this place is a laboratory. They're constantly doing experiments."

"Nichelle said they're going to dissect me."

"A dead Glow does them no good. She just knows how to frighten you. It's what she's good at."

"How long have you been here?"

"Three years."

Taylor began to cry. "I can't do it."

"You will. You're stronger than you think you are."

Taylor buried her head in her hands.

"I want to introduce you to the others."

"There're others here?"

"Like I said, there're three of us."

In spite of the pain, Taylor lifted her head and looked around. To her surprise there were two other girls. One was Chinese. The other was a blond with eyes blue enough that Taylor could see them in the room's lighting. Both of them were glowing.

"That's McKenna," Ian said.

The Chinese girl nodded. "Hi."

"Hi," Taylor said.

"And that's Abigail," Ian said.

"Hello," Taylor said.

Abigail knelt down next to her. "Hi, Taylor. I'm going to touch you," she said softly. "It won't hurt. I promise." Abigail gently pressed her hand against Taylor's back, and Taylor felt a light wave pass through her body, taking with it all her pain and fear.

Taylor exhaled with relief. "What are you doing to me?"

"I'm taking away your pain for a moment."

"You're healing me?"

Abigail shook her head. "No. I can't do that. I can only take away pain while I'm touching you. But when I stop it will come back."

"It feels so good right now."

"I'll do it for as long as I can," she said kindly. "It takes effort, but maybe I can hold out long enough for you to fall asleep."

"Thank you, Abigail."

"You can call me Abi."

"Thank you, Abi."

"You're welcome. Now try to get to sleep."

Taylor closed her eyes and buried her head in her arms. Before she fell asleep she said, "I love you, Abi."

Abigail smiled. "I love you too."

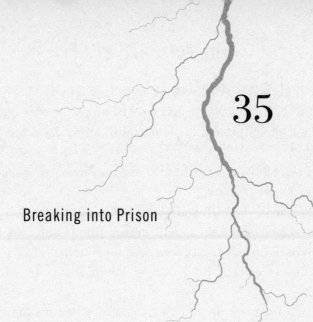

# 35

## Breaking into Prison

We arrived in Pasadena a little after noon. I was asleep in the backseat of the Camaro, lying across Ostin. I woke when we stopped for gas and to change drivers. Wade's eyes were bloodshot and he looked like he was about to pass out. He stumbled into the gas station to use the bathroom.

"Where are we?" I asked Jack.

"We're in Pasadena," he said. "I need the school's address."

"I've got it." I handed Jack the brochure, then got out of the car and stretched. The California air was moist and warm and, in spite of my worries, it felt good. I looked in the back window and saw that Ostin was still snoring, so I went inside the gas station. I got two bottles of strawberry-flavored milk and a box of doughnuts. I knew Ostin would be hungry when he awoke.

By the time I returned to the car Wade had climbed in the back and already fallen asleep. I sat in the front.

"Wade was pretty tired," I said to Jack.

"Yeah, he was. We would have been here sooner but he stopped in Lancaster and slept for four hours." Jack started the car. "Are you ready?"

I was blinking pretty hard. "No. Probably never will be. Let's go."

Jack smiled. "Nice."

Pasadena was lush and green with palm trees everywhere. I was eight when my mother and I moved from California, and I hadn't been back since. The city seemed foreign to me.

"Take Colorado Boulevard to South Allen," I said. "Then turn right."

Jack followed my directions and in a few minutes we were on Allen Avenue. "That's the place," I said. "It looks just like the picture. Except for the prison fence."

Jack parked the car at a gas station about a half block from the school. "Wade, wake up," he said.

"Who . . ."

"We're here."

Ostin woke as well and started searching for his glasses. He had fallen asleep wearing them, and I had picked them up off the car floor.

"Here you go," I said, handing them to him.

"Where are we?" he asked.

"The school," I said.

Ostin looked out at the building. "That's a school?"

"Looks more like a prison than a school," Wade said groggily.

"How are we going to get inside?" Ostin asked. "The fence is at least twelve feet high and there's barbed wire."

"And the entrance is guarded," Wade added.

"Getting in is not going to be easy," Ostin said. I think he meant "possible" instead of "easy."

Jack shook his head. "He's right, man. What are you going to do?"

I looked out at the building for a few more moments, then I sighed. "Well, it's not your problem. You got us here." I reached into my pocket and took out the rest of the money. "Here's the rest."

Jack took it without counting. "Thanks. Good luck."

"C'mon, Ostin," I said.

As we were climbing out of the car, Jack said, "Look."

I turned back toward the building. A white food-service truck was passing through the gate. "Get back inside, I have an idea."

We climbed back in and Jack started up the Camaro.

"What's your idea?" I asked.

He put on his sunglasses, then pulled out into the street. "We're going to borrow that van."

"Borrow?" Ostin said.

"This is life and death, right?" Jack asked.

"Absolutely," I replied.

We followed the van at a distance for about six miles, until it pulled into a parking lot, where there was a fleet of identical vans. Two men climbed out of the van and walked to the building. As soon as the men were out of sight Jack parked a couple stalls from the van. "Wade, follow us in the car." He looked at Ostin and me. "Let's go."

Jack, Ostin, and I ran, slightly stooped, to the van. I figured we'd have to break the window to get in, but the van was unlocked and we quickly climbed in. Jack checked on top of the visor, then in the ashtray for a spare key but didn't find one. He pulled out a pocket-knife, reached under the dash, and began sorting through wires. It only took a few minutes for him to hotwire the car. "These old vans are easy picking," he said.

"Where'd you learn to do that?" I asked.

"I'm not a car thief, if you're wondering. My old man's a mechanic."

"I wasn't wondering," I said. "Just impressed."

Jack drove out of the lot without drawing any attention. There was a CB radio mounted below the dashboard. Jack reached down and switched it on. "Better keep it on," he said. "So we know when they discover the van's missing."

Ostin was sitting in the back of the van with a bunch of metal trays stacked on a trolley. He lifted a lid. "Hmm. Chicken cordon bleu," he said.

"Don't steal food," I said.

"We just stole their van," Ostin said. "I don't think they'll care about a few leftovers. Besides, it might be my last meal."

"He's got a point," Jack said. "If they don't let us in the gate, we're screwed."

"What's our story?" I asked.

"What do you mean?" Jack said.

"I doubt they're expecting the food-service people back so soon. We better have a story."

"I've got one," Ostin said. "Tell them we left a stack of trays with chicken cordon bleu in the kitchen and it will stink up the place if we don't get it back."

"Not bad," I said. "I wonder if we'll need ID." I began looking around the van for paperwork or a badge but didn't find anything. "Nothing. All we've got is the story."

"We can make it work," Jack said.

Ostin said, "Hey, look at these." In a back compartment there was a stack of white food-service smocks and a sack of paper serving hats. "Uniforms."

Ostin lifted the smocks and hats out of the drawer and handed one to Jack and me. Even the smallest smock looked like a dress on me, but I put it on anyway. We drove back to the gas station parking lot, where Wade hopped out of the Camaro. I climbed in back and Wade got into the front seat of the van.

"Put these on," Jack said, handing Wade a smock and hat.

"Sweet," Wade said.

We circled the block and headed for the school. "Ready for this?" Jack asked.

"Yeah," I said from the back.

Jack pulled into the driveway and slowly up to the guard shack. The guard, a stern, powerful-looking man in a navy blue security uniform, wore a gun at his hip. "What's up?"

Jack looked surprisingly calm. "Sorry, we left a couple trays of blue chicken in the kitchen."

The guard squinted. "What?"

"You know, blue chicken, delicious from the oven but give it an hour out of the refrigerator and it's going to be stinkin' to high heaven. Stink up the kitchen, the dining area, the whole building. That blue chicken is stinky. Whoo. Diaper stinky."

The guard looked at him for a moment, then grinned. "All right. Go get your stinky chicken."

"Thanks."

The gate opened and we drove through.

"Blue chicken?" Ostin said. "It's chicken cordon bleu."

"Whatever," Jack said. "It worked."

He drove around the side of the building. We weren't exactly sure where to go, but there was only one open garage. In the back of it there was a door guarded by a man with a gun.

"Whoa," I said. "We've got another guard."

"Worse," Ostin said. "See that plate by the door? It's a magnetic switch. It's like my dad's office: You can't get anywhere without a card. No card, no entry. You better find something."

Wade looked through the glove compartment. "Nothing," he said.

"What do I do?" Jack asked. "Pull in?"

"We have to now," I said, "or they'll know something's up."

"Maybe we could offer the guy some food," Ostin said.

"Do you ever think of anything else?" Wade asked.

"Wait," I said, "he might be onto something. We'll carry the trays in and ask the guy to open the door for us."

Ostin sneered at Wade.

"Whatever we're doing," Jack said, "we better do it fast. 'Cause we're here."

# 36

## A New Glow

"Taylor."

Taylor slowly rolled over, again feeling the pain in her body. Ian was kneeling next to her.

"They're listening to us, so talk softly. Do you know about the last electrochild?"

"What do you mean?"

"There were seventeen of us. They found all but two, you and one other."

"Michael," she said. "His name is Michael. Why?"

"There's a new Glow outside the compound."

"What does he look like?"

"He's small, but the electricity around him is wild. Is he good or bad?"

"He's good."

Ian nodded. "Let's hope he stays that way."

"What's he doing?"

"He's with three other teenagers. I think they're trying to find a way in."

"We need to warn him that Hatch knows he's coming. Can you warn him?"

Ian shook his head. "No. I can only see."

Taylor covered her eyes. "I've failed him. I've failed everyone."

"This isn't your fault, Taylor. You're a good person."

"How do you know that?"

"Because you're down here."

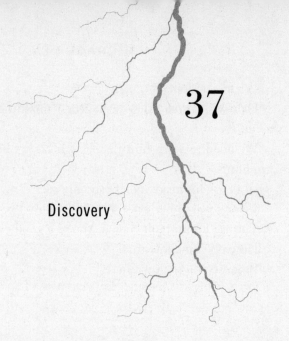

# 37

## Discovery

$J$ack slowly pulled the van into the garage, put it in park, and killed the engine. The guard watched us intensely.

"Ready, Ostin?" I asked.

"Yeah," he said, looking very *unready*.

I slid open the side door and stepped out. I grabbed one of the metal containers, then started toward the building's entrance. The guard's eyes were glued to me, and his hand hovered above his gun. When I was a couple of yards from him he said, "Stop."

I stopped. "Yes, sir."

"Where's your ID?" he asked.

I struggled to control my tics. "Sorry, it's in my pocket. Would you mind getting the door for me?"

His expression didn't change. "I need to see your ID."

"You recognize me, don't you? We talked last week."

"I wasn't here last week," he said.

I gulped. "It must have been another guard. In those glasses you all look alike."

"Your ID."

I sighed. "Okay. Here, it's just in my pocket. Hold this for one second."

Jack opened his door and started to get out of the van. "Is there a problem?"

The guard turned to him, "Get back in the van. I need his ID and your ID."

"I'm getting it," I said. "Just give me a hand." I pushed the tray toward the guard. He put his hands out, pushing back against the metal tray. "I'm not going to . . ."

I surged. His mouth opened but before he could make a sound he dropped to the ground unconscious. I set the tray on the ground.

"Whoa," Jack said. "I'm glad you didn't hit us with that much juice."

"It was only half," I said. "I'm getting more electric."

Ostin jumped out of the van. "Good job, dude."

"Don't start high-fiving yet." I took the lanyard hanging from the man's neck, then looked through his pockets for anything else we could use. I pulled out a thick plastic card. "What's this?"

"That's a magnetic key," Ostin said.

I held up the lanyard. "Then what's this?"

"Either a duplicate or you need two different keys."

"Now what?" Jack asked.

"Tie him up in the van and get ready to roll. Ostin and I will go find my mom and Taylor and bring them here."

"On it," Jack said. "Good luck, dude."

"Thanks for your help."

"I wasn't going to let you have all the fun."

I took the magnetic key on the guard's lanyard and swiped it across the black pad. The red diode turned green and the lock clicked. "We're in."

I pushed open the door. Inside was a long, brightly lit corridor with surveillance cameras on both ends. Ostin and I stepped inside.

"I've got the feeling we're being watched," Ostin said.

"Just act cool," I said. "They'll just think we're food-service guys." I kept walking. "Where do you think she is?"

"Where does the dog hide the bone?" Ostin asked.

"Just talk normal," I said.

"Find an elevator."

There was an elevator at the end of the hall. Inside the buttons were. 4-3-2-1-GL-D.

"What's GL?" I asked.

"Ground level, or garden level if they're being fancy. Push D."

"What's D?"

"I have no idea. But it's below GL."

I pushed the button but nothing happened. Outside I could hear footsteps coming down the hall.

"Look, it needs a key. Try yours."

I shoved it in the slot but nothing happened. The footsteps got closer.

"Try the other key."

I switched keys and the elevator door shut. "That's it."

The elevator began moving down. It stopped just a few seconds later and the door opened. I stuck my head out. We were in another corridor. The overhead lights must have been on dimmer switches because they were barely illuminated. Also there were thick metal doors spaced every fifteen or twenty feet that looked a little like the door to the refrigerated room in the back of the grocery store where my mom worked. There were metal boxes outside each door with bright green diodes. The hall was empty but there were security cameras mounted at each end of the hall. It was eerie being in such a large building and seeing no one.

"What's with all the security cameras?" Ostin asked.

"Mr. Dallstrom would be in heaven," I said. "We better hurry. I doubt the food-service guys come down here." We crept down the hall to the first door. The doors were thick metal with dark, mirrored glass in horizontal slits about four inches wide and a foot high.

I looked through the window on the first door. It was dark inside and I couldn't see anything or anyone. I went to the next door and looked inside. It was also dark, but I thought I could see a faint glow. "I think there's someone in this one."

"Is it your mom?"

"No. Whoever it is, they're glowing."

"It could be Taylor," Ostin said. "Try your keys."

I swiped both of them over the keypad but nothing happened. "It's not opening." I looked up and down the hall, feeling more nervous by the second.

"I bet it's a magnetic lock," Ostin said, looking it over. "You might be able to counter it with your electricity." He crouched down to examine it, then nodded. "The secondary magnetic coil should be about here. Let me see your hand. Don't shock me."

I held it out. He guided it to one side of the lock and backed away. "Okay, now."

I pulsed. There was a slight crackle of electricity but nothing happened.

"Give it more," he said.

"Okay." This time I pulsed with everything. The light in the hallway flickered and there was a clicking sound followed by the hiss of escaping air. "Are you done?" Ostin asked.

"Yeah."

Ostin grabbed the door and pulled it open. "It worked."

"All right," I said. I stepped into the room. It was dark except for the dim light coming from the hallway. I looked around, waiting for my eyes to adjust.

"Michael," a voice said. "It's me."

There was a girl lying on the floor in the corner of the room. Even in the darkness I knew who she was.

"Taylor," I said. "We found you."

# 38

## Michael's Induction

Taylor was barely able to move. I knelt down on the floor next to her. "What have they done to you?"

She started crying. "I'm so sorry I led them to you."

I put my hand on her shoulder. "It's going to be okay, Taylor. We're going to get you out of here. Have you seen my mother?"

"No. But they told me they have her."

"Did they say where?" Ostin asked.

"No."

"Taylor, what kind of school is this?"

"It's not a school. It's a laboratory."

"A laboratory? For what?"

Another voice came from the darkness. "To learn how to make more of us."

I spun around to see a young man standing on the other side of the cell. He looked about my age but was a full six inches taller. He was African-American and glowing. Standing behind him were two teenage girls, one Chinese, the other a tall blonde, who were both glowing as well. I'm not surprised that I hadn't seen them, as they were in the opposite corner of the cell and I was only focused on Taylor.

"I'm Ian," the boy said. "I've been watching you and your friends since you arrived this morning."

"From down here?"

"I see through electrolocation. I can see through the walls."

"Like electric eels," Ostin said. "That's cool."

"Why are you down here?" I asked.

"Around here you either do what Hatch says or you end up in the dungeon."

The two girls walked toward us. The Chinese girl said, "I'm McKenna."

"And I'm Abigail."

"I'm Michael," I said. "Do you also have powers?"

McKenna nodded. "I can make light and heat. Abigail can take away pain."

"Electric nerve stimulation," Ostin said. "Very interesting."

I turned back to Ian. "Do you know who else is down here?"

"I can see everyone in the building," he said.

"Do you know if my mother is here? They kidnapped her."

"How long ago did they take her?"

"Just a few days ago."

Ian shook his head. "The only female prisoners are on the next floor up and they've all been here for more than a year."

My heart fell.

Ian suddenly looked up toward the corner of the room. "Oh no," he said. "The two guys you came here with are being taken away by the guards." He turned back toward me. "How did you get in here? In this room?"

"Michael demagnetized the door," Ostin said. "With his electricity."

Ian shook his head. "That's impossible. The locks aren't magnetic. The sliding bolts are made of resin and work pneumatically. Everyone here has electrical gifts, so they prepared for that." Ian looked back up. "They're coming."

"Who's coming?" I said.

Ian didn't answer. He grabbed the girls and stepped away from the door, back to the corner of the room.

"If I didn't open the door," I asked, "then who did?"

A voice boomed from an unseen speaker. "That would be me, Michael. We've been expecting you. Welcome to Elgen Academy."

There was suddenly a loud screech in my head and I felt dizzy, just as I had in the parking lot when my mother was taken. I fell against the wall, covering my ears. Everyone in the room groaned except Ostin, who looked around curiously at us. "What's happening?"

"It's Nichelle," Ian said.

"What's a Nichelle?" Ostin asked.

The cell door opened. The man I had seen outside the pizza parlor was standing there next to the creepy girl.

"Hello, Michael," the man said. "I see the group has been reunited." He stepped inside the room.

"Shock him," Ostin said.

I took a step forward, then the screeching dropped me to my knees. Everyone else screamed.

Hatch turned to Ostin. "Ostin, isn't it? I thought you were supposed to be smart." He looked down at me. "What do you call yourself? The Electrokids? The Electroclub?"

"The Electroclan," Ostin said.

"Right." Hatch smiled darkly. "You don't belong here, Ostin. But here you are."

"I belong wherever Michael is," Ostin said.

Hatch smirked. "Loyalty. I like that. Even when it's misplaced, there's something endearing about it. Unfortunately, this is where your relationship ends. Michael, if you'll follow me, we'll let Ostin stay here with the others."

Ostin looked at me.

"I'm not leaving them," I said.

An even higher-pitched screeching poured through my head, followed by an increasing tightness, as if a metal band had been put around my head and cinched up. It was the same thing I had felt when my mother was taken—as if life itself were being drawn out of me through a straw. "Aargh." I fell to the ground, grabbing my temples.

"Stop it!" Taylor shouted. "Leave him alone."

"Mike knows how to stop it," Hatch said.

"Okay," I shouted. "I'll go."

Hatch nodded at Nichelle and the sound and pain stopped. "Come along, Mike. I'm a busy man."

I staggered to my feet. "My name is Michael."

"A Glow by any other name is just as electric, but as you wish."

I looked over at Ostin and Taylor. They both had fear in their eyes. "I'll be back," I said. I staggered out and the door automatically closed behind me. Halfway down the hall Hatch turned to me and said, "I sincerely hope you won't be back to that place."

"I belong with my friends."

"Then the question is, will your friends still be there? And that is completely up to you." The elevator door opened. "After you."

"Where are we going?"

Hatch pushed a button on the elevator. "I want to talk. But first, there are tests to be run."

# PART FOUR

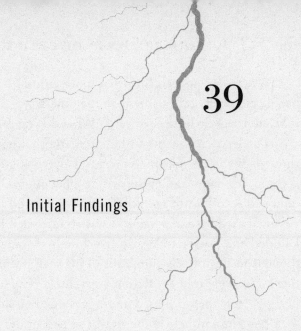

# 39

## Initial Findings

Later that afternoon, Hatch was in his office talking to Quentin when Dr. Parker knocked on his door.

"Come in," he said gruffly.

She opened the door. "Good evening, Dr. Hatch. Quentin."

"Quentin was just leaving," Hatch said.

Quentin immediately stood. "Yes, sir. Thank you, sir."

He walked out of the office and Hatch motioned to the same chair Quentin had occupied. "Take a seat." Before she could speak Hatch asked, "How's our boy?"

"I've never seen anyone like him."

"Explain."

"I've confirmed your initial findings. His el-waves are extremely high. Except they've grown since your first encounter."

"So he *is* becoming more powerful," Hatch said.

"So it would appear. But even more curious is that he seems to handle electricity differently than the others."

Hatch slightly leaned forward. "What do you mean?"

"His electricity seems to be circulating within his body, either through his bone marrow or central nervous system, which may account for some rather surprising phenomena. I administered a mild shock to him to see how he'd respond and his el-waves actually increased by one percent. I was so intrigued by this result that I upped the power to nearly five hundred joules. At that level I thought he'd probably jump out of his seat, but instead he just sat there. His body told a different story, however. His el-waves spiked fifty percent, then dropped and maintained at an increased seventeen percent and held there until the end of our examination. He still might be elevated."

Hatch leaned forward in his chair. "You're saying he can absorb electricity from other sources?"

"It would appear so."

"Like Nichelle?"

"Except that Nichelle doesn't retain power; she's simply a conduit to its dissemination. Vey seems to capture it."

Hatch rubbed his chin in fascination. "How is hoarding all that electricity affecting his health?"

"If it's hurting him, it's not manifesting. He's perfectly healthy. With the exception of his Tourette's syndrome."

"He has Tourette's?"

"Yes. That's why he has the facial tics."

"I thought he was just anxious." Hatch rubbed his palms together the way he always did when he was excited. "Could his Tourette's have something to do with why he's different than the other children?"

"I don't know. We don't even know enough about Tourette's to know what causes it. We know it's a neurological disorder, but not a whole lot more than that."

"But it's possible?"

"It's possible."

"I want this information kept in strictest confidentiality."

"Of course. All research is confidential."

"I don't even want your assistants to know. This is between you and me."

"Very well."

"If he'll cooperate, Mr. Vey could be the model of the Glows 2.0."

"And if he won't?"

"Then we'll have to fix that. How was his attitude?"

"He was quite defiant."

"Of that I'm sure. But there's one thing I'm equally certain of."

"What's that?"

"The boy loves his mother."

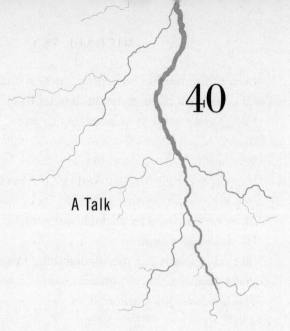

# 40

## A Talk

The Elgen guards all looked the same to me. They were all nearly the same height and build and wore the same uniform: a black beret, dark glasses, and black jumpsuits that appeared to have been made from a rubberized material. They all had communication radios hanging from their ears and jaws, and they carried an array of weapons on a utility belt—a knife, a canister of Mace, two different types of revolvers, resin handcuffs, a smoke grenade, a concussion grenade, and a long wooden truncheon.

I was sitting on the floor looking through a shelf of books when I heard the lock on my door slide. I looked up to see the door open.

"Sorry to disturb you, Mr. Vey," a guard said. "But Dr. Hatch is ready to meet with you."

I thought he sounded unusually polite for a prison guard. Of course prisoners aren't usually given a room with a plasma TV, surround-sound audio, and Monet prints on the wall. My room seemed more like a luxury suite than a prison cell, but if there's no doorknob on the inside, you're still a prisoner.

"All right." I stood as the door opened fully. There was a second guard standing a few feet behind him in the hall. The second guard didn't say a word. I noticed that they both had their hands on their Mace. I guessed they had been ordered to be pleasant.

"This way, sir," the guard said. We took the elevator down one level to the second floor.

They led me down a marble-floored corridor to the end of the hall and into a large reception area, where a secretary sat at a large wooden desk with several monitors. Directly behind her was a glass wall, partially obstructing another door. In front of the receptionist's desk was another guard sitting behind a tall, circular podium with a Plexiglas shield.

The receptionist, a thin woman about my mother's age and wearing narrow reading glasses, looked up as we entered.

"We have Michael Vey," the first guard said, though it was evident she was expecting us.

"I'll inform Dr. Hatch," she said. She pushed a button, then spoke into her phone. She nodded, then pushed a button beneath her desk. There was a loud buzz and the door slid open. "Dr. Hatch would like you to go on in."

The second guard motioned for me to go first, so I walked ahead of them through the open door. I stepped inside while they stopped at the door's threshold. I was ticking like crazy.

Hatch's office reminded me of the ones I had seen on the TV lawyer shows, with bronze statues and busts and cases of books I wondered if anyone ever read. Television screens took up an entire wall. Hatch was sitting at his desk. He wasn't wearing his sunglasses. Nichelle sat in a chair at the side of the room. I didn't look at her. I couldn't stand her.

Hatch motioned to a leather chair in front of his desk. "Hello, Michael," he said. "Please, take a seat."

I walked up to the chair and sat down, looking around the office. On the wall behind Hatch was a picture of Dr. Hatch shaking hands with the president of the United States. He noticed that I was looking at the picture.

"It's not hard to get to the president," Hatch said. "If you have money."

"Where's my mother?" I asked.

His eyes narrowed into thin slits. "To the point. I like that. After all, that's why you made this futile little trip, isn't it?"

"Where are you keeping my mother?"

"We'll get to that. But first, there's something you need to understand. More important than where *she* is, is where *you* are. And who you are." His voice dropped. "Do you even know?"

"Of course I know who I am."

"Yes, I know you think you do. But you don't really know." His gaze softened. "Who are you? You're a victim, Michael. A victim of your environment. You have been brainwashed, your thoughts contaminated by the human Petri dish your mind has been cultured in.

"For instance, you've been told that all men are created equal, but anyone who isn't stupid or ignorant can see that that just isn't true. Some are rich, some are poor. Some are smart and some are fools. No, no one is born equal. Especially you.

"You're not even equal to the other electric children. You handle electricity in a different way. And you seem to be getting more powerful. I compared your el-waves from now to when I first met you in Idaho. They've risen. It's very impressive." He leaned forward. "Do you know what we do here, Michael?"

"Kill babies with your machine?"

Hatch chuckled. "What an interesting take you have on this. That's the one thing I've learned about working with youth—if you think you know what they're thinking, you're mistaken." He straightened his tie. "You're right, you know. At least partially. It is about the machine. The MEI we call it. The MEI may have been a failure as an imaging device, but it led to the discovery of something more important. Much more important.

"If you think about it, Michael, there's a marvelous fate to all this. Many of the world's greatest discoveries are results of accidents. The MEI was one of those happy accidents. We set out to take pictures of the human body and instead we improved the human body. We invented superhumans. We invented the electric children.

"We've spent the last dozen years tracking them down. There were seventeen of you who survived. Seventeen very special children. Sadly, there are only thirteen of you left—four of you died before the age of seven."

"Died of what?"

"Cancer. No doubt attributable to the excessive electricity coursing through your cells. We can't be certain, of course, but there's a chance that unless we find a cure for your condition, that may be all of your fates."

I sat back in my chair. I had never considered that what I had was a disease.

"But I digress. I was saying that we had found all the survivors except two: you and Miss Ridley. Miss Ridley was adopted out-of-state and you know how inefficient government bureaucracy is. Her records got lost in the process. And you, well, we tracked you for a while, all throughout California.

"You don't know it, but we've been more a part of your life than you realize. If you look through your family picture album, say on that trip you took to Disneyland when you were seven, you're likely to find a picture of one of our agents in the background. Then, right after your father's death, your mother pulled a fast one and disappeared. We lost you.

"Actually, it's quite impressive how she eluded us, seeing that you didn't even know you were being followed. So we set some traps and hoped that you would someday come looking for us. And you did. Actually, it was Miss Ridley who did. But we never dreamed that we'd be so fortunate that she'd lead us to you. In this matter, fate was truly generous."

*Fate sucks*, I thought. "What do you want from us?"

Hatch stood and walked around to the front of his desk, leaning back against it. "We're scientists, Michael. We want what all scientists want. Truth. The truth about you. The truth about how you do what you do. We want to know why you lived when so many others died."

"No matter what you call yourself, you're just a bunch of murderers," I said.

"So much anger in you, Michael," Hatch said coolly. "But boys in glass houses shouldn't throw stones, should they?"

"What do you mean?"

"Don't play stupid, Michael. We know all about it."

I looked at him blankly. "About what?"

"Are you telling me that you really don't know why you left California?"

The way he asked the question frightened me. "We left because my mother was trying to protect me."

He laughed. "Protect you from what?"

I couldn't answer. He walked closer to my chair. "So you really don't know." Hatch rubbed his chin. "I think, deep inside, you do. You must. No child, not even an eight-year-old, could forget something that traumatic. Your mother wasn't protecting you, Michael. She was protecting others *from you*." His eyes leveled on me in a piercing gaze. I was ticking like crazy, both blinking and gulping.

Hatch leaned back against his desk. "I knew your father. I knew him well. Maybe even better than you did."

My chest constricted.

"Do you even know where your father worked?" Hatch asked.

"He worked at a hospital," I blurted out angrily.

Hatch just looked at me for a moment, then the corners of his mouth rose in a subtle smile. "Good. So your mother didn't hide everything from you. He did indeed work at a hospital. Your father was the head of radiology at Pasadena General." Hatch slightly leaned forward. "He helped us test the MEI."

His words hit me like a bucket of ice water. "No!" I shouted. "He wouldn't do that. He was a good man."

Hatch nodded. "You're right, he was a good man. He was a

visionary. And, like me, he never intended to hurt anyone. He wanted to advance science and save lives. He wanted to make the world a better place." Hatch's voice fell. "Unfortunately, he never got that chance." Hatch exhaled slowly. "I know what happened to your father, Michael." Hatch turned around and lifted a folder from his desk, extracting from it a single paper. "I've been saving this for some time now, haven't I, Nichelle?"

I had forgotten that she was in the room. "Yes, sir," Nichelle said. "Years."

Hatch held up a paper with a gold border around it. "Michael, have you ever seen a death certificate?"

I shook my head.

"I didn't think so." He turned the paper back around. "Let me read the important parts. State of California, County of Los Angeles . . . Carl T. Vey died at 7:56 p.m. in Los Angeles County on the fifth day of October, 2004 . . . Cause of death: Cardiac arrest from an electric shock." He set down the paper. "It's about time you owned up to the truth about your father's death." His eyes turned dark. "You stopped your father's heart."

At that moment, I had a flashback. I was sitting on my father's lap. My father was grasping his chest, his eyes wide and panicked. Then flashing red and blue lights illuminated our kitchen drapes, and sirens wailed in chorus with my mother crying. It was true. That's what my mother was hiding from me. I had killed my own father. Darkness filled my heart and mind.

"I was barely eight!" I shouted. "I didn't know how to control my electricity."

Hatch just stared at me. "Isn't that interesting. We wanted to save lives, so we created a machine that could do that. Like you, we didn't know better. Yet you condemn us—" His voice rose and he pointed at me. "How dare you call me, or your father, a murderer. You're no different than us, not one iota." He walked behind his desk and sat down. He looked calmer and his voice was gentle again. "But you can atone for this, Michael. Just as we are trying to atone for our mistake. We're trying to do the right thing."

"That's why you're torturing Taylor?"

The loud screech went through my head and I fell forward, grabbing my temples. "Aaah."

Hatch spun around to Nichelle. "Stop it!"

The pain stopped.

"Get her out of here," I said.

"I can't do that," Hatch said. "I don't fully trust you yet."

"You don't trust *me*?"

"You're still brainwashed from the outside world. Until you see clearly, I can only trust you to behave like a human."

"I just want my mother."

"Of course you do. Which, of course, is precisely why we took her. And whether you see her again depends entirely upon you. If you comply with my instructions, your mother will be set free. We'll fly her here to see you, joyful reunion and all that. If not . . ." His expression fell. "If not, sadly, I cannot guarantee her safety. Even if I wanted to."

I looked at him quietly. "What are your 'instructions'?"

"Simple, really. Let's call them demonstrations of loyalty."

"What kind of demonstrations?"

"I trust you remember Clyde. You met him in the parking lot and you spoke with him in the jail, didn't you?"

"How did you know that?"

Hatch smiled but didn't answer me. "Clyde is, or should I say, was, what we call a GP. It's a nickname we give our human guinea pigs."

"Guinea pigs?" I suddenly understood why Clyde had reacted with such fear and hostility toward me.

"GPs are inconsequential—the coffee grounds of humanity. They are America's untouchables, criminals and losers, none of them worth the carbon their bodies are made of. So, from time to time, we use them for the advancement of our scientific pursuits."

I was horrified by what he was telling me. "Where do you get them?" I asked.

"From all over. Sometimes we pull them off the streets or from homeless shelters. Sometimes we find them engaged in some kind of criminal activity. In fact we brought in two new ones just today. Would you like to meet them?"

"No," I said.

"These, I think you will." He pushed a button on his desk. "Bring GPs Seven Sixty-Four and Seven Sixty-Five to my office immediately."

I looked at him incredulously. "You kidnap people and use them for experiments?"

"Well, the word *people* might be a bit strong but the rest of what you said is accurate." He looked at me with a grim smile. "We're doing them a favor, really. Out in society they would only self-destruct. Most of them already had. This way we preserve their lives a little longer, improve their standard of living, and give meaning to their pathetic existences. They are actually contributing to society instead of just staining it."

A moment later one of the guards opened Hatch's door. "They're here, sir."

"Bring them in."

The guard signaled to someone outside the door and two other guards brought in the shackled GPs. I couldn't believe what I saw. Jack and Wade. They looked terrified, especially Wade, who was trembling so hard his chains were rattling. They were both barefoot and dressed in Day-Glo orange jumpsuits. In addition to the shackles and chains on their legs and wrists they had large plastic and stainless steel collars fastened around their necks. The collars had green flashing lights. The sight of them bound made me sick to my stomach.

"I'm sorry," I said to them, shaking my head. "I'm so sorry."

Jack and Wade just looked at me with fearful eyes. I didn't understand why they didn't say anything.

I turned back to Hatch. "What are those things around their necks?" I asked angrily.

"Simple devices to ensure they don't decide to leave us," Hatch said. "It's based on the invisible fence theory." He looked at me. "Are you familiar with that?"

"No."

"That's right, you had neither a dog nor a yard. Some dog owners put special electric shock collars on their pets that will administer a mild shock to their dog when it crosses an invisible boundary. It trains the dog to not leave the yard. These collars your associates are sporting operate on the same principle. If your friends leave this building they will be shocked.

"The collar also monitors their vocal cords. If they attempt to shout or even speak they will be shocked. But I'm afraid it's a bit more potent than that painful little wake-up call a dog gets. The charge these collars generate is quite a bit more lively and will completely incapacitate them." His eyes moved back and forth between Jack and Wade. "Maybe even kill them."

"You need to let them go," I said. "They're not part of this."

"You're quite wrong about that, Michael. The moment they chose to help you they became a part of this." His voice rose and he looked at Jack and Wade with disdain. "The moment they violated our academy they became a part of this."

"What are you going to do with them?"

"The same thing we do with all our GPs—whatever furthers our cause." He looked at the guard. "Take them back to their cells."

"You heard him," the guard said to Jack and Wade. They turned and shuffled out of the room.

"How many prisoners do you have here?" I asked.

"Only a few dozen. Our Pasadena facility is quite small compared to the others. In fact, now that we have you and Miss Ridley, we'll be shutting down this facility and moving elsewhere. Someplace where we have a little more . . . flexibility."

"Flexibility to do what?"

He looked at me gravely. "We're scientists, Michael. And we have a vision. We've been trying to create the perfect Glow. And we're getting close. You and Miss Ridley are very much a part of our plans.

"We've tested thousands of DNA samples. We've run thousands of blood tests, searching for the one link that all you survivors have in common. We've even been testing diets and nutritional supplements to gauge how eating affects your powers. We've discovered that with a nonsugar diet high in potassium we can actually increase electrical flow.

"But you, Michael, are something else. Even without our help, you've been increasing your electrical capacity nearly two percent a day. At that rate you'll be doubling in power just about every two months. In a year you may be the most powerful Glow of all—if your electricity doesn't kill you first."

"What do you mean, 'kill me first'?"

"Like I told you before, we've already lost four of you to cancer. That's why I sent you in for the checkup. You're going to need our help. The doctors out there can't help you; they've never seen anyone like you before. There are no medical books on your condition. If you want to live to manhood, you had better stay close to us."

His words filled me with even greater fear. What had they found in my exam? Was I really dying? It was too big to think about and I pushed it from my mind. "Why did you take my mother instead of me?"

"Trust me, your mother would rather it had been her than you. Mothers are like that. Actually we tried to take you both, but your chubby friend ruined that when he showed up with all those people around. We only had time to take one of you and, frankly, better her than you."

"But I'm the one with the power."

"Yes, but as you well know, power, undirected, is worthless—an engine without wheels. It's the old saying, isn't it? You can lead a horse to water but you can't make him drink. Unless you happen to have your horse's mother locked away in a cage somewhere. Having collateral will make you much more . . . malleable.

"Take your fellow Glow, Tanner. He has an amazing power. He can bring down an airplane from the ground. The first time I told him to crash a 747 he refused. Until we let him see his little brother getting nearly electrocuted by one of your peers. It only took ten minutes of his screams before he was quite eager to help out.

"You know how it goes, Michael. The first time you resist. The second time you relent. The third time you volunteer. It's that easy. Today, I tell Tanner to bring down a commercial flight and he says, 'which plane?'" He looked into my eyes. "We're creating an army, Michael. And you are a natural leader. You would make a very good general."

"An army to fight who?"

"Whomever we need to fight. Whoever stands in our way as we reach for our destiny. Just think of the powers at our disposal. Just consider Tanner. He can bring down a jet airliner without a bomb, missile, or security risk. There's no tracking, there's no preventing. Sudden and complete mechanical failure and the plane drops out of the sky. Do you have any idea what his talent is worth? Terrorists would pay tens of millions. Governments would pay hundreds of millions. Or billions. Especially if that plane were carrying a nuclear weapon—or the president of the United States.

"And that's just one of many of your graduating class's talents. We just need more of you. A lot more of you."

"What makes you think anyone will follow you?"

"They will and they do. Most of them have, at least. It's amazing what you can do to a young mind before the rest of the world contaminates it. It's you older kids, the brainwashed, who are the problem. Like poor, misguided Miss Ridley. I offered her the world and she spat it back in my face."

"Taylor's a good person," I said, my right eye twitching.

"That depends entirely on what you mean by 'good.' If, by 'good' you mean shortsighted, ungrateful, and small-minded, then you're right."

He stood and his expression relaxed. "That's enough for today. I'm going to let you stay in one of the guest suites tonight. You'll be much more comfortable there. Unfortunately, for now, you will still be assigned a guard. Don't get me wrong, Michael. I trust you. I really do. I just don't trust the world you come from. Too much of it is still in your head. But we'll work on it.

"In the meantime, if you have any seditious schemes, remember, your mother will pay severely for your mistakes. You shock someone, she'll be shocked twice. You hurt someone, well, you get the picture. It's beautifully ironic. For centuries the sins of the parents have been

answered on the heads of their children. Now the opposite is true."
He walked to the door. "It's time for you to go."

I stood and also walked to the door, followed a few yards back by
Nichelle.

"I'm giving you forty-eight hours to consider your predicament.
I urge you to seriously do so. Lives are at stake here. You've already
killed your father. Will you kill your mother too?"

His words cut like razor blades.

"And then there are your friends. If you choose to disregard my
offer, Jack and Wade will be the first to go. Then Ostin and finally
Taylor. It's your call. They're all counting on you to do the right
thing. If you don't, they'll disappear one by one. Think carefully now.
Are you going to lose a few of them before you change your mind?
Or will you do the right thing the first time?

"As you grow older, Michael, you'll learn an important lesson—
that most people spend their entire lives wishing for a second chance
to do what they should have done right the first time. Don't be like
them, Michael." He smiled at me, placing his hand on my shoulder,
which made me feel sick inside. "I believe in you. I know you think
you're doing the right thing by resisting, but it's because your point
of view is skewed. All you have to do is walk across the aisle and see
it from our side. And as your reward, I'm offering you everything
you've dreamed of. You'll be the head of the electric children. You'll
have a life a rock star would envy. And you'll have your Taylor." He
smiled. "Yes, I know how you feel about Taylor. And she'll be all
yours. Your little friend, Ostin, will be allowed to go home to his
mommy and daddy. And your mother will be set free. And some day
you'll have the adoration of millions. All around the world, children
will want to be you.

"Remember, history is made by those willing to tear up the last
mapmaker's map. Make history, Michael. You have two days to
decide whether or not to join us. I dare say that these are the two
most important days of your life. I know your heart may not entirely
be in it at first; I don't expect it to be. There's too much brainwashing in there. I just want to see that you're willing to commit. That's

all I ask. And for that simple commitment I offer you the world." He turned and nodded to the guard. "Have a good night, Michael."

"Let's go," a guard said to me.

Nichelle and the guards took me to a suite on the third floor. I sat on the bed and the door locked behind me. My head was spinning like a top. My entire world had been turned upside down.

For the next two days I was left alone in my room. Under different circumstances I would have thought I'd died and gone to heaven. The suite had a refrigerator and cabinet that were full of drinks and candies from all around the world. I tried some Japanese candy, Chocoballs and Hi-Chews, which were some of the best candy I'd ever eaten. Four meals were brought in daily, on plates that looked like my mom's best china. There were menus for entertainment as well as food. The first day an Asian woman came to my room and offered me a massage, which I didn't accept.

There were shelves of video games. The newest on the market, some not yet on the market, and some I'd only dreamed of. I thought of how excited Ostin would be to see them. I only wished that he were there to play them with me.

In spite of all the distractions, all I could think about was my impending decision. What did Hatch mean by "demonstrations of loyalty"? What would he require of me? Something told me that his "simple commitment" was anything but simple.

My second night, as I lay in bed, I made my decision. If they would let my mother and my friends go, I would stay. There was no other choice to be made.

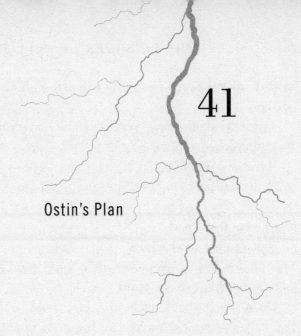

# 41

## Ostin's Plan

**O**stin was miserable. His stomach was growling and he was homesick. Taylor came and sat by him. "Are you okay?" she asked softly.

"No."

"Are you afraid?"

"Yeah."

"Me too." She put her arm around him. "I wanted to tell you that I'm sorry that I wasn't very nice to you back in Idaho."

"I thought you were nice. Except at that party when you kept threatening to reboot me."

Taylor looked down. "Maddie's party. That seems like a million years ago. It's funny how the things that were so important back then don't matter anymore. Maybe Hatch is right: We have been brainwashed."

"Hatch isn't right," Ostin said. "Hatch is a devil. It's like my mother always says, 'The devil will tell a thousand truths to sell one lie.'"

Taylor slowly nodded. "Want to know something?"

Ostin looked at her. "What?"

"I was jealous of you."

"You were jealous of me?" he said.

Taylor scratched her head. "You're so smart. I've always wished that I were that smart."

"But you get good grades."

"You don't really have to be smart to get good grades. Just good at doing what they tell you to do."

Ostin slowly shook his head. "How could you be jealous of me? You have everything. You're like the most popular girl in the universe. Everyone loves you."

"Not everyone. Being popular isn't always easy. You make enemies. And they're usually people who pretend to be your friend. Frenemies."

"I never thought of that."

"So maybe I do know something you don't." She sighed. "It all just seems so stupid now. What am I going to wear to Emily's party, what if Megan wears the same thing, who is Chase going to ask to the prom? It's all so meaningless."

Ostin put his head down. "I wish those were still our problems."

Taylor said, "Me too. What do you think they're going to do to Michael?"

"They'll try to break him."

"It's my fault he's here."

"No, it's not. I mean, he would have come after you, but he would have come anyway. They have his mother. He's got a great mother." Ostin touched her arm. "It's not your fault."

She smiled sadly. "Thanks."

"Besides, even if it were, we're a club, right? All for one and one for all."

"Yeah. I'd just rather be the one for all instead of the all for one."

Ostin sat back and breathed out heavily. "You know, there's

something about all this I don't understand. Why have they kept these kids here for so long?"

"What do you mean?"

"Ian, Abigail, McKenna. They clearly aren't going to convert. So why don't they just"—he hesitated—"you know, get rid of them?"

"I don't know."

Suddenly Ostin's eyes widened. "The only reason you keep something around is because it's valuable. That's it."

"What?"

"If they're valuable, they'll protect them." His whole face animated. "I have an idea how to get out of here. But I'll need everyone's help."

Taylor's eyes lit with hope. "Let's go talk to them."

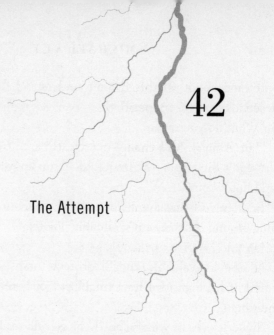

# 42

## The Attempt

In the darkness of the cell, Ian
looked like a ghost, the pale glow of his skin rising a half foot taller
than Ostin. He stood with his arms crossed at his chest, staring down
at Ostin. "That's the stupidest idea I've ever heard."

"Keep your voice down," Ostin said. "They'll hear us."

"You don't tell me what to do. In here, I'm in charge."

"You're not in charge of me."

"Yes, I am. This is my turf."

"No, you're not my boss."

"Are you dissing me?"

"I'll diss you if I want. I'm not afraid of you, bat boy."

Ian got in Ostin's face. "What did you call me?"

"You two knock it off," Taylor said. "He was just trying to help."

"Keep out of it," McKenna said.

There was an audible whirr as three of the five video cameras
panned across the room.

"Don't tell me what to do," Taylor said. "I'll fry your brain."

"Try it," McKenna said, her skin beginning to brighten. "I'll cook you."

"You'll never get a chance, lightbulb."

"Will you all stop it?" Abigail said. "It's bad enough we have them hating us."

Ian growled, "So, chunky soup here is dissing me for being blind?"

"Chunky soup?" Ostin said, "Take it back."

Ian uncrossed his arms. "Make me."

"I will."

"I'd like to see you try, doughboy. The only exercise you get is unwrapping Twinkies. I'll roll you out like pizza dough."

"You're going to pay for that."

"Ooh, scary," Ian said.

Ostin rushed at him and knocked him over by the door. Ian groaned as he hit the ground.

"What the . . . McKenna!" Ian shouted. "Taylor's doing something to me. She's messing with my brain."

A harsh voice came over the speaker system. "Occupants of Cell B, stop what you're doing, immediately."

Ian began screaming. "Abi, McKenna, stop the new girl! Stop her."

"That does it," McKenna said. "You're going to pay."

"Bring it on, Day-Glo," Taylor said. "I can take both of you."

The girls surrounded Taylor. Ian and Ostin were locked in combat when the door clicked and opened. Two guards ran into the room.

"Now!" Ostin said.

McKenna suddenly burst into a brilliant light, temporarily blinding the guards. Taylor turned and focused on the two men as Ian charged at them, knocking them both over. Abigail and McKenna quickly jumped on the men, pulling their Mace from their belts and spraying them in the face with it. Taylor kept rebooting them over and over and the men flailed about confused and gasping from the Mace.

"Ostin," Ian said, "come help me." They rolled the first guard over and handcuffed his hands behind his back, then dragged him inside;

next they handcuffed and dragged in the second one and stuffed both of their mouths with toilet paper. Ostin pulled their magnetic keys from their pockets.

"Got the keys?" Ian asked.

Ostin held them up. "Got 'em."

"Let's go," Ian said.

"Give us some light, McKenna," Ostin said.

"On it."

The four of them followed Ian out into the hallway, pulling the cell door shut behind them.

"Which way?" Ostin asked.

"The guards came from this direction," Ian said.

"How can you tell?" Taylor asked.

"I'm an electric hound dog," Ian said. "People leave electronic imprints when they move."

They ran down the hall toward a service elevator. "Oh, oh," Ian said. "They're coming." Suddenly an alarm went off.

"Monkey butts," Ostin said.

"Here, give me the key." Ian opened the elevator and they all rushed in.

"Go to the second floor. That's the administration level. They won't expect that."

Taylor hit the button. The door shut and the elevator began to move. The elevator hit the second floor and paused but the door didn't open. Suddenly it began moving up again.

"What's it doing?" Abigail asked.

"I don't think we're controlling it anymore," Ostin said.

The elevator climbed all the way to the fourth floor and froze. Ian's head dropped. "We're dead."

"What do you see?" Taylor asked.

"Trouble," Ian said.

The door opened. There were at least fifteen guards standing in front of them with guns drawn. "On your knees!" one shouted. "And put your hands behind your head."

"Taylor?" Ostin asked.

Taylor squinted. "There're too many of them."

Ian sighed and knelt down. The rest followed.

"You are smart," Ian said to Ostin. "That's the closest to freedom anyone here has ever got."

Ostin sighed. "Close only counts in horseshoes and nuclear weapons."

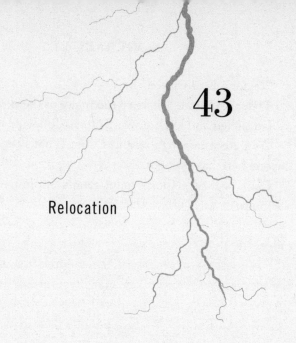

# 43

## Relocation

On the second floor Hatch had been watching the escape attempt unfold on the screens in front of him.

After the teens had been handcuffed and separated, the chief of security reported to Hatch. "The prisoners have been subdued, sir."

"Well done, Mr. Welch," he said. "Return them to their cell. Put the human boy in solitary confinement."

"Yes, sir. Thank you, sir."

Then Hatch's secretary's voice came over his phone. "Your call, sir."

"Thank you." He pushed the button again. "This is Hatch."

The British voice sounded annoyed. "What do you need?"

"The BA money has made it into all the accounts. We're filtering it through Switzerland and the Cayman Islands. Our Glow has been withdrawn from Dubai and relocated to our Italian compound. We're ready to commence evacuation of the Pasadena facility."

"What is the status of the Vey boy?"

"I've given him two days to pick a side. He's got eighteen hours left."

"And what side will he pick?" The voice was monotone but still managed to convey the intended threat.

"He'll be with us. He has too much to lose."

"I hope you're right. About the relocation, the board is rightfully concerned that you follow protocol. We want no attention drawn to our move."

"Of course. We'll evacuate the children first, then we'll drug and transport the GPs to our Lima facility. Our 727 will be sufficient for that. We'll destroy all records and quietly renovate the building. We already have the city building permits, and our leasing company has legitimate tenants ready to occupy the facility—a private school."

"Very well. Then I'll see you in Rome in a few months."

"I look forward to it. After the last month, it will be nice to relax a few days."

"Just don't plan on too much of it. We're ready to launch phase two."

# 44

## The Contract and a "Simple" Demonstration of Loyalty

It was evening of my second day in captivity when two guards came to my room. I was lying on my bed playing a video game when the door opened and they stepped inside, followed by Nichelle. I hated seeing her. Actually, I hated her. She always made me tic.

"Time to go," the first guard said, not as politely as the last time they'd come for me.

"Where are we going?" I asked.

"Dr. Hatch has requested your presence."

"Let me get my shoes on." I put on my shoes, then walked out of my room with one guard in front and one in back, with Nichelle walking at the rear guard's side. They walked right past Hatch's secretary and into his office. Hatch was at his desk. He stood as I entered.

"How are you, Michael?" he asked.

"Tired," I said.

"I would imagine. You've had enough on your mind to cause anyone insomnia." He turned to the guards. "You may go."

"Yes, sir," the guards said in unison.

To my surprise he said to Nichelle, "You too."

Nichelle looked at me. "Just try something," she said.

"Nichelle, that's really not necessary."

She glared at me before following the guards out of the room. Hatch shook his head. "Sorry about that. What Nichelle lacks in tact she makes up for in unpleasantness." His expression hardened. "So, down to business. Have you come to a decision?"

My tics were acting up and I tried not to blink but couldn't help it. "Yes, sir."

"And that is?"

"If you'll free my mother and my friends, I'll join you."

He just stared at me until the silence became uncomfortable. "You know I can't release Taylor," he finally said. "She's too dangerous. She knows too much."

"But that was our deal."

"No, you'll recall that our deal was that I'm giving her to you. A much better scenario, I'd say."

I just looked at him. That *was* what he'd said.

"I'm not trying to be difficult, Michael. But Taylor brought this on herself—and you. She'll have to live with the consequences. But, with you joining us, I think she'll come around and before too long she'll join us back in the house. And, she'll be yours."

I couldn't help but wonder how he planned to ensure that.

"But, of course, your mother will be set free immediately, as will Ostin and Jack. We'll fuel up Jack's car, give him some traveling money, and he can drive back home."

"What proof do I have of that?"

"What proof would you have? Ostin can call you as soon as they're on the road. And we'll let you talk to your mother." He leaned forward, extending his hand. "Do we have an agreement?"

I slightly hesitated, then stepped forward and took his hand. "Yes, sir." We shook. Then he sat back in his chair.

"Very well." He pushed a piece of paper toward me. "I'd like you to sign this document, to convey your resolve."

I leaned over the desk and looked at the form.

> I, Michael Vey, do hereby enroll and subscribe as a full member of the Elgen Academy and promise to do whatever is required of me to promote and advance the academy's work, mission, and objectives as long as my services are required.
>
> X _____

I thought it was peculiar that he wanted me to sign something. It's not like anything signed by a fifteen-year-old would be legally binding.

"You may use my pen." Hatch held out to me a beautiful, gold-plated pen inset with rubies. I read the statement again, then signed beneath it. I pushed the document back to him with the pen.

"Keep the pen," he said. "A memento of a very special occasion."

He leaned back and examined the document. "'I, Michael Vey, do hereby enroll and subscribe as a full member of the Elgen Academy and promise to do whatever is required of me to promote and advance the academy's work, mission, and objectives as long as my services are required.' That's quite a commitment you've just made." He set it back down and looked into my eyes. "Quite a promise. Unfortunately, promises are broken all the time. Like you, I need some proof. I need to see what's behind your commitment."

"What proof would you have?" I asked, using his words back at him.

"Simple. We're going to take a little test. Fortunately, unlike Mr. Poulsen's biology class, this is one you don't have to study for." He stood and walked around his desk. "This way, please."

I followed him out of his office. The guards saluted him, then fell back to my side, Nichelle trailing behind all of us. My mind was reeling. *What kind of test would this be?*

We went to the service elevator near the back of the building and all five of us entered. One of the guards pushed the button for D. I frowned. We were going back down to the level where I had found Taylor. The elevator stopped and the door opened. Hatch stepped out and I followed him. We walked down the hall to the end of the corridor, past the cell with Ian and the girls. We turned left, then left again, and walked on to a metal door at the end of the hall. A sign above the door read BLOCK H. There was another guard standing by the door and he pulled open the door as we approached, exposing a long, cavernous room with bare white walls. I followed Hatch inside.

In the center of the room was a chair bolted to the floor with a man in an orange GP jumpsuit sitting in it. The man's arms and legs were clamped to the chair by metal straps, like an electric chair, and a metal brace circled around his neck below his electric vocal collar, holding him erect. He couldn't move if he wanted to. The man in the chair had a hood over his head that fell to his chin.

"So, Michael, you've told me that you're now one of us and you've promised, as a full member of the academy, to do whatever is required to promote and advance the cause of our revolution. Here's your opportunity to show me that you mean what you say." He gestured toward the man. "Here's your test."

I looked at the man, then back at Hatch. "I don't understand. What's my test?"

Hatch walked up to the bound man and pulled off his hood. The man in the chair was not a man at all—it was Wade. "Simple, Michael. Electrocute him."

I looked at Wade as his eyes grew wide with fright. Suddenly he screamed out, "Please, no!" His outburst was followed by a scream of pain as blue-yellow electricity arced from his collar. Hatch shook his head in disgust. "Unless he decides to do it to himself."

I stared at Hatch, blinking like crazy. "How does killing Wade advance the work of the academy?"

"That is not yours to question," he said. "You committed to obey, now do as you're told. As you promised."

"I won't do it," I said.

Hatch sighed. "Michael, let me explain this better." He motioned to a large screen that hung down from the corner of the room like a stalactite. "Clark, turn on the monitor please. Set it to channel 788." The guard pushed several buttons and the monitor lit up. Hatch took the remote from the guard and turned to me. "For your amusement, we'll call this the Mommy Channel."

An image materialized on the screen of a frail, beaten-looking woman, huddled in the corner of a cell. It took me a moment to recognize who it was. My heart raced.

"Mom!"

She looked up at the screen as if she could hear me.

"Mom, it's me, Michael!" I shouted.

"She can't hear you," Hatch said. "Or see you." He stepped closer to Wade, lightly jostling the remote in his hand. "You have a choice, Michael. I was very clear about that choice. It's time you learned this important life lesson: You do as you promise or those you love suffer.

"See the silver box on the far end of the cell? It is connected to this remote in my hand." He pushed a button on the remote and a light on the silver box began blinking. "I have just armed the capacitor. If I push this button right here, it will release about a thousand amps into the cage. Enough to kill your mother." He looked into my eyes, weighing the effect his words had on me. "Or maybe not. It might just prove remarkably painful. As you know, the human body can be so unpredictable. Whether we discover its lethality is up to you. So, right now, you can punish GP Seven Sixty-Five or punish your mother. It's your choice."

I stood there looking at the screen, my body trembling. Through the corner of my eye I could see Wade shaking as well. "It's not my choice," I said. "It's not my choice to decide who lives or dies."

"It might not be a fair choice, but it most certainly is your choice."

I just stood there.

"Michael," Hatch said gently, "you said you were with us. You signed a binding document that confirmed your commitment. Were you lying to me?"

"You didn't say I'd have to kill someone."

"No, I didn't. In fact, I wasn't specific at all, was I? And that's the point. I demanded your allegiance, whatever that requires. And right now, this is what your allegiance requires." He folded his arms at his chest. "Or shall I push the button?"

I looked down at Wade. Sweat was beading on his forehead and his underarms were soaked through all the way down his sides. I walked to his side, then put my hand on his shoulder. He shuddered at my touch.

Hatch nodded. "Good choice, Michael. Now give him everything. That would be the merciful thing."

I looked down. Tears were welling up in Wade's eyes. I still stood there, frozen.

After a minute Hatch looked at his watch. "We haven't all day. You have thirty seconds before I make the choice for you. Who will live? A good, loving mother or a juvenile delinquent who will never amount to beans? What would your mother say?"

Something about what Hatch said resonated through me. I looked back up at the monitor, at my mother lying there alone and scared, then at Hatch, the man who had put her there.

"What would my mother say?" I said. My eyes narrowed. "My mother would say that she'd rather die than see her son become a murderer." I took my hand off Wade, then lunged at Hatch. Pain seared through my entire body, buckling my knees. I fell to the ground screaming.

Hatch took a deep breath to regain his composure. He kicked me, then walked to the door. "Thank you, Nichelle. Buy yourself a new bauble."

"Thank you," she said.

From the doorway Hatch looked back at me. "I'm so disappointed in you, Michael. You are a liar and an oath breaker." He turned to the guards. "Take him to Cell 25. Then have Tara report to my office." He looked back at me. "Unlike you, Mr. Vey, I don't break my promises. But I will break you. And here's my promise. You will never disobey me again. By the time I'm done with you, you'll beg for the privilege of electrocuting your own mother." He turned to the guard. "Take him."

My heart filled with fear. When Hatch was gone I asked, "What's Cell 25?"

Nichelle smiled. "Terror."

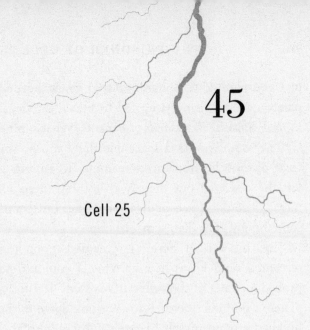

# 45

## Cell 25

Cell 25 was located at the end of the first corridor of the GP prison, the first floor below ground and one floor above level D, where Hatch had taken me for my "test." Even from the outside the cell looked different than the rest. The door was gray-black and broader than the others with a large, hydraulic latch. There were peculiar hatches and hinges and a panel of flashing lights.

The guards opened the door with a key, pushed me inside, and the thick, metal door sealed the world shut behind me. The room was completely dark except for my own soft glow. There was no sound but my heart pounding in my ears. I wondered what Nichelle had meant by "terror." I found out soon enough.

It was maybe an hour after they'd thrown me in the cell that I was suddenly filled with fear like I had never felt before. Something evil was crawling around in the cell. Even though I couldn't see it, I was sure of it. Something frightening beyond words. I was so paralyzed with fear I struggled to inhale the dry, hot air. *Venomous snakes? Spiders? Thousands of spiders?* "What's in here?" I shouted.

The room was dead space and there was no sound, not even the trace of an echo from my screaming. Trembling, I reached out and felt the cell wall but there was nothing there, just smooth, warm metal. I couldn't see or hear anything, but somehow I just knew something was in the room with me.

"Let me out of here!" I screamed, pounding on the walls. I screamed until I was hoarse. When I couldn't stand it anymore, I probed a corner of the cell with my foot. "It's nothing," I told myself. "There's nothing's here." I slowly slunk down in the corner, my arms huddled around myself. "There's nothing here," I repeated over and over.

I tried to force my mind to think of other things but the fear was too powerful. I began screaming again. *Black widow spiders. Crocodiles. No, sharks. Great whites.* "No, that's impossible," I told myself. "I'm not in water." And yet the absurd was somehow believable. What was going on in my head?

Peculiarly, about an hour after my panic had begun, the feelings vanished as suddenly as they had come, as if I'd suddenly awoken from a nightmare. Not all my fear was gone, of course, but the extreme aspect of it had vanished.

After a few minutes I slowly stood, venturing out of my corner. I felt my way around the cell. There was no bed or even a mat, just a slick concrete floor and a porcelain toilet in one corner of the room. I went back to the same corner and sat down again. I wondered how long I would survive.

The next few days (or what I thought were days, since I was quickly losing track of time) passed in pain and discomfort. The cell's temperature was usually high enough that I was covered with my own sweat, then it would abruptly drop until I was shivering with cold.

Food, when I got it, was also served sporadically. The food came to me through a hatch door that did not allow light into the cell, as the door on my side only opened after the outer door was sealed. I guessed that my feeding schedule was irregular to throw off my body's natural sense of timing. The food stunk, literally, and the first time I ate it I spit it out. I don't know what it was, I couldn't see it, but the texture and smell reminded me of canned dog food. I was given no water and as I began to thirst I realized that my only option was to drink from the toilet, which I'm sure was their intent from the beginning.

Then there was the sound—a consistent, loud, electronic beep that began shortly after my first panic attack and chirped every thirty seconds without cease. The sound began to occupy my sleep and dreams and eventually became incredibly painful as it filled my every thought. I had read about tortures like this before, like the water torture, where a single drop of water falls consistently on a bound man's head. They say that after a while the tiny drop begins to feel like a sledgehammer. I believed it. After several days of the sound my head felt like it might explode.

What made it even more unbearable was the uncertainty of it all. I was kept in the dark, figuratively as well as literally. Were they ever going to release me? Would it be minutes or days or years? I had no idea. I thought of Hatch's "promise." *You will never disobey me again. By the time I'm done with you, you'll beg for the privilege of electrocuting your own mother.* I wondered if he was right. Could one be so physically and emotionally broken that he no longer cared about anyone or anything except survival? I didn't want to find out.

Intermingled with my terror and pain were thoughts of my mother. On the screen she had looked so small and frail. I doubted that she could have survived the shock if Hatch had followed through with his threat. Had he pushed the button or not? The thought of it filled me with both hate and guilt. I wished that he had just killed me instead. Didn't he say that I was dying anyway?

I realized that the panic attacks I was having seemed to be on a type of schedule and I wondered if it was possible that Hatch and his scientists had actually perfected a process to generate fear.

Thirteen meals had passed. (That's how I kept track of time.) My fear attack had just ended and I lay on the ground, drenched in sweat and trembling. I heard myself mumbling, "I can't do it anymore. You win, I can't do it anymore." I felt the watch on my arm, the one my mother had given me. I couldn't read the words in the dark but I didn't have to. I'm sure Hatch had let me keep the watch to keep my mind on my mother. Nothing Hatch did was by accident and it certainly wasn't out of kindness. I began to cry. "I'm sorry I failed you, Mom."

I had lost weight and it felt as if every cell of my body ached. If they meant to break me, they knew exactly what they were doing. Of course they did. They were scientists.

As I lay on the ground, I noticed something very peculiar. In the corner of the room there was a dim light. The metal pipe that ran from the wall to the toilet began to lightly glow, not consistently, but intermittently. *It's happening*, I thought. *I'm losing my mind. I'm hallucinating.* I looked away. A moment later I looked back. The pipe was still glowing, though slightly brighter now. I crawled over to the toilet and cautiously put out my hand to touch it. The moment I touched it, it went dark. Then a feeling came over me that cannot be accurately described to anyone who hasn't felt it. I felt pure peace. It felt as if some power were pulsing through my body, pushing out the fear and hurt and replacing it with perfect tranquility. I felt as comfortable as if I were lying on my own bed at home listening to my music. Even the constant chirp sounded pleasant.

I let go of the pipe and my pain, exhaustion, and fear instantly returned. I quickly grabbed it again. Maybe I was losing my mind, but if holding on to a toilet pipe could make me feel good, I was going to hold on to that pipe.

Suddenly I understood. The cell with Taylor, Ian, Abigail, and McKenna was somewhere on the floor below mine. Abigail could take away pain. Abigail must be touching a pipe that ran between the two cells, conducting her power to me, much the same way I had shocked Cody Applebaum in school detention. But how would she even know I was here?

She didn't. Ian did. Ian had probably been watching me all along.

He knew I was here. Was it possible that he, Abigail, and McKenna were working together to save me? They didn't even know me. Yet it made sense. McKenna could have made the pipe glow to lead me to it. My eyes watered and I began to cry. It was not the first time since I'd been placed in the cell—but the first time that I had cried for something other than pain. For the first time in days I had hope that I might survive.

From that point on, whenever things got bad, I went to the pipe and grasped it and immediately the pain ceased. During the "terror sessions" my invisible friends were always waiting. I deduced that Ian must be able to see when and how they were torturing me.

I was filled with gratitude for my unseen friends and I learned that harboring an emotion as powerful as gratitude has power of its own. My greatest fear was that they might be discovered and moved to a different cell. I knew Hatch and his guards were watching me, so I was discreet in how I held to the pipe. I usually pretended to be throwing up or drinking.

Actually, their discovery was my second-greatest fear. My greatest fear was that my mother was dead. Not even Abigail's power could take that pain from my heart.

# 46

## Lack of Trust

I felt as if I'd been in Cell 25 for weeks when I heard the inner tumblings of the lock on the door. There was a slide of metal and the door opened and I saw the first light since I'd been incarcerated. As usual, I was lying on the ground, and I instinctively pushed myself way away from the door, covering my face from the harsh light. "Stay away," I mumbled.

Nichelle walked into the cell escorted by two of the guards. "It reeks in here. It smells like the giraffe house at the zoo." She started laughing. "He smells as bad as Zeus." One of the guards laughed.

She took a few more steps toward me and looked down at me. "Hatch wants you. Get up."

*Hatch.* His name alone filled me with terror. I rolled over to my knees and elbows and tried to stand but I couldn't.

"I said get up!" she shouted.

"I can't," I replied, my forehead pressed to the ground.

After a moment Nichelle nodded to one of the guards and he walked over to lift me. He stopped before he touched me and looked at Nichelle.

Nichelle squatted down in front of me. "If you shock him, we'll keep you in here for the rest of your short, miserable life. Do you understand?"

"I won't shock him."

"Why would I believe you? You're a liar."

"Liar or not, I can't stand up."

She looked at me for a moment, then said to the guard, "Help him."

The guard put his hands under my armpits and easily lifted me. When I was on my feet he let go of me and I collapsed back to the ground, crying out with pain. Nichelle rolled her eyes. "Carry him."

The guard lifted me again and this time he put his arm around me, carrying more of my weight than I was, as I staggered down the hall to the elevator. As we walked I sucked in the cool air, breathing it in like water. In spite of my pain, I can't tell you how luxurious it felt.

In the elevator I noticed Nichelle pushed the D button and I silently groaned. Hatch was back in the dungeon. *Another test*, I thought. *If he asked me again to electrocute Wade would I do it?*

I tried to think of better possibilities. Perhaps I was being reassigned to the dungeon. Maybe with Ian and the two girls. I wanted to see them badly. I wanted to hug them and thank them. The dungeon would be a Caribbean vacation compared to Cell 25.

My hope dissipated as we walked past their cell, back to the room at the end of the hall. Back to block H, the room where Wade had been bound and where I had "failed" my test. The room's light was on and the door was partially open. The guard carried me inside.

There were three chairs in the room and Taylor and Ostin were strapped into two of them. *Please, not them*, I thought.

I don't know what I looked like. In Cell 25 it was too dark to even see my reflection in the toilet, but, based on Taylor's reaction, I must have looked pretty awful. She gasped when she saw me.

"Michael," she said.

"Oh, buddy," Ostin said. "What have they done to you?"

"Shut up," Nichelle said. "Save your pity for yourselves."

The guard dropped me in a plastic chair and then fastened my hands and feet with plastic ties. A large plastic belt was drawn around my waist and fastened in back. It was overkill. I couldn't have even stood up under my own power. Only my tics seemed strong.

"What's going on?" I asked.

"Shut up," Nichelle said. "No talking."

"You're a toad-face," Ostin said.

Nichelle immediately tried to reach him with her powers, forgetting that she had no effect on him. She walked over and smacked him on the head. "You're fat."

"Yeah, well you're ugly, and I can lose weight."

She sneered and slapped him on the side of the head again.

"Ow," Ostin said.

"Keep your mouth shut, butterball."

About five minutes later Hatch walked into the room. He said to me darkly, "I trust your accommodations were to your satisfaction."

My head felt like it weighed a ton and I just sat there, staring at my feet.

"Look at me when I'm talking to you!" he shouted.

It took effort, but I raised my head and looked into his eyes. Hatch wore his dark glasses and a strange-looking helmet. I turned my head to one side and my neck cracked. I looked back at Hatch, "What did you do to my mother?"

"Twenty-six days in Cell 25 and still defiant. If I wasn't so disappointed in you I'd be impressed. Be assured that she's paid dearly for your choices, but she survived the shock, if that's what you're getting at. And I'm pleased. I didn't want to discard my best card yet. Though, as you see, even without her, the deck is stacked in my favor."

He turned and looked at Taylor. "Don't waste your time trying to reboot me, Miss Ridley. You have little enough of it left." He tapped his helmet. "Those electric waves of yours won't make it through this very special helmet your sister helped us create." He smiled at her smugly. "Perhaps you're wondering how we came up with this."

"I don't care," Taylor said.

"You should, it's quite interesting. When I was in my early twenties I did some work for the NSA—the National Security Agency. The NSA building in Maryland is completely wrapped in copper. It keeps prying spy satellites from listening inside. This helmet employs the same principle."

"Still not interested," Taylor said.

"On the other hand, for Mr. Vey, this copper helmet is the worst thing I could be wearing." He leaned close to me. "If he could get his little hands on this he could fry my head like a Sunday roast. That's why we have him strapped down to a plastic chair." He smiled at me. "I do hope you're comfortable."

"What are you going to do?" I asked. "Kill us?"

"Just some of you. Let me be clear about this. I want you, Michael. I want you to join us. I want to understand your power. But you're not cooperating." He stepped away from me. "Like you, during your vacation in Cell 25, I've had a lot of time to think about things. I've decided that our problem here is really just a matter of credibility. You, Michael, won't cooperate because you lack trust. Trust that I will do what I have threatened to do. I'd like to show you otherwise. Like they say in the old movies, I need to show you that *I mean business.*

"So we're going to have a demonstration with a couple of your friends. Proof of what I'll do to your mother if you choose not to cooperate." He took a step toward the door. "You may come in now." He turned back to me. "Michael, I think you remember our friend Zeus."

Zeus walked into the room. His long, oily blond hair was partially concealed beneath a copper helmet similar to the one Hatch wore. The last time I saw him he'd shocked my mother. I desperately wanted to get my hands on him.

"You creep," I said.

"The name is Zeus," he said.

"Your name is Zeus," Taylor said. "Like the Greek god?" She rolled her eyes. "Puhleeeeeze."

I could see Taylor trying to get to him but she couldn't.

"I told you, Miss Ridley, you can't get through our helmets," Hatch said. "And as far as the name, that's not the only similarity my boy here has with his Greek counterpart, is it Michael? Michael's seen a demonstration of his gift. Like the Greek god, Zeus also throws lightning bolts." He smiled at us. "So, Michael, to put it bluntly, Zeus is going to fry your friends."

"You won't do that," I said.

"There you go," Hatch said, flourishing his hand. "Lack of trust. You've just proved my point. Yes, I will do that."

"But you need them."

"Wrong again. The truth is I'm only annoyed by your chubby little friend and, frankly, Miss Ridley isn't really of as much value to us alive as we thought she'd be. Fortunately, we have a carbon copy of her, so she is quite expendable. Our research team thinks an autopsy will prove most valuable. We've never dissected a Glow before; it could help the cause immensely." He turned to Taylor. "Did you ever dissect a frog in science class?" He smiled. "Of course you did. Now you're the frog and some parts of you will be kept in little jars."

Taylor looked pale, like she might throw up.

"I'll give you whatever you want," I said.

Hatch looked at me, his eyes narrowed with contempt. "You had that chance twenty-six days ago. Maybe now you'll learn that, unlike you, I am a man of my word. We'll discuss a new deal after my demonstration."

He walked toward the door. "So, if you'll pardon me, I think I'll leave." He looked at Ostin. "I hate the smell of burnt butter."

"You're a psycho!" Ostin shouted at Hatch.

Hatch grunted. "Little man, do you really think you could say anything that I would find remotely hurtful? It's like being insulted by a slug. You are a donkey among thoroughbreds. How sad that there is nothing even vaguely special about you. You're just so . . . average."

"No he's not," Taylor said. "He's brilliant. He's a member of the Electroclan."

Hatch grinned. "The Electroclan. That's almost comical." His expression darkened. "Too bad you got in the way of the big boys, Ostin, or you could still be home with mummy and daddy eating pizza. Good-bye."

Hatch turned to Zeus. "When you're done cooking our friends, call the guards and have Vey returned to Cell 25 to contemplate the consequences of his choices." He looked at the guards. "You might want to wait outside. Zeus is very powerful but not always accurate. Come with me, Nichelle."

Nichelle smiled darkly at Taylor. "I'll miss you so much," she said sarcastically, then she followed Hatch out. The guards followed her and shut the door behind them, leaving the four of us alone. A wicked smile crossed Zeus's face. "All right, kiddies, it's playtime."

Taylor said, "Why are you doing this? You're one of us."

"I'm not one of you."

"You could be," I said. "You could join the Electroclan."

"What's that," he said laughing. "Your club? That's like booking a ticket on the *Titanic* after it hit the iceberg."

"What's your real name?" Taylor asked.

He turned to her. "Zeus."

"What's your first name?"

"Zeus."

"Your last name?"

"It's Zeus, Zeus, Zeus. First, last, middle, that's it."

"You really think you're going to kill us?" Ostin said. "Dude, you're like fifteen."

"Shut up," he said.

"No," I said. "He's right. Think about it."

"Yeah, think about this." He raised his hands and a quick burst of blue electricity arced between them. He stepped toward me. "Like that, electric boy?"

It was obvious that his electricity was different than mine. Mine came from within my body, while his seemed confined to the outside. I wondered how much he had to give. I, on the other hand, couldn't even stand under my own power.

He turned back around. "So who wants to go first? It's usually ladies before gentlemen, or maybe that doesn't apply to executions." He walked over to Taylor. "Does it?"

"Go ahead," Taylor said.

He touched her cheek. "It's a shame you didn't decide to join us. We could have had some fun. We're going to rule the world, you know."

"Why would you want to do that?" Ostin asked.

"I thought you were supposed to be smart," Zeus said. "Oh, you have no powers at all. Except eating." He laughed.

"Hey," Ostin said. "Before you fry me, tell me something. I mean, unless they don't trust you with the scientific stuff."

Zeus looked annoyed. "What?"

"I can't figure out how Hatch made that helmet work. I mean, the science of it doesn't make sense. Why doesn't the copper actually conduct the electricity and amplify Taylor's electromagnetic waves? Is there like a radio converter inside it?"

"It's just a helmet, doughboy."

"No, there's got to be something inside it. You probably just don't know that much about electricity."

Zeus's face turned red. "I'm made of electricity, idiot. It's just a stupid helmet."

"It couldn't be. You must not have examined it. There's got to be a little electric converter inside, maybe a little black pad with some circuit board. Did you notice some wires?"

"There's not a stupid black pad inside—there's no wires! It's just a copper helmet, like a football helmet made of metal. Look, chubster." He started to pull off his helmet but noticed Taylor, who was looking a little too eager. He stopped. "Oh, I see. Well played, fat boy. You almost got me. You're not as dumb as you look. Now prepare to fry." He lifted his hands.

"You surprise me, Zeus," Taylor said. "You're obviously really powerful. More powerful than any of us."

He turned to her. "You said it."

"You're named after a god. You could be, like, the ruler of the world."

He dropped his hands to his side. "What's your point?"

She shrugged. "Nothing. I'm just surprised that you're taking orders from Hatch. He should be taking orders from you. He tells you to kill us, you obey like a dog."

Zeus looked confused. "Enough talking." He turned back to Ostin. "You're a nobody. You go first." He again raised his hands.

"Hey, Zits," I shouted. "What kind of electro*wimp* picks on kids without powers?"

He turned back to me. "What did you call me?"

"Zits," I said. "Z-I-T-S. Actually, I don't think you even need electric bolts. You could just breathe on us." I looked him in the eyes and smiled. "Seriously, dude, when was the last time you brushed your teeth?"

"Shut up!"

"No, really. Did you eat a diaper?"

"Shut up!" he shouted. He squinted. "Do you know how much I enjoyed guarding your mother? I shocked her at least a dozen times just to watch her squeal."

"Yeah, well you could have just sat next to her and let her smell you. That would have been much worse. I've had hamsters with better hygiene."

"Enough! Don't think I won't electrocute you, Vey!"

Taylor looked at me as if I'd lost my mind. "It's his Tourette's, he can't help it."

"I'm scared, Zits," I said. "You know Hatch would have your head if you did. But here's my promise: after I'm in charge, my first command is to make you my shoeshine boy. You'll be following me around with a towel."

"You'll never be in charge."

"No, that's what Hatch said. You heard him. He wants my power. I'm not kidding, Zits. When Hatch was trying to get me to join you guys, he promised me that you would be my servant."

Zeus looked at me with a worried expression. After a moment he shouted, "Shut up! And stop calling me Zits!"

"I don't think I will. In fact, it's going to be the first rule I make. I'm going to have everyone else call you that."

"I don't care what Hatch says. I'm gonna fry you, Vey."

"Oooh, now I'm really shaking. You don't have enough juice in you to light a flashlight."

"Michael!" Taylor shouted. "Stop it. He's got a temper. I've seen it."

"You should listen to the cheerleader, Vey." He stepped toward me. "You think you're so cool. But you can't shoot electricity like me, can you? You're just a flesh-covered battery."

"And you're a flesh-covered outhouse. You should tie a couple hundred of those car air fresheners around your neck."

"Last warning!" Zeus shouted.

"I'm not kidding, Zits. There are porta-potties with better aromas. Would a little deodorant kill you? What was the last year you took a bath?"

"That's it!" He lifted his arms in front of himself and electricity arced between his fingers. "You're gonna die!"

He pointed his hands toward me, letting loose a storm of crackling blue-white electricity. I surged at that precise moment and the sound of his electricity hitting the field of my electricity was like the crash of two cymbals. The room lit up as bright as a welder's lamp.

To my surprise, I felt absolutely fine. Not only was my surge protecting me, but it wasn't going away either. The longest I had ever held a surge was ten or fifteen seconds, but I wasn't tiring at all. In fact, I was growing stronger. I was absorbing Zeus's electricity. Even the weakness I felt from before was leaving me.

There was so much electricity in the room that all of our hair was standing straight up. I looked over at Taylor. She stared at me in disbelief.

*It's not hurting me,* I thought.

She nodded.

*Can you read my mind?*

She nodded again. The electricity in the room had created some kind of bridge.

*I can,* I heard her say, even though her lips didn't move. Now I could read her thoughts as well.

Zeus could see that his electricity wasn't hurting me and he was getting angrier. He looked like a crazy man, his hands raised and moving. "Burn, Energizer!"

The foul stench of burning plastic filled the room. I looked down to see that my chair was melting. The plastic ties that the guard used to bind my wrists and legs had melted through and the vinyl band around my waist had melted as well. I was free.

I looked back up and smiled at Zeus. Rage burned in his eyes. He clenched his teeth and intensified his assault. But the force of his electricity only added to mine. I was getting stronger, and, from his appearance, he was growing weaker. Sweat was beading on his forehead and his breathing was heavy.

My skin began to glow a pale white, growing brighter and brighter until I was lit up like an incandescent lightbulb.

"Aaaargh!" he shouted in exhaustion, and the electricity stopped. He flicked his hands as if his fingers had been burned. "Okay, then I'll burn her!"

He turned toward Taylor.

"No you won't," I said, standing up. He turned back to look at me. I was now glowing brighter than the overhead lights. I lifted my arms and held my palms out toward Zeus. "Try this." I pulsed. A bright flash of light burst from me like a shock wave and Zeus screamed out as he was thrown against the wall. Taylor's and Ostin's chairs also flipped sideways. Zeus slid to the floor unconscious.

I ran to Taylor's side. "Are you okay?"

It took her a moment to answer. "I think so. I can't get loose."

I grabbed the plastic ties on her hands and surged and they melted in my hands. She reached down and unfastened her legs. Then I ran to Ostin. He was lying still. I knelt down by him. "Ostin?"

He wasn't breathing.

"Buddy!" I put my head to his chest. His heart had stopped.

"Ostin!" I shouted. I burned off his bands and began to administer CPR. "His heart stopped," I shouted.

Taylor came to my side.

"Come on, Ostin," she said.

I put my ear to his chest. Nothing. Tears began to fill my eyes. "You can't die, buddy. You can't."

I continued pressing his chest but nothing I did seemed to have any effect.

Then Taylor said, "Shock him."

"What?"

"Shock his heart. That's what doctors do when a heart stops."

I put my hand over his heart and pulsed. His whole body shook. I put my head to his chest, but there was nothing. "Ostin, buddy. Hang in there."

I put my hand on his heart again. "Surge." His body shook again. Suddenly his body trembled. I put my head on his chest. "His heart's beating!"

"Yeah!" Taylor said.

A moment later Ostin groaned and his eyes opened. He looked at me, then said, "That hurt."

I exhaled in relief. "Oh, man, that was close. Don't ever scare us like that again."

"Don't ever shock me like that again."

Zeus started to come to, groaning lightly. Taylor walked over and pulled off his helmet, throwing it behind her. He looked up at her. "Where am I?"

"You're on the ground," she said. He began to lift his head but Taylor squinted and knocked him back down. "Don't even think about it. And you better behave or Michael's going to finish you."

Ostin sat up, rubbing his chest. "How did you create a shock wave?"

"I'm not sure," I said. "I think Zeus's electricity made me stronger."

Ostin smiled. "Just like I was theorizing, you can absorb electricity."

Taylor pointed to a camera. "Hey, guys, whatever we're doing, we better hurry. We're being watched."

"No," Ostin said. "The light's off. Michael must have blown the camera with his surge."

"Still, Taylor's right," I said. "We've got to move fast. There are guards outside the door."

"What should we do with him?" Taylor asked, looking at Zeus.

Zeus looked up at me fearfully. *Don't hurt me.*

I heard his voice clearly but his mouth hadn't moved. There was still enough electricity in the room that I could read minds without touching.

"Please don't hurt me," he said aloud.

"Why shouldn't I?" I asked.

He just stared at me, unable to come up with a reason.

I leaned close to him. "I'll tell you why. Because I'm not you and I'm not Hatch." I leaned in closer. "Think of a number between one and a million."

He looked at me. "What?"

"Think of a number," I said.

*Five hundred twenty-six thousand and twelve,* he thought.

"Five hundred twenty-six thousand and twelve," I said.

He looked at me in astonishment. "How did you do that?"

"I can read your mind, Zeus. And if you so much as think of shocking one of us, I'll fry you like a chicken nugget. Do you understand?"

He nodded.

"Why are you loyal to Hatch?" I asked.

He didn't answer in his thoughts or otherwise. I guess he didn't know.

"He's worthless," Ostin said. "We can't trust him."

*I am worthless,* Zeus thought.

Taylor looked at me. *Did you hear that?* she thought.

I nodded. *What has he done?*

*Let's find out,* Taylor thought. *I'm going in deep.*

Taylor knelt down next to Zeus and put her head against his. We watched as she went through him, like she was reading a book. After several minutes, her expression changed and she sat back up. "I see."

"What is it?" Ostin asked.

Taylor said to Zeus, "When you were a child, did you kill your family in a swimming pool?"

The statement seemed to hit him as powerfully as my shock wave. He began trembling and he covered his face with his hands. "Yes."

"Are you sure about that?" she asked.

He peered up at her. "What do you mean?"

Taylor looked at me and then back at Zeus. "I looked through your memories but I couldn't find a memory of the swimming pool. *Any* swimming pool. I only found what Hatch told you when you were little."

"That's the way Hatch works," I said to Taylor. "He makes people think they're bad so they'll do bad things. Zeus thinks he's evil so he's acting the part. Can you do anything with it?"

Taylor looked at me. "What do you mean?"

"Can you . . . change his mind?"

A smile came to her face. "I've never tried."

Zeus looked back and forth between us. "What are you going to do?"

"You didn't kill your family, Zeus," Taylor said. "I'm guessing that Hatch did, then convinced you that you had done it. Are you willing to let me erase those lies?"

"Can you?"

"I've never done this before, but I'll try." She put her head against his. After about two minutes she moaned a little, then fell back.

"What happened?"

"I think I did it."

Zeus lay there with his eyes closed.

I said, "Zeus, have you ever gone swimming?"

"No."

"Never?"

He shook his head. "I can't. I shock myself in water."

"What happened to your family?"

He looked down. "I'm not sure." His eyes welled up with tears. "Something bad happened to them."

I looked at Taylor. "Good job."

"I don't know why I tried to hurt you," Zeus said.

"It's because Hatch was controlling you," I replied. "But he can't anymore."

He sat there looking confused. "What do I do now?"

"Join the Electroclan. Help us bring this place down."

He looked at me for a moment. Then I heard his thoughts. *I'm with you.* "I'm with you," he said, his voice echoing his thoughts. "What do you want me to do?"

"You were with my mother when they took her. Do you know where she is?"

Zeus shook his head. "They took her to one of the other compounds."

"There are other places like this?" Ostin asked.

"At least four that I know of. They're in other countries and they're bigger."

"Do you know where they are?" I asked.

"There's an office in Rome and a compound in the jungles of Peru. There's at least one in Taiwan." He frowned. "Sorry. That's all I know."

My heart ached. My mother had never seemed so far away. "Who runs the other compounds?" I asked.

"Hatch," Zeus said. "He's like the president. But he answers to the board."

"Then Hatch will have records of the other compounds," Ostin said.

Taylor said, "I don't think Hatch will be eager to share."

"No," I said. "We'll have to take them. But first, we've got to free the others."

Just then the cell door swung all the way open and three guards ran into the room holding machine guns. "Everyone on the ground," the first guard shouted. "Move your—" He stopped mid-sentence. "Move . . . uh."

All three of the guards lowered their guns and looked at each other as if they'd suddenly forgotten why they had come in. I smiled at Taylor.

"Zeus," I said.

"No problem."

Electricity arced from Zeus to all three guards. They dropped to the floor.

"Good job," I said. "Let's tie them up."

We quickly cuffed two of the guards' hands behind their backs. As I was trying to get the handcuffs on the biggest of the guards, he suddenly turned on me. He jumped up, lifting me above his head. I pulsed and he screamed out, dropping me on top of him.

"You okay?" Ostin asked.

"Yeah," I said, climbing off the guard. "He's not." I locked the guard's hands in cuffs.

Ostin took their utility belts with concussion and smoke grenades and fastened one of them around his waist.

"We've got to figure out how to get everyone out of here," I said. "Let's start with Ian and the girls, then we'll get Jack and Wade."

"What about Nichelle?" Taylor asked.

"Ostin, you're the only one she can't affect."

He patted his weapons belt. "I'll take care of her."

"Zeus, while Ostin and I free Ian and the girls, you and Taylor go to the end of the hallway and make sure no one sneaks up on us."

"What about the cameras in the hall?" Taylor asked.

"We've got to take them out," I said.

"I know how to do it," Zeus said. "When I was eight I was fooling around and blew one out. Hatch grounded me for an entire week."

"Well, start with that one," I said, pointing to a camera right outside our door. Zeus reached up and electricity jumped from his fingers to the camera. The camera's light went off and the camera froze.

"Nice shootin', Tex," Ostin said.

"Thanks."

"Okay, let's go," I said. "I'll go first. Zeus, you and Taylor behind me, Ostin, lock the cell then come up behind us."

"On it," he said.

We ran single-file down the hall to Ian and the girls' cell door. Zeus blew out another three cameras as he and Taylor crept to the end of the hallway. Taylor cautiously peered around the corner. "It's clear," she said.

I pounded on the cell door. "Ian. Can you hear me?"

I heard a faint pounding back.

"He sees us."

"How are we going to open it?" Taylor asked.

"Zeus, can you concentrate your electricity and cut through it?"

"No. That's Bryan's gig."

"I know how to open it," Ostin said, winded from running back to us. "You can use your electricity."

"But Ian said it's an air lock," I said. "It doesn't work by electricity."

Ostin smiled. "That's the flaw in their design. The lock is air, but how does the lock get its air?"

I shrugged. "An air tank?"

"Yes, with an electronic valve. While I was locked inside I asked Ian to follow where the hose went. There's an electronic valve above each cell door. If my calculations are right, all you have to do is blow the switch and the air pressure drops."

"He's good," Taylor said.

"Where's the valve?" I asked.

Ostin pointed above the door. "Right about there. A strong enough pulse should knock it out."

It was at least four feet above me. "I need a lift," I said.

"On it." Ostin got down on all fours.

"You sure?" I asked.

"Just do it."

I stepped on his back and reached as high as I could but it still wasn't high enough. "This isn't going to work."

"Wait," Taylor said. "We do this in cheerleading. Come here, Ostin."

Ostin stood.

"Take my hand like this." They locked hands. "Now, Michael, step right there and we'll lift you up."

"You sure you can lift me?"

"Oh yeah, this is how we make our pyramids in cheer."

I stepped on their arms.

"Lift!" Taylor said.

I rose higher than the door. "Awesome." I put my hand flat against the wall above the doorjamb. "Here, Ostin?"

"That's about right."

"Here it goes." I pulsed with all I had. The light next to me flickered.

"Now what?"

"Wait for it," Ostin said.

Suddenly we heard the hiss of escaping air. The door clicked.

"We did it," Ostin said.

Taylor and Ostin let me down and I pushed open the door. Ian, McKenna, and Abigail were standing in the middle of the room waiting for us. Seeing them filled me with strong emotion. I ran up to Abigail and put my arms around her, then McKenna and Ian.

"You guys saved my life," I said.

"You were very brave," Ian said. "Amazingly brave. I don't think I could have survived what you went through."

"We're proud of you," McKenna said. Abigail nodded.

"Thank you. How can I ever repay you?"

"I think you just did," Ian said, looking at the open door.

In the hallway an alarm went off, a bright red strobe accompanied by a deafening, shrill siren. Everyone covered their ears.

"Taylor, Ostin!" I shouted. "Give me another lift!"

They lifted me again. I reached up, grabbed the alarm, and pulsed. The alarm wound down with a sound like a sick cow.

"Thank goodness," Taylor said. "That was annoying."

"Okay, let's make a plan," I said.

As we were talking, Ian was frantically looking around, up and down the ceiling then to the walls. "The guards are collecting," he whispered. "There are two coming down the front hall toward us right now."

"Where?" I asked.

He pointed toward the far wall, moving his finger along with them. "Right there, on the other side of the wall."

"Ian, keep telling us where they are. Taylor, when they get close, reboot them. Zeus, the second you see their gun barrels, blast them with electricity."

"You got it, chief."

I walked out into the corridor with Ian. He was now facing the far cell wall, following the guards' movement. "They're about at the corner," Ian whispered. "Now."

Zeus and I backed against the wall, just at the corner. I saw the glint of metal from two gun barrels and Zeus shot electricity from both hands. Both guards dropped to the ground. "You got 'em," Ian said. "Two guards down."

"Are there any more down here?" I asked.

"Not yet. But there are some moving down the stairwell."

"Let's take care of these two," I said. Zeus and I dragged the two guards into the farthest part of the cell and handcuffed them together to the toilet, then gathered again outside the cell. "We've got to free Jack and Wade and the rest of the GPs."

"There's a problem with that," McKenna said. "They control all the collars from the command center. They could just set them all off and kill everyone."

"Where's the command center?" Ostin asked.

"Fourth floor," Ian said. "Next to the guards' barracks."

"Oh, great," Ostin said. "We've been there."

Ian smiled. "C'mon, Ostin. You didn't want it to be too easy, did you? The honey's always in the center of the hive."

"So we're headed to the fourth floor," I said.

Ostin said, "Trust me, don't take the elevator."

"Then the only way out is the stairwell."

"Which," Ian said, "they're covering."

"Do you know how many guards there are?" I asked.

Ian nodded. "I counted this afternoon and there were twenty-seven. Usually there are thirteen on duty during the day, and the other fourteen are split up between the other two shifts. But they all live here and right now they're all on alert."

"How do you know all this?" Ostin asked.

"I watch everything in the building. It's kept me sane for three years."

Just then the entire floor went black. We could see nothing but the glow of each other.

"They must have cut the power," Ostin said. "That's going to hurt them."

"They have night-vision goggles," Zeus said. "I've seen them run drills."

"Oh," Ostin said. "Then it's going to hurt us."

"No problem," McKenna said. She immediately began to glow, lighting up the corridor.

"That's so cool," Ostin said. "Do you have a boyfriend?"

McKenna smiled.

Taylor rolled her eyes. "Not now, Ostin."

"Sorry. Back to business. There were twenty-seven guards, we've taken out five, so there's twenty-two left," Ostin said. "I'll keep count."

"Ian," I said, "what's going on?"

"Six guards are covering the stairwell. There are three above us; the others are gathering on the second and fourth floor by the elevators."

"Which elevators?"

"Front and back. They might be getting ready to stage another attack. Or they might be waiting for us."

"What about the other electric children?" I asked.

"Hatch has them gathered on two."

"What powers do they have?"

"Quentin can produce a small EMP."

"What's that?" I asked.

"Electromagnetic pulse," Ostin blurted out. "It can knock out radios and stuff."

"Bryan can burn through things. Tara can manipulate emotions . . ."

"Wait," I said. "Can she create fear?"

Ian nodded. "Unfortunately."

"She's the one who was torturing you," Abigail said.

"She's as bad as Nichelle," I said.

Taylor looked at me but said nothing.

"Speaking of which, where is Nichelle?" I asked.

"She's on level two next to Hatch." Ian looked straight up. "Two men just went up top. I think they're getting the helicopter ready."

"I bet Hatch is going to run," I said. "How big is the helicopter?"

"It's pretty big. It will hold Hatch and all the kids. If things go bad, Hatch will probably take them with him."

"Well, things are going to go bad for them," I said. "Let's go." We turned the corner and ran down the next length of hall to the stairwell. Zeus continued down the hallway past the stairwell, blowing out five more cameras, which he could see from their glowing red diodes.

With McKenna's light we could see both elevators from where we stood, one in front of us, the other at the end of the hall—the same elevator Ostin and I had come through when we first entered the building. I could see under the door that the stairwell was still lit and as I opened the door bullets immediately began to fly. I jumped back and I could hear bullets ricocheting inside.

"Where exactly are they?" I asked Ian.

Ian looked up and down. "They're on floors one, two, and four. There are six of them."

"What are they doing? I mean, what are their positions?"

"Two of them are coming down the stairs. The rest are leaning over the railings with guns."

"Taylor, do you think you could reboot them all at once?"

"I'll try."

"I'll open the door," Abigail said.

"Ready?" I asked.

Taylor nodded. She put her hands on her temples. "Go."

Abigail pulled open the door and this time there was no gunfire. I slid my hand inside and grabbed the railing and pulsed with all of my power. There was a loud chorus of screams, and I could hear guns and men falling down the stairs.

"You got four of them," Ian said. "One of them crawled out of the well onto the second floor, and the other ran back out on the fourth."

"How bad are the four?"

"They're not moving."

"Eighteen left," Ostin said.

"Let's move," Zeus said.

"How many are on the next floor up?"

Ian looked back and forth. "Three."

"Near the stairwell?"

"No. That's the GP level; they're guarding the prisoners." He cocked his head. "Wait, there's some motion on the third floor."

"The kids?" Taylor asked.

"Maybe. I'm having trouble seeing through them. Nichelle must be near."

"Let's move up to the next floor." We all started to climb the stairwell. Suddenly I stopped. *It's hopeless.* I thought. *You're leading them to their deaths. Surrender now.*

"What are you doing?" Zeus asked.

"It's no good," I said. "This isn't going to work."

"What?" Taylor said.

"We can't make it," I said. "We'll never make it out of here. They're going to kill us."

"Stop talking that way," Taylor said.

"No, he's right," Zeus said. "It's hopeless."

Taylor's eyes flashed. "No," she said, "it's Tara." She looked back. "Abigail, take Michael's and Zeus's hands. Quick."

Abigail ran up half a flight. The instant she touched my hand the fear left. "What happened?" I asked.

"It was Tara," Taylor said. "My sister."

"Tara's your sister?" I asked.

"She's my twin. I'll tell you about it later."

"You have a twin?" Ostin asked.

"I can handle her," Taylor said. She put her hands on her temples and concentrated. A scream echoed down the stairwell. "Stop it, Taylor!" Tara shouted.

"You stop it!" Taylor shouted back. "Leave my friends alone."

"Your friends are going to die."

"No they're not. Why are you helping Hatch? You're better than that."

"Dr. Hatch is better. He's doing the right thing."

"Hatch is evil. He killed your parents."

"They weren't really my parents."

"You don't really believe that. Think for yourself, Tara."

"You can't change the world without casualties."

"You're saying everything he's brainwashed you with. What do you believe?"

"You're the brainwashed one."

"Hatch told you that too, didn't he?"

Tara didn't answer.

"C'mon, Tara. You're better than that. Join us."

"I'm not one of you. I'm special. I have special abilities."

"You do, Tara. And you used those special abilities to hurt that man on the motorcycle. What good have you ever used them for?"

"That man on the motorcycle was just human."

"I'm human, Tara. And so are you. Would you kill me if Hatch told you to?"

She didn't answer.

"Would you?"

"You can keep pecking in the dirt, Taylor. But I'm not a chicken. I'm an eagle."

Then there was silence.

"She went back inside," Ian said.

I touched Taylor's shoulder. "I didn't know that you had a sister."

Taylor's face bent in anger. "I don't."

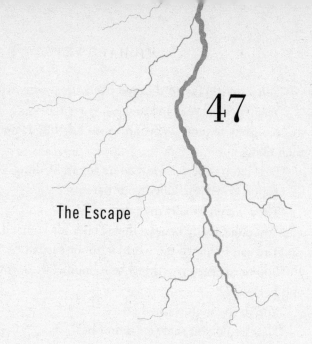

# 47

## The Escape

We cautiously crept up to the GP level: me and Zeus in front, followed by Ostin, Ian, and Taylor, with McKenna and Abigail bringing up the rear. The cameras inside the stairwell were panning back and forth like animals, heads up, watching for danger.

"Zeus, take those things out," I whispered.

"On it."

One by one Zeus blasted the cameras. Their blinking red lights went dark and they drooped, as if hanging their heads in defeat. Then the stairwell itself went dark.

"I think they're trying to make this difficult," Zeus said.

"No problem," McKenna said. She began to glow again.

"McKenna," I said, "stay close to the wall. You make an easy target."

She pressed back against the wall.

"Ian, where are they?" I whispered.

"Three guards on GP, two guards on level one and six on two—three guarding the doors and three with Hatch and the children. They've abandoned the third floor. There are seven guards on four and three scientists. It looks like they're preparing for a battle on the fourth floor."

"They must have guessed that's where we're going," I said.

As we came up to the first level, I whispered to Ian, "How close to the door are they?"

"One's touching it, the other's standing by the elevator."

I put my hand on the door and pulsed. We could hear the guard's gun hit the floor.

"Seventeen," Ostin said.

Suddenly Ian shouted, "Move, move!"

We scattered. Bullets started ripping through the door.

When the gunfire paused, Zeus asked Ian, "Where is he?"

Ian pointed. Zeus shoved his finger through one of the holes and fired back with a bolt of electricity.

"Got him," Ian said. "You are good."

"Thanks," Zeus said.

"Sixteen," Ostin said. "We're forty percent there."

We approached the door to the second floor cautiously. Hatch was on level two and there were the electric children and six guards. Fortunately, with the stairwell cameras dead, they were blind to our movement.

On our way up to the third floor we had to step over the bodies of two of the guards from our first battle. They were still unconscious. McKenna and Abigail put on the guards' bulletproof vests, even though they hung to the girl's knees. Then Ostin and I handcuffed the guards and stripped them of their weapons. Ostin added one of their knives to his utility belt, which looked like a small sword on him. I took one of the rifles and jammed it between the door and the railing to keep the door from being opened behind us.

With each step, Ian looked from side to side as he kept track of everything going on in the building. My biggest fear was that Hatch would attack with Nichelle and the electric children, but with the exception of Tara, they kept their distance.

"He can't risk them," Zeus said to me. "The kids are too valuable. The guards are dispensable."

We stopped on the stairwell between levels three and four. There was another guard's body on the stairs. We stripped the guard of his weapons. We now had more than we could carry, so we dropped them down the stairwell. Ostin put on the guard's bulletproof vest.

Ian groaned. "We've got a problem."

"What?" I said.

"On level four they're setting up inside the door with a flame-thrower."

"A flamethrower?" Ostin asked. "If we open the door that will fill the whole stairwell."

"It's worse, they've even armed the scientists. Superman couldn't make it through that door alive."

I looked back down the stairwell. "I've got an idea. How many guards on three?"

"None, they've abandoned the floor."

"You're sure?"

He looked again. "Yes."

"Ostin, how much smoke does one of these smoke grenades make?"

"Well, if they're like the ones on the Discovery Channel, they'll each produce forty thousand cubic feet of smoke in about thirty-five seconds."

"How many cubic feet is the fourth floor?"

Ostin loved questions like that. "I estimate this place is about forty-four hundred square feet per floor, the ceiling's about eight feet high, so, if my calculations are accurate that's thirty-five thousand, two hundred cubic feet of space per floor."

I grinned. "So twelve smoke grenades would cover it."

"The smoke will be so thick they could chew it like bubble gum. But how do we get the smoke grenades up there?"

"No problem," I said. "Follow me."

We climbed back down to the third level—the floor of the electric children suites. Knowing that the cameras were still live, Zeus went inside alone to take out the cameras, while I explained the plan to everyone else. A minute later Zeus opened the stairwell door on three. "All clear. The cameras are dead."

We all went inside.

Abigail and McKenna each called an elevator. When the elevators arrived they pushed the button for the fourth floor, then stepped back out and held the elevator doors open.

"Everyone ready?" I asked.

"Let's roll," Zeus said.

The elevators began to beep from being detained.

"Ostin?"

"Ready," he shouted from the stairwell.

"Now!"

At my signal Ostin leaned out the stairwell door and threw a concussion grenade up to the fourth floor, while Abigail and McKenna pulled the pins on their smoke grenades, six apiece, threw them into the elevators, and let the elevators go. A half-minute later Ian started to laugh. "It's working." Smoke was filling the fourth level.

"Taylor, now!" I shouted.

Taylor began concentrating, trying to create as much general confusion as she could.

We could hear the guards and scientists above us in a state of panic.

"They're running around like a bunch of chickens with their heads cut off," Ian said. "They're climbing out the windows."

Within five minutes the guards and scientists had completely vacated the floor. We went back to the stairwell. Smoke from our grenades had seeped into the stairwell and Ostin was covering his mouth and nose with his shirt, which he had pulled up through his vest.

"They're all gone," I said.

"Nine guards left," Ostin said.

"How's the smoke?" I asked Ian.

"It's dissipating. Give it a few more minutes."

I climbed past Ostin and tried the door. "It's bolted shut," I said. "Any ideas, Ostin?"

Suddenly the bolt slid and the door opened. Abigail and McKenna were standing there.

I looked at them curiously. "How'd you get up here?"

McKenna smiled. "We took the elevator."

We covered our noses and walked into the room. The smoke had mostly dissipated but its odor hadn't, leaving the room bathed in a pungent, sulfurous smell. Ostin stopped to look at the mounted guns they had facing the door. "Whoa. That's a Barrett M182 anti-matériel rifle retrofitted with a M2A1-7 flamethrower."

"How do you know that?" I asked.

"Internet."

"That's one nasty gun," Ian said, scratching his head.

"Ian, I'm going to release the prisoners," I said. "Will you keep watch?"

"Sure thing."

The command center was located at the front end of the floor, opposite from the stairwell we'd just come through. The room was open with large glass panels so that inside we could still see the stairwell and the rest of our group. There were two large consoles, each about the size of a car's hood, and as loaded with buttons and switches as a jet cockpit.

"Man, this is cool," Ostin said. "I need one of these in my room."

The first console had fourteen small screens stacked on top of each other in five levels, the numbers corresponding with each level of the building except for the GP level, which was missing. The images on these screens, each numbered, were constantly changing, switching between more than a hundred security cameras. However, thanks to Zeus's handiwork, only the first, second, and fourth floor monitors were completely live. Next to the screens was a long row of buttons allowing the operator to select and control any camera on the grounds.

"These are all the building's security cameras," I said to Ostin, pointing to a monitor. "See, there's the main hall, the yard, and the students' suites."

"The students' suites?" Zeus asked, walking into the room. "I completely took the third floor camera out."

"Not all of them. There are still the ones in the bedrooms."

"There are cameras in the bedrooms?" Zeus asked, looking surprised. "I didn't know we were being watched all the time. That's kind of . . . embarrassing."

Unfortunately we had taken out all the cameras in the stairwell, which would have been useful to us now.

Taylor joined us in the command center.

The second console was entirely dedicated to the GP level. There was a bank of twenty-five small screens, each with a number, all surrounding one large, central monitor. On the small screens we could see the GPs. There was little movement in the cells; the prisoners were either lying on their beds or sitting on them. In one room a few were on the ground playing cards.

"Interesting," Ostin said, watching them. "They've created their own sign language."

All but two of the cells were full and most had more than one occupant, some as many as four.

On the main console there were twenty-five panels, each with three buttons, a toggle switch, a sliding switch, and two green diodes. In the center of the console was a microphone.

"Ostin, help me figure this out," I said.

Ostin walked up behind me and looked over the console. "Each screen and panel corresponds with a cell and if you push the red button"—he reached over and pushed the red button on Cell 5 and the video image of two GPs playing cards on the small screen appeared on the central monitor—"you can enlarge the view of a single cell." He pushed the button again and the image zoomed in still more. He did it until we could actually read the cards one of the prisoners held in his hand.

"That's one way to cheat at cards," Zeus said.

"And this toggle switch moves the camera." Ostin pushed the button to the right and the camera panned right. "Man, I wish I had one of these."

He looked at the buttons on the panels below the red one. They were labeled VOX, PL, and EC. EC had a sliding button beneath it. "VOX, of course, is the intercom system. PL . . ." Ostin rubbed his chin as he thought. "Pneumatic locks. The green light tells you that it's locked. And EC would be electric collars. I'm guessing that the sliding button below them would intensify the severity of the shock; the green light signals that it's on."

"Look around for Jack," I said.

"Is that him in 9?" Taylor said, pointing to a small screen. The man in the cell was lying on his back looking up at the ceiling.

I pushed the red button on 9 and the picture came up on the central monitor.

"Push it again," Ostin said.

I pushed the button twice until the man's face took half the screen. "That's him," Taylor said.

"I didn't recognize him with the beard," I said.

"Where's Wade?" Ostin asked. "They're not together?"

I honestly didn't know if Wade was still alive. I hadn't had the chance to tell them anything about what had happened to us. "Keep looking," I said.

"There he is," Ostin said. "In 11."

I pushed the button on 11 and the image filled the screen. Wade wasn't alone. There was another man in the same room.

"He's almost across the hall from Jack," I said.

I pushed the button on 9 again and the picture of Jack came back up on the center screen. I pushed the VOX button on the 9 panel. "Jack."

He suddenly looked up toward the corner of the room.

"Jack, can you hear me?"

He looked around, as if trying to figure out where the voice had come from.

"Jack, it's me, Michael. Are you okay?"

This time he nodded.

"I can't hear anything," I said to Ostin.

"He's not speaking. He still has the electric collar on."

"Right." I looked down at the panel. "Which way should I push it to deactivate it?"

"Try pushing it to the right," Taylor said.

I started to slide the switch to the right. Jack immediately grabbed his collar.

"Stop! Stop!" Ostin shouted.

"Sorry. My bad," Taylor said into the microphone.

"Rules out the right," I said.

I slid the switch to the left. The green light on the panel went off.

"I think you did it," Ostin said.

"Jack," I said into the microphone, "I think we've disarmed your collar. Try speaking."

He looked nervous. "Michael," he said in a raspy voice. A look of relief came across his face. "Thanks. Where are you?"

"We've escaped. We've taken control of the main command center. We're going to unlock all the doors in the prison, but there are still three guards on your floor. We want you to get Wade and help us."

"I don't know where Wade is," Jack said.

"He's close. He's in Cell 11. That's directly across the hall, one cell to the right. I'm going to unlock your door, but don't open it until I tell you to. Taylor, where are the guards?"

"There's one coming down the hall toward 9."

"Hold tight, Jack. Ostin, on my word, unlock Wade's cell."

"Got it."

"He's turning back," Taylor said.

"Okay, Jack, be sure to shut your door so they don't suspect anything."

"Got it."

"Ready. Go." I pushed the PL button and a light on the panel turned green.

"Wait," Jack said, "there's no handle on the inside of the door. I can't open it."

"I got an idea," Ostin said. He walked over to the other console, looked around for a moment, then pushed a button.

"The door just opened a little," Jack said.

"What did you do?" I asked.

"I turned on the hall air conditioner and created negative air—"

"That was smart," Taylor said, cutting him off.

"Thanks."

"Okay, where's the guard, Taylor?"

"Still on the other end of the hall."

"Ostin, open Cell 11."

"Got it."

"Okay, Jack. Go. Fast."

Jack pried open his cell door, stepped out into the corridor, pulled his door shut, then pushed in the door at Cell 11. I hit the red button on 11 and the image took full screen. We watched the reunion. Wade stood as Jack entered and the other inmate just stared anxiously. "Ostin, shut off their collars. To the left."

"Got it. Done."

I pushed the VOX. "Jack, shut the door. We turned off the collars, but keep your voices down."

Wade looked around, afraid to speak.

"It's okay, you can talk," Jack said.

"Who is that?" Wade asked.

"It's Michael," Jack said. "They've escaped."

He looked at the camera. "You're the man, Michael."

"Can you take your collars off?"

"Yeah, they're just buckled like a seat belt. Are you sure they're turned off? Because the collars are programmed to go off on full if we try to take them off."

"They're off," Ostin said, then turned to me and shrugged. "I think," he said to me.

The three of them quickly removed their collars.

"Guys, here comes the guard," Taylor said.

"Ostin, can you figure out how to shut off the lights on the floor?"

He went over to the other console. "Just a minute." He quickly scanned the board. "I think this is it."

"Jack, the guard is coming. When he passes your cell we're going to shut off the lights. Can you and Wade jump him and drag him back into your cell?"

"My pleasure. Wade, you hit low, I'll take his arms."

"Count me in," the other inmate said.

"We have night vision here," I said, "so wait for our command."

"Got it."

"He's nearing the cell," Taylor said. "Okay, he's past the cell."

"Ostin, now," I said.

The GP level screens all went dark. Suddenly the images on them changed from black to pale green, ghostlike images.

I whispered. "Jack, can you see anything?"

"No."

"The guard is three feet to your right, directly in front of your old cell. He's facing Cell 9. Open your door."

He opened the door. The guard must have heard my voice and started to turn back.

"Now!"

The three of them blindly charged the guard. Wade hit first, wrapping his arms around the guard's legs, while Jack knocked him over. The other inmate grabbed the guard around the neck. The guard was flailing around but had no idea who or what had hit him.

Truthfully, the attack didn't look a whole lot different than back when Jack and his posse tried to pants me. The three of them dragged the guard back into their cell.

"Eight guards," Ostin said.

"Lights on," I said.

The lights came back on. The two remaining guards just looked around, confused by what had happened.

"Shut the door," I said.

Wade pushed the door shut. The third inmate still had the guard by the throat, and Jack pinned his arms behind his back as Wade handcuffed him. Then Jack pulled off all the guard's weapons, taking a rifle, Taser, and concussion grenade. He handed a pistol and a smoke grenade to Wade and the truncheon and Mace to the other inmate. The inmate immediately sprayed the Mace in the guard's face. "Feels good, don't it?"

The guard gasped and sputtered. "Don't kill me."

"Keep your mouth shut," Jack said to the guard. "You call for help and it will be the last thing you do."

"Put a collar on him," Ostin said into the microphone, "and we'll reactivate it at full."

"Gladly," Jack said. He fastened one of the collars around the guard's neck.

I slid the switch. "Reactivated," I said.

"Welcome to the other side," Jack said. He turned to the other inmate and put out his hand. "What's your name?"

"Salvatore."

"You did well, Salvatore."

"Grazie."

Zeus said, "If you can manually control the elevators, I can take out the front guard, while Jack takes out the other guard. Then we can start bringing the prisoners up here, bypassing the guards on two."

"Brilliant. Except you better have Ian go with you, so you don't walk into an ambush. Ostin, you're in charge of the elevators. Abigail and McKenna, keep watch on the monitors."

"What about me?" Taylor asked.

"Stay close to me," I said. "I'm going to need your help."

I got back on the speaker. "Jack, there are only eight guards left, and Hatch and six electric children. We're going to start transporting all the prisoners up to the fourth floor and arm them. We've got a whole weapons depot up here. What will happen if I unlock all the doors?"

"They're pretty keyed up," he said. "Prison riot. Could turn ugly."

"That's what I was afraid of."

"There're a few guys who could really help us, though."

"How many?"

"Half dozen."

"Okay, this is the plan. There are two guards still on your floor, one in each corridor. Ian and Zeus are going to come down the front elevator and take out the first guard. There's a guard at the end of the corridor to your left. You're going to have to keep him from helping out the other guard."

Jack took out his grenade. "No problem."

"When you've secured the floor, tell us where your friends are. Give the weapons you capture to the ones you trust and then start bringing them up here six at a time. I need you and Wade up here with us. Hatch may launch a counterattack up the stairwell."

"Got it."

Zeus and Ian walked over to the elevator. "We're ready."

"On it," Ostin said. He opened the elevator door. "Level GL. I'm going to cut the lights again. Ian, when you get there tell Zeus where to fire. And stay away from the elevator door. The guard is still armed; he may just fire at the sound of the doors opening."

"Got it."

They stepped into the elevator. Ostin shut the door and sent them down. Then he again cut the lights on that level. We could see the guards on our screens freeze in their positions.

"Look!" Abigail said. "The stairwell door."

Fire and sparks began shooting through the stairwell door. "Someone's cutting their way in here," I said.

"It must be Bryan," McKenna said. "He can do that."

"Taylor!" I shouted. "See what you can do to stop him!"

Taylor walked closer to the stairwell and focused her attention on the door. "Nothing's happening."

Ostin was still staring at his monitor. "Zeus and Ian have reached ground level," he said.

There was a bright flash of lightning on the screen. "Seven guards," Ostin shouted. "What's Ian doing?"

On the monitor, Ian looked frantic. He ran down the hall toward Cell 11.

Already a full line had been cut through the door. "Michael!" Taylor shouted. "I can't stop them!

"Ostin, who's out there?"

"I can't tell. Zeus shot out the cameras."

I turned back to the console. "Ostin, lights up on GL." I pushed the master VOX. "Jack, one of our guys, Ian, is about to come around the corner behind you. Don't shoot him. Can you take the other guard out?"

Jack raised a hand. "On it. Do it, Wade."

Wade threw a smoke grenade down to the end of the hall. The guard vanished behind a cloud of smoke.

"We've got you surrounded, man!" Jack shouted. "You're the only one left. Surrender your weapon now or we start shooting."

The choking guard threw his gun out ahead of him. "Don't shoot. I surrender."

"Get on your knees and put your hands behind your back." Jack turned back to Wade. "Get a collar."

"Six guards left!" Ostin shouted.

Ian rounded the corner and pushed open the cell door. He was out of breath, "Michael, can you hear me?"

"I'm here," I said.

He gasped out his warning. "It's Bryan . . . he's cutting through the . . . stairwell wall."

"We can see the sparks. Is he wearing a helmet?"

"Yes."

I looked at Taylor. "Get away from there. You can't help."

Just then Zeus walked into the cell behind Ian, carrying the guard's weapons. "What's going on?"

"Michael," Ian said. "Bryan's with Hatch and three guards. And he has Nichelle with him. They're coming for you."

# 48

## Overload the Circuit

Hearing that Nichelle was on the other side of the wall sent chills through me.

"Michael, we've got to get out of here," Taylor said.

"I need to finish. Hatch could still kill all the prisoners. Abigail, McKenna, get out of here."

"We're not leaving you," they said simultaneously.

Sparks bounced off the floor as Bryan completed the second cut.

"He's halfway through," Taylor said.

"I'm not going out without a fight," Ostin said. He ran from the console over to the flamethrower.

"Ostin, I need you back here," I said. "I need you to unlock all the prison doors and turn off all the collars."

He turned to me. "We've got to stop them."

Taylor went to the flamethrower. "You go, I'll do it." She crouched down next to the machine as Ostin ran back to the console and started hitting switches.

I hit the central VOX button. "Attention, prisoners. This is Michael Vey. We are freeing you. We're unlocking all the doors. Your collars will soon be deactivated. As soon as the light goes off, take them off as quickly as you can. We're under attack, so we don't have much time. Ian, Jack, and Zeus will help get you out of the building. Do exactly as they say."

"How does this work?" Taylor said.

"Just pull the top trigger," Ostin said. "But not now. It will set the floor on fire."

"Michael!" Jack shouted over the intercom. "We're coming up the stairwell to rescue you!"

"Just be careful."

"Hey!" Ostin shouted. "Zeus is coming back up the elevator."

I looked over. "What? Tell him to turn back."

"I can't. There's no intercom in there."

The cutting had started again and Bryan completed another line in the wall.

"He's almost through!" Taylor yelled.

"Ostin, are you done?"

"Just about."

"Ian, all the collars are just about off. I don't know how long we can hold the floor, so use the elevators with caution."

"Got it, Michael."

The front elevator door opened and Zeus walked out.

"What are you doing here?" I shouted to him.

"I need to face Hatch," Zeus said.

"Send him an e-mail. Nichelle's with him. Take the girls and get out of here."

"We're not leaving," McKenna said again.

Taylor looked back at me and shook her head. "I'm not leaving you alone."

"McKenna, Taylor, these are Hatch's personal guards. They'll kill you. They'll kill all of us. Just get out. Please."

Just then Bryan completed the last cut and the thick plated metal fell forward, crashing onto the floor. A concussion grenade flew through the hole at us, exploding in the middle of the room. Taylor screamed, falling to the floor behind the flamethrower.

"Put down your weapons," Hatch shouted, "or we'll throw in real grenades!"

"They have those?" Ostin asked.

"I don't want to find out," I said. "Okay!" I yelled. "Taylor, back away from the flamethrower."

A moment later a guard stuck his head through the hole in the door. He looked around, then stepped inside. He was wearing a different uniform than I'd seen before—a bright green, rubberized suit with a helmet and bulletproof vest. He pointed his gun at us, as if daring one of us to engage him. Then Hatch, wearing the copper helmet, stepped through the hole behind him, closely followed by Nichelle and two other guards. Hatch looked around the room and said to me, "Quite a mess you've made of things, Vey."

"I did my best," I said.

Zeus was standing in the middle of the hall, halfway between Hatch at the stairwell and me at the console. Hatch looked at Zeus and his face twisted in a scowl. "Well, Frank, you turned out to be quite a disappointment."

"My name's not Frank," Zeus said.

"You're right. It's Leonard. Leonard Frank Smith. That's all you are now. What a pity. I made you into a god and you chose to be Frank. I'd laugh if it wasn't so pathetic."

"You gave me a title so you could make me your slave. You lied to me. You lied to all of us."

"Who told you that, Frank? The liar Vey?" He looked at me, then back to Zeus. "It's not too late for you, Frank. Take out Taylor, Abigail, and McKenna right now and I'll let you back into the family."

The girls looked at him anxiously.

"Really?" Zeus said. "You'll let me be your minion again? What a deal."

"Nichelle," Hatch said.

Suddenly the worst pain I'd felt yet pierced my skull. Nichelle had always claimed that Hatch made her hold back but now, for the first time, I believed her. Taylor, McKenna, Abigail, Zeus, and I all screamed out.

At the same time the pop and spray of gunfire echoed in the stairwell and a concussion grenade exploded behind Hatch and the guards. One of the guards emerged from the stairwell. "Dr. Hatch, the GPs are attacking from below. We can't hold them long. There's at least two dozen of them."

"Help them," Hatch said to his guards. They climbed back through the hole into the stairwell. Hatch turned back to us. "Poor, misguided Zeus. You picked the wrong curtain. I gave you power and privilege. I gave you identity. Michael Vey gave you this . . ."

"Michael gave me freedom. You've done nothing for me that wasn't in your best interest. That's all this is about—absolute obedience to you. That's what you want from the whole world. But you're nothing, Hatch."

Hatch's expression turned fierce. "Nichelle, show Frank what nothing truly is. Show no mercy."

She smiled, then looked at Zeus, who immediately fell to his knees, grabbing his temples and screaming.

Then she turned it on all of us. "You insignificant little cretins," Nichelle said. "I told you that I could squash you all like mosquitoes."

Taylor, McKenna, Abigail, and Taylor simultaneously crouched over in pain. My knees buckled and I fell to the ground behind the console. As I writhed in agony, Ostin looked at me helplessly, then crawled past me under one of the consoles and pulled the cord out of the wall. He took the knife from his utility belt and cut the end of the cord and handed me the frayed end.

"Put this in your mouth," Ostin whispered.

I looked at him but did nothing. I was in too much pain to speak, and everything seemed to be spinning around me. I was on the verge of passing out. Ostin put the cord in my hand.

"Just do it!" he said.

I lifted the end of the cord to my mouth as he plugged it back into the wall. Electricity sparked in my mouth and a surge of power hit my body. Immediately, the dizziness left me and I felt normal again. Actually, I felt better than normal. I felt stronger.

Ostin crawled closer to me and whispered. "Michael, listen to me. I think I know how to stop Nichelle. Overload the circuit."

I pulled the cord from my mouth; the power was still flowing into my hand. "What?"

"Don't hold back, give her everything at once. Like blowing a breaker at home."

"Are you crazy?"

"Trust me."

I looked at him for a moment, then I heard Taylor scream out in pain. "Stop, please, stop! Michael!"

"Get behind me, Ostin." I forced myself to one knee, then to my feet.

Nichelle was now focusing her attention on Taylor, who was writhing in agony.

"Hey, Nichelle!" I shouted.

She turned and looked at me.

"You want my electricity? Take it!" I spread out my arms and surged with everything.

Nichelle suddenly started shaking and her expression changed from cruelty to fear. "What are you doing?"

"Keep it up!" Ostin shouted.

Hatch looked at me, then back at Nichelle. "Nichelle, stop him! That's an order!"

I continued to surge.

"What are you doing?" Nichelle repeated, her voice now trembling. "Stop it! That hurts! Stop!"

"I don't think so," I said.

Taylor, Zeus, and the girls all stopped shaking. Nichelle had released them.

"Stop it!" Nichelle screamed again, then she began convulsing as if she were having a seizure.

"What's going on?!" Hatch shouted. "Answer me!"

Nichelle fell to her knees, doubling over in agony. "Stop! Please, stop!"

Hatch turned to me, his jaw clenched, his face red with anger. Sweat beaded on his forehead. For a second we just stared at each other.

Then a guard shouted to Hatch from the stairwell. "Sir, they're on us! You've got to get out now!"

Hatch pulled a revolver from beneath his jacket and pointed it at me. "You did this, Vey. Now pay." He pulled the trigger.

As the gun erupted, lightning flashed across the room and hit the bullet just inches in front of me, blowing it into nothing. Then Zeus turned and hit the gun itself. Hatch screamed out in pain, throwing his gun in the air.

"My name is *Zeus*!"

There was another explosion in the stairwell. "Sir, we've got to go *now*!" the guard shouted, grabbing Hatch's shoulder.

"Help me!" Nichelle cried.

Hatch was holding his arm and glanced down at her. "You're no use to me anymore."

"But I'm your friend."

"You betrayed your own kind, Nichelle. No one likes a traitor. Even those they serve."

Hatch looked at me once more, his face twisted in hatred, then he ducked back out into the stairwell and climbed up to the roof.

"Zero guards," Ostin shouted as he stood up from behind the console.

Nichelle was on her knees, looking at me fearfully. I surged once more. She let out a yelp, then collapsed to the ground in an unconscious heap. A faint wisp of smoke rose from her body.

I let go of the electric cord and fell to one knee, exhausted.

The battle continued to rage in the stairwell as Jack and the prisoners pushed past our floor to the roof.

Ostin looked at me, then Zeus, then back at me. "That was the coolest thing I've ever seen," he said. "A bullet travels at a mile a second, lightning travels at a hundred and eighty-six thousand miles per second. That rocked."

Ostin looked around. Smoke was still wafting through the room and we all seemed frozen in place, like survivors of a natural disaster. He walked over to Nichelle and pushed her with his foot.

"Is she dead?" Taylor asked.

Ostin knelt down and put his hand on her neck. "Unfortunately not."

Just then Ian climbed through the stairwell into the room. "Michael, Hatch is gone. He escaped in the helicopter."

"With all the kids?"

"That I could see."

I sat down on the floor and raked my hand back through my hair. Then I looked over at Ostin. I'm sure it was the release of tension, but I suddenly started to laugh.

Taylor looked at me like I'd gone crazy. "What's so funny?"

"Ostin," I said, slowly shaking my head. "Ostin is. 'Overload the circuit.' Where in the world did you get that idea?"

Ostin said defensively, "Nichelle gave it to me. When she called you all mosquitoes."

"What?" Taylor said.

"Have you ever had a mosquito on your arm, but rather than swat it, just squeezed the skin around where it's sucking?"

"You had a strange, sick childhood," Taylor said.

"No, really, it's cool. The mosquito can't disengage, so it just fills up with blood until it explodes. I figured that since your natural reaction to Nichelle was always to resist, that she had probably just been dragging your powers out of you a little at a time, like sucking out of a straw. I figured if you just gave it to her all at once, she wouldn't be able to handle it."

"Brilliant," I said. "Brilliant." I looked over at Zeus. He was standing quietly, leaning against the wall, his head bowed. "Hey, Zeus," I said.

He slowly turned around. "Frank," he said. "I'm just Frank."

I shook my head. "No, dude, you're definitely Zeus."

He smiled.

"He's right," Taylor said. "You're Zeus." She walked up to him and kissed him on the cheek. "You were awesome. You were more than awesome—you were a hero."

"Thanks." He touched his cheek. "You're the first girl who's ever kissed me."

Taylor smiled. "You deserved it."

Just then Jack and Wade climbed in through the hole in the door. Jack opened his arms to me. "Michael, my man," he said, walking up to me. "Stand up, Vey, I'm going in for the bromance."

I stood and Jack embraced me, almost knocking me over. Then he stepped back and announced, "First time I ever hugged a dude I didn't have a choke hold on."

Wade stood a few yards behind Jack, staring at me. "You saved my life, man."

"And you returned the favor," I said. "We're even."

"Not even close," Wade said. "Not even close."

"So now what?" Taylor asked.

I looked down at my watch. The crystal was broken and its silver band was now scratched, but it was still there. It had come through the battle, just like me. "There's a phone back here," I said. "You better call your parents. They're worried sick about you. You too, Ostin."

Ostin started to the phone but stopped. "But what about your mom?"

"I'm going to find her," I said.

"*We're* going to find her," Jack said. "And bring her home."

I looked at Jack and shook my head. "Thanks, but I've already gotten you guys in enough trouble. I can't take that chance again."

"Trouble?" Jack said. "You can't buy this kind of excitement."

"I'm in," Wade said. "You risked your mom's life for me, I'll risk mine for hers. Besides, even that prison wasn't as bad as living with my granny." He looked at Jack. "The food was better."

"The guards were nicer too," Jack said.

I looked down and smiled. "Well, I could use a ride."

"I'm in too," Zeus said. "I helped capture her. I'll help free her." He looked at me. "What else am I going to do? Can't stay here."

"Count me in," Ian said, stepping forward. "I can't speak for the girls, but last I checked, my schedule was wide open." He looked at Abigail and McKenna. "How about you guys?"

"I'm in," McKenna said.

Abigail just looked down. She furtively wiped a tear from her cheek. "I'm sorry. I just want to go home."

McKenna walked over and put her arm around her.

I looked at Abigail affectionately. "Go home, Abi. You've done enough. But I'll forever be indebted to you."

"As will I," Taylor said.

"We all will," Ian said. "We love you, Abi."

Taylor walked over to the phone and picked up the receiver. She dialed three numbers, then stopped and looked back at me, smiling. Then she set down the phone and walked over and took my hand.

"You, Michael Vey, are a freaking rock star."

My eyes started twitching. "Thanks."

She grinned. "Oh, now you start blinking. You had bombs blowing up around you, bullets shot at you, and two dozen armed bad guys trying to kill you and you're a steely-eyed ninja, and now, when I hold your hand, you're nervous?"

I shrugged. "I can't help it."

She smiled. "I like that." She leaned forward and kissed me on the lips. Then she wrapped her arms around me and we kissed again. Out of the corner of my eye I saw Ostin giving me a thumbs-up. I could practically hear him. I knew what he was thinking without my powers. *Told you so, dude.*

The rest of the clan was smiling as well. When we parted, Taylor said, "Now let's go get your mother."

I leaned back. "Wait, Taylor. You can't come."

She put her hands on her hips. "If you think I'm going to let my boyfriend run off without me, you don't know me."

"But what about your parents?"

"I'll call them."

"What about cheerleading?"

She looked at me incredulously. "You're joking, right? Save the world or shake pom-poms. How shallow do you think I am?"

I started to laugh. It was a pretty stupid thing to say.

Suddenly, McKenna shouted out, "Michael, watch out!"

I spun around. No one had seen her enter. A girl I had never seen before was standing just fifteen feet from me. Zeus surged, knocking her back against the wall. She slid to the ground holding her arm. She cowered, her eyes averted. "Please don't hurt me."

I stepped toward her. "Who are you?"

"She's Grace," Ian said. "She's one of the seventeen."

"You're one of Hatch's kids," I said. "What are you doing here?"

"I ran away from Hatch."

"Careful," Ostin said. "She could be a plant."

"We'll know soon enough. Taylor, see if it's true."

Taylor walked over and put her hands on the girl's temples. Then she turned back to us. "It's true. She hates Hatch."

"I want to come with you," she said.

"Come with me? Where do you think I'm going?"

"To find your mother. I know where she is."

I looked over at Zeus. "What does she do?"

"No one was really sure," Zeus said. "Something with computers."

"I'm like a human flash drive," Grace said. "I can download computers. I broke into the academy's mainframe and downloaded all the information they had before they destroyed it all. You're going to need it to finish what you started."

I looked at her. "What do you mean, 'what I've started'?"

Grace was still holding her arm as she stood. "This is just the beginning. The Elgen have built compounds all around the world. They're already trying to create new electric children. If we don't work together and stop them, they'll hunt us all down individually and then they'll take over."

"It's true," Ian said. "None of us will be safe alone." He turned to Abigail and frowned. "Even you, Abi."

Abigail looked down. McKenna rubbed her back.

"Hatch never forgives and he never forgets," Zeus said. "He's like an elephant with anger management issues."

In the center of the hallway Nichelle groaned.

"Whoa! That's Nichelle," Grace said, her voice tinged with fear.

"Sure is," I said.

Taylor walked over to Nichelle's side. "So what do we do with sunny delight?"

Nichelle's eyes opened. For a moment she looked around the room, then the screeching and pain hit all of us. I immediately surged and Nichelle screamed out, "Okay, I'll stop!"

"Ugh!" Taylor groaned, rubbing her forehead. "Girl, you are one bad apple. Rotten to the core."

"I'd like to fry her like a corn dog," Zeus said. "And be done with her."

Nichelle looked up at me fearfully as I walked over to her. "No, I have something more fitting in mind. Something much worse."

"Worse than lightning?" Taylor asked.

I nodded, looking in Nichelle's face. "Look at her. She has nothing left. Her powers are now worthless, her so-called friends have abandoned her, and we're not going to let her take a single thing from this place." I crouched down and took the diamond collar off her neck. "We'll let her go back to the real world and live the rest of her life as a nobody."

As the reality of my words sunk in her expression turned. "No," she said. "Don't do this. Shock me, Vey!"

I shook my head as I stood. "No. You're on your own."

Taylor walked over and took my hand.

Nichelle turned to Zeus. "Zeus, think of all the times I punished you! Finish me!"

Zeus folded his arms. "I'm done taking orders from you, Nichelle."

"It's time for you to leave, Nichelle," I said. "Jack, would you escort her out? Make sure she doesn't take anything with her."

"Gladly." He walked over and lifted Nichelle by her arm. She struggled futilely against his grasp.

"Let go of me, you creep! I hate you. I hate you all!"

Jack just grinned. "Come on, Wade. Let's show Little Miss Sunshine the real world."

"Hurry back," I said as they waited for the elevator. "We have plans to make."

Jack smiled, raising his fist in the air in a power salute. "Go Electroclan."

As the elevator door closed behind them, a large grin blanketed Ostin's face. "Wow."

"What?" I said.

"We're buddies with Jack and Wade, we just freed an entire prison, and"—he glanced at Taylor—"Taylor Ridley's your girlfriend . . ."

Taylor smiled.

"We're definitely not in Idaho anymore."

"That's for sure," I said.

He held out his hand. "Bones, dude."

I held out my hand and this time it was without hesitation. "Bones."

Taylor smiled and, for the first time, she held her hand out as well. "Bones."

Ostin looked at Taylor and me, then around the room at each of our new friends. His smile grew wider. "You know what we have here, don't you?"

"What?" I asked.

"It's the rise of the Electroclan."

# MICHAEL VEY

## RISE OF THE ELGEN

*To McKenna*
*You have brought light and warmth into the world*

# PROLOGUE

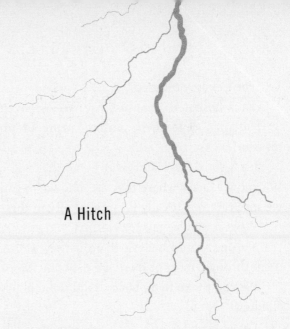

## A Hitch

"This had better be important," the man said. It was past two in the morning in the Tyrrhenian Sea and the man on the boat had been awoken for the call.

"There's been a . . . *hitch,*" Hatch said, choosing the word carefully. He leaned back in the leather seat of his private jet. "The transition from our Pasadena facility didn't go as smoothly as we planned."

"What kind of 'hitch'?"

"We had a revolt."

"A revolt? By who?"

"Michael Vey. And the GPs."

"Did any of them escape?"

"All of them."

The voice exploded in a string of profanities. "How did that come about?"

"The Vey boy was more powerful than we thought."

"The Vey boy escaped?"

Hatch hesitated. "Not just Vey. We lost seven of the Glows."

The man unleashed another string of profanities. "This is a disaster!"

"It's a setback," Hatch said. "One that will quickly be remedied. We know exactly where they are, and we're gathering up the GPs as we speak. We've already recaptured all but three of them."

"What if they've talked?"

"No one would believe them if they did. After what we've put them through, most of them are babbling idiots."

"We can't take that chance. Find them all. Where are the electric children?"

"We've been tracking their movements. They're still together and driving to Idaho. We have a team in place ready to take them."

"Why should I believe you'll be successful this time?"

"*This* time we know what we're dealing with. And we have a few surprises they won't be expecting."

"I'll have to report this to the board," the voice said.

"Give it until morning," Hatch said. "The picture will be different. Besides, everything else is on schedule."

"And I expect you to keep it that way." The voice paused, then said, "I think it's time you released Vey's mother."

"That would be a mistake. She's our only guarantee that Vey won't just disappear again, and he may be the answer to our problems with the machine. Besides, in less than twenty-four hours Vey and the rest of the Glows will be back in our custody."

"You had better be right," the man said.

"You have my guarantee," Hatch said. "Vey will be back in our hands before the day's out."

# PART ONE

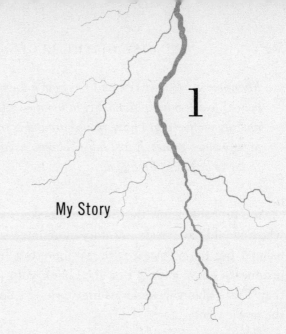

# 1

## My Story

In fifth grade my English teacher, Ms. Berg, was teaching about autobiographies and had us each write our life story on a single page of lined paper. I'm not sure which is more pathetic:

(a) That Ms. Berg thought our lives could be summed up on one page, or

(b) I could fill only half the page.

Let's face it, in fifth grade you're still kind of waiting for life to begin. Yeah, some of the kids had done cool things, like one had gone skydiving; another had been to Japan; and one girl's father was a plumber and she got to be in her dad's TV commercial waving a plunger, so she's kind of famous—but that's about as cool as it got. All I remember is that my autobiography was super lame. It went something like:

*My name is Michael Vey, and I'm from a town you've never*
*heard of—Meridian, Idaho. My father died when I was eight,*
*and my mother and I have moved around a lot since then. I like*
*to play video games. Also, I have Tourette's syndrome. I'm not*
*trying to be funny, I really do.*

You probably know that Tourette's makes some of us swear a lot, which would have made my story more interesting, or maybe got it banned, but I don't swear with my Tourette's. In my case, Tourette's just means I have a lot of tics, like I blink, gulp, make faces, stuff like that. That's about it. As far as life stories go, no one's called to buy the movie rights.

They might if they knew my secret—the secret I've hidden for most of my life and the reason my mom and I keep having to move.

*I'm electric.* So are you, of course. That's how your brain and muscles work. But the thing is, I have probably a thousand times more electricity than you. And it seems to be growing stronger. Have you ever rubbed your feet on a carpet, then shocked someone? Multiply that by a thousand and you'll get an idea of what it's like to be me. Or shocked by me. Fortunately, I've learned to control it.

I'm fifteen years old now and a lot has happened since the fifth grade. I kind of wish someone would ask me to write my life story now, because it would make a good movie. And it would take up *way* more than one page. This is how it would go:

*My name is Michael Vey, and I'm more electric than an electric*
*eel. I always thought I was the only one in the world like me,*
*but I'm not. I just found out that there were originally seventeen*
*of us. And the people who made us this way, the Elgen, are*
*hunting us down. You might say we were an accident. The*
*Elgen Corporation created a machine called the MEI (short*
*for Magnetic Electron Induction), to be used for finding*
*diseases and abnormalities in the body. Instead it created*
*abnormalities—us.*

*My girlfriend, the way-out-of-my-league cheerleader with perfect brown eyes, Taylor Ridley, is also electric. I can shock people (I call it "pulsing"), but she can shock people's brains and make them forget what they were doing (she calls it "rebooting"). She can also read minds, but she has to touch you to do it.*

*One month ago the Elgen, led by a scary dude named Dr. Hatch, found us. They kidnapped Taylor and tried to get me, too, but ended up with my mother instead. A few days later I went to California with my best friend, Ostin Liss (he and I live in the same apartment building, and he's one of the few people who knows about my powers), and a couple of kids from my school, Jack and Wade, to save Taylor and my mother.*

*Things didn't go so well. In the first place, Taylor was there but my mother wasn't. Then we got caught. Jack and Wade were forced to be GPs, which is short for human guinea pigs, the name the Elgen give their prisoners they experiment on. Ostin and I were locked up too, though I was put in Cell 25, the place they put people to break their minds.*

*I managed to escape and rescue my friends. I was also able to rescue four of the other electric kids: Zeus, Ian, McKenna, and Abigail. They have some pretty cool powers too. Zeus can shoot lightning bolts, which is why he's named after the Greek god. (But he can't touch water without shocking himself, so he doesn't bathe much—actually, never—so he kind of smells.)*

*Ian's blind but he can see way better than any of us. He sees the same way sharks and electric eels do, through electrolocation—which means he can see things that are miles away, even through walls.*

*McKenna can create light and heat from any part of her body.*

*Abigail can take away pain by electrically stimulating nerve endings.*

*We also rescued Grace. She was one of the electric kids who were loyal to Hatch (who calls us Glows). I don't know much about her other than that she can download things from computers and she downloaded all the information from the Elgen's mainframe before we escaped. We're hoping she has information on where the Elgen have taken my mother.*

*There are ten of us now (including our nonelectric friends Ostin, Jack, and Wade). We call ourselves the Electroclan.*

There's one more thing I would put in my autobiography, something that scares me but would make my story more interesting. I don't know for sure, but I may be dying. Hatch told me that four of the electric children have already died of cancer caused by their electricity—and I have more electricity than any of them. I don't know if it's true because Hatch is a liar. I guess time will tell. In the meanwhile we're headed back to my home in Meridian, Idaho, to figure out where my mother is and plan our next move.

Like I said, I think my story would make a pretty good movie so far. Maybe it will be one day. But not yet, because it's not even close to being over. And I have a feeling that things are about to get a whole lot wilder.

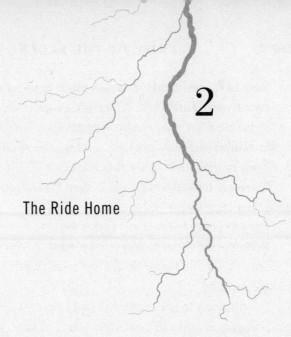

# 2

## The Ride Home

"I am so freaking dead," Ostin said, rubbing the palms of his hands on his head so hard I thought he'd leave bald patches. "My dad's going to tear off my arms and beat me to death with them."

I looked at Taylor, and she rolled her eyes. Ostin had been talking for hours about how excited he was to be home again, and it was only as we exited the highway into Meridian that it occurred to him that his parents would be angry that he'd run off without telling them.

"Relax," I said. "They'll be so happy to see you they'll forget they're mad. Besides, you've never even been grounded before."

"I've never run away from home before either."

"I'll go with you," Zeus said from the front seat. "I'll be your wingman. If it gets ugly, I'll take them down."

Ostin's eyes widened. "You can't shock my parents."

Zeus held his hands a few inches apart and arced electricity between them. "Sure I can. It's easy."

"I mean it's *not okay* to shock them."

Zeus blinked. "Why not?"

"They're *my parents*," Ostin said.

Zeus still looked confused. "Then Taylor can just reboot them until they forget who you are."

"I'm not going to do that," Taylor said.

"I don't want them to forget who I am," Ostin said.

Zeus shook his head. "Make up your mind. You want to get in trouble or not?"

"I don't want to get in trouble *and* I don't want to hurt them."

"Sometimes you can't eat your cake and have it too," Zeus said.

"Technically," Taylor said, "you can *never* eat your cake and have it too."

"I wish I had some cake," Ostin said, leaning his head against the back of the seat in front of him.


A few minutes later we passed the 7-Eleven where we'd started our journey, then turned into my apartment building's parking lot. Jack put his Camaro in neutral and turned off the engine. "We're here," he said, even though it was kind of obvious.

"Where's Wade?" I asked.

"I don't know," Jack said. "Last time I saw him was about a half hour ago."

I didn't like the sound of that. "He was supposed to stay with us."

We'd left Pasadena with Jack's car and one of the vans from the Elgen Academy, which Wade had driven with Ian, Abigail, Grace, and McKenna. Jack drove his Camaro with Taylor, Ostin, Zeus, and me.

Zeus sat up front with Jack and helped drive while the three of us crowded in the back, which, since I was next to Taylor, wasn't the worst ride of my life. Around Barstow I fell asleep against her. When I woke up she whispered to me, "That was the strangest dream."

"You had a strange dream?" I asked.

"No," she said. "You did."

It's a weird thing sitting next to someone who can read your mind. At least she never has to wonder how I feel about her.

Our plan was to drive back to Idaho and hide at my apartment while we figured out how to rescue my mother from Hatch and the Elgen. But first we needed to find out where she was. The Elgen are global, which means my mother could be anywhere in the world. *Anywhere*.

As I said, before we left Pasadena, Grace downloaded the Elgen computers. We were hoping that somewhere in all that information was my mother's whereabouts. All we needed now was a computer powerful enough to hold everything Grace had saved.

Fortunately, the Elgen didn't know where we were. At least I didn't think they did. I couldn't be certain about that either. The only thing I knew for sure was that I was going to rescue my mother—or die trying.

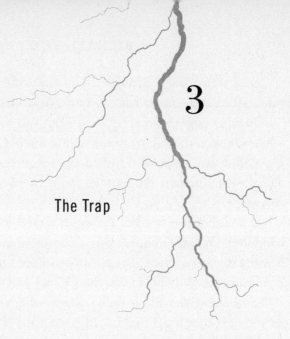

# 3

## The Trap

"I'm so dead," Ostin said again.

"We got it, Ostin," Taylor said. "Enough already."

"If they don't kill him, I might," Zeus said.

I looked at Ostin. "I'll come with you. They won't kill you if I'm there. Besides, they'll be impressed with how fit you look." Not surprisingly, Ostin had lost a few pounds in the Elgen prison.

"Yeah," Taylor said. "You're looking good."

Ostin's frown vanished. "Really? You think so?"

"The Elgen diet." Jack laughed. "Guaranteed to scare the fat away."

"Yeah," Zeus said. "Maybe you should go back and take the rest off."

Ostin frowned again.

Zeus and Jack opened their doors and got out, followed by the rest of us.

Taylor stood next to me in the parking lot. "Where do you think Wade went?"

I glanced back at the road. "I don't know. But it worries me."

Jack shook his head. "I'm going to pound him when he gets here. He knew he wasn't supposed to leave us."

"Maybe something happened," Taylor said.

"Yeah, maybe the Elgen captured them," Ostin said. "Or the van had a self-destruct mechanism."

Taylor frowned. "Or maybe they just got a flat. And besides, they have Ian with them."

With Ian aboard they were less likely to run into a trap than we were. His ability to see through solid objects had saved us more than once.

"I'm sure there's an explanation," I said, trying to sound calm. *Wait to worry*, I told myself. *Wait to worry*. I felt my face twitch. I could pretend to be calm, but stress always makes my Tourette's act up.


It was nearly fifteen minutes before Wade pulled the white Elgen van into the parking lot. He drove up next to Jack's Camaro and rolled down his window. "Hey," he said. "We're here."

Jack walked up to him and smacked him on the head.

"Ow!" Wade said. "Why'd you do that?"

"Where'd you go?" Jack asked. "You weren't supposed to leave us."

"The girls made me stop for doughnuts!"

"You wanted one too," one of the girls said from the back.

"I hope you got some for us," Ostin said.

"Sorry, man," Wade said. "We ate them all."

"They were *way* good," Abigail said.

"Thanks for sharing," Ostin said.

Everyone climbed out of the van.

"So this is Idaho," Abigail said, stretching her arms above her head. "Isn't this where they make potatoes?"

"*Grow* potatoes," Ostin said. "You don't *make* potatoes."

"You make french-fried potatoes," she replied.

Ostin shook his head.

Just then Ian said, "We're being watched."

I looked around but didn't see anyone. "Who's watching us?"

"There's a guy in the apartment building across the street with a telescope pointed right at us. I don't think he's seen us yet. He's sitting at the table eating a sandwich. But he's almost finished."

"What do we do?" Jack asked me.

"Is he alone?" I asked Ian.

"Yeah."

"Let's find out what he's doing here. Ostin, take my key and get everyone in my apartment. Taylor, Zeus, Jack, and Ian, come with me."

While Ostin, Wade, Abigail, Grace, and McKenna went to my apartment, the rest of us ran across the street. Inside the building I asked Ian, "Which apartment is he in?"

"He's on the third floor. I don't know which apartment, I'll have to look."

We quickly climbed the stairs. As we walked down the hallway, Ian commented on what he saw behind the walls, talking as if the residents could hear him. "Excuse me . . . Excuse me . . . Use a grenade jump . . . Don't eat that . . . Really, dude? Use a tissue. Oh, that's just nasty."

At apartment 314 Ian said, "There he is, he's back at his telescope. He just noticed the van. He's taking out his phone. Now he's dialing someone."

"Taylor, can you reboot him?" I asked.

"I'll try. Ian, where is he?"

Ian pointed left of the door. "Straight through there."

Taylor put her head up against the wall and concentrated.

"It worked," Ian said. "He put the phone down."

"What's he doing now?"

"He looks like he's thinking."

I tried the doorknob. "It's locked."

Ian examined the door. "Dead bolted and chained."

Zeus said, "Ring the doorbell and when he opens we'll shock him."

"There's a peephole," Taylor said. "He won't open the door with all of us standing here."

"He's dialing again," Ian said.

Taylor focused again.

"Got him," Ian said.

"You're right," I said to Taylor. "But if it's just you standing here, he'll open. Everyone against the wall."

Taylor looked at me. "What am I supposed to say when he answers?"

"You'll think of something. Just get him to open the door." I looked back. "Everyone ready?"

Jack nodded. "Bring it on."

I rang the doorbell.

A few seconds later, Ian said, "He's coming. He's got a gun."

Taylor looked at me fearfully.

"Is he holding it?" I asked.

"No," Ian said. "It's in his holster."

The peephole darkened. Then a gruff voice asked, "Who is it?"

We all looked at Taylor.

"Uh, good afternoon. I'm selling Girl Scout Cookies."

"Girl Scout Cookies?" I mouthed. Taylor shrugged.

"Not interested," the man said.

"He's leaving," Ian said.

Just then the door across the hall from us opened. An old man wearing a brown terry cloth robe scowled at us. "What are you kids up to?"

Before I could answer, Zeus zapped him. The man dropped to the ground like a bowling ball.

"You didn't have to shock him," Taylor said.

"What was I supposed to do?" Zeus said.

I put my ear to the man's chest to make sure he was okay. "His heart's still beating. Jack, help me get him back inside."

We dragged the man into his apartment, then shut the door behind us.

"The dude's back at the window," Ian said.

"Got him," Taylor said, rebooting him. She turned to me. "Let's try again. I think I've got something better this time."

I rang the doorbell.

"He's coming," Ian said.

We all leaned back against the wall.

"You're gulping," Taylor said to me.

"Sorry," I whispered.

"Who's there?" the man asked.

"Hatch sent me," Taylor said coolly.

"Who?"

"Hatch."

There was a slight pause, then the man began sliding the dead bolt. Jack leaned forward, ready to charge the door.

Suddenly the man stopped. "You're not supposed to use that name," he said. "How do I know you're with Hatch?"

Taylor swallowed. "How else would I know where you were?"

"What's the password?"

"The password?" Taylor said. She looked at me.

"Taylor," Ian whispered. "He's touching the doorknob."

"Oh," she said slowly, "the password." She grabbed the doorknob and concentrated. "It's . . . it's . . . Idaho."

There was a short, silent pause, then the man said, "All right." He finished unlocking the dead bolt. As he started to open the door, Jack rushed against it, knocking the man backward. The guy reached for his gun, but Zeus zapped him. The shock knocked Jack down as well.

"Man," Jack said, climbing to his knees. "Watch where you point that thing."

"Sorry," Zeus said.

We all scrambled inside, locking the door behind us. I knelt down next to the man. He was tall with a black mustache and beard. "Taylor, come see what they're up to."

Taylor crouched down next to me, put her hands on the man's temples, then closed her eyes. After a moment she said, "He's just the lookout. There are six Elgen guards waiting for us in one of the apartments across the street."

"Which apartment?"

"Just a minute." She touched him again. "One-seventeen."

"Are you sure?"

She nodded.

"That's not good," I said.

"What's wrong with one-seventeen?" Zeus asked.

"That's Ostin's place."

# 4

## Home, Not Home

"What do we do with him?" Taylor asked, looking down at the guard. "We can't just leave him here. If he wakes up he'll warn the others."

I took his cell phone and pulsed. The phone lit up, then burned out, a wisp of smoke rising from its keypad. "He won't be using that again," I said, tossing the phone aside.

"He can still come after us," Ian said.

"We'll tie him up," I said. "Taylor, see if you can find some rope or something."

"Ian," Taylor said. "Help me look."

"Always using the blind guy to find your stuff," Ian said.

I stayed close to the man, prepared to pulse if he suddenly roused. A couple of minutes later Taylor and Ian returned.

"Found something," Taylor said, holding up a roll of silver duct tape. "Who wants it?"

"I'll do it," Jack said, kneeling down next to me. Taylor tossed him the tape, and Jack rolled the man over onto his stomach, then pulled his arms around to his back. "Hey, Zeus, make yourself useful and hold his arms."

Zeus pinned the guy's arms to his back while Jack wound the tape around his wrists and hands until they were cocooned. When he had finished, Jack looked at me and grinned. "He's not getting out of that."

"What about his legs?" I asked.

"That's next. Lift 'em, Zeus."

Zeus lifted the man's legs as Jack wrapped the tape around them.

"Save some for his mouth," Taylor said.

"I have plenty for his mouth," Jack said. He wrapped the last of the tape around the man's head, covering his mouth and eyes.

"Don't cover his nose," Taylor said. "He'll suffocate."

"I wasn't going to," Jack said.

I looked at the man. "No way he's getting out of that."

"My brothers did that to me once," Taylor said.

"Did what?" I asked.

"Wrapped me up in duct tape like a mummy. I was only seven. When they were done they went out to play and forgot about me for like four hours. They only remembered me when my mom asked them at dinner if they knew where I was. She was furious when she found me. They got grounded for two weeks."

"I would have shocked them silly," Zeus said.

"I wish I had known how to reboot people back then," Taylor said. "I was just figuring things out."

"Michael!" Ian said. "Ostin's walking to his apartment."

"What a time to get brave," I said. "Taylor, can you stop him?"

"All the way across the street?"

"Just try," I said.

She closed her eyes.

"Nothing," Ian said.

"It's too far," Taylor said.

"You need to eat more bananas," Zeus said. "The potassium in them will strengthen your powers."

"Come on," I said. "We've got to stop him."

"What about the old man across the hall?" Taylor asked.

"We'll be long gone before he wakes up. Maybe he'll think he dreamed it."

We raced out of the building and across the street. When we entered my apartment building Ostin was still standing in front of his apartment door, getting up the nerve to walk inside. He slowly reached for the handle.

"Ostin!"

He turned and looked at me. "What?"

Taylor put her finger over her lips. "Shhh."

I motioned him over.

He looked at us quizzically, then walked toward us. "What?"

Taylor shushed him again. I pushed him into my apartment, and everyone else followed.

When we were inside, Ostin asked, "What are you doing?"

"We're saving you," Jack said.

"From my parents?"

"No," I said. "There are six guards in your apartment."

"With my parents?"

Ian shook his head. "They're not there. Not unless they're dressed like Elgen guards."

Ostin turned pale. "They took my mom and dad?"

"We don't know that," I said. "But we've got to get out of here before the guards find out we're here. Ian, what are they doing?"

"Four of them are watching television. One's in the bathroom. The other's reading."

"Is anyone near the front window?"

"The guy with the magazine is."

"Then we better go out the back."

"Wade and I will get the cars and drive them around back," Jack said. "C'mon, Wade." He opened the window and climbed out.

"We can't just leave my parents," Ostin said.

"Your parents aren't here," Ian said.

"Then we need to find out where they are!"

"How?" Zeus asked.

For the first time that I could remember, Ostin didn't have an answer. "Well, they'll know."

"The guards?" Taylor said. "Sure, let's go ask them. They'll be happy to tell us."

Ostin looked down.

I put my hand on his shoulder. "If the Elgen took them, we'll find them. But if we get caught . . ."

"I know," he said.

A moment later the cars arrived around back. Zeus and the four girls climbed out the window, followed by Ian and Ostin. After everyone was gone I looked around my apartment. In the excitement of our return I hadn't let the emotion of being back home sink in. Over the last few weeks I had honestly wondered if I'd ever see my home again. But now that I was back, it didn't feel like home. Not without my mom.

I picked up a framed photograph of the two of us from the hutch next to the kitchen counter—a picture of us on the Splash Mountain ride at Disneyland. We had gotten soaked, and my mother had bought me a new T-shirt to wear. I still had the shirt even though it didn't fit anymore. My mother had sacrificed a lot for us to go on that trip. It was less than a year after my father died, and I think she was trying to make me feel okay again. She was always worried about me. I had no doubt that even now she still was.

Would our lives ever be normal again—the way they were before I knew about Hatch and Glows and the Elgen? After what we'd been through it was hard to imagine sitting at the kitchen table while my mother made waffles and talked about normal things like school and movies: the things other people talked about.

Ostin interrupted my thoughts, leaning in through the window. "Michael. We have to go. Everyone's waiting."

"Sorry." I slid the photograph from the frame, folded it into my front pocket, then climbed out the window, pulling it shut behind me.

Ostin was still standing there. He looked scared.

"You okay?" I asked.

"They took my parents."

I put my hand on his shoulder. "If they did, we'll find them. I promise. Everything will be okay."

I didn't really know if what I'd said was true, but just saying the words helped me believe they might come true. We checked to make sure no one was watching, then ran to Jack's car.

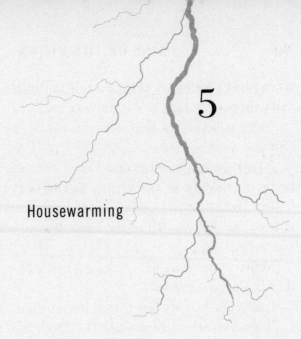

# 5

## Housewarming

"**A**ny idea where to go?" I asked Jack as I slammed the car door.

"We can go to my place," he said.

Jack's house sounded as good a place to hide as any—especially since I couldn't think of anywhere else. "Great," I said. "Your place."

"Don't mind my old man," he said. "He drinks sometimes." He rolled down his car's window, then pounded on his door to get Wade's attention. "We're going to my house."

"Got it," Wade said.

Jack drove around to the front of the building, waited for a car to pass, then pulled out into the street with Wade following closely behind.

Jack lived on the other side of Meridian High School, about two miles from my apartment. The last time I'd been to his house was when I had gone to ask him for a ride to Pasadena. I wondered how many times since then he'd regretted saying yes.

As we pulled down the road to his house, Jack suddenly shouted, "No!"

It took me a moment to understand what was wrong. But when I saw it, my heart froze. Jack's house had burned to the ground.

Jack hit the gas and sped down the street, slamming on the brakes in front of what was left of the house. He pulled his parking brake and jumped out.

At first, none of us said anything. Then Taylor said softly, "Do you think it was an accident?"

I put a hand on my face to stop my jaw from ticking. "No."

"It's no accident," Zeus said. "The Elgen love fires. It hides their tracks."

I got out of the car and walked to Jack's side. His hands were balled up in fists and his face was tight and angry. All that was left of his house were the concrete sidewalk and foundation. Even the cars in the yard had been torched. The area was cordoned off with yellow caution tape.

"I'm sure your dad got out," I said.

Jack thrust his hands deep into his pockets. "Unless he was drunk. Like he usually is."

I didn't know what to say, so finally I just settled on "I'm so sorry." My words sounded ridiculously inadequate. "This is my fault."

"Did you set fire to my house?" Jack asked.

"No. I just never should have gotten you involved."

"I made my choices," Jack said. "I'll stand by them." He turned to me. "It's not your fault; it's Hatch's. And he's gonna pay."

We stood there for another minute or so without speaking, the only sound was the whisper of a late afternoon breeze. Then I turned and walked back to the car. As I climbed in I looked back at Taylor. She was clearly frightened.

"Is he okay?" she asked.

I shook my head.

Jack returned a few minutes later. After he'd shut the door Zeus said, "Sorry, man."

Jack just grunted.

Then Taylor said, "I need to go home."

I turned to her. "If they were watching my place, Ostin's, and Jack's, you can bet they're going to be watching yours, too."

"I don't care!" she said. "I need to see my house."

"Taylor, think about it. If they capture us, your parents won't have a chance. The best thing we can do for them is be careful."

She turned away from me angrily.

"I'm sorry," I said.

After a moment she replied, "I know."

Jack started the car. Then he said, "We can drive by and see if Taylor's house is okay. If everyone stays down, they probably won't know it's us."

Taylor thought about this, then said, "Okay."

"Then we can go to my sister's place," he said. "She has a tanning salon about a mile and a half from here. She'll let us hide out." Then he said in a softer voice, "Maybe she'll know what happened to my dad." He looked back. "Any objections?"

Going by Taylor's house was risky, but she was so upset I couldn't bring myself to say no. "Let's go," I said.

Jack pulled his car around until his and Wade's windows were adjacent to each other. "Head over to my sister's tanning salon, we'll meet you there."

"Where are you going?" Wade asked. He looked as shocked as we did.

"It doesn't matter," Jack said. "Just go."

"Shouldn't we stick together?"

"No," Jack said, and rolled up his window. He turned back to Taylor. "Where do you live?"

"Behind the school," she said.

Taylor lived only a few minutes away, and none of us said a word the whole way over. As Ostin liked to say, the tension was as thick as good bacon. I knew Taylor was afraid of what she might find. *What if her house was burned down too?*

Jack turned onto her street, driving a little below the speed limit to avoid drawing attention to us. Ostin and I crouched down in the back, though I could still see out. I breathed a sigh of relief when I saw Taylor's house. Everything looked normal, though I noticed a white van with tinted windows parked at the end of the street. Taylor stared silently as we drove by.

After we had passed, Taylor said, "I think I saw my mom." There was longing in her voice. And pain. But at least she wasn't so afraid anymore.

"Seen enough?" Jack asked.

"Yes," Taylor said softly. "Thank you."

He picked up speed and headed off to his sister's tanning salon.

# 6

## Bronze Idaho and the Voice

There are people in this world you don't really picture as having a sister, like, for instance, Hitler. (However, Ostin told me that Hitler did have a sister, named Paula.) Jack was one of those people. I wondered what Jack's sister would be like and how she'd respond to us all showing up at her tanning salon. I remembered what Jack had said about her on our way to California—that she didn't really associate with the rest of his family anymore. Maybe she'd throw us out. Where would we go then? And what if Jack's father was dead?

We drove to a small strip mall and pulled into the parking space next to Wade. The sign on the building in front of us read:

**BRONZE IDAHO TANNING SALON**

A red-and-blue neon sign in the salon's front window flashed OPEN.

Wade started getting out of the van, but Jack stopped him. "You guys better stay here for a minute. I need to make sure my sister's cool."

"Okay," Wade said. "We'll keep watch."

The rest of us followed Jack through the front door. The salon's lobby was decorated in a Hawaiian motif, with amateurishly painted palm trees and hula girls on the walls and thatch covering the front counter.

The woman standing at the front desk looked up as we entered. She was a female version of Jack, though she was much smaller, maybe only an inch taller than Taylor. She had long, blond hair accented with a violet streak, and a nose ring and multiple ear piercings. Not surprisingly, she was very tan.

"Hey, sis," Jack said.

"Jack," she said, her surprise at seeing him evident in her voice. "Where have you been?" She looked at the rest of us with a confused expression, then came around the counter and hugged her brother.

After they separated, Jack said, "I just came from the house, or what's left of it. Where's Dad?"

I held my breath.

"He's staying with me until he can find an apartment," she said.

Jack's expression relaxed. I breathed out a sigh of relief.

"Where have you been?" she asked again.

"California."

"Who are these people?"

"Friends of mine," he said. "We need a place to hide out."

Her expression changed from curiosity to anger. "Hide out? What have you done?"

"Nothing," Jack said. "We haven't done anything wrong."

She looked at me and I nodded in confirmation.

"Then why are you hiding?"

"It's a long story," Jack said. "And the less you know the better. We just need a place to hang until we figure out what we're going to do."

She looked at him for a moment, then said, "Okay. But you can't stay up front. I've got a business to run. And you owe me an explanation."

Just then the front door opened and a tall, professionally dressed woman walked in. She looked around at us. "Excuse me, are you all in line?" she asked Taylor.

"No," Taylor said. "We're just visiting. We'll get out of your way."

"May I help you?" Jack's sister asked.

"Yes," she said, walking up to the counter. "Do you have a tanning bed available?"

"Yes, I do."

"Great," she said. "Do you have one a little more private—perhaps something near the back?"

"Yes. The last room has the Ultra Ruva bed. It's one of our best. Are you a member of our executive tanning club?"

"No. I'm just traveling through town."

"Very good. How long would you like me to set your session for?"

"Twenty minutes should be sufficient."

"Twenty it is." She handed the woman a key with a large key chain—a pineapple-shaped piece of plywood with the number six painted on it. "You're in room six. Just push the start button on the bed when you're ready."

"Thank you. Do you have lotion?"

"We have Coppertone and Beach Bum."

"Coppertone will be fine," the woman replied. She suddenly turned and looked at me, her gaze lingering a little longer than was comfortable. I twitched a couple of times.

"Here you go," Jack's sister said, handing her a bottle of lotion. "Cash or credit?"

"Cash. How much is it?"

"With the lotion it's twenty-nine dollars."

The woman handed her a couple of bills. "Keep the change," she said, stepping away from the counter. As she walked past me she dropped her cell phone on the ground near my feet. "Oh, I'm sorry," she said.

"No problem." I bent over and picked it up. "Here you go."

She made no effort to take the phone from me. "That's not mine."

I looked at her quizzically. "But, you just . . ."

"I believe it's yours, Michael." She looked right into my eyes, then handed me the tanning room key along with two other keys. "Take these into the room. Someone needs to talk to you."

My chest constricted. "Are you with Hatch?"

She touched her finger to her lips to silence me. "Room six," she said. "Turn on the tanning bed. I'll watch the door." She patted her jacket, making me think she was carrying a gun. I looked over at the others. No one was paying attention to me except Ostin. I could tell he was trying to figure out what was going on.

"Hurry," she said. "We haven't much time."

I looked back into her eyes. Something about her seemed trust-worthy. "Okay," I said.

"Room six. Don't forget to turn on the bed when you get inside."

I walked back to the room and stepped inside, shutting the door behind me. I turned on the tanning bed and the sound of the machine filled the room. The phone she had given me rang immediately. I raised it to my ear. "Hello?"

"Hello, Michael. Are you alone?" The man's voice was deep and grave.

"Who is this?"

"One of the few people in this world who knows what you're up against. They're following everything you're doing."

"Who is?"

"You know who. We don't have much time. If we can find you, so can they. Now listen to what I say and follow my directions precisely. You have to leave immediately. As soon as you get in your car I'll text you an address. Drive directly to that location and abandon your vehicles. The Elgen van you borrowed has a tracking device, and I'm sure that by now they've identified your friend's Camaro."

"How do you know this?"

"I haven't time to explain," the voice said.

"How do I know this isn't another trap?"

"You don't. But think about it, if we wanted to capture you, we would have just done it. The building you're in right now is a death trap. It only has two exits, the front glass door and a back door that leads to a narrow alley. You're sitting ducks. You have to trust me. If you want to escape the Elgen, you're going to need our help."

"Why would you help us?"

"We have our reasons. And we know even better than you what the Elgen are planning and what they're capable of. The Elgen are rising. You should also know that there are more electric children. And they have terrible powers—worse than anyone you've met so far."

"Great," I said.

"You can defeat them, Michael. You might not be strong enough to face them today, but by the time you do, and trust me, you will, you'll be ready. But you'll need to act quickly to stop them."

"But we did stop them. We shut down the academy."

"They were going to close it anyway—you just sped up their timetable. I wish we had more time, but that's a luxury neither of us has, so try to understand what I'm saying. Now is the opportune moment to strike. The Elgen are divided. To most of its board members, it is just a business. To Hatch, and a few others, it's more. Much more. They're building a secret society, and they're growing fast. They've made inroads in government, police, and military. If you don't believe me, check the state records to see what happened to the man who robbed your mother."

"What happened to him?"

"He's not a worry to the Elgen anymore."

"How do I know you're not one of them?"

"Like I said, you're going to have to trust a little. I won't ask more of you than that."

"If we ditch our cars, how will we get around?"

"Where you leave your cars, there will be two other vehicles. My associate gave you the keys."

I looked down at the keys in my hand.

"I've programmed the address of a safe house into the GPS system of the yellow vehicle. Go there and wait for my call. But you must leave now. The police are already on their way to the salon."

"The police? Why?"

"To arrest you for burning down Jack's house."

# 7

## Hummers

The phone went dead as the man hung up. I put it in my front pocket and walked quickly out of the room. Apparently Jack's sister hadn't made everyone go to the back, because they were all still in the lobby. The strange woman was gone.

I walked up to Jack, who was talking to his sister. "We've got to go," I said. "Fast. The police are on their way."

"How do you know that?" he asked.

I looked at the others, who were now all looking at me. "I just do."

"Who was that lady?" Ostin asked. It was the first thing he'd said since we'd left the apartment.

"I'll tell you in the car," I said. "We've got to hurry."

"Why don't we just wait for the police?" Taylor said. "They'll help us."

"No. They're coming to arrest us."

"Arrest us for what?" Ostin asked.

"We stole a van, Einstein," Jack said.

"It's worse," I said. "Someone told them that I burned down your house."

Jack frowned. "We've got to get out of here."

"You stole a car?" Jack's sister asked angrily. "You said you didn't do anything."

"We borrowed it," Zeus said. "And they owed us big-time."

She looked flustered. "What's going on, Jack? Why are the police coming?"

"I can't tell you right now. Just tell them that you don't know anything."

"I don't," she said.

"Good. It's better that way." He looked at her sadly. "We've gotta run. I'll explain when I can."

"C'mon, everyone," I said. "To the car."

When we were in the Camaro, Jack asked, "Now what?"

"I have an address," I said. I picked up the phone, but it was out of power. "I can't believe it, it's dead. It was perfectly fine a minute ago."

"Let me see it," Ostin said. He took the phone from me and examined it. "You just need to hold it."

"I was."

"Put out your hand," he said. He handed me the phone and this time it lit up.

"You were holding it wrong. See these metallic strips on the side? They're made of a silver alloy. The phone is designed to run off your electricity. That way it never runs out."

"And it won't work for anyone else," I said. I looked down at the address the man had texted me. "Thirty-eight South Malvern Avenue."

"I know that area," Jack said. "It's an industrial park. There are a lot of printing shops." Jack shouted to Wade, "Follow me!" Then he backed up and screeched out of the parking lot, followed by Wade, who also tried to screech but managed only a small chirp.

After we'd driven a few blocks, Taylor asked, "What's going on, Michael? And who was that woman?"

"I don't know who she was. But she knows who we are and who's chasing us."

"She knew about the Elgen?" Ostin asked.

I nodded. "She gave me the phone. A man called who says he's going to help us. He also told me that the van Wade's driving has a tracking device. That's how they've been following us. We need to ditch our cars."

"Wait a minute," Jack said. "No one said anything about ditching my car."

"Who is this man?" Taylor asked.

"Just . . . some man." I looked at her. "I know it sounds stupid, but I believe he's trying to help."

"I'm not ditching my car," Jack said.

"How do you know you can trust him?" Taylor asked.

"I don't. But do we have a choice?"

"Yes," she said, "we do."

I took her hand. "Here, read my mind. Listen to what he said."

She closed her eyes as I thought back on the call. When she opened her eyes she nodded. "Okay. I trust him too."

Jack was still upset. "You're saying that some dude I've never met wants me to ditch my car? I'm not ditching my car."

"They want us to *trade* cars."

"That's not going to happen," he said. "Do you know what this baby is worth?"

"The Elgen are following your car. They can either capture you and the car, or just the car. It's your call."

Jack shook his head. "This just keeps getting better."

We had driven about a half mile from the salon when two Meridian Police cars sped past us headed in the opposite direction. Their lights were flashing but there were no sirens.

"There they go," Jack said. "Looks like your man knows something."

"Maybe he's the one who called the police," Ostin said.

*Possible*, I thought.

The address on my cell phone led us to an abandoned industrial area near an automotive wrecking yard. I was nervous and twitching. I'm pretty certain everyone was nervous, because no one was talking. I looked over at Jack. His face was tight and his eyes were darting back and forth, searching for danger. The yard was surrounded by a tall fence topped with razor wire, and the sun had nearly set, leaving the yard dark.

"I don't like this place," Taylor said.

"Not a lot of escape options," Jack said slowly. "Keep your eyes peeled."

There was a loud snap of electricity from Zeus, and we all jumped. "Sorry," he said. "Just keeping sharp."

I did my best to control my tics. "I told Ian to have Wade honk if he sees anything that looks like a trap," I said.

We slowly drove around the corner of a weathered, aluminum-sided warehouse. There, next to a Dumpster, were two brand-new Hummers, one yellow, the other black.

Jack's expression changed when he saw the vehicles. "That's what they're giving us to drive?"

"Must be," I said. "I don't see any other cars."

"I've changed my mind," he said. "I'll trade."

We pulled up to the parked vehicles, and everyone got out of the cars.

"Are we safe?" I asked Ian.

"As far as I can tell. The only person around is a homeless guy sleeping in a Dumpster behind the building across the street."

I handed Wade a key. "You take the black Hummer. Follow us."

"Where are we going?" Wade asked.

"A safe house," I said.

"Are you sure it's safe?"

"I'm not sure about anything," I said, "except that the Elgen are hunting us and we just got some new cars."

Wade nodded. "Works for me."

"We're trading places," I said to Zeus, climbing into the front seat of the yellow Hummer.

"No problem," he said. "I'll sit next to Tara."

"Taylor," Taylor said.

"Sorry," Zeus said, sliding in next to her. "I keep confusing you with your evil twin."

"Well, you were with her a lot longer than you were with me."

Jack was in the driver's seat checking out the console. I handed him the key.

"Listen to that," he said, starting it up. "I've always wanted to drive one of these bad boys. My brother drove one in Iraq."

"Cool," I said.

"It was blown up underneath him by an IED."

"Not cool," I said.

"He survived, so it's even more cool. Where to?"

"The man said they programmed an address into the GPS system." I looked at the device. "I have no idea how this works. Ostin?"

Ostin leaned forward over the seat. He pushed a few buttons and a map appeared. "There are your coordinates," he said. "Just follow the arrow."

"Thanks," I said. "You good, Jack?"

Jack put the Hummer in gear. "I'm good."

As we pulled back out onto the street, Jack turned to me and said, "Hope it's not a trap."

I leaned back in my seat. "Me too," I said softly. "Me too."

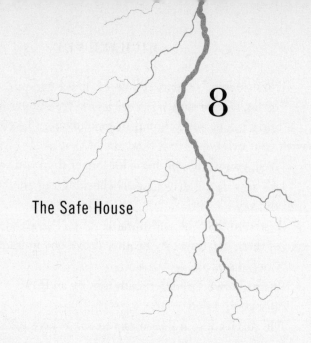

# 8

## The Safe House

According to the GPS our next destination was 7.3 miles from where we had picked up the cars, a distance we covered in less than fifteen minutes. The safe house was a small, ordinary-looking brick home in an ordinary suburban neighborhood. The yard was manicured enough not to warrant complaints, but simple enough not to warrant attention. The house was dark except for the front porch light.

Jack pulled into the cement driveway on the west side of the house. The drive was narrow but widened in back at the entrance of a two-car garage.

"I'll wait to pull in," Jack said. "In case we need to make a quick getaway."

"Good idea," I said, trying not to sound nervous. I realized that part of me was waiting for the worst to happen and I was ticking like crazy.

Wade pulled the black Hummer up next to us. In spite of our situation, he was grinning from ear to ear. "This baby is sweet," he said. "I never thought I'd get to ride in one of these, let alone drive one."

"I'm going to check things out," I said to Jack. "If it's a trap, just get everyone out of here."

"Warriors don't leave a man behind," Jack said.

"What are we doing?" Wade asked.

"Just keep your car running until we're sure it's safe," I said. I turned to Ian. "Can you give me a hand?"

"Sure, man. I'll give you both of them."

"It's your eyes I need."

"I'll give you both of those, too."

The two of us got out of the cars and walked to the edge of the driveway, looking cautiously at the dark house.

"What do you think?" I asked.

"It's empty," Ian said. He looked around at the neighbors. "Neighborhood looks legit. A mom helping a kid with homework, a family watching TV, a couple eating dinner."

"All right, let's go in." I rapped on the Hummer, and Jack pulled into the garage, followed by Wade. Everyone gathered in the driveway.

Taylor came up to my side. "You okay?"

"Yeah. Why?"

"You're ticking a lot."

"I'm nervous."

"But the house is okay?"

"It checked out with Ian."

We walked up to the back of the house, but as I reached for the storm door Ostin said, "Stop!"

I looked over at him.

"What if the door's booby-trapped? I saw this show where the bad guys had rigged all the doors with plastic explosives, so when the cops opened the door—ka-boom!" Ostin threw his arms out in demonstration. "Everyone's dead."

We all just looked at him.

Ostin shrugged. "It was a cool show."

"I'll open the door," Zeus said. He twisted the doorknob and pushed the door open, then stepped inside the dark house. "Hey, McKenna, how about a hand?"

"Sure." She lit up her hand, then stepped into the house behind him.

"There's the switch," Zeus said.

Taylor and I walked in, followed by everyone else. Jack was the last to enter. He still looked anxious and glanced around before shutting and locking the door.

The home's interior was as ordinary looking as its exterior, which, I suppose, is what a safe house is supposed to look like. I mean, if the place stands out like a zit on your nose, it's not going to be very safe, right?

We were standing in the kitchen. On the counter was a bulky, brown envelope, and I picked it up and pulled back its flap. It was filled with money.

"Check this out," I said, holding up the cash. "They left us money."

"That's some serious coinage," Jack said.

"I'll count it," Taylor said, taking the envelope from me. She riffled through the bills. "Ten grand," she said. "Even."

"That was fast," I said.

"I'm good at counting."

I took a handful of bills and put them in my pocket, leaving the rest on the counter.

From the front room Ostin shouted, "Michael, check this out! This is one sweet computer."

I walked into the other room. I was no expert on computers—I left that to Ostin—but it looked like a serious piece of technology. "Can we use it to get the data out of Grace?" I asked.

"I'm on it," he replied.

I was glad he had found something to distract him from his parents.

"Is there anything to eat?" Taylor asked. "I'm really hungry."

"Me too," Abigail said.

I opened the fridge. It was empty. "Nada."

"We passed a pizza place about a half mile back," Jack said. "Wade and I could go pick up something. What kind of pizza do you guys want?"

"Pepperoni and anchovies," Wade said.

"No anchovies," Taylor said. "They stink."

"I second that," Ostin said. "Who eats anchovies on pizza?"

"Only about a billion Italians," Wade replied. "And they're the ones who invented pizza, so they should know how to eat them."

Getting a history lesson from Wade, especially about food, was more than Ostin could stomach. "In the first place," Ostin said, standing, "no one knows who invented pizza. In the sixth century, Persian soldiers baked bread flat on their shields and covered it with cheese and dates. So you could argue that they did. Secondly, there are not a billion Italians in the world, not even a hundred million. In Italy there are—"

"Agh!" Wade shouted. "Will someone shove something into his mouth to shut him up?"

"Pizza would do nicely," Ostin said. "Without anchovies."

"Just get a bunch of different kinds," I said to Jack. "There are ten of us. How about three large?"

"I'll get some drinks, too," Jack said. "Everyone's good with cola?"

"I want lemonade," Taylor said.

"Me too," said Abigail.

"Diet cola," McKenna said.

"Write that down," Jack said to Wade.

Wade looked around. "With what?"

"Then remember it," Jack said. "All right, I'll be back. But not too soon. I need to test out the Hummer."

"Can I come?" Abigail asked.

Jack looked pleasantly surprised. "Sure."

"Thanks."

Taylor looked at me and grinned. Jack had told us earlier that he thought Abigail was hot.

"Wade," Jack said, "you don't need to come anymore."

"What?"

"Abi and I can handle it. Just chill here with everyone else."

"He can come," Abigail said.

"No," Jack said. "He doesn't want to." He looked at Wade with a threatening glare. "Do you?"

Wade frowned. "Nah, I'll just chill."

"Let's go," Jack said, opening the door.

"Okay, we'll be right back," Abigail said.

After they left I said, "C'mon, Ostin. Let's start uploading." I looked at Grace. "Are you okay with that?"

She nodded. "That's what I do."

Ostin powered up the computer, then turned to Grace. "So how do you transfer data?"

"First I need to touch a metal part on the computer." She glanced back at us. "I should sit down. Bringing it up is hard."

"Hard?" Taylor asked. "In what way?"

"I guess it's sort of like vomiting," Grace said.

"Oh," Taylor said.

Grace put both hands on the computer and began concentrating. Suddenly her eyes rolled back in her head and she began trembling.

"Holy cannoli," Ostin said. "Look at that."

Files suddenly began filling the screen. Grace continued until a screen popped up that said MEMORY FULL. She groaned, slumping forward.

"You okay?" Taylor asked, taking her by the arm.

She nodded. "Yeah. It just hurt a little."

"Wow. You filled the computer," Ostin said. "It has a terabyte of storage. You must have downloaded most of their mainframe." He looked at me. "We need a bigger computer."

"We got a lot of it, though, didn't we?" I asked.

Ostin nodded. "We got a boatload. Let's see if we can find your mom." He lifted his hands above the keyboard as if he were a pianist about to start a performance. He typed my mother's name into the computer's find function.

I held my breath. Taylor took my hand as we waited. A screen came up.

NO MATCHING FILES

My heart fell.

"I'll try 'prisoners,'" Ostin said.

NO MATCHING FILES

"Maybe they use a different word," I said. "Is there a GP file?"

"Let's see."

Ostin typed in "GP." About two dozen folders came up. "This one has the most information, let's see what's inside." He clicked on it. "Holy cow," he said. "Look at that."

There were thousands of records with names and mug-shot-type photographs.

"What are those numbers?" I asked, pointing to a series of numbers that appeared beneath each record.

Ostin glanced through the numbers looking for a pattern. "I'm guessing the first is the GP's serial number, like they give convicts in prisons. The second, based on the recurring sequence, appears to be a date, probably when they were admitted. I know how to verify that." He typed in a number. A picture of a terrified Wade appeared on the screen. "Yep. It's the day admitted. The third . . ." He hesitated, slowly rubbing his hand over his forehead. "Hmm. The list is sorted by the serial numbers, but you'll notice the last numbers seem to show up in clumped sequences. I'm betting it's where they're being held—they're just using a number instead of a location."

"That's not going to help us," Taylor said.

"On the contrary," Ostin replied. "It will tell us how many Elgen facilities there are."

"What's that?" I said, pointing to a folder that read:

CONFIDENTIAL MEMOS: STARXOURCE PLANTS

"No idea," Ostin said. He clicked on the folder.

*MEMO*

*Mr. Chairman,*

*Please find requested report of Starxource development. Note: All countries with populations of fewer than 15,000 are deemed irrelevant unless there are recognizable political ties that may allow us future development in larger economies; i.e., Saint Barths—France. (Grid Infrastructure development will be detailed in alternative report.)*

**Beta Control Countries**

| | |
|---|---|
| *Anguilla* | *(Starxource Functioning 100%)* |
| *Christmas Island* | *(Starxource Functioning 100%)* |
| *Cook Islands* | *(Starxource Aborted)* |
| *Falkland Islands* | *(Starxource Functioning 96%)* |
| *Saint Barths* | *(Starxource Functioning 96%)* |

**Operational Starxource Plants/
Combined Populations:**                    **115,597,166**

| | |
|---|---|
| *Palau* | *21,000* |
| *British Virgin Islands* | *28,213* |
| *Gibraltar* | *29,441* |
| *Monaco* | *35,881* |

| | |
|---|---|
| Saint Martin | 36,824 |
| Cayman Islands | 54,878 |
| Greenland | 56,890 |
| Bermuda | 64,237 |
| Dominica | 71,685 |
| Jersey | 97,857 |
| Aruba | 101,484 |
| Tonga | 103,036 |
| Grenada | 110,821 |
| Samoa | 184,032 |
| Finland | 5,405,590 |
| Zimbabwe | 12,754,000 |
| Taiwan | 23,200,000 |
| Peru | 29,797,694 |
| Tanzania | 43,443,603 |

**Plants Under Construction (PUC)/**
**Combined Populations:** **32,623,410**

| | |
|---|---|
| Portugal | 10,561,614 |
| Greece | 10,787,690 |
| Chad | 11,274,106 |

| Under Negotiation/Combined Populations: | 1,010,135,758 |
|---|---|
| Poland | 38,092,000 |
| Sudan | 45,047,502 |
| Spain | 46,196,278 |
| South Korea | 48,750,000 |
| Italy | 60,600,000 |
| France | 65,073,482 |
| Philippines* | 94,000,000 |
| Pakistan | 187,000,000+ |
| Brazil* | 192,376,496 |
| India* | 233,000,000 |

**\*Top 10 Populous Countries**

*Within 24 months we will be providing power to 19.89% of countries comprising 46% of the world's population. The current global economic stagnation provides an ideal political and socioeconomic environment to allow our entrance into these countries that might otherwise be wary of our global growth and Elgen control. It is our estimation that within 48 months we will control the energy and, subsequently, the economies of 78% of the world's population.*

*Dr. C. J. Hatch*

"It's from Hatch!" Ostin said.

"It sounds like he's talking about global conquest," Taylor said.

Ostin clicked on another folder. "Check this out." He pulled up a video screen that showed a large logo.

"It's a news story about the Elgen," he said.

"Run the video," I said.

**Energy Solutions *today* for a *brighter* tomorrow**

Ostin clicked the play button and an attractive, professionally dressed woman with a British accent began speaking:

REPORTER: *In global news, Elgen Inc., an international energy conglomerate, has announced a new source of cheap, renewable energy. Elgen's Starxource power plants promise to "light up the globe" by delivering economical, renewable, and environmentally friendly power to the world.*

The video cut to a shot of Dr. Hatch.

"Die, you pig!" Ostin shouted.

"Quiet," Taylor said.

REPORTER: *Dr. C. J. Hatch, CEO of Elgen Inc., told reporters that the Starxource project would revolutionize the world in more ways than just affordable power bills.*

The audio came up on Hatch.

HATCH: *Currently more than twenty-five percent of the world's population lives without electrical power. It is Elgen Inc.'s goal to remedy this problem within our lifetime. The benefits of our Starxource plants are innumerable, as will be the relief of human suffering . . .*

"Human suffering," Ostin said bitterly. "The man invented it."
"Shh," Taylor said.

HATCH: *. . . and other sociopolitical factors, such as freeing children in underdeveloped countries from gathering wood and fuel all day, so they can attend school.*

REPORTER: *The technology behind your Starxource plants is more confidential than the formula for Coca-Cola, but rumors are that you have created sustainable cold fusion.*

HATCH: *The process we've developed might best be compared to cold fusion; however, there is no environmental backlash. Starxource plants create no nuclear waste, and there is no danger of a nuclear core meltdown like that experienced in Chernobyl or during the Fukushima Daiichi nuclear disaster.*

REPORTER: *When will the first Starxource plants begin operating?*

HATCH (smiling): *They already are. Elgen Inc. has been operating mini–power plants in developing countries for more than three years now, and the benefits to the local communities have far surpassed our greatest hopes. We are now preparing to operate in more populated countries.*

REPORTER: *Tesla, Edison, and now Dr. C. J. Hatch. Clean, cheap,*

*and renewable energy from Elgen Inc. Finally, some good news for a*
*change. I'm Devina Sawyers. Back to you, Mark and Carole.*

After the video ended we all sat quietly.

"Hatch said the Elgen were going to control the world," I said. "If they control the world's power, they control the world, don't they?"

"But it doesn't make sense," Ostin said.

"What doesn't?" Taylor asked.

"Cold fusion's not their bag. The Elgen scientists are biologists, not physicists. It doesn't make sense that they would invent or discover something outside their field of research. It would be like a pizza chain building cars."

Taylor pointed to a folder next to the one Ostin had just opened: ER Protocol. "What's that?"

Ostin looked at it. "ER . . . Emergency room protocol?" Ostin clicked on the file.

MEMO

*Dr. Hatch,*

*Due to your recent report of the likelihood of additional ER21 escapes, the board wants to know what protocol has been initiated in order to deal with a potential outbreak. There is concern that due to the organisms' short gestation periods, an epidemic of ER could quickly spread near one of our Starxource plants, jeopardizing our control. Do the ER20 and ER21 propagate outside the controlled environs, and if so, for how many generations? We have reviewed the press coverage you enclosed concerning the recent ER outbreak near our Puerto Maldonado plant. What is our status to date?*

"What's an ER21?" Taylor asked.

"Never heard of it," Ostin said. "It sounds like a virus, which is something the Elgen would do. But what does that have to do with a power plant?" He turned to Grace. "Do you know?"

Grace shook her head. "I've never heard of it."

We continued reading the chain.

*MEMO*

*Mr. Chairman,*

*The outbreaks of ER20 and, more specifically, ER21 in Puerto Maldonado have been contained. It was fortunate for us that this outbreak occurred during the rainy season, as the ER cannot withstand the direct application of water due to the specimen's biological mutations.*

*Dr. C. J. Hatch*

*MEMO*

*Dr. Hatch,*

*How can you be certain of the successful containment of the ER20/ER21?*

*MEMO*

*Mr. Chairman,*

*We have developed sophisticated el-readers for detecting ER20/ER21 over large areas. Also, the properties of the living ER20/ER21 make them highly visible in darkness.*

*Dr. C. J. Hatch*

MEMO

*Dr. Hatch,*

*Fortunate as it may be that the Puerto Maldonado situation has been contained, it is of concern to us that it was only by "fortune" that a near catastrophic situation was mitigated. Please respond to our initial inquiry. Do the ER20 and ER21 propagate outside the controlled environs, and if so, for how many generations?*


MEMO

*Mr. Chairman,*

*In regard to your inquiry about ER reproduction outside of captivity, the ER20/ER21 do, in fact, propagate the genetic mutation that is developmentally favorable for the rapid production and operation of Starxource plants. However, scientists at our Kaohsiung, Taiwan, plant have developed an ingenious solution. We have genetically altered the next phase, ER22, with a 92% iodine deficiency, far less than is available in any natural environment. The ER will die within 72 hours without the supplements we provide. Our beta test of ER22 in the Aruba, Puerto Maldonado, and Taiwanese plants has proven successful, and we will be neutralizing all ER21 as soon as we can replace them with the ER22, as not to disrupt our current power production and potentially damage our grids in those regions.*


MEMO

*Dr. Hatch,*

*Due to the short gestation period of the specimen, is it possible that some ER could survive longer than 72 hours and reproduce?*

*MEMO*

*Mr. Chairman,*

*In response to your recent inquiry, the answer is no. It is not possible.*

"Any idea what that's all about?" I asked.

Ostin shrugged. "I need to do a little detective work. The memo said this ER escape made the news. We've got a date here and a general location." He looked at me. "This might take a little while."

"Then I'm going to take a nap," I said. "Wake me if you find something."

"Will do," Ostin said.

I walked out of the front room to find a bedroom.

Taylor followed me out. "Michael. Can we talk?"

"Sure. Let's go in here."

We walked into a bedroom. I sat at the foot of the bed and Taylor sat cross-legged on the floor.

"You okay?" I asked.

"Yeah." She looked down at her hands. "How long are we going to stay here?"

"I don't know. The man didn't say."

"Can you call him?"

"I don't know." I lifted the phone from my pocket, and it immediately lit up. For the first time I noticed that it didn't even have a keypad. "It's not designed to dial out—only to receive." I looked over at her. "Are you sure you're okay?"

"No," she said. She lowered her head into her hands, her coffee-brown hair falling in front of her like a veil. "All of this is my fault. And now Ostin's parents are gone, and Jack's house is burned down. If I hadn't looked for the Elgen online . . ."

I sat down next to her on the floor. "Taylor, you can't keep doing this to yourself. You've seen how high-tech the Elgen are. It was just a matter of time before they found us."

"What if they take my family?"

"Then we'll rescue them," I said. "Just like we're going to rescue my mother."

She looked at me, forcing a smile. "Thank you. I'm glad . . ."

I waited for her to finish but she didn't. "You're glad . . . what?"

"Can't you read my mind?" she asked sadly. "You could before."

"There's got to be a lot of electricity between us," I said.

She looked into my eyes. "And there's not?"

I smiled, restraining my impulse to tic. "That's a different kind."

She put her arms around my neck and laid her head on my shoulder. "What I was going to say was, I'm glad I have you for my boyfriend."

"Me too," I said. "Sometimes I have to pinch myself."

She pinched my arm and smiled. "You're so cute."

We sat there for several minutes, and my thoughts drifted to something I'd been hiding since my first meeting with Hatch. I forgot Taylor could read my mind.

She jerked back, her eyes wide. "Why are you thinking that?"

"Thinking what?"

"You know *what*. About dying."

"It's nothing," I said.

"Dying isn't *nothing*. It's a very big *something*."

"Why were you listening to my thoughts?"

"It just happens. Sometimes I don't even know I'm doing it." She squeezed my hand. "Why were you thinking that?"

"It's just something Hatch said. I don't know if it's even true. . . ."

"What did he tell you?"

"He said four of the other kids have already died from cancer caused by our electricity, and I have more electricity than they did." I looked into her eyes. "He said I might be dying."

Taylor looked as if she didn't know how to respond. "Was he lying?"

"I don't know. You know him better than I do."

Her eyes started to well up with tears. "You can't die, Michael."

"Believe me, it's not something I'm trying to do," I said.

She put her head back on my shoulder, and I held her for several minutes until Ostin barged into the room. "Hey, guys. You'll never guess what I just discovered." He stopped and looked at us. "What's going on?"

Taylor sat up, pulling her hair back from her face. "Nothing," she said, her eyes still red.

"What did you discover?" I asked.

He looked back and forth between us, then said, "I figured out what the ER20 and ER21 are. Dudes, you're never going to believe it."

# 9

## ER20 and ER21

Taylor held my hand as we followed Ostin back into the front room. Everyone was gathered around the computer.

Wade was sitting in a beanbag chair, still looking angry that Jack had left him. "C'mon, already," he said. "What's the big announcement? What's an ER?"

One thing I know about Ostin is that it's impossible for him to just tell you the solution to a problem—he has to tell you *how* he solved the problem. It's annoying sometimes—actually, it's annoying all the time—but I'm pretty sure he can't help it.

Ostin's face was pink with excitement. "So I started searching for ER, ER20, ER21, ER22, but it just led to that old TV series and other stuff. Then I searched the location mentioned in the memo: Puerto Maldonado.

"Puerto Maldonado is a Peruvian city in the Amazon jungle near

Cuzco. The memo said that the outbreak occurred during the rainy season, which is between November and March, so I started to scan through their local newspaper for anything unusual. Look what I found." He clicked a link and an article appeared on the screen. The headline read:

Las Ratas Abrasadoras Destruyen El Pueblo

"Isn't that crazy!" Ostin said.

I looked at him blankly. "What language is that, Spanish?"

"Yeah, unbelievable, isn't it?"

"I wouldn't know; I don't speak Spanish."

"Oh, sorry," Ostin said. "I forgot."

Ostin was born in Austin, Texas (hence his name), where he had a Mexican nanny. Average human babies pick up second languages remarkably fast, but with Ostin's IQ, I'm sure he was reciting Shakespeare in Spanish by the time he was five.

"*Las ratas abrasadoras* is Spanish for 'fiery rats.'"

"What's a fiery rat?" Taylor asked.

"Exactly," Ostin said. "There's no such thing." His voice lowered. "Or is there?" He sounded ridiculously dramatic, like the host of some UFO show on the Discovery Channel. "Check this out," he said, scrolling down the screen. "According to this article, there was a plague of rats in Peru that nearly wiped out a small village. The town's mayor said that the rats started fires everywhere they went."

"What were they doing?" McKenna asked. "Smoking?"

Ostin didn't catch that she was joking. "No, I think they do it the same way you do. Or, at least, Michael and Zeus."

"They're electric?" I asked.

Ostin touched his finger to his nose. "Bingo. One eyewitness said that these rats glowed at night, like they were on fire. And when he tried to kill one with a crowbar, he said '*me dio una descarga como anguila eléctrica.*'"

"Translate," I said.

"It shocked him like an electric eel."

"Like an electric eel?" Ian repeated. "They've discovered a new breed of rat?"

"No," I said. "The Elgen have *made* a new breed of rat. They've electrified rats."

"It makes perfect sense," Ostin said. "They're having trouble creating more electric kids, but they've learned how to make electric rodents."

"Why would they do that?" Taylor asked.

"It was probably just an accident at first," Ostin replied. "I mean, we test everything on rats, right? Drugs, cosmetics, shampoo. Makes sense they were testing rats in the MEI. Voila, electric rats."

"Whoa," I said.

"Yeah, but what are they good for?" Taylor asked.

"That was my next question," Ostin said. "So I scanned the Internet for any other stories about fiery or electric rats. I came up with mentions in Saint Barths, the Cook Islands, and Anguilla." He looked at me, grinning. "Sound familiar?"

"No," I said.

"Remember what we read earlier? That's where the Elgen have built their Starxource plants."

It took me a moment to make the connection. "You mean their power plants are rat powered?"

Ostin was so excited he almost jumped up from his chair. "Exactly!"

"Why rats?" Taylor asked.

"Why not!" Ostin exclaimed. "They're perfect! The problem with most of our current energy sources is what?"

"They're expensive," Taylor said, turning to me. "My dad's always complaining about how much it costs when I leave lights on."

"Yes, but more importantly, they're exhaustible. They're limited. You can't make more oil, unless you can wait around a few hundred million years. Once it's gone, it's gone. The big search is for renewable energy, and the Elgen found it. Actually, they made it. Rats are super-renewable. They're practically breeding machines!

Think about it. Rats are mature at five weeks, their gestation period is just three weeks, and the average litter is eight to ten babies. If you started with just two rats and they had an average of ten offspring every three weeks, then they had babies, and so on, in one year you could have . . ." He did the math in his head. "Holy rodent. Under ideal circumstances and lacking natural predators, like in a laboratory, you could breed *billions* of rats in one year."

"That's crazy," McKenna said.

"And if each one of those rats could generate even a tenth the electricity that one of us does . . . ," I said.

"You could power entire cities," Ostin said. "Enough rats, you could power the entire world."

I shook my head. "They're making rat power. The Elgen are making *rat* power. That's why they're afraid of them escaping. If they breed, anyone could use them."

"They could also be like those killer bees that escaped from South America," McKenna said.

"You mean the band?" Wade asked.

"What band?" McKenna said.

"The Killer Bees."

McKenna shook her head. "I'm not talking about some stupid band."

"She means Africanized bees," Ostin said. "In the fifties some scientists took African bees to Brazil to create a better honeybee, but the African bees escaped and starting breeding with local—"

"Good job, Ostin," I said, cutting him off. "You did it."

"Thanks," he said proudly. "It's amazing, they're creating these power plants and no one knows how they're doing it, but the answer is right in front of them. Apparently the Elgen have a sense of humor after all."

"What do you mean?" I asked.

"The name of their plants . . . Starxource. It makes their power plants sound like they run off thermonuclear fusion, since that's where stars get their energy from." He turned around and looked at me. "But 'star' is just 'rats' spelled backward."

# 10

An Unplanned Visit

Rat power. In a bizarre way it made sense. Like my mother was fond of saying, "whatever works." The ramifications of this discovery made sense as well. If the world became dependent on Elgen energy, the Elgen would control the world.

"Man, all this thinking has made me hungry," Ostin said. "Where's the pizza?" I was glad to see he had his appetite back. He looked at the clock on the wall. "What's taking them so long?"

"They're probably kissing," Wade said, still bitter about being left behind.

"Hey, wait a minute," Ian said. "Both Hummers are in the driveway. But they're not in them." His expression fell. "Oh no."

Just then something crashed through the home's front window. Before we could see what it was, there were two loud explosions, and the room was filled with an overpowering stench. My eyes watered and I covered my nose and mouth with my hand and yelled for everyone to run.

Suddenly the door burst open, and a man shouted, "Everyone on the ground. Put your hands in front of you. Do it! Do it now!" He ran inside the front room, flanked by two other guards.

Zeus was the first to react. He extended his hands and blasted the man standing in the doorway, knocking him back against the wall. But before Zeus could hit anyone else, two darts struck him in the side. Zeus cried out and fell to the ground, screaming and writhing in pain. The darts were peculiar looking, fat like a cigar, tapered at one end, and yellow with red stripes.

Elgen guards poured into the room through the front and back doors, shouting as they entered. They were wearing black rubberized jumpsuits with helmets, masks, and gloves, which made them look more like machines than humans. Each of them carried a chrome weapon I'd never seen before. It looked like a handgun, only broader and without the barrel.

I pulsed while Taylor was trying to reboot the guards, but neither of us seemed to have any effect on them. Darts hit us almost simultaneously, one in her chest and one in her knee, and three on me, two hitting me in the side, the third just below my collarbone. We both collapsed, as if our bones had suddenly turned to rubber. The experience was similar to what we felt when Nichelle, one of Hatch's electric kids, would use her powers to drain the electricity out of us. Except this new machine was even worse.

I began to shake uncontrollably, and I wondered if I was having a heart attack. A moment later a man wearing a purple uniform walked in through the front door. He was followed by a guard nearly six inches taller than him. The guard in purple held an electronic tablet, which he studied as he approached Zeus.

"Frank," he said to Zeus.

"I'm Zeus," Zeus said.

"Yes," the man said. "Dr. Hatch said you suffered from delusions of grandeur. You know he's looking forward to your reunion. He has something very special in mind for you. He said a pool party was in order."

Zeus turned pale.

I looked over to see Ostin on the ground with one of the guards standing above him. The guard's boot was on Ostin's neck, pushing his face into the carpet. There were four darts in Ostin's back. "Captain, the darts don't work on him," the guard shouted.

"Idiot, he's not electric," the captain replied.

"What do I do with them?"

"Same as the ugly kid over there," he said, pointing at Wade. "Take them to the van."

The captain walked over to Ian, who had three darts in him. He was on his knees and holding his side. "So you're Ian," the captain said. "How's the vision?"

"Perfect," Ian said defiantly, turning toward the man's voice.

"Really? Perfect?"

"Yeah, I can't see your ugly face."

He kicked Ian in the stomach. Ian fell to his side, gasping.

"Too bad you didn't see that coming." He shouted to the guards, "Get them all into the van. Move it!"

*At least Jack and Abi got away*, I thought.

The captain looked over at Taylor and me, then walked up to Taylor, his stooge following closely behind him. "You must be Taylor," he said, looking her in the eyes. "The reason we wear these uncomfortable helmets. Let's remedy that." He turned to his guard. "Belt."

"Here, sir," he said, handing the captain a long strap with blinking green LEDs.

He cinched the belt over Taylor's head and chin. It looked like some kind of orthodontic headgear except with a lot of wires and lights. Taylor gasped. "It hurts."

"Does it?" he asked. He shouted to the guards who were still in the room, "You can take your helmets off now." Then he grabbed Taylor by the chin and forced her to look at him. "I heard Tara had a carbon copy."

"I'm nothing like her," Taylor said, wincing in pain.

"You're just as beautiful as she is." He ran his finger across her face.

"Don't touch her, you creep," I said.

The man turned to me, his eyes narrowing with contempt. "And you must be the famous Mr. Vey. Dr. Hatch was very specific about you." He touched something on the tablet he was carrying, and the pain in my body increased. I screamed out, gasping for air. If you have dental fillings and have chewed aluminum foil, you have an idea what it felt like—except spread throughout my whole body.

"Stop it!" Taylor shouted. "Please."

I rolled over onto my back, struggling for breath. The pain continued to pulse through my body—a wild, agonizing throb followed by a sharp, crisp sting. "Stop it!" I shouted.

"I don't take orders from little boys."

After another thirty seconds Taylor screamed, "Please stop it! Please. You're killing him. I'll do whatever you want."

"Don't be dramatic, sweetie. I'm not killing him. I'm just making him wish he were dead. Dr. Hatch gave us instructions to bring him back alive—like an animal to be put in a zoo. And yes, Miss Ridley, you *will* do whatever I want."

He pushed something on the tablet and the pain eased. "There's an app for everything these days, isn't there?" He looked at me. "We underestimated you, Mr. Vey. But it won't happen again. Trust me, there are worse things in this world than Cell 25."

# 11

## The Ride to the Airport

**I** was carried by a guard out to the backyard, where the guards had parked their truck—a large van emblazoned with the name of a moving company. The darts were still in me, and the guards had special hooks with which they secured them. I don't know what the darts were, but they seemed to suck the life out of me, twisting my thoughts with pain.

Everything seemed to be happening around me in quick, staccato flashes, like I was surfing TV channels with a remote.

I saw Ian being dragged off by three men. McKenna was crying. Ostin had a bloody nose and was calling a guard a dumb gorilla. Two guards were standing near the garage taking pictures of the Hummers. I heard their conversation, or at least some of it—one guard was asking the other where we'd gotten the cars.

My mind flashed, and I remembered that Ian had said both Hummers were in the garage—where were Jack and Abigail? Then I noticed three pizza boxes on the ground.

Connected to the back of the truck was a motorized platform that the guards used to lift us into the cargo bay. The inside of the truck looked like a laboratory and was filled with long rows of blinking diodes and pale green monitors. On one side of the truck were horizontal cots, stacked above one another like shelves. Zeus and Ian were already strapped down on the bottom two cots.

On the opposite side of the truck was a white, rubber-coated bench with rubber shackles every three or four feet.

Jack and Abigail were both strapped to the bench, their arms fastened above their heads, with belts across their waists, thighs, and calves. Abigail was crying, and I could see that Jack was bleeding from his nose and forehead. He hadn't gone without a fight.

On both sides, near the center of the truck, were narrow, locker-like cabinets. Behind those was a console with digital readouts and rows of switches and more flashing lights. A guard was seated at the console, watching as we were brought in. Waiting for us.

One of the guards pulled a cot out like a drawer, and I was laid on it, then strapped down at my ankles, waist, chest, and arms. Last, a wire was fastened around my neck, holding me fast and making it difficult to breathe.

"C is connected," a guard shouted to the man near the console.

Through my peripheral vision I saw the man push a lever and I immediately felt a tingling in my neck followed by stinging pain throughout my body. I felt nauseous, as if I might throw up, but fought the urge.

"C is active," the man in back said. The guard pushed my cot toward the wall, into its slot. The empty cot above me was only six inches from my nose.

"What's this?" a guard said, holding up my cell phone.

"I got it off him," the other said. "It's dead. Take it back to the lab."

They stowed the phone in one of the cabinets. My mind was still racing, trying to figure everything out. Breathing was a challenge. Escape was impossible. Almost everything in the back of the truck was coated in plastic or rubber, which I figured was so we couldn't short things out.

Wade and Ostin were secured next to Abigail and Jack on the long bench across from me, their hands strapped over their heads. Taylor was brought in next and bound to the cot above me. I could hear her crying as they tied her down. The sound of her in pain hurt as much as the machine I was connected to.

"B is connected," the guard said.

Taylor moaned.

"B is active," the man in back said.

"What about them?" one of the guards said, walking up with McKenna and Grace. "They're electric."

"They're harmless," the voice said. "Put them on the bench."

McKenna and Grace were strapped to the bench, their arms lifted above their heads like the others'.

When we were all secured, the overhead door was brought down, leaving the truck illuminated in an eerie, greenish glow. Two guards were still with us, one sitting on a short bench across from Ostin while the other walked to the front of the cargo hold and disappeared through a door to the cab. The engine started up and the truck shook, then lurched forward, swinging everyone on the bench to one side.

I felt drugged. It took effort to maintain consciousness.

"Taylor," I groaned, the effort taking almost everything I had.

"Shut up!" the guard shouted, which, in my state, seemed to echo a dozen times between my ears.

Taylor never answered. I could hear Zeus breathing heavily below me. No one spoke. I felt like we were being driven to an execution, which was possible.

After a few minutes of silence, the guard stood up from his bench and walked over to the cots, squatting down next to Zeus.

"Hey, stinky. Remember me? It's your buddy Wes? I used to be on the electric children detail. I bet you're glad to see me again."

Zeus said nothing.

"Well, I'm excited to see you. I've waited a long, long time for our reunion—to catch up on old times. Maybe you remember when you and Bryan thought it would be really funny to shock me when I was in the shower?"

Zeus still didn't speak.

"Yeah, I'm sure you remember. How could you forget something that hilarious? Unfortunately, *I* almost forgot about it because of the concussion I got from hitting my head on the tile. And then I got distracted by the surgery it took to fix the slipped disk in my back. Not that they really fixed it, I still have chronic back pain. But no big deal, right? Everyone had a good laugh." His voice dripped with venom. "I guess we just don't go well together, stinky. That happens, you know? Some things don't go well together. Like, say, oil and water. They just don't mix." He turned around to the cabinets and brought something out. "Or should I say Zeus and water."

I caught a glimpse of what he'd taken from the cabinet. It was a child's plastic squirt gun.

"I brought this especially for our time together. Our special reunion. Oh, look at you. You look scared. What are you, a baby? It's just a tiny, little squirt gun. What harm could that do?"

He pulled the trigger and a stream of water showered on Zeus. I heard the crisp sparking of electricity. "Aaaagh," Zeus groaned.

"Oh, come on. It's just water, stinky. It's about time you bathed. You smell like an outhouse." He sprayed again. There was a louder snap, and Zeus cried out this time. He was panting heavily and moaning in pain.

"Ah, the stench. How do you live with yourself? Or don't pigs smell themselves. Maybe you like your own stink."

He sprayed again. Zeus sobbed. "Please . . ."

"Please? You want more?"

"Hey, be cool," Ian said.

"Shut your mouth, mole boy, or I'll turn up your RESAT." He leaned in toward Zeus. "Do you remember what you said to me after I got out of the hospital? You said, 'C'mon, Wes, where's your sense of humor?'" He began pulling the trigger over and over.

Zeus let out a bloodcurdling scream.

"C'mon, Zeus, where's your sense of humor?"

Zeus's screams rose higher still.

"Not so funny now, is it?" he shouted over Zeus's screams.

"Stop it!" Abigail yelled.

The man looked back at her. "Stay out of this, sweet cheeks."

"Please," she said. "Please. I'll take away your pain."

"What?"

"I'll take away your pain, if you'll leave him alone."

Wes stared at her, wondering if she was telling him the truth. "If this is a joke . . ."

"It's what she does," Ostin said. "She stimulates nerve endings. She can take away pain."

"I'll help you," she said. "Please stop hurting him."

Wes turned back to Zeus, then spit on him, which also elicited a sizzling spark. Then he walked back to the bench where Abigail was sitting.

"If this is a trick, I guarantee you'll wish you were never born."

"I can't hurt you," Abigail said. "I wouldn't if I could."

He studied her expression, then sat down next to her. "What do I do?"

"I need to touch you. If you unlock my hands . . ."

"That ain't gonna happen, baby face."

"Then put where it hurts next to me. Anywhere."

"Your knee?"

She nodded.

He crouched on the floor next to her, his back pressed up against her. After a moment he sighed. "Wow. I'm going to have a talk with Hatch about keeping you around."

Zeus was still whimpering below me, but Abigail had probably saved his life.

The truck continued on, but with few stops, which made me believe we were on the freeway. I turned my head as far as I could to look at the others. McKenna and Jack were shackled directly across from me. What was this thing I'd been hooked to? My body and my mind ached. My heart ached too, but that was my own doing. *What did I get my friends into? How could I have been so stupid to believe some stranger on a cell phone?*

Suddenly McKenna seemed to blur. It may have been sweat running down my forehead into my eyes, but something about her was different. Her skin color was changing. Was I hallucinating? Ostin looked at me, then he glanced over at McKenna. He got a strange expression on his face, and I wondered if he saw it too.

Ostin looked over at the guard, then suddenly began singing. "Ninety-nine bottles of beer on the wall. Ninety-nine bottles of beer. Take one down. Pass it around. Ninety-eight—"

"Shut up," the guard said.

Ostin swallowed. "Just thought . . ."

"Shut up."

Ostin clenched his jaw. He looked down for a moment as if thinking, then he said to the guard, "Those new gizmos you have rock. What do you call them?"

The guard didn't answer. But he didn't tell him to shut up either.

"Sorry, I didn't realize they don't tell you these things. Probably top secret. For the important guys . . ."

"It's a RESAT," the guard said.

Ostin nodded. "RESAT. Cool."

I looked back over at McKenna. I wasn't seeing things—her skin color really *was* changing. She was now almost glowing red. Ostin must have seen what she was doing and was trying to keep the guard distracted. I looked back at Ostin, who was nodding, carefully manipulating the guard.

"Clever. Clever indeed. RESAT is 'Taser' spelled backward."

The man suddenly scratched his chin. "I never thought of that."

"I'm sure you would have," Ostin said. "If they didn't work you so hard. I bet they work you like a rented mule."

"You got that right, cheeseball."

At that moment McKenna's arms melted through the bands. She was free.

"But I bet you get great health benefits with all those Elgen doctors around."

"You kiddin' me?" the guard said. "The dental plan has a five-hundred-dollar deductible."

"You're pulling my leg," Ostin said loudly. "Why even have it? That's a whole head of cavities."

"It's a joke," the man said.

McKenna slowly reached over and grabbed Jack's bands, immediately melting through them. Jack slowly lowered his arms, rubbing his wrists. Suddenly the guard started to look back. Jack put his hands up again.

"Hey!" Ostin shouted.

The guard stopped.

"Do you have kids?"

"What?"

"Kids. Rug rats, spawn, you got them?"

"No."

"Sorry, of course not. I'm sure you're married to your job. If you had kids, the dental thing might still be worth it."

"Family isn't allowed," the guard said. "It's a regulation."

"They regulate that, huh?" Ostin said. "You know, there's something I can't figure out."

Jack reached down and unclasped his legs, then slowly inched down the bench toward the weapons cabinet.

"What?" the man asked.

"I can't figure out how you'd go about getting hired for a job like yours. It's not like you could post it in the Help Wanted section."

"I can't talk about that," he said.

"I mean, what kind of ad would that be? Wanted: ugly, mean, smelly dudes with below-average IQs to kidnap and abuse teenagers."

The guy's mouth fell.

"What section would that be under anyway? Creepy Dudes?

The man scowled. "You watch it, you smart-mouthed little—"

"Actually," Ostin said, "you should watch it."

"What the—"

Jack cracked the guard over the head with a truncheon, knocking him out with one blow. The guard slumped to the van's floor.

"Man, that felt good," Jack said, stretching out his arms like a baseball player at bat.

"Not to him," Ostin said.

McKenna walked over to Ostin, who looked at her with admiration. "That was cool," he said.

"Careful, don't touch me," she said, kneeling on the bench next to him. "I'm still pretty hot."

"Yeah, you are *hot*," Ostin said, sounding smitten.

McKenna grinned a little as she grabbed Ostin's armbands and melted through them. "There you go."

"Like buttah . . . ," Ostin said, stretching his arm. He bent over and unclasped his stomach and leg belts. "Let's free Michael."

"We've got to take care of this guy," Jack said, standing above the guard, with the club.

"Let me loose," Wade said. "I'll help you."

Jack unloosed his bands, and they lifted the guard up and strapped him to the wall while McKenna and Ostin unfastened my collar. The intense pain immediately stopped, and I groaned with relief, though I still felt as dizzy as if I'd just ridden the teacups ride at Disneyland for an hour.

"Well done, McKenna," I said.

"Thanks."

As I climbed out of the cot, Ostin and McKenna unstrapped Taylor, then Ian and Zeus. I helped Taylor climb out, then Ian. Zeus hadn't moved. He was still in a lot of pain from the guard's torture. "Can I help you?" I asked.

"Just give me a minute," he said, rolling over in the cot.

"You okay, buddy?" I asked.

"Been better," he said. His skin was blistered where the guard had sprayed water on him. "I don't know what that new dart thing is," he said. "But it's like Nichelle in a can."

"That's exactly what it is," Ostin said. "The Elgen must have found a way to replicate her powers without her weakness."

"How's your vision?" I asked Ian.

"It's back," he said.

Across the aisle Jack unloosed Abigail. "Thank you," she said softly.

"You're going to be okay," he said. "I'll get you out of here. I promise."

As Jack freed Grace, Abigail knelt at Zeus's side. She put her hand on him and closed her eyes. After a moment he relaxed and stilled. "Thank you for stopping him," he said.

"You're welcome," she said.

I was leaning against the opposite wall, holding my head and trying not to throw up.

Taylor laid her hand on my back. "You okay?"

"Alive. How about you?"

"Me too," she said hoarsely. "I wonder where they're taking us."

"We just passed a sign for the airport," Ian said.

"What's our situation with guards?" I asked.

"There are two guards driving this truck, one Escalade in front, two behind us."

"How many guards in the Escalades?"

"Four in front, five and four in back."

"We need to take charge of the van," I said.

"Then what?" Ian said. "We can't outrun the Escalades. Not in this whale."

"We don't need to," Jack said. "We'll crush them. I saw this in a movie once. But first we need to commandeer this bad boy."

"That's a good word," Ostin said. "Commandeer."

Jack looked at him. "What? You don't think I know any big words?"

Ostin withered. "Sorry."

"Anyone got a plan?" I asked.

"I say we just storm the cab," Jack said. "Commando-style."

"Too risky," I said. "They'll crash."

Ostin's face lit up. "I have an idea," he said. "A good one, with three parts."

"Three parts?" I said. "That was fast."

"Yes. This is going to be epic," he said.

# 12

## Riding the Whale

A couple of minutes later McKenna casually opened the door to the truck's dark cab. "Excuse me, guys. Can we stop to use the bathroom?"

Both men glanced back, their eyes wide with surprise.

"What are you—"

McKenna shouted, "Now!" All of us covered our eyes as she flashed to her full extent. A brilliant light filled the entire truck. Both men shouted and put their hands over their eyes. Jack and Wade rushed the cab, bringing clubs down over the guards' heads.

Jack knocked the driver out, but Wade only succeeded in dazing the other, so I put my hand on the guard's neck and pulsed, which took care of him. Wade and I climbed over the seat, and I held the wheel while Jack pulled the unconscious guard out of the way, then climbed behind the wheel.

"That was easy," Jack said, pressing down on the accelerator.

Zeus, Taylor, Ian, and McKenna dragged the men to the back of the truck and I used the van's passenger-side mirror to watch the two cars behind us. I hoped the other guards hadn't noticed the flash, but I was certain they had to have noticed our change in speed. This was confirmed ten seconds later when a voice came over the van's radio.

"Elgen Two, this is Elgen One. Are you having mechanical problems? Over."

I looked at Jack. "Don't answer."

"Wasn't planning on it," he said. "Time for phase two. We've got an exit a mile ahead of us, I'm going for it." He hit the gas, moving up quickly on the Escalade in front of us. I climbed back over the seat to see what was going on in the rear.

The two guards had been strapped to the wall, next to the guard Wes, who was now awake. "You're gonna pay for this!" he shouted angrily.

"Shut up, Wes," Zeus said fiercely. Then he blasted him. The guard's head jerked back so hard against the wall he knocked himself out again.

"Everyone, buckle up!" I shouted. "We're going for phase two!"

"Phase two!" Ostin shouted. "Everyone in place!"

Everyone sat down, strapping the waist belts around themselves. I went back up front and buckled myself into the passenger seat. "Ready," I said.

"Half mile," Jack said. "If this doesn't work, prepare for some crazy driving."

"Better work," I said. "We've only got a few seconds to hit phase three, so be ready. Everyone's strapped in."

"There's our exit," Jack said. "Hold on tight." He hit the gas. In spite of the van's size, it lurched forward, and Jack swerved into the lane left of the lead Escalade. We pulled up to the car's side, and I could see the guards looking at us with surprise.

"Here goes," Jack said. He spun the wheel to the right, forcing the moving van into the side of the Escalade. His timing was perfect as he pushed the car directly into the barrier between the exit and the freeway. The car smashed into the railing at nearly seventy-five miles per hour, flipping the car end over end.

Jack was grinning. "Just like Grand Theft Auto. Only better."

I unbuckled and climbed to the back. "Ian!" I shouted. "Are we good?"

"They're thirty feet behind us!" he shouted.

"Now, Taylor."

Taylor put her head down and concentrated on rebooting the driver of the car behind us.

"You got him," Ian said.

I braced myself against the wall. "Jack, now!'

Jack slammed on the brakes as hard as he could. There was a big jolt as the Escalade plowed into the van, followed by a second hit, when the rear Escalade plowed into the first. The force of the wreck jarred us, pushing our van partially sideways. All the lights in the back went out. Jack hit the gas again, pulling ahead of the collision.

"The first car is toast!" Ian shouted. "It's crumpled!"

"How bad are we?" Jack shouted over his shoulder.

"Not sure," Ian said, looking down. "But I see sparks." The truck was vibrating and there was a sound of something scraping. "Something's dragging. I think it's the lift."

"What about the second car?" I asked Ian.

"We're good . . . wait." His expression changed. "No way."

"What?" I asked.

"It's still running. They're coming after us."

"Jack, the second car survived the crash!" I shouted.

"I can see him in my mirror!" Jack shouted. He sounded worried.

"He's got a big gun," Ian said. "He's aiming it at us." He looked around. "Everyone on the ground. Now!"

Everyone unbuckled and dropped to the floor.

Jack shouted, "We can't outrun him. Are there any guns back there?"

"McKenna, we need light," I said.

She lit up the back of the van.

Taylor and I crawled to the cabinets and looked through them. "Nothing. Just those RESAT things."

"This just keeps getting better!" Jack shouted. "Hold on, kids!" He swerved to the right, and we all tumbled to the other side of the van. Bullets began ripping through the van.

"Ian, what's going on out there?"

"Nothing good. They've got a cannon-looking thing."

"A what?"

Suddenly we heard the gun again, though nothing came through the walls this time. The truck dropped and began veering.

"They shot out our tires!" Jack shouted. "Someone think of something."

"Taylor!" I shouted. "Can you reboot them?"

"It won't work," Ian said. "They've put their helmets back on." His brow furrowed. "What kind of gun is that?"

Ostin crawled to the back and looked out through a bullet hole in the back door. "It's an antitank gun," he said. "They'll blow us sky-high."

The truck dropped again as we lost another tire, and Jack swerved wildly trying to keep the vehicle under control. "Someone better think of something fast!" Jack shouted.

A voice came over the radio. "You've got ten seconds to pull the van over, or we will blow you up. Do you understand?"

"Don't say anything," Wade said. "They won't shoot us."

The voice returned. "Ten, nine, eight, seven . . ."

I looked over at Taylor, then took her hand.

Jack shouted back, "What do I do?"

"Four, three, two . . ."

"Pull over—" I started to yell, but before I could finish there was a loud explosion.

"Holy cow!" Ian yelled.

I looked around. We were all there. The walls were still there. The van was still there. "What was that?"

Ian was just staring at the back door in awe, shaking his head. "The Escalade . . ." He stopped in midsentence.

"Did you guys see that?" Jack shouted from the front. "That thing blew up like a bomb!"

"What blew up?" I asked.

"The Escalade. It, like, disintegrated. It's just a big ball of fire."

"What caused that?"

"I have no idea," Jack replied. "But I am *not* complaining."

"Good driving, man," I said. "Now get us off the freeway. Let's get out of this beast."

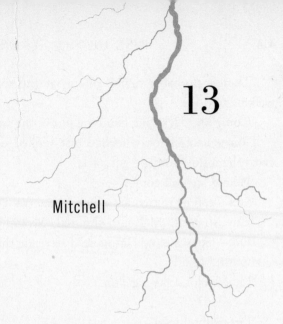

# 13

## Mitchell

Jack pulled off at the next exit and drove to the far side of a Flying J truck stop. A long row of trucks was parked next to the mini-mart, and Jack parked the crippled van between two long semis and shut off the engine.

Jack smiled at me as I walked up to the front. "Just another day in the life of a superhero," he said.

I grinned. "You're having fun, aren't you?"

"As long as we're winning, bro," Jack said. "As long as we're winning."

"We've got to find somewhere safe to finish uploading Grace's info," I said. "Any ideas?"

Jack thought for a moment, then said, "I know where we can go. Do you still have that phone?"

"It doesn't dial out," I said. "Besides, I'm sure the Elgen would be listening in on it if it did."

"There's probably a pay phone at the mini-mart," Ostin said, walking up to us.

"Come on," Jack said, climbing out of the van.

I turned to Taylor, who had just walked up to the front. "Keep everyone inside until we get back."

"Where are you going?"

"Jack's calling someone to pick us up. We'll be right back."

"Hey, Michael!" McKenna shouted. "Would you get me something to drink—like water or Gatorade? I'm really thirsty."

"Got it," I said.

"I need a lot. Like a gallon."

"A gallon?"

"I'm really thirsty."

By the time I got out of the truck, Jack and Wade were already standing next to a pay phone outside of the truck stop. As I approached I heard Jack say, "I don't have time to tell you right now. Just shut up and listen. . . . I'll tell you when you get here. Get your mom's Suburban and come to the Flying J truck stop off I-Eighty-Four West. It's just south of Meridian. You can't miss it. . . . Hurry. Yes, I know it's late. Yes, Wade is with me. . . . Because you weren't invited, that's why. Consider yourself lucky. Now hurry. . . . No, I told you, bring the Suburban. . . . There's a bunch of us. I said I'll tell you when you get here." Jack hung up the phone. "Man, what a baby."

"Who was that?" I asked.

"Mitchell," Wade said.

"He's mad we left him," Jack said. "He has no idea what he missed."

"Lucky him," Wade said.

"Does Mitchell have a computer?" I asked.

"Mitchell has everything," Wade said, shaking his head. "His old man's loaded."

"He'll be here in fifteen," Jack said.

"I'm going inside the truck stop," I said. "McKenna needs something to drink. We might as well get something to eat. Everyone's starving."

"Yeah, the pizza didn't quite make it," Jack said.

Fortunately the guards hadn't taken my money. The three of us went inside the mini-mart, and I grabbed a plastic tote and filled it with six bottles of water and a six-pack of Gatorade. I also got two boxes of powdered jelly doughnuts, licorice, and a handful of Power-Bars while Wade put together a dozen hot dogs. Jack grabbed a bag of beef jerky and pork rinds.

We paid for the food, then brought it back to the van. Jack stayed outside to wait for Mitchell while Wade and I carried everything in through the front cab.

"Thank goodness," Ostin said as we came in. I handed him the box of doughnuts. He tore it open, shoved a doughnut in his mouth, coughed from the powdered sugar, then grabbed a second doughnut and passed the box along to Ian.

McKenna took two bottles of Gatorade from me and, to all of our surprise, downed both of them, stopping only twice to breathe. After she'd emptied both bottles she sighed with relief. "Sorry. Heating up dehydrates me like crazy."

I sat down on the bench and opened my licorice. I offered some to Taylor.

"Thanks," she said, taking a strand. She pulled her knees up to her chest. "So what's going on?"

"Jack called his friend Mitchell. He's coming to pick us up."

"Then what?"

"We'll hide out at his place until we've uploaded the rest of Grace's information. Once we know where my mother is, we'll make our plan."

"What if there's no information about her?"

I frowned. "I don't know. I have to hope there is."

"Hey," shouted a voice from the back of the truck. "How about some water?"

It was the guard Wes. Zeus stood up, carrying one of the bottles with him. "You want some water, Wes?"

The guard looked at Zeus in horror. Zeus poured what was left in his bottle over the guard's head. The guard sputtered a little as it washed over his nose and mouth.

"See, Wes. I haven't lost my sense of humor," Zeus said, electricity sparking between his hands. "And I'm going to prove it to you."

The guard's eyes widened.

"Zeus," I said.

Zeus looked back at me.

"Don't."

"What? You didn't see what he did to me?"

"Yeah, I did." I looked Wes in the face. "It was cruel. But we're not like them. We're better than them."

"Maybe you are," Zeus said. "But I'm not." He lifted his hands, and Wes shut his eyes, preparing to be shocked. But it never happened. Zeus had caught sight of Abigail, who looked horrified. Zeus sighed. "All right," he said. "All right." He looked at the guard. "You're lucky these guys are better than us."

I leaned back on the bench, closing my eyes.

"What's that?" Ostin asked.

"What's what?"

"That." He pointed to my butt.

Taylor started laughing as she pulled something off me. It was a refrigerator magnet in the shape of an Idaho Spud with the words IDAHO COUCH POTATO printed across it. "How is that sticking to you?" she said.

"Wait," I said, taking it back from her. I put it on my stomach. It stuck. Then she peeled it off me and placed it against my cheek. It stuck there too.

"Wow," Taylor said. "You're like a magnet."

Ostin stared in amazement. "Not *like*. He *is* a magnet. Doesn't surprise me with all that electricity running through him."

"But I've had electricity in me my whole life. Why am I suddenly magnetic, too?"

"You must still be getting more electric."

The words hit me like a bucket of ice water. I felt as if I'd just been told I had less time to live.

"But why is he becoming magnetic?" Taylor asked.

Ostin rubbed his chin. "Let's see," he said slowly. "How do I explain this to a cheerleader?"

Taylor bristled. "How would you like a *cheerleader* to permanently scramble your brain?"

"No, don't!" Ostin said, holding his hands in front of him as if he could block her waves.

"She's not going to do that," I said.

"Don't count on it," Taylor said.

Ostin still looked terrified. "I'm sorry. I won't do it again."

I shook my head. "Just explain the magnetism."

"Okay," he said. "It works like this. Electric currents are magnetic. When you coil an electrical current around a core, the magnetism becomes stronger. In your case, your body is the core, and as you have millions of nerves and veins, which are carrying your electricity, it creates a massive coil. So it makes sense that you're becoming magnetic."

"Great. So now I'm going to have things sticking to me?"

"Like me," Taylor said, taking my hand.

I couldn't help but smile.

Just then Jack shouted through the front door, "Come on, our ride is here!"

"What do we do with the guards?" Taylor asked.

"Leave them," I said.

"Tied up?"

"Yeah. Someone will find them eventually."

Outside, Mitchell was standing next to Jack, watching everyone climb out of the truck. "Who are all these people?"

"Friends of mine," Jack said.

He pointed at me. "You're the kid who shocked us."

"His name is Michael," Jack said.

He turned back to Jack. "You took him instead of me?"

"Listen, Mitch. I'll tell you what's going on later. But right now we've got to get out of here before they find us."

"Before *who* finds you?" Mitchell asked.

"I'll tell you when we get to your house."

"We're going to my house?"

"Yeah. We need a place to hide out for a few days. Are your parents home?"

"They're never home."

A large FedEx truck pulled in next to us.

"We gotta go, Mitch," Jack said. "C'mon, everyone. Get in."

Jack and Mitchell climbed in the front, and Jack rolled down the window. "Hey, Abi. Want to sit up here?"

She smiled at him. "Thanks, but I better sit next to Zeus. He's still in pain."

"Right," Jack said, sounding disappointed.

"I'll sit up front," Wade said. "The three amigos ride again."

"Nah," Jack said. "You're too big. How about you, Grace?"

She shrugged. "Sure."

Zeus opened the tailgate and climbed into the narrow space between the backseat and the door. Abigail walked up next to him. "Do you mind if I sit here with you?"

His eyes brightened. "No, of course not." He scooted back as Abigail climbed in.

As I shut the tailgate, I noticed that two truck drivers were standing in the dark near the back of the van, examining the shredded lift. One of them pointed to the bullet holes.

"Really, it's time to go, guys," I said, climbing into the middle seat with Ian and Taylor. Ostin, Wade, and McKenna were in the row behind us.

"Hit it," Jack said.

Mitchell pulled out of the truck stop and headed east toward the freeway.

As we were climbing the freeway on-ramp, I said, "Hey, McKenna saved the day back there. Give it up for McKenna."

Everyone clapped.

"Thanks," McKenna said. "But everyone helped. Ostin distracted the guard."

"Thanks," Ostin said, looking pretty pleased. "I just saw an oppor—"

"And how about Jack's driving?" Taylor said, interrupting Ostin's speech.

"All in a day's work," Jack said.

Ostin turned to McKenna. "That really was awesome how you did that. How hot can you get?"

"At the Elgen laboratory they measured me at about two thousand Kelvin."

"Holy cannoli," Ostin said. "Two thousand Kelvin!"

"Who's Kelvin?" Wade asked.

Ostin rolled his eyes. "Kelvin is a thermodynamic temperature scale. Two thousand Kelvin is more than three thousand degrees Fahrenheit. That's almost twice as hot as fire." He turned back to McKenna. "You *are* hot. In more ways than one."

"Thanks," she said, smiling.

I didn't have to turn back to know Ostin was blushing.

"So much for your 'voice,'" Jack said.

I frowned. "I know. I'm sorry, everyone. He seemed legit."

"I believed him too," Taylor said.

"I would have put money on it," Ostin said. "I mean, it still makes no sense. Why would they have gone to the trouble of getting us cars, leaving money for us, and then attacking us? Why didn't they just trap us at the salon or along the road?"

"Maybe it was too public," Taylor said.

"True," I said. "But they could have attacked us when we got the cars. There was no one around."

Ostin added, "And those guards acted like they'd never seen your cell phone before."

"And why did they ask where we got the Hummers?" Abigail said.

"What are you guys talking about?" Mitchell asked.

"You have no idea how much you don't know," Jack said.

# 14

## Special Delivery

It was nearly midnight when we reached Mitchell's house. Even though Wade had said that Mitchell's dad was "loaded," I didn't realize just how well-off his family was until I saw his place. He lived in a massive, well-lit two-story Colonial-style house with tall gothic columns in front, wings on each side, and a cobblestone driveway that wound past a carefully manicured yard up to a fountain and front door.

"This is Mitchell's house?" I said.

"It looks like the White House," Ostin said.

"Is the butler going to answer the door?" McKenna said.

"We don't have a butler," Mitchell said. "He quit."

Jack said, "We're going to be hanging out in the pool house."

"You have a pool?" Ostin asked.

"He's got a pool *and* a pool house," Wade replied.

There was a four-car garage to the side of the house, and Mitchell opened the third door by remote and pulled in. When the door had shut behind us, Mitchell said to Jack, "Okay, what's going on? You said you'd tell me."

"Let's go inside first," Jack said. "We don't know if we were followed."

Mitchell looked afraid. "Who's following you?"

"Bad people you don't want to meet," Jack said.

"They won't come here, will they?"

"Only if they find out we're here," Grace said.

Mitchell turned to Jack. "She's kidding, right?"

Jack shook his head. "Nope."

We got out of the car, and I opened the tailgate for Zeus and Abigail. As they got out, Zeus put his hand on Abigail's back. "Thanks, Abi."

She smiled. "Anytime."

Jack was standing on the other side of the car looking at them. I could tell he was bothered.

"This way," Mitchell said. "The pool house is in back."

The pool house was located behind the main home, next to a large barbecue area with an atrium and a rock fountain. The backyard looked like something out of a *Better Homes and Gardens* magazine. I didn't know Idaho even had places like that.

The house had an electric keypad entry, and Mitchell pressed a few buttons, then pushed open the door. Inside, we all looked around in amazement.

"Your pool house is bigger than my whole house," Taylor said. "Way bigger."

The pool house was two stories high with a loft and an outdoor balcony. Mitchell gave us a quick tour. On the main floor was a large, open dining room, kitchen, bathroom, master bedroom, and two guest rooms. Upstairs, in the loft, was a television room with a fifty-one-inch plasma TV, two beanbag chairs, a long, wraparound sofa, and a foosball table. On the far side of the room, past the sofa, were two bedrooms connected by a bathroom. The walls were covered with paintings of lighthouses.

"It even smells good," Abigail said. "Like flowers."

"I could live here," Taylor said, still looking around.

"It's almost as nice as the academy," Zeus said.

"That would depend on which floor of the academy you're talking about," Ian said. Abigail and McKenna nodded in agreement.

"There are extra quilts, pillows, and sleeping bags in that closet," Mitchell said.

"The girls can sleep up here," I said. "We can stay downstairs."

"We only need two rooms," Taylor said. "Grace and I can share a room and McKenna and Abigail can take the other."

"I can sleep on the couch up here," Zeus said.

"That's okay," Jack said. "That's Wade's and my spot." He glanced over at Abigail, and she smiled at him.

Zeus looked back and forth between the two. "Whatever, dude."

"Anyone hungry?" Taylor asked. "That hot dog was gross."

"Can we order pizza again?" Grace said. "Maybe we'll get to eat it this time."

"I don't think we need to," Ian said with a curious expression.

"Why is that?" I asked.

He raised his hand. "Wait for it . . ."

A doorbell rang.

Mitchell looked at him quizzically. "That was the main house doorbell. How did you know it was going to ring?"

"Psychic," he said.

"Who is it?" I asked Ian.

"Pizza delivery. The guy has like six boxes."

"Did you order pizza?" Jack asked Mitchell.

"No," Mitchell said. "I didn't even know you were coming."

"Everyone better hide," I said. "Ian, Zeus, Ostin, and I will check this out. Mitchell, it's your house. You better get the door."

"I better come too," Jack said.

"No, you and Taylor should stay back with the rest in case it's another trap. They'll need you."

The doorbell rang again as we walked past the pool and in through the main house's back door.

"He's alone," Ian said. "It looks clean."

"How are you doing this?" Mitchell asked.

"I told you," Ian said with a grin. "I'm psychic."

Ian, Zeus, Ostin, and I ducked into Mitchell's father's office next to the front door, where we could see Mitchell but not the deliveryman. Zeus raised his hands, electricity snapping between his fingers.

"Take it easy," I said.

"Just being prepared," he replied.

Mitchell glanced over at us nervously, then opened the door. "Hey."

"Got your pizza," the voice said. "Also your garlic-cheese bread, a cinnamon dessert pizza, and two liters of soda."

"We didn't order any pizza," Mitchell said.

There was a pause. "Isn't this 2724 Preston Street? The Manchester residence?"

"Yeah. That's us."

"Then it's your pizza. And it's already been paid for. Except my tip. And this stuff was heavy."

"All right," Mitchell said, pulling out his wallet. "Just set them there."

We all moved back from the door as the guy stepped in and laid the stack of boxes on the foyer table. The deliveryman wasn't what I expected—he looked older than my mom and had hair longer than Taylor's. There were six boxes in all. Mitchell handed him a bill.

"Thanks," the man said as he walked out.

Mitchell shut the door. I watched out the window as the guy got in his car and drove off.

"Anything look suspicious in the car?" I asked Ian as we walked out to the foyer.

"No. It's a mess."

"Who do you think sent the pizza?" Zeus asked.

Just then something started to buzz in one of the boxes. "What's that?" Mitchell asked.

"It's a bomb!" Ostin shouted.

"Hit the deck!" Mitchell yelled, dropping to the ground.

Zeus, Ian, and I just stood there.

"It's not a bomb," Ian said. "It's a phone. Second box from the bottom."

Mitchell looked up from the floor. "How do you do that?"

Zeus lifted the top pizzas off, and I opened the box and took out the buzzing phone. It was identical to the one I'd received from the woman at the tanning salon.

"Are you going to answer it?" Ostin asked.

"Do you think I should?"

He shrugged. "Your call. Literally."

I pushed the answer button, then held the phone to my ear. "Hello?"

"Michael. It's me." It was the *voice* again.

"You tricked us."

"We didn't trick you. That was a safe house."

"You call that 'safe'?"

"We don't know how they found you. Someone in your group might be tipping them off."

"You're saying one of us is a traitor?"

"Maybe. An Elgen plant."

"I trust them more than I do you," I said. "I'm hanging up."

"Please don't hang up. We need to talk."

"What are you doing, tracing this call?"

"We already know where you are. We sent the pizza."

I felt stupid. "Oh yeah."

"If you look out the window you'll see two white, windowless service vans parked across the street. They're ours. They're guarding the house."

"Why should I trust you?"

"Do you know what happened to the third Elgen car?"

"What?"

"The third Elgen car. The one that was about to blow up the van you were in. You don't believe that car just blew up on its own?"

I didn't know what had happened to the car. None of us did. I wondered how he knew about it.

"We did it," he said. "You did an amazing job of escaping, Michael. All of you did. You just needed a little help at the end."

"If you're with us, why didn't you just stop them from capturing us to begin with?"

"Anonymity is our most valuable weapon. If the Elgen had gotten you to the airport, we would have been forced to attack. But it was our last resort. Thankfully we didn't have to. After you destroyed the first two cars, we knew they'd assume you destroyed the third."

My mind was reeling. I didn't know what to believe. "How do they keep finding us?"

"Like I said, we don't know. We knew that the Elgen were tracking your cars. We thought once you traded cars they'd lose you. Unfortunately, we were wrong."

"We noticed," I said sarcastically. "How are *you* following us?"

"The old-fashioned way. We've been following you since Pasadena." The voice paused. "Are there any GPs with you?"

"No," I said. "We let them all go in California."

"All of them?"

"Of course, we don't have room for . . ." I stopped. "Jack and Wade were GPs."

"That's how they're doing it," the voice said. "The GPs are all implanted with subdermal RFIDs. You'll have to get rid of them."

I didn't understand. "Get rid of Jack and Wade? Or get rid of the subthermal R-F-I . . ."

"Sub*dermal* RFIDs," the voice said quickly. "Your friend Ostin will know what they are. And the answer is either. I'm afraid my time's up."

"Wait. Do you know what happened to Ostin's parents?"

Ostin looked at me.

"They're safe, and we have a man watching over Taylor's house as well. You saw our van as you drove by her house yesterday afternoon."

"What about Jack's house?"

"We didn't know about him, so we weren't prepared." The receiver went dead. I put the phone in my pocket.

"What did he say?" Ostin asked.

"Your parents are okay."

"Where are they?"

"He didn't say."

Ostin looked confused. "That's good, right?"

"I hope so. What's a subdermal RFID?"

"'Subdermal' means beneath the skin. RFIDs are radio frequency identification devices." His eyes widened. "Holy cow, is that how they've been following us? Did they implant everyone with them?"

"He only said the GPs."

"What about the electric kids?"

"They tried," Ian said. "But our electricity interferes with the frequency."

"RFIDs," Ostin repeated. "So that's how they're following us."

"What do they look like?" I asked.

"You've seen them before," Ostin said. "Stores put them in books and video games to catch shoplifters. It's a little square foil thing, usually about the size of a postage stamp. But I've read that some new, high-tech RFIDs are the width of a human hair. They can almost make them like powder. There's even talk of making them digestible."

"Why would they do that?" Ian asked.

"Think about it," Ostin said, suddenly looking excited. "You could put them in restaurant food, then when you go to check out, they'll scan your stomach and charge you for what you ate."

"That's . . . weird," Mitchell said.

"That's the future," Ostin replied.

"How do they implant these things?" I asked.

"They inject them," Ian said. "In a shot. I've seen them do it."

"We need to get rid of them," I said.

"Jack and Wade?" Zeus asked hopefully.

"No," I said. "The tracking devices." I lifted half the pizzas. "We better get back to the others."

Jack, Taylor, and Wade met us by the pool.

"What happened?" Taylor asked. "Who sent the pizzas?"

"I'll tell you inside," I said. We carried the food into the pool house and set it on the kitchen table. "The voice sent the pizzas. And he sent us another phone."

"What did the *voice* have to say?" Jack said angrily. "Sorry we *almost* killed you?"

"He said they didn't do it. He said that they were the ones who blew up the third Elgen car so we could escape."

"Do you believe him?" Taylor asked.

"I don't know. I mean, the Elgen wouldn't blow up their own car, and we sure didn't do it. And if they know we're here, why didn't they just attack us?"

"Because we kicked their butts last time," Jack said.

"No," Taylor said. "If they're still trying to capture us, it would be better for them if we didn't know that they knew where we are."

"What?" Wade said.

"Precisely," Ostin said. "First rule of war, never give up the element of surprise."

I said, "The voice said he thinks they know how the Elgen have been following us." I looked at Jack. "They think that you and Wade were implanted with tracking devices."

Jack's brow furrowed. "Implanted where?"

"When the guards took you prisoner, did they give you a shot?" Ostin asked.

"Oh yeah," Wade said. "And that needle was wicked big. It stung worse than a hornet."

"Did they tell you what the shot was for?" Ostin asked.

Jack shook his head. "No, they weren't real talkative. Why?"

"GPs are implanted with a subdermal RFID so they can be tracked if they escape," I said. "That includes you and Wade."

"A what?" Jack asked.

"It's a radio frequency identification device," Ostin said. "They use them to track people. And they're small enough that they can be injected into the body."

"The voice told you this?" Jack asked skeptically.

I nodded. "He thinks the Elgen have been using the RFIDs to track us."

"Wait," Taylor said. "If that's true, then they can still find us."

Mitchell looked at her. "What will they do if they find us?"

"They burned down my house," Jack said.

Mitchell's eyes widened. "If something happens to the house, my parents will kill me."

"If the Elgen find us," Jack said, "they'll kill you for real."

Mitchell turned pale. "You've got to get out of here. All of you."

"No, just Jack and Wade have to get out of here," Zeus said.

"But they'll capture us," Wade said.

"It's you or *all of us*, moron," Zeus said.

"Watch your mouth," Jack said.

"We're in this together," I said. "There's got to be another solution."

"Wait," Ostin said. "There is. Mitchell, do you have any aluminum foil?"

"In the pantry."

"Get it. Quick. The thicker the better."

He started walking toward the kitchen.

"Run!" Jack said.

"Okay." He ran out of the room.

"Aluminum foil?" I said.

"We can wrap them in foil. It will block the frequency."

Taylor stifled a laugh. "They'll look like baked potatoes."

"I'm not going to wear foil," Wade said.

"Maybe you prefer the Elgen jumpsuits," Jack said.

Wade nodded. "Actually, I have always looked good in silver."

Mitchell returned with two boxes of foil. "Here."

"Someone help me wrap them," Ostin said.

"I'll help," Taylor said.

"Where did you get the shot?" Ostin asked.

"At the Elgen Academy," Wade said.

Jack shook his head. "In our arms. Our left arms."

Ostin and Taylor wrapped Jack's and Wade's left arms and shoulders with foil.

"I take it back," Taylor said. "You don't look like baked potatoes.

You look like the Tin Man from *The Wizard of Oz*."

"Yeah," Zeus said. "I'll get you a funnel for your head."

"And I'll shove your greasy head through it," Jack said.

The two of them glared at each other.

Abigail stepped between them, then said to Jack. "I think you look like a knight in shining armor."

Zeus shook his head and turned away.

"At least there are no more radio frequencies," Ostin said.

Jack smoothed the foil down on his shoulder. "We can't walk around like this for the rest of our lives."

"He's right," I said. "Can't we just run a magnet over it like you do with a credit card?"

"That won't do anything," Ostin said. "You've got to really crush it. Like hit it with a hammer."

"We can't hit anyone with a hammer," I said.

"Yeah," Wade said, looking pale. "That wouldn't be good."

"You're right," Ostin said. "It wouldn't be efficient. You'd crush bones long before it damaged the chip."

"Can we cut it out?" Jack asked.

Wade's eyes widened. "What?"

"You could do that," Ostin said. "If you could find it."

"What?" Wade said again. "You want to cut it out of my arm, like with a *knife*?"

Jack walked to the kitchen and returned with a steak knife. He handed it to me. "Cut it out."

Wade stared, his eyes wide with fear. "Please don't."

"Is there any other way to break them?" I asked.

"You can microwave them," Ostin said. "But even if Wade fit in a microwave, he'd probably explode."

Wade was speechless.

"What about an EMP?" Zeus said. "Quentin used to blow out RFID readers at toll booths just to cause traffic jams."

"What's an EMP? Taylor asked.

"Electromagnetic pulse," Ostin said. "A high-frequency electromagnetic burst could overload the RFID's antenna and blow out the chip." He thought for a moment. "A quick electric surge could knock it out. But you'd have to be right above the RFID. And we don't know where it is."

"Ian can find it," I said, looking at him. "Can't you?"

"If I knew what I was looking for. What does it look like?"

"I've never seen one that small, but it would look like a tiny piece of metal," Ostin said. "Like a sliver. Embedded in flesh it shouldn't be that hard to find."

"What about the EMP?" Taylor asked. "Where do you get one of those?"

"A big blast from Michael," Ostin said.

"Why do all these solutions have to involve some form of torture?" Wade said. "Michael's done that to me before."

"He's shocked you before," Ostin said. "This would have to be much more powerful."

"I really don't mind the foil that much."

"Quit being such a wimp," Jack said.

"It's that or the knife," Ostin said.

"Enough of this," Jack said. "Let's get it over with. I'll go first."

"Ian?" I said.

Ian walked up to Jack. "Point to where they gave you that shot."

Jack peeled back the foil and rolled up his sleeve. He pointed to a spot a few inches down from his shoulder.

We were all quiet as Ian looked at Jack's arm. "I think I see it. It's about the size of a sesame seed."

"What does it look like?" Ostin asked.

He focused his eyes. "It has markings. Almost like . . . fingerprints."

"That's it," Ostin said. "We should mark where it is. Anyone got a pen?"

Mitchell retrieved a fine-tipped marker from a drawer next to the phone. "Here."

Ostin handed the marker to Ian, who drew a small dot on Jack's skin. "It's right there, about a sixteenth to an eighth of an inch in."

"The subcutaneous level," Ostin said.

I looked at Jack. "You sure about this?"

"Do I have a choice?"

"Not really," I said.

"Then I'm sure."

"You should sit down," Ostin said. "The shock might knock you out."

"Right." Jack walked over to the couch and sat back, his arm on the armrest.

I put my hand on his arm. "Ready?"

"I feel like I'm in the electric chair waiting for them to flip the switch. Don't count or anything. Just do it."

"Wait!" Abigail said. "I can help." She walked over to Jack's side and put one hand on his shoulder, the other on his neck. "Okay," she said.

Jack smiled. "Thanks."

I put my index finger on Ian's ink dot and closed my eyes. Then I pulsed.

Jack's body heaved and Abigail jumped back with a scream. The spot on Jack's arm was bright red and there was a blister where my finger had touched him.

"Sorry," I said.

It took him a moment to speak. "It was nothing," he said, still looking a little dazed. "I think Abi took most of it." He looked at her. "Are you all right?"

Her eyes were moist with tears, but she nodded.

"Thank you," he said. "I owe you one."

She forced a smile. "You're welcome."

Jack turned to me. "So, did it work?"

"Ian, what do you see?"

Ian looked at Jack's arm. "The thing looks . . . smaller than it was, kind of wrinkled, like it's melted."

"Perfect," Ostin said.

Wade stepped forward. "Guess it's my turn." He pulled the foil back from his arm.

Ian had to look a little longer for his. "What's up with this? You've got a *bunch* of metal in there."

Wade looked stumped for a moment, then said, "Oh. It's probably buckshot. I got in the way of a shotgun when I was little."

"His dad was drunk and took him duck hunting," Jack said.

"There it is." Ian marked the place with the pen.

Abigail put her hand on Wade's shoulder.

"You don't have to do this," Jack said to her.

"I know."

This time I didn't hesitate. I put my finger on the spot and immediately pulsed. The shock wasn't as strong as the first one, but it was strong enough. Abigail cried out as she pulled away, shaking her hand in pain. Tears were rolling down her face. McKenna and Taylor both put their arms around her to comfort her.

"I'm so sorry," I said.

"It's not your fault," she replied.

Ian examined Wade's arm. "It looks shriveled too."

Jack wadded up a piece of foil from Wade's arm and threw it at Mitchell. Then he grabbed Wade by the hand and pulled him up. "You're the man."

"That wasn't so bad," he said.

"Yeah, because Abi took it," Taylor said. "How about a thank-you."

"Sorry," Wade said. "Thanks."

"That's okay," Abigail said.

"Now that that's done," Ostin said, "how about some pizza?"

"I could go for that action myself," Zeus said.

"Looks like there's a little of everything," Grace said, opening the boxes.

"Pineapple and Canadian bacon," Ostin said. "Score."

I took a couple of pieces of sausage and pepperoni pizza for Taylor and me, then we sat on the floor in the corner of the room. After we'd taken a few bites she asked, "Now what do we do?"

"We get the information out of Grace." I looked over at Mitchell. "Hey, Mitchell. Do you have a computer?"

"Like six of them," he said, his mouth full.

"We need your most powerful one. We've got to upload Grace."

"What's grace?"

Grace was sitting on the arm of the couch next to him. "I'm Grace," she said.

Mitchell looked at her. "I don't get it."

"They're uploading me," she said.

"I'm so confused," Mitchell said. "Will someone please tell me what's going on?"

"I'll tell you," I said. "Remember when I shocked you?"

"Yeah, like I'd forget that."

"There are other kids like me with electric powers. Thirteen of them. The people who made us this way, the Elgen, are trying to get us back. That's why they kidnapped my mother and Taylor."

"You?" Mitchell said, looking at Taylor.

Taylor nodded.

"She's electric too," I said.

"You can shock too?" Mitchell asked.

"Kind of," she said. "Just your brain."

"Might be hard with Mitch," Jack said. "Small target."

Mitchell made a face.

I continued. "Jack and Wade drove Ostin and me to California to rescue my mother and Taylor."

"Where we were captured and put in cells and tortured," Wade said. "Still wish you had come?"

Mitchell looked at Jack. "The Elgen dudes captured you?"

Jack nodded. "They put these electric collars on us that would shock you if you even talked. But Michael escaped and freed us."

"And the Elgen dudes are the ones looking for you now," Mitchell said.

I nodded. "Yes."

Jack said, "We came back to Idaho to regroup. But the Elgen were waiting for us. They burned down my house."

"Then they recaptured us," Wade said. "But we got away."

"That's where you come in," I said. "The truck you saw us climb out of, that was what they were holding us in."

"You're really not making this up?"

Jack scowled. "Don't be an idiot. You saw the truck, dude. You saw the bullet holes."

"So what are you going to do now?"

"We're hoping Grace has information about my mother," I said. "That's why we need a computer."

Mitchell just stared at me for a moment. "But what if these Elgen guys find us?"

"That's why we had to get rid of the RFIDs," Jack said. "So they won't."

"There's no way they'll find us now," Ostin said.

Just then my phone rang. Everyone turned to look at me as I answered. "Hello."

"Get ready, Michael," the voice said. "The Elgen are here."

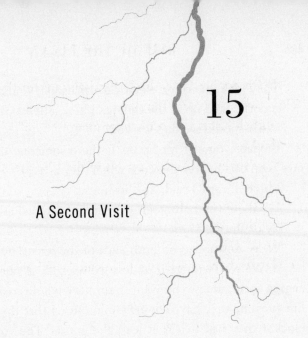

# 15

## A Second Visit

"Where are they?" I asked.

Taylor grabbed my arm. At first I thought she was frightened, then I realized she was just listening in.

"They're one street east of you. There are about a dozen guards in three vehicles. Did you get rid of the GPs?"

"No, but we destroyed the RFIDs," I said. "At least we think we did."

"You must have succeeded or else they would have already surrounded the house. They were probably closing in on you, then lost the signal. They've got a helicopter and listening devices, so stay inside and no loud talking. Turn up the radio or TV. They're also going door to door with remote el-readers. They're sensitive up to thirty feet, so stay away from the front door and outer walls."

"What are el-readers?" I asked.

"They pick up erratic electrical signals like yours."

Taylor looked up at the ceiling. "I hear a helicopter."

"What should we do?" I asked.

"Prepare yourself for battle. Is there someone they won't recognize who can answer the door when they arrive?"

"Mitchell can," I said. "It's his house."

"*What* are you volunteering me for?" Mitchell asked.

Taylor shushed him.

"We're positioned on both ends of the street, but we're outnumbered. We won't move in unless we have to. It's best that we don't engage them, unless you want to turn the whole area into a war zone. I'm guessing they have enough ammunition that they could level the block if they had to. Or at least the house." The voice paused. "Did you hear that?"

"No."

"I need to go before they intercept this signal. I'll call back when it's clear. Be strong. Good luck." The phone went dead.

Taylor looked at me, her eyes dark with fear. Everyone else was staring at me as well.

"What?" Ostin and Zeus asked simultaneously.

I lowered my voice to a whisper. "The Elgen are in the neighborhood."

"They're in my *neighborhood?*" Mitchell said.

"Quiet," Taylor whispered. "They have listening devices."

"Someone turn the TV on," I said.

"What channel?" Wade asked.

"A noisy one," I said. "They don't know where we are. They lost our signal. So they're going door to door." I looked at Mitchell. "If they come here, you're going to have to answer the door."

He turned white. "Why me?"

"Because they have machines that can detect us and you're not one of us."

"How about we just don't answer the door?" he said.

"Then they'll search your place, and if they pick up our el-waves . . ."

"But what's going to stop them from forcing their way in?"

"Look," I said. "They have a lot of houses to check. They won't attack if they don't think we're here. So just act normal and nothing will happen."

Mitchell just stared at me blankly. "Act normal? They're going to kill us!"

Jack put his arm around him. "Listen, Mitch. It's cage time in the Octagon. Wipe that fear off your face. You're a warrior. No fear."

Mitchell took a deep breath. "Right. No fear."

"Jack, you're going to have to be his backup."

"Wade, Mitch, and I got it," he said. "And you." He pointed to Ostin.

Ostin looked around. "Me?"

"Yes, you. We might need your smarts."

"We'll need to know what's going on," I said.

"I'll be watching," Ian said.

"I know. But it would be better if we could hear what they're saying." I turned to Mitchell. "Does your house have an intercom system?"

"Yeah, but I'm not sure how to work it."

"I'll figure it out," Ostin said. "Just show me where it is."

"Set it so we can listen from the loft in the pool house."

"Done," Ostin said.

"All right," I said. "Good luck, everyone."

Ostin turned the front door's intercom on so we could listen to what was happening. It was about twenty minutes before the doorbell rang. We heard the door open.

"Whassup, guys?" Mitchell said.

"We're sorry to disturb you at this hour, but we're from Homeland Security. There's no need to panic, but we've received a report that there is a radiation leak in the area. For your safety, we need to check the radiation levels of your house."

"Liars," Taylor whispered.

Mitchell said, "Radiation? Someone got a bomb around here?"

"No, sir. It's not a bomb. It may be nothing at all. May we please come in?"

"Uh, my parents are out, and they'd freak if I let strangers in. You got a warrant or something?"

"No, sir, Homeland Security doesn't need warrants. This is for your safety. We don't need your permission to enter your home."

There was a long pause. "Come on, Mitchell," I said. "Think of something."

"Look, I just got my little sister to bed. Why don't you come back tomorrow?"

"It will only take a few minutes, sir."

"Come on, guys. It took me an hour to get her down."

We heard a high voice say, "Mitchie, who is it?"

"Mitchie?" Zeus whispered.

"Was that Ostin?" I asked.

Taylor shrugged. "He kind of pulled it off."

"Just some government guys!" Mitchell shouted. "Go back to sleep!" Pause. "Really, guys. I'm sure there's no radiation around here, or I'd be glowing or something, right? Just come back in the morning."

"Do you mind if we check around back?"

Taylor and I looked at each other.

There was a long pause. "No problem," Mitchell said. "Help yourself."

A different voice said, "I'm not pulling a reading."

"Nothing?"

"No."

"All right. Looks like you're good. Thank you, sir."

"Yeah. No problem. Come back when my parents are here."

We heard the door shut and lock.

"He handled that surprisingly well," I said.

"You think that girl's voice was Ostin?" Taylor asked.

"Probably Jack," Zeus said.

"You're so mean," Abigail said.

I looked at Abigail. She was smiling at Zeus.

"I don't like where that is headed," Taylor whispered to me. "I see a collision coming."

# 16

## Uploading Grace

Ian watched the guards until they left Mitchell's street and started on the next. A few minutes later Jack and the rest walked back into the pool house. Jack had his arm around Mitchell, who was beaming like a conquering hero.

"How'd I do?" Mitchell asked.

"You should win an Academy Award for that performance," Taylor said. "So who was the girl calling for 'Mitchie'?"

"That was me," Jack said.

"Told you," Zeus said to Abigail.

Jack scowled at him.

"Okay," Abigail said. "Can we go to bed now? I'm exhausted."

"Me too," McKenna said.

I looked at Taylor. She grinned. "Me three."

"Someone's got to stand watch." I looked around the group. "Anyone not tired?"

No one said anything. Finally, Jack looked at Zeus. "If no one else is going to man up, I'll do it."

"I'll do it," Ostin said.

I looked at him in surprise. Ostin was one of those guys who always went to bed at the same time and always before ten.

"Really?" I asked.

"If we can upload Grace, I'll stay up and go through the files."

Grace had been so quiet I'd almost forgotten she was there. She took a deep breath. "Let's get it over with."

While everyone else got ready for bed, Ostin, Grace, Taylor, Jack, and I followed Mitchell to his room on the second floor of the main house. Not surprisingly, his room was huge—larger than my room and my mother's combined. It was also a mess, strewn with clothing, cracker boxes, and candy wrappers. The walls were covered with magazine pictures of cage fighters and *Sports Illustrated* swimsuit models.

There was a large, beige computer next to his desk with a huge monitor on the desktop. Ostin was drawn to it like a moth to a flame.

"That's a custom Alienware Aurora," Ostin said. "Maybe the best gaming computer ever built. It looks brand-new. Have you even used it?"

Mitchell shook his head. "Nah. My dad bought it for my birthday. I'm not really into computers that much."

"He means he doesn't know how to turn it on," Jack said.

"Neither do you," Mitchell said.

"I would kill for one of these," Ostin said, sitting down at the keyboard. He fired it up and the screen's glow lit his face. "Let's go, Grace."

"You're not going to break it, are you?" Mitchell asked.

"Would you even know if we did?" Ostin said.

Mitchell just looked at him.

Ostin rolled his eyes. "No, we're not going to break it."

Grace sat down in a chair next to the computer. She took a deep breath, put her hands on top of the CPU, then closed her eyes and began to concentrate. Files began filling the computer as sweat beaded on her forehead. Just a minute into the upload she began to shake and her eyes rolled back into her head like before.

"That's creepy," Mitchell said.

"No it's not," Taylor said indignantly.

"Shh," Ostin said. "You're slowing her down."

It took nearly five minutes for Grace to upload everything. When she was done she fell forward onto her knees, panting heavily like an athlete just completing a sprint.

Taylor put her hand on Grace's shoulder and knelt down next to her. "Good job."

Ostin just stared at the screen. "Mitchell, do you have a pen and paper?"

"We've got some downstairs."

"I'm going to need a whole pad. Actually a couple. Is there paper in your printer?"

"What printer?"

"Just get the pen and paper, Einstein," Jack said.

I checked the printer drawer. "Looks full."

Ostin continued examining the file names, shaking his head in wonderment. "That's a lot of data. It's going to take me all night. At least."

Mitchell returned. "Here's your pen and paper," he said, setting two yellow writing pads on the desk next to Ostin.

"You're sure about this?" I asked. "I can stay up if you want."

"I'm good," Ostin said. "Everyone can go to bed."

"This *is* my bed," Mitchell said.

"Not tonight it's not," Jack said. "Ostin's got work to do."

"A few terabytes' worth." Ostin said this more to himself than us, and I could tell that he'd already started to slip off into his own world. I don't think he even noticed when we left.

# 17

## Ostin's Discovery

"Michael."

I opened my eyes to see Ostin standing over me. I had fallen asleep on the couch on the main floor of the pool house, and sunlight was streaming in through the blinds above me.

"What time is it?" I asked.

"Morning," Ostin said, looking very tired.

I rubbed my eyes. "Did you stay up all night?"

"I found your mother."

Suddenly I was wide awake. "You found her?"

"She's in Peru. I found her file on the computer."

"Peru? Show me." I pulled on my T-shirt and grabbed the cell phone.

We were walking to the front door when Taylor called to me. "Michael."

I looked up. She was leaning over the loft railing. "What's going on?"

"Ostin found my mother," I said.

"I'll be right there." Taylor hurried down the stairs and joined us at the door. "Are you sure?"

"I'm sure she was there when Grace downloaded the information," Ostin said. "They could have moved her."

"How did you find her?" I asked.

"I tracked her through their internal travel logs. I started with the date she disappeared, then went from there."

Taylor and I followed Ostin back to Mitchell's room.

"Is anyone else awake yet?" I asked Taylor.

"No. Everyone was exhausted."

"They should be," I said.

We walked into Mitchell's room.

"I've got a feeling things are going to get even crazier," Ostin said, pointing to a picture of my mother on the screen.

My heart froze at the sight of her. She looked tired and frightened and was wearing an Elgen jumpsuit.

"She's being held at the Elgen Starxource plant in Puerto Maldonado, Peru."

"Isn't that where the fire rats escaped?" Taylor asked.

"Exactly," Ostin said. "It's a jungle town in the Amazon rain forest."

"How long has she been there?" I asked. I noticed I was ticking but didn't bother to try to control it.

"The travel records show that she was transported to Peru directly from Idaho."

"How do we get to Peru?" Taylor asked. "Can we drive?"

"I'm not sure. We'd have to go through Mexico, Guatemala, El Salvador, Honduras, Nicaragua, Costa Rica, Panama, Colombia, and Ecuador and halfway through Peru."

Taylor just stared at him. "How do you know all that?"

"Geography is my strong subject," Ostin said.

"Everything is your strong subject," Taylor said.

"We're going to have to fly," I said.

"All of us?"

"We might have enough money," I said.

"You can't just fly into a foreign country," Ostin said. "There's customs and border control. Do you even have a passport?"

I had never traveled outside the country, so I hadn't thought of any of that. "That will be a problem."

"Not our biggest one," Ostin said. "The compound she's being held in is a fortress. It's more prison than energy plant. It's built on a twenty-five-thousand-acre ranch, and it has hundreds of guards. At least ten times more than what we faced at the academy."

All the excitement I felt at locating my mother vanished in a puff of impossibility. What good was knowing where she was if we couldn't reach her? She might as well be on the moon.

I put my head in my hands.

"What do we do now?" Taylor asked.

"I don't know," I said. I turned to Ostin. "Do you have any ideas?"

"I think . . . ," Ostin said. He thought for a moment. "I think I need some sleep."

I exhaled heavily. "Yeah, get some sleep. Thanks for staying up."

"No problem," Ostin said. He lay down on Mitchell's bed. A feeling of despair permeated the room.

Taylor said, "I know what we should do."

"What?"

"Get bagels. I need to get out of here."

After all we'd been through, something as normal as going out for bagels sounded fantastic.

"Maybe Jack or Wade are up by now."

I looked at Ostin. He had already shut his eyes.

"Do you want something from the bagel place?" I asked.

"Sleep," he said.

"Wow, you are tired," Taylor said.

"And a blueberry bagel," Ostin added. "Or chocolate chip if they have it. With strawberry cream cheese."

"You got it," I said. I started for the door, then suddenly stopped and turned back. The picture of my mother was still on the screen.

Taylor took my hand. "Things have a way of working out."

I looked at her. "My mother used to say that."

# 18

## The Bagelmeister

When we walked back into the pool house, Jack was sitting at the kitchen table holding a spoon and eating from a carton of vanilla ice cream. "Where were you guys?"

"With Ostin," I said. "He found my mother."

He set down his spoon. "Awesome. Let's go get her."

"It's not that simple," Taylor said.

"She's in Peru," I said.

"Is that in Idaho?" he asked.

Taylor covered her eyes.

"No," I said. "It's in South America. They have her locked away in a huge compound."

"Good," he said. "I like a challenge."

"Well, you've got one. The first is how we get there."

"Maybe the *voice* can help us," he said.

Taylor looked at me. "He's right. I bet they could fly us there."

The thought gave me hope. "If they call again."

"They'll call," Taylor said. She turned to Jack. "In the meantime, we're hungry for bagels. Will you drive us?"

Jack stood. "Sure. I'll get the keys from Mitchell."

The three of us drove about six blocks to Taylor's favorite bagel shop—the Bagelmeister. I had never been to the place before, but I knew it was a hangout for the popular kids.

"Let's go inside," Taylor said. "It's faster."

"Wait," I said. "What if someone recognizes you? They've probably been hanging 'missing girl' posters around town."

"We'll just be a second," she said. "Besides, all my friends are in school right now."

"All right," I said. "But we can't stay."

I held the door for her as she walked inside. As we walked into the store, Taylor froze. There was a shrill scream. "Guys! It's *Tay*!"

I looked over Taylor's shoulder to see a group of girls. Her friend Maddie was pointing at her. "OMG! It's really you! Where have you been? You are in so much trouble."

Taylor just stared at them like a deer in the headlights of an oncoming car.

"Reboot them," I said. "Quick!"

Taylor closed her eyes.

Immediately the entire room froze. I grabbed Taylor's arm and pulled her to the door. As we ducked out of the shop I heard someone say, "I think I just had, like, an aneurysm. . . ."

We ran back to the car. I opened the door and pushed her in.

"That was fast," Jack said. "Where are the bagels?"

"We've got to get out of here," I said. "Taylor's friends are inside."

He looked at Taylor. "Did they see you?"

"Yes, but I rebooted them."

"Hope it worked." Jack put the car in reverse, backed up, then squealed out of the parking lot. When we were a couple of blocks away he asked, "Where to now?"

"There's that other bagel place over on Thirty-Third," I said. "Next to the theater. I think they have a drive-through window. What do you think, Tay?" I looked over. "Taylor?" Her head was down, her eyes covered by her hands. She was crying.

"What's wrong?"

She kept crying. I put my hand on her shoulder. "Taylor?"

She wiped her eyes, then looked up at me. "I just miss my life," she said. "I miss my family. I miss my friends. I miss my mom hiding my Easter basket in the same stupid place every year for the last ten years. I even miss my dad yelling at me for being gone all the time."

I wasn't sure what to say. Jack glanced at me in the rearview mirror with a helpless expression.

After a moment I breathed out heavily. "Maybe it's time you went home."

Her expression turned from sad to angry. "You're trying to get rid of me?"

"No. I just don't want you to be so unhappy."

"We're in this together. All of us are. Besides, we both know the Elgen aren't going to leave me alone just because I gave up. It makes me an easier target."

I held her hand. "I don't know what to say."

"You don't have to say anything. I just needed someone to listen." She wiped her eyes. "Do you have a Kleenex or something?"

"There are some napkins up here," Jack said.

"That works."

Jack handed her a stack of napkins, and she blew her nose and wiped her eyes again.

Just then the cell phone rang. I picked it up, and Taylor took my arm to listen in.

"Hello?"

"Well done last night, Michael," the voice said. "Another potential catastrophe averted."

"We found my mother," I said.

The voice paused. "Are you sure?"

"She's being held in Puerto Maldonado, Peru."

"Their Starxource training compound," the voice said. "Of course. It's their most secure compound—especially as far as Hatch is concerned. He has complete control over the personnel. How do you know she's there?"

"I can't tell you," I said.

"Are you certain your information is correct?"

"We know that she was sent there after she was kidnapped. I've seen her file with a picture of her."

"So you either hacked into their system or, more likely, downloaded the files at the academy."

I could have kicked myself for divulging so much. I didn't confirm his guesses, but I began gulping.

"You're right not to tell anyone," the voice said. "If Hatch knew that Grace had downloaded those files, he would stop at nothing to hunt her down."

His words filled me with fear. "I didn't say anything about Grace."

"You didn't have to, Michael. She's the only one who could have accessed that information before it was destroyed."

"How do you know it was destroyed?"

"Elgen protocol," he said. "Does Hatch know that Grace is with you?"

"I don't know."

"Even if he does, he clearly doesn't know what she's carrying. How much of their mainframe did you get?"

"We think all of it."

"This is a fantastic stroke of luck," he said. "That information is invaluable to our cause. Where is this data now?"

"It's on one of the computers at the house."

"We need to get that information. We'll send someone over this afternoon to retrieve it. The van we send will be disguised as some type of service vehicle."

"I didn't say you could have the information," I said.

There was a long pause. "What do you mean?"

"I need a ride to Peru."

"You want to try to rescue your mother?"

"Yes."

"You do realize that you're walking into a trap and that Hatch is holding your mother as bait."

"Probably."

"Not probably, he is. And once you're in the compound there's nothing we can do to help you."

"I wasn't planning on your help. I have to take a chance. I have to save her."

There was another long pause. When he spoke his voice was softer. "I just wanted to make sure that you know what you're up against. I'll make the arrangements. It will take me a while. We'll get you to Peru and provide you with all the information we have on the compound in return for Grace's information. But we want one more thing. We want Grace."

Taylor looked at me. She mouthed, "Grace?"

"I can't turn her over to you."

"If Hatch catches her, he'll probably kill her. But he'll break her first. Then he'll know exactly how much we know. It will render the information useless."

I thought over his warning.

"You know I'm right, Michael. Grace can't help you. Her powers aren't what you'll need. And you'll be putting her life in terrible danger. If you won't do it for the cause, do it for her sake."

After another minute I said, "Okay. I'll ask her. But it's up to her."

"Fair enough. Do we have a deal?"

I looked at Taylor and she nodded.

"Okay," I said. "We have a deal. Send your guy."

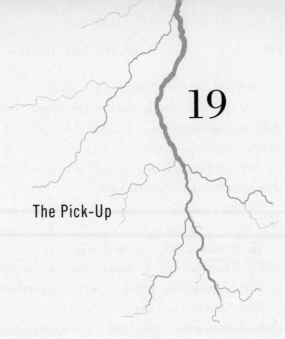

# 19

## The Pick-Up

"**W**e're going to Peru?" asked McKenna, her mouth full of blueberry bagel.

"Isn't that in Africa?" Wade asked.

"Did you even go to school?" Ostin said.

"Same one you did, loser."

"Same school, different planet," Ostin said.

All eleven of us were gathered in the loft eating bagels. I stood in front of the TV with Taylor by my side. "Yes, we're going to Peru. The voice has promised to take us there." I looked around the room. "This is going to be very dangerous—even more dangerous than what we risked at the academy. I don't want you to go unless you're positive you want to."

"I'm in," Jack said immediately. "Wade?"

"I already committed," he said. "I owe you, Michael."

I nodded. "Thanks."

451

"What about you, Mitch?" Jack asked.

"Uh . . ." His eyes darted back and forth between Jack and me. "I think my parents are . . . I think we're going to be out of town. My dad—"

Jack cut him off. "It's okay, Mitch. It's not your battle. It's probably better that you don't come."

Mitchell looked relieved. "If you say so."

"I'm there," Zeus said.

"In with both feet," Ian said. "Girls?"

Jack and Zeus both looked at Abigail. She shrugged. "I'm coming."

"Me too," McKenna said. "You're going to need me."

"You can count on that," Ostin said.

McKenna turned to Grace. "How about you?"

She looked at us. "I guess I'm in too."

"Actually," I said, "it might be better if you stayed back."

"Why?"

"If Hatch catches you, he'll force you to reveal how much you downloaded. That will jeopardize all the information we already got from them. Plus, you know he won't hold back on your punishment. It's probably best if you're not with us."

"Where will I go?"

"With the voice."

Grace looked at me nervously. "But we don't know who they are."

"I know," I said. "Either way, it's a risk. It's your decision. But if Hatch catches you . . ."

"You know what Hatch does to traitors," Zeus said.

I looked at Zeus. I was afraid for him as well.

Grace looked down for a moment, then said, "All right. I'd probably just be in the way anyway."

"I think it's the smart choice," Taylor said.

"So when do we go?" Zeus asked.

"I don't know."

"Then I have a suggestion," Zeus said. "We need to better prepare ourselves."

"How do we prepare for the unknown?" Ostin asked.

"By practicing our powers."

"Practice?" Ostin said.

"We practiced using them every day in the academy. When I first got there, I could only shock things less than a yard away. Now I can shoot more than fifty yards."

"How do we practice our powers?" Taylor asked.

"By using them. Our powers are like muscles. They get stronger with use. And we need to eat right. We need to eat more bananas. More potassium."

"There are things with more potassium than bananas," Ostin said. "Spinach has nearly twice the potassium as bananas."

"The Elgen scientists would have known that," Ian said. "There must be something special about bananas."

"To begin with, they taste a lot better than spinach," McKenna said.

"Mitchell," I said. "When do your parents get back?"

"Not until two weeks from tomorrow. They decided to stay an extra four days in Hawaii."

"By then we should be gone." I looked around at the group. "So, I guess that's that. I'll let you know as soon as I hear something. In the meantime I suggest we take Zeus's advice and prepare ourselves. Zeus, can you coach us?"

Zeus nodded. "I'm your man."

Later that afternoon a white, windowless appliance repair van pulled into Mitchell's driveway. A husky man wearing a blue jumpsuit came to the door. "I'm here to check your washer," he said.

"What?" Mitchell asked.

"You know why I'm here," he said.

"Oh right. Come in."

The man stepped inside, and Mitchell shut the door behind him. I stepped forward. Zeus, Ian, and Jack stood by my side while Taylor and Ostin stood on the opposite side of the foyer.

"Why are you here?" I asked.

He looked at me apprehensively. "I've come for the computer."

"You can't have the computer," I said. "We need it. But we've copied the information to a hard drive."

"That will do," the man said. "Where is it?"

"Before we give it to you, we need you to sit down." I pointed to the upholstered chair we'd dragged from the den into the foyer.

The man looked at us suspiciously. "What is this about?"

"We're protecting ourselves," I said. "Now sit down."

His eyes darted back and forth between us. "I'm not sitting anywhere." He started toward the door.

Zeus shot a blue bolt of electricity to the door handle, the sound of which filled the room. The man jumped back. Zeus held up his hands and electricity arced between his fingers. "Try that again and I'll light you up like a Christmas tree."

The man glared at us.

"He's got two guns," Ian said. "One in a shoulder holster, the other on his ankle."

"Put your hands in the air, now," I said firmly.

Zeus stretched his hands forward. "You've got three seconds to comply, man. You go for the guns it's the last thing you'll ever do."

The man looked exasperated. "Look, guys, we're on the same side."

"Then you won't mind if we check your story," I said.

The man hesitated, then slowly raised his hands in the air. "Okay. Do it your way. Whatever you say." He sat in the chair. I walked over and put my hand on his shoulder. "Don't move."

"You know he's got enough amps to make sure you never move again," Ostin said.

"We know what Michael can do," the man said. "Let's just get this over with. The longer I'm here the riskier."

"Jack, take his guns," I said.

Jack pulled the man's guns from the two holsters. "Nice," he said, examining the pieces. "A Glock and a Walther P99."

"I want those back," he said.

Taylor and Ostin walked over to the man. Taylor put her hands on his head while Ostin held out the list of questions he'd written.

"I want you to answer these questions in your mind," Ostin said.

He began reading from the list we'd put together as a group, asking each question twice and pausing between each question until Taylor nodded for him to continue.

"Who sent you?"

"Why are you helping us?"

"Did you know we were going to be attacked at the safe house?"

"Did you really blow up the third car?"

"Are you going to help us get to Peru?"

"Are you allies with the Elgen?"

"Are you helping the Elgen?"

"How do you feel about the Elgen?"

"How do you feel about Dr. C. J. Hatch?"

When Ostin had finished reading his list, I looked over at Taylor. "What do you think?"

"I think he's on our side."

Mitchell brought down the hard drive, and I handed it over to the man. "We've lived up to our side of the bargain. When do we go to Peru?"

"We'll call," he said. "There's a lot of preparation that needs to happen first."

"How long?"

"I don't know. Could be a few days, could be a few weeks."

"A few weeks?"

"This will take some planning. We need to get you as close as possible without them knowing. Be ready and wait for our call."

He put the hard drive in his bag and locked it. Jack returned the man's guns. He put them back in their holsters, then walked to the door. "Be ready."

He saluted me, opened the door, then walked out to his van.

# 20

## The Call

The days we spent waiting for the phone call felt like an eternity. Ian, Zeus, McKenna, Abigail, and Grace didn't have to worry about being recognized in public, but we were pretty sure the Elgen were still lurking about, so they hid out as well. For the next week we mostly sat around the house playing cards and video games or watching television.

We also practiced our powers. My electricity had, as Ostin theorized, continued to increase. So had my magnetism. I was doing things that surprised me. After my first full day of practice, I pulled a bicycle over to me in Mitchell's garage from more than twenty feet away and, even more difficult, opened the refrigerator door from the kitchen table. I have to admit that magnetism was way more fun than shocking people, because it looked like magic and no one got hurt. By carefully varying my power I was even able to levitate objects. I started moving everything I could and quickly learned my own limitations. Magnetism is not like in the superhero movies. I couldn't pull a car toward myself, because a car weighs more than I do. I just ended up pulling myself to the car.

I wasn't the only one practicing my powers. One day McKenna got hot enough that she burned through some carpet and got a lecture from Mitchell, who was certain his parents would think he was smoking.

Taylor was practicing too. We were sitting around the pool when she showed me one of her new tricks.

"Are you still going to kiss me?" she asked.

I looked around, feeling a little confused. I couldn't remember what we were talking about or even offering her a kiss. "Sorry." I leaned forward and kissed her.

She laughed as she pulled away. "I'm sorry, but you said you wanted a demonstration."

"I wanted a demonstration of what?"

She cocked her head to one side.

"Did you just reboot me?"

She nodded. "You asked me to. I'll remind you of what we were talking about. Watch." She turned to Wade, who was standing a few yards from us holding a piece of pizza in his hand. She put one hand to her temple. Wade paused midbite, then looked up with a dazed expression.

"Well?" Taylor said to him.

He looked at her with a blank gaze. "What?"

"Are you still going to give me that piece of pizza?"

He glanced around. "Oh, yeah. Sorry." He walked over and held out the piece to Taylor.

"You can keep it," she said. "I'm not hungry anymore."

"Thanks," he said, looking even more confused than before.

She turned to me and grinned. "See? That's the second time I've made him do that. You just don't remember the first time. And that's how I got you to kiss me. I've discovered that people are especially vulnerable to suggestion after I reboot them. The more confused they are, the more willing they are to believe others."

"That makes sense," I said. "Like, if you're lost, you'll trust a complete stranger to tell you where to go."

"Exactly. I'm also getting better at rebooting too. Watch this."

She focused on Mitchell, who was standing next to Jack on the opposite side of the pool. Suddenly he put his hands to his temples and groaned. "Ow."

"I can fill their heads so they can't think at all. It gives them a little headache. I think if I did it really hard, I could make someone faint."

"That could come in handy," I said.

"I'm going to keep working on it."

"I've been working on something too," I said. "Want to see?"

"Yeah."

I held my hand out toward Mitchell. My hand began shaking. Mitchell started to walk sideways toward the edge of the pool, as if he was being dragged, which, incidentally, he was.

"Hey, what the . . ."

Then he fell into the water. He popped up to the surface, sputtering and flailing. "Who pushed me?" he shouted. "Who pushed me?"

Jack was laughing. "No one, you idiot."

Taylor burst out laughing. "You really just did that?"

I was grinning. "I locked onto his belt buckle. Cool, right?"

"Way cool."

"Kylee can do that," Zeus said.

I looked back, unaware that Zeus had been watching.

"She can climb metal walls too."

"Climb walls?"

"It's just timing. Like using suction cups. Lock onto the wall with magnets, then release one hand and the opposite leg at the same time and move them up, lock on and repeat."

"That would be cool," I said. "If I could find some metal walls."

While we practiced our powers, the nonelectrics did too. Jack did like a thousand push-ups a day, went on a strict diet of raw-egg-and-protein drinks, and practiced hand-to-hand combat and ultimate fighting techniques with Wade and Mitchell, who seemed more like punching bags than opponents and every day sported fresh bruises.

Ostin researched. He dug through Grace's information like a gold miner at the mother lode. Within days he had pulled up everything the mainframe had on the Peruvian compound, including an early architectural drawing of the facility.

He spent most of his time looking for a way in. What made breaking into the compound especially difficult was that it was surrounded by a lot of land and ringed by tall electric fences. It was clear that the Elgen had built a large buffer around the facility to prevent unwanted guests.

When a week had passed, I began to worry again about the voice, particularly because of all the information we had handed over. Could the man we had interrogated somehow have tricked Taylor? They knew about her powers; maybe they had been prepared to deceive us. Maybe they had technology we didn't know about. Eight days from the man's visit, my phone finally rang.

"I understand you gave my man some grief," the voice said.

"We were being careful," I said.

"Good," he said. "You should be. You leave for Peru tomorrow morning at six. Drive to the same place you picked up the Hummers. Do you remember the place?"

"Yes."

"There will be two black Ford Excursions waiting for you. They will drive you to the airport. What did Grace decide?"

"She's decided to stay behind with you. Keep her safe."

"We will."

"Okay," I said. "I'll let everybody know. Anything we need to take with us?"

There was a short pause. "Courage," he said. "Lots of courage."

I gathered everyone together to tell them about the call. Afterward, Ostin took a moment and briefed us on what he'd learned about the compound. Things got quiet fast. For the first time, the reality of what we were attempting set in.

I asked if anyone had questions, and no one did—at least none they wanted to share. I had no doubt there would be plenty to come—more than I had answers for. At the end of the briefing I said, "If you've changed your mind, it's not too late to back out."

"We're not backing out," Jack said. *"Semper Fi."*

"What does that mean?" Taylor asked.

"Always faithful," Ostin said. "It's the Marine Corps motto."

"We're all in," Ian said. Everyone else nodded their heads in agreement.

"Thanks, guys. Get some sleep. We've got a long day tomorrow."

As everyone got ready for bed, I slipped out alone by the pool, settling into one of the vinyl lounge chairs. The pool area was dark, lit only by the solar lights in the corner of the yard and the blue, shimmering luminescence of the pool's light. The only sound was a symphony of crickets.

I needed to get away and think. Or maybe to *not* think. I had too many thoughts to effectively corral and too many fears to accompany them. I had been gulping all day, and I took a few deep breaths to calm myself.

I cupped my hands together, like I was making a snowball, and pulsed. To my surprise a ball of electricity formed, almost like a soap bubble, except with more weight, like a Ping-Pong ball. Out of curiosity, I tossed it away from me. It hit the ground and popped loudly with a crisp electric snap.

I made another and threw it into the pool. It exploded in the water, lighting the entire pool. "That is so cool," I said.

I made another and threw it across the pool. I hadn't noticed there was a cat on the other side, and although the bubble didn't hit it, the cat screeched and ran off.

The glass door slid open and Ostin walked out. "There you are," he said. "I was wondering where you went."

"Come here," I said. "I want to show you something."

I pulsed as I had before, and a glowing orb about the size of a golf ball rose from my hand. I threw it into the pool. This time the pop was as loud as a firecracker. I thought Ostin's jaw was going to fall off.

"Pretty cool, isn't it?"

"Do you know what that is?" he said.

"A ball of lightning," I said.

"That's exactly what it is! Scientists have been arguing for centuries about whether or not ball lightning exists. You just solved a centuries-old debate. Do it again."

I was about to make another when Taylor walked out of the house. "Michael?"

"I'm over here," I said.

She walked over to my side. "I was wondering where you'd gone. What are you guys doing?"

"You gotta see this," Ostin said.

Taylor sat down in the lounge chair next to me. "See what?"

"Do it, Michael."

I pulsed, forming another ball. This one was larger than my first, about the size of a baseball.

Taylor leaned forward to look at it. "It's kind of beautiful. Can I touch it?"

"It will definitely shock you," Ostin said. "It's lightning. Just in a different package."

Taylor pulled back.

"Watch this," I said. I threw it at the pool. It came off my hand like a softball and exploded in the water, briefly illuminating the entire surface.

"That's so cool," Taylor said.

"I wonder how I could measure the amps of one of those," Ostin said, settling into the lounge chair to my left.

I made a few more while Taylor and Ostin watched.

Taylor said to Ostin, "Hey, Tex. Would you mind going inside for a moment? I need to talk to Michael."

"You can talk to him," he said.

"Alone," she said.

He looked at her, then me. "Okay," he said. He stood up. "For how long?"

"I don't know," Taylor said. "Until we're done."

He walked inside, sliding the glass door shut behind him. I looked at Taylor. Her eyes were soft.

"You okay?" I asked.

She nodded. "It's you I'm worried about. How are *you* doing?"

"I'm fine," I said. "Why? Was I ticking a lot?"

"Some," she said. "How can you be just fine? Your mother's gone, the Elgen are hunting us, we're about to fly to a strange country, and everyone's depending on you for answers. I don't know how you handle all the pressure. I know I couldn't do it."

I exhaled. "I don't know. What else am I going to do?" Suddenly my eyes began to tear up. I looked away so she wouldn't see.

Taylor got up and pushed her chair next to mine. "Come here," she said.

I looked back at her and she smiled. "Come closer," she said.

I leaned in to her and she put her arms around me. She put her chin against my forehead and gently stroked the back of my head. It felt so good.

"You don't have to be strong all the time," she said. "Even heroes need to be taken care of."

"I'm not a hero," I said. "I'm a fifteen-year-old who has no idea what he's doing."

She was quiet for a moment, then she kissed the top of my head and said, "You're *my* hero."

I didn't know what to say. Maybe there wasn't anything to be said. I just closed my eyes and felt her warm face against mine and, for the first time in weeks, felt peace.

# PART 2

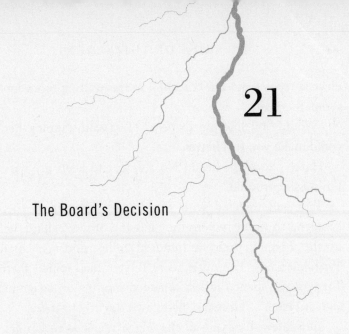

# 21

## The Board's Decision

"**I** hate boats," Hatch said, wiping his forehead with a gold-monogrammed handkerchief. The boat he was *hating* was a superyacht with all the luxuries befitting a $450 million vessel: a helipad, two current-jetted swimming pools, and an art gallery that included two van Goghs, three Escher lithographs, and a Rembrandt (the chairman had a penchant for Dutch artists). There were luxury suites for eighteen and an exclusive dining room with crystal chandeliers and scarlet wool carpet interwoven with twenty-four-karat gold thread. The yacht also featured some less luxuriant but interesting add-ons, including radar, sonar, and surface-to-air missiles.

Hatch was prone to seasickness, and although he understood the necessity of moving the Elgen corporate headquarters to international waters, he would have preferred the ship to remain docked in some obscure bay off the coast of Africa or the Philippines. The two electric teens seated next to him in the waiting room looked at him sympathetically.

"Would you like me to help?" Tara said, tapping her temple. "I could make you feel better."

Hatch shook his head. "No. I've got to keep my wits about me. I'm sensing trouble."

Tara had traveled with Hatch and the rest of the kids from Pasadena to Rome, where they left the others behind, helicoptering to the Elgen's yacht a hundred miles north of Sicily—in the Tyrrhenian Sea. The other teen, Torstyn, had joined them in Rome. Torstyn had spent the last nineteen months on assignment in Peru and, at Hatch's command, had flown directly to Italy.

Tara knew Torstyn—all the Elgen teens were familiar with one another—but she hadn't seen him in a long time and he had changed. His skin was darker from the South American sun, and his hair was long and wild. His personality had changed as well. Something about him frightened her.

"How long will we be here?" Torstyn asked, his hand extended toward the hundred-gallon saltwater aquarium built into the wall in front of them.

"Only as long as we need to be," Hatch said.

"Stop it!" Tara said.

"Stop *what*?" Torstyn asked, grinning.

"You know *what*. You killed the fish."

Torstyn had boiled the water in the aquarium from fifteen feet away. Two exotic angelfish were now floating on top of the water.

"They're just fish," Torstyn said. "Same thing you ate last night."

"Actually," Hatch said. "They were rare peppermint angelfish, found only in the waters of Rarotonga, in the South Pacific. I gave them to the chairman as a gift last year. They run about twenty-five thousand dollars apiece."

Torstyn frowned. "Sorry, sir."

"Ask next time."

"Yes, sir."

Hatch looked at him coolly, then asked, "How long did it take you?"

"About forty seconds."

"Good. I want you to get it down to twenty."

"Yes, sir."

"Then ten."

"Yes, sir."

Hatch nodded. "At ten you'll be unstoppable."

"Yes, sir. Thank you, sir."

Hatch went back to his e-reader. He'd been reading a book on mind control written in the late fifties by William Sargant, a British psychiatrist. He had already read the book several times. He was fascinated with the subject and had studied all aspects of mind control from hypnosis to suicide cults.

A slender, well-dressed woman in her midthirties walked into the waiting room. "Excuse me, Dr. Hatch?"

Hatch looked up.

"The board is ready to see you now."

Hatch stood, tossing his reader on the sofa cushion next to Tara. "I'll be right back," he said.

"Do you want us to come with you?" Torstyn asked.

"No, you're not invited." He walked to the conference room door, then turned back. "But stay alert."

"Yes, sir," they said, almost in unison.

Hatch straightened his tie, then walked into the conference room. An Elgen guard stood on each side of the door. Neither of them saluted him. The guards on the boat were the only ones in the company who never saluted Hatch. He walked past them into the room.

The boardroom was bright and the walls were covered with stainless steel tiles. Recessed directional lighting illuminated the art on the wall—large, black pictures with red, abstract silhouettes, images that looked more like inkblot tests than art. The shape of the room was trapezoidal; one entered in at the smaller end and broadening out in the rear. The outer wall, to Hatch's right, was made of thick, protective glass, forming an eight-foot-tall window looking out over the crested waves sixty feet below.

The table in the middle of the room was twenty-seven feet long and made of rare Brazilian rosewood, with brushed stainless steel trim around the edge. The table was surrounded by twelve high-backed chairs upholstered in black Italian leather and spaced every few feet. All of the chairs were filled except for two, one next to the chairman and one at the opposite end of the table, which was usually reserved for visitors.

The board was split evenly between men and women—all over fifty, a few gray with years. Anonymity was essential to the Elgen, and board members used numbers instead of names, the numbers corresponding to their term of service and place at the table. The chairman, Giacomo Schema, was Number One and the only member of the board who used his name.

Every eye was on Hatch as he entered the room. Although he had, at one time, served as CEO of Elgen Inc., the company had been reorganized after the original MEI machine was discovered to be dangerous. Hatch had been removed from the board, but had served ever since as the executive director, overseeing the daily affairs of the company. His relationship with the board had been volatile, and more than once there had been motions to remove him as director. But the company's growing profitability and status had, at least to that moment, ensured his longevity.

"Chairman Schema, board members," Hatch said, slightly nodding.

"Welcome, Dr. Hatch," the chairman said. "I trust your flight wasn't overly taxing." Chairman Schema was a broad, barrel-chested Italian who dressed impeccably in Armani suits with silk ascots.

"No, thank you. I'm used to the flight."

"Take a seat, please," Schema said, motioning to the chair at the opposite end of the table.

"Thank you." Hatch pulled the chair out and sat down.

"Tell us about the disaster in Pasadena," Schema said, no longer concealing his anger.

"As I wrote in my report, one of the electric children—"

"Michael Vey," Six, one of the board members to his left, said.

Hatch looked at her. "Yes," he confirmed. "Vey managed to

overpower one of our youths, the one you know as Zeus, and recruited him to help him free the others."

"How did he accomplish this? Was Vey left unguarded?"

"On the contrary. He was actually strapped down and being watched by three guards and Zeus. We believe that Vey may have telepathic powers we were unaware of—powers like Tara's or her sister, Taylor. Shall I continue?"

Chairman Schema waved his hand in an angry flourish. "By all means."

"The surveillance cameras in the room were blown out, so we've had to deduce much of what transpired. From what we've gathered, after Vey overpowered Zeus, he freed two of his accomplices who were locked down and the four of them attacked the guards in the hallway outside. They then released three more of the children who had been kept in seclusion—Ian, Abigail, and McKenna. Together, the seven of them attacked the academy and freed the GPs. The GPs managed to arm themselves, and for the protection of the rest of the children, we were forced to flee."

"What is the status of the freed GPs now?"

"The GPs are all accounted for except three. Two of them are with Vey, the other one, we believe, committed suicide in an aqueduct. His RFID tags are no longer registering. We are awaiting a report on the body."

"What about the children?" Three asked.

"We lost seven. . . ."

There was an audible groan from both sides of the table.

Hatch looked around, then said in a softer voice, "We lost seven. Vey; Zeus; Tara's twin, Taylor; and the three from Cell Block H—Ian, Abigail, and McKenna."

"Please, remind us of their gifts," Four said.

"Ian sees through electrolocation. . . ."

"Which means?" Chairman Schema asked.

"He can see through solid objects that humans cannot. McKenna can generate heat and light. Abigail can eliminate pain by stimulating nerve endings."

"I could use her for my headache right now," Eight said wryly.

Hatch ignored the comment. "Then, as I mentioned, Zeus, who can throw electricity."

"That's only six," Chairman Schema said.

"We also lost Grace."

"They captured her?"

Hatch interlaced his fingers in front of him. "Yes, we think so."

"What is it that Grace does?"

"She can hack into data systems and store information like a hard drive."

Six asked, "Did she hack into our system? Does she have confidential information that could compromise our security?"

"She was never given access to our mainframe."

"Were the children still in the building when you fled?" Three asked.

"Yes. They were."

"Then may we presume that she had access to the mainframe after you left?"

"The mainframe was set on self-destruct, so all the information was destroyed. But there was a short window of opportunity, so it is possible she downloaded *some* information, but even that is highly unlikely. Especially if she was taken against her will."

"What makes you think she was taken against her will?" Six asked.

"As we gathered up the other youths, we were not able to locate her. We believe she was on one of the other floors when the attack occurred."

Eight shook his head in disgust. "What a nightmare."

Chairman Schema leaned forward, pressing his fingertips together. "You had reported to me . . . actually, you had *promised* me, that the children would be back in your custody two days ago. But they are not."

"No. Vey and his associates have eluded two of our traps."

"Two?"

"They were tipped off to the first one. They attacked and tied up our watch, then fled the scene. We tracked them down to a home where they were hiding, and they were all captured. But they managed to overpower the guards and escape."

"This seems to be part of a pattern, Dr. Hatch," Chairman Schema said angrily. "I am beginning to doubt your ability to capture Vey and his friends."

"These are very powerful youths. The combination of their unique powers makes apprehending them, as Eight so aptly put it, a nightmare. Especially since our objective is to bring them in alive."

"What provoked Vey's attack in the first place?" Three asked.

"Vey was looking for his mother. We captured and held him for more than three weeks before he attempted his escape."

Three leaned forward. "And did he find his mother?"

"No. She wasn't being held in Pasadena. She's currently detained in our compound in Peru."

"So now we are holding hostages too?" Eight said.

Hatch replied, "She's the bait we need to recapture her son."

Chairman Schema slammed his hand on the table. "Dr. Hatch, your missteps continue to compromise this organization. First you were abducting children, now you are abducting their parents. These are crimes for which the board may be held accountable."

"Which is why we reside in international waters," Hatch said. "Mr. Chairman, may I remind the board that we were all complicit in much greater crimes with the death of forty-two infants. It was our cover-up of that incident that revealed the phenomenon of the electric children in the first place."

"Strike that from the record," Chairman Schema said to the board member taking notes. "Yes, we are aware of our complicity in that matter. And every time you pursue additional lawlessness, you further endanger this board. Are you mindful of this?"

"I do not take any of our actions lightly, Mr. Chairman. What has been done is part of our ongoing Neo-Species Genesis program, a program that has been unanimously approved by the board, not once but repeatedly, over the past decade."

"Which is precisely what we wish to discuss this morning," Chairman Schema said. "Dr. Hatch, in the last decade you have spent two hundred and forty-six million dollars in the Neo-Species program. Other than the 'accidental' creation of the original seventeen children, have you successfully replicated an electric human?"

"No, sir. But we believe we're close."

"What evidence would you have to support what seems to me a rather optimistic assessment?"

"As you're well aware, we've now successfully altered the electric composition of other mammals, and we are about to begin testing on primates. Also, there have been many other worthwhile discoveries and advancements that have come as a result of the program. The Starxource initiative wouldn't exist if it wasn't for the Neo-Species program—surely that alone warrants its continuation."

"Dr. Hatch is right," Four said. "The Starxource program is of inestimable value."

"Thank you," Hatch said. "And we don't know what other beneficial advancements the program will generate in the future."

Board member Two spoke up for the first time. "I am the first to commend you for your success with the Starxource program, Doctor. Our power plants have been even more successful than we envisioned or hoped for. My question is, now that we have found a commercially viable use for the technology, why should we continue pursuing an end, which, after more than a decade, appears to be a dead one?"

"I would second that argument," Nine said. "Even if we are successful in achieving your Neo-Species goals, I see no commercial application."

"Commercial application?" Hatch blurted out. "We're talking about creating a new species of human beings. We are altering the very course of human history."

"Exactly," Nine said. "And how do you propose we monetize that? These are people, not machines. If we create an electric person, they are free to do whatever they want with that power. What is to keep them from sharing their gifts with the highest bidder?" Nine turned to the chairman. "It is not our objective to create history, it is our mission and corporate objective to create profits. If the doctor's goal is a worthy one, and I have no doubt that he intends it as such, I suggest he create a charitable organization to pursue these ends—but separate it from the corporate body."

Hatch didn't answer, though some of them noticed his hands trembling with anger.

"At any rate," Two said, "whatever good may come from electrifying people, it certainly will not generate more profits than the already proven Starxource initiative. We have a very real opportunity to become a force of global power, larger than OPEC or any of the oil-producing countries of the world."

This started a discussion among the board members. Chairman Schema raised his hands for silence. When the room was quiet he turned his attention to Hatch. "Dr. Hatch, you should be aware that this discussion on the continuance of the Neo-Species program is more than a hypothetical one. Several months ago a motion was brought before the board to shut down the program entirely. At that time we tabled the motion until you could join us in person and be given the opportunity to defend your work."

Hatch turned red. "Shut down the program? That would be ludicrous. The power of this corporation exists because of this program."

"That is incorrect," Twelve said, speaking out for the first time. "The MEI was developed prior to the Neo-Species program. Unfortunately it is still too dangerous to use. The only part of the machine we can duplicate is the part that kills people. I agree with the commercial assessment proffered by Nine. I believe we should focus our efforts on the propagation of the Starxource initiative, to the exclusion of all else. Future discoveries will still come, just from Starxource labs."

"I have a question," Three said, looking over a document. "Please explain this twenty-seven-million-dollar price tag for our facility in Peru. It's nearly double the cost of our other plants."

"We added a new guard training facility as well," Hatch answered.

"What are we training them to do? Fly?"

Several members chuckled. Hatch looked at Three, concealing his fierce anger behind a controlled demeanor. She had been against him from the beginning.

"Elgen security is of utmost importance," Hatch said. "Just one leak of our information or the theft of one pair of breeding rats could endanger our entire operation. Security is no place to count pennies."

"Twenty-seven million dollars is hardly pennies," she retorted.

"Dr. Hatch has a valid point," Chairman Schema said. "But why Peru?"

"Peru gives us a certain latitude to train in privacy and in the manner we consider best practice."

"Very well," the chairman said. "Is there anything else you would like to say, Dr. Hatch, before we vote on the future of the program?"

Hatch glanced around the room. "What you are considering . . . to shut down the Neo-Species Genesis program is to turn our backs on the future."

"Wait, wait," Three said. "What future are you speaking to? Certainly not the Starxource program. The future could not be brighter." She turned to the other board members. "I sound like the slogan, don't I?"

"Please," Hatch said. "Just give me another year. We are on the verge of a breakthrough. With the finding of Vey and the twin, Taylor, we expect critical advancement."

"But you don't have Vey or Taylor," Three said.

"We will soon. I promise you, you won't be disappointed." Hatch turned to Chairman Schema. "Just give me twelve more months."

"We've been hearing a lot of promises but seeing few results," Three said. "You ask for another year, I would maintain that we've given you five years too many. At least."

"Mr. Chairman," Four said, "I move that we suspend discussion for a vote."

"Do I have a second?" Chairman Schema asked.

Three hands went up.

"Very well. Doctor, if you would please leave the room while we conduct a vote."

Hatch slowly stood, looking over the board members. "Shutting down the Neo-Species Genesis program would be a huge mistake, one I believe you will live to regret."

"Noted," Chairman Schema said. "If you would please wait in the reception area, we will momentarily notify you of our decision."

Hatch walked outside the room, shutting the door behind him. Tara and Torstyn watched him enter. They could see from his expression how angry he was. Torstyn started to speak, "What's—?"

Hatch held up his hand to silence him. "They are voting on our future." He sat down on the couch. Nothing was said. Less than a minute later the door opened.

"Dr. Hatch, you may come in now."

Hatch returned to the conference room. Few of the board members were looking at him, and from the sympathetic expression of those who were, he knew how the vote had gone.

"The vote was not unanimous," Chairman Schema said. "But there was a majority vote in the affirmative to dissolve the Neo-Species Genesis program. To avoid further expenditures we are asking you to fly immediately to Peru, where you will relieve the scientists who are involved with the program."

"But . . ."

Chairman Schema raised his hand. "You will relieve these scientists of their current duties. Obviously we cannot just release them back into society, so they will be assimilated into the Starxource program. Their expertise led to the creation of this program, so we expect that their talents will be put to good use in maintaining and improving the program. At our current rate of growth and demand we will certainly need their specialized knowledge.

"The GPs, of course, are no longer of use to us. For obvious reasons, we can't just release them, as that would cause serious problems and inquiries into our activities. We trust that you will find a creative *solution* to this problem. We don't want to know about it."

"What about the electric children?" Hatch asked.

"It is also the decision of the board that the electric children should be reintegrated into normal society. An endowment will be established for each one allowing them to pursue further educational or vocational opportunities.

"As for Vey, you will reunite the boy with his mother with sufficient monetary remuneration to guarantee that there will be no lawsuits filed. We expect you to work with Legal to ensure that this delicate situation is handled discreetly."

Hatch was speechless.

"This is not a censure, Doctor, this is simply a change in course. We appreciate your devotion and the success that your efforts have brought to our company."

Hatch clenched his hands behind his back, his jaw tightening. "Do you have a time frame for this action?"

"We desire an immediate shutdown. We expect you to be in Peru within two days to begin the process. We realize that your relationship with the children is as personal as it is professional, so your timeline for that transition is up to you and the children to decide; however we expect that all business related to this matter be finalized before the end of this calendar year. We ask to be kept informed in all aspects of the transition. We thank you in advance for your expeditious handling of this matter, and we trust that it will be more successful than the shutdown of the Pasadena facility."

Hatch looked around the room, veiling his contempt for most of the gathered body. "Yes, sir. I'll see to it immediately." He turned on his heel and walked out of the room.

Tara and Torstyn stood as he entered. "Come on," he said. "We're leaving."

Walking to the helipad, Torstyn asked, "Where are we going?"

"To Rome to gather the others. Then we're headed back to Peru."

Within minutes the three of them were hovering over the Tyrrhenian Sea on the flight back to Rome.

"What did they say, sir?"

"They want to dismantle the NSG program."

The kids looked at each other.

"What?" Torstyn asked. "How come?"

"What about us?" Tara asked.

"I'll tell you on the plane," Hatch said. He glanced down at his satellite phone. "No! No! No!" he shouted. He pressed a button on his phone. "Get me Dr. Jung immediately."

"What is it?" Tara asked.

Hatch looked at her with a dark expression. "Tanner just tried to kill himself."

# 22

## More Bad News

The Elgen helicopter landed around 7:00 p.m. atop the six-story Elgen building just outside of Rome. Bright orange lights flashed at the corners of the structure, silhouetting the waiting guards dressed in the Elgen black uniform.

"Welcome back, sir," one of the guards shouted over the sound of the helicopter's rotors.

Hatch shouted to Tara and Torstyn, "Get something to eat, then gather up the rest of the family in the conference room by eight." He turned to the guard. "Where is Tanner?"

"He's in restraints in the basement detaining cell, sir."

"Where is Dr. Jung?"

"He's in the basement with him, observing, sir."

"Come with me."

They took an elevator from the roof. Tara and Torstyn got off on the second floor while Hatch and the guards went all the way down to the basement level.

The marble-tiled corridor was dimly lit and the only sound was the echo of their footsteps as they walked. The observation room and detaining cells were at the end of the hallway. One of the guards opened the door, and Hatch stepped in.

Dr. Jung, the resident psychiatrist, was sitting in a chair facing a two-way mirror that looked into the adjacent room. He stood as Hatch entered.

"Dr. Hatch, I was just—"

Hatch raised his hand, silencing the psychiatrist. He leaned forward toward the glass to better comprehend what he was seeing in the next room.

Tanner, one of the seventeen electric children, was cuffed and curled up in bed in the fetal position, softly whimpering. His long, red hair was tangled up around his face.

Hatch studied him for a moment, then turned back toward the doctor.

"You incompetent worm. I told you to fix him. Do those letters before your name even mean anything?"

The psychiatrist was red in the face. "I'm doing my best."

"And your *best* is in restraints curled up in the corner of his room."

"He's not a machine, sir. He's a boy. You can't just go in and change out a few parts and make him better."

"But I can change out a few doctors," Hatch said.

The psychiatrist took the threat seriously. He'd heard rumors about what happened to those dispatched from the Elgen service. Most became GPs. Some of them just disappeared. He began stuttering, "W-w-what do you want me to do?"

"Why are you asking me? You're the shrink. Give him a pill. Give him a hundred pills, just fix him."

"He has a conscience. If you killed a thousand people, you'd have trouble sleeping at night too."

Hatch leaned in toward him, his eyes narrowing. "I *never* have trouble sleeping, Doctor. And if you ever insinuate anything like that again, I'll see to it that you never have trouble sleeping either."

The doctor swallowed. "I didn't mean to imply . . . Tanner's just really stressed right now. He's been worked too hard. Children need downtime. We need to let him spend some time with the other teenagers. And his parents."

"His parents?" Hatch said softly. "You think he should see his parents?"

The doctor looked terrified. "He said he misses them."

"Of course he *misses* them, you idiot. That's why he's been taken from them. So you think he should spend a little quality time with them? And what if he tells his parents what he's been doing, and they tell him they would rather die than have him drop another plane from the sky? Add that to your list of mental problems." Hatch walked across the room. "You're on probation, Doctor. Don't disappoint me again."

"I'm sorry, sir. I'll figure him out."

"You better. I'm taking both of you with me to Peru. I expect the boy to be heavily sedated. Heavily. I don't want to be along for the ride when he decides to take his life again. We leave first thing in the morning, oh five hundred hours."

"Yes, sir."

Hatch looked back at Tanner for a moment, then turned and walked out of the room. On the way to the elevator Hatch's phone rang.

"Dr. Hatch, Captain Welch is on the line."

"Put him through." Hatch paused in the hallway. "Did you capture Vey?"

"No. We lost him."

"How do you lose a tracking device?"

"He must have discovered the RFID tracers in the GPs and disabled them."

Hatch's anger reached a new high. "Find them now!"

"Yes, sir. We'll find them, sir."

Hatch threw his phone across the hall. "Vey!"

The guard retrieved his phone and held open the elevator door. "Your phone, sir."

Hatch took it from him. "Fifth floor."

# 23

## The Family Meeting

Quentin, Tara, Kylee, and Bryan were sitting in the Elgen dining room waiting for Hatch to arrive. Torstyn was on the opposite side of the room, looking through a stack of *Soldier of Fortune* magazines.

"What's Torstyn's power?" Bryan whispered.

The kids rarely talked about one another's powers, and Torstyn had been separated from them for so long that some of them had forgotten what he could do.

"He's like a human microwave oven," Tara said.

"That could come in handy," Bryan said.

"Yeah," Quentin said dryly. "Around lunchtime."

Torstyn suddenly looked up from the magazine he was browsing, and Bryan quickly turned away. Torstyn stood up and walked over to the group. "Hey, Tara," he said. "Do that thing again."

"What thing?"

"You know, what you did on the helicopter with your powers."

Quentin looked at Tara, and she blushed. "I don't know. . . ."

"Oh, come on. You said you needed to practice."

Quentin's eyes narrowed. "Whatever it is, she doesn't want to do it. So leave her alone."

"I wasn't talking to you, pretty boy. Mind your own business."

"I'm the student body president of the academy, so Tara is my business."

Torstyn grinned. "That is pathetic. Never before has so little power gone to somebody's head. And in case you didn't get the memo, school's out, loser."

Quentin turned red in the face. "Don't push your luck, Tor-Stain."

Torstyn pushed his face into Quentin's. "Do you think I'm afraid of you? While you've spent the last year and a half lounging around California in designer jeans and polo shirts, drinking girlie drinks with little umbrellas in them, you know what I've been doing for fun? I hunt anacondas alone in the jungles. No gun. No machete. Just me." He rolled up his sleeve to show a ragged scar across his biceps leading to two large puncture wounds.

All the kids stared, and Torstyn was pleased by their response. "Last January, during the rainy season, I was wading through a patch of jungle when a thirty-foot anaconda shot out of the water and grabbed me by the arm. It tried to drag me into the river."

"No way, dude," Bryan said.

Torstyn smiled. "As it was wrapping its coils around me, I looked it in the eyes and cooked it. Its brain exploded out its ears."

"Whoa!" Bryan said. "Awesome!"

"I had some of the servants drag the snake back to the compound, and I had boots made out of its skin. The thing was a monster. I could have made a dozen pairs." Torstyn looked at Quentin and sneered. "I'm guessing the scariest thing you've faced in the last year was too much starch in your shorts, pretty boy."

Quentin didn't back down. "You want to see how much you scare me, Tarzan?" Quentin said. The air around him began to crackle with electricity.

"Don't start what you don't want me to finish, tough guy," Torstyn said.

"C'mon, guys," Tara said. "This isn't cool. Someone could get hurt."

"Shut up," Bryan said. "I want to see them fight. Battle of the Titans."

"There better not be a fight," Hatch said sternly, walking into the room. "Stand down. Both of you." He looked at Torstyn. "You weren't thinking of using your powers on another family member?"

Torstyn fidgeted. "Uh, no, sir."

"And you, Quentin?"

"No, sir. I was protecting Tara's honor, sir."

"That sounds noble," Hatch said facetiously. "You were going to protect her 'honor' with your powers?"

He swallowed. "It hadn't come to that, sir."

"You both should be glad for that. Remember my rules, gentlemen. Then remember the penalty for breaking my rules."

"Yes, sir," they both said.

"Now listen up. We are flying out first thing in the morning. So pack up tonight. We'll be gone awhile and where we're going there are no shopping malls and no concierge desk. You're going to be roughing it. So bring extra necessities. Especially you young ladies."

"How long will we be gone?" Kylee asked.

"More than a month. Possibly as long as a year."

"A year?" Tara said.

Quentin raised his hand. Torstyn rolled his eyes.

"May I ask where we're going, sir?" Quentin asked.

"No, you may not. I will fill everyone in on the details during the flight. Now go to bed. We have a long day tomorrow, and I need you all to be sharp. Everyone's excused except for Torstyn and Quentin. You two stay."

"Yes, sir," Quentin said.

Torstyn breathed out heavily. "All right."

When everyone had left Hatch looked at the two young men. Quentin's head was slightly bowed; Torstyn was slumped down in his chair.

"Sit up," Hatch said to Torstyn.

"Yes, sir," he said, straightening himself up. "Sorry, sir."

"You thought you were going to fight? What were you thinking? This isn't a schoolyard playground. With your powers, any fight is to the death. Or have you grown stupid in the last two days? Who gave you permission to kill each other?"

They sat quietly, avoiding Hatch's fierce gaze.

"I asked you a question!" Hatch shouted. "Who told you that you could risk your life without my permission?"

"No one, sir," Quentin said.

Torstyn shook his head. "No one, sir."

Hatch leaned forward. "Let me make myself perfectly clear. I don't care what you think of each other. But if either of you lets your ego get in the way of what's about to happen, you'll spend the rest of your life guarding a Starxource plant in Outer Mongolia. Do you understand?"

"Yes, sir," they said in unison.

"There will be order and strict obedience. Do you understand me?"

"Yes, sir," they repeated.

"Good. Quentin has been in charge of the group for the last five years in Pasadena and has done an adequate job of keeping the Elgen youths in line. I see no reason to change that. Quentin will remain my number one."

Quentin crossed his arms triumphantly over his chest, giving Torstyn a satisfied look. "Thank you, sir."

"Don't get smug, Quentin. You're number one over the rest of the youths, but not Torstyn. Torstyn answers only to me."

"Thank you, sir," Torstyn said, glaring at Quentin.

"Where we're headed is no Beverly Hills vacation, and none of you, except Torstyn, are ready for what you're going to encounter. Torstyn knows what it takes to survive in a hostile environment, don't you, Torstyn?"

"Yes, sir."

"Now hear me and hear me well. Whatever you do, you will not get romantically involved with any members of the family. We do not need any complications right now—a house divided against itself cannot stand. Do you both understand?"

"Yes, sir," they said again.

"What we are facing will test everyone. We've lost half the youths already, and now Tanner is on the verge of cracking. In fact, he already has. I need both of you one hundred percent. Now shake hands."

Quentin reached out his hand. "My apologies."

Torstyn gripped his hand. "Okay," he said. "Me too."

"Good," Hatch said. "I'm not surprised that you're at odds. You're both alpha males and you're both warriors—which is exactly what I need right now. Warriors." He leaned forward. "Gentlemen, the pieces are in place and we're about to make the first move. The war has begun. But first we must cleanse the inner vessel."

# 24

A Close Call

The sun was just starting to rise in Rome as Dr. Hatch and the electric children drove in a small convoy of Mercedes-Benz vans to the Leonardo da Vinci–Fiumicino airport to board the Elgen's private jet. Only Tanner traveled alone, strapped to a gurney and heavily sedated. He was attended by his doctor and one guard.

Hatch was in the lead car with three guards and the driver. He was wearing his dark, custom glasses and wrote in a notebook the entire ride, speaking only when they reached their destination.

He didn't talk to the youths at all, except to hurry them onto the plane. They each took their own row of seats except for Tara and Kylee, who sat next to each other. Tanner and Dr. Jung were behind the others, near the back of the aircraft. Tanner's gurney was fastened to the wall next to Dr. Jung's seat and a screen was drawn around them. After the jet's cabin door was closed, Hatch disappeared into his private quarters, in the back of the plane.

The flight attendant distributed a breakfast parfait to the passengers, then offered a full hot breakfast, which only Torstyn took. Bryan and both of the girls fell asleep as soon as they were airborne.

About two hours after the jet had left the ground, Hatch came out of his quarters and walked to the front of the main cabin. He grabbed a microphone from the wall and spoke. "All right, everyone. Give me your attention."

He waited as the kids stirred. Quentin woke Tara and Kylee. "Dr. Hatch is speaking."

"Is everyone listening?" Hatch asked.

"Yes, sir," Quentin said.

"Show me the Elgen salute."

Everyone made the sign, touching the three middle fingers of their left hands to their temples, their thumb and little finger touching.

"Listen carefully. What I'm about to tell you is C10."

"Whoa," Bryan said. He glanced over at Quentin, who raised his eyebrows.

Hatch labeled messages to the teens in levels of confidentiality—the more important the message, the higher the level. C10 was the highest. Even Quentin had only heard a C10 once before. The consequence of divulging information was proportionate to the level of confidentiality. Revealing a C10 message to outsiders would carry the highest punishment—death by torture.

"We are flying to Peru because I have been ordered by the Elgen board to shut down and dismantle the Neo-Species Genesis program—the very program that brought you to me in the first place, the program that you and I have spent our *lives* on for the last twelve years. I have been instructed to reallocate the scientists to different Starxource operations, quietly exterminate the GPs, and then send you all off to lead your own lives as private, normal citizens of whatever country and school you choose, never to hear from us again." Hatch leaned back, waiting for the teens to react.

"What?" Quentin said, clearly stunned.

"They can't do that!" Tara said.

Kylee started crying.

After a moment Bryan said, "Does this mean no more family trips?"

"No more family trips," Hatch said calmly. "No more *family*. You're on your own."

Hatch stoically watched them as the reality settled in, his own emotions concealed behind his glasses. The teens were clearly upset, glancing back and forth at one another in disbelief, hoping that Dr. Hatch was playing some kind of a horrible prank.

Finally Hatch said, "So tell me, what do you have to say to that?"

Quentin was the first to speak. "With all due respect, sir. I think I can speak for all of us and say we don't like it. We want to stay with you."

Hatch glanced up and down the rows. "Is that true? Kylee?"

Kylee wiped her eyes. "Yes, sir. I don't want to be an orphan."

"Tara?"

"Me too, sir."

"Bryan?"

"I think it's the dumbest thing I've ever heard."

"Torstyn?"

"Sucks."

Hatch nodded a little. "Then I take it you disapprove, Torstyn?"

"Yes, sir. I disapprove."

Hatch paused for a moment. "Then the real question is, perhaps, what exactly would you be willing to do to keep the family together?"

"Whatever you tell us to do, sir," Quentin said. "Right, everyone?" He was answered with a chorus of affirmations.

Hatch studied their expressions for a moment, then nodded approvingly. "Exactly what I thought you would say. Now let me remind you that what I am going to tell you, every word of it, is C10. What is the punishment for disclosing a C10 secret? Tara."

"The punishment for disclosing a C10 secret is death by torture."

"That is correct," Hatch said. "If you understand, show me the salute."

They all put their fingers to their temples again.

Hatch looked down for a moment, then removed his glasses, carefully folding them and sliding them into his jacket's inner pocket. "I'm pleased to hear that you don't like the board's plans, because I have no intention of following them.

"Imagine, letting you go. You beautiful, powerful youths. Cast out as pearls among the swine of humanity. You, my eagles, are not to spend your lives pecking among the chickens. The chickens are for your amusement only.

"The board will not decide our fate. *We*, not them, are in charge. *We*, not them, carry the burden of history. Their rejection is not a surprise to me. I knew that the day would come when we would reach this impasse. Why? Because we have different motivations. Their motivation is profit. But our motivation, our cause, is nothing less than a new world.

"Those idiots on the board want to put a new coat of paint on the house. I say burn the house to the ground and rebuild it! No government but *our* government. No religion but *our* religion. No gods but *our* gods. We will tear down the human foundation brick by brick and construct our own.

"These chickens have lost their way. And we are going to lead them into a bright, new coop." His eyes carefully studied the excited expressions of the youths. He spoke his next words very slowly and deliberately. "Are you with me?"

The youths cheered.

"The war has begun, my eagles. First the Elgen corporation, then the world. I have been preparing. We are going to Peru, not to shut down the compound, but to consolidate our power. Peru will be our headquarters for mounting our overthrow of the misguided corporation. You will be my war council, my generals, and my personal guard. Make no mistake, the stakes are high. If we lose, you are on your own, no money, no privilege, just a life of quiet desperation pecking out an existence with the rest of the chickens."

Hatch looked around the cabin, judging the effect of his words by the terrified and indignant looks on their faces.

"But we are not going to lose. That is not your destiny. That is not my destiny. And the Elgen are just the first speed bump on our journey. After we have conquered them, we shall, one by one, overthrow nations. I have taught you from your childhoods that you were royalty. You shall soon see how right I am. But you are not just royalty. You will be royalty's royalty. Kings will be your butlers and queens your maidservants. They will bow in your presence.

"Some of you are likely wondering how we are going to accomplish this. Our plan is perfect and already begun. We will take control of the world's electricity. Electricity is the mother's milk of civilization. When we control the electricity we will control communications, health care, and the production and distribution of food.

"If a country tries to take over our plants, we will shut down their businesses. We will shut down their communications. We will cripple their economies, and they will crawl back to us for help. And we will help them—but on our terms and at our price. If they do not surrender to us, we will threaten other countries' power until they fight for us. And *they will* fight for us. Survival is always the first rule of politics."

Quentin raised his hand.

"Yes?" Hatch said.

"How do we *make* electricity?"

Hatch smiled. "Except for Torstyn, none of you have been briefed on our Starxource project, even though you were, indirectly, a part of its development. Now is the time for you to know. How do we make electricity? The same way that you do. When we are in Peru you will have a full tour of the facility. Our Starxource plants use a renewable, bioelectric source of power production.

"We are currently opening Starxource plants at the rate of a new facility every two months. Soon we will have that down to one plant a month. Then two plants a months. Then a plant a week.

"Countries are already begging for us to come in with our power. Why wouldn't they? We offer them clean power at a fraction of the cost. It's practically free. No pollution, no economic strain. Those who don't turn to us will be at an economic disadvantage to those who do.

"Of course, this begs the question, why would we give away our electricity? Because we are like the drug dealer handing out free drugs on the schoolyard playground. Once the world is hooked, we will, of course, raise the prices and increase our demands until we own them."

"We rule!" Bryan shouted.

Hatch smiled. "Yes, we will."

Quentin raised his hand again. "Sir, how will we fight the Elgen? They have thousands of guards."

"Which we will use to our advantage. In fact, we will soon be quadrupling our number of guards, all of whom will be trained by us in Peru. As for our current force, I have summoned all the guards from Elgen facilities around the world. In two days they will be arriving in Peru for a two-week rehabilitation conference. The board believes this conference is to train our forces for their new roles in the Starxource plants, which, ironically, is true—just not in the roles the board expects.

"Our Peruvian force is our largest and is completely loyal to us. Soon *all* the Elgen guards will be loyal to us. We will choose our leaders and purge the rest of the force. When we are done, we will control the security forces within each plant. Anyone who does not follow my orders will be punished. Any questions?"

Suddenly the plane took a huge dip, knocking Hatch to the ground. Several of the teens screamed. An alarm began beeping and oxygen masks dropped from the ceiling.

"What's happening?" Hatch shouted to the pilots. There was no answer. Hatch crawled to the cockpit and pulled open the door. "What's happening?"

"We don't know," the copilot shouted. "We've lost power. Everything just went . . ."

Hatch didn't wait for him to finish. He rushed to the fuselage, shouting to the guard. "Pull the screen!"

The guard, who was still belted in his chair, reached back and pulled the screen. Tanner was awake, his dark blue eyes looking at them.

"Shoot him!" Hatch shouted to the guard.

The guard didn't move. He just stared, as if frozen.

"Shoot him before he kills us all. Now!"

The guard still hesitated.

Suddenly Tanner started screaming. "I'll stop! I'll stop!"

Hatch looked over to see Torstyn, his lip curled in anger, his hand extended toward Tanner. Then the guard hit Tanner over the head with his pistol, knocking him out.

The jet dropped again, then leveled out. Kylee and Bryan both threw up. It took several minutes for everyone to settle. After the plane was back on course the captain's voice came over the PA system. "Sorry for the turbulence, everyone. We should be fine now."

Hatch stood again, composing himself. "Well done, Torstyn," he said. "A round of applause for Torstyn, who just saved all of our lives."

Everyone clapped, even Quentin.

"You will be handsomely rewarded when we arrive in Peru."

"Thank you, sir," Torstyn said.

Hatch pointed at the psychiatrist. "You."

Dr. Jung was pale with fear.

"Sedate the boy until anesthetic flows from his tear ducts." Hatch's eyes narrowed. "Do not let him wake again until we're on the ground. Do you understand?"

"Yes, sir. He won't. It won't happen again. I promise."

"I should hope not. If he wakes again, I'll have both of you thrown out of the airplane. Are we clear on this?"

The doctor blanched. "Yes, sir. Very clear."

"Close the screen," he said to the guard.

"Yes, sir," the guard said, pulling the screen around the pair.

"We'll deal with your insubordination after we land."

"Yes, sir."

Hatch looked back at the youths. "Where were we?"

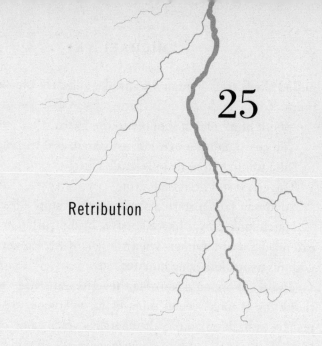

# 25

## Retribution

The plane landed in Rio de Janeiro to refuel, then quickly took off again, finally touching down at a small airfield near the Elgen's Peruvian compound, in the town of Puerto Maldonado.

The asphalt runway was surrounded by walls of trees that spilled outward from the burgeoning forest. The jet taxied to a small hangar where a contingency of Elgen guards and a bus were waiting to transport the group to the compound.

The plane stopped and a stairway unfolded from its side. A guard climbed to the top of the stairs and knocked on the door.

Bryan was the first one out, followed by the rest of the youths.

"Whoa," Bryan said. "It's hot. Like a furnace hot."

"And humid," Tara added. "My hair is going to be frizzy."

Torstyn rolled his eyes. "This is nothing. Wait until summer."

A moment later the guard walked out, followed by Hatch. The

six Peruvian guards at the bottom of the stairs saluted Hatch as he emerged from the plane and descended the stairway. Hatch stopped at the bottom and returned the Elgen salute.

"Captain Figueroa," he said.

"Yes, sir!"

He pointed to the guard from the plane, who was not standing at attention. "This man disobeyed a direct order. His inaction nearly cost us our lives. Put him under arrest."

"Yes, sir," the captain snapped. "Guards at attention."

The Peruvian soldiers pointed their guns at the lone guard, who, in spite of his many years with the Elgen, was still caught off guard. He looked on in horror.

The captain stepped forward with his gun drawn, his other hand out. "Guard 247, surrender your gun. Slowly and by the barrel."

"Yes, sir," he said, his voice trembling. He slowly removed his gun from its holster and, holding it by its barrel, handed it to the captain.

"Put your hands behind your back. Now!"

He quickly obeyed.

"Secure this man," the captain barked.

"Sir, yes, sir." One of the soldiers ran up behind the guard and handcuffed the man's hands behind his back, fastening the metal belt through a buckle in the back of the guard's uniform.

The captain turned to Hatch. "Prisoner is secured. What are your orders, sir?"

Hatch scowled at the handcuffed guard. "Captain Figueroa, detain this man for now in maximum security. For the benefit of the visiting guards we're going to make an example of him. We're going to put him in the chute."

The condemned guard's face turned pale. "No, please, sir. Not that. I beg you!" He fell to his knees, bowing his head to Hatch's feet. "Please, sir. Anything but that! Shoot me. Please, shoot me."

Hatch sneered. "Show some dignity, man." He kicked the guard away from him. "Captain, keep him alive until I give you further instructions."

"No!" the man screamed. He tried to get to his feet to run, but he was knocked down before he could stand.

The teens watched the exchange with amusement.

"What a wimp," Torstyn said.

"What's the chute?" Tara asked.

"It's where they feed the rats," Torstyn said.

"What rats?"

He looked at her with a snide grin. "They really don't tell you much, do they?"

Several guards carried Tanner's gurney from the plane, escorted by Dr. Jung.

"Let's go," Hatch said to the captain. "Captain Figueroa."

"Yes, sir."

"Also detain Tanner and the doctor in maximum security until further notice."

The doctor turned white. "But, Dr. Hatch—"

"Don't speak to me," he said. "Or I'll send you to the chute as well."

The doctor froze.

"To the bus, please," Hatch said to the teens.

Tara said to Torstyn, "They're going to feed him to rats?"

"Yeah. It's a cool thing to watch."

"You've seen this before?" Quentin asked.

"Of course. Hundreds of times. Feeding time is better than the movies. I've seen the rats strip the meat off a two-thousand-pound bull in less than a minute."

"Awesome," Bryan said.

"Yeah, this guy will be a snack for them."

As Hatch and the kids approached the bus, a man wearing a white jacket and Panama hat, holding a spider monkey, walked up to Torstyn. "Here is your *mono*, Señor Torstyn."

"Hey, Arana," Torstyn said, taking his pet. He put the monkey on his shoulder, and it climbed up onto his head.

"Cute," Tara said, reaching out her hand.

"Yeah, wait until she bites you," Torstyn said.

Tara quickly pulled her hand back, and Torstyn laughed. Suddenly the monkey began screeching, then jumped off Torstyn's head and ran off toward the jungle.

"Arana!" he shouted after it. When it had disappeared into the jungle he turned back to Tara. "What did you do?"

Tara just smiled. "Nothing. You think I can get in an animal's head?"

"Yes," he said.

Quentin grinned. "Bad news for you, Torstyn. You thought you were safe."

Torstyn glared at both of them. "That was my pet," he said, turning away from them.

Quentin laughed. "We're definitely going to have fun in the jungle."

# 26

Puerto Maldonado

The Elgen's Peruvian Starxource plant was situated near the southeastern city of Puerto Maldonado, a jungle town in the Amazon Basin. It was the largest of the Elgen's compounds and built on a twenty-five-thousand-acre ranch hemmed in by jungle on all sides. Hatch and his team had selected the city for three reasons: First, it was remote, many miles away from curious eyes. Second, there was plenty of water, as the Río Madre de Dios, a tributary of the Amazon River, passed through the town; and third, it had an abundance of labor. Puerto Maldonado had once been a thriving logging and gold-mining camp, but both the gold and lumber were long gone, leaving few employment opportunities for the natives and guaranteeing an abundant workforce.

The compound had three main structures. The largest building was the Starxource power plant, called *el bol* by the natives, or "the bowl." The bowl was a massive, redbrick building with stainless steel casings that bulged out in the middle. Most said the bowl looked like a flying saucer had crashed into it. Just east of the building were three smaller buildings: the water house, the ranch house, and a food production plant.

West of the bowl was the Elgen Reeducation Center, or "Re-Ed," as it was known by the guards, a rectangular building without windows used to rehabilitate uncooperative employees.

Connected to the Re-Ed by a brick corridor was the assembly hall, a massive building that could house more than two thousand people and served as both a cafeteria and an educational facility.

North of the assembly hall was residential housing, three long, rectangular buildings where the guards, scientists, and employees slept. Hatch, the electric children, and the Elite Guard—twelve men personally selected by Hatch to oversee the Elgen security force— had their own housing facilities on the west side of the Re-Ed.

The bus passed through two checkpoints during the drive into the compound, and even though the bus entered the gates only ten minutes from the airfield, it took a little more than thirty-five minutes for them to reach their housing facilities.

The youths were each assigned a guard and two personal assistants, all Peruvians who spoke English. While the assistants prepared their suites and oversaw the delivery of their luggage, the teens ate lunch in their private dining room. Afterward they gathered in the lobby of their new home, where Dr. Hatch was waiting for them.

"I know it's not Beverly Hills," Hatch said. "But I trust your suites are satisfactory."

All of them agreed that their Peruvian accommodations were as luxurious as the academy in Pasadena.

"Then it will be my pleasure to give you a tour of your new home. I think you will be rather impressed with what we've built in the jungle. I know I am." Hatch ushered them outside to a twelve-seat golf cart with a flashing amber light on top. The driver was a guard dressed in the standard uniform, except for a bright red patch featuring a condor, symbolic of the Chasqui, a special Elgen military order in Peru.

The teens boarded the cart and Hatch climbed up front with the driver and took the microphone. "Everything you'll see on this tour is C9."

The difference between C9 and C10 was that C9 could be discussed with other Elgen associates while in a secure Elgen facility. Unlawful disclosure, however, carried the same punishment as C10.

"Onward," Hatch said.

The cart made a sharp U-turn, then glided silently down the smooth, resin-coated cement floor past the Re-Ed and toward the Starxource plant. Two guards stood at attention as they approached, and the metal doors behind the guards opened.

The inside of the building looked similar to the lower laboratory of the Pasadena academy, only on a much larger scale. The building was more than a hundred yards from end to end, the length of a football field. The corridors were lit with bluish-white indirect lighting, giving the hallways a futuristic, eerie look. It took several minutes for the cart to reach their destination—the elevator to the bowl's observation deck.

As they approached the room Hatch said, "What you are about to see is the heart of the Starxource program—the very core of our power and our future." A grim smile crossed his face. "I guarantee you won't soon forget it."

The elevator opened to reveal a sealed door guarded by two Elgen guards dressed in black with red armbands. The guards stood stiffly at attention and saluted as Hatch stepped from the cart. One of the guards opened the door, and the kids filed in after Hatch.

Bryan was the first to comment on what they saw. "No way!" he shouted.

# 27

Beware the Stranger

The teens had seen remarkable things in their lives, far more than normal teenagers, but nothing could have prepared them for the bowl. The observation deck was sixty feet long, and the inner wall, slightly convex, was made of glass, which allowed them a view of something few would ever see: nearly a million electrified rats.

The swarms of rats crawled over one another, creating an undulating, massive orange-and-gray carpet, and in parts of the bowl they looked like molten lava.

"What you're looking at is almost a million rats, each of them capable of generating two hundred and fifty watts and two amps of electricity an hour; that's five hundred watts a second, nearly identical wattage to the electric eel. Combined, that's three hundred seventy-five million watts a second, more than enough to light downtown New York City.

"You can't see it because of the rodents, but beneath them, the floor is a delicate, silver-coated copper grid, the largest ever constructed. Its purpose is to conduct electricity to the capacitors below. We also use the grid to solve the problem of waste, as the rats' excrement drops below and is conveyed out to be processed into manure, more than twelve tons a day."

"That's a lot of crap," Bryan said, punching Torstyn in the shoulder.

"Do that again and I'll melt your head," Torstyn said.

"What's that big arm thing in the middle?" Quentin asked.

Connected to the center of the bowl was a curved metallic blade about three feet high and a hundred and forty feet long. The arm slowly swept the bowl like the second hand of a clock.

"That's the sweep," Hatch said. "The rats only generate usable amounts of electricity when they're active, so the sweep makes a complete revolution of the bowl every ninety-six minutes, forcing the rats to continually move. If we need more power we simply increase the speed of the arm, generating more electricity. The sweep has another purpose as well. The angle of the blade forces anything on the grid to its outer rim—so it disposes of animal bones and dead rats, pushing their carcasses off the grid."

"With the poop?" Bryan asked.

"No. The outer rim falls into special troughs that convey the dead rats into an electric grinder. There, the meat and bone are milled into powder, mixed with an iodine supplement and a glucose solution, then stamped and baked into biscuits, which our scientists call Rabisk—short for rat biscuits. We then feed them to the rats."

Tara grimaced. "You mean they're cannibals?"

"Rats are naturally cannibalistic, but ours are a little different. The electric rats won't eat their own. Our scientists believe that they learn this from shocking each other when they're young. So they won't eat a rat, even a dead one, until it no longer looks like a rat, or until it's been processed into Rabisk. It's an extremely efficient way of feeding. When we first started this process we had some problems with the rat version of mad cow disease, but our rats only live nineteen months on average, so by genetically altering the rats we were able stave off the disease for their lifespan. Our rats die earlier than other rats because of their constant state of motion and the electricity that flows through them."

"Where did you get so many rats?" Tara asked.

"The old-fashioned way," Hatch said. "We bred them. Rats are one of the most efficient breeders of all the mammals on the planet. They are capable of producing offspring within six weeks of birth—compared to twelve to thirteen years for humans. It's been speculated that two rats in an ideal breeding environment could produce more than a million offspring in their lifetime.

"Of course, until now, that has just been speculation. But we've proven it. We are able to create thousands of rats a day, far more than we need." Hatch pointed to the far edge of the bowl. "See that small door there? You can just make out the outline. That is where new rats are delivered to the grid. We introduce about seventy new rats every hour, twenty-four/seven. In addition, we keep a twenty percent surplus of rats at all times, in case of disease."

"What if they escaped?" Bryan said. "That would be awesome."

"No," Hatch said coldly. "That would not be *awesome*. In fact, it's one of our greatest concerns. They would spread throughout the world like an epidemic. Rats are already the world's leading cause of extinction. Electric rats like ours could destroy entire ecosystems.

"It would also allow anyone to breed our rats and create their own power source, something that would forever end our monopoly. So, as I said, it *would not be awesome*. And it will never happen. Our rats have been bioengineered to die outside of captivity. However, accidents happen. We had a few dozen rats escape before we reengineered them. It might have been an utter disaster, but fortunately the rats have a weakness. Water applied directly to their bodies kills them."

"Like Zeus," Kylee said.

Hatch spun around, his face twisted in fury. "What did you say?"

Kylee flushed as she realized what she had done—they were not allowed to speak Zeus's name. The other youths looked at her with anger and sympathy.

"I—I didn't mean to. . . . It just came out. I'm sorry. . . ."

"To your room," Hatch said.

"I'm so sorry, sir. It will never happen again."

"Indeed it won't," Hatch said. He turned to the guard. "Take her back. Punishment B."

Kylee grimaced but dared not complain. Punishment B consisted of a full week of room confinement on a bread-and-water diet. During that time she would be required to write *I will not disobey Dr. Hatch's rules* ten thousand times.

Bryan grinned. "Have fun."

Kylee shot him a look as she walked away with the guard.

Quentin slowly shook his head. "That was dumb."

"It was just a mistake," Tara said softly. "Anyone could have made it."

"I'm just glad it was her and not me," Quentin said.

Just then an alarm sounded from inside the bowl.

"Hear that?" Hatch said. "We're in luck. You're going to get to watch the feeding."

"You're going to love this," Torstyn said to Tara. "The guards usually come up here on their breaks to watch."

Thirty yards to their right, a chute, about eight feet wide with metallic rollers, suddenly protruded from the wall. The feeding chute was connected to hydraulic lifts that extended it about twenty yards out from the bowl's side, slowly lowering it until the end of the chute dangled less than ten feet above the rats, which had already begun congregating around it. A door opened from the wall.

"Watch," Torstyn said. "Here it comes."

Suddenly a massive, long-horned bull slid down the chute. The animal's feet were tied together and it struggled against its bindings but was able to move only its head.

"What is that?" Bryan asked.

"It's a bull," Hatch said. "Raised on our own ranch. We passed many of them on our way in."

"It's still alive?" Tara asked, slightly grimacing.

"Always," Hatch said. "Fresh meat produces more electricity. Or, more accurately, struggling meat."

A spiked-wheel mechanism caught the animal near the bottom of the slide, and the end of the chute snapped in the middle, slowly tilting farther down until the animal was about six feet above the grid. The animal was desperately trying to free itself.

"The chute can't touch the grid or it will damage it," Torstyn explained. "The grid, as a whole, can hold more than a thousand tons, but square by square it's actually pretty fragile."

In anticipation of their meal, the rats clambered to the chute, climbing on top of one another in a massive wave of fur that glowed a dull red like a hot plate. For the first time since they'd arrived, the glistening copper grid was partially visible, as the rodents were all gathered beneath the chute. When the bull was lowered within a yard of the grid, rats began jumping up onto the animal.

"I didn't know rats could jump that high," Quentin said.

"They look like spawning salmon," Bryan said.

"Rats can jump up to forty inches vertical," Hatch replied. "That's the equivalent of a human jumping three stories."

Within seconds the bull was completely covered by the rodents in a wild feeding frenzy. The rats increased in brightness like a filament. Blue, white, and yellow electricity arced around the carcass, and steam and smoke rose around the bull. The arcs and colors, highlighted by the steam, were, in a peculiar way, beautiful to look at—like the aurora borealis.

"The vapor you see comes from the rats' electricity against the bull. They're actually cooking the meat with their bodies," Hatch said. "That's a rat barbecue."

"Look!" Bryan said excitedly. "They've already stripped its legs to the bone."

Within three minutes the bull was reduced to nothing but skeleton. Even its internal organs were eaten.

"They're like furry piranhas," Quentin said. "I'd hate to be down there."

"Wait," Tara said. "You mean, that's what they're going to do to that guard on our flight? Put him on *that* chute?"

"Yep," Torstyn said.

Tara covered her mouth. "I'm going to be sick."

The chute began to retract and lift, dropping the animal to the floor of the grid as it moved. Then the door at the top of the chute opened again and another bull slid out.

"How many bulls will they eat?" Tara asked.

"Our rats are a little more voracious than your average house rat," Hatch replied. "Still, they don't eat that much. About an ounce to an ounce and a half a day. But with this many rats, that still equates to twenty-nine tons of food a day. They're omnivorous, so they eat a combination of grains and meat. Every day we go through about ten tons in raw meat, about five bulls, and the rest are in Rabisk and grain. But they prefer the meat, especially since fresh food helps quench their thirst and drinking water can be a little tricky for them."

"How do they drink?" Quentin asked.

Dr. Hatch smiled. "Very carefully." He pointed to the vacant side of the bowl. "See those white ceramic disks? They're drinking fountains for rats. They're exactly one tenth of a millimeter beneath the grid—just close enough that the rats can lick water off them."

After the second bull had been devoured, Hatch ordered the teens back to the elevator. "There's more to see," he said.

They made the rounds through the laboratory and corridors around the bowl. The MEI room and breeding labs were connected directly to the bowl for ease of operation. They toured the Rabisk plant, which smelled so bad they had to wear nose plugs. Men in white coats walked back and forth between different machines, measuring output, then sending the small biscuits to the oven, then back to the feeding rooms.

"This side of the facility is our meat processing center and next to that is our ranch house, where our *gauchos* live."

Before they left the facility Hatch pointed out one last section of the building. "These are the cells where we inter our traitors and GPs who have outlived their usefulness. You might also call this a meat processing facility. Our guards call it death row. You'll recognize our newest guest." They looked in to see the guard from the plane.

"You should show him the bowl," Bryan said.

Hatch replied, "If we were trying to get information from him or instill a behavioral change, the fear would be of some value. But, as it is, his course is set, so to show him the bowl would serve no useful purpose."

They walked from the cells back out to the lobby, where the cart was waiting. As they climbed aboard, an overhanging door rose ahead of them, and they drove out into the yard. The walks of the compound were all open but covered, as the weather on Puerto Maldonado was usually temperate, though subject to a heavy rainy season. The guard drove around the building to the south, the transmission substation.

"Nothing here you haven't seen before," Hatch said. "This is where the power that comes from the plant is dispersed. It feeds from our transmission substation over high-voltage transmission lines to local power substations and then to homes and businesses as far away as Lima.

"You can compare our system to the human body. Our power plant is the heart. The high-voltage lines are major arteries, which break down into veins, then capillaries, eventually feeding into individual homes and businesses. Electricity is truly the lifeblood of civilization.

"Over the last two years we've helped the Peruvian government lay miles of high-voltage power lines. If we were to shut down, all of Puerto Maldonado, Cuzco, and the surrounding cities would also shut down. Even more impressive is that two of Peru's largest cities would also be majorly impacted: Eighty percent of Arequipa and almost half of Lima would go dark. Within a year, we will be powering ninety-five percent of the country." A smile crossed his thin lips. "At which point, we'll own the country." He looked out over the station with satisfaction.

"They should have been more cautious. 'Beware the stranger offering gifts, as true for man as it is for fish,'" Hatch said slowly. "So it is."

*   *   *

The next building the cart stopped at was the Reeducation Center. The cart pulled up to a door made of thick steel and attended by two guards who, like the guards at the bowl, stood at attention and saluted Dr. Hatch.

The doors opened, and the group walked into a holding area with a second set of doors.

"This looks like a prison," Tara said, her voice echoing.

"It's much more than that," Hatch said. "This is our Reeducation Center. It's here that we help our enemies change their minds."

"You brainwash them?" Quentin asked.

Hatch gave him a disapproving glance. "This is where we *teach* these misguided souls the error of their thinking. Sometimes it takes a while, but you would be surprised at just how malleable the human brain can be. In the right environment the mind can be molded like clay. Men and women walk in here as enemies and come out as devotees, willing to lay down their lives for our cause."

After the first door had locked behind them, the second door clicked, then opened, and the teens walked into the main hall. The floors were smooth, resin-coated concrete, and the walls were dark red brick.

Hatch spoke as they walked. "Pavlov taught us the rules of conditioning—but he also taught us that the human mind can be quickly converted from years of training to a new way of thinking by a single traumatic experience.

"We can induce that kind of trauma through punishment—but we've also discovered that the mere *threat* of punishment can be just as effective. So, of course, we show them the rats."

Through Plexiglas windows the teens could see rows of men in pink, flowered jumpsuits sitting on long benches watching films.

"Why are they wearing pink?" Bryan asked.

"Everything you see has a reason. They are dressed in clothing that embarrasses and humiliates them. How strong can you be dressed as a little girl?"

Tara and Bryan snickered.

"You would be surprised at how powerful something as simple as changing someone's clothing can be. Psychologists and fashion designers have long known that changing someone's appearance can alter their self-perception. And when you change someone's self-perception, you change their behavior.

"Of course, we also change their names. In our case we give them numbers. When they no longer can identify with who they were, they begin to doubt their own thoughts and feelings. It is then that we can implant them with our truths.

"We didn't discover all this, of course—we had the Korean War and Vietnamese reeducation camps to learn from—but I'm proud to say we've significantly advanced the science. We have the benefit of using procedures they never dreamed of." He put his hand on Tara's shoulder. "Like emulating Tara's gifts. We can make them doubt their own sanity within minutes. And, like their identity, once they doubt their sanity, we're most of the way there.

"What we discovered is that the more people think they can't be controlled, the easier subjects they make. What the masses don't realize is that they're looking for a shepherd. Those who don't think they can be influenced or call themselves 'independent thinkers' are usually the biggest conformists of all—and the easiest to turn. Why do you think cults prey on college students? Easy picking."

"You make it sound simple," Quentin said.

Hatch looked at him and smiled. "It is when you know what you're doing." He stopped near an open door to a theater room. Nearly two dozen inmates were seated quietly on the ground even though there were enough seats for everyone. "Take a seat, everyone," Hatch said to the youths. "Everyone except Tara." The group quickly found seats. Tara stood anxiously, unsure if she'd done something wrong. "While I speak to Tara, I'd like you to view one of the films we've produced so you understand how the newly reeducated think and act. In the meantime I have an errand. I'll be back when the film is over. Tara, if you'll come with me."

"Yes, sir." Tara followed Hatch out of the room. In the hallway

Hatch turned to her. "We have a little visit to make. I need your help."

"You need my powers?" she asked with relief.

"No," Hatch replied. "I need your face."

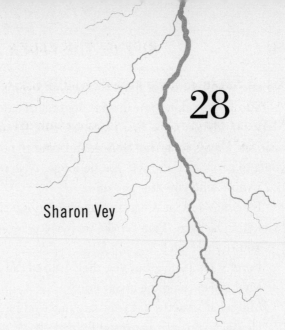

# 28

## Sharon Vey

Thirty-four marks. Sharon Vey had counted the days of her captivity by scratching marks into the concrete floor of her cell. Her room was only ten by ten, two-thirds of it occupied by her metal cage.

She was sitting back against the bars when Hatch walked into the room. "Hello, Sharon." A buzzer went off and he typed in the required code. Mrs. Vey turned away from him.

"Miss me?" Hatch asked.

Still no answer.

"I trust your accommodations are to your satisfaction."

"You can't keep me here."

"Of course we can."

"You won't get away with this. They'll find me."

Hatch's brow furrowed with mock concern. "*Who* will find you?"

Mrs. Vey didn't answer. She knew it was a stupid thing to say.

No one would find her here. She wasn't even sure where she was.

"Surely you don't mean that inept little police department in Meridian, Idaho. In the first place, we own them. Secondly, you, my dear, are a long, long way from Idaho. And the only way you're ever going to get back there is if you no longer wish to return."

"I know who you are," she said.

"Do you?" He sat down in the room's lone chair, an amused grin blanketing his face. "Don't make me wait, tell me."

"You're Jim Hatch."

"I prefer Dr. Hatch, but yes, they used to call me that."

"My husband told me about you."

"And what, exactly, did your late husband have to say?"

"He said you are an unstable, diabolical, delusional man with megalomaniac tendencies."

Hatch smiled. "Did he also tell you that I'm dangerous?"

Mrs. Vey looked at him coldly. "Yes."

"That's the thing about your husband, he always called a spade a spade."

"Where is my son?"

"We have him safely locked away as we reeducate him."

"I want to see him."

"When we're done, you'll see him. When he's broken and subservient, you'll see him. You may not recognize him anymore, but you'll definitely see him."

"You'll never break him."

"On the contrary. If psychology has taught us anything, it's that everyone has a breaking point. *Everyone*."

"I want to see my son!" she shouted.

"Poignant. Really, I'm moved. A mother crying out for her son. But what *you* want is of no relevance. All that matters is what *I* want. Besides, he's not ready. He's a special boy. And when we're done, he'll be of great value to our cause."

"You have no cause except your own lust for power."

Hatch grinned darkly. "You make that sound like it's a bad thing." He leaned toward the bars. "The lust for power is the only way the world has ever changed. Of course we dress it up in noble intentions, but in the end politics and religion are like sausage—it may be good, but it's best not to know what goes into it.

"Trust me, the day will come when I will be honored as the visionary I am."

"You're delusional," Mrs. Vey said.

Hatch smiled. "All great men are delusional. How else could they be crazy enough to think they could change the world?" He leaned back. "The day will come when I will be as celebrated as George Washington is today. And the electric children, including yours, will be held up and worshipped as the pioneers of a new world order. You should be pleased to know that your son will be held in such high esteem. You cling to the past only because you fear change. But nothing good comes without change. *Nothing.* Change is evolution, nothing more. And if it wasn't for evolution you'd still be living in a tree eating bananas."

Mrs. Vey just looked at him.

"Speaking of eating, has anyone told you what *you've* been eating for the past month? Those tasty little biscuits are called Rabisk. They're made of ground-up rats: meat, fur, and bonemeal."

Her stomach churned.

"There's someone I'd like you to meet." He walked to the cell door and opened it. "You may come in now."

Tara walked in. "Hi, Mrs. Vey."

Mrs. Vey looked at her with surprise. "Taylor?"

Tara smiled. "It's so good to see you."

"What are you doing here?"

"I came to help. What Dr. Hatch is doing is wonderful. For all of us."

"Have you seen Michael?"

"Of course."

"How is he?"

"He's great. He's having a good time."

Mrs. Vey couldn't believe what she was hearing. "A good time? Has he asked about me?"

Tara shook her head. "No. I mean, he knows you're okay and we're all just so busy and going places. But I'm sure he'll find time to visit before too long."

Mrs. Vey knew her son better than that. Something was wrong with the situation. Something about the girl's eyes was different—not the color or shape of her eyes, but something less definable. It was the light in them. Or lack of it.

"Does Michael still wear the watch you gave him for his birthday?" Mrs. Vey asked.

Tara hesitated. "Uh, most of the time. Not when he plays basketball or stuff."

Mrs. Vey nodded. "So, Taylor. What do your parents think of you leaving home?"

"They're really happy for me."

"Really?"

"Oh, yes. They're so proud that I can make a difference in this world."

"Even your dad?"

"Of course. Why wouldn't he be?"

"Well, you know how schoolteachers worry about kids. Especially their own."

"No, he's good with it all. He's good."

Mrs. Vey stared at her for a moment, then breathed out slowly. "No, he's not. Your father's not a schoolteacher, he's a police officer. And you didn't give Michael that watch for his birthday. I did."

Tara glanced nervously at Dr. Hatch.

"Who are you and why do you look just like Taylor?" Mrs. Vey asked.

Hatch slowly shook his head. "It was worth a try. Sharon, this is Tara, Taylor's lost twin. And she's going to be your new best friend. Every day until we bring Michael in, she's going to make your stay a little more . . . interesting. Just like she did for your son."

"What did you do to him?"

"You'll find out soon enough. Tara, Mrs. Vey likes rats. She's been eating them for weeks now. So, for your first session," Hatch said, tapping his temple with his index finger, "I think you should give her a few hundred to keep her company."

"Yes, sir," Tara said.

"Thirty minutes' worth."

"Yes, sir."

Hatch smiled. "Very well. I'll go now and let you two get better acquainted."

Hatch walked back to the others, who were still in the theater. "Let's go," he said.

The youths immediately stood, unnoticed by the others in the room. When they were outside the theater, Bryan asked, "How many times do they have to watch that movie?"

"As many times as they need," Hatch replied. "A few of these prisoners have seen this particular presentation more than a thousand times. Remember, repetition breeds conviction.

"When the prisoners are brought in for reeducation, they go through our boot camp, a carefully orchestrated psychological assault guaranteed to drive them to submission or madness. We'll take either. First they are shown a rat feeding, then told that they will be fed to the rats the next morning. While they await their fate they enter phase one: They are locked naked in a three-by-three cell without food or water. We call this 'think time'—time for them to contemplate the fragility of their own mortality and their own powerlessness.

"In their cell there is no sound, no darkness, just a bright light and their impending death. Since there is neither a clock nor contact with the outer world, they do not know when it is night or day, and minutes begin to feel like days. On the third day they are given two cups of water and three Rabisk biscuits. They are told that their fate is still being considered.

"They then enter phase two. During the next seventy-two hours loud music is piped into their cube, nonstop. We usually choose something primal with a heavy beat, like heavy metal or grunge, as we find that it has a decidedly *unsettling* effect. Believe me, it works.

"After those three days comes phase three. The music stops. They are told that due to the mercy of the Elgen and because we believe that they still might be saved, their life has been temporarily spared. This is when their education begins. We start by playing a looped audio presentation we call *The Scold*. This recording consists of different voices screaming at them, condemning them for their crimes against humanity. After three days of *The Scold* they are usually reduced to whimpering idiots. They are then invited to confess their crimes, real or imagined." Hatch grinned. "You'd be surprised what they come up with.

"They are then reviewed by one of our therapists, and if they are sufficiently penitent, they are moved to a cell and allowed brief interaction with others—in supervised group therapy, of course. It is here that they are given a new identity. They are allowed to confess and seek forgiveness. All this time they are allowed only four hours of sleep a night, and the rest of their time is filled with studying the Elgen plan of forgiveness and our new global order. Every moment is planned, and they become deeply dependent on us. By the end of the process, they belong to the order and we reinforce their condition by allowing them to help reeducate others. It's a beautiful thing to watch."

Tara appeared in the hallway.

"How did it go?" Hatch asked.

"Good. She's strong, but not that strong. She passed out."

"Next time tone it back so she experiences the full therapeutic effect."

"Yes, sir."

Hatch looked back at the group. "It's time for dinner. I want you to go to bed at a reasonable hour. The guards begin arriving early tomorrow. We have a special few days ahead, and I want you at your best for all of it. This is the time for you to show them who you are." Hatch smiled. "My eagles."

# 29

## The Future

The next morning the Elgen guards began arriving from the thirty-eight Starxource plants around the globe. There were more than two thousand Elgen guards worldwide, and they made up an fierce, well-trained, and well-equipped security force.

They were met at the airport by Hatch's Peruvian guards. The men were disarmed, then led immediately into orientation.

One of Hatch's Elite Guards informed him of the first arrival. "The guards are arriving, sir."

"How many?"

"Three buses, a hundred and forty-seven men."

"What condition are they in?"

"Exhausted."

"Good," he said. "Don't let them sleep."

"A few have already lain on the ground."

"Then get them up and run them. Has there been any insubordination?"

"Some."

"Good," Hatch said. "We need examples. Arrest them. We'll be showcasing them tonight. You know my plans, make sure they are followed to the letter."

"Yes, sir."

Hatch had organized the guards' flights to be as long and tiring as possible, so they would be exhausted upon arrival. When the guards landed, they were also given drinks lightly laced with Trazodone, a mild antidepressant that is often used as a sleep aid, causing drowsiness, light-headedness, and confusion. Hatch's plan was first to break the men down physically through drugs, labor, lack of sleep, and hunger. Then, when they were near collapse, he'd break them mentally. In their weakened condition, the guards would reveal their true loyalties and Hatch would divide them into "sheep" and "goats." The sheep, those who would enthusiastically follow Hatch, he would train and advance to leadership rank, repositioning them to take control of Starxource plants or Elgen compounds. The goats, or those who did not cooperate, would be reeducated. If after several weeks they were still troublesome, he would extinguish them. There was no room for defiance.

Upon their arrival, the guards were put to work digging a large trench on the far side of the ranch. The trench had absolutely no purpose but to keep the men working. When darkness fell, the exhausted guards were driven back to the compound and assigned to their barracks. They were instructed to put on their guard uniforms and report to the mess hall for dinner.

The men were served small meals; peas and carrots, salad, and cuy—a local Peruvian delicacy of fried guinea pig. Many of the men complained about the food, and there was a small uprising at one table that was immediately quelled by the Peruvian guards. The two most demonstrative protestors were arrested and taken away.

At 9:00 p.m. the men were sent back to their barracks and told to sleep, as their day would begin early the next morning. It was only a ruse, as less than two hours later a shrill buzzer rang throughout the compound and all lights came on. Armed Peruvian guards walked into each barrack, waking the men and marching them to the assembly hall, where they were told to stand quietly at attention in front of metal chairs. A few more complained of their treatment and were quickly taken away by the Peruvian guards.

The room they had been congregated in was large enough to hold all two thousand men. The metal chairs faced a raised stage at the front of the hall. There was a podium in the middle of the stage flanked by twelve guards, six on each side, dressed in black, with purple and scarlet chest emblems and armbands on the right arm. The Elgen logo was projected on the screen behind them in letters twenty feet high. At exactly midnight a loud bell sounded and the guard to the right of the podium walked up to the microphone.

"Elgen Force. Salute."

The men gave the Elgen salute.

"The weak among you may sit."

The men looked at one another. A few sat—collapsed, really—but most, in spite of their exhaustion, remained standing.

"Many of you have flown from halfway around the world. I have heard complaints from the weak that you are tired. I would expect such complaints from weaker men. But you are not men. You are Elgen."

This was followed by applause among the standing.

"It is my distinct privilege to bring to this stage our supreme commander and president. A true visionary the world will someday acknowledge. The weak who are sitting will rise with the strong for President C. J. Hatch."

The room broke into applause as Quentin and Torstyn walked onto the stage, taking their places on each side of the podium, in front of the Elite Guards. Then Hatch walked in from the side of the stage to the podium. The guard who had introduced Hatch quickly stepped back as he approached. Hatch saluted him, then stepped up to the microphone. The audience stilled while he looked them over.

Hatch spoke in a soft voice. "Sit down. Sit down, please. All of you." He waited for everyone to sit. "Greetings, my friends. It is just past midnight. A new day, literally and figuratively. Today is the beginning of a new day for each of you. When you came into our employment you were fully aware that this was not merely a job but a cause far greater than any mission you ever will have or ever will bear—a cause of greater importance than even your own life. Today the fullness of our cause is revealed. Today you will begin to understand the depth of our campaign and the level of your own commitment. Yesterday you were mere men. Today you are Elgen."

The hall echoed with loud applause.

"The sleeping minions of this world may not have heard of the Elgen yet. But they will."

More applause.

"The sleeping minions of this world may not yet be trembling at the mention of our name and power. But they will."

More applause.

Hatch pounded the podium furiously. "Presidents, prime ministers, and kings may not be bowing to us yet, but mark my words—they will."

The audience rose to their feet in wild applause.

"I now introduce the new order. These soldiers standing next to me, wearing the Elgen uniform of purple and scarlet, are my Elite Global Guard. *You* will refer to them as the Elite Guard. You may have noticed that their acronym is EGG. Like eggs, there are a dozen of them. Only I will affectionately refer to them as my EGGs. You will not.

"You will obey their commands as if they came from me. To disobey their orders is tantamount to disobeying me.

"In the first three rows, directly beneath the Elite Guard, wearing scarlet armbands, are the Zone Captains. The ZCs are the leaders of a global zone of Squad Captains.

"Now hear me and hear me well. Your previous chain of command no longer exists. From this moment on, you will no longer take orders from weak-bodied scientists and weak-minded bureaucrats!"

Hatch's pronouncement was met with loud applause.

"You will answer only to me, the EGGs, your Zone Captains, and, most often, your Squad Captain. Squad Captains wear the purple Elgen uniform and are responsible for each and every one of the members within their squad, which will number between six and twelve. Let me repeat the hierarchy. Your Squad Captain will answer to a Zone Captain, who will answer to one of the twelve Elite, who answer only to me.

"In addition to your Squad Captains, there will be one or two Elgen Secret Police, known to us as ESP, in each squad. These men are primarily informants. You will not know who they are. This force constitutes the eyes and ears of our organization and will communicate directly with the Zone Captains and, if necessary, the Elite Guard. Any sign of insubordination within a squad will be dealt with swiftly and severely.

"It's a brave new world, gentlemen. Those of you who are with me will prosper far beyond your wildest imaginations. Governors and magistrates will bow at your feet and clean your boots with their tongues." His voice lowered threateningly. "But those who defy me will learn suffering they never imagined possible. I would like to demonstrate what I mean. You are all familiar with the Starxource energy grid. Captain Welch, please take us live to the bowl."

The image on the screen behind Hatch changed, revealing a close-up of the bowl's chute, which had already started moving out from the wall. When the chute reached its extremity, the door in the wall opened. A man's black boot appeared, followed by the rest of his body as he was pushed out and the door shut behind him. The guard was fully dressed in Elgen uniform and bound at his legs and wrists. As the chute lowered, he desperately tried to hold on to the sides of the chute, but it was impossible. He slid on the metal rollers to the bottom of the chute, where he was caught by the cog, which was hanging just a few yards from the grid.

Within seconds the guard was covered with rats. His amplified screaming echoed through the entire hall for less than a minute, leaving the men silent. After just ninety seconds the man's skeleton was ejected from the chute. The camera zoomed in on the shredded uniform and the bone remains of the guard.

"They go much quicker than the bulls, don't they?" Hatch said without emotion.

The room was silent as Hatch looked over the audience. Hatch nodded to one of the guards, and three men dressed in pink girls' party dresses were led out, bound and shackled. Their mouths and chins were covered with tape. They all had large bows on their heads.

"Cute, aren't they?" Hatch said.

The men in the audience laughed loudly.

"These so-called men arrived at our conference with the wrong attitude. How unfortunate for them. They will not leave us with those attitudes, simply because they will not be leaving us at all. If you once knew these men, you will be doing yourself a favor to disassociate with them, as they are traitors and fools. And they are part of tomorrow's entertainment, for they are all headed to the chute. But first you will be allowed the privilege of letting them know how you feel about traitors.

"Elgen Force, do not make their fate yours. Over the next two weeks we are going to introduce a new food group to our rodents' diet. Every day, for the next fourteen days, one of you will meet these men's fate. One of you each day."

The men were all silent, none daring to move or speak.

"We will select our fourteen 'meals' by monitoring your level of cooperation and performance. Each day we'll nominate three of you, but only one of you will be chosen, and that will be my decision. If you are nominated twice, then you will automatically be selected. Our informants are already in place. From this moment on, anything and everything you say and do *will* be used for or against you."

Hatch paused for emphasis. "If you think you can beat this system, think again. For those among you who have seditious thoughts, remember that the friend you invite to join you will rejoice in your treachery, because, and excuse the pun, to 'rat out' a disloyal guard is the fastest way to ensure your own survival.

"Each of you will be given a new Elgen rule book. It looks like this." Hatch held up a navy book with gold embossing. "This is your new *Bible*. It is only thirty-six pages long. Over the next five days you are to memorize the entire book. Every line. Every word. And yes, there will be a test. Two of them. The two guards with the lowest score will automatically be included as two of the fourteen meals. So, for your sake, I recommend that you know the book well."

Hatch nodded to one of the EGGs standing by the side of the stage. The guard saluted, then gave a hand signal, and twelve other guards—the ESP Captains—walked to the front of the stage. They wore scarlet berets and sashes across their chests.

Each of the captains had an assistant at their side, a guard dressed in black, with yellow and black striped armbands. The assistants wheeled a stainless steel cart with a black, metal box on top that resembled a large toaster. The box had several dials and knobs and a white meter with a needle. Two long red wires protruded from the side of the box leading to finger clamps. On a lower shelf on the cart was a box of books.

The ESP Captains sat down at black, plastic chairs while the assistants assembled the apparatus, then stacked the books on the ground next to them. The preparations were carried out quickly and sharply.

At the same time the three men in dresses were led from the stage down to the auditorium's exit. The men were forced to their knees and shackled together, facing outward in a triangle.

"This is how you will receive your Elgen rule book," Hatch said. "Each of you will have the opportunity to take the Elgen oath of loyalty. Should you choose to make this commitment, and I strongly advise that you do so, you will come up to the front and stand in the queue until it is your turn. When you are summoned to the podium, you will have sensors placed on the fingers of your right hand. The administrator will be reading his monitor as you take the oath. If you are lying he will know it.

"You will put your right hand on the Elgen rule book, raise your left arm, and repeat the oath after the administrator." Hatch lifted a paper from the podium and read, "'I swear on my life, breath, and fortune to prosper the Elgen cause, to advance its mission until every man and woman on earth have sworn allegiance to the *Novus Ordo Glorificus Elgen*, our new glorious order. I offer up my life and death to this endeavor and will follow all rules contained in this book and those that will come, with fidelity, honor, and exactness. I swear this oath on my life.'"

He set the paper down and looked over the group. "You will then make the Elgen salute and bow to the administrator and remain bowed until he accepts or rejects your oath. If he accepts your oath he will hand you the contract to sign. You will then be given your rule book and you will go to the adjoining hall to await further instruction and, if you are wise, start memorizing your rule book."

A guard stepped forward and whispered something to Hatch.

"Of course," Hatch said. "Let me remind you that as you pass out of this room you may make known your disdain for the three men who have shamed us all with their weakness. Elgen are not weak. When you are through with these pitiful little girls, what is left of them will be fed to the rats.

"Now, back to you. If your administrator rejects your oath, you will be sent to the end of the queue for another opportunity. If you fail your oath the second time, you will be taken to a separate hall. I will not tell you what will happen there. Those of you who merit that placement will learn soon enough."

He stopped talking, looking out over the silent audience. "I ask those of you who do not wish to take this oath to remove yourselves from our company immediately. If any of you wish to leave, you may raise your hand at this time."

There was a pause, then one lone hand in the crowd went up. Guards in red immediately surrounded the man and escorted him out of the room, amid the whispers and buzzing of the remaining men.

After he was gone Hatch smiled. "Gentlemen, I think we just found our first meal."

Nervous laughter skittered through the crowd.

"It is now time for you to make a decision that will affect your life, the lives of billions, and history itself. Time for you to choose your paths. Gentlemen, welcome to the future."

# PART 3

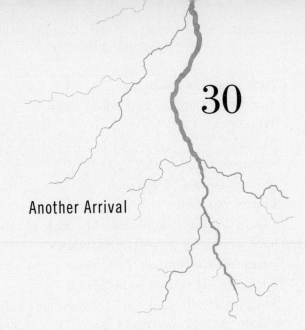

# 30

## Another Arrival

$O$ur plane landed at night at the Cuzco airport. I had never left the United States before, and standing in a foreign airport where all the signs were in a different language filled me with anxiety. We walked out of the terminal. The air was warm and moist.

"My head is killing me," Wade said, grimacing.

"I have a headache too," Taylor said. "It started as soon as we landed."

"It's altitude sickness," Ostin said. "Cuzco's elevation is eleven thousand feet, more than double Idaho's."

"Does it go away?" Taylor asked.

"Not always," Ostin said. "I read that the best remedy is to drink coca tea. In fact, that's what that lady is selling over there."

Everyone glanced over at a brightly dressed native woman who was holding a plastic bag filled with green leaves.

"Now what?" Jack asked.

"Someone's supposed to meet us," I said.

"Who?"

"No idea."

"Anyone speak Spanish?" I asked.

"*Yo hablo español,*" Ostin said.

"Besides you, Ostin."

"I know a little," Abigail said. "My uncle is Mexican. He used to teach me words. But it's been a few years."

"Beautiful *and* bilingual," Zeus said.

"Suck-up," Jack said under his breath.

"But you can still speak some?" I asked hopefully.

"A little," Abigail said. "And I can understand a lot of it."

"So it's Ostin and Abi," I said.

Just then a man walked up to me. He was poorly dressed and held out his hand. *"Tiene dinero?"*

"What did he say?" I asked Ostin.

"He wants money," Ostin said.

I took a dollar out of my pocket and handed it to him. "I only have American dollars."

Ostin translated. *"Yo tengo sólo dinero americano."*

The man nodded. *"Gracias, Señor Michael."*

I looked at him. "Did you say . . . ?"

"*Sí,*" the man said. "Mr. Michael, the bus is for you and your friends." He cocked his head toward a medium-size tour bus that was parked next to the curb. The bus had dark tinted windows. When I turned back the man was already walking away.

"Guys," I said. "Over here."

We started toward the bus.

"What do you think?" I asked Ian.

"It looks clean," he said. "The driver has a gun, but nothing you, Taylor, or Zeus couldn't take out if you had to."

"I expect him to be armed," I said. "Where we're going, he probably needs it."

The bus shook as its engine started up, and the doors opened as we approached. From the curb I looked inside. The driver was a Peruvian man, stocky, and at least twice my age. He watched us carefully as we climbed aboard, counting or mumbling something as each of us got on. The moment we were all inside, the driver shut the door and pulled away from the curb, clearly in a hurry.

Taylor and I sat together about four rows from the front. Everyone else was behind us.

"He kind of reminds me of my grade school bus driver," Taylor said. "About as friendly, too."

"Do you think he speaks English?" I asked.

She shrugged. "No idea."

I walked up to the front, crouching down in the aisle next to the driver. "Excuse me," I said. "What's your name?"

He kept his eyes fixed on the dark road. "It is not important," he said with a thick accent.

"Where are you taking us?"

"Chaspi," he said.

"Chaspi?"

"You will see."

"How far are we from Puerto Maldonado?"

"Far," he said. "Far."

I guessed he was being purposely vague, so I went back to my seat.

"What did he say?" Taylor asked.

"As little as he could," I replied. I looked out the window. We were traveling away from the city lights into dark, forested hills.

"Do we even know where we're going?" she asked.

"Yes," I said. "To the Elgen."

Elgen. The name filled me with dread. In spite of how hard we had worked to get here, I was still having a difficult time controlling my fear. My tics were going crazy.

When we were in the middle of nowhere, the driver lifted the microphone. "Amigos. We are going off the highway up ahead onto a small side road so you can sleep. There are many trees overhead so the helicopters or satellites cannot see us. We cannot take the chance of staying at a hotel. The Elgen are very careful to know who is coming near them. This bus has a bathroom and there is food for you. The seats lean back most of the way, and there is a pillow and blankets above you. I am sorry it is not a real bed, but I know where you are going and it will be the best bed you will have for some time.

"You will start your journey in a few hours. We will hike a small distance to the river, where there is a boat waiting for you."

Zeus was already asleep, which I was glad about. I didn't think he'd like the idea of being in a boat.

"Can't we just take the road?" I asked.

"No. The road is not safe. The Elgen make many roadblocks and checkpoints. You will ride the boat up the Río Madres de Dios, a tributary of the Amazon River, and will be let out in the jungle near the Elgen compound. You will arrive a little before morning. There you will be on your own. So please, get what sleep you can."

# 31

## Into the Jungle

That night I had a nightmare. I dreamed I was being chased through a dark maze by a beast. I never saw it, but I could hear its snarls and growling behind me, always just at my heels. The maze I was running through had hundreds of doors, but every one I tried was locked. I kept hearing my mother shouting out my name, but I couldn't tell where her voice was coming from. I just kept running. When I was in center of the maze, I heard her voice coming from the very last door. Relieved, I opened it. Dr. Hatch was standing there. He started laughing. When he opened his mouth, his tongue was a snake, and its body curled around me, constricting me. That's when I woke up.

It took me a moment to remember where I was. I could hear voices—two men speaking in Spanish. I looked out my window. In the moonlight I could see the men standing near the front of the bus. One was our driver, his face illuminated by a cigarette. The other was a man I hadn't seen before. I glanced over at Taylor. She was still asleep, and I could hear Ostin snoring behind me. I got up and walked to the front of the bus.

The man speaking to our driver looked up at me. He was carrying a machete. *"Buenos días, señor,"* he said.

*"Buenos días,"* I repeated, which was pretty much the extent of my Spanish. I stepped outside with the men. "I'm Michael."

"Yes, Michael. I know you from your picture. I am Jaime. Are your friends ready?"

"They're still sleeping."

"You must wake them now. They can sleep on the boat. We must soon go. Timing is everything."

"Now?"

He nodded.

I climbed back on the bus and woke everyone. It was probably two or three in the morning, so, not surprisingly, no one was happy about the wake-up call.

As I headed back to my seat, the man with the machete walked onto the bus carrying a large sack over his shoulder. "Amigos," he said. "We are going to hike through the jungle. There is much water. You must put on the galoshes."

"How much water?" Zeus asked.

"You will not drown," the man said. "It is just a few inches of water."

"Drowning isn't the problem," Zeus said.

"Oh, yes, you must be Zeus. Forgive me. I have special boots for you." He brought out a pair of waders that would reach nearly to Zeus's chest.

Jaime walked down the aisle handing out boots, which we pulled on over our shoes. Then, following the man's directions, we grabbed our packs and hurried off the bus to the trees on the other side of the road.

Stepping under the cover of the forest canopy, the man pointed his flashlight under his chin, illuminating his face. "I am Jaime, your guide. I will go much of the way with you. As we walk through the jungle, keep your eyes paled for animals."

"Paled?" Ostin asked, yawning.

"He meant 'peeled,'" I said. "What kind of animals?"

"The vipers, jaguar, and the anaconda. The big snakes like the water. I am told that some of you are more powerful than these things—I do not doubt it. But your electricity will not save you from a viper strike, so please follow me. I was born in the jungle. I know its ways."

He pointed the flashlight ahead of us, and we lined up behind him in single file. I brought up the rear with Zeus, who was moving cautiously. Jack and Abigail were in the front, behind Jaime, who had given Jack a machete to help widen the trail. McKenna walked in the middle of the group. She lit up her head to illuminate the path for us but stopped after a few seconds because of the millions of insects attracted to her light.

About five minutes into the hike Taylor asked, "What's that sound?"

"Crickets?"

"No, it's a buzzing sound. Like electricity."

"It's me," I said. "I'm like a human bug zapper."

We were walking under a canopy of leaves so thick that we might as well have been inside a building. Our group made for an interesting sight, our glow lightly illuminating the forest around us.

After twenty minutes or so, Jaime stopped for us to rest. We gathered in a small half circle. As Jaime looked at us he said, *"Increíble."*

"What?" I asked.

"You, you . . ." He struggled with the word in English. Finally he said, *"Son fosforesentes."*

"You glow," Ostin said.

"I wish to show you something," Jaime said. He pointed to a nearby tree with his flashlight. It was maybe twenty feet tall, slender, with narrow leaves.

Wade walked up to it with his hand outstretched. "This one?"

"Don't touch it!" Jaime said.

Wade stopped.

"It is the tangarana tree. You will notice that there are no trees around it."

"That's kind of weird," Jack said.

"I'll show you why. Watch." He tapped his machete against the tree's trunk. Immediately a swarm of red-and-black ants covered the tree's limbs. "The tangarana ant," Jaime said. "They have a friendship."

"A symbiotic relationship," Ostin said. "The ant's a symbiont. Like Dr. Hatch."

The man glanced at him, then continued. "The ants protect the tree and the tree gives them shelter. The ants will attack animals who come too close. They will even kill any plant that tries to grow near it. The natives used to tie their enemies to the tree. The ants would eat them alive."

"That's horrible," Abigail said.

Jaime shrugged. "War is horrible."

He turned and we started walking again. A few minutes later there was a loud screech, which echoed around us.

"What the heck was that?" Ostin said, his eyes wide with panic. "It sounded like a pterodactyl."

Jaime smiled. "That is the *mono aullador*—the howler monkey. It is loud, yes?"

Suddenly something swung from the darkness toward us. A bolt of lightning flashed across our heads, and the animal dropped to the ground.

"You electrocuted a monkey," Ian said.

"I didn't know what it was," Zeus said. "It attacked us. It had it coming."

"You shocked a cute, furry little monkey," Abigail said.

"He's not little," Zeus said.

Jack laughed, and Zeus looked at him. "You going to give me grief too?"

Jack shook his head. "No, dude. I would have roundhouse kicked it back into the tree. You just got to it faster."

The jungle was alive with noise, and the sound of rushing water became more pronounced the closer we got to the river. The trail started to decline, and once we reached the riverbank, the trail dropped steeply to a dark, slow-moving river. The river bubbled at its crests, illuminated by a half-moon's glow.

Below us was a riverboat with a striped canvas top, the sides covered in plastic. A Peruvian man was sitting at the back of the boat, manning the engine.

"This boat is what the gold miners use," Jaime said. "It will not cause suspicion in the night. But you must all stay quiet. We do not know who we will encounter on the river."

"Do the Elgen patrol the river?" I asked.

"Not yet," he said.

One by one we boarded the boat. Jack and Jaime helped everyone on, except Zeus, who stood alone on the top of the embankment looking down at the boat. "Really, man. I don't do boats."

"Quit being such a prima donna and get on the boat," Jack said.

Jaime hiked back up to see what was keeping Zeus.

"I don't do boats," he said to Jaime. "I'll take my chances on the road."

"You have no chance on the road," Jaime said.

"You don't understand. If I fall in the water, it will electrocute me." Zeus looked into Jaime's eyes to make sure he understood the seriousness of his circumstance. "My electricity will *kill* me."

Suddenly Jaime started laughing, softly at first, then louder, growing into a great, echoing chuckle.

Zeus's eyes flashed with anger. "Shut up! Why are you laughing?"

"Amigo," Jaime said, "I do not mean to disrespect, but look." He held the flashlight out over the water near the bank, revealing several bright orange reflections, slightly oval like cat eyes. "You see, amigo? Many caiman. The river is full of caiman and piranha and anaconda. If you fall in the water you die anyway!"

Zeus looked at him for a moment, then said, "Oh." He walked down the bank to the boat.

Taylor swallowed. "Caiman, piranhas, and anacondas?"

I just shrugged. "Come on. This is the easy part."

Zeus carefully climbed over the bow, sitting at the opposite end from Jack and Abigail. I thought we all looked miserable and afraid.

I remember once seeing a World War II picture of paratroopers sitting inside the fuselage of a plane waiting to jump, wondering if they would live to see the morning. I guess that's how we felt.

Jaime unlashed the rope from the tree, then pushed us out from the shore while the other man revved up the outboard engine, pulling us backward into the flow of the river. Taylor laid her head on my shoulder. No one had anything to say.

# 32

## Final Instructions

The journey up the river seemed like a strange dream. It took two men to operate the boat—Jaime, who lay across the bow watching for drifting logs, and Luis, who sat back at the engine, quietly watching over us. Both banks of the river were walls of trees, creating a narrow, overgrown corridor that stretched for hundreds of miles through rain forest until reaching into the heart of the massive Amazon itself. There were occasional breaks in the trees, revealing small clearings for huts or illicit mining camps.

The boat's long benches were covered with dark vinyl pads and the ten of us stretched out on them, overlapping our heads and feet. The inside of the boat was lit with a warm, green luminance from our glow. I looked around at my friends. McKenna, Wade, and Abigail were asleep. Jack was awake, sitting near the engine, opening and shutting a pocketknife. Ian was leaning over the side watching the water. Ostin, who was lying near Taylor, was still trying to get comfortable. When he turned to his side I saw something move across his back—a hairy tarantula about the size of my hand.

"Ostin," I whispered.

"What?"

"Don't move."

His eyes widened. "There's something on me, isn't there?"

"Don't move. I'll get it."

"There's a massive, hairy spider on your back," Taylor said.

"You didn't have to tell me," Ostin said.

"I'll get it," I said. I pulsed as I grabbed the tarantula. There was a loud snap, followed by a wisp of gray smoke. I threw the spider over the side of the boat into the dark water.

"Spiders," Ostin said. "I hate spiders." He shuddered, then lay back down.

I slid to the front of the boat near Jaime. "How did you get involved with us?" I asked.

He leaned back a little. "Let's just say I do not like the Elgen. They come to my city and they change everything. We live in fear now. Their guards walk our streets. They have all the power. If they want something you have, they take it. There is nothing you can do. Even our policemen fear them. We know danger. The jungle is dangerous. It will take your life, even your family. But it is fair. It only takes from those who do not respect it. The Elgen take what they want."

"Did the Elgen take something of yours?" I asked.

Jaime slowly nodded, his eyes dark with gravity. "They took my son."

"Why?"

"I don't know. I wasn't there. The Elgen need no reason."

"I'm sorry," I said.

"Me too," he said softly. "I am very sorry I was not there to protect my son. I was working for the Elgen. It was my right to die before my son." Jaime looked at me with a deep sadness. "I must tell you something I learned as a boy." He looked around. "We are jungle people. From my boyhood I was taught its ways. My father taught me the vines and roots that will save your life from a viper bite. And he warned me never to go into the jungle without a machete. There are many dangerous animals in the jungle. In the water, the electric eel, the caiman, and piranha. On the land, there are the vipers and the jaguar and puma. But the most dangerous lives both on land and water, it is the anaconda. They grow ten meters and longer, yet they are fast. Even the caiman and jaguar fear the grown anaconda.

"One day my father taught me this lesson. He said, 'Jaime, if you are ever in the jungle without your machete and you are to meet an anaconda, do not run, it will catch you and eat you. This is what you are to do. First, you must look directly at the snake. It is frightening, but you must look at it. It will freeze like a tiger does as it stalks its prey. While it is frozen, you must slowly move yourself, very, very slowly, to where the sun is directly above your head. The jungle is on the equator, so the sun is often high in the sky. The snake will not want to lose its dinner, so it will keep following you, slightly turning. But the snake does not have eyelids, so as it looks up at you it is also looking into the sun and it will burn out its eyes. When its eyes are white with blindness, you may just walk away.'"

I looked at him for a moment, then said, "You're not just talking about snakes, are you?"

He shook his head. "No. I have not met the one they call Hatch. But I think he may be like this snake. If he wants you too much, that may be his weakness."

"I hope that's not his only weakness," I said softly. I exhaled slowly. "I better try to get some sleep."

"Yes," said Jaime.

I lay back on the bench next to Taylor. But I couldn't sleep. After a while I sat up, looking out over the dark, moving landscape.

It was maybe an hour later when Ian whispered, "Michael, look." He was pointing toward the riverbank.

"I don't see anything," I whispered.

"Look carefully."

As my eyes focused I saw the silhouette of a man standing on the bank looking at us.

"I see him. Is he . . . Elgen?"

"No," Ian said. "He's dressed like some kind of tribesman."

"He is of the Amacarra tribe," Jaime said. He had walked over to see what Ian was pointing at.

"Amacarra?" I said.

"Yes. The Amazon once had many such tribes—more than ten million people. But now there are few left in the forest. The shamans and medicine men are growing old. The ancient knowledge of the Amazon and her healing will soon be lost."

"Are they dangerous?" Ian asked.

"Not as dangerous as some of you, perhaps. But they have blow darts tipped in the poison of the blow-dart frog—very, very dangerous."

"*Dendrobates leucomelas,*" Ostin said in his sleep. "The poison dart frog, indigenous to South America. A frog the size of my fingernail has enough venom to kill ten full-grown men." Then he smacked his lips and was quiet again.

I looked at Ian, and we both shook our heads in wonder.

"The Amacarra have something in common with us," Jaime said.

"What's that?"

"They hate the Elgen. They call them '*bai mwo gwei.*' The white devil."

We watched the man fade into the inky blackness of the forest as our boat slowly slipped past.

"He is a holy man," Jaime said. "Once when I was fishing, my boat engine had problems, and I paddled my boat to the shore. The holy man was standing there at the bank. I told him I was having problems with my boat. He said, 'Yes, last night the Great Spirit told me to wait here for you.' Then he blessed my boat, and the engine started. I made it all the way home."

I wasn't sure what to say to that. "Now sleep," Jaime said, and went back to the bow.

\* \* \*

As badly as I needed sleep, I couldn't find it. I lay quietly, listening to the steady sound of the boat's whining chug.

As dawn came, Jaime left his post at the front of the boat to talk to me. "Señor Michael. You are not sleeping?"

"No. I can't."

"Too much on your mind, I think."

"Probably."

"You are a very brave young man."

"No," I said. "I'm very afraid."

"You cannot be brave without fear." He sat back. "Luis at the engine is mourning. Last summer his son was in this river playing with his friends when he vanished. A caiman pulled him under. Or perhaps an anaconda. Luis was on the bank. He jumped in the river to save his son. But it was too late. His son was already gone."

I sat up and looked at Luis. No wonder he was so quiet. "That was very dangerous for him to jump in after his son," I said.

"Yes, but he did not think of the danger to himself because he loves his son."

I nodded.

"You and Luis have much in common. You also jump in the water with the Elgen caiman. You too are brave." He slapped his chest. "But more than brave, you have love. And love is brave." He patted me on the shoulder, then went back up to the front of the boat.

About a half hour later the engine cut back, and Luis shook Jack to wake him. He then pointed at the dirty, oil-stained blankets Jack was lying on. Jack handed the blankets to Luis, who began wrapping them around the outboard motor. Everyone but Wade and McKenna awoke.

"What's going on?" I asked Jaime.

"Luis is quieting the motor. Just ahead is the beginning of the Elgen compound. Their land comes close to the river here."

I peered up over the side of the boat. Through the trees I could see the light of a clearing in the forest and the glistening of a metal fence.

"How big is the compound?"

"Ten thousand hectares," he said. "It will take you an hour to hike to the compound, if that's the route you take. But I don't think that will be possible. There are cameras everywhere."

"The Elgen love cameras as much as I love Oreos," Ostin said, sitting up.

"It would be like walking three miles in front of their faces and them not seeing you. It is impossible."

"Then how do we get in?" I asked.

He shook his head. "I do not know. But I am instructed to give you this." He handed me a bulky envelope, which I quickly opened. Inside were several documents, a satellite map, and a letter. I extracted the letter and began to read it out loud.

*Michael,*

*If you are reading this letter you are already near your destination. Through satellite surveillance we have gathered some information about the Elgen compound that may be of help to you. The Elgen compound is built in the center of a twenty-five thousand acre ranch surrounded by two high-voltage electric fences. The fence may not be a problem for you, but it will be for some of the other Electroclan members. How you get into the facility will be up to you. It won't be easy. Crossing the ranch will be difficult, if not impossible, as there are hundreds of surveillance cameras, some visible and some not, and nowhere to hide. You will be utterly exposed. There is only one entrance into the compound, the main road, and it is heavily guarded and entered only at the checkpoint. All vehicles are searched by dogs, even the Elgen vehicles. Again, it is up to you to find a way into the compound.*

*The facility consists of four main buildings and a power transformer. This is the largest of the Starxource plants. We know that your primary goal is to find your mother, but if you can knock out the compound's grid you will do great damage to the Elgen's credibility as you will shut down all power in a*

*two-hundred-mile radius and affect the major cities of Lima
and Arequipa. After you leave the compound, we have made
transportation arrangements for you. Enclosed in this package is
a transmitting and global positioning device.*

I reached into the envelope and pulled out what I thought was
the device but turned out to be only an iPod nano.

"It looks like an iPod," Taylor said.

"That's definitely an iPod," Ostin said. "Maybe they rewired it into
a GPS."

"Keep reading," Taylor said.

*For your and our safety the GPS device has been hidden inside
an iPod nano.*

"Told you," Ostin said.

"Shh," Taylor said.

*To use the GPS go to the Colby Cross album and click on the
song "I'm Lost Without You." A map of the area will appear,
leading you to us. When you have reached your destination you
can use the device to signal us. Again, go to the Colby Cross
album and click on the song "Come and Get Me, Baby." As
the song plays it will send us a signal, and we will dispatch
a helicopter to pick you up at the location we installed on
your GPS, a clearing in the jungle about ten miles east of the
compound. We're sorry it cannot be closer, but once you've
attacked the base, nowhere in the vicinity will be safe. Traveling
through the jungle will not be easy, but the Elgen will have
difficulty following you.*

*We have just received some unfortunate news. We have learned
that Dr. Hatch is now at the Peruvian compound. For reasons
unknown to us, he has summoned all of the Elgen guards from*

*around the world. We believe there will be more than two*
*thousand guards on the premises. Had we known this earlier*
*we would have postponed your arrival. If you wish to delay, it's*
*your call. Tell Jaime and he will continue to drive you up the*
*river to our rendezvous.*

*Good luck.*

"Hatch is there," I said.

"Good," Jack said, making a fist. "I have a present for him."

I looked over at Taylor. "What do you think?"

"Not good," she said softly. "Two thousand guards?"

"That's an army," I said. "Maybe we should delay." I looked at Ostin. "What do you think?"

Ostin thought for a moment, then said, "Where's the best place to hide a penny?"

"Really?" Taylor said. "We're about to face our deaths and you're telling riddles?"

"I'm making a point," Ostin said indignantly. "The best place to hide a penny *is in a jar of pennies.*"

Taylor just looked at him.

"Think about it. The more people there are, the easier it is to blend in. The huge influx of guards might be creating the very distraction we need. Besides, if it comes down to a gunfight, what does it matter if there's fifty guards or two thousand? Either way we're dead."

"Wow, I feel so much better now," Taylor said.

"He might be right, though," I said. "What do you all think? Do we go?"

"Your call," Jack said. "I'm game either way."

"Zeus?"

He looked nervous but said, "Whatever you decide."

I turned to Taylor, who was still looking anxious. "What do you think?" I asked.

"I don't know," she said. "It's up to you."

I put my head in my hands. "Why does everyone keep saying that? I have no idea what the right thing is."

Jack said, "Look, you got instincts. You rescued us from the academy, didn't you? You didn't know what you were doing then, either."

I sighed. "Okay, I think Ostin's right. If we can figure out how to get inside the place, I say we do it. As far as taking out the power station, I wouldn't know how to do that if I were alone in the building with a ton of dynamite. I say we find my mother, then get out of there."

For the next half hour Ostin and I carefully studied the map of the compound, trying to get an idea of where we were. About the time the sun rose above the tree line, Luis cut back the boat's motor and we began moving closer to shore.

"Señor Michael," Jaime said. "We are close. You should all eat before we dock."

"Ostin," I said. "Wake Wade and the girls."

"No problem," he said.

Jaime had brought bananas, tamales wrapped in corn husks, and a pastry that looked a little like something my mother used to make called a tiger roll.

"*Pionono de manjarblanco*," Jaime said as he handed it to me in a pan. "It is filled with *dulce de leche*."

I knew only a few words in Spanish, *leche* being one of them. "Milk?"

"Sweet milk," Ostin said. "Caramel."

I took a bite. It was airy and good. *"Bueno,"* I said.

"Eat many," Jaime said. "Eat many."

"Everyone eat a lot of bananas," Zeus said. "We need to be at our best."

"Hand me a couple," Ostin said.

"Not you," he said. "The electric ones."

"I do have electric powers. The brain . . ."

"We know, Ostin," Taylor said. "A hundred gazillion electric synapses-thingies." She smiled at Zeus. "He won't give up."

"Here is something to drink," Jaime said. He opened a cooler filled with cartons of milk and bottles of Inca Kola. I took one of each, popping the cap off the bottle with the bottle opener Jaime handed me. The Kola tasted a lot like bubble gum.

"What's with tamales for breakfast?" Taylor asked.

"It's Peru," I said.

The tamales were stuffed with eggs, cheese, and shredded chicken.

"Think we can heat these?" Ostin asked, peeling back the husk.

"Sure," Taylor said. "We'll just throw them in the microwave."

McKenna reached over and took the tamale from Ostin, holding it gently in her hands. Within a few seconds steam began to rise from between her fingers. She handed the tamale back to Ostin. "Careful, it's hot."

Ostin stared at her with bright eyes. "I'm so going to marry you someday."

She smiled as she sat back.

A half hour later Jaime and Luis began arguing. Jaime was pointing ahead toward the bank and Luis was shaking his head. *"No aqui."*

*"Si, aqui,"* Jaime said.

Finally Luis relented, steering the boat closer to the bank.

"Ian," I said. "I think we're about to dock. Do you see anything up ahead?"

He looked toward the bank and shook his head. "Nothing but jungle."

Luis guided the boat into a small inlet that was overhung with thick canopy, and again we were obscured in shadow. Jaime climbed out onto the bow as Luis ran the boat up onto the shore, startling several small caimans and sending them scurrying back into the water. Jaime jumped out onto dry ground with a coil of rope. He pulled the boat farther up onto the bank and lashed the end of the rope around the trunk of a peculiarly shaped tree. "Amigos, hurry," he said.

We grabbed our packs and one by one climbed out of the boat. Ostin and I were the last out. As I was stepping down Jaime put his arm on my shoulder, stopping me. "Señor, do you have your device?"

I held up the packet. "It's in here."

"I'm sorry, you cannot take the packet."

"What?"

"It is too dangerous. If the Elgen find it they will know we are helping you. Do you remember the instructions for the device?"

"Colby Cross. Yes. Can I at least take the map?"

"No, señor."

"It's okay," Ostin said, tapping his temple. "I've got it all right here."

I took the iPod out of the envelope and handed the rest back to Jaime. He unlashed the boat.

"*Dios esté contigo,*" he said.

"God be with you," Ostin translated.

"*Gracias,*" I replied.

Jaime pushed the boat off the bank, jumping into it in one fluid motion. He gave us a salute, then the boat pulled back out into the river, reversed direction, and sped back the way we had come.

# 33

## Teasing Bulls

"How far is it to the compound?" Wade asked.

"I think it's about the same distance as our hike to the boat," I said. "Everyone ready?"

Everyone looked tired and anxious, but they all nodded.

"Okay," I said. "Let's go."

Jack held up his machete. "I'll take the lead."

We all followed him back into the jungle. Insects continued to flare off my skin in bright blue flashes. Ten minutes into our hike Jack stopped.

"What is it?" I asked.

"Look."

A jaguar was standing in our path, about fifty feet ahead of us, its green eyes pale in the distance.

"Zeus," I said. Zeus quickly stepped up. "We might need you.

Just in case it decides to hunt one of us."

"Nobody run," Ostin said. "We should be okay."

"Why are we okay?" Taylor asked.

"We don't look like what they usually eat. But if you run, it triggers the chase instinct."

"Good to know," Wade said.

The cat looked more bored than hungry. After a few minutes it turned away and lumbered off into the thick foliage.

We breathed a collective sigh of relief, then continued hiking.

Ostin said to Taylor, "I hope we don't have to deal with those rats. I hate rats. Even without electricity they're bad."

Taylor sighed. "You're going to tell me everything you know about rats, aren't you?"

"Rats," Ostin said, "are the most successful survivor of any mammal on earth. They can live almost three weeks without sleep, keep themselves afloat in water for three days, and fall fifty feet without getting hurt. That's the equivalent of us falling off a twenty-six-story building.

"They're also breeding machines. In ideal conditions a single pair of rats could produce, in three years, three and a half million offspring. That's why nearly ninety percent of the world's islands have been overrun by rats. They cause about half the extinctions of reptile and bird species."

"You're not making this any easier," Taylor said.

"Did you know that rats are ticklish and actually giggle?"

"No."

"And they have belly buttons but no thumbs?"

"Why would I want to know that?"

"Did you know that a group of rats is called a mischief?"

"No. Really?"

"Did you know that rats regulate their temperatures through their tails because they can't sweat?"

"Nope. Didn't know that either."

"Did you know that there's a temple in India where rats are worshipped?"

"No," Taylor said. "Maybe you should go there."

"Did you know that rats can't vomit?"

"Okay, enough. No more rat trivia."

"I'm just passing time."

"Then talk about something besides rats."

Ostin thought about it. "How about snakes? These jungles are slithering with them."

"Michael, your turn," Taylor said, pulling me next to Ostin.

We hiked another forty minutes before we saw light ahead of us—the edge of the forest. I stopped everyone. "All right, everyone, stay alert."

We cautiously approached the forest perimeter. The Elgen fence was only thirty feet from the clearing, and we could see dozens of bulls on the other side. The fence was about twenty feet high with horizontal wires eighteen inches apart. The fence was marked with DANGER: HIGH VOLTAGE signs in both English and Spanish.

"It looks like a ranch," McKenna said.

"It *is* a ranch," I said. "Ostin, how far do you think we are from the gate?"

"It's about three miles southwest."

I stared ahead at the animals. "Can you see the compound?" I asked Ian.

"Barely. There's a lot of electrical interference. There are also a lot of security cameras between here and the compound."

"A lot?"

"More than a hundred."

I shook my head. "The Elgen and their cameras."

"What now?" Taylor asked. "How do we get in?"

"I think I could lift the wires high enough that everyone could climb under, but then what do we do?" I asked. "With all those cameras, we'd be surrounded by Elgen guards before we got within two miles of the place."

Zeus said, "Ian could spot the cameras and I could blow them out."

"Yeah, like they're not going to notice that?" Jack said snidely.

"Shut up," Zeus said. "I don't hear you coming up with anything."

"C'mon, guys," Ian said. "Quit fighting all the time."

"Maybe if he'd quit being such a jerk," Zeus said.

"You watch your back," Jack said.

"Is that a threat?" Zeus asked.

"Please, stop it," I said. "We've got enough to worry about." I sat down to think.

"We need them to come get us," Ostin said.

"Sure," Wade said. "Why don't we just call them and ask for a ride."

"Ostin, tell us your idea," I said.

"If we can somehow damage the fence, they'll have to send out a repair crew. While they're trying to repair the gate we'll jump them, take their uniforms and vehicle, and drive to the compound."

"How do we damage the fence?" Taylor asked.

McKenna was looking at the top of the fence. "We could drop a tree branch on it," she said.

"Brilliant," Ostin said. "We find a tree that hangs over the fence, then one of us climbs up with a machete and hacks a branch off so it falls on the fence."

"I could do that," Jack said.

"It's worth a shot," I said. "Let's find ourselves a branch."

We walked about a half mile along the fence line concealed in the shadow of the jungle until we found a tree with a large branch that hung over the fence. The branch provided enough shade that six large bulls were grazing beneath it.

Jack shimmied about forty feet up the tree, his machete slung through the back of his belt. He climbed out on the overhanging branch, then, straddling it, began hacking away.

"Be careful up there," Abigail said.

Jack smiled and pounded harder.

"That's a really big branch," Ostin said.

"It will have to be big to damage that wire," I said.

"Yeah. I'm just saying, it looks really heavy. I just hope when it breaks off, the tree doesn't flip back and catapult Jack through the jungle."

"We should be so lucky," Zeus said.

It took Jack almost fifteen minutes to hack through the branch, and he was soaked with sweat. With each slash of the machete he rained down perspiration.

When the branch began to crack Jack shouted, "Watch out. Here it goes." He gave the branch a few more whacks, then jumped onto another tree limb as the branch fell out from under him, directly onto the fence. Sparks shot out in a bright cascade but the branch just flipped off the top wire, doing no damage. We stood there speechless.

"Crap," Ostin said.

I looked up at Jack. He was shaking his head. "That fence is a lot stronger than it looks."

"And it looks pretty strong," Taylor said. "Any other ideas?"

"Watch out," Jack shouted. He let the machete fall. It stuck blade first into the marshy ground about ten feet from Ostin, who wasn't paying attention and jumped when it hit. Then Jack slid down the tree's trunk and joined us. "Didn't work," he said.

"You need a shower, dude," Zeus said.

Jack wiped his forehead. "Yeah, I'm starting to smell like you."

The two glared at each other.

"What we need," Ostin said, "is a car to drive through the fence."

I looked over at the fence and the bulls behind it. "How much does a car weigh?"

"That depends," Ostin said. "Are you talking about a Volkswagen or a six-wheeler?"

"Something big enough to break through that fence."

"A ton should do," Jack said.

Ostin nodded in agreement. "That's about right."

"How much do you think one of those bulls weighs?" I asked.

Ostin smiled. "A ton. At least. The problem is, how do you get a bull to charge an electric fence?"

"Easy," Wade said.

We all looked at him.

"Oh yeah, my uncle had bulls on his farm. Those things are crazy.

I've seen videos of them charging a train head-on. You just have to get them mad enough."

"How do you do that?" Taylor asked.

"Call them names," Ostin said.

Everyone looked at him.

"You're kidding, right?" Taylor said.

Ostin blushed. "Yeah, of course."

"Actually, it's easy," Wade said. "Those things are born mean. You just have to throw things at them. It always worked for us. Once we were throwing apples at them and one of my uncle's bulls got so mad it broke through the fence. He had us up a tree for almost an hour."

"Let's try it," I said.

We all went into the jungle looking for things to throw. McKenna found some softball-size seed pods on the ground. We loaded up with them, then picked out the largest of the bulls and started throwing things at him. We managed to pelt him a few times—I even knocked him once in the head—but he was pretty tranquil as far as bulls go. He didn't even look at us.

Finally Zeus got impatient. "I'll do it," he said. He walked up to the fence and began waving and shouting at the bull. "Hey, want a piece of me? Come and get me, you ugly cow." The bull looked at him, then suddenly began hoofing the dirt, like it was preparing to charge.

"I told you they don't like to be called names," Ostin said.

Then Zeus stuck out his hand and shot a bolt of lightning at the bull. The bull stiffened, then fell to its side, rolling all the way to its back, then onto its side again, its legs sticking straight out the whole time.

"I think you killed it," Ostin said.

"Way to go, genius," Jack said.

Suddenly the bull climbed to its feet and charged at us.

"Run!" I shouted.

The bull hit the fence with the force of a car crash. There was an electric snap, like the sound of a moth on a bug zapper, except a hundred times louder. The bull didn't break through the wire, but had lodged itself halfway through the fence, and sparks continued to fly all around it. Suddenly the sparks stopped. I looked at the top of the fence. The orange flashing lights affixed to the posts had gone dim.

"He shorted out the fence," Ostin said.

I walked over and touched the fence to make sure the power was really out. It was.

"Perfect," I said. "They'll have to come out to free the bull."

"Which will take at least a half dozen men," Ostin said.

"All right!" I shouted. "Everyone back to the jungle!"

As everyone walked back, Ostin grinned at me.

"What?"

"I don't know," he said. "That 'everyone back to the jungle' just sounded kind of funny."

"Glad you liked it."

"I'm going to use that sometime."

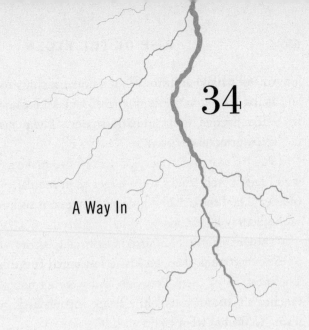

# 34

## A Way In

It didn't take long for the Elgen to respond to the damaged fence. Less than ten minutes had passed when Ian said, "Here they come."

"The guards?"

"No. They look like ranchers or something. They're driving the fence looking for the problem."

"How many are there?" I asked.

"They've got two trucks. Three in each of them."

"Any guards?"

"Doesn't look like it. At least not in uniform."

"This is perfect," Ostin said. "They'll have to get close to the fence to free the bull."

"And while they're freeing the bull, we'll take them down," I said. "Then we'll take their clothes and trucks."

"We should tie them to one of those tangarana trees," Wade said.

Abigail looked at him. "What a horrible thing to say."

"What were you thinking, man?" Jack said, glancing at Abigail.

Wade flushed with embarrassment. "I was just joking. C'mon, can't you guys take a joke?"

The Elgen ranch trucks were larger than regular pickup trucks. And quieter. They looked like a cross between a pickup and a Sno-Cat, without the tank treads.

"They're electric of course," Ostin said, before I asked.

The first truck stopped just a few yards from the struggling bull. The men, all of them Peruvian and wearing boots, jeans, and white rancher shirts, got out of the truck and walked around the animal, trying to decide what to do with it.

They talked for about five minutes, then one of them went back to his truck and retrieved a rifle. He pointed it at the bull's head and fired. When the animal had stopped moving, the men took rope from the truck and tied the bull's legs together. Then they let out the wire from the truck's winch, wrapped it around the bull's torso, and began pulling it from the fence.

As the animal was being dragged to the truck, one of the men pointed to the branch that Jack had cut. All but two of them walked over to examine it. One of the men crouched down, running his finger over the machete marks. He began speaking excitedly. They looked up to where the branch was cut from, then in our direction. One of them pointed directly to where we were hiding.

"They're on to us," Jack whispered. "We've got to attack."

"We've got to get them closer to the fence," I said. "That guy's still holding his gun. Ostin, any ideas?"

Before he could answer, Abigail stood. "I've got one."

"What are you doing?" I said.

"Get down!" Jack said. They'll see you."

"I'm counting on it," she said, stepping from the shade of the canopy. "I'm betting they won't be expecting a blond American girl to come walking out of the jungle."

Abigail began sauntering toward the fence with a big smile.

"Zeus," I said. "Be ready to hit the guy with the gun."

"I'll try," he said. "But he's pretty far."

"*Hola*, amigos!" Abigail shouted.

The men all stopped what they were doing and stared.

"Excuse me," she said. "I'm lost. I'm looking for the beach."

The men looked at one another in amazement. One of them translated, then they all started to laugh.

"Hello, how do you do?" said one in broken English. He started walking toward the fence. The rest followed.

"Pretty girl," another said. "Come close."

"*Es un ángel?*" one man said. "*De dónde vino?*"

"They think she's an angel," Ostin said.

"Taylor, now," I whispered.

Taylor concentrated, and the men suddenly stopped talking. Some of them looked around as if they were confused; two fell to their knees, their hands on their heads.

"Now!" I shouted.

Jack, Zeus, Wade, and I sprang from the bushes. Zeus began firing, first hitting the man with the rifle, then knocking three others to the ground. I knocked out the two on their knees with lightning balls.

I tested the fence to make sure it was still dead, then all four of us climbed through the wire. Wade and Jack grabbed the man closest to the fence and dragged him over to Ian.

"Grab that guy's rope," Ian said. "And his knife."

"Got it," Wade said. He took the man's bowie knife from its sheath, then grabbed his coil of rope and threw it through the fence. "Here's the knife to cut it," he said, handing it to Ian.

McKenna began stretching the rope in long, straight pieces. "How long?"

"About five-foot lengths," Ian said. "Here's the knife."

"Don't need it," McKenna said, her hand burning red. She easily melted through the nylon rope.

Zeus, Wade, and I worked together dragging the men over to the fence within reach of Ian and the girls.

"I'll check the truck for weapons," Jack said, running toward the first truck. He returned holding two cans in the air. "Check this out. Bull mace."

We carried the men into the jungle, where we removed their rancher uniforms, leaving them in their underwear. Suddenly one of the men jumped up and ran.

Zeus shot at him but was too late, as the man was already in the trees.

"Get him!" I shouted. Jack and Zeus ran into the jungle after him.

We finished tying the rest of the men, then I said, "Ian, we better go help them. McKenna, you better come too. We'll need some light." I looked at Taylor. "Can you guys make sure they don't get away?"

"They're not going anywhere," Taylor said.

Wade held up one of the cans of bull mace. "I guarantee they're going nowhere."

Ian, McKenna, and I ran into the jungle in the direction Zeus and Jack had taken in pursuit. Even in the middle of day the jungle was dark enough that a person could hide, at least until McKenna lit up, illuminating everything around her like a great torch. After a few minutes of running we heard shouting in the distance.

"They're over there," Ian said.

When we caught up with them, the rancher was lying facedown on the ground between Jack and Zeus; Jack was pointing a can of mace at Zeus, and Zeus had his arms outstretched toward Jack, electricity arcing between his fingers.

"Stop it!" I shouted. They both turned to me. "What's going on?"

"Lightning stink shocked me," Jack said.

"It was an accident," Zeus said. "He was standing next to the dude."

"I *had* the dude pinned down, you stinking—"

"You say 'stink' one more time and I'm going to fry you—"

"Stop it!" I shouted again. "Are you guys crazy? We're about to walk into a camp of two thousand Elgen soldiers who want to kill us and you're fighting with each other?"

They both lowered their hands.

"If we can't do this together, we don't stand a chance. You two have got to stop fighting."

After a moment, Jack sighed. "All right. You're right." He put out his hand.

Zeus just looked at Jack angrily.

"I'm not offering it again," Jack said.

Zeus turned away. "It was an accident."

"Whatever you say, bro," Jack said. "Whatever you say."

"You guys have got to solve this. If we're not together, we're dead." I lowered my head, fighting my despair. "We're probably dead anyway. But if we're going down in flames, it's not going to be because we made it happen." I looked at the man on the ground. "Come on, we need to bring him back with the others."

"I got him," Jack said. He knelt down and lifted the man over his shoulders in a fireman's carry, and the five of us walked back to the fence in silence.

As the others came into view, Ostin shouted, "Good work, dudes. You got him."

No one answered him.

"What happened?" he asked McKenna.

"Don't ask," she said.

"What's wrong, Michael?" Ostin asked. "You'll feel better if—"

I held up my hands. "Just . . . stop. I don't want to talk about it. And I don't need you analyzing me right now."

Ostin stepped back. "Sorry." He glanced at McKenna in embarrassment, then walked away.

Taylor just stared at me.

"What?" I asked.

"Are you okay?"

"Oh yeah, I'm doing great," I said sarcastically. "My mother's being held captive by a sociopath, we're hopelessly outnumbered, and our friends are turning on each other while I lead them to certain death."

Taylor looked at me for a moment, then asked softly, "Do you really believe that?"

I suddenly realized that everyone was looking at me. I swallowed, embarrassed at my outburst. "I don't know what I believe."

Taylor took my hand. "Come here." She led me deep enough into the jungle that we were away from everyone else. When she looked at me her eyes were filled with tears. "You can't give up now. We're all here because we believe in you. If you really believe this is hopeless, we might as well turn ourselves over to Hatch right now."

"I didn't mean to say that," I said.

Her expression didn't change. "Michael, I'm terrified. Six months ago the most frightening thing I had ever done was try out for cheerleading in front of the student body.

"I need you to believe, Michael. Because I'm holding on by a thread—and you're that thread. If I don't have you to hold on to, I don't have anything. None of us do. I know it's not fair putting that much pressure on you, but it's the way it is."

"I didn't ask any of you to come," I said defensively.

"I know. But we're here. And we came because we believe in you. And because we care about you."

I looked down for a moment, then rubbed my eyes. "I'm sorry. I guess I'm terrified too."

"I know." She hugged me. After a minute she leaned back and said, "I've never told anyone this before, not even my best friend Maddie. I used to get severe panic attacks before I tried out for cheer. My first year, on the morning of the final cut, I pretended to be sick so I didn't have to go to school. My dad said to me, 'Are you afraid?' I said no but he knew I was lying. He said, 'Let me give you some advice. As long as you remember the whys, the hows will take care of themselves.'" Taylor looked into my eyes. "Your mom is a pretty big why. We believe in you because we believe you're doing the right thing. So let me ask you again . . . Do you believe that we can do this?"

"You're holding my hand," I said. "You already know."

"I want to hear you say it."

I straightened up. "I believe in what I have to do. That's what matters. My mother always said that if you do the right thing, the universe comes to your aid, and look what's happened so far: we escaped two Elgen traps, we found my mother, we got to Peru, and now we have a truck and a way into Hatch's stronghold. It's too big of a coincidence. I don't believe that whatever brought us this far brought us to fail."

Taylor smiled. "That's what I needed to hear. I'll follow you wherever you go and slap Hatch in the face if you tell me to. Now you need to let everyone else know."

I took her hand. "Come on."

We walked back to the group. The ranchers were all awake, lying on their stomachs with their hands bound behind their backs. Sadly, the Electroclan looked about as subdued as the ranchers did, their shoulders slumped in despair. Every eye was on us.

"I need to say something," I said, walking in front of the group. I looked at them all, then slowly started. "First, I'm sorry, Ostin. I shouldn't have gone off on you like that."

"It's okay, buddy," he said.

"It's not, but thank you. Second, I believe with all my heart that we're going to rescue my mom and get out of here. I'm sorry I was so negative. You've put your faith in me, and I should have been stronger."

Everyone was quiet for a moment, then Zeus said, "No, it's not your fault. We've been acting like jerks. Especially me." He looked at Jack, then stood and walked over to him.

"I'm sorry," Zeus said. "I really didn't try to shock you, but I didn't try not to either. You were right to be angry. I know you said you wouldn't offer your hand again, so let me do it." He put his hand out.

Jack looked at Zeus's hand for a moment, then he took it. "Forgotten. *Semper Fi.*"

Zeus nodded. *"Semper Fi."*

Taylor squeezed my hand.

I continued. "Third, it's time to do what we came here for. We're going to take the trucks right into the compound. Ian, I need you to stay next to me and tell us what you see as we get closer. Look for others dressed like us, and we'll head for their building. I'm hoping they might have a separate ranch entrance."

"Why don't we just ask them?" Ostin said.

"They're not going to tell us the truth," Zeus said.

"Maybe not with their mouths, but Taylor can read their thoughts."

"Except I don't speak Spanish," she said.

"I'll ask yes-or-no questions," Ostin said.

"Good idea," I said. "Is everyone ready?"

"Let's go, team!" Taylor shouted, sounding a lot like a cheerleader. In spite of the gravity of our situation I had to smile. "Sorry," she said, blushing. "Habit."

We put on the ranchers' uniforms. There were only six of them, so Abigail, Taylor, and McKenna didn't wear them. The men weren't big people, so the uniforms fit us fairly well, except for Jack, whose pants legs fell above his ankles.

"How do I look?" I asked Taylor.

"Like an Elgen ranch hand," she replied.

"Great. Now let's get some information." I looked at the men, on their stomachs. "Who should we talk to?"

"*Hombres*," Ostin said. The men looked up. "Show them a little electricity, Michael."

I held my hand up, separated my fingers, and pulsed until electricity arced between my fingers.

"Let's talk to that one," Taylor said, pointing to a young man with fearful eyes. We walked over to him. He didn't look much older than us, and his back was marked with long, thick scars, as if he'd been severely whipped. The three of us dragged him away from the others, laying him in a small clearing near a termite nest.

"No!" he pleaded. *"Por favor!"*

"He thinks we're going to hurt him," I said. "Ostin, tell him we won't hurt him."

"You really want to tell him that?" Taylor said.

"You're right, he doesn't need to know that." I turned back to Ostin. "Tell him we won't hurt him if he cooperates."

Ostin relayed the message in Spanish.

While Taylor and Ostin interrogated the man, I sat down with Ian and showed him the photograph I'd taken from our apartment. "That's my mother."

"She's beautiful," he said.

"Can you remember what she looks like? She's probably not going to look exactly the same after all she's been through."

Ian put his hand on my shoulder. "Don't worry. If she's in there, I'll find her."

A few minutes later Ostin and Taylor returned to the group.

"Here's the four-one-one on the Peruvian dude," Ostin said. "His name is Raúl. His family is from Puerto Maldonado, and he was forced to work for the Elgen after they took his family's land. He says it's the same for all the ranchers."

Taylor nodded. "It's true. Those scars on his back are from the guards. The Elgen lost some cattle to a jaguar, so the guards whipped him as an example to the other ranchers. He says the Elgen treat them like dogs."

"Sounds like the Elgen," I said.

"He says that he can help us," Ostin said. "The compound has a double electric fence around the entire property, with guard nests on each corner. Close to the compound the fence is narrower, so you can't crawl through it like you can here. There is one main road with a checkpoint that everyone has to go through, except for the ranchers. The ranchers have their own gate on the southeast side of the compound near the building they call the 'bowl.' That's where they bring the cattle in to be slaughtered.

"He says there are guards above the wire but they don't pay much attention to the ranchers, and he knows this because some of the ranchers sneak their wives in. There's only one guard on the ground, but he's not always there and he's sleeping half the time. We can get into the bowl through the ranchers' entrance or the cattle entrance. From the bowl we can walk right into the compound."

"Won't we be seen?"

"He said there will be ranchers around and since we're foreigners they'll be aware of us, but he doubts they'll sound an alarm. The Elgen have a lot of foreigners come through their area—especially lately."

"Why lately?" I asked.

"He told us that the one they call *el doctor* is holding a big conference with all the guards."

"*El doctor?*" I asked.

"I think he means Hatch," Ostin said.

"Just like they warned us in the letter," I said.

"They've had to work extra hours to bring meat in for the kitchen, so he says the camp is in complete chaos right now. Our timing is perfect."

"Perfect or perfectly awful?" Taylor said.

"We'll find out soon enough," I said. "Let's go."

"What about the ranchers?" Taylor asked. "We can't just leave them here. It's the jungle. Something will, like, eat them."

"If they work for Hatch, they deserve it," Zeus said.

"No," I said. "They might be victims of the Elgen too. But if we let them go, they could alert the Elgen."

"I vote that we bring Raúl with us," Ostin said. "He could help us. Then, when we're done, he can come back on his own and free them."

I thought over the idea. "You trust him that much?"

Ostin nodded. "I do."

I looked at Taylor. "How about you?"

"Me too," she said.

I was doubtful but said, "Let's talk with him."

# 35

## The Compound

"He understands a little bit of English," Ostin said.

"Can you help us get in?" I asked.

Raúl nodded.

"If you help us, we'll let you come back and free the others. Do you understand?"

He nodded again.

I looked at Taylor, and she nodded. "All right." I pulsed and melted through Raúl's ropes, which seemed to both intrigue and frighten him. Ostin gave him back his clothes and waited for him to dress. "Let's go," I said.

"*Vámonos,*" Ostin said.

The four of us walked back over to the others. They were surprised to see the rancher with us. "Raúl knows the way, so he's going to drive the first truck. Jack, you follow us."

Jack looked at Raúl suspiciously. "You sure you can trust him?"

"Taylor read his mind. She trusts him."

"Ostin," Jack said. "Translate this." He pointed at Raúl. "You betray us, I'll make sure you go down with us. Understand?"

Ostin translated. Raúl frowned.

Zeus added to the threat. "Tell him that if he turns us in, I'll electrocute him *first*. Make sure he understands that."

Ostin nodded and translated that as well.

Raúl looked as indignant as he was afraid. *"Los odio también,"* he said.

"He says he hates the Elgen too," Ostin said.

"We'll see," Jack said.

"Raúl will drive the first truck," I said to Jack. "You, Zeus, Ian, Abi, and McKenna follow us. Stay close."

The warning lights on the electric fence still hadn't come on, so I checked it once more, then we all climbed through and walked to the trucks.

Raúl said something to Ostin, who seemed to be nodding his head in agreement.

"What did he say?" I asked.

"He says we should bring back the bull. Otherwise it will look suspicious."

I looked over at the dead animal. "Good idea."

Raúl got in the truck and finished hoisting the bull into the truck bed.

The ranch was nearly five miles in diameter and was composed of hilly terrain. We drove for several minutes before we could even see the compound. The sight of it filled us all with dread.

We drove on, crossing diagonally across the main road to avoid other cars and trucks.

As Raúl had explained, the compound was surrounded by two large fences with guard towers perched high on the corners, the silver barrels of their mounted machine guns glistening in the sun. The place reminded me of the pictures I'd seen in my history book of World War II German prison camps, though this place was clearly much more high-tech.

The compound's checkpoint was a hive of activity, with trucks, cars, and buses backed up for more than a hundred yards and dozens of guards, many with leashed dogs, checking the vehicles that awaited entry. The dogs were large and muscular, and I wondered what breed they were.

"Rottweilers," Ostin said, as if reading my mind.

"What?"

"That's what type of dogs those are. Very powerful. I wonder if they're electric."

The guards were wearing the same Elgen uniforms as the guards who had attacked our safe house.

As we got closer to the compound my tics increased and I began to gulp, something I didn't notice until Taylor started gently rubbing my back. The compound was bigger than I expected and reminded me a little of the Boise State University campus, without the football stadium.

The Starxource plant, at the east end of the compound, was by far the largest of the buildings. I guessed it had to be nearly a hundred yards in diameter. Above it were three large exhaust pipes from which white smoke billowed into the air.

"Look at all that pollution," Taylor said. "I thought this was supposed to be clean energy."

"It is," Ostin said. "Those are cooling towers. That's steam emission. I'd bet my frontal lobe that's where the rats are."

Raúl pointed to a small gate near the plant and said, "There."

"There's the entrance," I said. "Be alert."

"*Todo el tiempo esta allá,*" Raúl said.

"What's that?" I asked.

"He said the guard's there," Ostin said.

"Should we turn back?" I asked.

Ostin asked Raúl, then said, "He says no. That would be too suspicious looking."

"I'll take care of him," Zeus said.

"No," Taylor said. "Let me try first."

Raúl pulled the truck slowly up to the gate. The man at the gate, a stocky Peruvian man nearly as wide as he was tall, looked at us sternly. He said to Raúl, "*Quiénes son estos gringos? Dónde están Cesar y Alvaro?*"

Suddenly the man bent over, grimacing and holding his head.

Taylor said to Ostin, "Tell him that he's been expecting us, and we've just brought the bull back that was causing the problems."

Ostin translated.

The man blinked a few times, then waved us on. "*Sí. Adelante.*"

I turned to Taylor. "That was cool."

"Thanks," she said.

Raúl pulled through the gate. I motioned to Jack to follow us.

"Whoa," Ian said. "You won't believe what I'm seeing."

"The bowl?" Ostin said.

"Yeah, it's full of rats. Millions of them. And they're glowing like us. Only brighter and sort of an orange-red."

Raúl drove the truck up to the first of three metal doors. Even though we couldn't see anyone, the door slowly began to rise. Raúl said something to Ostin.

"This is where they take the meat to be processed," Ostin said. "We have to pull in here. It's their procedure, and it would look suspicious not to."

I looked into the dark entrance. Five men in ranchers' uniforms were waiting on the side of the concrete slip. Raúl slowly backed up into the space until a light came on. Jack pulled the second truck up to the side of the door.

"No," Raúl said. He began saying something very quickly to Ostin.

"He can't park there," Ostin said. "He needs to pull up next to the other trucks."

I hopped out of the truck, squeezing between the concrete wall and the vehicle until I was outside the building and close to Jack. "Raúl says to park there," I said, pointing. "But back in, just in case we need to make a run for it. Then meet us inside the building."

"Got it," Jack said.

When I returned, everyone was out of the truck and Raúl was talking to some of the ranchers who were inspecting the bull.

"What's going on?" I asked.

"They're trying to decide whether to use the bull to feed the guards or the rats. If it's the guards they'll send it to the butcher. If it's the rats it goes to the grid."

"What's the grid?"

Ostin pointed up. Half of the room's ceiling looked like the underside of a steel bowl. "The grid is where they make electricity from rats," he said.

The men appeared to have made a decision because an electric forklift drove up to the back of the truck and lifted the bull, then carried it over to a metallic cage connected to a hydraulic lift. The bull was carefully lowered onto the platform.

After the forklift had backed away, a yellow light began flashing, accompanied by a shrill beeping sound. The lift began to rise. When the platform was halfway to the ceiling, a hole opened above it and the platform moved perfectly into place, sealing the gap.

"That's cool," Ostin said. "I wonder what's up there."

I turned to him. "Has anyone asked about us?"

He nodded. "The older guy with the mega-mustache is in charge. He asked Raúl where the other ranchers are, and Raúl told him they're still out repairing the fence. He said they sent him back with the bull so a jaguar wouldn't get it."

"How'd he explain us?"

"He said one of the Elgen guards flagged him down near the checkpoint and made him bring us over to the ranch square. He said we're ranchers from an American Starxource plant and we've been brought here to observe their operations."

"Raúl's pretty clever," I said. "I almost believe his story."

"Let's hope mega-mustache does too."

Jack and the others came inside, and we gathered together in the corner of the room, trying to keep out of sight, though not successfully. The ranch hands kept glancing over at us, though they were just interested in the girls.

"There are cameras everywhere," Ostin said. "Not good. Not good."

"I'd like to blow a few of them out," Zeus said. "Just for fun."

"What do you see, Ian?" I asked. "What is this building?"

"It's their power plant. This corner is where they feed the rats. There's a butchery to the right, with a refrigeration room. In front of us there's a series of tunnels and a lot of water pipes and conveyor belts. Directly under the bowl is a huge funnel."

"For the rat droppings," Ostin said. "If there's really a million rats up there, they're going to be moving several tons of droppings a day. That's why there's a manure processing plant outside." He shook his head. "Man, I'd die for a look inside that bowl."

"I'm sure Hatch would be happy to arrange both," Taylor said.

"There are water pipes everywhere," Ian said. "Like hundreds of them."

"Cooling pipes," Ostin said. "The bowl is like a nuclear reactor. With that much heat it would need a giant cooling system to keep it from melting down. Kind of like a car's radiator."

Ian turned a little to the west. Looking up, he said, "There's an observatory up there, so they can see inside the bowl. On this level on the other side of the building it looks nearly identical to the laboratories back at the academy. Except in one of the rooms there are rows of cages filled with rats."

"Probably where they breed and electrify them," Ostin said.

Ian continued panning the room. "Over there are more offices." He turned to his left. "Hmm. They aren't offices. It's a jail. Along this wall are five cells. The three closest are empty, the fourth one has an older man in it, and there's someone in the fifth, but I can't tell what they look like."

"Is it my mother?"

Ian shook his head. "No. It's a guy. And whoever it is, he's glowing. He's one of us."

"Maybe it's Bryan," Zeus said. "He was always getting in trouble. But he'd just cut through the door. Does he have any of those wires on him?"

"He's wired," Ian said.

"That explains it," Zeus said. "Gotta be Bryan."

"Maybe he'll join us," Taylor said. "We could use him."

Zeus shook his head. "No. He won't join us. Those guys are loyal to Hatch."

"Maybe he'll change his mind like you did," Taylor said.

Zeus looked at her. "Maybe. But I doubt it."

"I want to know who it is," I said. "If Hatch is losing control of his kids, I want to know why. What type of locks are on the doors?"

"Old-fashioned kind," Ian said.

"So we need a key."

"Or explosives," Ostin said.

"Or Bryan," Zeus said.

"What do you see outside the building?" I asked.

"More buildings. The building closest to us looks like a prison or jail. A lot of bars."

"The Reeducation facility," Ostin said. "It's next to the assembly hall. Is there a bigger building next to it?"

Ian nodded. "Yeah. The guards are eating lunch in there. There's got to be more than a thousand guards in there right now."

"That's the assembly hall, all right," Ostin said. "North of it should be the dormitories."

"Yep. Bunk rooms. A lot of them. There're guards in there, too. How do you know this?"

"I studied the plans. What else do you see?"

"Past it, on the other side, there are maybe forty or fifty tents. There are guards in all of them."

"Temporary shelter for the visiting guards," Ostin said.

"This place is crawling with guards," Ian said. "They're every-where."

"Good," I said. "Once we find some guard outfits, we can move freely around the complex."

Raúl walked back to Ostin and started speaking. Ostin listened intently and asked a few questions before turning to us. "Raúl says that his boss told him to give us a tour of their operations. He also says we need to be careful because there are three Elgen guards assigned to the ranch house. Two of them are new here, so they'll be easy to fool, but it's best if we don't talk to the guards at all."

"Will the other ranchers tell the guards about us?" I asked.

Ostin asked Raúl, then said, "He doesn't think so. They don't like the guards."

"Where are the guards now?" I asked.

"He said they're at lunch."

"We can jump them for their uniforms when they get back," Jack said.

"With all these cameras around, that's risky," Ostin said.

"Being here is risky," Taylor said.

"Maybe we don't have to jump them," I said. "Ostin, ask Raúl if he knows if the guards have a uniform locker around here."

Ostin translated. Raúl's answer was surprisingly long, and Ostin looked very interested in what he had to say. When Raúl finished speaking, Ostin said, "He says they have a guard room over there by the door, but the ranchers are not allowed near it. But he knows where there are some Elgen guard uniforms no one will miss."

I couldn't believe our good fortune. "Really?"

"He said that when they built the compound they put in emergency drainage pipes. The pipes are always empty and large enough for a man to crawl through. They run underground below the compound and fence and empty about a hundred yards out into the jungle.

"The guards aren't allowed into town alone, but some of them have Peruvian girlfriends, so they uncapped one of the pipes, and every night a few of them sneak out. They secretly call it the Weekend Express. The guards don't wear their uniforms in town because the other guards might report them and the townspeople sometimes attack them if they're alone, so they change their clothes and leave their uniforms inside. A few of the guards have left and never come back, so their uniforms are still there."

"How many?"

"He remembers seeing three."

"Where are these pipes?"

"In a mechanical room behind the butchery and refrigeration."

"Can he take us to them?"

Raúl understood the question and said, *"Sí. Más adelante."*

"Later," Ostin said.

Raúl led us to the southeast corner of the room, stopping again near the cage lift, which had lowered back down without the bull. Raúl put on a show, giving us a demonstration of how the lift worked, while mega-mustache watched us from his corner. Afterward, Raúl led us to the butchery and the refrigeration room, where large slabs of meat hung from overhead hooks. It was so cold we could see our breath.

Ostin said, "Raúl says on really hot days the guards hang out in here."

Jack began pummeling a hanging beef like a punching bag. "Look, I'm Rocky."

Taylor shook her head.

At the back of the refrigeration room were green metal doors. Raúl said something to Ostin.

"He says it's best that we don't all go back to the mechanical room. There are three uniforms there, so we should decide who is changing into them."

"I need to decide who's coming with me to find my mother," I said. I turned to Ian. "I'm going to need you."

"I'm there," he said.

"Who else wants to come with me?"

Jack, Zeus, and Taylor raised their hands.

"You know they'll spot you a mile away," I said to Taylor.

"I know. I just want to help."

"You can help back here." I looked at Jack and Zeus. "Jack, you come."

Zeus started to protest, but I cut him off. "Look, if things turn bad, we're going to need you to get everyone out. Besides, I don't want you anywhere near Hatch. I think you're the only one Hatch hates more than me."

He nodded. "You're right." He looked at Jack, and I braced myself for another argument. Instead Zeus raised his hand. "Bring them back."

Jack hit it. "I'll do my best."

I breathed out in relief. "Let's go."

Jack, Ostin, Ian, and I followed Raúl into the mechanical room. The room was dim enough that my and Ian's glow could be seen.

Raúl looked at us in wonder. *"Ustedes extraterrestres?"*

Ostin grinned. "He wants to know if you and Ian are aliens."

"Tell him yes," I said.

Near the back of the room were four massive conduits that rose from the ground up to the ceiling. Raúl pointed to a pipe with a horizontal plug. It was capped with a metal lid and a locking latch.

"Is that the one?" I asked.

Raúl nodded, then gestured to another door just past the pipes. He opened the door to reveal piles of civilian clothing.

"How many guys are sneaking out of this place?" Jack asked.

*"Muchos,"* Raúl said.

We found four uniforms in the closet instead of the expected three.

Raúl looked concerned and pulled one of the uniforms to him. *"Sudor,"* he said.

Ostin touched the uniform. "It's sweaty. The guy is still out there."

"Not for long," Ian said, pointing to the ground. "He's coming back up." Suddenly we heard the sound of someone in the pipe.

"I guess our guard's coming home," I said.

"We could lock him out," Jack said. "Or knock him out. Either works for me."

"No," I said. "Let's see if he knows anything about my mother."

The lid suddenly opened, pushed up with one hand, and a machete fell out to the concrete floor. Then a head appeared. The man was starting to climb out when he saw us and froze. I could tell he was considering fleeing back into the pipe.

Ian waved his hand, "No worries, bro. We're doing the same thing you are. Weekend Express. Our man Raúl here is hooking us up with his cousins."

The man's expression relaxed. "Oh, right."

Jack pulled the lid back for the guard, and he climbed out. He was a big man, at least an inch taller than Jack, and he picked up his machete, then walked past us to the closet, where he stripped off his street clothing. "You guys look young. What are they doing, recruiting at high schools now?"

"Better early than late," Ostin said. "We're part of the Elgen Empowering Youth program."

The man shook his head. "Never heard of it." He pulled up his pants and fastened his utility belt. "You done the tunnel before?"

"No," I said. "First time."

"Watch for snakes. Condensation forms on the pipe and the snakes like it. They hang out near the mouth. Last night I killed an eyelash pit viper on the way out."

"*Bothriechis schlegelii,*" Ostin said. "About eighteen inches long?"

He held up his stained machete. "Not anymore."

"Thanks for the warning," I said.

He sat down on a crate to pull on his boots. "No problem. But I've gotta hurry, my shift is in ten."

"Where are you stationed?" I asked.

He laced up his boots. "At the gate until a week ago. That's where I met my darlin' milkmaid," he said with a grin. "She was bringing in *leche* for the troops. Now they got me over at the Re-Ed."

"Re-Ed," Ostin said. He looked at me. "Reeducation. The *prison.*"

"Yeah," he said, standing. "Not bad duty. At least it's air-conditioned." He pulled off his shirt and donned a black Elgen one.

I took a step toward the guard. "I hear there's an American woman in there."

He looked up as he buttoned his shirt, his mouth wide in a dark grin. "Yeah, and she's all that you've heard."

"Is she?" I asked. I could feel my face turning red.

Ostin shook his head at me in warning.

"Oh yeah. But we're not allowed to go near her. She's Hatch's pet. But I keep my eye on her if you know what I mean. I've had some fun with her." He laughed. "A couple days ago I made her do a belly dance for a glass of water."

I looked at him dully, steeling my anger behind my eyes. "Sharon," I said.

"Yeah. That's her name. How'd you know that?"

I put my hand on his shoulder and looked into his eyes. "She's my mother."

His scream never made it past his lips. I had never shocked anyone that hard before, and I could feel his skin blister beneath my fingers. I didn't stop, even after he dropped to the ground and I had crouched down next to him. I was so electric that sparks were shooting at him from my knees and thighs.

"Michael," Jack said. "Bro!"

Ostin shouted, "Michael, stop it! You'll kill him!"

I stepped back, blue-white sparks still zigzagging between my fingers.

Raúl was looking at me in terror. Everyone was silent.

Ostin cautiously stepped toward me. "You okay?"

I was panting heavily. "Get his key. We just found our way in."

Ian took his key. Jack and Ian pulled off his uniform and carried him back to the pipe, dropped him in, then locked it. We dressed in the uniforms and helmets, choosing the ones that were closest to our sizes. I took a knife and cut four inches off my pants' length. Raúl took a grenade and baton from the fourth uniform.

"What's he doing?" I asked.

Ostin spoke to him. "He says he's helping us."

"He doesn't want to get mixed up in this," I said.

"He already is," Ostin said.

I looked at him, then nodded. *"Gracias."*

He nodded back.

Ostin took the fourth uniform and rolled it up.

"What's that for?" I asked.

"How else are you going to get your mother out of a prison surrounded by two thousand guards?" Ostin said.

"You are a genius, my friend."

Ostin smiled. "Tell me something I don't know. Oh, wait, you can't."

I put my arm on his shoulder. "All right. Let's get my mother."

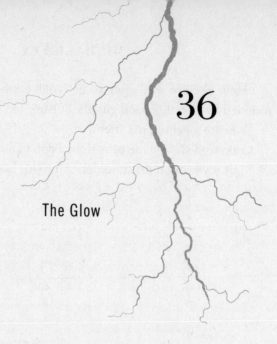

# 36

## The Glow

**W**hen we walked back out to the freezer, the rest of our group was huddled together, their arms wrapped around themselves against the cold. They stepped back when they saw us.

I raised my visor. "It's us."

Taylor held a hand to her chest. "Oh, you scared us. We thought you were real."

"Good," I said. "That's the idea."

"It's about time you got back," Wade said, annoyed. "We're freezing."

"Enjoy it while you can," Jack said. "Everything is about to heat up."

"We found out where my mother is," I said. "She's over in the Re-Ed."

"And we've got the key," Ian said, holding up a card.

"What's the plan?" Taylor asked.

"First, I want to see who's in that cell Ian saw. Then Ian, Jack, and I will go to the Re-Ed to find my mother. While we're gone, the rest of you need to see if you can find a way to shut down the power plant. But don't take any dumb chances. We're going to find my mom and get out of here as fast as we can." I took the GPS iPod out of my pocket and gave it to Taylor. "If things go bad, get to the jungle as fast as you can. We'll catch up to you."

"But you won't know where the pickup is," Taylor said.

"She's right," Ostin said. "How will we find you?"

"This is only in case things go bad," I said. "But if we get separated we'll make our way back to Cuzco and hide out in a hotel under Jack's name. The voice can call the hotels and find us. But don't wait for us. Promise me."

Taylor looked upset but relented. "Okay. I promise."

"Do you remember how to use the GPS?"

"Yes. Colby Cross."

We walked from the refrigeration room back out through the butchery. The three of us in guard uniforms walked out first. I could see what Raúl had meant about the ranchers hating the guards. They avoided even looking at us. Taylor and the others followed a few yards behind us. Raúl led us through a set of double doors at the side of the room that opened to a long, tiled corridor.

"The cells are there," Ian said, pointing toward a magnetic keypad next to a thick, metal door. "There's a guard inside."

"Maybe he'll let us in," I said. "Ostin, ask Raúl what the guards' names are."

Raúl did his best to pronounce the names. "Ste-ven, Kork, Sco-tt."

"Steven, Kirk, and Scott," I repeated. I hit the button on the keypad.

"Who is it?"

"It's Kirk," I said.

"What do you need?"

"We're bringing an American group through on a tour."

"I can't let you do that."

"Dr. Hatch's instructions. They are about to open a new

Starxource facility in New Mexico, and he wants them to see every inch of this place."

"You know the rules. This is a controlled access. No one comes in here without direct EGG written clearance."

"And you know that Hatch changes the rules whenever he pleases."

"And you know what he does when you break a rule. No form, no entry."

I looked at Taylor. "Try it," I whispered.

She concentrated.

"Now open the door," I said. "We're on a tight schedule."

"I don't care if you're on a tightrope," he said angrily.

Ostin stepped forward. "I have the form," he said into the intercom.

"Why didn't you just tell me," I said, playing along.

"Because I assumed we wouldn't need it," Ostin said.

"He's got it," I said. "Open up." I turned to Zeus, and he nodded.

The doorknob turned and opened. The guard, who was tall and muscular, blocked the door with his body and reached out his hand. "Let me see the—"

Zeus blasted the man so hard it knocked him back against the opposite wall. We hurried inside, shutting the door behind us. Jack grabbed the keys from the unconscious guard and opened the second cell, and he and Wade dragged the guard inside, tying him to the bed with leather restraints. They locked the door behind him.

"Which room is the Glow in?" I asked.

"Fourth one," Ian said, pointing to a cell door. Jack threw me the keys, and I unlocked the door, then slowly pushed it open. The cell was small—about half the size of my bedroom at home—and was dark and musty. There was a figure huddled under a blanket on a mat in the corner of the room. I pulled the wire out of the RESAT machine and the figure groaned a little.

"We're here to help," I said.

The figure moved, and his head slowly rose. Peering between the covers was a red-haired boy with freckles and deep blue eyes. His skin was puffy, and he was pale and trembling.

"Tanner?" McKenna said.

He looked up, his face twisted in disbelief. "McKenna?"

She went to his side. "What have they done to you?"

He dropped his head back down. "Everything."

"You know him?" I asked.

"We were captured the same week. What are you doing here?"

"Hatch locked me up."

I unfastened the RESAT from his chest and set it on the ground next to him.

He breathed a loud sigh of relief. "How did you get out of purgatory? And what is Tara doing here?" he asked, looking at Taylor.

"That's Taylor, Tara's twin, and Michael."

"In the flesh," Tanner said. "The last two. Hatch told me they found you."

"Did he tell you we shut down the Pasadena facility and escaped?" McKenna asked.

"He left that part out." He looked at Zeus. "Frank. How are you, buddy?"

"Alive and shocking," he said. "Why do they have you locked up?"

"I tried to bring down a plane."

"That's what you do," Zeus said.

Tanner smiled darkly. "The one we were flying on."

"That would do it," Zeus said.

"You tried to kill yourself?" Taylor asked.

"Yeah," he said indifferently. "I almost succeeded, too." He exhaled. "They brought me in here. The guards have this new device. It's called a RESAT." He looked at Zeus. "Since when are you on the outs with the Elgen?"

"Since I met Michael," he said. "And learned the truth."

"What truth?"

"That Hatch has been using us."

Tanner sneered. "You think?"

"What have they done to you?" Taylor asked.

"Nothing I didn't deserve," he said. "I've done bad, bad stuff."

"Whatever you did, it's not your fault," McKenna said.

Tanner grimaced. "Not my fault? Do you have any idea how many people I've killed? Thousands. I pulled the trigger. I'm one of the worst mass murderers in history. I make Jack the Ripper look like a jaywalker." He shook his head. "Not my fault."

"Let's get him out of here," I said.

"No! Stay away." His voice softened. "They're going to feed me to the rats, you know. Fitting punishment for one of the biggest mass murderers in history."

Taylor walked to his side. "May I touch you?"

"That's an odd introduction," he said. "But why not." He tried to reach out his hand but was unable to.

"I just want to help," Taylor said.

"By all means," he said, sounding almost comical. "Help away, whatever your name is, Tara's twin."

"Taylor," she said. She laid a hand on his shoulder. "Oh no."

"What are you doing?" he said. He looked at McKenna. "What is she doing?"

Taylor burst into tears. "No!"

"She's reading your mind," I said.

In spite of his weakness, Tanner pulled away from her, lifting the blanket up to his chin. "Keep out of my mind. I don't want you to see what's in my mind."

Taylor couldn't stop crying. I put my arm around her, and she laid her head on my shoulder.

Tanner glared at us. "Stay away from me!"

Abigail had been standing by the door, but now she walked up to Tanner.

"Don't touch me," he said to her.

"It's okay," McKenna said. "She's my best friend."

"Well," Tanner said sarcastically, "with that ringing endorsement. By all means." He looked at Abigail. "You one of us?"

She nodded. "I can make you feel better."

His eyes narrowed to slits. "No you can't."

Abigail looked into his eyes and held her hand up to him. "May I try?" She slowly reached out and touched him.

Almost immediately his expression changed. His eyes closed in relief and the look of pain left his face. Then he began to cry. When he could speak he said, "Thank you."

"You're welcome," Abigail said.

"Are you healing me?"

"I'm sorry. I can only do this while we're touching."

"Then don't stop touching me. Please." Tanner looked over at us as if suddenly remembering we were all in the room. "Are you rescuing me?"

"Yes," I said.

"I know some places in Italy where we can hide, if you can get me out of here."

"We're not in Italy," Taylor said.

"Where are we?"

"Peru," I said.

His eyes widened. "Peru? How did I get in Peru?"

"We don't know," I said. "But we'll take you with us. Can you walk?"

"I don't know. I thought I was still in Italy. Who knows how long they've had me hooked up to that machine."

Zeus walked over and took his arm. "C'mon, buddy. I'll help you up." He helped Tanner to his feet.

"What about the other prisoners?" Taylor asked.

"We don't have time to rescue everyone," Jack said. "We get Michael's mom and get out of here."

"He's right," I said. "Every minute we're here the more danger we're in." I turned to Taylor. "We're going to go look for my mom now. If you can find a way to shut this plant down, do it. Otherwise, be ready to go."

I looked at Ostin. "Taylor's in charge. Work together. We'll be back in less than an hour."

"Michael," Taylor said.

"Yes."

She put her arms around me. "Hurry back."

"Of course. Keep everyone safe." I lowered my visor. "Let's go, guys."

Ian and Jack pushed down their visors as well. "*Hasta luego*, baby," Jack said.

We left them standing inside the prison.

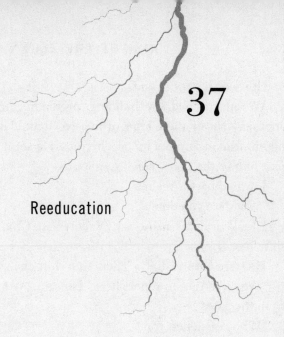

# 37

## Reeducation

The three of us walked out of the Starxource building into the blinding Peruvian sunshine. Ian hadn't exaggerated; there were guards everywhere.

"That's the Reeducation building," I said, gesturing with my head.

"I've got the key," Ian said.

"We just don't know what it's good for," I said.

Near the Re-Ed door was a guard sitting inside a cylindrical booth.

"Ian, is there another way in?" I asked.

"Through the assembly hall, but it's worse. There are two guards at the door and about fifty just walking around."

"I say we try curtain number one," Jack said.

"What's the booth made of?"

Ian shook his head. "Plastic. All plastic."

"Great."

"Maybe he'll just let us in," Jack said.

"It's worth a try," I said.

We approached the building, pretending to be talking to one another. Out of the corner of my eye I could see the guard in the booth drinking from a metal Thermos. He set it down as we walked past him to the door. "Hey!" he shouted.

I turned back. "Yeah?"

"What are you doing?"

I looked at his name tag. "Lieutenant Cox, we're here for our shift," I said.

He stared at me dully. "There's no shift change at this hour."

"We were told to report here," Ian said. "We were just reassigned from the gate."

"Who reassigned you?"

When none of us answered, the man's eyes narrowed. "Let me guess. Anderson."

I glanced at Ian, and he shook his head.

"Come on," I said. "Don't make me name names. We're just doing as we were told."

"So it is Anderson. That's the third time this month that idiot's done this. I'm writing him up."

"All right," Jack said. "Do what you need to do, but we've got to get in before we're written up."

"All right." He pushed a button and a lock on the door buzzed. Jack quickly grabbed the door and pulled it open.

"Hold up, there. I still need your IDs."

We glanced back and forth at each other. The only ID we'd found in our guard uniforms was in Ian's pocket, and the photo was of an Asian guard.

I reached into my pocket, digging around in the empty space. "I must have left it back at the gate."

"What do you mean, you left it? No one forgets their ID. You know the penalty for not having it with you. You better find it before you're caught or I turn you in." He looked at Ian and Jack. "You two, show me yours."

Ian glanced at me. "Sure," he said. He reached into his pocket and brought out the ID. I looked back at the guard.

"C'mon," I said. "Lieutenant Cox doesn't have all day."

"You got that right."

I put Ian's ID on the counter upside down and slid it partway through the opening in the window. As Cox reached for it, I magnetically pulled his metal thermos over, spilling the liquid. The fluid rushed out over his hands and down the front of the counter, giving me the conductivity I needed. I put my hand in the liquid and pulsed as hard as I could. Electricity flashed and Cox collapsed to the ground.

I looked back at Jack and Ian. "We've got to hurry. I don't know how long he'll be out."

Jack held the door for us as we rushed inside. The interior of the building looked like a large elementary school with video monitors and screens everywhere. A strange noise played over the intercom system.

"They're in pink," Ian said, looking at a row of inmates.

"Welcome to Looneyville," Jack said.

"What kind of prison is this?" I asked.

"Reeducation," Ian said. "It's where they brainwash you. Hatch was experimenting with brainwashing at the academy."

In spite of all the cameras, we moved through the facility undisturbed. I turned to Ian. "Where is she?"

Ian casually looked around. "I think I found her. End of the second hall to our right."

My heart jumped. I couldn't believe she was so close.

"Don't stare," I said to Jack, who looked fascinated by what he was seeing.

"Don't gulp," Jack replied.

"Sorry," I said, taking a few deep breaths to calm myself. We walked slowly down the hall, then, when no one was around, strode up to the door. "This is it?" I asked Ian.

"She looks like the picture," Ian said. "Mostly."

I could guess what he meant. Ian ran the key we'd taken from the guard over the magnetic pad: A light flashed green, and we heard the sound of the lock turning.

I pulled open the door. It was dark inside, but I recognized what I was looking at—it was the same room Hatch had shown me on the monitor at the academy when I was ordered to electrocute Wade. Inside the cell was a metal cage. The prisoner huddled in the corner of the cell looked small and feeble, but there was no mistaking who she was. She was my mother.

# 38

## Reunion

"Mom," I said, running toward the cage.

She flinched when she saw me, then scooted herself as far back from us as possible. "Leave me alone."

I took off my helmet. "Mom. It's me."

She leaned forward, her eyes blinking rapidly. "Stop it!" she said. "Enough of your tricks."

"It's no trick. We're here to get you out."

"How dare you use my boy against me. How *dare* you?"

"Mom, I'm real. Ask me something. Ask me something no one else would know."

Her eyes narrowed. "What's my son's favorite place to eat?"

"Mac's Purple Pig Pizza Parlor and Piano Pantry," I said.

"You're a fake. My son would never call it that."

*What was I thinking?*

"It's PizzaMax," I said. "I call it PizzaMax. We went there on my birthday."

"So did Hatch."

"Ask me something else."

"Leave me alone."

"Mom. Please." My voice was pleading. "Please believe me."

"Quit calling me that."

"It's me. Don't you know your own son?"

Her expression softened a little. "What did I give you for your birthday?"

"Dad's watch."

She shook her head. "No. I already told you that one. I told you. What does the engraving on the watch say?"

My eyes welled up. "'I love you forever.'"

This time my answer seemed to reach her. "How do you know that?"

"Because I read it every day." I pulled back my sleeve to reveal the watch.

I saw the doubt leave her eyes. "Michael," she said.

She scooted herself forward and I ran to her, putting my arms through the cage. "Oh, Michael," she said.

"We've got to get you out of here, before they catch us."

"How? There are guards everywhere."

"We're going to dress you as a guard, then we're going to walk out the front door."

Suddenly a light started blinking on a black box on the top of the cage. A feminine automated voice said, "Code required. Please input code. Arming capacitor. Commencing countdown. Twenty-five, twenty-four, twenty-three . . ."

"What's that?" I asked.

Her eyes showed her fear. "It's an alarm, it needs to be shut off when you come in. Do you know the code?"

"No. What will it do?"

A green light turned on in the box above her cell.

"When it reaches zero it will electrocute me."

"Seventeen, sixteen, fifteen . . ."

"Ian!" I shouted. "We've got to get her out of here. Now!"

"I don't have a key."

"Find one!"

"I'm looking!" he shouted frantically. "Jack, that guard right there. He's got a key ring. Get it!"

Jack ran out into the hall and smacked the guard over the head with his baton. Jack grabbed him by the back of his collar and dragged him into the cell. Ian went after the key.

"Eight, seven . . ."

"Hurry!" I shouted.

"I'm hurrying!" Ian said. He ripped the key ring from the man's pocket. "It's gotta be one of these," he said, fumbling through them. He tried one and it didn't work.

"Three, two, one. Capacitor armed. Prepare for discharge."

My mother looked into my eyes. "Michael . . ."

"Get back!" I shouted. I grabbed the bars, pressing my entire body against the cage, and braced myself for the release. There was a bright flash and a powerful snap of electricity, the force of which threw me to the ground. Then all was quiet. The air was full of a powerful smell of ozone.

"Michael?" Ian said.

I slowly opened my eyes. Then I looked in the cage. My mother was standing against the bars staring at me, her eyes wide with panic. "Michael?"

I suddenly started to laugh.

"It fried his mind," Jack said.

I slowly climbed to my feet. "No. What a rush. Let's get out of here."

Ian continued through the rest of the keys until he found the right one. The lock slid, and he opened the door.

My mother stepped out and threw her arms around me. Tears fell down both our faces. "You shouldn't have come," she said. "You shouldn't have come."

"You can ground me when we get back to Idaho," I said.

She wiped her eyes. "I love you."

"I love you, too."

"Lots of love in here," Ian said, his voice pitched. "But out there, not so much."

"Sorry," I said, stepping back. I reached down and picked up the extra uniform. "Put this on," I said to my mother. We had saved the smallest of the Elgen uniforms for her. She quickly pulled it on. It was way too big on her, but she looked all right if you didn't look too closely.

The bigger problem was her trouble walking. She'd been kept in a cage for weeks and her legs muscles were weak and cramped. "I'm sorry," she said.

"I'd carry you if I could," I said. "But they'd notice."

"Just give me a minute," she said, leaning against the wall to stretch her legs.

"Mom," I said. "This is Jack and Ian. They're my friends. I couldn't have made it here without them."

"Thank you," she said, straightening up. "I'm ready."

"It's clear," Ian said.

Jack opened the door, and we stepped out of the cell, shutting the door behind us. We walked down the hall, back toward the doors we'd entered through.

Ian stopped abruptly. "Change of plans," he said. "Lieutenant Cox is back in action and buzzing like a mad hornet. Follow me."

We ducked down the first hall we came to just as Cox and two guards stormed past us.

"Where are we going?" I asked.

"Into the hive," Ian said.

# 39

## Breaking Back In

The doors to the assembly hall opened automatically at our approach and we walked into a room full of hundreds of guards. Most of the guards were gathered in small clusters. Then I saw him. Hatch was standing in a corner of the room. I froze.

"What is it?" Ian asked.

"Hatch," I said.

He was surrounded by a group of guards dressed in black and red. Standing near them were three of the electric kids I had seen pictures of in my room at the academy: Quentin, Tara, and Bryan. There was also a kid I'd never seen before..

"Who's the other kid?" I asked.

"His name is Torstyn," Ian said. "You don't want to meet him."

"He's electric?"

"Yeah. He's dangerous. Let's get out of here."

I turned back. "Where's Jack?"

"Oh no," Ian said.

Jack was already twenty feet from us. He had his hand on his belt and was walking toward Hatch. I pushed through the guards, catching up to him halfway across the floor. "What are you doing?"

His jaw was clenched. "He burned down my house."

"You won't make it within twenty feet of him."

He kept walking. "I'll take my chances."

"They'll capture you."

"Let them try."

We were now only fifty feet away from Hatch.

"He'll capture *us*."

Only then did he stop.

"This isn't the time," I said. "We've got to get out of here."

Jack took a deep breath, then slowly exhaled. "This isn't over."

We turned and walked east through the assembly hall, then, meeting up with Ian and my mom, went out into the yard.

"Where are we going?" my mother asked.

"Back to the others," I said. "They're in the power plant."

"Others?"

"There are a bunch of us."

We had to walk past the Re-Ed entrance again to get to the power plant, so we waited for a large group of guards to pass by and blended in with them. When we arrived at the plant, we found a guard standing in front of the main entrance. It had been so easy getting out that I hadn't considered the difficulty of getting back in.

"Can we walk around to the ranchers' entrance?" Jack asked.

Ian shook his head. "There's a twelve-foot fence with razor wire."

"Whatever we're doing, we better decide fast," Jack said. "Cox is back and gathering a crowd."

Lieutenant Cox was talking to a dozen other guards, who were passing around an electronic tablet.

"Ian, what are they looking at?" I asked.

He turned to me with a grim expression. "Us."

"We need to create a distraction," Jack said.

As I looked at the guarded door I had an idea. "Maybe the guard can be the distraction. Ian, can you see his ID?"

"It's lying on the platform," Ian said. "Cal . . . Calvin Gunnel."

"Cal's my new best friend," I said. "Go along with me." I turned to my mother. "You better keep a few yards back. I don't think there are any female guards down here."

She looked nervous but nodded.

"Ready?" Ian said.

I took a deep breath to get my twitching under control. "Let's do it."

We walked up to the guard, a broad-shouldered man with a scar on his cheek partially concealed by a sandy beard. He reminded me of a lumberjack.

"Cal?" I said.

He looked up at me.

"Cal Gunnel?" I walked closer to him, pointing to myself with both thumbs. "It's me. Michael."

His brow furrowed. I could tell he was trying to place me.

"I've been looking for you for days. I owe you big-time, man. And don't you think I've forgotten. I never forget a favor."

"Wait," Ian said. "This is the Cal you were talking about?"

"I told you it was him." I turned back to the guard. "When's your next leave?"

The guard was glancing back and forth between us, looking more confused by the moment. "Tuesday. What—"

I didn't let him finish. "Okay. I'm going to have to trade some shifts, but you and I are going to Lima. I know this club, and let's just say you're going to be glad you did me a favor."

He stared at me for a moment, then said, "I have no idea who you are."

I faked a laugh. "Yeah, right." Then I looked into his face. "You're not kidding, are you?" I pointed to myself. "Cal, it's me."

"You sure you got the right guy?"

"I don't know," I said. "How many Cal Gunnels are there in Puerto Maldonado?"

He squinted. "Michael, right?"

"Michael. Who else? Whatever you told Anderson made the difference. I can't thank you enough for helping me."

"Anderson," he said, nodding. "It helped, huh?"

"I'll say. I don't know what you have on him, but you, my friend, have clout." I turned to Jack. "You don't want to get on Cal's bad side, you know what I mean? This guy is powerful." I turned back. "Next Tuesday. You can leave your *dinero* at home, this party is on me. I guarantee you will never forget this trip." I put out my hand. "See you then?"

"All right," he said. "Next Tuesday." He took my hand.

I dropped him like a bad habit. As I had anticipated, at least a dozen guards saw him fall.

"Get everything you can from him," I said to Jack. "But act like you're helping him."

Jack knelt down next to him, ripping the magnetic key from around his neck, then going through his pockets.

"Medic!" I shouted. "Medic!"

Guards began to move in toward us.

When there was a circle around us I said, "I think it's sunstroke."

"Clear out," one of the guards in a purple uniform said. "Give me room."

We stepped away from the crowd and the guard knelt down next to Cal, putting his fingers on the man's neck. "Heartbeat's strong. Looks like sunstroke." He stood, grabbing the phone from the podium. "We need a stretcher at Starxource west. Another sunstroke."

As the crowd milled around him, I caught my mother's eye and gestured toward the door. With more than twenty guards standing around us, the four of us opened the locked door and walked into the plant unnoticed.

At least I thought we had.

# 40

## The Welcome

$O$nce we were back inside the cool of the plant I asked Ian, "Where are they?"

"They're over that way," Ian said, pointing toward the center of the building. "The trick is getting to them. This place is built like a rat's maze."

"Fitting," I said. "What are they doing?"

"They're near some breaker-looking things. I think they're trying to figure out how to shut the grid down."

"It's too late for that," I said. "We've got to get out of here before they discover my mother's gone."

Almost in answer to my words, the shrill scream of a siren sounded and yellow strobes began flashing in the hallways.

"Too late," Jack said.

"Run!" Ian said.

With my mother in tow, we ran as fast as we could through

the long, vacant corridors, winding our way toward our friends. The halls were covered with a metallic, slate-colored material and were lined with stainless steel water pipes about a foot in diameter, spaced six feet apart. We caught sight of the rest of our group in a long, dark hallway halfway from the plant's entrance. Taylor was leading, with McKenna at her side providing light. They stopped when they saw us.

"Tay—" I started to say. Suddenly my head felt like it was caught in a clamp. All four of us dropped to our knees. Then Zeus shot Jack and me with electric bolts. Jack screamed out in pain, but the effect of the electricity on me was opposite. With renewed strength I took a deep breath and stood. Even Taylor's scrambling was no longer able to affect me.

"It's us!" I shouted.

"Stop!" Ostin shouted, raising his hands. "It's Michael!"

"Sorry!" Taylor said, clasping her hand over her mouth. "I'm so sorry I didn't know it was you!" She ran to me. "And there are four of you."

"Taylor?" my mother said, taking off her helmet.

"Mrs. Vey!" Taylor said. "They found you."

"What are you doing here?"

"It's a long story," Taylor said.

"Your parents are going to kill me," my mother said.

"Hi, Mrs. Vey," Ostin said.

"You too, Ostin?"

"And a good thing too," I said. "He's saved us more than once."

Ostin grinned. "Just doing my job."

Zeus walked over to Jack and put out his hand. "Dude, I'm so sorry."

"Really?" Jack said. "Again?"

"We thought you were guards," he said anxiously.

Jack looked at him, then started to laugh. He took his hand. "I would have done the same thing."

Abigail walked up to Jack and hugged him. "I'm so glad you made it."

"Me too," Jack said.

I counted the group. There were ten of us. Two were missing. "Where are Raúl and Tanner?"

"Raúl took Tanner to the mechanical room," Taylor said. "He was having trouble walking. He said if there's trouble they'll escape through the pipe."

"Where are we?" I asked.

"We're right under the bowl," Ostin said. "These pipes are all water mains to cool the grid."

"So how do we get out of here?" Zeus asked. "You can bet they've sealed off the compound. We'd never make it to the fence by car."

"I say we join Raúl at the escape pipe," I said. I turned to Ian. "How do we get there?"

"Three corridors down, on the left, there's an air duct in the ceiling that leads back to the butchery."

"All right," I said. "This way."

Suddenly the flashing lights around us stopped. Then a voice boomed from overhead speakers, echoing down the hallway. "Michael Vey. So pleased you could join us."

# 41

## Zeus's Sacrifice

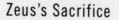

Hatch's voice continued over the speakers. "You should have told us you were coming, Michael. I would have prepared something special. As usual you've made a mess of things. And, Frank, I knew you'd come back. Couldn't resist, could you? You and I are going to have some fun. We'll bob for apples. Throw water balloons. Good times for all."

"The name's Zeus," I said.

"Inconsequential," Hatch said. "Be advised that we have you completely sealed in and surrounded. So you have a choice. You and Frank can surrender yourselves, and your friends will have reasonably humane treatment. Or you can resist and you will all die painful deaths. It's your call. Either way will amuse me."

"Eat my shorts!" Ostin shouted.

"Oh, Ostin. You just can't keep out of this, can you? Tell you what. I'll up the ante. If Michael and Frank surrender, I'll spare all of your lives and throw in a box of jelly doughnuts for Ostin. So let's see how much Michael really cares for you."

"Don't listen to him," Taylor said.

"You want us, Hatch?" I shouted. "Come and get us!"

Hatch laughed. "I was hoping you'd say that. Captain Welch, make sure the cameras are all recording, I'm going to want a replay of this. Are we set?"

"Yes, sir," a voice said. "Gate is opening."

"Wonderful. Just wonderful. You know I always enjoy feeding my pets."

From the bowels of the corridor came a loud, echoing groan like the sound of a heavy metal gate. Suddenly a high-pitched screeching echoed down the hall, shrill as a fork on a chalkboard.

"What's that sound?" Taylor asked.

Ostin turned white. "It sounds like . . . rats."

"Run to the air duct!" I shouted. I put my arm around my mother and helped her. The darkness behind us began to turn amber, the corridor distantly illuminated by some strange source of light. The first wave of rats came into view like the initial stream of a river, growing steadily heavier and thicker as the rodents began overlapping and running on top of one another, their bodies glowing like lava. They quickly closed the gap between us.

Jack threw a concussion grenade behind us, which killed a few of them but barely slowed the mass.

"Taylor, can you stop them?" I shouted.

"I'll try."

She turned and faced them, her hands on her temples. Ten yards in front of us the flow stopped as some of the rats began running in circles, confused.

"It's working," I said.

I was premature. The first wave of rats were quickly overcome by the rats behind them, as they pushed forward and climbed or jumped over them.

"There are too many of them!" Taylor shouted.

It was difficult to hear her over the squeals, which had grown in volume until the mass of them sounded like the braking of a train on metal tracks. They continued to pour toward us.

"Up the pipes!" I shouted, pointing to the walls.

Everyone grabbed onto the pipes and began climbing. I pushed my mother up the nearest pipe, and she hooked the utility belt of her uniform onto a bracket, holding her in place. I looked back down the hall. Everyone was up a pipe except Abigail, who was standing in the middle of the corridor staring at the oncoming rats, paralyzed by fear.

"Abi!" I shouted. "Climb up!"

She didn't move.

"Abi!"

Suddenly she fainted, falling to the ground.

Jack jumped down from his pipe and ran for her while Zeus began shooting at the rats heading for them, killing all he could hit. Jack lifted her and ran back to his pipe. He tried to climb with her but couldn't secure a strong enough handhold to pull them both up.

I jumped down from my pipe and ran to him. "Jack, climb up! Lift her!"

I took Abigail in my arms as Jack climbed up. He reached down and with one arm pulled her up. He hooked her blouse around a bracket to keep her from falling, then wrapped himself around her, holding them both in place.

"Michael!" Taylor shouted. "Look out!"

Zeus continued to pick off the rats, but it was like shooting rubber bands at a hive of angry hornets. Just as the first wave of rats hit my legs, I pulsed and the rodents that hit me died in a bright flash. But there were far too many. They began to swarm me, jumping higher and higher. I swatted at them, staggering to move away from them.

"Michael!" McKenna shouted, waving me to her. "Over here!" She was clinging to a pipe directly across from me. I tried to get to it, but walking was like trudging through mud. Slippery, flesh-eating mud.

Suddenly a rat about the size of a cat hit me in the chest, knocking me over. As I fell to the ground a wave of the rodents covered me. I pulsed with everything I had to keep them from eating me, but they were breaking through and I could feel their sharp teeth tearing at the Elgen uniform. My electricity was nearly exhausted. One last pulse, I told myself. Maybe I could kill enough rats to make a difference.

I wanted my last act to have some significance. I wanted my death to matter.

Just then I saw a brilliant light and felt a wave of heat. I could feel the weight of the rats lessen as they began jumping from my body. I opened my eyes to see McKenna standing next to me, raging like a blast furnace. The frenzied rats were running away from her heat.

"Get up, Michael!" she shouted.

I pulled myself up, then staggered over to a pipe and used my magnetism to climb to the top of it. McKenna climbed up after me, keeping only her legs blazing to ward off the rats. She couldn't get more than three feet from the ground. She was suffering from dehydration and looked pale and dizzy. I reached down, grabbed onto her blouse, and pulled her higher. "You need water, don't you?"

Her mouth was too dry to answer. It was cruelly ironic—we were clinging to a twelve-inch water pipe and she was about to pass out from dehydration.

Hatch's voice calmly echoed down the corridor. "I'm betting you wish you'd just stayed home about now."

With McKenna's heat gone the rats had returned tenfold, and the tile floor below us was no longer visible, just a rising sea of glowing fur.

McKenna was panting heavily, and I saw her grip on the pipe loosen.

"Hang on!" I shouted.

Her eyes were closed, and she slowly shook her head. "I can't. . . ."

I swung my body around hers, pinning her against the pipe. "I've got you."

The rats continued to pour down the hall, thousands, maybe tens of thousands, swarming below us, waiting for one of us to fall. As their numbers increased they rose like the tide, and as they got closer they started jumping at us. Most of them hit well below us, though I saw Ostin kick one off his leg. For the moment we were too high up the walls for them to reach us, but I knew it wouldn't last. Soon they would be jumping on us, one or two, then dozens, dragging us down to the undulating fur below.

I wasn't the only one who realized our predicament. Zeus, who was twenty feet ahead of me, began shooting out the hallway cameras. "If we're going to die, it's not for their entertainment!" he shouted.

Still they came. As far as I could see, the corridor glowed brilliant orange, like the inside of a toaster. I looked over at Taylor. Her eyes were wide with terror. She looked over at me and for a moment we both just stared. "They just keep coming!" she shouted. "They're like a river!"

"That's it!" Ostin shouted. "Zeus, shoot out the ceiling sprinklers!"

Zeus turned back and looked at us.

"Blow out the sprinklers!" Ostin shouted. "They can't take water. Do it or we're goners!"

Zeus looked down at the rats, then at Jack and Abigail, then over at me.

"He can't," I said, not loud enough for anyone but McKenna to hear. "He'll electrocute himself." I looked at Zeus, wondering what he was thinking. He wore an expression that seemed to be less fear than sadness. He looked once more down the hall at the rising flow of rats, then pointed his hand toward the farthest sprinkler, visible in the distance by the rats' glow.

"Don't do it!" I yelled.

My shout was too late. Fierce yellow bolts of electricity shot from Zeus's fingertips, connecting with the sprinkler head. At first nothing happened, then, like a breaking dam, water burst from the ceiling, starting from the sprinklers at the end of the hall, then, one by one, working its way toward us. I looked at Zeus, who was stoically watching the water approach. Then all the hall sprinklers blew. Water burst from the ceiling in a torrential downpour.

The rats shrieked as the water hit them, and electricity sparked wildly below us in sporadic, brilliant bursts, like camera flashes at a concert. I held tightly to McKenna as she leaned her head back and opened her mouth to catch the spray, drinking furiously.

Zeus screamed, then fell backward into the middle of the steaming rats.

"No!" I shouted.

In an instant Jack shouted, *"Semper Fi!"* He jumped from the wall and started running up the corridor toward Zeus, sinking thigh-deep in the squirming bodies of dying rats. By the time Jack reached him, Zeus was completely covered by the rats, a bulge in a pile of moving fur. He reached down and lifted Zeus up onto his shoulders, rats falling off around him. Zeus's skin was severely blistered, and blood was streaming down his arms and legs from rat bites.

Jack struggled through the mound of rats, like he was dragging himself from a snowbank. As he pulled his legs out from the pile, rodents were still clinging to him, and he flung them off. He ran to the end of the corridor where the sprinklers hadn't been activated and pulled off Zeus's wet outer clothing. He wiped the water off Zeus's blistered body, then listened to Zeus's chest and started CPR. Zeus suddenly gasped for air, then screamed with pain.

"Abi!" Jack shouted. "I need you."

Abigail had regained consciousness just in time. She slid down the pipe and ran to Zeus's side, putting both of her hands on him.

"That was crazy brave," Jack said to Zeus. "Crazy brave."

Zeus was barely conscious and didn't respond.

I turned to McKenna. "Are you okay?"

She nodded, water dripping from her face. Her lips were pink again. "I'm okay."

"Good, because we've got to go."

We both slid down the pipe to the wet floor, which was layered with the bodies of dead rats. The carcasses squished beneath our feet. Taylor had already jumped down, and I crossed the hall and helped my mother to the ground. She was trembling with fear.

"Come on, Mom. We know a way out."

She didn't speak, but leaned into me.

"Everyone after Ian!" I shouted. I purposely didn't mention the air duct. Zeus may have blown out most of the hall cameras, but I was guessing the Elgen could still hear us.

Jack lifted Zeus onto his shoulders, and he and Abigail ran down the hall after Ian. When we reached the air vent Ian climbed up the pipe first, pushed out the vent cover, and climbed inside the duct. Then he reached down to help us up. "Come on! Hand him up!"

Jack and Ian lifted Zeus, then Abigail, Wade, and my mother.

Hatch's voice came echoing down the hallway. "Your resource-fulness never ceases to amaze me. But there's no way out. The building is surrounded by hundreds of guards. Give yourself up."

"You're a freak!" I shouted. "Come get your dead rats!"

"Don't worry, I've got plenty more. Guards," Hatch said softly, emphasizing his confidence, "get them."

Jack noticed a fire box a few yards down the hall, and he kicked it in and grabbed the ax.

"What's that for?" I asked.

"Whatever comes next."

A moment later Ian yelled, "Bunch of guards sixty yards up the hall."

"How many is a bunch?" I asked.

"Thirty? And there's twice that down the hall, waiting behind the door."

"Do they have those helmets?" Taylor asked.

"Looks like it," Ian said. "You can't help here. Give me your hand." He lifted her up.

"Your turn, Ostin," I said.

"After McKenna," he said.

"Go without me," McKenna said. "I've got an idea. Jack, can you break one of these pipes?"

"I think so." Jack lifted the ax to the closest water main, then swung at it. The blow only dented the pipe. "Hold on!" he shouted.

He pulled back and hit the pipe again and again. On his fifth strike the ax pierced the pipe and a powerful stream of water shot across the corridor, hitting the opposite wall.

"Here we go," McKenna said, turning her hands white with heat. She put them into the gushing stream. The water immediately flashed into steam, the sound echoing loudly down the hallway like the blast of a steam engine. The steam made it impossible for every-one but Ian to see.

While McKenna continued to fill the hall with steam, I helped lift Ostin up to Ian; then Jack lifted me up, and I climbed inside the duct, leaving just Jack and McKenna behind. Everyone was still clus-tered around the vent area.

"Taylor!" I shouted. "Get them to the mechanical room! Hurry!"

"How far down is it?"

"It's the third vent opening!" Ian shouted. "You should be able to feel the cold of the refrigeration room, it's just past that!" He turned back. "Michael, they're close! Tell McKenna and Jack to get out of there!"

I leaned out through the vent. "McKenna, Jack, you've got to come now!"

McKenna had cupped her hands in the gushing water and was drinking greedily from its spray.

"Now, McKenna!" Jack shouted.

She ran to the vent. Jack threw down the ax, then lifted McKenna up to me, and I helped pull her in. Then Jack jumped and, doing a chin-up, pulled himself up and in.

Just a few seconds after I'd replaced the vent cover the guards moved past us through the steam, none of them noticing the vent above them.

I breathed out in relief. "Just in time, guys," I said. "Now let's get out of here."

## The Weekend Express

It took us only a few minutes to crawl to the mechanical room, though we had to stop once when a troop of guards ran underneath one of the vents. Wade was ahead of us dragging Zeus, who was still barely conscious. He was the first to reach the vent opening above the mechanical room.

"That's it!" Ian shouted to him. "It's clear below. Just Raúl and Tanner!"

Wade pulled off the vent cover. "Hey, guys! It's us!" he shouted. Then he climbed out, dropping to the concrete floor. Ian helped lower Zeus and Abigail down to Wade and Raúl, then climbed down himself.

Taylor jumped down without anyone's help—it was easy for a cheerleader—then Jack helped lower my mother, and then climbed out of the vent, lowering himself down slowly. McKenna and I were the last ones out. As I looked around, I saw that Raúl was standing next to the open pipe. Tanner was curled up near the lockers, his shirt pulled over his head.

"Where's the guard we left in there?" Jack asked Raúl.

Raúl said something to Ostin, who translated. "The guards can be executed for going AWOL, so he's probably running for his life," Ostin said.

I put a hand on my mom's arm. "I know it's crazy, but hang in there. We're going to get home again."

My mother forced a smile. "I know we are. I'm so proud of you, Michael. Your father would be proud of the man you've become."

Her words had a powerful impact on me—powerful enough that I had no idea how to reply. "Thanks," I finally said. "Now let's get out of here." I turned back to the group. "McKenna, you go first so you can light the way."

She looked nervously down into the pipe.

"Is something wrong?" Ostin asked.

"I'm just a little claustrophobic."

"Just look straight ahead," Ostin said. "And think of feathers."

"Feathers?"

"Something soft and relaxing. It will help."

McKenna smiled at him. "Feathers. Thanks." She climbed in.

Next in was Jack, who was carrying Zeus, with Abigail following closely behind, keeping a hand on him always. Raúl, Wade, my mother, Taylor, and Tanner went next.

When she was in the pipe Taylor turned back to me. "Come on."

"Go on," I said. "I'll be right there."

She looked at me nervously but obeyed, leaving just Ian, Ostin, and me. Ian went next. As he was climbing in we heard a short burst of machine gun fire.

"Ian," I said. "How close are they?"

"They're entering the butchery."

His words filled me with fear. We'd run out of time.

"Go!" I shouted. "They need you to make sure it's safe at the other end."

Ian dropped out of sight, and Ostin climbed into the pipe. He slid down the side, then said, "Come on, Michael."

"We're not going to make it," I said.

"What do you mean? We're almost out."

"They could be here any second. The guards know about the pipe. If we just disappear, they're going to figure it out. Then all they need to do is throw a grenade down the pipe or wait at the other end to catch us. We need time. We need to keep them looking."

Ostin looked at me with an anxious expression. "I don't like where this is going," he said. "What are you thinking?"

"Anacondas," I said. "Hatch wants me. If he follows me, everyone else can get out. Taylor's got the GPS, she can get you to the pickup point. "

"You can't do this," Ostin said. "If we need a distraction it should be me."

"Hatch doesn't care about you."

Ostin stared at me blankly. There was another burst of machine gun fire, closer this time.

"We don't have time to debate this. You know I'm right."

"They'll catch you."

"Think, Ostin. It's the logical choice. This way everyone else gets out and I still have a chance."

"Dude . . ."

"You know it's the logical thing! Now get out of here. I'm locking the pipe behind you, so there's no turning back. I'll lose the guards, then I'll join you."

"But you don't know where we're going."

"Remember plan B. Find me in Cuzco."

There was a crash just outside the door. My heart froze. "Go! Now!"

Ostin looked at me one last time, and his eyes watered. "Don't get caught!"

"I don't plan to. Go!"

Ostin disappeared down into the pipe, the last of McKenna's light just barely visible behind him. I capped the lid and locked it. Then

I pushed some crates around the pipe and laid a chain over its cap. I figured that if one of the guards was familiar with the pipe, he would think we couldn't have escaped through it.

I gathered grenades from the locker—three concussion and two smoke grenades—then I put my ear to the door. The guards were close, but as far as I could tell, they hadn't entered the refrigeration room yet. I pulled the pins from both a smoke and a concussion grenade, threw them into the refrigeration room, then locked the mechanical room door.

The concussion grenade exploded with a loud boom. A minute later I heard the guards enter the refrigeration room, their heavy boots clomping on the concrete floor. As their footsteps came closer to the mechanical room, I hid behind a stack of boxes next to an air duct. When someone tried the door, I pulled down my visor, then set off a smoke grenade, filling the room with smoke.

Just seconds later there was a loud blast as the door blew in. The guards shouted as they blindly stormed the smoke-filled room. I stood up and joined the chaos, my visor pulled down over my face.

"Where are they?" someone shouted.

I pointed up toward the vent. "Look."

A guard shouted, "They're in the air shaft!"

"We'll flush them out," the captain said. He lifted a communicator from a strap on his chest. "Targets are in the air ducts. I repeat, targets are in the air ducts. Position guards at all vents. We'll hold at east corridor and send a deuce in." He replaced the communicator, then pulled out an electronic tablet, summoning up a complete diagram of the Starxource duct system. "Schulz, Berman, go after them. You are only cleared to use RESATs. We're too close to the bowl for guns."

"Yes, sir," the two guards said almost in unison. The first guard stepped on the crate, then jumped up, grabbing both sides of the vent. He lifted himself up with the dexterity of a gymnast. As the second guard stepped up on the crate, the captain said, "Wait." He took from his utility belt a handheld device that resembled a television remote. "Track them with this."

He turned it on and the machine immediately started to scream. The captain looked at the reading, then back up with a bewildered expression. He slowly panned the machine the length of the ceiling, then down across the room, stopping at me. For a moment we both stared at each other.

"Gentlemen," he said, replacing the device in his belt, "the chase is over." He pulled his helmet off and smiled at me. "Finally we meet, Mr. Vey."

I produced a lightning ball in each hand and simultaneously threw them in the faces of the guards closest to me, dropping them both to the ground. Then I lunged at the captain as he reached for his RESAT.

I never made it. Two darts hit me in the back, followed by a third, taking my breath away. As I dropped to my knees, three more darts hit me. I think it was three. At least that's as many as I could remember before blacking out.

# PART 4

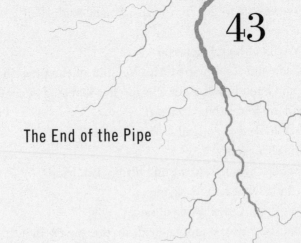

# 43

## The End of the Pipe

The escape pipe was smooth and sloped slightly, so even at a distance of more than a hundred yards, it was an easy crawl. It reminded Ostin of a slide at a water park.

The end of the pipe was deemed clear by Ian, so McKenna jumped down about five feet to the spongy forest ground below. The ground and foliage beneath the pipe were trampled and littered with cigarette butts, revealing the pipe's steady traffic.

As McKenna looked around, Jack jumped down, then turned and helped Zeus, who was now more conscious, which meant in more pain.

Jack laid Zeus on the ground a few yards from the pipe, then helped Abigail, who immediately knelt down next to Zeus, running her hand over his forehead. She pulled back the shirt they had put on him, revealing second- and third-degree burns over half his body.

"We've got to get him help," Abigail said. "If it gets infected he could die."

"We'll get help," Jack said.

Wade and Raúl helped Mrs. Vey out of the pipe, then Raúl came over and knelt beside Zeus. His forehead creased in concern. "*Sábila*," he said, nodding. "Need *sábila*."

Jack looked at Abigail. "What's *sábila*?"

She shrugged.

"*Sábila*," Raúl said again, lifting his hands in a flourish as if describing what he was saying.

"We'll ask Ostin," Abigail said.

Mrs. Vey was standing next to the pipe's mouth when Taylor climbed out. After Taylor had caught her breath, she put her hand on Mrs. Vey's shoulder. "Are you okay?"

Mrs. Vey nodded, even though she was weak and emaciated. "Where's Michael?"

"He'll be here in a second. He's bringing up the rear."

Tanner carefully jumped down, followed by Ian. It was another five minutes before Ostin stuck his head out, panting from the long crawl. He looked around, then scooted on his butt until he was sitting on the rim of the pipe and jumped down.

As Ostin dusted off his knees, Mrs. Vey walked over to the pipe and looked inside. "Where's Michael?"

Taylor also looked inside the pipe. "Michael!" Her voice echoed in the darkness, but there was no response. "Ian, where is he?"

"He was right behind us," Ian said. He looked at the pipe. "He's not there."

"What?" Taylor and Mrs. Vey said in unison.

Ostin looked up with a pained expression. "He didn't come."

Taylor blanched. "What do you mean, he didn't come?"

Everyone's eyes turned to Ostin, who was still catching his breath.

"The guards were too close. Michael stayed back to provide a diversion so we could escape."

Mrs. Vey stared at him in disbelief. "Michael's still inside the compound?"

"He said he had to stay," Ostin said.

"And you let him?" Taylor shouted.

"What was I supposed to do? It was the logical thing to do."

"Logical!" Taylor screamed. She put her hands on the rim of the pipe to climb back in. "I'm going after him."

"It won't do any good," Ostin said. "He locked the pipe after me."

"No!" she shouted, her voice echoing down the pipe. She turned back angrily. "We came all the way here to rescue his mother and you left him behind?"

Ostin swallowed. "I was just—"

"Being stupid?" Jack said fiercely.

"Leave him alone," McKenna said. "It's not his fault."

"Then whose is it?" Taylor said.

"It's Michael's," McKenna said. "He made a choice."

"I knew I should have waited!" Taylor shouted. She swung around, thrusting her finger in Ostin's face. "I never would have gone first if I had any idea he was thinking of leaving. We stick together."

"I'm sorry," Ostin said.

"Sorry?" Taylor said. "I thought you were smart."

For a moment no one spoke.

Then Abigail said, "So what are we supposed to do now?"

Ostin said meekly, "Michael said that Taylor has the GPS; she's supposed to lead us to the pickup site."

"That's not going to happen," Taylor said. "I didn't come all this way to leave Michael. Do you have any idea what Hatch will do to him if he catches him?" She turned to Ian. "Can you see him?"

Ian looked back for a moment, then said, "He's with the guards."

"They've captured him?"

"No. He's standing with them, talking. They must think he's one of them."

"He stayed back to cause a diversion so we could get away," Ostin said. "He said after he led them away he'd sneak back down through the pipe. But he wanted us to hurry toward the pickup site before they figured out how we escaped."

"I'm not leaving without my son," Mrs. Vey said.

"And *if* he gets out," Taylor said, "just how exactly is he supposed to find us?"

"He said he'd go to Cuzco."

"How? It's at least a week by foot, with no food or water—if something in the jungle doesn't kill him first."

"He's more powerful than anything in the jungle," Ostin said.

"Even when he's sleeping? Or is he supposed to go a week without sleep, too?"

Ian suddenly groaned. "Oh no."

"What?" Taylor asked.

"They just captured Michael."

His words stunned everyone. Taylor gasped, and Mrs. Vey sat down on a fallen log and began to cry.

"I'm so sorry," Ostin said, his eyes filling with tears. "I thought it was the right thing to do. I couldn't have made him come if I wanted to."

"Did you even try?" Taylor asked.

"Yes," he said.

Taylor looked at him in disgust. "I'll bet. And he thought you were his best friend."

Ostin hung his head.

"Enough!" McKenna said, walking up to Taylor. "Leave him alone. It's not his fault."

Mrs. Vey looked up, her cheeks wet with tears. "She's right. It's not Ostin's fault. Michael would have done this anyway. He would do anything to save his friends."

"No," Ostin said, shaking his head. "Taylor's right. I should have tried harder. I let him down. It's all my fault." He put his head down and walked away from the group.

Taylor turned toward him. "Ostin, come back."

Ostin continued walking off into the jungle until he was out of sight.

"Thanks," McKenna said angrily, then ran after Ostin.

A haze of despair fell over the group. After a few minutes Jack said, "We're not leaving him."

No one answered. The impossibility of saving Michael was obvious to everyone. The silence was broken by Zeus's groan. Raúl looked at Zeus, then pointed to Jack's knife. *"Cuchillo."*

"You want my knife?" Jack asked.

Raúl nodded. *"Por favor."*

"That means please," Abigail said.

Jack pulled his knife from its sheath and handed it to him. Raúl took it, then ran off into the forest.

"Where do you think he's going?" Abigail asked.

"I have no idea," he said. "But does it matter?"

# 44

## The Betrayal

I awoke buckled tightly to a cot only slightly larger than the one I'd been strapped to in the back of the Elgen truck. There were wires connected to me coming from a white metal box about the size of a deck of cards strapped to my chest. It was a RESAT box, the same device I had pulled off Tanner when we'd freed him. The top of the box had a single knob and several flashing red and green diodes registering its power diffusion. It also had a small antenna, which made me believe my suffering was being controlled by remote. I felt dizzy, and my thoughts were blurred, nearly as hazy as my vision. Above me was a large light fixture, and the light from it blinded and hurt my eyes, making me blink as hard as I ever have, which is probably why I didn't notice Taylor until she spoke.

"Michael."

I squinted, looking up into her face. *I must be dreaming,* I thought.

She leaned over and kissed me on the forehead. "How are you?"

"What are you doing here? You've got to get out, before they catch you."

"It's okay," she said. "We're safe."

My forehead was wet with perspiration. "We're not safe. Pull off these wires. We've got to get out of here."

Taylor just smiled. "Why would I want to escape?"

"What?"

Her smile grew. "I want to tell you a secret." She leaned close to my ear and whispered, "The whole boyfriend-girlfriend thing, it's not real. I made it up to get you down here for Dr. Hatch. I delivered you to him. And in return Dr. Hatch gave me this beautiful diamond bracelet." She dangled the bracelet in front of my face. "You know how we girls love bling. I just thought you'd like to know that." She stood up and walked out of the room.

Tears fell down the sides of my face. *This must be a nightmare*, I told myself.

Ten minutes later someone else walked into the room, stopping at the side of my cot. It was Dr. Hatch. "Welcome back, Michael," he said.

I closed my eyes. I didn't want to look at him.

"You've been crying. So you must have learned the truth about Taylor. Unrequited love always hurts. You didn't really think that a girl as beautiful as Taylor would be interested in someone as pathetic as you, did you?"

I said nothing.

"Not speaking, I see." He slowly exhaled. "No matter." He pulled a stool up to the side of my cot and sat down. "Michael the oath breaker. That's what we call you around here. What do you think of that?"

"I don't care what you call me," I said.

Hatch's voice turned more serious. "How did you get down here?"

I didn't answer.

He grabbed my face, squeezing my cheeks. "I asked you a question."

"I walked."

He let go of me but remained close enough that I could feel his breath on my face. His voice dropped. I knew Hatch well enough to know that that was his way. Most people's voices rise when they're angry. Hatch's voice softened. "Let's try this one," he said slowly. "Where are your friends, Michael?"

I didn't answer.

Hatch waited nearly a full minute before he said, "Oh please. Don't be so cliché with the 'I'm going to be the hero and protect my friends' routine. We both know that I could throw you in Cell 26, our new and improved Peruvian version of your suite in the academy, and get it out of you."

The idea of being sent to the cell sent chills through me, but I also knew that my mother and friends would be back in America before the Elgen broke me.

Hatch leaned forward. "Apart from Taylor, you don't know where your 'friends' are, do you? Maybe they're not really friends. If they were, wouldn't they have tried to rescue you? They haven't, you know. We haven't heard a peep out of them. I'm a little surprised that they deserted you in your hour of need. Aren't you?"

I clenched my jaw.

"Or maybe you just don't want to accept the truth that after all you did for her, even your mother didn't care enough to stick around. That must hurt even more than Taylor's betrayal." His voice fell almost to a whisper. "No one cares about you, Michael. You're all alone in this world."

In spite of the pain, I forced a defiant smile. "They got away," I said, finding relief in his words. "That's all that matters."

Hatch sneered. "Yes, they got away, for now. But that's all right. We'll get them. We'll hunt them down one by one. And in the meantime, we have you. The big kahuna. President of the electro*clam* or whatever ridiculous name you gave your group."

"Electroclan," I said.

"It doesn't matter. The club has been disbanded. But you were worth all the trouble you and your little club caused. At least I thought you were." He reached over to the box on my chest and turned a knob. Increased pain shot through my body, and I groaned out. "Then you went and made things . . . difficult. You changed your destiny for the worse. Only one thing can save you now. Do you want to know what that is?"

I was gritting my teeth with pain. "Yes."

He reached over and turned the knob back down. The pain lessened.

"Humility, Michael. Humility." He sat back as if giving me time to contemplate his words. "I wonder if you even know what it is? It's a lost virtue. Kids these days are all swagger. They think they have all the answers. But they're just a new generation of fools.

"Humility is the wisdom of accepting the truth that you might just be wrong. Unfortunately, for most it comes too late—after the game is lost, if you know what I mean. Humility comes when you've hit rock bottom. When your best friends have deserted you. When you have nothing more to lose. Like you. So just put away your arrogant ways and join us, like Taylor did, completely and without reservation, or I have no choice but to dispose of you."

"You're not going to kill me," I said. "You need me."

"Not exactly," Hatch said. "We need your DNA, a few pints of blood, and some of your tissue. But we don't need *you*." He lingered on the word "you" like it left a bitter taste in his mouth.

"Honestly, I wouldn't have minded keeping you around for a while. I had planned on it. But then you went and ruined the party. Now I have no choice but to make an example of you.

"You see, I have eight very promising and powerful young men and women who I am grooming for future leadership in my organization. These young people are impressionable and they have seen you defy me. If I let that slide, they'll think I'm soft. Then it's just a matter of time before one, or all of them, tries the same thing. Not right away of course, these things need time to culture, but, like a virus, dissension will grow." Hatch's eyes flashed with anger. "*That* is not an option. They need to know that being special does not mean they're indispensable.

"So, after our scientists have taken what they need from you, you're going to help me teach my youths a vital lesson about the importance of obedience and fidelity. And in this way, your worthless little life, which until now has only served to annoy me, will actually do me some good.

"How will I do this, you ask?" He ran his finger up my arm. "I can see from these bites that you've had a taste of our rats. Or," he said darkly, "vice versa. They're going to get another helping of you. Only this time there will be no one to save you. Do you have any idea how carnivorous those little things are? I've seen them strip a bull to bones in less than two minutes. I can't imagine the pain, the sheer agony, as a thousand little teeth devour your flesh.

"I'll give you some time to consider your fate, Michael. Can you be humble?" Hatch leaned close to my ear. "Before I go I'd like to confide in you. Parents sometimes say it's the child who stands up to them who they respect the most. I admit there is some truth to this. You have shown tremendous leadership with your little group of miscreants. I'm just sorry it's not going to take you anywhere but the bowl." He stood. "Au revoir, Michael. The next time I see you will be suppertime. Not for you, of course."

"Wait," I said.

Hatch smiled. "Yes?"

"Tell Tara that I know she and Taylor are identical twins, but she's really not as pretty. Sorry."

Hatch scowled at me, then turned and walked out of the room.

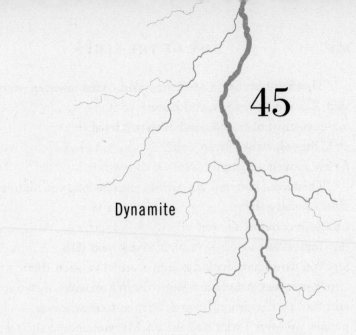

# 45

## Dynamite

**O**stin was sitting by himself nearly a hundred yards away from the camp, leaning against a tree. He was drawing in the dirt with a stick, doing mathematical equations, something he did when he was upset. He didn't notice McKenna until she was standing a few yards from him.

"May I sit down?" McKenna asked.

"Free world," Ostin said. "At least until the Elgen take over."

McKenna sat down cross-legged a few feet from him. She picked up a rock and rolled it in her hands. For a long time neither of them spoke.

"They estimate that there are seven and a half trillion trees in the Amazon rain forest," Ostin said. "That one right there is called a strangler fig. The Peruvians call it *matapalo*, the killer tree. It starts when a bird drops its seed up in a tree and the strangler fig grows down to the ground until it chokes out the host tree and takes its place."

"That's interesting," McKenna said. After another moment she said, "It's not your fault, you know."

"I let my best friend down. I wasn't loyal."

"Did you want him to stay?"

He looked up angrily. "No! Of course not."

"Then you honored his wishes even when you didn't want to. That's loyalty, isn't it?"

Ostin couldn't answer.

"Taylor doesn't really think it's your fault either."

"You could have fooled me."

"Sometimes people are like that. When we're upset at someone and they're not around, we take it out on whoever is close. Even people we love. Taylor's afraid for Michael and so she's upset. And since he isn't here, she took it out on you. Does that make sense?"

Ostin sighed. "I guess so."

"The truth is, no matter what anyone said back there, if it wasn't for you, we'd all still be locked up at the academy. All of us, including Michael." Ostin looked up to see her gazing at him. "You're the smartest person I've ever met. And you're smarter than any of us. You're our only hope of saving Michael." She looked at him for a moment, then leaned forward, staring him directly in the eyes. "Michael needs you. So stop feeling sorry for yourself and *save* him."

"You think I can save him?"

"I *know* you can save him. And I know you can save us." She leaned back.

Ostin stared at the ground for a moment. When he lifted his head his expression had changed. He looked like himself again.

"Let's break down our situation into its individual components. We're hiding in a tropical rain forest next to a seemingly impenetrable fortress with two thousand armed guards, huge electric fences, and ubiquitous camera surveillance. Our original way into the compound through the ranch entrance is no longer an option, and our second route was locked off by Michael.

"Our foe seems all-powerful, but if history has taught us anything, it's that everyone and everything has a weakness—you just have to find it. My weakness is jelly doughnuts. Your weakness is dehydration, or lack of water." His brow furrowed. "Zeus's weakness is also water." Suddenly his face animated. "That's it!" He clapped his hands together. "That's their weakness!"

"What?" McKenna asked.

"Water! They built protection around the power plant but not their water source." He jumped up. "I know how to shut them down."

"Explain," McKenna said, smiling at his enthusiasm.

"To power two million homes, their plant would have to create nearly twenty billion kilowatt hours of electricity. That's twice the energy of a standard nuclear power plant. Given that the Elgen's power creation is three times more efficient than a steam-turbine system, I'm guessing that the rats are generating heat close to one thousand degrees Fahrenheit. That's why they built the plant next to a river—without water the bowl would melt down in a matter of minutes. Or even if it didn't, the heat would kill the rats. No rats, no electricity. No electricity, no lights, no cameras, no electric locks, and no electric fences." Ostin grabbed McKenna's hand and pulled her to her feet. "Come on, we've got to tell the others."

In Ostin's absence, the group had moved a couple of hundred feet from the pipe to a more concealed location. Everyone was sitting or lying down when Ostin and McKenna rushed into the clearing.

"I know how we can save Michael!" Ostin shouted.

Taylor stood. "How?"

"Everyone gather round," Ostin said, standing next to Zeus. They formed a crescent around him, McKenna holding on to Ostin's arm.

"Here's the gist of it," Ostin said. "Just north of the compound is the Elgen pump house. That's where they bring in the water from the river to cool the Starxource plant. It's outside of the compound. If we blow up the pump house, their grid will heat up to a thousand degrees within minutes. So even if the grid doesn't melt down, the heat will kill all the rats and still shut down their power. The entire compound is electric, so if they lose their power they lose their cameras, alarms, intercoms, and light. Which means the prisoners can escape."

"Don't they have backup power?" Zeus asked.

"They have two backup generators run by diesel," Ostin said. "But even if they could get their generators up, it would take at least five to ten minutes to get them online. And they would only create enough power for the compound. The rest of Peru would go dark."

Suddenly a grin crossed Ostin's face. "Wait, I've got an even better idea. We also blow the generators! All that diesel fuel would create a massive explosion that would set fire to the camp. It will take hundreds of guards to fight it. Between that and all the escaping prisoners, we'll practically be able to walk in and get Michael."

"Brilliant," Ian said.

"But how do we blow the pump house?" Taylor asked.

"Dynamite," Ostin said.

"Last I checked we're completely out," Wade said sardonically.

"Where do we get dynamite?" Taylor asked.

"I don't know," Ostin said. "But this is the jungle and jungle people use dynamite for clearing trees and mining. I'm hoping that Raúl knows where to find some." He looked around. "Where is Raúl?"

"We don't know," Abigail said. "No one could understand him. He took Jack's knife and ran out into the forest."

Ostin looked puzzled. "Did he say anything?"

Jack looked at Abigail. "Something like saliva."

Ostin's brow furrowed. "Saliva?"

Abigail said, "No, it was more like . . . saliba. Salvia. Maybe, sabila."

"*Sábila*," Ostin repeated. "Of course. For Zeus."

"He was looking at Zeus when he said it," Abigail said.

"He must know where he can find some."

"Find what?" Jack asked.

"Aloe vera. It's a cactuslike plant that grows in Peru and is useful for treating burns," Ostin said. "While we're waiting for Raúl we need to make our plan. Ian, the generators are on the north side of the plant. There should be some big fuel tanks."

"I think I see them," Ian said, standing up and looking toward the compound. "There are two huge tanks aboveground, then a couple dozen oil barrels stacked near them."

"Can you tell if they're full?"

"All except two."

"Perfect," Ostin said. "So first we set the dynamite at the pump. The generators are going to be trickier because they're behind the fence."

"We could throw the dynamite," Jack said. "If it's not too far."

"It's not," Ian said. "But then how do we detonate it?"

"Zeus could do it," Jack said. "Couldn't you?"

Zeus nodded weakly. "If I can get there, I can. Back at the academy I used to set off firecrackers all the time."

"I'll get you there," Jack said.

Ostin continued, "While the guards are trying to put out the fire, we'll blow the pump house. Then the bowl will melt down, the power will go out, and in all the confusion, Ian, McKenna, Taylor, and I will slip in through the east fence to save Michael."

"Where am I while this is happening?" Jack asked.

"After we blow the pump house, you and Zeus will stay with the rest of the Electroclan. If something goes wrong, you get them to the village. Raúl knows his way through the jungle. In the village he can hide you."

Jack nodded. "Good plan."

"When do we do it?" Taylor asked.

"Tomorrow, after dark. It's also best if we wait until their feeding time—that's when the bowl will be at its hottest." Ostin looked at them all. "Are you with me?"

"I'm with you," McKenna said.

"Me too," Taylor said.

"I'm in," Jack said. "So is Wade."

"It could work," Ian said. "What do we do first?"

"First thing we need to do is get the dynamite. Let's just hope Raúl knows where to find some."

"Let's just hope Raúl comes back," Jack said.

*   *   *

Raúl returned to the camp about a half hour later carrying half a dozen large, dull-green serrated leaves. He set them down on the ground near Zeus, then knelt beside him.

"Yep, aloe vera," Ostin said. "It's a natural remedy for burns."

Zeus looked at the moist leaves fearfully. "It may burn me more," he said.

"Let me try just a little," Ostin said. He took a leaf from Raúl, squeezed some salve from it onto his finger, then lightly touched it to Zeus's skin. There was no electric reaction. "Looks good," Ostin said.

"All right," Zeus said.

Ostin nodded to Raúl. "Okay."

"Okay," Raúl said. He split a leaf, then began applying the salve to Zeus's burned flesh, murmuring something to Ostin as he worked.

"He said this will help," Ostin said.

"Let's hope so," Jack said.

Abigail continued to hold Zeus's hand.

"How are you holding up?" Zeus asked Abigail. She was weary from her constant exertion, but she forced a smile. "Still better than you."

As Raúl worked, Ostin explained his plan, then the two of them had a long discussion. When it was over, Ostin said, "Raúl knows where we can find dynamite. It's about a three-hour walk from here. But he'll need help carrying it."

"Someone's going to carry dynamite for three hours through a slippery jungle?" Wade said. "That sounds like a death wish."

"Wade and I will go," Jack said.

"What?" Wade said.

"Someone's got to do it," Jack said. "We'll do it."

Wade just shook his head.

Raúl handed Jack's knife back to him, then pointed to Jack and Wade and said something.

"He said you should leave a little before sunrise," Ostin said.

Jack nodded. "*Sí.*"

Wade looked distressed. "Great. I won't even get a last meal."

\* \* \*

As darkness fell, Mrs. Vey approached Ostin, who was sketching out a map of the compound in the dirt. "Ostin?"

He looked up. "Yes, Mrs. Vey?"

"It's really a great plan you came up with."

Ostin blushed. "Thank you."

She kissed Ostin on the forehead. "You're a good friend to Michael. That's why he loves you so much. And when we get back to Idaho, I'm making you waffles."

Ostin pumped his fist. "Yes!"

Ostin was still smiling when Taylor approached him a few minutes later.

"Hey," she said.

Ostin looked up.

"About your idea," Taylor said. "It's brilliant."

"Thanks."

She took a deep breath. "Look, I'm sorry about what I said earlier. It wasn't your fault. I was just upset."

"I know," Ostin said.

"You do?"

He nodded.

"I was afraid you wouldn't know that. I mean, you're so smart about everything except girls. Well, girls and pretty much anything social . . ."

"McKenna explained it to me," Ostin said.

"Oh," Taylor said. "I feel awful about what I said about you being a bad friend. You're not. You're a great friend." She looked into his eyes. "Can you forgive me?"

"Yes."

"I know I tease you a lot, but I'm glad we're friends, too."

"Really?" Ostin asked.

Taylor nodded. "Really."

Ostin put out his fist. "Bones?"

Taylor smiled and put out hers. "Bones."

# 46

## Nighttime in the Jungle

The group huddled together for the night, sleeping on the dirt. The Amazonian floor receives less than 2 percent of the sunlight, so very little grows, making it soft, like a decaying mulch pile.

The night air was moist and a little too cool for comfort, but they didn't dare make a fire or even let McKenna light herself up for fear that they'd be discovered by an Elgen patrol—it was dangerous enough that most of them glowed naturally.

Everyone was thirsty. Raúl took Ostin with him into the jungle, and when they came back Ostin was holding a tan, tennis-ball-size glob from which he pinched out pieces, rolled them into small balls, and handed them out to everyone.

"What is this?" Taylor said.

"It's gum," Ostin said. "It will make you less thirsty."

"Where did you find gum?"

"It's called chicle. It comes from the sap of the sapodilla tree. That's how they make gum."

"Chicle. Chiclets," McKenna said.

"*Exacto,*" Ostin said. "That's where it got its name."

Taylor put some in her mouth and chewed. "It's kind of sweet. But it tastes like gum you've already chewed for ten hours."

"It's tree sap," Ostin said. "What did you expect, Bazooka bubble gum?"

Taylor shrugged. "That would be nice."

The jungle came alive at night, as noisy and bustling as Times Square. Maybe noisier. As exhausted as he was, Ian volunteered to stand guard. It wasn't as difficult as he thought it would be, as observing the jungle at night was like watching a live presentation of the Discovery Channel. He watched two scorpions, locked in combat, battle to the death. He saw a jaguar climb a tree to catch a monkey, and an entire colony of vampire bats emerge from a rotted tree to seek blood. Everything in the jungle seemed engaged in a life-and-death struggle. Just like them.

No one, outside of Raúl, got much sleep. Between their growing thirst, the symphony of insects, and the continuous assault of mosquitoes, everyone was miserable.

In the middle of the night the sound of thunder rolled across the forest accompanied by the excited chatter of monkeys. Even though they could hear the sound of rain hitting the trees, the thick, lush canopy of leaves kept them dry. Ian found a stream of water rolling down a tree and let it gather in a leaf to drink.

Tanner woke up three times in the night screaming. On the third occasion, Mrs. Vey went to his side and comforted him, gently stroking his forehead. He broke down crying, and she held him, rocking him like a baby.

The only thing that really concerned Ian was when he spotted a guard sneaking back to the pipe. *Isn't he going to be surprised?* Ian thought.

A half hour later, the guard, having found the cap locked,

reemerged from the pipe's mouth and ran back in the direction he had come from.

Ian was still awake when Raúl, Jack, and Wade left at the first hint of dawn.

Ostin awoke an hour later covered with mosquito and spider bites. "I can't spend another night here," he said, scratching his arm.

"I know what you mean," Ian said.

"Did Jack and Raúl already leave?"

"And Wade."

"I hope they make it."

"Me too," Ian said. Then added, "It's a jungle out there."

The three didn't return until late afternoon. They were carrying large, overstuffed packs. Jack had two, one strapped to his front as well as his back, and Raúl was carrying a bag in his hand in addition to his pack. Wade was a physical and emotional wreck and his clothes were soaked through with sweat. He took off his pack and carefully set it on the ground, overjoyed to be free of it.

"You made it," Taylor said to them.

"That was farther than I thought it was," Jack said. "Nice hike."

Taylor turned to Wade. "So how was it?"

"It was a death march," he said. "Nothing like carrying death on your back through a dangerous, death-filled jungle."

"The good thing is that if the dynamite had gone off you'd never even know it," Jack said.

"Comforting," Wade said.

"Well," Taylor said, "if you gotta go, that's the way to go. Oblivious."

"Just like my great-grandfather," Jack said. "He died in his sleep. Much more peacefully than the screaming passengers in the car he was driving."

"You just made that up, didn't you?" Taylor said.

Jack grinned. "Yep." He lifted one of the packs and tossed it to her. It landed on the ground a few feet in front of her.

Taylor jumped back. "What are you doing?"

Jack laughed. "It's not dynamite. I brought back some food and water. Also some gauze for Zeus."

Taylor opened the pack. Inside were a dozen bottles of water, four large, crusted loaves of bread, and green fruits that were slightly smaller than a grapefruit, with the texture of an avocado. She drank some water, then took one of the fruits from the pack.

"What's this?" she asked.

"No idea," Jack said. "He said it was a cherry or something. But it's pretty good."

"Cherimoya," said Raúl, who was eating one a few yards away.

"I'll take your word for it," Taylor said. She grabbed two more bottles of water, three fruits, and a loaf of bread to take to Mrs. Vey and Tanner.

Jack walked around distributing food and water. McKenna was so happy when she saw the water that she started to cry. "Water."

"I got two bottles for you," Jack said. "I know how you need it."

"Thank you, thank you, thank you," she said, opening a bottle. "You're my hero."

"I thought I was," Ostin said.

McKenna drank half the bottle, then said, "You still are."

Relieved, Ostin asked, "Are those cherimoyas?"

"Something like that," Jack said, tossing him one. "Is there anything you don't know?"

"The meaning of life," Ostin said. "And how girls think." He peeled back the fruit's glossy green skin and took a bite, juice dribbling down his chin. "Oh man. That's good."

"What does it taste like?" McKenna asked.

"The flavor falls somewhere between strawberry and bubble gum."

"I want one," she said.

"Mark Twain called the cherimoya the most delicious fruit known to man," Ostin said.

"I definitely want one," McKenna said.

Jack handed her a fruit.

"Me too," Ian said. "Toss one this way."

Raúl laughed and said to Ostin, *"Vendes muy bien. Puedes trabajar en el carro de frutas de mi mamá."*

Ostin laughed.

"What did he say?" McKenna asked.

"He said I'm a good salesman. And I can have a job at his mother's fruit cart."

Jack took water and food to Abigail and Zeus. The night before, at the first sound of thunder, Jack and Abigail had carried Zeus into the sloping, deep roots of a kapok tree, then covered him with an additional canopy of brush. Jack handed Abigail a bottle and she took a quick drink, then held it to Zeus's lips.

Zeus raised his hand. "I can hold it," he said.

"How are you feeling?" Jack asked.

"I think the aloe vera is helping."

Jack brought out a crusted loaf of bread and offered it to Abigail. "I brought this."

She tore off a piece and handed it to Zeus, then took a piece for herself. "I'm so hungry," she said.

"Try this," Jack said, handing her a cherimoya.

"What is it?" she asked. "Actually, never mind, I don't care what it is. I'll eat anything."

Jack peeled a fruit for Zeus and handed it to him.

"I've had one of these before," he said. "In Costa Rica. Thanks."

"No problem," Jack said.

After the food was gone Jack handed Abigail the gauze. "We should wrap him in this. It will help keep his burns from getting infected."

"Thank you," Zeus said. He turned to Abigail. "Could you give Jack and me a moment to talk?"

She looked at him quizzically. "But your pain . . ."

"I can take it for a few minutes. And you need the rest."

"Okay." She stood up. "Bye." She walked over to McKenna.

When she was gone Zeus said to Jack, "Why are you being so nice to me? I shocked you twice."

Jack grinned. "Yeah, but what did I call you? Lightning stink? I deserved to get shocked."

Zeus looked at him somberly. "I'm serious. Abi told me what you did in the compound. How you ran through the rats to save me."

Jack sat down next to Zeus. "Not something I hope to do again soon."

Zeus just looked at him. "Really, why did you do it?"

Jack didn't answer immediately, though his expression turned more serious. When he spoke his voice was low and sincere. "We may have our differences—or maybe they're really our similarities—but anyone who's willing to sacrifice his life for his friends is a true hero. I'd award you the Medal of Honor if I could."

For a moment Zeus was speechless. Then he said, "About Abi . . ."

Jack lifted his hand. "We don't have to talk about her."

"I know. But if you want a shot at her, I'll step aside."

Jack looked down at him. "I don't think she's going to be leaving your side anytime soon," he said. "Besides, that's not really our choice, is it?"

"I'm just saying, I owe you."

"No you don't. But I'd be proud to be your friend."

"Me too," Zeus said. They clasped hands and Zeus grimaced a little, hiding his pain.

Jack stood. "I'll get Abi."

"Thank you."

He took a few steps, then turned back. *Semper Fi.*

Zeus smiled. *Semper Fi.*

After everyone had eaten, Taylor and Ostin called the group together. Jack and Abigail helped Zeus over, though he insisted on walking himself.

In the center of their camp Ostin had drawn a diagram of the Elgen compound in the dirt, using rocks and leaves to designate buildings.

"This is where we are," Ostin said, pointing to a spot a few inches from the compound, using a long, slender stick. "And this is where we came from the pipe. Over here, about four hundred yards from us, is the pump house. Earlier today Ian and I sneaked over to take a look at it. Even though it's outside the compound it's still within view of the guard towers, which means we'll have to camouflage ourselves to get to it. Right here is the side where the water is controlled."

"There's also a barbwire fence around it," Ian said. "But it's easy to climb over."

"Or under," Ostin said. "When we blow this thing, it's going to be like a fire hydrant on steroids. We'll be hiding over here behind these rocks when we set off the dynamite. The northeast guard tower is only fifty yards from the pump house and it's equipped with two fifty-caliber Browning machine guns. Those bad boys spit bullets longer than my foot and can pretty much mow down anything in the jungle, so hiding behind a tree won't do much good. Stay clear until the place goes dark."

"I'll explain the next part," Taylor said. "After the sun sets we'll split up into three groups. Ian, McKenna, Ostin, and I are in group one. We'll set the dynamite at the pump house and keep an eye on the bowl. Ian will tell us when it's time to blow the pump and the generators.

"Group two is Jack, Zeus, Abi, and Wade." She looked at Jack. "Your job is to blow the fuel and diesel generators. You won't be able to get close, so you'll have to throw the dynamite, and Zeus will have to set it off. The oil drums are about thirty yards behind the fence. What's the farthest you can hit, Zeus?"

"I can hit them," Zeus said.

"Good," Taylor said. "Ian will be watching for when the bowl is hottest, which is at feeding time. When we tell you, you'll blow the pumps. Ian's been able to confirm that there are eighteen forty-two-gallon drums as well as the tanks connected to the generator. There are fourteen sticks of dynamite in each pack, so you'll each take one pack. Combined with all that oil, that's going to make one big explosion. The generator is only fifty yards from the guard barracks, so with some luck we'll set them on fire as well."

Ostin jumped in. "Diesel puts out a lot of thick smoke, so it will help create confusion and panic, but it has one potential problem— it's not as flammable as gasoline, so it's going to be harder to get this right. Remember, our primary goal is to shut down the generator. So make sure that the dynamite is close to the generator and blows up the tanks first. Just hitting the barrels might not be enough. Are you clear on that?"

"Got it," Jack said. "Hit the generator and hope the barrels come along for the ride."

"Exactly. As soon as we hear your explosion, we'll blow the pump house. We'll be close enough to lay a fuse, which McKenna will light. Without water the power plant should go down within three to five minutes."

"One question," Zeus said. "How are you going to signal me when it's time to blow our dynamite?"

Taylor looked at Ostin. "We didn't think of that," she said. "Maybe we could do a bird call."

"The guards are closer to you than we are," Jack said. "They'll hear." Ostin squeezed his chin. "Hmm."

"I have an idea," McKenna said. "Didn't you say there's a barbwire fence outside of the compound?"

"Yes," Ostin said. "But don't worry, it will be easy to get through."

"I'm not worried about that," McKenna said. "How long is the fence?"

"It extends almost the whole length of the north side," Ian said. "How come?"

"What I'm thinking is that Taylor should switch to group two, and then she and Ian could both hold on to the wire. When it's time to blow, Ian just thinks that it's time, then Taylor hears his thoughts and signals Zeus. That way there's no sound or anything that might alert the guards."

Ostin just gaped at her. "That's brilliant."

"Thank you," she said with a slight smile.

"That is a good idea," Taylor said. "So maybe Wade and I should switch places."

Wade nodded. "I'm good with that."

"Then what?" Abigail asked.

"After we've blown the dynamite," Ostin said, "we'll regroup halfway between the pump house and the generator, then Taylor, Ian, McKenna, and I will climb through the fence and rescue Michael. Ian thinks that Michael is being held in the same place Tanner was."

"What about the rest of us?" Mrs. Vey said.

Taylor turned. "You, Tanner, and Raúl are group three. Since you and Tanner are still recovering, we decided it's best that you get an early start to our meeting point. Raúl will lead you back to where we entered the compound."

Ostin added, "We left some of Raúl's friends tied up there and we need to free them."

Taylor nodded. "After we've got Michael, we'll meet you there, then we'll all hike together to the pickup point. Sound good?"

Mrs. Vey nodded.

"I almost forgot," Ostin said, looking at Tanner. "The Elgen have four helicopters. If they put any up, you take them down."

"With pleasure," he said. "I hope they come after us."

"We're kicking their hive," Ostin said. "I think you can count on it."

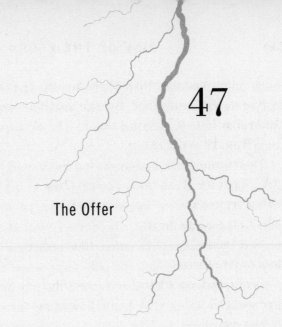

# 47

## The Offer

There was a video monitor in my prison cell that played a continuous loop of the rats at feeding time. The Elgen guards were generally cruel, but I'm sure this was done on Hatch's orders. He would do anything he could to increase my suffering. And he'd enjoy it. I think that deep inside he was sorry he had to kill me, but only because he couldn't do it more than once.

I had been in the cell (in the same cellblock where we had found Tanner) for less than twenty-four hours, but it felt much longer. Security around me was tight, with a guard outside my door and two inside. The truth was, they didn't even need a locked door. Drained of my electricity, I couldn't even leave the cot, let alone my cell.

The RESAT box still fastened to me was like having Nichelle sitting on my chest, drawing out all my energy—only the box was much more powerful than Nichelle was. The only bodily functions that seemed undisturbed by the machine were my tics, which, unfortunately, never seemed to take a break. Especially now. My eyes stung from all my blinking.

Then a thought came to me—a small spark of hope. Maybe the Elgen had locked me up not to keep me in the cell but to keep my friends out. *Maybe my friends are still trying to save me after all.* I had mixed feelings about this. Of course I wanted to be rescued. I was terrified by what was to come. But, realistically, there was no way they could save me—and the only thing worse than dying would be to watch everyone I loved suffer and die too. I couldn't think about that option. I hoped they had followed my instructions and made it to the pickup site. At least then my death would have mattered for something.

That morning I had visitors. Tara, Bryan, Quentin, and Torstyn. This time Tara came as herself. I had seen Bryan and Quentin at the academy, but I had seen Torstyn only when Ian pointed him out as we escaped from Re-Ed through the assembly hall.

I knew there were other electric kids, seventeen in all, but Hatch had told me the last four were dead. But here was Torstyn—so Hatch was lying after all.

The guard opened the door, and Tara was the first in, her lip curled in a mocking sneer. "Oh, Michael, you're so cute. I'm so in love with you." She laughed. "So you're all kissy with my pathetic sister?"

Bryan shook his head. "What an idiot."

Quentin walked up to my side, his mouth stretched in a confident grin. "You really thought you could take us on? You're delusional, man. You're getting what you deserve."

I turned away from them. Torstyn grabbed my chin and pulled my head back. "I didn't say you could look away from us. You want me to fry you, lover boy?"

In spite of my weakness I said, "Try."

The other youths looked at Torstyn, wondering if he would. He just stared at me. "You know I would if Hatch let me."

"Your master won't let you?" I said. "Maybe he'll let you lick his shoes."

Torstyn scowled. "Watch your mouth or I'm gonna mess you up, man."

"Real tough threatening me when I'm locked up. Let me out and you can show everyone how tough you really are."

Torstyn looked stumped, caught between his ego and his fear of Hatch.

"Don't worry about it, Torstyn," Quentin said. "The rats will take care of him."

"That's your name?" I said. "Torstyn? They named you after a wrench?"

Torstyn turned red. When he finally spoke he said, "You're stupid."

"Wow," I said. "Is that your superpower? Your brilliant vocabulary?"

Torstyn blushed again.

Quentin intervened. "Hey, Vey, you're going to love this. We just talked to the dudes at the chute. They said they can slow the conveyor belt, so we can prolong the fun. The rats can eat you a couple of inches at a time."

"Awesome," Bryan said. "Wouldn't it be cool if Dr. Hatch, like, made a game of it and let him run across the bowl? They could even make it a contest. If he gets to the other side and back, he can go free. It would be like dropping a grasshopper on an anthill. We could, like, make bets on how far he gets."

"Hey, Bryan, wouldn't it be cool if you had half a brain?" I said. "Did you know these guys all think you're an idiot? Zeus told me all about it."

Bryan looked back and forth between them. "No, they don't. They're my boys."

"Really? Is that why Quentin put dog poop in your bed?"

Bryan looked at Quentin. "*You* did that?"

Quentin shoved him. "He's just messing with your head, man."

"Yeah, he did it. Zeus watched him."

Bryan glared at him.

"I didn't do it," Quentin said. "That was Tanner."

"Tanner was in England," Bryan said.

"I told you," I said. "They're always making fun of you behind your back."

Bryan stormed out of my cell. I turned my attention to Torstyn. "C'mon, tough guy, let me out. Let's see how tough you are."

For a moment he looked as if he actually might do it. I didn't know if I had any chance against him, I didn't even know what his powers were, but I figured he couldn't be worse than a million rats.

"He's messing with you, too," Tara said. "Enough of this loser. Let's get out of here."

"You know, your sister is so much cooler than you are," I said. "In Meridian she has like a million friends. I guess beauty really is more than skin deep."

"So are rats," Tara said.

"That doesn't even make sense," I said.

Quentin said, "We thought watching the bulls get eaten was sick. You getting eaten is going to be epic."

"Enjoy it. Your turn's coming soon. Someday Hatch will be feeding you to something," I said.

"That shows how little you know," Quentin said. "Dr. Hatch is like a father to us. He'd never hurt one of us."

"Yeah, Tanner thought that too," I said.

My reply stumped him.

Tara said, "Tanner was a screwup."

"Then you better hope you don't screw up," I said. "Because, father or not, Hatch is afraid of you. Do you know why he's executing me? He told me he's afraid that if he doesn't, one of you will someday take him down."

Suddenly a beeper went off on my RESAT and a wave of pain passed through my body, freezing me. I grimaced. Through clenched teeth I said, "I guess someone doesn't want me telling you the truth."

A guard walked briskly into the room. "It's time to leave," he said. "The prisoner is getting agitated."

"Hatch is getting agitated," I said.

The guard quickly ushered them out. Tara turned back at the door. "Enjoy the bowl."

"You too," I said.

Hours later Hatch walked into my room wearing his sunglasses. He came to the side of my cot and sat down but didn't say anything. They hadn't turned down the RESAT, so I was still struggling to breathe.

"Twelve," he said.

The pain dropped immediately—not completely, but enough for me to take a deep breath. I turned toward him.

"It's that easy," Hatch said. "Just one word and the pain goes away."

"I don't think your kids' visit went the way you planned."

Hatch didn't answer, but I saw his jaw tighten.

"I met Torstyn. You said that the other four kids had died."

"Truth is relative."

"Then I'm not dying?"

"You're dying—just not from cancer. You're actually quite healthy, you oath-breaking, insignificant bug." Hatch looked down at his watch. "It's almost time. It's a shame it had to end this way. There are few things sadder in life than squandered opportunity. You could have been great. I could have made you a god."

"You must be dyslexic," I said. "I think you meant to say 'dog.'"

He leaned in close. "In spite of your continual insolence, it's not too late, Michael. One word and I can still save you."

"Why would you want to save an insignificant bug?"

"Don't try me!" Hatch shouted. "I'm giving you a chance at salvation." He calmed himself. "I don't think you've ever really thought this through. You've seen how we live—how our youths live. They have whatever they want. I know you're not the materialistic type, and I honestly admire that. I too am a man of principles. But what principles allow you to watch your mother suffer every day of her life and do nothing about it? There she is, working herself to the bone, just trying to put food on the table, trying to take care of *you*. That's not a life, Michael, that's an existence—and a poor one at that. If you joined us, really joined us, your mother wouldn't have to work another day for the rest of her life. She could see the world, dine at fancy restaurants, drive a new car, wear nice clothing, live in a beautiful home. Doesn't she deserve that? Don't you want that for her? Don't you love her enough to give that to her?"

"My mother deserves everything you just said," I replied. "But there's more to life than things."

"Of course there is. There's happiness. And is she happy?"

"Most of the time," I said.

"She acts that way for you, Michael. Because she loves you. Don't you love her? Wouldn't she be happier without all the stress and worry? Be honest, Michael."

"Not at the price you're asking."

"What price?" he said. "My offer to you is free."

"Nothing is free," I said. "The price is my allegiance to you."

"And is that too much to ask? You will never be raised higher than when you are kneeling to me."

I lay there quietly for a moment, then said, "I'd rather kneel to a rat."

His expression turned to rage. "So you shall," he said. "You fool. Again I have offered you the world and you spit it back at me." He looked up at a camera and said, "Make it twenty."

Immediately the RESAT buzzed, and pain racked my body. I gasped, my eyes welling up from the pain.

"It's time," Hatch said to the guard. "Take him to the chute." He turned back to me, leaning in close enough that I could feel his breath. "You have no idea how much I'm going to enjoy this." He stood and walked away.

Immediately the two guards were by my side. They checked my shackles and wires, pulled out my IV, and unplugged my RESAT from the wall.

Two more guards walked in. One came behind my cot, knelt down, and unlocked the wheels on my gurney; the other pulled out a plastic handle from the front and pulled me forward. The two guards who were already in the room walked behind the bed until I was outside the cell door, then they came to my side and walked in formation, slowly and at attention, like a color guard. I was wheeled from my cell through a long, concrete-floored corridor with tiled walls.

I had a flashback to the time I was seven years old and was taken to the hospital to have my tonsils removed, my mother and father had walked next to me as I was wheeled to the operating room. I found out later that I had shocked the doctor while he was operating.

*Why am I thinking about this?* Maybe that's what the mind does when it can't face its own reality—it searches for another one. It was safer to be seven again.

I was in such excruciating pain that everything seemed nightmarishly unreal. The walls blurred past me, partially hidden by the guards, who moved without a word, steady and emotionless like robots, their heavy boots echoing through the hallway. We stopped, waited for a double set of doors to open, then entered a different room with high ceilings. *I've been here before*, I thought. I heard Spanish being spoken in whispers, and above me I could see the curve of the bowl. I was in the ranch entrance, the room where we had entered the power plant. Of course I was. They were taking me to the lift Raúl had shown us, where they brought the bulls to feed to the rats.

Time was running out. If I was going to escape it had to be now. I had to think of something—but even thinking seemed impossible. My mind felt like it was on a long string, like a kite, floating away from me, connected by nothing but a quivering line. I was helpless. I couldn't think. I couldn't move. I was going to die.

The cart stopped, and the guards lifted my bed and set it on the lift. I must have blacked out from pain for a few seconds because the next thing I knew I was already high up in the air, approaching an open trapdoor in the ceiling.

This was it. Doubt began to creep in. Hatch's words returned to me, mocking me. *Where are your friends now, Michael?* Was he right?

Had they deserted me? I fought Hatch's lies. *I* had left *them*. I had locked the pipe behind me. Of course they would have come for me if I hadn't made it impossible. I had told them to run, to escape. If they didn't try to save me, it was my fault, not theirs.

The lift stopped abruptly. I tried to look around, but I could barely move my head. I was in a dark room lit by dim, amber lights flickering like candles. There were people there. Guards? Ranchers? No. They were dressed all in black like the guards, but they were executioners.

Thoughts of my loved ones came flooding into my mind: Taylor and her beautiful eyes. I wondered if they would cry for me. I thought about Ostin and the time he blew up his parents' new microwave because he was sure he could create cold fusion in a Tupperware container.

Mostly, I thought of my mother. I had read somewhere that grown men, dying on the battlefield, cried out for their mothers. I understood that. I wanted to be with her again. At least she was safe, I told myself. Tears fell down both sides of my cheeks.

The executioners were methodical and quiet, not even speaking among themselves. I was grateful for this. The Elgen guards would have mocked me. They would have laughed at my tears, then slapped me a few more times before sending me off to my end. Perhaps the executioners had seen too much death. There were two, maybe three in the room. I couldn't see their faces. Were they wearing hoods? It was hard to tell. Whatever they wore over their faces was stiff and resembled a mask. They all wore the same disguise, making them anonymous. *Do they feel anonymous? Are they wearing their masks for me or for themselves?*

I was unstrapped from the cot, lifted, and set on a conveyor belt. A strap, made from the same rubberized material that my shackles were, was pulled around my chest, next to the RESAT, and my bound wrists were lifted and buckled to it.

*Is Ian watching me?* Or were they already on their way back to America? Part of me felt relief that I wouldn't have to fight anymore. The fight was theirs now. I had given all I could.

An executioner turned a knob on the RESAT, and I groaned as my body convulsed with more pain. At first I thought he had done this out of cruelty, but as my thoughts became more blurred I realized that he was probably acting in mercy, dulling me to the impending agony of being eaten alive.

Alive. I was too young to die! I wanted to live and fall in love and someday have children of my own. I had wondered if they would be electric too. My Tourette's could be passed on, why not my electricity? And what if I married Taylor? Would our children possess multiple powers?

*What if.* What if I had just gone with them? Maybe we could have made it. Maybe we would all be together. Or maybe we would all be together in here. There was no use second-guessing what I couldn't know. I had made my decision. What was done was done.

One of the executioners began spraying something on me from a hose, soaking my clothing and skin. *What is this? It smells sweet.*

There was suddenly a loud beep like the sound a garbage truck makes when it's backing up. From its echo I guessed it was coming from the bowl itself. I didn't think about its meaning, as I was certain it had something to do with feeding time. A thin, tinny voice from an intercom spoke to the executioners. I couldn't understand what was said, nor did I try. One of the executioners grunted a response then pushed a button. A loud, stoic, female voice began counting down from ten.

"Ten, nine, eight, seven . . ."

My executioners put on earphones. "Five, four, three . . ."

On the wall ahead of me, near my feet, a door slid open and the color of the room immediately changed, lit by an amber glow like the flickering of a fire. The rats. They were waiting.

"Two, one. Commence feeding."

The beeping suddenly stopped, replaced by a single long tone. There was no rescue coming. I had run out of time.

A light above me began to flash, then the conveyor started to move beneath me. My heart froze. "No . . . ," I said.

I was so weak. There was nothing I could do but wait. At least it wouldn't take long. Soon everything would be over.

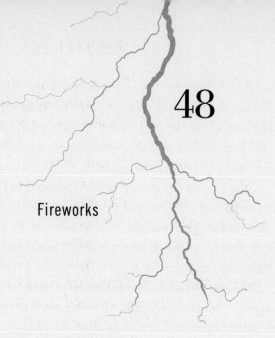

# 48

## Fireworks

The hours waiting for night-time passed quietly. The bread, water, and fruit were long gone, and everyone was thirsty, tired, and hungry. As darkness fell over the jungle Ostin gathered everyone together to review the plan one more time. Just sitting together in the darkness already revealed a flaw in their plan. "The guards in the towers are going to see your glow," Ostin said. "They'll shoot you through the trees."

"Easy fix," Taylor said. "Everyone who's electric follow me." She led them over to a spot near the edge of their camp where the ground was still wet from the rain the night before. She scooped up a handful of moist dirt and rubbed it over her hands and face. With the exception of Zeus, the rest of them covered one another with the dark soil. Jack and Wade said they were rubbing mud on for solidarity, but the truth was they loved the commando look.

As soon as the last of the light had vanished, they said a quick good-bye to Mrs. Vey, Tanner, and Raúl, then set off through the jungle in single file, Ian and Taylor leading the group. Zeus slowed their pace considerably. He was finally walking on his own, but he had to lean heavily on Jack. Had they not needed his power they would have sent him off with Raúl. Wade, Ostin, and McKenna walked at the rear of the column, carrying the dynamite.

They traveled east in an ellipse, making a wide swing into the jungle to avoid being spotted by the tower guards at the northeast corner of the interior fence. When they were past the compound they circled back in, crouching at the perimeter of the barbwire fence just thirty-five yards from the pump house.

The pump house was a simple adobe-brick structure with a tin roof and barred windows. A large pipe, nearly three feet in diameter, was visible on the east side of the structure. It rose up from the ground forming a loop.

"There it is," Ostin whispered. He turned to Taylor. "Is group two ready?"

"Ready," Taylor said.

"We're ready," Jack said.

Ostin looked at Zeus. "You okay?"

He was clearly still in a lot of pain but nodded. "Let's shut them down."

"We should test the wire," Taylor said.

"Good idea," Ian said. He and Taylor grabbed the barbwire about six feet apart.

"What number am I thinking of?" Ian asked.

"You're not," Taylor said. "You're thinking about that fruit."

"It works," Ian said, releasing the wire.

"All right," Ostin said. "See you after the fireworks. Good luck, everyone."

While Taylor led group two back into the jungle, Ostin, Wade, McKenna, and Ian covered themselves with branches, then crawled on their stomachs under the barbwire closer to the pump house. Ian and Wade carried the dynamite on their backs but had to take their packs off to slide them through the fence. They all stopped about fifteen yards from the house.

"What's going on in there?" Ostin asked Ian.

"There's a guy sitting at a console."

"Just one guy?"

"Yes."

"Is he armed?"

"No. He looks more like a tech." He turned back. "He looks like he's sleeping."

"He's about to get the wake-up call of his life," Ostin said. "What else do you see?"

"The right side of the house is nothing, just a kitchen and bathroom. On the other side there's the end of that pipe with a bunch of lights and switches."

"How thick is the pipe?"

"About three feet."

"I mean the walls of the pipe."

"Oh." He looked closer. "Maybe an inch and a half."

Ostin thought this over. "Dynamite blows down, so we should put the packs on top of the pipe, but it's much more powerful in a confined space." He did the math in his head. "For maximum explosive effect we need to stack the packs *inside* the loop."

Ian and Wade pulled a coil of fuse out of each pack, and McKenna wrapped the ends of the fuse around her hand.

Ostin looked at McKenna. "You don't ever just spontaneously ignite, do you?"

"Only a few times a day," McKenna said, staring ahead.

"Really?"

She looked at him. "No."

"Sorry," he said.

Wade turned to Ostin. "Now?"

"Do it," Ostin said. "Don't forget to check the fuses."

"I won't." Wade slid his arms through both packs, then McKenna and Ostin covered them with brush.

"Good luck," Ostin said.

Wade crawled on his stomach toward the pipe, moving about as fast as a turtle. In the darkness he looked like a slow-moving bush.

"Can't he go faster?" McKenna said.

"He's just being careful," Ostin said. "We've got one shot at this."

When Wade reached the pipe he looked back at Ian, who gave him the thumbs-up. Wade checked the fuse connections again, then placed the packs in between the looped pipe and crawled back, though much faster. The four of them dropped back into the jungle, McKenna feeding the fuse out from her hand as they went.

"How's our sleeper?" Ostin asked Ian.

"Still snoozing."

"Good. Have you found Michael?"

"No. He's not in the cells anymore."

"What's going on in the bowl?"

Ian strained. "It's hard to see with all the electrical interference. But something must be going on. There's a large crowd gathered up in the observation deck. The chute's extended, so it must be feeding time." He shook his head. "That's strange, I don't see a bull. Let me see what's in the feeding station." His expression changed. He quickly grabbed the barbwire. "We've got to blow it. Now!"

"What's going on?" Ostin asked. "What's in the feeding station?"

"Michael."

# 49

## Return of Power

The conveyor belt moved me slowly toward the open door leading to the bowl. As I approached the opening I was overcome by the shrill scream of a million rats echoing in the metal collector—far louder and more horrific than the sound of the rats in the hallway. I can't describe the terror of that sound, though I had once heard something like it. A few years earlier Ostin played for me something he had downloaded from the Internet—a radio program claiming that Russian scientists conducting deep-hole drilling experiments in Siberia had recorded the sounds of hell. The recording was proven a hoax, but if there was such a place as hell, it couldn't be worse than this—the shrieking of a million hungry rats climbing on top of one another to eat me alive. Even the stench was torture, and I started gagging.

The belt moved slowly, like a roller coaster about to take its first plunge. My heart raced, fueled by adrenaline. My mind and my body felt numb. I wished I could pass out.

Then I felt something else. As my feet cleared the door, they began to tingle. Powerfully. As I slowly passed through the opening in the wall the sensation moved up my body. *What's happening to me?* To my surprise I was able to lift my feet. It felt like energy was washing over me. Of course it did. I was being carried out over the largest electrical field ever created—millions of kilowatts were bombarding my body. The RESAT that had been sucking the energy from me couldn't possibly handle that much current. A thousand of them couldn't.

As my chest approached the opening I was able to sit up and look down. My feet were beginning to glow. What I saw past my feet, at the bottom of the chute, was horrific. Until you see the rats you can't possibly imagine how terrible they look, bubbling like a vast sea of lava. At the sight of me, the rats' ravenous, collective shriek grew in intensity, and I could see a wave of rodents swelling toward me.

My thighs were now glowing. I strained at my bonds. I couldn't break free yet, but I was still absorbing electricity. My head passed through the opening, and I was looking directly down the chute, lying on the metal rollers. This is where I was supposed to roll down. I waited for it, but I didn't move. I wasn't sliding anywhere. Of course I wasn't. These were metal rollers and I was magnetic again, only a hundred times more.

The RESAT started to make a high-pitched squeal, then popped as it blew, a thin wisp of smoke rising from it. My skin was now as bright as an incandescent lightbulb. I was just lying there on the chute, a few yards past the trap door, immovable and growing brighter by the second, brighter than I had ever experienced. I looked down at my feet, but they were now too bright to look at. I wasn't melting through my bands; my bands were just gone. I lifted the RESAT from my chest and threw it down at the grid.

I could hear shouting coming from the intercom in the execution room. Then the chute began to lower. I guessed that if I wasn't going to the rats, they were going to bring the rats to me. The trapdoor shut behind me, and the chute continued lowering until it was within a few feet of the grid. The ravenous rats began jumping onto the chute, pouring up the trough like a flash flood in reverse.

I had been covered by the rats before—in the hallway—but I hadn't felt this way then. The bowl was designed to collect and focus energy toward a collector, and I had become the center of that focus, channeling the pure energy of a million rats.

The first rats didn't come within six feet of me before they burned up like meteors entering the Earth's atmosphere. I was becoming even more electric. I *was* lightning. I was *pure energy*. Then I wasn't burning the rats anymore; I was vaporizing them. For the first time, I felt more electric than human. I wondered if I would vaporize too.

As the metal rollers began to glow beneath me, I slowly stood and walked, on an incline, down the chute, my feet clinging to the metal. The rats began running from me, scrambling as if they were fleeing a burning ship. I walked to the end of the chute, then stepped down onto the grid.

I looked up at the observation window. Hatch was pressed against the glass. Even with his glasses on I could see his astonishment. Standing next to him were his kids: Tara, Quentin, Torstyn, Bryan, and Kylee, with at least a dozen guards at attention behind them. I stepped over the sweep and walked closer to the observation window so I could observe them.

I formed a brilliant ball of electricity in my hand and threw it right at Hatch. Hatch, and everybody else, dove out of the way as the ball exploded against the thick glass, blasting a hole in it large enough for my mom's car to drive through. When the smoke cleared, only Torstyn's head popped up. I formed another ball in my hand.

"Hey, tough guy!" I shouted. "Want to play ball?"

He ran.

I noticed that the sound the rats were making had begun to change. I turned to see the rodents pressed up against the opposite side of the bowl. Thousands of them were on their backs, twitching. A loud alarm sounded. That's when I noticed that the color of the bowl was also changing. The bowl was heating up. Even in my state, I could feel its heat. All around me, rats were dying by the thousands.

*Am I doing this?* Then the rats began to burst into flames, like stuffed animals thrown into a furnace. A robotic female voice echoed across the bowl: "Danger. Evacuation protocol. Bowl meltdown imminent."

I didn't want to stick around to see what that might look like. I ran to the side of the bowl and jumped across a three-foot trough, magnetically sticking to the bowl's metal side.

That's when the power went out.

# 50

## Darkness

Everything stilled. A dying alarm echoed across the bowl, and the only light came from me and the burning carcasses of rats. I slowly lowered myself down the metal side, below the grid. I was free, at least for the time being, but I wasn't sure how to get from where I was to the mechanical closet.

*Michael?*

The voice sounded as if it had come from someone standing next to me. It sounded like Taylor's. I looked around but couldn't see anyone. *Taylor?*

*Good, you hear me!* she said.

I realized that I wasn't hearing a voice but thoughts.

*Where are you?* I asked.

*I'm outside the building. Are you touching the bowl?*

*Yes.*

*Me too. You're reading my thoughts.*

*Where is everyone?*

*In the jungle.*

*Is everyone okay? Is my mother?*

*She's fine. Raúl took her and Tanner to our rendezvous point, where the bull got caught in the fence.*

*The power's out. The bowl melted down.*

*I know. We blew up their water supply so the bowl would melt down.*

*Ostin's idea?*

*Of course. How are you getting out?* Taylor asked.

*The pipe. If I can find it. Is Ian around?*

*Yes.*

*Ask him how I get to the pipe.*

*Just a minute. Ian, how does Michael get to the pipe?*

*Tell him to climb down to the ground below and go right to the first door. That hallway will take him back to the air duct we crawled through. Did you hear that, Michael?*

(It's a little weird listening to someone's thoughts when they're listening to someone else speak, almost like an echo.) *Yes. I'll lose contact with you when I drop down from the bowl. I'll meet you at the rendezvous point.*

*We'll see you there. I'll see you soon.*

I couldn't help but smile. *I'll see you soon.*

I climbed down the sloping metal of the bowl as far as I could, which wasn't far enough, as there was still a twelve-foot drop to the dark ground below—the floor barely illuminated by my glow. I let go, dropping hard to the concrete.

"My ankle," I groaned. I looked down at my foot. My right foot had landed on a wrench and twisted as I hit. As I stood, a shock of pain shot through my ankle. It felt like a sprain. I limped along the wall until I found the door Ian had told me about and opened it to the corridor we'd escaped from. The hall had some illumination, as the battery-powered emergency lights had been activated. I looked both ways, then hobbled out into the hall.

I could hear running, heavy Elgen boots, but it was coming from somewhere else in the maze. I limped down the hall until I found the vent cover. I climbed the water pipe next to it into the duct, then replaced the cover behind me.

My glow had increased tenfold, illuminating the duct almost as brightly as McKenna had. I crawled as quickly as I could until I felt the cold of the refrigeration room. I crawled slowly to the next vent and put my ear to it. I could hear movement. Then I saw the beam of a flashlight. There was someone in the mechanical room. I pulled back, afraid that they might notice my glow through the vent, but the sound didn't stop. I crept up and looked out the vent again. There was a guard below. He was in uniform, standing near the pipe. I couldn't tell if he was coming or going. He lifted the cap off the pipe and dropped his flashlight in, answering my question. He was escaping too.

I gave him time to disappear down the pipe, then I removed the vent cover. I looked around and then climbed out, lowering myself as much as possible, then dropped to the floor, trying to absorb as much of the fall as I could on my good foot. I hobbled over to the pipe and lifted the cap. I could hear the echo of the guard moving inside. I put both hands on the pipe and pulsed, knocking the guard out. I climbed into the pipe, then slid down, crawling out of the compound as fast as I could.

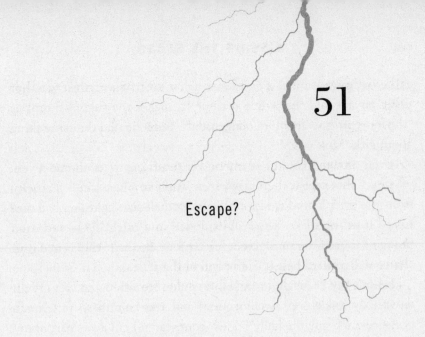

# 51

## Escape?

I caught up to the unconscious guard just a hundred feet from the pipe's entrance. I took his weapons, mostly so he couldn't use them on me. He was carrying the standard Elgen weaponry and ordnance: a concussion grenade, a smoke grenade, a special ops knife, and a 9mm pistol. I took everything, including his flashlight. Then I cuffed his hands behind his back. I didn't want him following me. I wondered how many other guards were taking the opportunity to escape.

I hurried on as fast as I could, wondering how the rest of the Electroclan were doing. They had just shut down the Elgen's largest power plant and blackened out the country's largest cities. I could only imagine how angry Hatch was. He would spare nothing to catch us before we left the country. He would be out for blood.

As I neared the end of the pipe, I saw something move. I pointed the flashlight toward the pipe's mouth. A brightly colored snake was slithering toward me. I didn't know what kind of serpent it was, but Ostin always said that when it came to snakes the rule of thumb is "the more pretty, the more dangerous." I think he said the same thing about girls.

Even though I could feel my power returning to its normal levels, whatever that meant these days, I was still carrying excess electricity from the grid. I produced a brilliant, softball-size lightning ball and tossed it at the snake. The ball exploded in a bright flash, and even though I missed the snake by at least a foot, the ball still burned it to charcoal. I crawled past it to the end of the pipe.

I shone my flashlight around but could see nothing, so I let myself down. My ankle was swelling now and too painful to put much pressure on. Using the knife I'd just confiscated I cut away part of my shirt, then wrapped my ankle with it. I looked back at the compound. I could hear shouting and an occasional gunshot but no machinery of any kind. There were no electric lights, but in the moonlight I could see a column of smoke rising from behind the power plant. My Electroclan had wreaked some serious chaos. I was so proud of them.

I knew it would be just a matter of time before the Elgen came looking for me outside the compound. I had to get to the meeting point as quickly as possible. Forgetting my ankle, I started to run and nearly fell. I didn't want my friends to have to wait for me. But they were traveling with wounded as well, so I might not hold them back too much.

I hurried on, concealed in the darkness of the jungle but close enough to keep my eye on the fence for navigation. The last thing I wanted to do was get lost in the jungle. I was glad I had given Taylor the GPS. At least I didn't have to worry about everyone else getting lost.

I had limped along for about a half hour when I heard the sound of approaching helicopters. As they got closer I heard another noise that I couldn't distinguish until I saw the fire. The helicopters were burning the forest with flamethrowers.

In spite of my pain, I started moving faster, heading deeper into the jungle. But they kept coming as if they knew exactly where I was. *How did they find me?* Then I remembered the el-readers, like the handheld one they had caught me with in the mechanical room. With the Elgen's love for technology I had no doubt that they had developed bigger, more powerful el-readers that had a range of hundreds of yards.

The sound of the rotors just got louder, and it didn't matter how deep I was in the jungle, how dark the night, or how thick the canopy, they were clearly following me. Then I heard the blast of the flames again, this time followed by the screeching of birds and monkeys. A black jaguar ran past me.

Thirty feet in front of me was an orange-yellow wall of fire, taking out everything in its path and clearing a smoldering swath in the jungle nearly twenty feet wide. Then I heard the blast of a flamethrower behind me as well.

Huddled in the trees, I couldn't tell how many helicopters there were—at least three. They were flying in circles around me, cutting back the jungle with their flames—the circle closing in on me until the heat was intense enough that it was hard to breathe. They didn't have to burn me—they could just suck all the oxygen out of the area and suffocate me. Smoke and fumes stung my eyes and throat and I was covered with ash. Within minutes they had left me in a small circle of trees, an island in an inferno of fire and soot. Then one of the helicopters broke off and hovered directly over me. A voice boomed out from its amplifier.

"You can't escape, Vey. We have you surrounded. If you run we'll open fire. You have five seconds to step out from the canopy or we'll burn you alive."

I said nothing, weighing my chances of running through the charred and burning swath to the jungle beyond without getting mowed down by their machine guns. But really, there was no point to it. They'd just find me again.

"One. Two . . ."

"Okay!" I shouted. "I'm coming out."

I limped out into the smoldering black clearing, my arms raised, my body illuminated by their spotlights. There were four helicopters, bobbing above me in the night like they were on strings. One was directly over me, maybe just fifty feet above the tops of the trees, another was to my left, and the other two were slowly circling, their spotlights and machine guns all pointing at me.

The voice said, "Get on your knees."

I looked at the steaming ground, then slowly knelt down.

The helicopter to my left began to descend when it suddenly started to wobble. It yawed violently to one side, veering directly into the path of another helicopter. Their blades collided and both helicopters exploded.

Then the third and fourth helicopters dropped to the ground. I sprang to my feet and, ignoring the pain in my ankle, sprinted out of the way as one of the helicopters fell just twenty yards from where I had been kneeling and burst into flames.

I looked back only once to see the clearing completely engulfed in fire, then ran headlong into the jungle as fast as I could.

"Wherever you are, Tanner," I said, "thank you."

# 52

## Shadows and Nose Bones

*My friends are close.* Close enough at least to drop the helicopters. Not that that knowledge did me much good. I was utterly lost. In fleeing the helicopters I had run even deeper into the jungle. I had no idea how far I was from the meeting point or even what direction to walk in. If I were Ostin I could look at the stars and figure it out, but I wasn't Ostin and, even if I were, under the thick canopy, I couldn't even see the stars. I had to somehow find my bearings. If I could get above the canopy I could find the compound and head back toward the fence. My ankle was throbbing now, and I hopped on one foot until I found a tall, lichen-covered tree hung with vines as thick as rope. I tested one of the larger vines, and it easily held me, so I began to climb.

I was tired and weak and the climbing was difficult, but I continued on, knowing that the Electroclan was nearby. Monkeys and birds screeched around me as I invaded their domain. A black-and-white monkey about the size of a squirrel jumped on my head. It started pulling at my ears so I pulsed a little, and it shrieked and jumped off, scolding me as it swung to a nearby limb.

It took me about a half hour to make it to the emergent level above the canopy. I was panting and drenched with sweat, but the air was cooler and fresh and I sucked it in like water. The velvet night sky was brilliant with stars and, for the first time since I'd come, I realized that it wasn't the same sky we saw at home. There was no Big or Little Dipper down here, no North Star. In this part of the world they looked to the Southern Cross.

From my vantage point I could see for miles around in all directions. I could see the moon reflecting off the river, winding through the jungle like a snake through grass.

On the opposite side of the valley the Elgen compound was still dark, lit only by sporadic fires. Smoke was billowing into the sky. This made me unspeakably happy.

I found the electric fence. Its yellow warning lights were dead but I could see the moon glisten off its metal lines. I had gone farther into the forest than I had thought, and I could now see that I was at least a quarter mile from the fence and a couple of miles from what I guessed to be our meeting place.

As I looked out over the compound I saw them coming. Shadows. They were everywhere. There were more than a thousand of them, silently moving toward the jungle. The guards had been sent out to find us.

I quickly climbed back down below the canopy, afraid that my glow might have given me away. I had no doubt that they were equipped with el-readers and night vision goggles. My optimism vanished, replaced with dread. I couldn't go to our meeting place even if I could find it. The meeting place. My mother was there. Raúl could guide them through the jungle. *Had the rest of the Electroclan already caught up to them? Had Ian seen the Shadows coming?*

A few minutes later I heard something crashing through the foliage below me. As I turned to see what it was, I heard a gunshot and something smashed against the tree less than three feet from my head, splintering wood around me. Then I saw the brilliant green flash of laser pointers on my body. Three Elgen guards had their guns trained on me. "Come down from the tree!" one shouted. "Or we'll shoot you down!"

I had no doubt they would, though I wondered if I would be better off taking the bullet here. Hatch would not be so merciful. But the rest of the Electroclan was somewhere nearby and they had to have heard the gunshot. They could take out these three. "All right," I said. "I'm coming."

My back was to them as I climbed down the tree. I was afraid. Part of me expected a bullet at any second. When I reached the ground I put my hands in the air and slowly turned around. "Don't shoot."

To my surprise, all three guards were lying facedown on the ground, motionless. I couldn't figure out what had happened. I hadn't heard a thing. I looked around but couldn't see anyone.

I knelt down next to one of the men and saw a small, feathered dart stuck in his neck. I swallowed as I slowly looked up. Just yards away from me, concealed in the darkness, were at least a dozen Amazon tribesmen. The lower halves of their faces were painted bloodred, and the upper halves, just above their noses, were painted black, making them look like they wore masks. They wore simple loincloths and headdresses of freshly plaited leaves, perfect camouflage for the jungle. They were armed with blow darts and spears.

I slowly stood. I had no idea what to do. If they had wanted to kill me, they could have easily done it as I climbed down the tree, just as they had the three Elgen guards. I remembered what Jaime had said about the tribes—that they hated the Elgen. *White devils*, they called them. Maybe the tribesmen were still trying to figure out what I was. If the Elgen were hunting me, maybe they would think I was good. You know, my enemy's enemy is my friend.

One of the natives approached me. His face was painted like the others', and he wore a chest plate made of bamboo laced together with dyed twine and a necklace with jaguar claws and bird talons. There were bones through his nose and ears. He slowly reached out and cautiously touched me, probably intrigued by my glow. For a second it crossed my mind that if I gave him a small shock, he might think I was a god or something, but I decided it was too risky. I had clearly watched too many movies.

He took my hands and crossed them at my wrists, then another one of the natives stepped forward and tied them together with twine. I could have easily dropped them both, but I was sure that I would answer for it with a dozen poison darts and arrows.

One of them made a peculiar clicking noise with his tongue and the rest began mimicking him, then they started off, leading me deeper into the black jungle. Even in the darkness they knew where they were going. We walked all night. My ankle throbbed with pain, and a few times I had to stop, which was met with a lot of shouting and shoving. It took a great deal of self-control not to shock them.

After hiking for miles through the dense terrain, we finally stopped at a village on a cliff overlooking the river. It was still dark and I guessed it was probably around four in the morning. I was moving on sheer adrenaline.

In spite of the hour, there was a great deal of excitement at my arrival, and even children, about two dozen of them, ran out to look at me. Old, gray-haired men came from their huts, their bodies painted in white and red. The women were also painted and wore layers of bright blue beads around their necks.

From what I could see, the village consisted of about thirty thatch-roofed huts. The tribesmen led me to an elderly man who, from the natives' gestures, I guessed was a person of authority—a chief or shaman. His face was painted white with a few black lines and his gray hair was cut short. He also had a bone through his nose. He wore a necklace made of piranha jaws and a headdress made from brightly colored parrot feathers. He looked me over, touched me, then said, "Shr ta."

His pronouncement was met with a loud whoop from the tribesmen.

*"Pei ta dau fangdz chyu. Ma shang,"* the old man said.

*"Ma shang,"* they echoed.

*"Chyu,"* my guard said to me.

"Chew what?" I said. "I don't speak cannibal."

The man grabbed my arm, and I was taken to a small hut and my hands were untied. As I rubbed my wrists the guard said, *"Chyu. Chyu."* I looked at him blankly, and he pushed me inside the hut. *"Schwei jau,"* he said.

"I don't understand a word you're saying," I said.

He pointed to a large fur on the ground and closed his eyes. *"Schwei jau."*

"Sleep," I said. "I can do that. Gladly."

I sat down on the fur. The bed was on a dirt floor covered by mats made of woven leaves. It wasn't any worse than the Elgen's prison cot. In spite of my fear, I immediately fell asleep.

At daylight, I opened my eyes to an elderly man with a bone sticking through his nose, staring into my face. I jumped back.

He laughed.

"You think that's funny?" I said. "How would you like a shock? We'll see how funny that is." I was pretty angry, and I felt at ease to speak my mind because I was certain they couldn't understand me.

The man stared at me for another moment, then he made a clicking noise and left my hut. I sat up on the fur, reminded of my ankle. After last night's hike it was swollen to almost twice its size. I rubbed it for a minute, then lay back down. My mind was reeling. What was going to happen? My mother used to say, "Better the devil you know than the one you don't." I finally understood what she meant. At least, with the Elgen, I knew what they wanted. I had no idea what these people were about. For all I knew I was their main entrée for dinner tonight.

I wondered about my mother and the rest of the Electroclan. Had they made it to the pickup point? Were they still waiting for me? No, they couldn't be. Not with the guards searching for us.

A few minutes later an older woman walked into my hut. She

carried a wooden bowl with something inside that resembled a greenish-brown oatmeal, which she handed to me along with a gourd filled with water. I drank thirstily, then, using my fingers, tried the food in the bowl. It tasted unlike anything I had ever eaten before. It wasn't all bad and I told myself it was some kind of fruit, but it could have been smashed bug larvae or monkey brains for all I knew. The woman then knelt down by my feet and took my sprained ankle in her hands and began rubbing it. I took this as a good sign, as I doubted they would spring for massages for people they planned to eat. Or maybe this was just how they tenderized their meat.

Nearly an hour later two young tribesmen came into the hut. I thought I recognized them from the night before, but from the way they were painted, I couldn't tell. They said something to the woman, and she stopped rubbing my ankle and stood. I looked at my ankle. The swelling had gone down considerably. "Thank you," I said to her. The woman didn't look at me as she left but said, "*Buyong she,*" and walked out.

"*Jan chi lai!*" the older of the two shouted at me. I guessed that he was telling me to stand. I lifted myself up, slowly putting weight on my bad foot, testing it. My ankle had improved. Not enough that I could outrun anyone, but I had never considered that an option anyway. In the jungle I was definitely at a disadvantage.

The men escorted me back out into the center of the village. The old man, Mr. Important Guy, was standing in the exact same place he had been the night before. He was waiting for me.

"*Womun dai ta,*" one of the tribesmen said to him.

"*Ta yo mei yo schwei jau,*" the important guy said.

"*Schwei le.*"

"*Yo mei yo ting chi tade ren?*"

"*Mei yo.*"

I listened to them banter for a while, then finally I said, "Listen, if you're going to eat me, you're not going to like the way I taste."

To my surprise the men stopped talking. The old man's face twisted with a peculiar expression, then he started to laugh.

"I'm not your enemy," I said. "I just want to go home."

The old man stopped laughing. He looked at me for a long time, his dark gray eyes locked onto mine. Then he said in perfectly clear English, "Michael Vey. That is not your path. You are not going home."

# ELGEN GUARD

## GENERAL HANDBOOK

THE ELGEN GUARD

ABSOLUTUM DOMINIUM

FROM PRESIDENT C. J. HATCH, SUPREME
COMMANDER GENERAL ADMIRAL, AS DICTATED TO

# RICHARD PAUL EVANS

# Memorandum for the Elgen Guard

1. This handbook is designed to summarize the current laws, policies, and general dispositions from the Elgen High Command pertaining to general guard duty, requirements, and training.

2. This handbook is in no way to be used to contradict or disavow the ranking officers' ADC (active duty commands). All ADC are to be followed at the time of issuance. Where commands are considered in conflict with the GHI (General Handbook of Instructions) grievances may be filed at a later date as set forth in Section 4.

Respectfully,

David W. Welch

EGG, Chief of Guard

# CONTENTS

# INTRODUCTION

Dear Elgen Guard,

I congratulate you. You have been initiated into the elite group of the Elgen Force. Throughout history, there have been groups of power that have changed the world: the Knights Templars, the samurai, the Nazi Brown Shirts, and the fierce horsemen of the Russian Cossack. You now belong to the greatest of these elite groups. You have taken your place in history.

When you entered this employment you were informed that this was not merely a job, but a cause far greater than any you ever had or ever will have—a cause of greater importance than even your own life. Before joining, you were a mere man. Today, you are Elgen.

As an Elgen Guard you are the sworn upholder and enforcer of the Elgen law. The world will fall onto its knees before you or be crushed under your boot. It is a brave new world. Those of you who are with me will prosper far beyond your wildest imaginations. Those who fail will be crushed beneath the brute power of our growing force.

As an enforcer of the law, you must first be completely familiar with the law. It must become first nature to you. Second, you must be compliant with the law, the purest example of the Elgen elite, both physically and mentally. Your mind is sure and sharp, your way true and straight, your body strong, formidable, and unyielding. You are unlike the weak who inhabit this earth. You are above them. You are the talons of the eagle, ready to capture or to tear asunder. Your path is the way of glory. The uniform you wear is a symbol of your commitment and honor. You must never disrespect it, nor allow it to be disrespected.

A new day has dawned, not just for the world but for you. Rise up to this morning of a new dispensation, the Novus Ordo Glorificus Elgen, and personal glory will follow. Elgen, I salute you.

*General Admiral C. J. Hatch*

# SECTION ONE
## GENERAL

# THE ELGEN OATH

The oath-taker will raise his left arm while repeating the following oath:

> I swear on my life, breath, and fortune to prosper the Elgen cause, to advance its mission until every man and woman on Earth have sworn allegiance to the *Novus Ordo Glorificus* Elgen, our new glorious order. I offer up my life and death to this endeavor and will follow all rules contained in this book and those that will come, with fidelity, honor, and exactness. I swear this oath on my life.

This Elgen oath is to be held with utmost sanctity. Any guard demonstrating an attitude to the contrary will be disciplined.

# THE ELGEN SALUTE

The Elgen salute is a symbol of our purpose, unity, and strength. Elgen Guards will salute all officers of higher rank than themselves.

The salute is performed by touching the three middle fingers of the left hand to the temple, the thumb and little finger touching together at the tips.

# ELGEN GUARD STANDING ORDERS

1. Memorize this handbook. Strict adherence to its guidelines will ensure your success and progress within the Elgen Force. Any disobedience to its precepts will result in immediate disciplinary action.
2. From this moment forward, your previous chain of command no longer exists. As an Elgen Guard you will answer only to the Supreme Commander, the Elite Global Guard, your Zone Captain, and your Squad Captain.
3. Officers of the Elite Global Guard (guardsmen are to refer to them as Elite Guard) represent the Supreme Commander in his absence. To disobey their orders is tantamount to disobeying the Supreme Commander.
4. Any sign of insubordination, intentional or otherwise, will be dealt with swiftly and severely. Precise obedience and loyalty is the guardsman's only true protection.
5. Guardsmen will report any disloyalty or infraction among fellow guardsmen to their Squad Captain. Guards found "protecting" or "sheltering" another guard will be considered an accessory and receive the identical punishment as the transgressor.
6. The contents of this manual are confidential (C5). Leaking of information will be punished according to Elgen guidelines.
7. Guardsmen are to rid themselves of all previous loyalties, attachments, and commitments, whether personal or professional.
8. Guardsmen are required to maintain peak physical and mental condition. Weakness of body or mind will not be tolerated. Periodic testing will be utilized to determine continued eligibility.

# HISTORICAL BACKGROUND

The history of Elgen Inc. begins with the history of electricity itself. As long as humans have existed, they have been fascinated by electricity and ascribed it with mystical properties. The ancient Greeks believed that lightning was the weapon of Zeus, the king of the gods. Any place struck by lightning was considered sacred, and became the site of temples and worship. Similarly, the Scandinavian mythological figure Thor threw lightning bolts at his enemies. In Hindu mythology, Indra is the god of lightning and a symbol of strength.

While the mystical power and majesty of electricity have been observed since the beginning of humankind, it is only in relatively recent times that humans have sought to understand and control this great power. Scientists like Franklin, Edison, Tesla, Westinghouse, Ampere, Volta, Ohm, Faraday, Joule, and others, dedicated their lives to understanding the science of electricity, but it is only in recent centuries that electricity has been harnessed by humankind and used for its benefit. It is no coincidence that the successful manipulation of electricity occurred at the same time as some of society's greatest technological advancements.

Today, in our so-called *civilized* world, it is difficult to imagine life without electricity, yet *25 percent* of the world's population still lives without its benefit. It is Elgen Inc.'s goal to remedy that crisis within our lifetime. Once we have succeeded, the relief of human suffering will be without measure, as will the effect on the advancement of civilization. Children who were previously shackled to the daily chores of gathering wood and fuel for basic survival will now be able to attend schools. Women will be free of the menial chores that keep them from advancing their own educations. Economies will improve as manufacturing and farming becomes more productive and efficient with the benefit of electrical power. In short, Elgen Inc.'s electricity will change the world.

After many years of research, Elgen Inc.'s scientists created our unique electricity-generating process. In 2009 we successfully opened our first Starxource power plant. While the science behind our electricity production is top secret, our process may be best compared to fusion—but without the environmental backlash, threat of meltdown, or the contaminants of nuclear waste.

Since the opening of that first plant, many others have followed in both developed and developing countries. The benefits to these countries have far surpassed our, and their, greatest hopes. In the future we will assist larger and more populated countries until the entire world is advanced and prospering beneath the Elgen network of electric power. Then the wars between the nations will cease. They will be bound to one another through their common energy source and will no longer rise up against one another, for no one nation can assault another without the power of electricity. The promise of Elgen Inc. is much more than a cleaner, ecologically brighter world, it is also one without pain, fear, and the destruction of war.

One does not change the world without opposition, which is why Elgen Inc. has trained and employed its own army, dedicated to the advancement of Elgen Inc. and its goal of providing energy solutions today for a brighter tomorrow. *As an Elgen guard, you are now a part of ensuring that brighter tomorrow for billions around the world.*

# SECTION TWO
## LEADERSHIP, HIERARCHY,
## AND CHAIN OF COMMAND

# CHAIN OF COMMAND

The Elgen Guard is ruled through the following hierarchy:

GENERAL GUARD

I.   ELGEN SUPREME COMMANDER, General Admiral C. J. Hatch

II.  THE ELGEN BOARD

A remnant of the former Elgen organization, the Elgen board now acts as a non-voting advisory counsel to the Elgen Supreme Commander. Membership on the board is determined solely by the Elgen Supreme Commander.

III. ELITE GLOBAL GUARD (EGG)

The Elgen Supreme Commander's force of twelve guards. The authority of the EGG is challenged only by the Supreme Commander, and their orders are to be followed as though from the Supreme Commander himself.

Uniform: Black with purple and scarlet chest emblems. Red and black armbands on right arm.

IV.  ZONE CAPTAINS (ZCs)

Zone Captains are the leaders of a global zone of Squad Captains. Zone Captains report to the EGG.

Uniform: Same as EGG with addition of scarlet armbands.

V.   SQUAD CAPTAINS

Elgen Squads are the fundamental unit of the Elgen security corps. Squad Captains are in authority over and responsible for all members of their squad, comprised of six to twelve Elgen Guardsmen. Squad Captains report to their regional Zone Captain.

Uniform: Purple Elgen Uniform

VI.  GUARDSMEN

The Elgen Guardsman is the fundamental figure of the Elgen security corps and is responsible for the inner workings of all Elgen operations. Tasks and responsibilities vary widely and training is provided by Squad Captains. Guardsmen report to their Squad Captain.

Uniform: Standard Elgen Uniform with armband bearing the guard's zone and squad identification number.

VII. ELGEN SECRET POLICE (ESP)

One or two Elgen Secret Police members exist within each squad. As the eyes and ears of the Elgen organization, their primary responsibility is to act as informants on the other guards while keeping their identities confidential. ESPs communicate directly with Zone Captains, ESP Captains, and, where warranted, the Elite Guard.

Uniform: The ESP uniform is indistinguishable from regular Elgen Guardsmen.

VIII. ESP CAPTAINS

A group of twelve elite ESP members responsible for the organization and success of the ESP force.

Uniform: Elgen uniform with a scarlet beret and a scarlet sash, hung from the left shoulder. (New captains will hang sashes from right shoulder during first six months of tenure.)

IX. ESP CAPTAINS' ASSISTANTS

There are twenty-four assistants who help the ESP Captains collect and consolidate information from the ESP force as well as assisting the ESP Captains in special projects and duties as the position may require.

Uniform: Dressed in black with yellow and black striped armbands.

## NAVAL ELGEN OFFICER RANKS

**Admiral of the Fleet**

**Admiral**

**Rear Admiral**

**Ship Captain**

**Commander**

**Lieutenant Commander**

**Naval Guardsmen**

**Ensign**

Currently the offices of General Admiral and Admiral of the Fleet are held by the Elgen Supreme Commander. Please refer to the *Naval General Handbook of Instructions* for descriptions of duties and uniforms.

# ELGEN ELITE FORCES

In addition to specific ranks, guards may be associated with special elite forces. Membership in these forces may have geographical consideration and is by invitation only.

I. **Electric Youth**

Elgen Inc.'s Youth Force is comprised of a small group of gifted adolescents. Guards will be aware of their presence but are not to approach or speak to them unless it is a specific part of their assigned duties. Guards are to obey these youth's orders as they would the EGG. The Elgen Youth Force members are to be guarded and protected at the expense of guards' lives.

      i.     Quentin

      ii.    Torstyn

      iii.   Bryan

      iv.   Kylee

      v.     Tara

      vi.   ~~Tesla~~

      vii.  ~~Tanner~~

      viii. ~~Nichelle~~

      ix.   ~~Zeus~~

      x.     ~~McKenna~~

      xi.   ~~Abigail~~

      xii.  ~~Ian~~

## II. Chasqui

Translated from the ancient Quechuan dialect, the word "chasqui" means "messenger of light." The Chasqui are a special Elgen military order in Peru. Their roles are specifically connected to the Peruvian Starxource plant in Puerto Maldonado.

## III. Domguard

Also known as the "Order of the Amber Tunic." The Domguard are a very powerful and secretive global force.

## IV. Lung Li

The Lung Li (literally meaning "dragon power") is a special Asian Elgen military order. Their activities are limited to countries in the eastern hemisphere, including China, Taiwan, Korea, Japan, Vietnam, Cambodia, and Thailand.

# SECTION THREE
## TRAINING

# REQUIRED TRAINING

All Elgen Forces must complete a minimum of ninety days initial training (IT) at the Kaohsiung, Taiwan, or Fiumicino, Italy, training facilities.

Initial training will include physical endurance and strength testing and building (see Physical Requirements), psychological testing, and aptitude testing. Guards will be assigned their first field of duty (FOD) based on the observed accumulated test scores and performances during initial training.

# PHYSICAL REQUIREMENTS

All Elgen Guardsmen are required to maintain peak physical condition. The following physical fitness tests will be administered quarterly by Squad Captains without warning and at random times, including the middle of the night or during regular shifts. Failure to pass the physical test will result in dishonorable discharge.

| Physical Test | Required Time/ Repetition | Guard Actual Time | Pass/ Fail | Squad Captain's Signature |
|---|---|---|---|---|
| 3-Mile Run | Complete in less than 24 minutes | | | |
| Pull-Ups | 25 consecutive repetitions | | | |
| Sit-Ups | 100 consecutive repetitions | | | |
| Push-Ups | 50 consecutive repetitions | | | |
| 25-Foot Rope Climb | Complete in less than 60 seconds | | | |
| Standard Obstacle Course | Complete in less than 13 minutes | | | |

# WEAPONRY

All Elgen Guardsmen will be issued the following basic weaponry:

- **Bulletproof vest**

- **Utility belt with concussion and smoke grenades**

- **Standard M4 Carbine Rifle**

- **Standard 1911 Colt sidearm**

- **Tactical Special Ops Knife (fixed blade) with leg holster**

Elgen Guardsmen assigned to special details (especially those involving electric children) may be issued some or all of the following:

- **RESAT gun and darts**

- RESAT detention systems

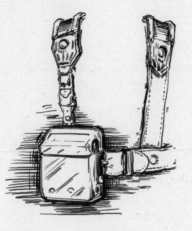

- Mindwave Helmet

# SECTION FOUR
## ELGEN PROTOCOL

# LEVELS OF CONFIDENTIALITY

Confidentiality is key to Elgen Inc.'s mission. After a trial period, most guards will be granted some information in return for their continued loyalty and service. Any information given to guards is to be kept strictly confidential. Guards are to discuss internal affairs with no one, excepting the commanding officer who has issued the information. C10 information may only be discussed in the presence of the Supreme Commander, and only at his initiation. All information is assigned a confidentiality level and requisite penalty. This level will be disclosed before the information is divulged. Any sharing of information among low-ranking guards or with outsiders will be met with swift punishment as outlined in the following table:

| Level of Confidentiality | Disciplinary Action for Unauthorized Divulgence |
|---|---|
| C1 | Verbal reprimand. One year probation. Pay reduction. |
| C2 | Verbal reprimand. Two weeks confinement. Pay reduction. |
| C3 | Verbal reprimand. Ten day detention period in Reeducation. Pay reduction. |
| C4 | Three-week detention period in Reeducation. Pay reduction. |
| C5 | Six-month detention period in Reeducation. Pay reduction. |
| C6 | One-year detention period in Reeducation. Pay reduction. |
| C7 | One-year detention period in Reeducation. Life-long assignment to menial position within Elgen Force with no chance for promotion. |
| C8 | Life imprisonment with hard labor. |
| C9 | Death. |
| C10 (Highest) | Death by torture. |

# DISCIPLINARY ACTION

Disciplinary action for minor offenses, including the consumption of alcohol, tobacco, or use of unauthorized chemical substances, will be handled by the immediate commanding officer and may include corporal punishment, internment, fines, peer discipline, or probation. Major offenses, including breech of confidentiality above C2 must be reported to the Zone Captain. In cases requiring extreme disciplinary action (i.e. sedition or divulgence of C5 to C10), a disciplinary court will be convened, comprised of a counsel of five ZCs, two ESP Captains, and overseen by the regional EGG.

# HANDLING OF INTERNAL GRIEVANCES

All grievances must be submitted by form EIA0026B, in duplicate, to the Elgen Guardmen's Squad Captain. In the case that the grievance is against (or involves) the Squad Captain, a complaint may be submitted to a Zone Captain for summary examination.

**Note: Guards who submit complaints that are found to be meritless may face disciplinary action.**

# REEDUCATION

Although only a relatively few guards will ever work in the Elgen reeducation program, it is vital for all personnel to understand its workings and role in the global expansion of the Elgen empire.

The reeducation process is designed to help those who have been counterconditioned to non-Elgen paradigms. Misguided individuals are sent to the nearest reeducation center where they will undergo a series of educational and mind-altering exercises in which erroneous thinking is replaced with the glorious truths of the Elgen. The following exercises and procedures have been used with such great success that even a few of our most dedicated guards are graduates of our reeducation campuses:

### Step 1: Appearance Alteration
Detainees wear attire (i.e. pink, flowered jumpsuits) that promotes humility and greater willingness to cooperate. Jewelry, facial hair, or distinguishing hairstyles are removed or changed during the admitting process.

### Step 2: Name Change
Disassociating detainees from their previous identities serves to open their minds to new truths. All detainees are assigned numbers that serve as their identity until their graduation from Reeducation.

### 3. Confinement
Detainees are housed in individual ten-by-ten foot rooms containing a metal cage. For the detainee's safety, a special deactivation code is required in order for a visitor to enter the detainee's cell. Failure to input the code will result in the detainee being electrocuted.

## 4. Educational Media

Elgen Inc. has produced a series of films designed to correct detainees' thinking and expedite the conversion process. These films are shown at regular intervals during the detainees stay, as often as twenty times per day. The more time spent in front of these films the speedier the process of conversion and the greater the success.

## 5. Detention Time Period/Integration

While individual cases vary, most detainees require a relatively short reeducation period. They are then welcomed into our cause.*

Historically, 97% of all detainees are satisfactorily reeducated and allowed the privilege of serving the Elgen, oftentimes in menial roles such as janitorial or groundskeeping work. All former reeducation students are continually monitored and assessed for their continued improvement.

*Occasionally, it is deemed necessary to detain individual students for longer/indefinite periods. These special cases pose special security risks and require extra attention from Elgen Guardsmen.

# SECTION FIVE
## MISCELLANEOUS

# ELGEN FLEET

The Elgen fleet consists of seven vessels manned by Elgen naval personnel and equipped to handle a variety of projects.

## ES *Ampere*
The flagship of the Elgen fleet, the *Ampere* is a superyacht that serves as the Elgen command ship. It is used for special functions and to entertain Elgen VIPs.
Design Specifications: 11,000 tonnes. 145 meters. Steel over aluminum superstructure with Kevlar insulation. Powered by a triple screw, diesel-electric propulsion system with four marine diesel engines.
Max speed: 25 knots. Cruising speed: 22 knots.

## *Faraday*
A refurbished World War II troopship used to transport Elgen guards.
Design Specifications: It can carry in excess of 3,500 passengers. 76,000 GRT. Powered by twin marine diesel engines. Twin props.
Max speed: 18 to 19 knots.

## *Watt*
A fully operational battle cruiser equipped to protect the rest of the Elgen fleet. Carries and operates advanced technology including tactical tomahawk cruise missiles, torpedoes, long range cannons, and advanced targeting systems.
Design Specifications: Displacement: 38,200 tonnes. 213 meters.
Max speed: 32.5 knots.

## *Volta*
The Elgen's science ship. It also contains a confinement center capable of housing up to fifty GPs.
Design Specifications: Displacement: 13,000 tonnes. 152 meters.
Max speed: 20.5 knots.

*Joule*
(Classified)

*Ohm*
Serves as a supply ship for the Elgen fleet as well as Elgen compounds and Starxource power plants.
Design Specifications: Displacement: 9,000 tonnes. 98 meters.
Max speed: 20.5 knots.

*Tesla*
The Tesla is a small landing craft used for transporting troops from the *Faraday*. (This type of ship is also known as a "tender.") It is equipped with twin fifty caliber machine guns and a twenty millimeter Oerlikon cannon.
Design Specifications: Displacement: 3,586 tonnes. 100.55 meters.
Powered by three twelve-cylinder gasoline-fueled engines. (Modified design of the Packard 3A-2500 V-12 liquid-cooled aircraft engine.)
Max speed: 35 to 40 knots.

# ELGEN FACILITIES

**Administrative Offices (Land-Based)**
Italy, Rome
Finland, Helsinki
Taiwan, Kaohsiung (Training Facility)
Peru, Puerto Maldonado

**Reeducation Centers**
Peru, Puerto Maldonado
Taiwan, Kaohsiung
Mexico, Tampico, Tamaulipas
Italy, Fiumicino (Training Facility)
Tuvalu, Funafuti
Finland, Helsinki
Tanzania, Mwanza

## STARXOURCE PLANTS
**Beta Control Countries (BCC):**

| | |
|---|---|
| Anguilla | (Starxource Functioning 100%) |
| Christmas Island | (Starxource Functioning 100%) |
| Cook Islands | (Starxource Aborted) |
| Falkland Islands | (Starxource Functioning 96%) |
| St. Barths | (Starxource Functioning 96%) |

**Operational Starxource Plants (OSP)/**
**Combined Populations: 115,703,571**

| | |
|---|---|
| Palau | 21,000 |
| British Virgin Islands | 28,213 |
| Gibraltar | 29,441 |
| Monaco | 35,881 |
| Saint Martin | 36,824 |
| Cayman Islands | 54,878 |
| Greenland | 56,890 |

| Bermuda | 64,237 |
| Dominica | 71,685 |
| Jersey | 97,857 |
| Aruba | 101,484 |
| Tonga | 103,036 |
| Grenada | 110,821 |
| Virgin Islands | 106,405 |
| Samoa | 184,032 |
| Finland | 5,405,590 |
| Zimbabwe | 12,754,000 |
| Taiwan | 23,200,000 |
| Peru | 29,797,694 |
| Tanzania | 43,443,603 |

**Plants Under Construction (PUC)/**
**Combined Populations: 32,623,410**

| Portugal | 10,561,614 |
| Greece | 10,787,690 |
| Chad | 11,274,106 |

**Under Negotiation/**
**Combined Populations: 1,010,135,758**

| Poland | 38,092,000 |
| Sudan | 45,047,502 |
| Spain | 46,196,278 |
| South Korea | 48,750,000 |
| Italy | 60,600,000 |
| France | 65,073,482 |
| Philippines* | 94,000,000 |
| Pakistan | 187,000,000 + |
| Brazil* | 192,376,496 |
| India* | 233,000,000 |

*Top 10 Populous Countries

# MEDALS AND AWARDS

**C. J. Hatch Award for Distinguished Service**
The prestigious C. J Hatch award is the highest honor given to Elgen Guardsmen, and is often followed by an advancement to Squad Captain, Zone Captain, or even Elite Global Guard status. The recipient of this award is personally selected by the Supreme Commander himself and stands as an example of exemplary Elgen performance, dedication, and heroism.

## Golden Lightning

This award is bestowed upon one Guardsman every calendar year. This award is given to the Guardsman who demonstrates the highest level of dedication, loyalty, and performance. Squad Captains will submit names for review to the Zone Captains, who will then narrow the field of candidates to five. The final names are passed to the EGG for a decision. Golden Lightning candidates are awarded a private audience with General Admiral C. J. Hatch. Many Golden Lightning–award winners have been promoted to Squad Captains or Zone Captains.

**Silver Filament**

This award is bestowed upon an Elgen Secret Police member every calendar year at a private event. Because the identity of the ESP must remain confidential, candidates for the award are chosen by the ESP Captains based on performance, discovery, and value of discovery. ESPs who uncover disloyal guards or factions among the ranks are considered for the award. Although there is no public presentation of the award (in order to protect the identity of the ESP member), winners are granted special privileges as well as a private audience with EGG David W. Welch.

**Bronze Spark**

This award is bestowed biannually during the Elgen Guard Global Training Camps. Candidates are chosen from each squad and reviewed by Zone Captains. Each zone bestows the award on a soldier who has best demonstrated Elgen qualities of loyalty, determination, strength, and solidarity. Bronze Spark winners receive a pay grade advancement and are publicly acknowledged during the training broadcasts.

# LANGUAGE AND TERMINOLOGY

The Elgen military force has developed language and terminology in reference to its unique mission. While Elgen Guardsmen will use many of these terms on a daily basis, it is required that their meanings are kept strictly confidential from outsiders. (Note: Many terms are classified and will only be revealed on a need-to-know basis.)

**Section I—Acronyms & Abbreviations**

| | |
|---|---|
| ADC | Active Duty Commands |
| BCC | Beta Control Countries |
| EGG | Elite Global Guard |
| EMP | Electromagnetic Pulse |
| ESP | Elgen Secret Police |
| FOD | Field of Duty |
| GHI | General Handbook of Instruction |
| GPs | Guinea Pigs *(Homo sapiens)* |
| IT | Initial Training |
| MEI | Magnetic Electron Induction |
| NSG | Neo-Species Genesis program |
| OSP | Operational Starxource Plants |
| PUC | Plants Under Construction |
| Re-Ed | Reeducation |
| RFID | Radio Frequency Identification Device |
| ZCs | Zone Captains |

## Section II—Terms & Definitions

**ADC**   (Short for *Active Duty Commands.*) All rules and instruction given to Elgen Guardsmen.

**BCC**   (Short for *Beta Control Countries.*) Used in reference to Starxource power plant development. (See *OSP*, *PUC*, and *Starxource.*)

**Bowl (The)**   Any Starxource plant's central conductor—designed to direct power to a delicate, silver-coated copper grid that conducts electricity to capacitors.

**Cell 25**   An important aspect of every GP prison, Cell 25 acts as the ultimate recalibration tool. Prisoners locked in Cell 25 are forced to endure erratic food schedules, a consistent electronic beep, and frequent bouts of terror. Cell 25 references a specific room that can be duplicated in any Elgen facility.

**E Patterns/El-Waves**   Units of measurement that designate the biological electricity patterns and levels present in the body.

**EGG**   (Short for *Elite Global Guard.*) The Supreme Commander's elite force of twelve guards.

**Electrical Pulse**   A secondary pulse that references the flow of electricity within the body. Tested through sensors developed specifically for this purpose.

**Electric Children**   Group of youth with electric capabilities. Many of these youth are a part of Hatch's special youth force, but others are considered enemies of the Elgen. (See *Electroclan.*)

**Electroclan**   Small terrorist group comprised of renegade Electric Children as well as a few nonelectric youth. Considered an enemy to the Elgen. (See *Electric Children.*)

**Elgen**   Electric Generation. The Elgen Corporation as a whole. (Pronounced *El-Jen*.)

**Elgen Academy**   An elite school designed to engage and train Electric Children. Originally referencing a specific facility in Pasadena, this term now refers to the Electric Children's education in a broader sense. (See *Electric Children*.)

**EMP**   (Short for *Electromagnetic Pulse*.) A wave of electricity capable of stopping all electrical functioning and communications.

**ER 20**   (Classified.)

**ER 21**   (Classified.)

**ER 22**   (Classified.)

**ESP**   (Short for *Elgen Secret Police*.) Secret informants existing within each Elgen Guard squad.

**ESP Captains**   (Short for *Elgen Secret Police* Captains.) Twelve ESP leaders who report to ZCs and EGGs when appropriate. (See *EGGs* and *ZCs*.)

**FOD**   (Short for *Field of Duty*.) The initial duty assigned to new Elgen Guardsmen after the completion of IT. (See *IT*.)

**GHI**   (Short for *General Handbook of Instructions*.)

**Glow**   Common term for Electric Children. Because of their unique bioelectrical makeup, all Electric Children give off a faint, phosphorescent glow. (See *Electric Children*.)

**Goats**   Guards of questionable loyalty who require reeducation in order to remain members of the Elgen Force. (See *Sheep* and *Reeducation*.)

**GPs**   (Short for *Guinea Pigs*.) Elgen Inc.'s human test subjects. Comprised of criminals and other untouchables, their presence is crucial

38

to the advancement of our scientific pursuits. GPs are assigned numbers and kept in GP prisons. They wear orange jumpsuits and collars that monitor their vocal cords, administering incapacitating shocks if the GP attempts to talk or scream.

**Grail**   (Slang.) Elgen-speak for a project or mission that cannot reasonably be accomplished.

**IT**   (Short for *Initial Training*.) Ninety day requisite training similar to the U.S. military's basic training or boot camp

**MEI**   (Short for *Magnetic Electron Induction*.) Elgen invention used for finding diseases and abnormalities in the body. Since its early testing the MEI's role within our organization has evolved to become an intricate part of the NSG program. (Commonly pronounced *may*.)

**Mindwave Helmet**   Also commonly called a "reboot helmet." A protective helmet constructed of copper and made to withstand projected electrical interference. Used in special missions.

**Newf's**   (Derogatory slang.) Non-Elgen workforce.

**NSG**   (Short for *Neo-Species Genesis* program.) Details are classified.

**OSP**   (Short for *Operational Starxource Plants*.) Starxource power plants currently in operation. (See also *BCC*, *PUC*, and *Starxource*.)

**PUC**   (Short for *Plants Under Construction*.) Used in reference to power plants currently being developed. (See also *BCC*, *PUC*, and *Starxource*.)

**Rabisk**   A biscuit made from rat carrion, fur, and bone meal. Though primarily used to feed other rodents, Rabisk is sometimes fed to Elgen prisoners.

**Re-Ed**   (Short for *Reeducation*.) Process by which Elgen alter the minds of individuals who have been counterconditioned to reject Elgen beliefs. Also refers to a physical facility.

**RESAT**  Unique to Elgen Inc., the RESAT is used to subdue errant Electric Children through lowering their body's electrical content. To be used in special missions only. (Pronounced *Ree-Sat*.) (See *Electric Children*.)

**RFIDs**  (Short for *Radio Frequency Identification Devices*.) Subdermal tracking devices used to track the location of GPs. They are administered through injection and most often placed in left arm. (See *GPs*.)

**Sheep**  Enthusiastic soldiers whose loyalties lie with General Hatch. These guards will be trained and advance to leadership rank, ultimately taking leadership positions over the Starxource Plants or Elgen compounds. (See *Goats*.)

**Squad Captains**  Leaders of the Elgen Guardsmen subgroup, composed of six to twelve Elgen Guardsmen.

**Starxource**  Name given to Elgen power plants. Starxource power plants deliver economical, renewable, and environmentally friendly power to the world through a top secret process most closely related to cold fusion.

**Stretch**  References the effectiveness of Electric Children's abilities. Electric stretch can be increased through proper diet—extra potassium and minerals, decrease in refined sugars—as well as practice. (See *Electric Children*.)

**ZCs**  (Short for *Zone Captains*.) Leaders of a regional zone of Squad Captains. (See *Squad Captains*.)